Copyright © 2022 by ALESSA THORN

All rights reserved.

No part of this book may be reproduced in any form or by any electronic or mechanical means, including information storage and retrieval systems, without written permission from the author, except for the use of brief quotations in a book review.

Editing and Proof Reading by Damoro Design

AUTHORS NOTE

To help readers keep up with the growing cast of characters in 'The Fae Universe,' I have placed a **Character List** at the back of this book. I have kept it as spoiler free as possible.

PROLOGUE

When the fae returned with their armies and their magic, everyone felt like the world had changed. It hadn't. Not if you were an Ironwood.

Sure, the other *normal* people got a taste of the supernatural, but it had always existed even if they were too blind to see it.

The great old families in the world, like the Ironwoods and the Greatdrakes, had been fighting against evil for centuries, their knowledge of magic and monsters never disappearing like it had for the other humans.

If anything, the return of the fae was a relief because there were never enough hunters or magicians in the world to keep the darkness at bay.

Morrigan's attack on Ireland woke the world up again, and even with the wounded goddess banished to the underworld realm of Annwn, she had left a hell of a mess behind her.

Ancient bloodlines could no longer operate alone to deal with the fallout of being invaded by creatures of the dread horde. But working together? Well, that was something that magicians, hunters, and fae had never been able to do well.

It was a good thing for the world that they had no choice.

1

Charlotte Ironwood believed in two things above all others—that getting a magical sigil perfect was like seeing the face of God and control over one's emotions was the utmost quality a human could possess.

Understanding magic and harnessing it were her lifelong pursuits that demanded perfection and were the highest calling one could have. In her world, magic entailed respect, discipline, and commitment.

For all those reasons, she found the magician standing before her utterly problematic.

Reeve Greatdrakes was the antithesis of everything she believed in.

Reeve Greatdrakes was a trash magician and human.

Reeve Greatdrakes was smiling at her like he knew everything she was thinking about him and didn't care.

Reeve Greatdrakes was smiling at her...

"Do you think she's stroking out or building up to throw a curse at me?" he asked Imogen. She waved a hand in front of Charlotte's face.

"Think she might be having an aneurism," her sister replied.

"Or she's wondering what you are doing in her laboratory *uninvited*," Charlotte said, tone dripping more acid than the overflowing beaker to her right.

Imogen flicked her long lavender braid over her shoulder. "Don't get all pissy, lil sis. We have a family meeting with the boys, did you forget?"

Charlotte rubbed at the tension already building in her temple. She *had* forgotten. She had woken with a new sigil for Bron glowing in her mind, and she had been focused on it ever since.

"If it is a family meeting, what are you doing here?" Charlotte asked Reeve. He was looking about her lab with curious eyes.

"I was invited, Charlie." Reeve gave her another one of his lazy, smug smiles, and her shoulders knotted with tension.

The pet name was like a razor blade to her nerve endings. A few years ago, she would have lit up on the inside if he'd called her that. Now it made her feel like a goddamn fool.

They were both older than the dumb college kids they had been, but he had somehow gotten even more attractive with age. His hair was out today, hanging in lazy, dark brown waves to his shoulders. With his trimmed goatee, studs in his ears, and layered boho look, he portrayed the magician love child of Captain Jack Sparrow and Will Turner. She hated him even more for that.

"Don't call me Charlie," she said, turning off her Bunsen burner.

"I thought fighting side by side six weeks ago made us friends again," Reeve replied. He reached out to turn one of her notebooks that had the new sigil on it, and Charlotte smacked his hand away.

"You thought wrong. Don't touch my stuff."

Imogen chuckled. "Charlotte's protective of her shit, Reeve. Maybe you should go on ahead, and I'll get her moving."

Reeve's smile slipped. "Of course. Ah, Charlie, that sigil is banging. Good—good job."

Imogen watched him go before turning to her. "You know, you really don't have to bust his balls so hard."

"It's none of your business, Gen. Don't bring him in here again," Charlotte said, pulling out her hairband and re-doing her ponytail. "Do I have anything on my face?"

"No, you look fine. Reeve is right, though. You guys fought together against Morrigan's horde. Whatever your secret vendetta is against him, it will have to take a back seat for the good of everyone," Imogen said.

She picked up Charlotte's black-framed glasses off the counter and wiped at them with the edge of her Nine Inch Nails T-shirt. They were even more smudged when she handed them over, but Charlotte didn't mention it. She knew when her older sister was trying to be helpful.

"It's not a vendetta. It's that I don't trust him. That's all." Charlotte didn't want to try and explain their history to Imogen, who was liked by everyone she met. "Come on, we better hurry. We wouldn't want to keep our brothers waiting."

Imogen grinned. "They are family now even if they are princes. They can wait."

It had barely been two months since Bron had officially become the mate of Killian, the Night Prince, but Charlotte was already used to having him as a part of the family. They had also inherited Kian, Bayn, and their mates by extension. Charlotte liked them all, which was a miracle because she rarely liked anyone.

Maybe you should have been trying to be friends with fae and not humans all along.

She might have if she hadn't been raised to hate all fae since the day she opened her eyes. They had all grown as a family recently in more ways than one.

The conference room table was packed with all the Ironwoods, including Bron and Killian. Moira wasn't technically meant to be there, seeing how she was only a child. Still, she was sitting on Kill's lap, whispering conspiratorially to him. She adored her new fae brother, and Killian indulged her in whatever mischief she was plotting. Like all of the fae, he loved children, and the princes were delighted to have one in their family. It was going to make Moira even more spoiled.

Reeve was sitting next to Lachlan, and he patted the empty chair beside him when she walked in. Charlotte ignored him and took the seat next to Bron before Imogen could.

Killian smirked at her. He covered Moira's ears and whispered, "Have you not given that poor lad his balls back yet, Charlotte love?"

Charlotte didn't get a chance to reply because the screen on the far wall turned on, and they were joined by Bayn and Kian.

Charlotte smiled up at the Blood Prince. She liked her new family, but she had a soft spot for Kian. He loved magic, and she never had to dumb down a single conversation she had with him.

Being the only one interested in magic over hunting in her family had made Charlotte always feel a little on the outside. Kian had changed that to a certain degree. He was always busy governing the fae, but he made time for her when he could. It meant the world to her.

"Are we all here?" Kian asked, and Kenna nodded. "Okay, let's get to the point of this meeting. Horde creatures are still being sighted throughout Ireland and Britain. We have confirmed that some managed to come through the portals here in Britain when Morrigan entered our world again. We don't know if it was a part of her plan to have them scout us or just to cause some chaos, but now that she is dead, they are making their own plans."

"I haven't seen any in Scotland yet, but that doesn't mean they aren't here. I got men on the lookout for any signs of them, and nothing has pinged my wards," Bayn said, tucking a long blue-black strand of hair behind his pierced pointed ear.

Charlotte was still a little wary of Bayn. Where Kian and Kill could hide their more feral, violent sides, Bayn wore his on the outside and didn't give a shit how uncomfortable it made anyone.

"They are probably staying away from you because we are in winter, and your power is strongest. They would know not to get your attention," Killian replied.

Bayn grunted. "Maybe. To be honest, I'm more worried about Aneirin still being on the loose. If anyone can get the horde creatures back under some kind of control, it would be him. The last thing we need is for the fucker to turn up with a new army."

"I thought he would have made some kind of appearance again by now. He seems to have just vanished like the little rat he is," Killian replied. "Just because he doesn't have all the extra power Morrigan was feeding him doesn't mean he's not dangerous. He was the strongest bard and battle magician of his time. It was what drew the old witch to him in the first place. He's still going to be a hard fucker to kill."

"How do we even know Aneirin is still in Ireland?" Layla asked, toying with a pen in her hand. "I was fighting with Arne and Torsten the night of the invasion, and we saw Aneirin step off the stage when

Morrigan started gloating over Kill. When Bron stabbed her with that sword, Aneirin just...vanished. I swear I blinked, and he was gone."

"He made a portal and got out of there," Ciara said with a firm nod. She had been fighting close with Layla that night too.

Charlotte never thought she would see the day that Ciara would willingly fight alongside one of the Úlfhéðnar wolf shifters, but she and Tor were almost friendly by the time he went back to Norway.

"We have tried to track him," Reeve spoke up. They all turned to look at him. "My brothers have returned to Ireland. They tried to get back before Morrigan attacked but missed it. Anyway, we have tried using magic to track Aneirin, but every time we get a glimmer of his presence, by the time we get to the spot, he is gone."

"Of course he is. He's not some hack magician. He's going to be able to keep himself hidden," Charlotte replied.

Reeve shrugged. "It was better than doing nothing. My brothers want to help."

"Are they magicians too?" Kian asked, raising a red brow.

"Yeah. All the Greatdrakes are. It's kind of our family gift or curse; however, you want to see it. Val, Apollo, and Bas were all studying abroad, and my father was in Italy on a research sabbatical. They are all here now in Ireland to help," Reeve replied. "Cosimo, my dad, says that Aneirin is still here because he can sense his presence like a miasma on the land."

"Interesting," Kian replied, steepling his fingers. "Do you think he's staying in Ireland for a purpose?"

"Dad has a theory that Morrigan has had followers here for centuries, and the ones who remain are helping keep Aneirin hidden while he gathers his strength back," Reeve explained.

"That's a good theory. They might be shielding Aneirin and doing his bidding. We need to find out more. Surely there will be people in the magical community who know who was a supporter of Morrigan before her return," Bron said, her hand flexing around the hilt of her sword.

Technically, it was Killian's blade, but he had let her keep it as a mating gift. Bron was still pouting that she hadn't cut the goddess's head off with the terrifying black blade.

"Charlotte can work with Reeve to hang around the magical underground in Dublin and see if we can find some information on who might be sympathetic to Aneirin's cause," Kenna said, thoughtfully.

"No," Charlotte replied, making the table go quiet.

"But you are the only one of us adept at magic, cuz. It has to be you. None of us will be able to get through the doors because we don't have powers," Lachlan said from beside Reeve.

"I think this is a good plan—" Kian was saying, but Charlotte was no longer listening. She got to her feet, their voices a buzz in her ears. She could tolerate Reeve's presence at these meetings, but she wasn't going to hang out and go on missions with him.

Not so long ago, Reeve Greatdrakes had broken her heart and made her life hell, and be damned if she was going to let him have the opportunity to do it again.

"I said no," Charlotte repeated and strode from the room before anyone could stop her.

2

One of the only benefits of being magically brilliant in a family full of hunters was that when Charlotte locked her room or lab with wards, no one could break into them.

The family could work out another plan without her input. She didn't see why Reeve couldn't go and investigate the Dublin magic workers himself. He knew most of them, for God's sake! Charlotte had better things to do than pretend she liked people enough to socialize with them. Especially with Reeve.

Charlotte opened her notebook and looked over the sigil she had been working on that day. Like all magic, there were many paths to shape an intention. Charlotte liked to draw, and she liked old language, so she had been attracted to any sigil work since she was a child. She had experimented with different traditions until she had finally made her own. Her intention was usually written in a modified version of the ogham alphabet known as the *Beith-luis-nin* before the dashes were connected and encircled within a Celtic knot.

She didn't know why some shapes called to her, but she would wake with the idea in her mind, see the sigil, and do her best to draw it out. The ones that she managed to get right were usually the most powerful.

Charlotte could fight with weapons like her sisters; she just preferred magic. Even the most basic object could turn into a magical weapon with one of her sigils on them.

In a fight, she always carried chalk to draw her battle sigils that she knew off by heart, but having pre-made sigils to use against whatever she was fighting was more practical.

Charlotte had experimented with different types of adhesive patches during the fight with Morrigan's creatures. She had been able to get close enough to throw one at a creature and then detonate it when she was out of the way. She was as lithe as a dancer and could move quickly when she needed to.

It was an adhesive patch that she had in mind for Bron because her sister was always on the move.

Charlotte was so lost in the task of drawing the sigil with silver-infused ink on the flax patches that she only felt the shudder in her warding when it was too late. She was readying something to knock over Reeve when Kian stepped through the lab door.

"What are you doing here?" she blurted out, confused to see the tall antlers and flame-haired prince.

"I've come for Bron and Killian's housewarming tonight, or did you forget that too?" Kian said with an amused smile. "Excellent wards."

"Not excellent enough, it seems." Charlotte put down her pen. "And I didn't forget. I just didn't realize how late it was."

Kian joined her at her worktable. "What are you working on that has your attention?"

"I'm making these as a present for Bron." She offered a patch to Kian, the only person she would allow to touch them before they had finished drying.

Kian hummed thoughtfully, turning the patch and studying the symbol closely. His golden eyes narrowed in concentration, and Charlotte fidgeted under the scrutiny.

"It's a glamour of some kind, isn't it?" he guessed, and she beamed. This was the exact reason she liked Kian.

"That's right. It's to help hide her wings so she's not so conspicuous and can blend into a crowd if she needs to. It should hold as long as it's sticking between her wings," she explained.

"Fascinating. She will appreciate such a thoughtful gift." Kian placed the patch back on her bench. "Is this project the reason you don't want to do some investigating for me?"

Charlotte's shoulders tightened. "No. It's because I'm not a good person for the job. I don't like being sociable with other magicians. Send Imogen. She will do fine. She probably knows the right people to talk to."

"And your fight with Reeve has nothing to do with it?" Kian asked, seeing right through her. He placed a hand on her shoulder to stop them from bunching up even further. "He is an ally in this fight, sister. We need all the help we can get. Can you tell me the cause of your animosity?"

If it had been anyone else but Kian asking, Charlotte probably would have told them to fuck off and mind their own business. Her brother was a prince and not the type of male you didn't answer even if you didn't want to.

"We actually used to be friends. At least, I thought we were," she began, the words hurting in her throat.

Charlotte had met Reeve while they both had been attending Trinity College. They had bonded over magic and the burden that came with hiding what they could do from other people. They both had come from old families that had high expectations of them. He had a natural affinity with magic, making it look so easy that she had been envious and curious. They had plenty of arguments on the nature of magic and how every person wielded it differently.

Reeve was handsome, charming, popular with everyone, and somehow, had befriended Charlotte when most hadn't given her a second glance. Her fragile young heart had fallen hopelessly in love with him. Sometimes she had been led to think that he might have a fondness for her too…right up to the point that she had built herself up to confess her feelings, only to overhear him in the library with one of his many friends Alex. Alex was telling Reeve that he was going to ask the 'sweet nerd with the long legs' out to a party that weekend, seeing how Reeve didn't seem interested.

Reeve had told Alex that he should aim higher than some plain Jane. Charlotte was too boring for the likes of Alex, then he proceeded to list all of her defects with scathing detail before claiming that he was only befriending her because her family had important connections and a library that no one outside of the family had been allowed in.

Charlotte had heard everything. She had turned and run from the library, mortified that she had been duped so completely, and had never spoken to Reeve again. She had left school. She had only been attending because Kenna had wanted her to have some connection with regular life, and she had refused to go back.

What did she care about a history degree when she had magic at her fingertips? As an Ironwood, it was not like she would ever have the chance to be a historian anyway.

"Reeve pretended to be my friend and was using me the whole time. It was humiliating, and I should have known better," Charlotte finished, her arms crossed so tightly that it hurt.

"And you never confronted him over what you heard?" Kian asked, red brows drawn together.

"No. I was too embarrassed. I know it was years ago, but how can I trust someone like that to have my back if we get into a fight with the other magic users? I can't believe anything he says," she replied. She was feeling the cringe all over again at how young and dumb she had been.

"I understand why you would feel that way, but Reeve does seem to want to try and make amends with you."

"He can try all he likes. I still don't trust him."

Kian sighed. "I know, but this fight with Aneirin is too important, and we are still going to need you to work with him. I don't trust anyone else to do this but you, Charlotte. You are highly sensitive to magic and suspicious of everyone. You have the clarity of thought and intuition to know when something isn't right, which will be invaluable." Charlotte opened her mouth to object, but Kian held up a hand to silence her. "I know I'm asking a lot from you with this, so let's make a deal. You help figure out who is supporting Aneirin, and you can come to England to work with me and study with the other fae mages. You can even use the crossing in and out of Faerie to work with them in both lands."

Work with the fae mages? Even having access to Kian's library would be something Charlotte couldn't walk past. She gnawed on her lip, fighting the urge to hold onto her refusal, but oh, she was so tempted by what he offered.

"You fae really know how to drive a bargain," she grumbled, making Kian smile.

"I'll even convince Kenna to let you come without a fuss."

"Now you're playing dirty, you fiend." Charlotte threw up her hands in defeat. "Fine! I'll work with Reeve just this once."

"We have an agreement." Kian took out one of his daggers from his suit and cut his thumb before offering the blade to her. Charlotte had never had an official deal before, but she knew it was Kian's way of showing how serious he was about it. He would never be able to back out of his end, and he trusted Charlotte to do the same. She cut her thumb and pressed it to his.

"It's a deal," she said, and the magical bond settled over her.

Kian took back his knife and straightened his cuffs. "Now, my brilliant sister, we have a party to attend."

Charlotte cringed at the state of her clothes. "I'll go get cleaned up and meet you there." She quickly finished off the patches and hurried to her room, wondering about how long it would take her to get annoyed enough to hex Reeve.

3

Reeve wasn't used to being hated. As a rule, he tried to be friendly to everyone he met and didn't lose sleep if someone didn't like him. He had lost *hours* of sleep over Charlotte Ironwood for a multitude of reasons, ranging from curiosity to worry, anger to outright horniness.

They had been close once, and Reeve had intended to get a hell of a lot closer. Before he could make his move, Charlotte had shut him out completely. He had tried reaching out to talk to her and figure out what he had done for her to utterly turn her back on him. She had never reached back.

For five years, he had taken the hint and left her the hell alone. He had tried dating other people and had done his best to forget about the brilliant girl with the smile that was so rare and so beautiful, it had made his heart stop every time he saw it.

As hard as he had tried, Reeve had never been able to forget the magical Charlotte Ironwood. He knew the Greatdrakes curse was to blame for it, but curses tended to happen when you had a dragon in the family.

The legend claimed that as one of the last great red dragons lay dying, he had passed his power onto Reeve's ancestor Darragh. He had been the dragon's closest friend and a magician. He took the name

Greatdrakes to honor the dragon and ensure no one of his bloodline forgot who they had to thank for their power.

All magic demanded a price, and the vast wellspring of power that had been surging through every generation of Greatdrakes ever since was no exception. The first curse was that at least one of the children got an extra helping of dragon magic in every generation and tended to lose their goddamn minds.

In Reeve's generation, everyone was betting that his eldest brother Valentine would be the crazy one. Hell, he was halfway there already.

The second curse was when their dragon side decided to choose a mate; the man had no say in the matter.

In the beginning, generations of Greatdrakes had investigated the phenomena but found no way to unravel the bond once it happened. Most didn't care because their dragon side always knew best, and the Greatdrakes family was full of happy marriages. They weren't the ones dealing with a pissed-off female magician from a family raised to kill men when they annoyed them.

Reeve had believed the mating thing was total bullshit and had spent five years trying to prove it. It hadn't worked one fucking bit. No matter how great the person he was dating was, they would never be enough because they weren't her. He had seen Charlotte in Trinity Library with her dark braids and knee-high boots, and every part of him had *known* that she belonged to him. It had scared the hell out of him.

Over the years, Reeve thought he had imagined that intensity and longing, right up until a pissed-off goddess had threatened Ireland, and he had found himself at the Ironwood estate. Charlotte had grown even more powerful in their years apart and more beautiful.

And she still hated the very sight of him.

You fucking blew it so hard and don't even know how, he thought.

Reeve had never seen a glare like the one Charlotte had given her mother when she had suggested that they work together. He wished that outright defiance didn't turn him on as much as when she smiled. She was such a force of nature, full of magic and wild beauty, that robbed him of all his self-preservation.

What a fucking mess.

Outside of the mansion, Reeve rolled a cigarette, cursing himself for giving in to the temptation. He was trying to quit, but Charlotte's fierce blue eyes and biting rejection were enough for him to ruin his three-week streak.

"Running off so soon?" Imogen asked, appearing out of nowhere. They had been friends almost as long as Charlotte had been angry at him. He'd met Imogen at a party and had instantly liked her. She was effortlessly cool with her pastel goth rock style and zero fucks attitude.

"I know where I'm not wanted, Gen. I shouldn't have come. Me and my brothers will do the digging, and I'll keep the rest of you in the loop," Reeve replied, placing the cigarette to his lips and lighting it.

"Wow, you suck on that pity cock any harder, and you'll choke," she replied with a roll of her eyes.

Reeve laughed. "Shut up. I'm lucky Charlotte didn't blast me across the other side of Dublin for turning up today."

"Just apologize to her already."

"I would if she told me what the fuck I did," Reeve argued, shoving his cold hands into his pockets. Snow was starting to fall, and he had forgotten his gloves in his hurry to see Charlotte again.

Dumb, pathetic bastard that you are.

Imogen bumped against him. "Don't worry. Kian and Bayn have just arrived through the ice. Kian will talk her into working with you, and that will give you plenty of opportunities to make it up to her."

Reeve had seen the way Charlotte got along with the Blood Prince and couldn't help feeling a stab of irrational jealousy. Kian had his own brilliant mate, but Reeve resented that his own mate preferred the prince too.

His mate. God, he had been hanging around the fae way too much. The Greatdrakes were careful not to mention the M-word, the term too animalistic, but they all knew what it was in their blood and bones. Fucking dragons and their fucking curses.

"You running off so soon?" Bron asked, appearing with Killian.

"Well, there's no point hanging about. Besides, I have some digging to do."

Killian snorted. "Why don't you dig yourself out of the hole Charlotte's put you in first, lad?"

"He doesn't know how," Imogen said with a mocking smile. "She won't tell him."

"Sounds like her. Whatever it is, she will just have to get over it. Will we see you tonight at our place, Reeve?" Bron asked, shaking out her green and black wings.

"We better," Killian added, his emerald eyes shining with trouble. "I'll get some alcohol into Charlotte, and you can apologize to her. Corner her if you have to, just get it done."

"Yes, my prince." Reeve gave him a mocking salute. Fucking pushy fae.

"Look at him, full of attitude where I'm concerned, but scared of wee Charlotte," Killian replied. He spread his wings, took Bron's hand, and they launched into the sky.

"God, I am so jealous of that," Imogen admitted, staring up with longing at their large, dark wings.

"Yeah, me too," Reeve replied. "I guess I'll see you tonight." He butted out his cigarette and headed for his car, eyes on the fading figures in the sky.

Imogen may have been talking about the wings, but he spoke of two mates accepting each other. One problem at a time. First, he needed to figure out how he would make Charlotte listen without blasting him.

THE TWO-STORY HOUSE in the Docklands was lit up with enough wards to have Reeve's magic itching. It was the only house in the area that wasn't covered in Christmas lights. The winter solstice wasn't far away, and all of Dublin seemed intent on enforcing a holiday spirit to pull them out of the terror that Morrigan and her horde had created.

Reeve stepped through the high wrought iron gate and into a lush garden, the kind only a fae could convince to grow so quickly. The couple had wanted privacy but to be close to the city, and the massive trees provided what cover the fence didn't.

Reeve gripped the neck of the expensive, old whiskey he found in the Greatdrakes cellar and knocked on the glossy green door. It swung open to reveal not Killian, but his brother Kian. He looked down at Reeve, and his eyes narrowed.

Well, shit. What had he done now?

"Mr. Greatdrakes, just the person I wanted to see. Do come in," Kian said, opening the door wider while his smile turned sharp. His instincts screamed that it was a trap, but he still stepped into it. He had barely made it through the door when he was suddenly pinned up against it, Kian's forearm angled over his throat.

"What the hell?" Reeve hissed, fighting the urge to release the magic in his fingertips.

"I'm going to make something very clear to you, young Greatdrakes," Kian whispered, his fangs showing. "I haven't had sisters for long, but I am very protective of them all, so appreciate the restraint I'm currently expressing. You have hurt my Charlotte very deeply, and you are going to apologize and beg her forgiveness, or gods help me, you will regret it."

Reeve's blood went hot. "Look, prince, I'm growing pretty fucking tired of people getting in my face about Charlotte. If I *knew* what I had done to her, I would apologize and make amends. It's not like I want her angry at me!"

Kian loosened his grip, but only a little. "She told me that you were a close friend, one of the only people who ever understood her. You betrayed her trust when you decided to list all of her flaws to your friend Alex, including saying you were only friends with her to gain access to the Ironwood library. What kind of idiot are you to do something like that to such a girl?"

Reeves stomach churned as a cloudy day in the university library flashed in his mind. "This is all a big mistake. Alex was a competitive asshole that was sniffing around Charlotte. He wanted to nail her because he thought I liked her and wanted to compete with me. It wasn't because he actually liked her. He only wanted whatever I had. I told him all that stuff so he would think I wasn't interested and leave her the fuck alone. She didn't deserve that piece of shit trying to get in her pants all the time. I swear, Kian, I'd never do anything to hurt her. She's my..." Reeve cut himself off, but it was too late.

Kian's golden eyes narrowed, his arm pressing harder against his throat. "She's your *what*?"

"She's—she's my mate," he wheezed.

Kian's whole demeanor changed instantly. He eased his chokehold on Reeve but didn't let him go. "Explain."

"We had a dragon bond with the family. It's a leftover echo of that."

"Gods. Dragons are even older than I am. I've never heard of them bonding with humans," Kian muttered thoughtfully. "We must talk more of this, but after you speak with her. I take it she doesn't know."

"No fucking way. And I want to keep it like that." Reeve straightened his shirt. "She would hate me even more. At least you know I'm telling the truth when I say I'd never do anything to hurt her. It wouldn't be possible."

Kian nodded. "That's true, but my threat still stands. She is my sister, and I'll kill you if you hurt her."

Fucking overprotective fae. Reeve smiled. "Of course you will, but it's not going to happen."

Kian took the bottle of whiskey from him and pushed him gently down the hall. "See that it doesn't, Greatdrakes."

Reeve managed to make it down into the central part of the house without any more threats. He wondered if the third prince would bail him up about Charlotte and make it a whole family affair.

Reeve stepped into a brightly lit lounge room and spotted Bayn on the couch. He was leaning forward, elbows on his knees, and listening attentively to Moira. The youngest Ironwood played with his long hair and told him about the trick she had taught her dog, King.

The Winter Prince's expression went cold as he caught Reeve's gaze.

And here we go, Reeve groaned inwardly.

Bayn's eyes flicked to Charlotte on the other side of the room and back to Reeve. Very slowly, he tapped the black hilt of a dagger sticking out of the top of his boot.

Reeve fought the urge to roll his eyes because he valued them in his head and gave the prince a curt nod. Message received. Bayn nodded and turned his attention back to Moira.

Reeve's guts unclenched and turned back to the task at hand. Charlotte was taking Bron into another room. The eldest Ironwood gestured at him with her head to follow.

Reeve took a steadying breath, rallied his courage, and went after them.

4

Bron was showing Charlotte her new study, so she took the opportunity to offer a wrapped packet to her older sister. "This is for you. Happy house, whatever," she said.

Bron took the present and smiled wide. "You didn't have to do that."

"I know, but you know how my mind gets when it has a challenge. I hope you find them useful."

Bron opened it and studied the patches and glittering silver with wide eyes. "I...what do they do?"

"They will make your wings invisible so you can blend in when you're on a hunt or trying to hide from someone wanting to catch a glimpse of the Night Prince's elusive mate," Charlotte replied with a teasing smile.

Bron wrapped her in a tight hug. "This is perfect. Thank you. Kill has been having to glamour them for me, and I can't always expect to have him around. Will my wings work fine even though they are invisible?"

"Of course they will. I didn't want to rob you of that advantage."

Bron held her by the shoulders. "You really are the best of sisters. That's why I hope you'll forgive me for this."

"For what?"

Bron turned Charlotte quickly and stepped out the door just as

Reeve stepped in. "Work it out, you two!" Bron said, and the door locked.

Charlotte's face turned red with anger at being trapped in a small room with *him*. Why did her sister want to torment her?

"Did you put them up to this?" she demanded, crossing her arms.

"No. We need to talk, Charlie. This has gone on for five years too long."

Gone was Reeve's mocking smile, and in its place was six feet of pissed magician on a mission. His power was radiating off him in soft waves as he stepped closer. Charlotte took a step back, her own magic burning in challenge.

"I'm sorry," he began. Charlotte's eyes narrowed, but he held up a hand to stop her from speaking. "I'm sorry I didn't try harder to stop you from walking away from me five years ago. I'm sorry you overheard Alex and me that day in the library. You have to understand that I was only saying those things to keep him the fuck away from you. He wasn't a good guy, and I was worried he would try and hurt you to get at me."

Charlotte's stomach clenched. "Kian told you?"

"Well, someone fucking had to because you sure as shit wouldn't do it yourself," Reeve replied. "I can't believe you never told me. Even to confront me."

"I had heard enough, that's why. I *trusted* you. You were my only friend in that place, and I didn't want you lying to me so you could get to the Ironwood library. I didn't need some fake friend," Charlotte snapped.

"I was trying to protect you from him!"

"I'm a goddamn Ironwood. I don't need protection. I could've handled the likes of Alex, but I never thought you had it in you to say such cruel..." she stopped herself before she said something she would regret. Reeve didn't need to know that she had fallen for him and that he had broken her heart.

Reeve ran his hands through his loose hair and paced the study. "I really am so sorry, Charlotte. I valued your friendship, and I should've just told Alex to fuck off. I never meant to hurt you, and all of that stuff I said was fucking bullshit. I was never interested in the Ironwood library. I liked you because you were so damn clever. You understood magic the way I've never seen before and—"

"Stop." Charlotte held up her hand. She didn't want to hear how much he had liked her. It would only open old wounds again. It had taken a long time to close the gaping hole that losing him had caused.

"You don't need to say it, Reeve. We aren't kids anymore, and I've made a deal with Kian. I'll work with you as much as we need to deal with Aneirin. I appreciate the apology, but it doesn't change anything. I don't owe you my friendship. I don't owe you anything at all," she said, swallowing the lump in her throat.

Reeve's jaw clenched, but he muttered, "Fine, Charlie. Whatever you want. Just come to the Greatdrakes mansion tomorrow, and I'll show you what we have been working on to find the bard."

He took a paper clip from his pocket, folded it quickly, and with a burst of his intoxicating magic, it was suddenly a key. He slid it into the lock and opened the door.

"You know, you weren't the only one that lost a friend that day. You walked away without even talking to me when we could've worked this out with one phone call. But you didn't. You let it die. That's how much our friendship meant to you. Fucking nothing," he said and slammed the door behind him.

Charlotte took a shaky breath, her knees giving away as she sank onto the small couch beside her. She tried to squash the guilt that was suddenly worming its way through her.

She shook herself. *No.* She was the injured party there. She wouldn't have been able to trust him again. Even if he had explained what she had heard, she would've always had that kernel of doubt that he didn't give a shit about her.

"Hey, sis, you in here?" Layla's blonde head appeared around the study door. "Fuck, what happened? Are you okay?"

"Yeah. Bron locked me in here with Reeve," Charlotte replied, the lump back in her throat. Layla's brown eyes softened with worry. She sat down next to her and put an arm covered in colorful tattoos around her shoulder.

"What a bitch move. Still, you guys probably needed to have it out, even if you feel shitty now," Layla said, squeezing her. "You okay?"

"Yeah, just pissed off."

"Well, use that energy to find Aneirin, and then you'll never have to deal with Reeve again." Layla looked around the study at Bron's weapons on the walls and books everywhere. "God, who would've thought Bron would shack up with a fae? If you had even suggested it six months ago, I would've laughed myself sick."

Charlotte managed a smile. "True. At least she chose well. I like having big brothers."

"Me too. And their friends are cool even if they aren't here," Layla said, pulling a displeased face.

"Who's not here? Arne?"

Layla's lips formed a red pout. "Kind of hoped he would be. I liked him and Torsten, and I've never met an elf before. I had lots of questions I wanted to ask."

"And the fact that Arne is gorgeous and dangerous with those two massive swords has nothing to do with it," Charlotte teased.

"I mean not *everything*," Layla admitted with a grin. "I wanted to see Ciara and Tor do their whole staring contest to see who's the bigger alpha too. You can't put a price on that kind of entertainment."

Charlotte laughed softly, and some of the hurt inside her eased up. "Well, she and Lachie are off on a hunt tomorrow in the Carpathians, so I'm sure she'll find another wolf or some other monster to fight."

"I'm so glad I'm not with her this time. She's bloody relentless when she's tracking. I've never been so tired and cold in my life, and it's like she didn't even feel it," Layla griped.

"I hoped she would stay and help us find Aneirin."

"You know Ciara. She isn't happy unless she's in a forest hunting something twice her size." Layla bumped her shoulder into Charlotte's. "There's plenty of us still around. And just think, after we get the bastard, you can put a hex on Reeve and won't get into trouble. Think of it is as a Christmas present just for you."

Charlotte laughed and hugged her little sister closer, grateful that Layla always knew how to pull her out of a mood. "You know, I might just do that."

5

Charlotte had never been to the Greatdrakes mansion in Dublin's medieval quarter. She knew it was near St. Audoen's Church somewhere, but that was the extent of her knowledge. Imogen, who *had* been at least to the outside of the house, had told her that it had no number and that she would have to feel it out.

Helpful as always, Gen. Charlotte couldn't give her too much of a hard time because Imogen was suffering through the mother of all hangovers.

From her sister's groaning mumbles, Charlotte had gathered that Imogen had gone out after Bron's party and had made out with some hot goth guy at a club before coming home at dawn.

It was so typical of Imogen. She had never felt the responsibility to the Ironwood name or reputation the way the others did.

Imogen had almost drowned when she was eleven, and after that near-death experience, her sister had changed. She was determined to fit as much life in between her hunting jobs as possible.

Imogen had always done whatever the fuck she wanted, wore what she wanted, said what she wanted, and didn't give a damn what anyone thought about her.

Charlotte envied her for all of that, more than she could possibly articulate.

She, on the other hand, had spent a full twenty minutes trying to figure out what to wear to the meeting with the Greatdrakes. Her opinions and feelings towards Reeve were complicated, but his father, Cosimo, was someone to be respected and feared. He had a decent enough acquaintance with Kenna and David, though Charlotte had never met him before.

Charlotte straightened her cream knit sweater over her cold hands and crossed the green grounds of St. Audoen's. She had put make-up on to hide her sleepless night. She didn't want Reeve to think that his apology or explanation had gotten to her.

It wouldn't change anything between them. Not unless she wanted it to. They were such different people now, and it was like they were starting everything new again.

"Focus on the house, not on Reeve's drama," she said under her breath.

Feel it out. What did that mean...Oh? Oh. Magic smacked Charlotte hard enough to cause her to stumble in her knee-high boots.

"Shit." Charlotte turned right, following the pulse of power. It was so strong that she was surprised that the ordinary people around her didn't feel it. In the corner of her eye, she saw a gold and red shimmer.

"There you are," she murmured. She stopped in front of a metal gate, set into an ancient stone wall. She wasn't sure it was even visible to a non-magical eye. Charlotte went to touch the gate and stopped before the wards flayed the skin off her hands.

"That's just rude," she muttered.

Reeve knew she was coming, had invited her, so why was the house still in battle mode? Maybe it was Reeve still being pissed off at her.

Or it's a test, Charlotte realized with a small smile. Well, she would show a house full of entitled male magicians exactly what she was capable of.

Charlotte pulled out a small patch of woven silver from her pocket and tossed it at the gate. Red and orange warding caught the patch, and they flashed in bright, fiery lines and sigils.

"Impressive, but not unbeatable," she whispered and allowed

herself a small cocky smile. Charlotte had many talents, but hacking into people's magic spells and overriding them was her rarest gift.

She placed two fingers to the silver patch still caught in the web of power and closed her eyes. Charlotte took three slow breaths and fell into the magic. She could feel the intention of the magician who had made them, the raw power and a touch of malice thrown in.

She didn't know how she did it and could barely explain it in simple terms, but she could always find the core knot, or holding point, in a spell. She let her own magic curl around the knot, and with one sharp pull, the warding unraveled like a broken spider web.

Charlotte opened her eyes and caught the silver patch before it fell to the pavement.

"Hmm, let's see what you are all hiding that you need such wards," Charlotte whispered. She opened the gate and walked up a stone path.

If she didn't know she was in Dublin, she would've thought she was at a country house. The trees and gardens surrounding the stone mansion were old and established.

The house itself was at least three stories, but it shone with so much magic that in some light, Charlotte thought she could see a tower or two.

You can't expect an ancient family of magicians to have an average house. Especially not a family that had inherited their magic from a dragon. Charlotte had always taken that story as a legend, but she was starting to have her doubts. It felt like the very air around her was pulsing with a strange, ancient power.

Everywhere she looked, dragons were carved into the stonework, curling around stained glass windows, and set as statues amongst the wild gardens surrounding her.

Charlotte stopped at a red door with a snarling dragon's head knocker. She checked it for any other nasty wards before she lifted the golden ring and knocked three times.

The door swung open to reveal a tall, young man in dark jeans, a navy waistcoat, and a deep purple shirt that matched his eyes. His hair was trimmed at the sides but had a mop of long dark brown curls on top.

"You must be the Ironwood," he greeted with a disarming smile.

"And which brother are you?" Charlotte replied.

"Basset. Bas. The second youngest to Reeve, the baby." He opened the door wider.

"Oh shit, she broke through the wards? Val is going to be *pissed*," a cheerful voice said, and a golden-haired man charged down a set of stairs. "Well, don't stand out there. Come in, cutie."

"Charlotte, not cutie," she said and finally walked in.

The golden one grinned like a fiend and looked her over.

"I'm Apollo. Damn, baby boy really is punching above his weight with you. How's Imogen? Haven't seen her in ages."

"Hungover," she said, with zero surprise that her sociable sister knew this Greatdrakes as well.

"How did you get through those wards? You should've been crisped from touching them."

"For God's sake, Apollonius, let the girl in and stop cornering her in the hall," another tall man said. He was lean and handsome like the other two Greatdrakes, with silver shot through his raven hair and the most vivid sapphire blue eyes.

"I apologize for these heathens, Charlotte. They were supposed to lower the wards for you, but it seems they don't know how to follow orders."

"Aw, come on, Dad! We wanted to see how good she was," Apollo said and flinched under his father's disapproving glare.

Cosimo Greatdrakes offered her a warm smile and held out a long hand. "It's a pleasure to meet you, Charlotte."

She found herself smiling back and shook his hand. His magic thrummed under his warm skin at the touch.

"Hello, sir. Kenna and David send their regards."

"It's been too long since we've caught up. We will have to change that. And please, call me Cosimo. Sir makes me feel a thousand years old," he replied. "Come this way, and we'll have some tea. Reeve and Valentine are waiting in the parlor."

Charlotte followed Cosimo through halls of dark wooden walls decorated with oil paintings of famous magicians. She did her best not to get distracted by the occasional magical artifact humming on stands or under glass.

Cosimo opened a set of double doors, and they stepped into a room bright with winter sunshine.

Reeve was lounging on a velvet chaise. His shoulders straightened, and his face lit up when he spotted her despite their spat the night before. His magic pulsed, and she felt its warmth from the other side of the room.

Charlotte told herself that the little flutter in her stomach was only nerves. She didn't know how someone so scruffy could be so attractive at the same time. Charlotte's eyes lifted to the raven-haired stranger in the room.

Charlotte had heard a lot of stories about the eldest Greatdrakes. The often repeated one was that he was the most powerful magician to be born in Europe, not just Ireland, in the last hundred years. Now she knew it wasn't a story.

Charlotte could feel the magic radiating in the man's aura, and she knew without a doubt that he was the creator of the wards.

Dressed in a black button-down shirt and expensive black jeans, he looked the most like Cosimo. He had his father's high cheekbones and dark hair but lacked his warm expression. Valentine's gray eyes narrowed as he looked her over.

"Nice wards," she said, trying not to straighten her shoulders at his scrutiny.

Valentine's mouth rose in the corners, but it wasn't exactly a smile.

"I'll make them stronger next time."

Charlotte looked down her nose at him. "You do that. I enjoy a challenge."

"Back off, Val. She's not an enemy," Reeve growled at his brother. He offered Charlotte an apologetic smile. "Thanks for coming, Charlie."

She didn't bother to correct him. She wasn't going to let the pet name or any of the Greatdrakes get under her skin. She sat on a comfortable antique chair that Cosimo offered her.

Bas went to the tea tray and started pouring. He gave Charlotte another charming grin, "How do you have it?"

"Just as it is. Thank you," she replied, accepting the cup and saucer. "Well, isn't this civilized?"

"I try my best, Charlotte, but honestly, they are about as well-mannered as tomcats," Cosimo said with a sigh.

Charlotte blew on her tea and tried not to make it too obvious she was sending her magic through the cup.

"It's not poison," Valentine said with a grin.

"Considering your wards were designed to flay me, you'll forgive me for being suspicious."

"Jesus, you set them up to flay? What the fuck is the matter with you?" Reeve snapped.

Valentine shrugged. "I wanted to see if she was as good as you claimed, little brother."

Charlotte ignored them and turned to Cosimo. "So is it a family thing to have you all named after magicians and occultists?"

Cosimo nodded. "Everyone except Reeve. He was named after my late wife's father. Also a practitioner, but not famous. Are you really the only Ironwood that does magic?"

"Yes. My sisters can use certain things I make for them, but none of them are actively practicing," Charlotte replied and sipped her tea.

Cosimo's eyes softened. "Kenna has no gift for magic either, so you've taught yourself? All alone."

Charlotte pushed her glasses up her nose, trying to hide her sudden awkwardness. "The Ironwood library had a lot of books, and what I couldn't find, I learned through trial and error. I love magic, so I didn't feel alone."

"Well, you certainly aren't anymore. You're welcome to ask me anything about magic that you like," Cosimo said with a firm nod.

"You can have my number and also call me whenever you like, Charlotte," Apollo added with mock seriousness. Reeve threw him a glare, and Bas turned red from stifling his laughter.

Cosimo frowned at them. "Let's get to business, shall we?"

6

Reeve thought he wouldn't be affected by Charlotte being in the Greatdrakes manor, but as usual, he was wrong.

He didn't think there had been a woman outside the family in the house since his mother died ten years ago. Cosimo had a strict 'do not bring your sleazy hookups into my house' policy, and his brothers preferred not to have permanent girlfriends due to their near-constant study.

It was rare for a magician to be interested in anything other than magic anyway.

Reeve was also doing his best not to show how much he loved that Charlotte had pushed aside Val's wards like they were no more than an inconvenience.

You are definitely showing it, little bro, Bas touched his mind. Having a telepath in the family could be a real pain in the dick, especially when he could stretch out his gift to include other people.

I can't believe you totally blew it with this chick. She's way more intelligent than you and positively vibrating with power, Apollo chimed in. *Even Val is impressed by her.*

Impressed is a strong word, came Val's deep voice. *But I can agree that she's definitely too good for you. Perhaps you should step aside and let another Greatdrakes win her over.*

Perhaps I should burn your precious tower to the ground. Reeve flipped off Val before he could stop himself.

Cosimo threw them an irritated glance. He always knew when they were communicating, even if they never said a word out loud. Reeve threw up a mental shield to keep them out of his thoughts.

Charlotte was looking between them with a curiosity she couldn't hide. She looked fucking adorable with her hair in a braid, long enough that it would wrap around his wrist.

At least twice.

He was a weak man for knee-high riding boots too, and that so soft-looking cream sweater that he wanted to rub his face over. It was like she had purposely worn an outfit designed to send him mad.

God, he couldn't entertain those thoughts when they were meant to have a serious meeting. It was like a strange dream to have her sitting with his family, drinking tea and talking about magic with his father.

"Let's get to business, shall we?" Cosimo said, knocking Reeve out of his increasingly lusty thoughts. "Now, the boys and I were out of the country when Morrigan attacked, so if you have any insight that you can give us about Aneirin, it would be helpful. We only know what Reeve does, and he wasn't in all of the action."

"He's also not the baby sister to three ancient fae that know more about Aneirin than any living being," Bas added.

Charlotte nodded. "I know that he was Welsh originally. Killian said that he was a battle bard that caught Morrigan's attention with his ability to whip men into blood lust. She made him immortal and gave him a place as one of her generals. He was sent to Ireland to be her harbinger and rally anyone who would support her."

"That much we've put together ourselves," Val said, but she ignored him.

"My sister Bron witnessed him coming through a portal from Tir Na Nog and said the ruins were packed with followers. He had communicated with them before even stepping foot into Ireland." Charlotte took a sip of tea before continuing.

"Bron said that Aneirin's influence was so strong that she wanted to *worship* him. Kill got her out of there, but I saw her afterward. She was white and shaking and utterly terrified. And before you even think of getting an attitude about weak women," she shot a glare in Val's direction, "my sister braved Morrigan's castle to get Kill out, and that didn't scare her like Aneirin did. She had no control when it came to him."

Bas's dark brow furrowed. "That kind of mental influence would take a lot of power. With Morrigan gone and her power broken, we can assume that Aneirin won't be working with the same amount of magic."

"He was still powerful enough when he was mortal to get the attention of a goddess," Reeve pointed out. "Even without extra juice from Morrigan's bond with him, he's not going to be some weak pushover."

Charlotte nodded. "Reeve is right. According to my sisters, Aneirin portaled himself out of the way as soon as Bron hit Morrigan with the sword. He wasn't even wounded, which means he's staying quiet for another reason."

"He must've known she was going to be fucked from that sword to just abandon her like that," Apollo mused.

"It's a god-killing sword. Even if Arawan came to take her before Bron finished the job, Morrigan was taken to the lands of Annwn. It's an underworld realm that not even the gods can escape from," Valentine added, his gray eyes darkening in thought.

"Not without help." Charlotte placed her empty cup and saucer down on the coffee table. They all looked at her curiously.

"What do you mean, Charlotte?" Cosimo coaxed.

"I've been going over and over this in my mind. If I was Aneirin, what would I want?" When they didn't answer, she said slowly, "I'd want to summon the other two generals and get enough power behind me to get my goddess and her god power back or carry out her original plan. According to Killian, the other two generals were still locked up in Tir Na Nog when she *died*, for lack of a better word, but we don't know they aren't free now. Her power shattered, which means any spells that she had active would've been broken too, and that includes the control she had on the Dread Horde."

"Damn. That does make a lot of sense. And it would take a lot of magic to open a portal to Tir Na Nog to get the generals here," Reeve said and got to his feet. "Let's take this to the library, and we can show Charlotte the tracking we've been doing."

Charlotte's big eyes lit up at the word *library*, and Reeve hid a grin. She might hate him now, but he was going to do everything he could to soften her up. And nothing made Charlotte happy like a library.

~

THE GREATDRAKES LIBRARY took up a whole tower of the house. It wound up and up until it reached an observatory at the top. Each level had a floor of work areas and tables. Charlotte bit her full bottom lip as she looked around.

"There have to be some perks with working with me," Reeve whispered to her.

"There is. I'm going to go to England to study with the fae mages," she replied. Reeve had wondered what Kian had promised her in order to convince her to help them. That sure was something that would've been irresistible to any human magician, not just Charlotte.

But she will be in England. Fuck, it was like a kick to his balls. He couldn't think of that now.

"That would be an amazing opportunity," he replied, forcing a smile on his face.

"He's playing it cool to hide his jealousy," Apollo said, ever the unhelpful bastard.

Val rolled out the map of Ireland that they had been working with. Reeve had used Bron's map of all the sacred sites to mark them in, so they knew what places to monitor.

"Everywhere you see a black cross are known sightings of Aneirin, before and after the attack," Cosimo said, folding his arms. Charlotte bent over to study the sites, and Reeve caught Bas giving her ass a look.

Get your dirty eyes off her! Reeve snapped at his brother.

Bas shrugged nonchalantly. *I'm a mere mortal with basic instincts, and she bent over right in front of me. And it's such a nice ass.*

You are a basic bitch, all right. We need her help. Don't be a creeper. Reeve ran a frustrated hand through his hair.

Something you should remember when you are looking at her like a kicked dog, Valentine added wryly.

"Reeve said that you have been trying to track Aneirin's magic and are having problems," Charlotte said, with a frown at the map. "What's the issue?"

"He moves too quickly. By the time we get a fix on him and get to the site, he's gone," Cosimo explained.

"Then he's using a spell that alerts him when someone is using magic to try and find him. We need to find a way to counteract that without him realizing it. Let me have a think about that," she said like it was the simplest thing in the world. "If we are right about his plan to summon the generals, the portal will need the power of a sacred site, which we have areas marked up and know of."

"He will also need a fuck ton of power," Bas added.

Charlotte's brows drew together into her thinking face. "When he came through the portal, he had worshippers there."

"The power of the faithful," Reeve said.

"Exactly. This time, he's going to need something more. He doesn't have Morrigan's dark power bolstering him anymore, so a few followers aren't going to cut it." Charlotte looked at them expectantly. "Magicians, gentlemen. He's going to need magicians. To take their power through a collective ritual or steal it from them. As discussed at the meeting yesterday, Aneirin is probably being hidden by people who supported Morrigan and him. They might be doing the recruiting for him to keep him out of our eye line."

Cosimo rubbed at his chin. "My gut tells me you're right, Charlotte. I'm just not sure how we can flush out any followers."

"Magicians are gossipy. Someone will let something slip. We just need to be at the right place at the right time," Apollo replied, and his eyes lit up with impish mischief. "Maybe we need to hit the Monkey Paw and see what the word is. I can whip up some party favors with something special that will loosen the tongue."

"Are you suggesting drugging a bar full of magic users?" Charlotte asked, slightly outraged.

"It would hardly be the first time," Valentine commented.

"Aw, come on. My party favors are natural, and they are feel-good. They aren't malicious or dangerous!"

"I do wish you would use your alchemy for something better than party drugs, but desperate times and all that," Cosimo conceded.

Reeve turned to Charlotte with a teasing grin. "You better dust off your party dress, Charlie."

Her expression narrowed but turned to Apollo. "How much time do you need to make them?"

"I should have a decent batch ready to go by tomorrow night if that's not too soon?" Apollo gave her a charming as hell smile. "If I make them extra good, I don't suppose you will save a dance for me, Ironwood? That is if a group of uptight hunters even *learn* how to dance up in that fancy estate?"

"Of course we learn how to dance. They would have to be spectacular to convince me," Charlotte said, looking him over. "And if you step on one of my toes, I'll break yours."

Apollo tossed his head back and laughed. "You got a deal, Ironwood."

"Wait, wait, he can't dance for shit, Charlotte. You should dance with me instead," Bas argued. Reeve prayed to all the gods to give him the strength to deal with his fucking brothers.

"We will have to see, Basset." Charlotte glanced at her watch. "If there's nothing else, I really should be going. I'll start working on a way to track Aneirin without alerting him."

"You really think you can do that?" Valentine asked.

Charlotte shrugged. "I've done something similar before, so I don't see why not. I have felt Aneirin's magic, and I should have enough to work with. It's not like I've never gone into a spell from behind and hacked it. I dealt with your wards easily enough, didn't I?"

Reeve took his phone from his pocket and snapped a photo of Valentine's disbelieving and outraged face. It made him love Charlotte a little more.

"Excellent, we have a plan," Cosimo said and took Charlotte's hand. "It has been a delight, Miss Ironwood. You will come back soon, yes? You are always welcome."

"I'm sure that by the time we get Aneirin, you will be sick of the sight of me," she replied, giving him a genuine smile.

All the Greatdrakes men decided they would walk Charlotte out to the gate.

"Do you need a ride? I'm happy to take you home," Reeve offered.

"No need. I have things to do around the city first." Charlotte hesitated and added, "Thank you for the offer."

"Any time you need a ride, you give me a call," Bas said with an innocent smile.

Reeve was going to kill his brothers as soon as she was out of sight.

"Text me the details for tomorrow night. My number is still the same, but if you need it..."

Reeve shook his head. "Nope. I still have it."

Charlotte opened the gate. "Until then. Keep me posted if anything interesting pops up." She gave them a small wave before disappearing down the street.

All five Greatdrakes men waved back, even Val, and watched her go.

"I don't need to tell you to protect that girl with your life, do I?" Cosimo said sternly.

"No, sir," Reeve replied and was surprised when the rest of his brothers mumbled the same thing.

7

Charlotte was in her favorite corner of the Ironwood library when Killian and Kian came in. She was busily scribbling down ideas on her morning and trying not to think too hard about all the books in the Greatdrakes house.

"How did the meeting go, little sis?" Killian asked, taking a chair beside her.

"Good, I think. Want to know our theories?" she said, putting her pen down.

"A house full of magicians ought to have some decent ones," Kian replied.

Charlotte broke down her visit, excitement in her voice that she couldn't hide. She had never had the chance to sit down with a group of expert magicians like that. She didn't mind their curious flirting and brotherly banter. Once she had gotten over her nerves, it had been almost...nice.

"Aneirin summoning the generals. Fuck, that is a nightmare waiting to happen," Killian groaned.

"Are you sure they were still locked up in Tir Na Nog? Why would Morrigan lock them up anyway?" Charlotte asked.

"Because she was a psycho who wanted to have her generals at her beck and call. Don't think of them in a cell. They weren't. They were bound to the castle because she didn't want them wandering too far from her. They were the ones that really kept the horde under control, too," Killian explained.

Charlotte tapped her pen on her notebook. "Do you think that without Morrigan's power holding them, they would have wandered off?"

"Doubtful. They have a lot of power and authority, and they wouldn't just pass that up even with Morrigan gone. If anything, they would be busy trying to hold the power base together," Kian replied.

"Or they will be putting their own nefarious plans into action," Killian added. His wings bristled a little in irritation. "I don't like the idea of either one of them being loose in the world again. Morrigan was a monster, but she kept them in check."

"Who are they? You always refer to them as *the generals*, but I've never heard their names. If I know them, it might help me get some kind of an idea on what magic they could be using." Charlotte watched Killian and Kian have a silent argument before Kian nodded.

"It used to be considered bad luck to talk about them, in case one of their agents overheard," he said and crossed his arms uncomfortably. "How well do you know Welsh myth?"

"I know a little? Why?"

"Aneirin is Welsh, and so is the second general, Hafgan. He was one of the kings of the underworld. He had a rivalry with Arawan."

Charlotte froze. "Arawan, who took Morrigan that night?"

"The very one. It's only a guess, but maybe Morrigan took Hafgan as some kind of deal with Arawan. That's why she summoned him and said he owed her a favor," Killian replied. "Hafgan was always at war with him, so Morrigan recruiting Hafgan would have gotten the fucker out of Arawan's hair."

"Do you think Arawan would know if Hafgan is loose? Could we find out?" Charlotte asked.

Killian laughed. "You really want to try and ask him? The Lord of the dead isn't exactly on speed dial, lass."

Charlotte shrugged. "You never know. He might want to tell us."

"No. We are *not* summoning Arawan. We can't even think to attempt it," Kian said firmly.

"Why not?" Imogen asked. She was leaning against a bookshelf with a frown on her face. Charlotte had no idea how long she had been standing there, listening in on their conversation.

"Because it's an insanely bad idea. You never, ever fuck with a death god…or a god at all! The price they ask for is always too high. Arawan isn't some benevolent Santa Claus that will come when called and be pleased about it. If he wanted to help us, he would," Killian argued. "Hafgan is the real problem. He's a fucker. And he's indestructible, in the very literal sense. His battles with Arawan are legendary because the bastard can continuously regenerate."

Charlotte rubbed at her temples. A legendary king that could regenerate was going to give her a migraine. She forced herself to ask, "And the third general?"

"He is a true mystery because there are so many rumors and stories about him. He was the only one that Morrigan recruited from another Otherworld," Kian said and started to pace. "Arne has been able to give us a little more information about him, and none of it is good news. The general's name is Vili, and he used to be a Dökkálfar king. A dark elf."

"His family claims that they are descended from Kvasir, the legendary being born of the saliva of both the Aesir and Vanir. Kvasir was the wisest being ever created, and he traveled through all Nine Realms spreading knowledge and his seed by the sounds of things before he was murdered, and his blood turned into the Mead of Poetry."

Killian's wings ruffled. "Which means, if it's true, this dark elf is insanely smart as well as being a king, a warrior, and my favorite part… He wields the cursed sword, Tyrfing."

"A cursed sword as well? Oh, come on, that's not playing fair at all," Imogen complained.

"What's the curse?" Charlotte asked.

"That it sheds blood whenever it's drawn. Vili has been the only one to wield it that can control the curse."

Charlotte chewed the inside of her cheek, mind ticking over. She needed to tell Reeve all of this, and maybe they could look in their library for other references.

"Okay, but why would a king give up his throne to serve a god not even in his pantheon?" she said.

"Who knows. Arne said that Vili was a scary, violent bastard who was going to get overthrown by a rival who made an alliance with a disgruntled faction of light elves. Vili had a light elf wife, a princess, and treated her like shit. They wanted her back and started a rebellion in Vili's kingdom," Killian explained. "Vili left with Morrigan, and if I had to guess, I'd say she promised him help to get his kingdom back, or she offered him a better one."

"So what you are saying is that we need to do everything we can to make sure the scariest bastards ever don't leave Tir Na Nog," Imogen said with a small laugh. "We are so fucked."

"No, we aren't. We just need to find Aneirin and stop him," Charlotte replied with way more bravado than she felt. "I'm going to a magicians' club with the Greatdrakes tomorrow night. We have a plan to find Aneirin's followers. We *will* find him. The world has changed since he was last here. No one can hide for long."

Kian smiled at her. "I hope so, little one. I'll talk to the fae mages and see if they can help with the problem of the spell Aneirin is using to warn him when he's being tracked."

"Here's hoping the bastard is only after the generals and isn't going to start a pissing contest with Arawan to get Morrigan back," Killian said, with a troubled frown. "That will get so messy, so quickly."

"Why? He might not care and kick her out of his realm to save himself the drama," Imogen said, toying with the end of her lavender braid.

"That's not how he works." Kian shared a loaded look with Killian before he said to Imogen, "Once Arawan claims something, he will never, ever give it back willingly."

"Oh, so scary," Imogen said irreverently. She nudged Charlotte with the toe of her boot. "I want to come tomorrow night too. It's been forever since I've seen the Greatdrakes brothers. Are they as good-looking and charming as ever?"

Charlotte didn't have to think about it. "Yes."

"How's their hot dad doing?" Imogen waggled her eyebrows.

"Still hot and absolutely brilliant. I want to pick his brain apart."

"What a coincidence. I want to pick his clothes apart." Imogen let out a filthy laugh. "Maybe you're my sister after all."

Charlotte was back in her lab, thinking about Aneirin and the other two generals and what it might take to defeat them if they did break out. Her phone buzzed, making her jump. She expected a meme from Lachie because he was the only one who ever messaged her. Instead, it was from an unknown number.

I'm sorry if my brothers were full on and made you uncomfortable at all. They haven't been home for a while and have gone feral in the wild.

Charlotte took a shaky breath. She had never thought that she would see the day that Reeve would be messaging her again.

The eternally hurt part of her wanted to lash out, but God, she was so tired of being angry, especially at him. She didn't think she would ever be able to trust him again with anything other than work. That didn't mean she had to be hostile.

Your brothers are all quite charming. I expected them to be more like you. Okay, so maybe she wasn't ready to let go of *all* of her hostility.

We have different ideas about what's charming. Val tried to flay you.

Tried is the correct word. He was only being cautious. I don't think he's as grumpy as he likes to portray.

He one hundred percent is that grumpy. I'm not going to tell them that you found them charming, or they'll become even more insufferable.

Charlotte smiled at the text before she wrote back, telling him an abbreviated version of what Kill and Kian had said about the generals.

Fuck. Here I thought you would give me some good news, Reeve shot her back with a line of crying emojis.

Sorry, too bad. Can you check out your library and see if there's anything on either Hafgan or Vili? I want to believe they are still locked up, but I doubt it. Knowledge is power. We need to be ahead of them if they do break into our world.

Will do. I'll let you know if we find anything.

Charlotte stared at the messages, and something ached in her chest. Texting Reeve had always been easier than talking to him, mainly because it had gotten to the stage where Charlotte couldn't hide the crush anymore, and she would turn into a sweating wreck.

Maybe texting him would make it easier to work with him again. She put her phone on silent, ignored the rush of warmth up her spine as she saved his number, and got back to work.

8

The Monkey Paw was a funky hipster club in Temple Bar. The front half was for normal humans and tourists; the back half had a secret alley entranceway for anyone and anything with a drop of magic in their veins. Unless you could see the glowing sigil marking the entrance, you would never find it.

Reeve hadn't been back to the club since before the fight with Morrigan. He had been involved in a messy breakup with a girl called Sarah and had gone to the Paw to drink away his sorrows. Most of his hookups and attempts at relationships ended up the same way. He was still too caught up in a girl who hated him.

A girl who was coming down a set of stairs at that second. Reeve's heart did a weird double beat. Charlotte had her thick, glorious hair out in dark waves that he wanted to bunch in his hands. Reeve registered black knee-high boots, a red skirt, and a black off-the-shoulder top. His brain hazed as he reached her red lips.

"You starting the party without us," Imogen teased, giving him a half hug as they joined him at the bar. "Where are your sexy brothers?"

"Apollo is buzzing like a social butterfly. Bas got caught up in generals research, and Val was too busy being a Byronic drama king to come along."

Imogen pouted. "Aw. I haven't seen V-plates in ages."

Reeve choked on his drink. "Fuck, Gen. Please call him that to his face."

"I would if he ever turned up." Imogen lit up. "Apollo!" She collided with him, and he spun her around.

"Imogen Ironwood, you foxy bitch. I'm so glad to see you." Apollo kissed her cheek. "What are you drinking?"

"Something strong."

"That's my girl. Charlotte, you look lovely."

"Thanks, Apollo," she replied, cheeks pinking. "How's the plan going?"

Apollo grinned. "It's going to be happening in about twenty minutes when those party favors kick in."

Imogen poked him. "Hey, where's my party favor?"

"They aren't for us, my sweet. They are going to loosen everyone up so we can get information out of them." Apollo gave her a shit-stirring smile. "Besides, last time we were together, and you had one of my treats, you—"

"If you finish that sentence in front of my sister, I swear to God, I will fuck your hot dad and become your new step-mom," Imogen hissed.

Apollo roared with laughter. "Fuck, I've missed you, Gen."

Reeve shook his head at their antics. He was trying not to stare at Charlotte, like the rest of the bar. It wasn't only because she was all long legs and glossy hair. She *radiated* magic, and that kind of power always drew people's attention.

"You still drink gin and tonics?" he asked, needing to say something useful.

Charlotte nodded. "That would be great."

Reeve waved at the bartender and ordered them all another round of drinks. He had thought for years about what he wanted to talk to her about, and now he had the chance, his brain was failing him.

"Do you think Bas is going to find anything?" she asked.

"If anyone can, it will be Bas. He'll be able to comb through the library quicker than all of us together. His magic is mostly telepathy and telekinesis, but his psychometry is unparalleled. He's working through each library level, touching books and searching. He'll be at it for a while," Reeve replied.

He passed her the gin and tonic, tapped his beer against it, and shot her a wink. She smiled a little, and his heart struggled again.

"That sounds amazing. I'd love to be able to read books and objects that way," she said. "He must have excellent control over it, so he's not swamped with information all the time."

"It's taken him years. When he was first learning, it was overwhelming for him. But then he got good at it, and he became insufferable because he could touch your hand and know everything you had done that day, good and bad. We all had to learn to block him in order to get any privacy."

Charlotte laughed and quickly stopped like she had surprised herself.

"I can't even imagine. I always wished that someone else in the family had magic. I never thought how bad that could be. Siblings are bad enough when they are non-magical. Speaking of, where did ours go?"

Reeve turned and spotted Imogen's bright hair on the dance floor with Apollo. They looked like they were having a great time.

"God, I hate that she can do that," Charlotte said and then flushed.

"Do what? Dance?"

"No, just...fit in. It's always been so easy for her."

"Imogen doesn't fit in, Charlie. She doesn't give a fuck, and it looks like the same thing." Reeve had a mouthful of beer to steady his nerves. "You're not made to fit in. You're too powerful, and everyone is always going to be jealous of that."

Charlotte shrugged. "I don't know if that's the reason. How would they even know?"

"They can feel it. I would say you need to shield it better, but it will give any dickheads a pause before they get all sleazy on you." Reeve did his best not to sound too happy about that. He could feel people watching her, even if she was oblivious to them.

Charlotte put her drink down and reached into her black clutch purse. "I've started working on this. Will you have a look at it and see what you think?"

Reeve took the piece of paper from her and tried to hide his smile. Magic was always going to be common ground between them. That she was even showing him something was better than Christmas.

He unfolded the paper and looked at the sigil. It pulsed with magic even if it was not activated. Charlotte's power always felt like electricity under his skin, a not unpleasant snap and tingle of static that he had missed.

"Woah, this is to help counteract whatever Aneirin is doing?" he guessed, tracing a finger over the lines.

"Yes. I want it to work as a web that will sit behind his spell. I don't want it to touch his because he will feel it."

"But if it's behind it, he will still feel his spell working, but yours will be catching the magic," Reeve said, blown away by her ingenuity.

"Exactly. With any luck, he won't even know it's there," she replied, excitement in her voice.

"It sounds amazing, Charlie. I don't know what you need me for."

She tapped the paper. "I'm bad at subtlety. Stop smiling. I'm trying to be serious. I need something that's going to lock it into the right spot. If I use it as it is, it'll be like a door slam, as opposed to a gentle click into place. Does that make sense?"

"Perfect sense. Okay, let me have a look," Reeve said, smoothing the paper out on the bar. "You have a pen?"

Charlotte passed him a pencil, which was so like her that he had to bite down his smile. He made a few notes, his own magic humming and guiding him as he broke the spell down. Reeve's power was always more intuitive, so he let it reveal what it would. Something about a corner loop in her knotwork made him pause.

"This is the problem here," he said, circling it.

Charlotte leaned closer, the heat of her body and her rose-tinted scent making him go tingly all over.

"How can you tell?"

Reeve was always bad at trying to explain his magic to other people, but Charlotte had always been interested and patient with his answers.

"It's the discordant note in the song. Everything else is like graceful strings, and this is a symbol clash. I can feel it."

Charlotte frowned and looked at the sigil again, turning it this way and that. "I'll have to look at it at home where I can think properly. Thanks—" she cut off as a tall blonde closed in on them.

Oh, Jesus, not tonight.

"Is this her?" Sarah barreled in. Reeve's ex looked at Charlotte like some kind of gross bug.

"Don't do it, Sarah," Reeve said softly. He had hurt her pride more than her heart with his rejection. Sarah wasn't the type of woman to get rejected.

"Can I help you?" Charlotte asked icily.

Sarah's lips curled into a sneer. "You've got some power. Maybe that's the appeal because fuck knows why he'd leave me for you otherwise."

"I didn't leave you for her, Sarah. I left because we didn't work."

"We could have if you weren't pining away for someone who doesn't want you," she said, voice rising. People were starting to look at them uneasily. Fuck, he didn't need this tonight.

"And you think that person is me?" Charlotte let out a laugh. "Reeve and I are barely even friends. He probably made that up to let you down easily. Go on, go bother someone else with your bullshit. We are busy."

Sarah went bright red. Her magic flickered at her fingertips, ready for a fight. Before Reeve could say a word, Charlotte had stepped between them. With her hunter swiftness, she caught Sarah's hands before she could lift them. Charlotte's power smothered whatever hex the witch was about to throw at him.

"Let me go, bitch!" Sarah snarled.

"You lost. Have some fucking dignity about it. Go away and stop bothering me before I get upset." Charlotte gave her a smile that was so chilling, it would've made Bayn proud. "And if you ever try to hex Reeve again, I'll rip out every ounce of magic you have and feed you to my dogs." Charlotte let her go with a hard shove that had Sarah stumbling backward in her heels. She glared at them and pushed her way back through the crowd.

Reeve's heart was pounding too hard, shock filling every part of him. Charlotte had stood up for him... Reeve took her hand.

"What?"

"Come and dance with me. Right now," Reeve tugged her onto the dance floor and put an arm around her.

Charlotte finished putting the sigil back into her clutch. "What are you doing?"

"We are drawing too much attention. Now put your arms around my neck and stop arguing with me," Reeve replied.

That little display had made Charlotte even more interesting to onlookers, and the fact she had just smacked down one of the most powerful witches in Dublin didn't help the matter. The dragon in him didn't like their hungry eyes coveting what was his.

Shut up, you don't get a say, he tried telling it. It didn't matter. She might not like him anymore, but she had just staked her claim whether she wanted to or not.

"So that was your ex? She seemed...pleasant," Charlotte said. She hesitated before her hands went to his shoulders, and they started moving slowly to the beat.

"She doesn't like losing as you can tell."

Charlotte made a soft snorting sound. "And to think that she imagined I was the one that had stolen you. Why do people need to be so ridiculous? You've never looked at me twice like that, even when we were friends."

"Yes, I have," Reeve admitted, his hands tightening in case she decided to run.

Charlotte only rolled her eyes. "Sure, Reeve. You don't need to say it. My ego isn't so fragile."

"I'm not trying to flatter your ego. I'm trying to tell you the truth." Reeve had a little bit too much alcohol in his system to keep his mouth shut. "Before we had our falling-out, I was... I wanted to ask you out. I was working up the courage, and then everything went wrong. If I hadn't totally fucking blown it, would you have considered it? Even for a second?"

Charlotte had gone pale, and he could see the hurt in her eyes. Hurt he had put there. Fuck, he shouldn't have said a damn thing. They swayed in silence for a few seconds before she leaned against him so she wasn't looking at him.

"Yes, I would've considered it," she admitted so softly, he almost missed it.

"I'm so sorry for everything, Charlie." Reeve braved her wrath and pressed a kiss to the top of her head. "Tell me how to fix it, and I'll do it. I don't want us to fight anymore. It sucks, and I'm tired of it."

"Me too."

Reeve pulled back, lifting her chin. "Yeah?"

"Yeah." She bit her full bottom lip, eyes full of uncertainty. "Truce?"

"Truce," Reeve whispered. His thumb brushed the curve of her cheek, and her breath hitched. He wanted to kiss her more than he wanted anything in his life.

A wave of dark power rolled through the club, and his steps faltered. Charlotte dragged Reeve to the ground, and the closest wall exploded into rubble.

9

Charlotte clung to Reeve, holding him down until the dust cleared. He stared up at her with wide, appalled eyes.

"What the *fuck*, Charlotte?" he demanded.

"You're welcome, asshole," she hissed.

They climbed to their feet before a horde creature roared and charged through the hole in the wall. Charlotte fought her instant panic and pulled some patches from her purse.

Imogen's battle cry echoed from the other side of the club, and a flaming bottle sailed through the air and hit the hard beetle-backed creature. It roared, whirling towards Imogen and giving Charlotte an opening to dash between its spider legs, slap a patch on its sticky body, and dive out the way as it swiped at her.

"Jesus, fuck, what are you doing?" Reeve cried, pulling her backward.

"This." Charlotte focused her power, and the sigil on the creature burned to life. It screeched in fury and confusion and then exploded into smoking hunks. They didn't have time to celebrate as another two scuttled in over the bloody remains.

"When we get out of this, we are going to have a discussion about you throwing yourself into danger," Reeve shouted. He grabbed a handful of toothpicks off the floor and threw them towards one of the creatures. His magic streaked hot in the air, and the tiny picks changed into five-foot-long wooden stakes and skewered the beast in its googly eyes.

Someone screamed as tall figures came through the hall. They looked like weird insect human hybrids. They snatched the closest magicians they saw, most of them too shocked to summon any of their power.

Charlotte bent down and sketched a symbol in the dead creature's blood. Concrete and bricks pelted at the creatures, but they only screeched and took their struggling cargo out through the broken wall.

A giant scarab-like monster put itself between Charlotte and the hybrids. She rolled out of the way, dodging its pincers as it seemed to zero in on her. Some other magicians tossed spells and debris at it, but it ignored them, its beady eyes fixated on her.

What the hell? She didn't have time to wonder why it was following her.

"Reeve!" She tossed him a patch. "Stick that to something and throw it at the creature!"

He caught it, stuck it to a beer bottle, and threw it towards the scarab. The creature caught it reflexively in its pincers, and Charlotte detonated it. Half of the scarab's head blew off, sending a shower of black blood over them. Its big dead body blocked the hole to stop any more from coming in.

Imogen grabbed her by the arm. "Come on! We need to get outside and follow them."

"Go! I'll get these people out before those creepy hybrids shift the body."

"Okay. I'll try and get a hold of Kill and Bron. Stay with Reeve and get your ass to safety." Imogen took off up the stairs and into the main club before Charlotte could argue.

"This way! You all need to stop hiding and get out," Charlotte shouted at the patrons cowering under tables and inside the booths. "Reeve, get them out."

He clapped his hands. "Get moving! There are more coming."

Charlotte grabbed a piece of glass off the floor and scratched a symbol into the scarab's shell. Magic shivered through it, and its shell and legs fused with the wall and the floor. She could feel other creatures shoving and screaming against it. She was trying to reinforce it when a hand wrapped around hers.

"Leave it, Charlie, we need to go," Reeve said, pulling her away. Charlotte hurried after him, taking the stairs two at a time. The front of the bar had been evacuated, screams and sirens roaring in the distance.

"We need to find Imogen," she said, looking around.

"Imogen's gone!" Apollo ran to join them. "The creatures just freaked all of a sudden and took off. She grabbed a motorbike and followed them. Kill and Bron are incoming. We need to get out of here before the cops arrive."

Charlotte shook her head. "We can't leave. What if they come back?"

"Kill will have called for backup. We need to get home and behind the wards." Reeve took her by the shoulders. "That thing came straight for you, Charlotte. It wanted you, and I'm not going to let them have you." He looked more panicked than she had ever seen him. He was covered in concrete dust and horde creature goo.

"Reeve, we can't just leave. What if Kill needs us? We—"

"No! He would want you safe first." Reeve brushed his mouth against hers in a trembling kiss that stole the argument out of her mouth. "Please, baby, you've done enough. Let someone else handle it."

Charlotte was too shocked to move, lips burning and brain dazed.

Apollo grabbed her other hand. "No time for that. Follow me. I know a way back home."

"Here, put this on. You're shivering." Reeve took off his leather jacket and helped her into it. Together they jogged all the way back to the Greatdrakes house near St. Audoen's.

Charlotte's whole body was aching by the time they got there. The front door opened as soon as they reached it.

"What the hell happened?" Cosimo demanded.

"The club was attacked, and fucking monsters stole people," Apollo babbled. "Fuck, Reeve, you told me about the horde creatures, but I've never seen anything like that before in my life."

"Quickly, inside all of you." Cosimo hustled them into the kitchen and pulled out a chair for Charlotte. "Sit, darling, you look spent."

She didn't have it in her to argue, just slumped down. Reeve looked her over with that same panicked expression.

"Apollo, mix up something that's going to help with her magic loss," Cosimo instructed. "I'll go call Kenna and let her know Charlotte is safe."

After they left, Reeve went to the fridge and took out a water bottle. He opened it and passed it to her.

"Drink this, Charlotte." She took it gratefully and drained it. He grabbed a clean kitchen towel from a draw and wet it.

"You're bleeding. Let me look," he grumbled. Charlotte could only sit dumbly as he wiped the remains of blood and creature gore off her head.

"How bad is it?" she winced.

"Bad enough to give you a headache and a nasty bruise, but it doesn't need stitches. Are you hurting anywhere else?"

"No, just tired."

Reeve washed out the cloth before starting to clean her hands. It was the strangest, most intimate thing she'd experienced. What the hell was the matter with him?

"I said I'm okay, Reeve."

"I know, but you're covered in crud and concrete, and you pulled me out of the way when a wall exploded and..."

"And you're freaking out."

Reeve's hazel eyes filled with anger. "You could've died, Charlotte! What the hell were you thinking?"

She hadn't been. She had felt the spell a second before it went off, and her body reacted on instinct.

"I was trying to protect you," she said far too softly.

Reeve crouched down in front of her, still working to clean her hands of grime and blood.

"Don't ever do that again. I'm serious. I'd never be able to live with myself if something happened to you," he replied, voice cracking as his knees hit the floor. "I can't lose you again, Charlie. I just can't."

Reeve's arms wrapped around her legs, and something finally broke inside Charlotte. She could feel his whole body shaking with emotion.

Swallowing the heavy lump in her throat, Charlotte rested a shaking hand in his disheveled hair, not knowing how to soothe him.

"Reeve, I'm okay. Just breathe," she said, stroking his curls back from his face. Her lips tingled in memory of that too brief, shaky kiss outside of the club. "Are *you* hurt?"

"No. Just shook up."

"Are you sure you haven't hit your head? You are starting to freak me out." Charlotte wanted it to sound like a joke, but it made Reeve's grip on her tighten.

"I'm sorry," he said, finally pulling back from her. "You really scared me. Then you just went straight for the first monster that turned up like it was nothing. I honestly don't know whether to be angry, impressed, or aroused."

Charlotte choked on a bubble of laughter. Going straight for a monster was her prerogative as an Ironwood.

"Or you could just say thank you for being a badass?"

Reeve took her face in his hands, and before she could stop him, he gave her a soft, silky kiss that made her fingers curl in his dirty shirt.

Reeve Greatdrakes is kissing me. Her brain couldn't make sense of it quickly enough to be offended. She only opened her mouth a little more and let it happen. It wasn't a quick, frightened thing like it had been outside the club. This kiss had the kind of intent that made her blood fizz.

Reeve murmured against her lips, "Thank you for being a badass, Charlotte Ironwood."

Charlotte's brain was still struggling to turn back online when Cosimo came into the kitchen. "Come quickly, we have a fae prince at our gate, and I don't think he's here for me."

Outside, Charlotte could see the twin silver horns of Killian's wings moving in the moonlight. He was pacing up and down the front fence like he was debating on whether or not to be rude and to rip down the wards in his way.

"Kill!" Charlotte yanked open the gate and had taken two steps before Killian crushed her in a tight embrace.

"Are you okay? Tell me you're not hurt?" he demanded.

"I'm a bit banged up but nothing serious. Where is Bron?" Charlotte asked, pulling back from him.

Emerald eyes flashed in the dim light. "She's with Imogen. They lost the trail and the creatures in the darkness."

"Would you like to come in?" Cosimo asked and made an opening in the warding for Killian to step through.

"Thanks. Bron is going to meet us back at the mansion. We can pick up the hunt from where we left off tomorrow." Killian gave Cosimo and Reeve a quick once over. "I think Aneirin isn't going to be subtle for much longer. Can you put out the word to the other magic users in Ireland to be careful? Imogen said his creatures were snatching people tonight. He might not be interested in willing recruits anymore."

"I will make some calls. Magicians rarely listen, but after tonight I can at least hope they will be cautious," Cosimo said.

"Charlotte! Wait, take this," Apollo called, coming down the path. He passed her a vial with bright purple liquid inside of it. "Here. It will restore your magic."

"Take it now," Reeve said. When they all gave him strange looks, he added, "So that by the time you get back to the estate, you can make the wards stronger."

Charlotte could see that the panic for her safety hadn't entirely left his eyes, so she uncorked the vial and drained it. "Thanks, Apollo."

"After watching you charge those creatures tonight, I owe you a lot more than a simple potion."

Killian's brows rose. "You charged horde creatures?"

"I'm an Ironwood." Charlotte gave a shrug. She didn't regret it for a second.

Killian only laughed and held out a hand. "Come along, fierce hunter. I have to get you home before Kenna gets antsy."

Reeve's hand brushed against hers. "Make the wards extra strong, Charlie. I don't like the way they came for you in particular tonight."

Charlotte wanted to roll her eyes and snap at him, but she didn't. Her lips were still tingling from the kiss in the kitchen, and she needed to get away from him to get her head clear again.

"I will, don't worry. I'll give you a call tomorrow, and we'll find where those hybrids went," she reassured him.

Killian picked her up easily, and they shot up into the sky. Cold wind rushed past them, and Charlotte tried not to cling in terror to her brother. She was grateful for Reeve's jacket that she was still wearing.

"Did something happen between you and trash magic?" Killian asked.

Charlotte flushed. "No. He's just overprotective because he's scared of you princes."

"Sure, that's the reason." Killian laughed. "Despite whatever is not going on between you, it is nice to see you working as a team."

"Kian promised me a trip to see the fae mages. I'd work with anyone for that." Charlotte didn't sound as confident as she hoped. She didn't know why Reeve had kissed her. It was probably just adrenaline from the fight and nothing else.

She stared up at the cold night sky. *It was nothing at all.*

10

Reeve watched the silhouette of Charlotte and Killian disappearing into the cloudy distance. He didn't even know his hands were balled into fists until Cosimo took them.

"She's okay, son. She'll be safe with Killian," he assured him. Reeve let out a shuddering breath and looked his father in the eyes. He wanted to tell him about the bond he felt and ask him how to control it. That would mean saying it out loud, and he didn't know if he had the strength that night.

"I know. It was just a bad night," Reeve managed, and his father let him go.

"You should've seen Charlotte, Dad. Like, I don't think she needs anyone's protection," Apollo said as they went back inside. He passed Reeve a vial, too, even though he hadn't used as much magic as Charlotte. He drank it anyway, knowing that it was Apollo's way of helping.

Reeve went to the kitchen to grab a glass and a bottle of whiskey. It probably wasn't the best idea, but his nerves were shredded. He didn't know if it was the dragon in his blood that was making him feel so crazy.

No, it was definitely Charlotte herself, jumping in to protect him like he was some kind of damsel. He was flattered that she would and also mad as shit that she had thrown herself into danger like that.

"Well, you look like crap. Fun night?" Valentine asked, walking into the kitchen with Bas.

"Fuck you, Val."

His elder brother held up his hands in surrender. "Sorry, but this has given us an advantage."

"Fuck the advantage." Reeve drained his glass. "People could have died. I'm pretty sure the ones the hybrids snatched are already dead."

"Yes, and that's not your fault," Cosimo said, coming in to break up the fight before it could start again. "Valentine, don't antagonize him."

"Yeah, Val, it was fucked up. Those horde creatures are terrifying as fuck." Apollo grabbed the whiskey and had a swig. "Things would've been worse if Charlotte hadn't been there."

Bas held his hands out to Apollo and Reeve. "Show me, and I'll show them."

It was one of Bas's creepier talents to be able to see memories and transfer them to others, but it had its uses. Reeve took his hand and showed him what had happened.

"Aneirin has fucked up," Valentine whispered, blinking rapidly at the images that had been dumped into his head. "Don't you think it's strange that the general has been silent for nearly two months and then decided to attack hastily while you were there?"

"It could've been a fluke," Apollo replied.

"No. I don't think so." Valentine poured himself a whiskey and had a sip. "Aneirin hates the Ironwoods because of what happened with Morrigan. Those creatures might have been tasked to nab a few magicians, but they were there for Charlotte. To kill her or to take her alive if they could. She has a lot of magic that could be useful to the general."

Reeve groaned into his whiskey. "What makes you so sure?"

Valentine nursed his glass, his expression thoughtful. "It's what I would do if I was him."

"And you saw that big scarab fucker go straight for her, Reeve. Nothing could distract it. It wanted her," Apollo said, nodding in agreement.

"Fuck, just what we need." Reeve rubbed at his tired eyes.

"There isn't anything we can do tonight. I suggest we all get some sleep and start everything fresh in the morning," Cosimo interrupted them. "Reeve, you can go with Charlotte tomorrow and see if you can find where the hybrids took those people."

"I will. There's no way in hell I'm letting her go alone." Reeve put his glass in the dishwasher. "I need a shower and sleep and time to think. A few months ago, those hybrids weren't a part of the horde attack. Aneirin might be opening portals already to get them from Tir Na Nog."

"Seems like a lot of effort for something he could make here with less power," Val replied. At their questioning glances, he added, "Who do you think would've helped Morrigan make them to begin with? He might not have her power anymore, but he has her techniques. He could've decided to make servants of his own."

"Annnddd now I'm not going to sleep at all," Bas complained, glaring at Valentine. "God, your brain is creepy sometimes."

Val didn't look the least bit offended. "We need to think like him to catch him."

~

UP IN HIS ROOMS, Reeve pulled off his wrecked clothes and dumped them into a bin. There was no way he'd be getting all that blood and horde creature out of them.

Charlotte's blood.

His stomach clenched, and he only just made it to the toilet before he was vomiting his guts up. It wasn't like he hadn't seen her fight before.

Their paths had collided during the fight with Morrigan. She had been with her sisters then, and they had her back. She had hated Reeve, and he hadn't spent any time with her again to realize those feelings he had for her hadn't gone away. Now he *knew* they hadn't. Not even a little.

Reeve sat on the cold tiles and thought about their night before everything had gone to shit. His mind drifted to his confession that he had planned to ask her out before everything had gotten fucked up.

Yes, I would've considered it. Her gentle reply was more than he'd ever hoped for. Had she felt their crazy connection too?

Reeve climbed into the shower on shaky feet. He soaped himself all over three times, determined to get the reek of sticky black blood off him.

Exhaustion was starting to close in on him by the time he dried off. His phone buzzed on the bathroom counter, his heart skipping when he saw Charlotte's name pop up.

Get your Dad or Val to tie this sigil into the wards. It's for those hybrids.

Attached was a complex design that was so powerful, it made his eyes blur.

Did you just slap this together? It's fucking incredible.

Yes. Try not to be too jealous.

Reeve laughed. Jealous wasn't what he was. It was like she kept him in a continuous state of awe. It was exhausting and exhilarating to be this impressed all the time. The three dots danced again.

Sleep well, Reeve.

You too, Charlie.

Reeve swallowed a lump in his throat. He wouldn't get his hopes too high; he knew better than that. It was another beginning, and he was going to do everything in his power to not fuck it up this time.

A small smile appeared on Reeve's face. He could still taste Charlotte's sweet mouth on his lips, and while he wouldn't ever push her, he was officially *done* with being subtle about what he wanted.

11

Charlotte and Imogen were barely through breakfast when Reeve arrived bright-eyed and looking way too good, considering the night they'd had.

"Good morning, Ironwoods," he greeted, coming into the kitchen.

"What has you so cheery this morning?" Imogen complained.

Everyone else was asleep, and if it wasn't pride driving her, Imogen would've still been in bed. She had been doing her best to make out with yet another cute goth guy when the club was attacked, and she felt guilty for not being more alert. And then she had lost their trail. That was too much for Imogen's pride to handle.

Charlotte did her best to hide how much Reeve's sudden appearance and easy smile affected her. She had thought way too much about their kiss the previous night, the phantom sensation of his stubble and warmth keeping her up too late. One kiss she could have dismissed as battle high, but two...

Reeve took out two yellow vials that pulsed with magic.

"Here, present from Apollo," he said, passing them over.

"This better not be pee," Imogen grumbled but downed it anyway. Almost instantly, her eyes lit up. "Holy shit, I love your brother. What is in this?"

"Who knows. He calls it *Morning Glory*."

Imogen choked on a filthy laugh. "I bet he does."

Charlotte shrugged and drank hers. It was like sunshine and honey, and her entire body woke up. "Wow."

Reeve helped himself to the pot of coffee. "So where are we going today?"

"We head for Swords. That's where I lost them last night. Fuck, those horde creatures can move when they want to. The hybrids were flying on the back of the scarabs, and the rest were running down the bloody roads. Even Bron couldn't keep up," Imogen explained with a shake of her head. "Let's hope we can find some sign of them."

"Someone must have seen something," Charlotte replied and finished her porridge. "Maybe Layla can do a scan of the police channels."

"If she bloody wakes up before noon," Imogen said with a touch of jealousy.

Charlotte left Reeve in the kitchen with Imogen and went to get her bag. She was determined to act like the kisses never happened. He didn't seem concerned. Perhaps he kissed people regularly enough that it was like a handshake?

Careful. He's starting to mess with your head, a voice warned her. It was like Reeve's life purpose. Charlotte wished she could go back to hating him, but it was too late. He'd gotten under her skin already.

It wasn't just the kissing. It was the dancing and the magic too. Especially the magic. Despite their magic affinities being completely different, Reeve had always been able to help her figure out magical problems. He understood her mind in a way that no one else did.

"Focus on the task at hand. Everything else can wait," she mumbled to herself as she brushed her teeth and grabbed her satchel bag. She banged on Layla's door on her way past.

"Fuc'ff," came the muffled reply.

Charlotte stuck her head in the door. Layla was a lump of pillows and platinum hair.

"Get up. We need you doing some digging to see if there is any chatter about horde creature sightings near Swords."

One tattooed arm waved at her from the depths of the blankets. "Yeah, yeah."

Charlotte left her to it and hurried downstairs. Reeve was waiting by the front door. She wished like hell that he didn't look so damn good in jeans and dark blue peacoat. She held out his leather jacket.

"Here. Thank you for letting me use it last night," she said.

"Any time, Charlie," he replied, folding it over his arm. "My car or yours?"

"Your car. I don't feel like driving," she said, stepping out into the cloudy day. Imogen was already sitting on her black motorbike, waiting for them. She finished braiding her lavender hair and put on her helmet.

"Try and keep up," she said, turning on the bike.

Charlotte got into Reeve's silver BMW and dumped her bag at her feet. Reeve got in, a strange grin on his face.

"What's that smile about?" Charlotte asked.

"Nothing. It's nice to see you in my car, that's all."

She frowned in confusion. "We are working together, Reeve. We were bound to share a car."

"I know. I still like it. You were barely talking to me, and now you're not going to be able to escape me unless I stop driving," he teased, turning on the car and waving at Imogen.

"I'm just going to smile and think of the fae mages," Charlotte mumbled. She didn't like the idea of not being able to escape.

Reeve only laughed, and Imogen took off down the driveway. They followed her through the city. Charlotte pulled out her phone and sent a message to Bron and Layla to make sure she had gotten up.

"Val and Dad were really impressed with the sigil you created for the wards last night," Reeve said after a while.

"I'll take it as a compliment. Cosimo seems like a hard man to impress."

"Not as hard as Val. You can always tell how impressed he is by how deep his scowl gets," Reeve replied. "They all like you."

Charlotte's ears went red. "They don't even know me."

"They know enough. I've gotten more lectures from them about keeping you safe in the last twenty-four hours than I've been lectured about anything in my entire life."

"That's kind of them, but as I proved last night, I don't need your protection."

Reeve winked at her. "I know, Charlie. I only told them I would so they would get off my back. I fully expect you to protect me in the next fight."

"So the usual?" she teased, surprising herself.

"I was taken unawares last night. It shook me up. Next time, I'll be ready."

"Shook enough to kiss me spontaneously." Charlotte bit her tongue. Fuck.

"Nothing spontaneous about either one of those kisses, Charlie Belle," Reeve replied firmly. "I've wanted to kiss you for over five years now. I just took the opportunity to follow through while I had the chance."

"Oh," she said, her mouth going dry. He had been thinking about kissing her for five years? *What the actual hell?*

"That's it? Oh? No shouting or lightning bolts?"

"Do I need to say anything else? It happened. You knocked it off your list, and now it's done," Charlotte replied as nonchalantly as she could manage. Her palms were sweating, and her chest was too tight. She couldn't fall for him again, no matter what he claimed.

Reeve's hand gripped the steering wheel a little tighter but didn't push it. He watched Imogen zooming through traffic, weaving about at dangerous speeds.

"God, she's got a death wish."

"Always has. I try not to watch because my heart can't handle the stress," Charlotte replied. "I used to worry about it, but that's just her."

Imogen pointed at the exit sign for Lanistown, and they followed her. Charlotte's phone started ringing, and she dug about in her bag for it.

"What's up, Layla?" she answered.

"I found something you might be interested in. A retiree put up on Facebook that some monster trampled her gardens and lawn last night and that the local police refused to do anything about it," Layla replied with a massive yawn.

"Where was this?"

"Her property is off Portrane Beach. I'll keep digging, but that's in your general area," Layla replied and hung up. Charlotte dialed Imogen and waited for it to connect to the Bluetooth in her helmet.

"Hey, baby sis. Are you and Reeve playing nice? Have you asked him to take your virginity yet?" Imogen replied.

"We both know my virginity is long gone," she said, and Reeve coughed awkwardly.

Charlotte might have given up on Reeve, but she still occasionally picked a guy up like the rest of her sisters. Imogen just delighted in teasing her that she didn't get laid enough.

"Layla found a report of something that could have been a horde creature. Head for Portrane Beach."

"Will do. Maybe they wanted to work on their tan?" Imogen hung up before Charlotte could tease her for her awful joke.

"I wonder why they were heading towards the ocean. As far as we know, they can't swim great distances," Reeve said, biting his bottom lip in a downright sexy way.

"Maybe they were reporting back to someone who was there?" Charlotte replied, transfixed. It was like he was designed to distract her with all of that dark hair and stubble. Even the spicy smell of his cologne was too much in such an enclosed space.

She refused to be reduced to a stupid teenager crushing on him again. Something had changed between them last night, starting with her admitting she would've gone out with him if he had asked and ending with his lips.

Charlotte had the horrible realization that as much as she had hated him for the things he had said, her feelings for him hadn't gone away. They had been buried and locked up in her fury, and he'd unsealed that Pandora's box by kissing her.

It would've been a lot easier to keep hating him if his glossy dark hair wasn't out and curling in the collar of his jacket. Her fingertips tingled, wanting to brush them back.

"Do I have something on my face?" Reeve asked, a grin appearing in the corner of his mouth. "Seriously, what are you looking at?"

"Nothing. I was thinking of something and happened to be looking in your general direction," Charlotte muttered.

"What were you thinking about, Charlotte?" he asked, voice dropping in a way that made her stomach clench not unpleasantly.

"Those strange hybrid horde creatures," she said, picking the first thing that popped into her head.

"Ah huh. Well, Val seems to think that Aneirin could've spawned them recently because he was probably the one helping Morrigan create the others in Tir Na Nog," Reeve replied.

"That makes a lot of sense. Otherwise, Bron or Kill would've recognized them. They were both at Morrigan's castle, so they saw a lot more than what came through to attack Dublin." Charlotte rubbed at the back of her neck. "Maybe, Aneirin realized having smaller ones that were more humanoid would be better than creatures the size of cars. Shit. If he can just *make* an army, we are fucked."

"He can't make them out of nothing. Val and Apollo are looking into what someone would need to make creatures like that. Apollo is an alchemist. He understands about transmutation processes when it comes to organic substances."

"Is there anything your brothers don't know?" Charlotte sighed. It must've been nice to grow up with so much magic around them. She couldn't help feeling a little jealous of it.

"How not to be assholes? We all have our areas of expertise, so it comes in handy," Reeve replied. "They think my magic is the most undisciplined thing they have ever seen."

"They are right," Charlotte said, and Reeve poked her in the ribs.

"Hey! You're meant to be on my side."

"Since when? Your magic makes absolutely no sense."

Reeve shook his head. "Come on, Charlie, you know better than that. All magic is energy and intention. You guys think you need all the fancy training and bells and whistles, but you're wrong. Magic is magic. It doesn't matter how you channel it. It's still the same force. I transform objects into what I need. I can feel the magic, and I create what I want using it."

Charlotte puzzled over his words for a minute and decided to go with the truth. "I think the main problem is because you make it look so easy. The rest of us have to work on it. It took me *years* to learn how to channel it properly and make any decent kind of sigil."

"You were teaching yourself. I grew up with generations of magicians," Reeve pointed out. "And magic *is* that easy. I bet if you really put your mind to it, you wouldn't even have to draw sigils out. You could just see them in your mind and release them, and magic would do the rest."

Charlotte laughed. "Sure, Reeve."

"I'm serious. You'll never know until you try it," he replied.

Ahead of them, Imogen slowed and pulled into a parking lot at the most northern part of Portrane Beach. They got out into the chill, damp wind, and Charlotte wrapped a scarf around her neck. There wasn't anyone around, the lousy weather dissuading anyone from a walk.

"Layla rang me and said the house where the complaint came from was only one street that way," Imogen pointed. "Let's head down the beach and see if there are any tracks."

They didn't have to go far before they found part of the sandy embankment that had been trampled into a mess.

"Well, well, what do we have here?" Imogen crouched down and pointed at a black smear. "One of them must've been wounded." She took a photo on her phone before tapping into a search engine. "We've only got an hour before the next high tide, and we lose the tracks. Do you have everything you need, Charlotte? We are on foot from here."

Charlotte tapped her satchel. "Got it."

Reeve bent down and pulled out a silver square that had been trodden amongst the black stains. "Perfect."

"What are you thinking, Reevey?" Imogen asked, watching him curiously.

"That there might be an easy way to track them because we have their blood," he replied. He started folding the dirty wrapper into a paper crane. His dark eyes flared gold, and the bird flapped its wings. It flew up into the breeze haphazardly before heading further up the beach. "Come on, they went that way."

"Nice one," Charlotte said with a small smile. Reeve flushed at the compliment but only nodded.

Imogen was already moving down the sand, looking entirely out of place in her motorcycle boots and leather pants. Charlotte hurried to catch up to her.

"Why on earth would they have come out here?" she said, looking about. There were only grassy banks, rocks, and water.

"I'm sure we'll find out. I don't see them coming all this way unless they were under Aneirin's orders," Imogen replied.

Twenty minutes later, they had cleared the beach and walked around the point into Rogerstown Estuary.

"Hey, ladies, I think I found something," Reeve called. They walked over to where he was on the grassy edges. There was a smashed phone smeared in blood.

"Do you think the humans they were carrying might have dropped it?" Charlotte reached into her satchel and pulled out a small zip-lock bag. She picked up the phone with it and sealed it.

"They might have tried to call for help," she said, her guts twisting.

"I have more blood over here," Imogen said, a few meters ahead of them. They moved to catch up with her in the knee-high grass. Charlotte stumbled, crashing to the ground with a thud.

"Fuck!" she groaned. She turned to see what she had tripped over. "Fuck."

"Let me help you up," Reeve said, taking her by the hand. "You okay? You're pale."

Charlotte pointed at the mauled arm she had stepped on. "Reeve..."

"Oh, God." He helped her up and shifted the grass back with one foot. "Imogen! We have an arm."

"We've got more than that," Imogen replied. She was further down the bank and looked like she was about to heave.

Charlotte and Reeve moved to join her, his hand still clasping hers tightly. Charlotte gagged violently when she saw what Imogen had found.

Arranged in the sand was a sigil made of blood and the bodies of humans and horde creatures alike. The dark, clawing intent of the magic hit her like a slap. Charlotte barely had time to turn away before she was heaving up her breakfast onto the grass.

12

Reeve had never seen something so horrific in his life as the torn bodies before him. He gently pulled Charlotte's hair back, fighting to keep his own breakfast down.

"We need to call Kian," she said, taking a tissue from her bag and wiping her mouth before downing some water from a bottle. "I swear if you tell anyone I threw up, I'll make you regret it."

"Would I do that?" he asked innocently. Charlotte gave him a withering look that he secretly loved. He pulled out his phone and video called Valentine.

"What do you want now?" his brother answered, black hair askew from his hands running through it.

"Look what we found." Reeve turned the camera around and showed him the sigil created from blood and bone, and fuck knew what.

"Jesus. Aneirin was definitely there," Valentine said, his eyes suddenly alert. "Take lots of photos. What does the vibe of it feel like?"

"Disgusting," Charlotte replied, toying with her own phone. "My magic is shuddering, and I want to wash myself with bleach."

"Fascinating."

"Don't be creepy, Val," Reeve chided. "It's a real fucking mess, and

I'm willing to bet money that those people that got snatched last night have ended up in this."

"He probably stole their magic as well as their blood in order to boost his power. The sacrifice itself would have generated a lot on its own." Valentine shook his head. "Send me all the photos, Reeve, and shoot a video too."

"Sure thing, bro." Reeve hung up and studied the spell again. The whole thing made him want to claw his skin off. He pushed down his nausea and started taking the photos.

"Talk to me, Charlotte. What did you find?" Kian's calm voice said, not far from him. Charlotte was taking her brother on a tour of the site too.

"It's like a messed-up triskelion in shape with smaller symbols in each of the three branches," Charlotte explained. "One looks like a sketch of a harp. I can't make out the other two. The spell isn't active, but it's still pulsing with the after-effects."

Kian leaned closer on the video like he was trying to get a better look. "Move over the image slowly for me, sister. I feel like there's something..." he trailed off, red brows drawn tightly together. "Show me the individual symbols again."

Reeve followed Charlotte, studying the sacrifice and trying to look past the carnage and to the spell underneath it.

"This one here looks like the Norse rune Teiwaz, the warrior," he said, taking a photo and sending it to Val. His rune lore knowledge had always been better than Reeve's.

"I think this one was a tree of some sort," Charlotte said about the third and put the phone closer for Kian to examine it.

"Fuck, it's the generals," Reeve muttered.

"What was that, Greatdrakes?" Kian demanded.

"It's the generals. Look, the harp for Aneirin, the battle bard, Teiwaz is Norse, so we can assume that is for Vili, and the tree could be a tree of life, for Hafgan, the undying lord." Reeve stepped back towards the water, looking at it as a whole.

"Why here, though? Why not try and use a sacred site to make a doorway like last time?" Imogen asked.

Charlotte joined Reeve at the water's edge. "An estuary is neither land nor sea but both. This was done just before dawn, a time between times. Both things would have made it a weak spot, an in-between place."

"What if he wasn't trying to make a portal but a call?" Reeve said, trying to catch up with her thinking. "He wouldn't need the power of a permanent weak place into Faerie. Just something strong enough."

"He also knows that we are watching the sites. He would be stupid to try and risk going to one without having the power to take us on," Kian added, and the three of them studied the sigils again.

"Hey, who's that?" Imogen said, making Reeve look up. A man was watching them from a distance. He turned and ran. Imogen took off. "I'll get him!"

Reeve bent down and picked up a piece of driftwood. Sending his magic into it, he hurled it after them. The wood sailed past Imogen and hit the fleeing figure in the back of his legs. He went down with a shout, and Imogen was on him, a gun pressed to the back of his neck.

"Gods below, I hope he wasn't some innocent onlooker," Kian muttered. "Charlotte, send me through what you have, and I'll alert the police about the matter. I'll send Bron and Killian out as the fae representatives, and they'll bag everything up."

"Will do, Kian. I'll let you know what we find." Charlotte hung up the call and rubbed at her arms. "Fuck, this gives me the creeps."

"Me too."

"Looks like we caught ourselves a little spy," Imogen said, returning with their watcher. She had him cuffed, the gun still pointed at him. "The fucker reeks of magic and horde creatures." He was covered in black stains that were unmistakably creature blood.

"You're one of Aneirin's acolytes," Charlotte guessed. The man spat in her direction. "I'll take that as a yes."

"Fuck you, Ironwood slut."

Reeve took a step towards him, but Imogen was quicker. She brought the butt of her gun down on the back of the man's head, and he toppled over into the sand.

"Right, let's get this fucker into the trunk of your car, Reeve. He's going to tell us exactly what Aneirin is up to," Imogen said, tucking her gun away.

Reeve sent a message to Cosimo, telling him what happened and to meet them at the Ironwoods estate in two hours. If they were going to be questioning the acolyte of a deranged general, they were going to need the best magical interrogators to help them.

13

The sun was setting when Reeve and Charlotte pulled in at the Ironwood mansion. They had waited until Bron and Killian had arrived at the site and left as soon as the local police cars started to pull up.

Charlotte didn't know what normal humans thought about the mess, and her heart felt too heavy about the magicians she hadn't been able to save the night before.

Reeve stroked her cheek lightly. "You okay?"

"I can't stop thinking if I had been quicker at sealing that hole in the wall at the club that I could've stopped those poor people from being taken," she admitted.

As soon as they stepped out of the car, she would have to put on her tough Ironwood face. She let herself have a moment of weakness and leaned into his palm.

"None of this is your fault, Charlotte. You were fighting for your life too. Those creatures went for you, and you did what you could. You stopped them taking anyone else," Reeve replied, voice firm but soft. "You saved *everyone* else last night, including me. It's not a hollow victory. This is Aneirin's fault, not yours."

Charlotte nodded slowly, fighting the urge to hug him. "I know. It still feels shitty."

"Only because you care." Reeve pressed a quick kiss to her forehead and dropped his hand. "Let's see what this asshole locked in the trunk knows, and we can work on stopping Aneirin from doing this to anyone else."

Reeve got out of the car, leaving her staring after him. She really had to stop this casual affection he was starting to show for her own good.

Starting tomorrow. Today had been too horrible.

Charlotte got out of the car as Cosimo and Valentine arrived. Reeve said he had called his father in to help, but she was surprised to see Val tagging along.

"Caught something interesting in the estuary, did you, baby boy?" Valentine asked with a teasing smile.

"It was a joint effort. Let's hope Imogen hasn't given him a concussion," Reeve replied and popped the trunk. The acolyte jumped out, kicking and screaming. A bright flash of light emanated from Cosimo, and the acolyte crumpled to the ground.

"She obviously didn't hit him hard enough," Cosimo said, straightening his cuffs. "Take his arms, Reeve. Val, his legs. Charlotte can lead the way to Kenna's lovely dungeon."

Charlotte let them in through the back entrance, so they didn't tread the estuary and drip horde creatures onto the floors. The acolyte reeked of blood, his light-colored hair and face smeared in it.

"Am I the only one that thinks this asshole turning up is too convenient?" Valentine asked.

"All depends if he was there to make sure nothing disturbed the sigil and lessen its power. You said that you could feel it still?" Cosimo questioned.

"Yes, it wasn't fully activated, but it was like it was still charged and thrumming. It felt...disgusting is the only word. It only stopped pulsing when Killian turned it off somehow so they could clear up the mess," Charlotte replied.

They went down a set of back stairs and into the manor's basement. She unlocked the heavily warded cell that had once kept Killian. Her phone in her back pocket buzzed, and she hurried to answer it.

"What did you find, Kian?" she asked, getting out of the way and putting him on speaker. "I have the Greatdrakes here with me."

"I looked over your photos and talked to one of the fae mages that are staying with me at the moment. It was definitely used to steal power through the blood of the sacrificed. They are still debating whether the point of it was to give Aneirin more magic or if it was used for something else," Kian continued. "If you have any trouble getting information out of the acolyte, wait for Killian, and he will take care of it."

"Thanks, Kian. I'll let you know if he says anything interesting," Charlotte said and hung up.

Cosimo dragged over a chair, and Reeve and Valentine shoved the acolyte into it.

Kenna appeared in time with a handful of iron cuffs to stop the acolyte from using any magic.

"Hey, Cos, didn't expect to see you here," Kenna said, kissing his cheek.

"It's been too long. When Reeve told me they had captured one of Aneirin's lackeys, I knew I had to see him for myself. You don't mind?"

Kenna shook her head and handed Reeve the cuffs. "Not at all. Have at him."

Once they got the acolyte secured, Cosimo lifted the spell, and he jolted awake. Kenna smiled coldly at him before punching him twice in the face.

"That's for the magicians you took, you son of a bitch," she snapped.

Cosimo laughed. "Oh, Kenna, don't ever change."

When Kenna gave Cosimo one of her rare smiles, Charlotte couldn't believe it. "I'm done. Let me know if the little piggy squeals anything good," Kenna said and paused. "Are you staying to watch, Charlotte?"

"Yes," she replied. No matter how squeamish she was, she was still an Ironwood and would do the job no matter how gross.

"Good girl." Kenna headed back up the stairs without another word. Those two words were like a month full of head pats from her mother. It made Charlotte feel a little better.

"Which one of you, pretty boys, thinks you are going to get information out of me, huh?" the acolyte chuckled, his nose bleeding freely thanks to Kenna. "Get your knives and pliers ready because you are going to be here a while."

"You really think that we would resort to such archaic methods?" Valentine's voice was like dark silk that brushed malice over Charlotte's skin. "Silly, silly boy. We are magicians, and there are far easier ways that won't ruin my nice clothes."

Reeve surprised her by taking a long knife from his coat. "I might take a piece or two off him for fun."

The acolyte didn't look nearly as confident as he had a moment beforehand. Cosimo smiled at him, and it was the warmest, most charming thing Charlotte had ever seen.

"I'm Cosimo. What's your name?" he asked kindly. Charlotte felt the glamour in the air like a warm hug. If he had aimed it at her, she would've told him anything he asked.

"My name..." the acolyte pulled at the cuffs before muttering. "Stephen."

"Stephen. Good. You seem like such a bright lad. What made you want to get involved with Aneirin?" Cosimo asked, leaning casually back against the bars.

"Aneirin..." Stephen's jaw snapped together hard, and he groaned in agony.

Charlotte frowned and studied him. There was something off about his aura. "I think he's got a spell on him, so he can't talk about the general."

"Would be a good idea to stop any loud mouths," Valentine said. He pulled out an object that looked like a small gold magnifying glass and looked through it at the acolyte. "Oh yes, definitely a muffling spell. It's well done actually like an invisible ball gag."

"See if you can figure out how he's done it, and we can use it on Apollo next time he huffs too much happy gas in his laboratory," Reeve said, making Charlotte laugh. She tried to smother it. She hated he could do that even in the middle of an interrogation.

Valentine's magic hummed in the air, and Charlotte wanted to take a step back from him. It wasn't evil, but it made a chill streak up her spine. It was subtle as a whisper of smoke and as dangerous as a dagger in the dark. She didn't know what he did, but it was like he cut the threads of the spell over the acolyte and peeled it back from him like a second skin.

"Gross, Val," Reeve complained.

The acolyte screamed. "No! No! Don't take him from me! My general needs me."

"Hush now. There's a good lad. Easy breaths," Cosimo crooned.

"You don't understand. He's my god. He is my all..."

"He is a mass murderer who sacrificed innocent people," Charlotte snapped.

The acolyte's crazed eyes turned on her, and he licked his lips. "So do all gods, pretty magician."

"Don't look at her like that, or I'll cut your eyes out," Reeve growled.

"Why shouldn't I? She's more pretty than what the master said she was. So pretty, so full of magic, so perfect for his plans," the acolyte rambled on.

"What plans?" Valentine demanded.

The acolyte shook his head. Cosimo raised a hand and put two fingers to the man's sweaty forehead. "Tell me, Stephen. What was the sigil at the beach for?"

"Ring ring ring," he chimed, sounding more deranged by the minute.

"He was contacting the generals?" Charlotte asked. "Hafgan and Vili?"

"Never say their names," he screamed. "The master rang for them, sent out the call to summon them. Ring. Ring. It's dinner time, and you're all fucking prey to be eaten!"

Reeve let a frustrated sigh. "This dude is cracked."

"It's only because I can see the truth, and you can't. You think too small, but the generals think wide and deep. They are going to fix this world. They will restore magic and the old gods to their rightful places. They are going to bring back the one who will sit atop a throne of bones."

Charlotte rubbed at her arms. She made sure her voice was steady and asked, "Do you mean Morrigan? Because where she's gone, the generals won't be able to go to retrieve her body."

"My goddess, my goddess, can you hear your magicians calling for you? They don't need to go to the dreaded Isle of Annwn to retrieve a broken body. They only need her soul." The acolyte's lip curled over his teeth, his attention still wholly focused on Charlotte. "Your body is going to be a lovely, lovely vessel for her to live in, pretty little witch."

They all froze as the acolyte laughed and laughed. Reeve's eyes shone with a strange golden light, and suddenly he was moving. He grabbed the man's hand and cut the fingers off one hand with one swipe of his blade. The acolyte screamed in agony, blood gushing to the floor. Valentine grabbed Reeve and dragged him away.

"Go and walk it off, Reeve!" Cosimo commanded, taking the knife from him. Reeve growled, his eyes glowing brighter before storming out.

"What was that?" Charlotte asked, too shocked to move at the blood and anger. She had never seen Reeve like that before. He was usually the easy-going one, not violent.

"Stop the bleeding, Charlotte," Cosimo said. Automatically, she pulled out some healing patches from her bag and stuck one on the man's bloody palm and one on his forearm. She whispered the activation word, and the acolyte screamed again as the flesh began to knit. With one last whimper, he fainted.

"Reeve did that to ensure he couldn't cast any magic again," Valentine said, looking at the severed fingers on the floor. "Brutal."

"What the fuck got into him?" Charlotte muttered.

"Only you can make him do something so stupid." Valentine gave her a pointed look. "You know our family has a dragon in it, right?"

Charlotte nodded. "Yes, but what does that have to do with anything?"

"Let's just say you bring out Reeve's dragon side."

"You can't be serious. Me? What do I have to do with anything?" Charlotte demanded.

"That's enough, Val," Cosimo hissed at him, making the other man shut his mouth with a snap. "We got what we needed from this poor sap, at least for now. We'll go and update Kenna. Charlotte, please go after Reeve. I doubt he'll listen to anyone but you right now."

"You two seriously overestimate my value to him. We are barely friends," Charlotte argued.

"You need to talk to him," Valentine shoved her out of the jail cell. "Off you go. Send him home when you're done with him."

Confused and pissed off at being dismissed, Charlotte strode up the stairs and out of the back doors. Night had fallen, and it was starting to rain. There was no sign of Reeve.

"Just perfect," she grumbled and went to look for him.

14

Charlotte pulled the collar up on her coat to stop the rain from dripping down her neck. Reeve wasn't hanging about under the house's awnings at all, which meant he was out on the grounds somewhere.

Charlotte pulled out her phone and sent him a message.
Where are you?
When he didn't reply, she let out a frustrated breath. Fine. *Fine.* She would do it another way. Charlotte closed her eyes and steadied her breathing.

Killian had taught her how to feel out magical signatures. She was good at it because she was already sensitive to magic and its vibrations.

Reeve wasn't doing any magic at that moment, but she could feel it, like a warm brush against hers, beckoning her towards the glass greenhouse. She had promised herself that she wouldn't ever let her power touch his again, and here she was, allowing it to pull it towards him like a siren song.

Charlotte wiped the rain from her face. She had broken a lot of promises to herself when it came to Reeve, but maybe they needed to see that the past years had been a stupid misunderstanding.

You wasted five years...a small voice said inside of her head. She didn't need to make herself feel worse, so she shoved it away.

Charlotte opened the door to the greenhouse and stepped into the warm, damp air. The greenhouse had slowly become Layla's purview. She was the only one that didn't kill the plants of all the sisters, and she somehow managed to keep everything green and healthy all year round.

"Reeve? Are you in here?" Charlotte called. There was no reply.

She bit back her anger and stepped through the lush greenery and headed towards the day bed and a small table that Layla had set up.

"I know you are in here, so stop hiding from me," she said, her feet finding the path in the scant light.

"Who said I am hiding?" Reeve's voice replied from the darkness. It was deeper than it usually was, a feral note in it that had the hair on her arms lifting.

"Valentine and Cosimo are done with the prisoner. Don't you want to go home with them?" she said, her voice nowhere near as steady as it had been a moment ago.

"No." There was a sheen of golden eyes through the leaves, and then it was gone. Charlotte froze. Reeve wasn't hiding. He was stalking her.

You bring out Reeve's dragon side, Valentine had said. Was that really a thing? Charlotte had no idea if the story of the Greatdrakes was true, let alone the mythical beast still having any effect on their ancestors.

Goes to show what you know.

Charlotte slowed her steps, her magic rising under her skin to try and protect her. She wasn't afraid. She knew Reeve wouldn't hurt her, but her heart was pounding hard in her chest.

"Come and talk to me, Reeve. Tell me, what's wrong? We have a truce, remember?" Charlotte licked her too dry lips. "We are almost friends, aren't we? Friends talk to each other."

"Friends," Reeve sneered. "We've always been more than that. You've just never wanted to admit it."

"Neither have you." Charlotte stopped in the center of the greenhouse. The day bed was empty and undisturbed. "You say that I threw our friendship away, but you did too. You didn't exactly show up on my doorstep and demand to talk to me."

"You say that like you would've listened. You were too angry."

"I was hurt, not angry." Charlotte crossed her arms. "You would've been too if you heard the person you were in..." she cut herself off quickly, "you were friends with saying terrible things about you."

"I told you my reasons for that," Reeve said from somewhere behind her. "We both were stupid about it, made mistakes. And I am done apologizing for it. Time to face facts, Charlotte."

She refused to turn around as warmth spread down her back. She gripped herself tighter to stop her leaning back into him.

"What facts are you talking about?" Charlotte said.

Reeve's breath was warm against her ear. "That you and I are fucking destined. You can fight as much as you want. I still know the truth. You woke up my dragon side, and it doesn't lie."

"You sound crazy right now. What dragon side? Why did you cut off that guy's fingers? What the hell is going on, Reeve?" she demanded. She turned around and stumbled back. Reeve was so close that he loomed over her, his eyes glowing. She went to move again, but his hands shot out and grabbed her by the biceps.

"Aneirin wants to use you as a vessel for Morrigan. What about that am I meant to be okay with?" he demanded, getting in her face. "That asshole would serve you up to him on a silver platter. How was I supposed to react?"

"M-Maybe not by cutting his fingers off?" she stammered.

"He's lucky I didn't cut off his fucking head."

Charlotte was shaking, but she wasn't trying to pull away. He was clearly not in control of himself. She placed her hands on his face and stroked his soft stubble.

"Reeve, I'm not going to be used as Morrigan's vessel. He was stupid and told us Aneirin's plan. This is a *good* thing," she said, thumbs caressing his cheekbones. "I'm not hurt in any way. You need to calm down."

Golden power flashed in his eyes, and her mouth went bone dry. "That's not what I need."

"N-No?"

Reeve bent his head and kissed the side of her neck. His lips dragged over her skin, and he inhaled deeply. "Your magic, your scent, your smile... I can't get enough. You are going to be the death of me, and I don't care."

"I don't understand what you want from me, Reeve." Charlotte's hands curled into the warmth of his shirt, neck tilting, her body following an instinct she couldn't name.

Reeve's teeth scraped against her skin. His hand rested on the back of her neck and gripped her gently. "I want everything, Charlotte Ironwood. Everything."

Reeve kissed her, pinning her to him as his tongue pressed against her lips, demanding access. Charlotte's mouth opened, and he swept inside, the feel of him overwhelming her. Her skin was tingling, everything going tight with desire. Her brain had stopped working, and whatever madness Reeve was under, she didn't have the will to fight it.

"God, you taste amazing," he growled. He stepped backward and sat on the day bed before tugging her gently into his lap.

"Reeve, are you sure you're okay? You're acting a bit crazy," Charlotte said breathlessly.

Reeve's hands slid under her jacket and sweater so he could touch the soft skin of her back. "This is the least crazy I've been for days." He went to kiss her again, but she moved back a little.

"I don't want to be something that you regret," she whispered, forcing the words out.

Reeve lifted her chin. "The only thing I regret was not kissing you five years ago and every day since." Charlotte's mouth popped open in a surprised O, and he took the opportunity to kiss her again.

Charlotte pressed her fingers through his silky, thick hair like she had always wanted to. She felt shaky, the yearning she had felt for years hitting her like a bus. She wrapped her legs around his waist, and he made a soft sound of approval at the back of his throat. She could feel the hard length of him press into her thigh, and she blushed hot all over.

Reeve Greatdrakes is turned on just from kissing you.

She didn't know what strange reality she was suddenly in, but she really didn't care. She kissed him harder, hands gripping his hair and tugging his head back to give her access to his throat.

"God, why do I want you so damn much?" she murmured against him.

Reeve's hands tightened on her hips, pulling her against him, so his erection ground up against the liquid heat pooling in between her thighs.

"The feeling is mutual, Charlie. Don't stop kissing me," he begged. She had never heard him use that tone before, so she took his mouth again. She rolled her hips against him again, groaning at the pressure building inside of her. She had never gotten off by dry humping anyone, but being this close to Reeve was undoing her.

"Can I touch you?" Reeve asked, kissing down her neck. "I'll give you exactly what you need, baby."

"Yes." Charlotte was on fire, a few kisses igniting a long-dead heat inside of her. Reeve slid his hand inside the top of her tights. His hot palm cupped her, and they both moaned. Charlotte kissed him, her hands gripping his shoulders tight as his fingers gently explored her, finding the slick heart of her. Her hips rocked gently against him, and he swore.

"Fuck, you are so hot and wet," he whispered against her lips. The tip of his finger circled her clit, and she whimpered.

"More, Reeve," she managed, her breath becoming shallow. Reeve slid a long finger inside of her, and she rose up on her knees so she could lower herself further down on it. Reeve added another finger, and her grip on him tightened.

"That's it, Charlie. Fuck, you look like heaven riding my hand," he said. He gripped her hip with his other hand, bringing her down harder. "Does it feel good?"

"So...good. Don't stop. I'm so close." Charlotte's vision was blurring, her orgasm shimmering closer. Reeve's head bent down to rub against the soft fabric of her sweater. He bit into her breast through the material, and she cried out.

Reeve's voice was a demanding, husky growl. "Come for me, Charlotte. Let me feel you lose control." His gentle thrusts quickened, and his thumb pressed down on her clit. Charlotte's whole body lit up and shook, her voice a broken cry in her throat. Her orgasm whited her vision, her sensitive inner walls gripping him tightly. She could feel the warm wetness dripping out of her and onto him.

"That's my good girl," Reeve said, kissing her forehead, her cheeks, and the corner of her eyes where a few tears had slipped.

She didn't know why, but his soft approval had her clenching up, and he toyed with her too sensitive clit again. Slowly, he removed his fingers from her. They glistened in the scanty moonlight, and with the feral gold glowing in his eyes again, Reeve licked them clean. Charlotte's eyes blew out wide, watching him.

"Every part of you is so fucking delicious," he said, not breaking the eye contact. "It might not be tonight, but I'm going to taste every part of you to prove it."

Charlotte gasped as he kissed her. She could taste herself on his lips and didn't know if she should be appalled or not. She didn't stop kissing him. Nothing could make her stop kissing him. Reeve pulled her down onto the bed, so he was spooning her.

"Do you... Should I..." she began, feeling his erection still pressing into her.

"Return the favor? Not tonight, Charlie. This was for you." Reeve propped his head up with one hand and kissed her again. "It'll be my day tomorrow."

Charlotte's cheeks went hot. "Tomorrow?"

"You think I'm going to let you go?" Reeve smiled down at her and brushed a finger over her full lips before dipping it inside her mouth for her to suck. "Oh, baby. I'm never going to let you go again."

15

Reeve woke before dawn, Charlotte still bundled up in his arms. He stared at the lightening glass roof above him, a grin splitting his face. He didn't expect his previous day to end how it had, but he was stoked about it.

"What's that goofy smile about?" Charlotte murmured. Her sleep-heavy eyes were only opened just a little.

"I don't know what you're talking about," he said, pressing a kiss to her forehead. "I should get out of here before everyone wakes up and realizes I never went home."

Charlotte grumbled something and buried her face into his side. Reeve laughed softly and stroked her hair. "One little orgasm, and you suddenly turned into a cuddler?"

"Wasn't little," she mumbled and huffed out a laugh. "Don't look so smug about it."

"I can't help it. You should really go and climb into your nice warm bed."

"That involves moving."

Reeve nibbled at her ear. "I could carry you. Imagine the uproar if we were caught."

"I'll walk," Charlotte said, wriggling out of his arms. Her braid was a mess, and she looked so gloriously bedraggled, his dick went hard again. He was positive he would have a permanent zipped mark in it after last night.

"Come over later when you wake up," Reeve said before he could second guess himself. "I think we need to see if we can find something that will stop Aneirin from using your body as a vessel. The library at home is bound to have something that will help."

"You would let me look about in the Greatdrakes library?" Charlotte asked, blue eyes sparking awake with excitement. God, he'd give her the damn thing if it was in his power and anything else she wanted.

"For as long as you want. I'm sure Valentine and Cosimo have caught everyone up on yesterday's interrogation. They are busy enough on the other research, we can find an answer to the possession," he said, knowing just what to offer her.

Charlotte yawned but nodded her head. "Sounds good. I just need a few more hours of sleep first."

Reeve walked across the grounds with her before giving her a soft kiss and heading for his car. He made sure she was inside the safety of the house before he turned on the ignition and headed home.

Reeve had never had his dragon side take over so entirely like it had the previous evening. As soon as the acolyte had threatened Charlotte, it had come roaring to the surface. He barely remembered cutting the man's fingers off or anything before Charlotte had found him in the greenhouse. He remembered unending rage at having his mate threatened, and nothing could calm him down except her.

You really need to talk to Kian. The prince understood what happened with mates. Killian would tease him, and Bayn would threaten to cut his balls off. Kian seemed like the safest choice.

Reeve wanted to talk to Cosimo about it but didn't want to open any old wounds. His father had almost lost his mind when his mother, Lisa, had died. If Cosimo hadn't had young sons to raise... Reeve didn't want to think about it. It had taken two years to even have his father be a glimmer of his old self.

Reeve didn't want to risk Cosimo's mental health by telling him about Charlotte. His father might even suggest having space from her, and that was something Reeve wouldn't be able to handle. Charlotte wouldn't be safe until Aneirin was dead, and he wanted to keep her close. Preferably on top of him. Just to be cautious.

"Fuck," Reeve groaned, horny all over again. His mind sent him some unhelpful visuals of the way she had felt clamped tight around his fingers. Her sweet pussy had been so drenched for him; he had never felt anything like it. And her taste...

Reeve pulled out his phone, and before he could second guess himself, he pressed Kian's number. Technically, it was only meant to be used for emergencies, but he needed information. He couldn't be losing his shit like the previous night.

"Mr. Greatdrakes, I had a feeling I would be hearing from you today," Kian answered, sounding fresh despite the early hour. "You cut anything else off the prisoner last night?"

Reeve flinched. "It might have been an overreaction."

"Or an under reaction considering the information he held. Is it true that Aneirin has singled out Charlotte for a vessel for Morrigan?" Kian asked.

"Yes. He threatened her, and I lost it. I was hoping you could give me some advice on handling the mates thing."

Kian made a sound that could have been a smothered laugh. "The *mates thing* isn't something that can always be handled. It is why the fae usually do it out of society if they can. I don't know how it is with you. Tell me, how did a dragon end up in your family?"

Reeve told Kian everything that he knew about his ancestor, the dragon, and the curses that had come through the family ever since. Kian asked questions about the mates, and Reeve told him about his mother.

"I don't want to trigger anything for my father if I don't have to, so I thought you might be the best person to ask," Reeve finished.

"I have honestly never heard of a dragon offering to bond with a human and give its power to them. It's a great honor, but I am sure your family knows that. From what you have said, it is similar to fae mating urges, especially the overprotective instincts," Kian replied. There was a long pause before he continued. "I don't think it is something that should be managed. You looking out for my sister's well-being while Aneirin is alive will be a boon. The only other advice I can give you, you aren't going to like."

"Let me hear it, prince," Reeve said with a sigh.

"You need to tell Charlotte."

Reeve laughed. "Kian, I've barely got her to like me again. I can't spring this on her."

"I understand your reluctance. Charlotte values her independence and won't like the idea. If things progress between you, it would be better if she knew. I don't know how dragon mating can work, but if she starts to get unusual abilities, it might frighten her."

Reeve ran a hand over his face. "I promise I'll tell her if that happens. I just need to let her warm up to me again first. We need to prioritize Aneirin, and I don't want this hanging over her head."

"Let me know when you do, and I'll get Elise ready to talk to her. She has a way of calming people down, and Charlotte will be able to ask her questions," Kian replied.

"Thank you, Kian. I appreciate that and your help. I know we don't know each other well, and you owe me nothing."

"Charlotte is family, and I know better than anyone that destiny rarely is wrong when it comes to mates. There will be no better person in the world for her," Kian replied. "And if you're not, I'll obliterate you."

Reeve felt a chill roll down his spine. "That's your right, but it's not going to happen."

"Good luck, Greatdrakes. Keep me up to date on Aneirin." And the prince hung up, leaving Reeve to wonder how he could tell Charlotte she was his mate without her blasting him.

The house was quiet when Reeve hung up his keys in the garage and padded upstairs to the kitchen. Basset was at the kitchen table, drinking coffee and reading the paper.

"Jesus, Bas, you scared me," Reeve started. "What the hell are you doing awake?"

Basset looked at him from over the top of his glasses. "And miss you doing the walk of shame?"

Reeve flipped him off and snagged a piece of his brother's toast from his plate. "Ain't no shame here, bruv."

"Didn't think so. Val said you went full dragon and cut off fingers yesterday. Not exactly my idea of a turn-on, but I suppose Charlotte didn't care. She is an Ironwood after all," Bas replied, going back to his paper. "You better get upstairs before Apollo wakes up and wants details."

"He's not going to get them. Wake me up in a couple of hours?" Reeve asked.

Basset waved him on. "Yeah, yeah, go get some beauty sleep. What time is Charlotte due?"

"What makes you think she's coming over?"

Basset gave him a genuinely glorious eye roll. "Call it brother's intuition."

∽

REEVE WOKE hours later to Apollo going through his wardrobe. His brother hated doing laundry and would help himself to Reeve's clothes whenever he could. Valentine had gone as far as putting a curse on his clothes, so if anyone but him wore them, they would break out into a horrible rash. That was pure Valentine, so Apollo had learned to steer clear.

"What are you stealing now?" Reeve grumbled.

"Nothing. Shhh, go back to sleep," Apollo crooned and pulled on one of Reeve's *Doctor Strange* T-shirts.

"Hey, you better not wreck that shirt. It's one of my favorites," Reeve said and rubbed at his face. "What time is it?"

"Eleven. What time is sweet Charlotte coming over?" Apollo waggled his eyebrows at him. "Did princess rock your world last night?"

Yes, and I didn't even get off.

"That's none of your business."

Apollo flopped down on the bed beside him. "Sure it is, baby boy. I'm so relieved you're not a virgin anymore."

Reeve hit him with a pillow. "You better not say anything to Charlotte when she gets here. I'm trying not to scare her away."

"Are you kidding me? She terrifies me. I wouldn't mess with her if you paid me to." Apollo's blue eyes sparkled. "You do know she's way out of your league?"

"I am aware."

"Like, physically, emotionally, magically..."

"Thanks so much. And yes, I know," Reeve said and sighed. "It's not going to stop me from trying to win her over."

"Well, if she's coming round after last night, then you must've done something right. Val said she brings out your dragon side. Does that mean what I think it does?" Apollo asked, suddenly serious. He didn't say the dreaded M-word, but they were both thinking it.

"Maybe? Or I'm just being overprotective. The guy yesterday was laughing about the idea of shoving a war goddess into Charlie's body, and I lost it. Fucking, Aneirin."

Apollo gave him a shove with his shoulder. "We'll get him. Don't worry. And all of us like Charlotte more than we like you, so we will keep her safe, Reeve."

"Not that she needs it, but thanks."

Apollo shrugged. "She's an Ironwood, but I think she's more of a magician like us than a hunter. She needs other magicians. People that get her."

"True. Valentine will have to get used to not being the smartest all the time," Reeve said, and they both laughed.

"Worth it to watch her smack him down a peg or two. Don't fuck this up, Reeve. There hasn't been a girl in this house for too long. It'll do us all good."

Reeve studied his brother's profile. He wasn't usually so severe. "I won't. You know, you could always bring home a girl occasionally."

"Never met one that I wanted to. None like Charlotte. She's beauty, brains, and magic. Those are rarer than unicorns. She fits with us and isn't intimidated by our bullshit." Apollo got up again and kicked the edge of Reeve's bed. "Come on, you better get up before she gets here. Or I'll steal her from you."

"You got no chance."

"You hope I don't, baby bro," he said, leaving Reeve's room with a backward wave.

Reeve pulled himself upright. He needed all the coffee and to tidy up the mess Apollo had made rummaging through his wardrobe.

Reeve's smile turned sly as he thought about getting Charlotte into his bedroom.

Despite inviting her over to study, Reeve fully intended to continue what he had started with Charlotte the night before and take his sweet time doing it.

16

Charlotte managed to get into her room without being spotted, set her alarm, and had gone back to sleep. She was usually awake by dawn and up first, so it wasn't a surprise when Layla came in to poke her.

"What?"

"Just wanted to see if you were still alive," Layla said and placed a steaming mug of tea on Charlotte's bedside table. "What did you get up to last night?"

Charlotte rolled over and sipped at her tea. She didn't particularly want to tell anyone about Reeve, but she needed advice. Layla was always a safer bet than Imogen because Imogen would tell Bron; Bron would tell Killian, and then all Dublin would know.

"Promise not to tell anyone?" Charlotte asked.

"Geeze, a promise? That sounds serious." Layla sat down on Charlotte's desk chair and propped her feet up on the edge of the bed. She was wearing her Lord of the Rings pajamas and somehow still looked effortlessly cool despite her fair hair being a total riot. "Okay, okay, I promise. What happened?"

"Made out with Reeve in the greenhouse," Charlotte mumbled quickly into her mug.

Layla's brown eyes went wide in shock. "You're kidding me!"

Charlotte shook her head. "He wasn't quite himself. Something to do with the dragon in his family, apparently. I went to calm him down to stop him from killing our prisoner and may have ended up with my tongue in his mouth."

Amongst other things, the sweet ache between her thighs reminded her.

"May have." Layla's full lips broke into a wild smile. "I'm proud, sis. Good on you."

"Seriously? I thought you would be giving me a hard time about this."

"Why? Reeve is awesome and has obviously been into you since forever. I was more surprised that you didn't hook up in college," Layla replied and lifted her coffee to her lips. "Was it good at least? He always struck me as someone who would kiss like a demon."

More like a dragon.

Charlotte couldn't stop her smile. "Yeah. He was good. I mean the kissing." She wasn't about to tell her any more details about what happened. She was still having difficulty believing that Reeve had made her come so hard just by using his fingers.

Layla chuckled. "If he can kiss well, it's a good sign he'll be great at giving head."

"Layla! Jesus, we aren't that far along," Charlotte said, her cheeks turning hot.

Aren't you, though? Charlotte's thighs pressed together at just the thought of it.

Layla's grin only widened. "Yeah, sure you aren't. When are you going to see him again?"

"Today. We are going to do some research in his library," she replied. "You should see their place. It's wild. Their library is in one big tower and..."

"And your nerdy heart loves it. I can tell." Layla got to her feet. "Okay, you little hussy. You have a shower, and I'll make you some breakfast. You deserve to have lots of sustenance for your big day of *research*."

"We *are* doing research," Charlotte claimed. She thought back to Reeve's hot promise the night before.

It'll be my day tomorrow...

Oh, God, how would she concentrate with that hanging over her head? Maybe his temporary bout of dragon crazy would have calmed down, and he was having second thoughts on what they had done.

"Hey! Whatever you just thought, unthink it," Layla said, snapping her out of her sudden anxiety. "Reeve is good people, Charlotte. He's not the type of guy to fuck about, so don't freak out over it."

Charlotte unraveled her messy braid. "Yeah, that's not how it works. I can't help it. My brain doesn't function like yours on unlimited self-esteem."

Layla was gorgeous, with curves that Charlotte envied and the warmest heart of all the Ironwood clan. People liked her, but more importantly, Layla liked herself just the way she was. Charlotte had days when she could barely look at herself in the mirror.

"Don't make me smack you," Layla said, a hand going to her hip. "You are fucking beautiful and amazing, and everyone knows it. Not just Reeve. He's lucky that you're giving him another shot. He's not going to fuck that up. So get your ass out of bed and into the shower and stop pouting that you got to make out with a ridiculously hot guy last night. Some of us only went to bed with a vibrator, so be grateful."

Charlotte screwed her nose up. "Eww, Layla. Stop it."

"You stop it. Reeve is hot, and I'm jealous." She turned on her heel and headed for the door. "If I'm cooking you breakfast, you better hurry up because you know I don't do it for just anyone."

"Okay, I'm up," Charlotte said, picking up her tea and heading for the shower.

～

CHARLOTTE WAS in a surprisingly good mood by the time she made it to the Greatdrakes house. Valentine had done a number on the wards, making them twice as vicious and intricate.

Charlotte couldn't help but smile. It told her that he had a begrudging sort of respect for her. It was almost a shame to rip them apart.

Charlotte knocked on the front door, her stomach filling with butterflies. Reeve pulled open the door, and the butterflies threatened to escape out of her throat. He had his hair out and was dressed in shredded jeans and a maroon knit sweater stretched over his broad chest. It even had a hole in it. How did he make scrappy look so fucking gorgeous?

"Hey," she said, trying not to sound awkward as hell.

"Hey yourself," Reeve replied, closing the door behind him before taking her face with both hands and kissing her. It wasn't a quick peck. It was a slow exploration of lips and tongue that made her body light up quicker than a shot of caffeine.

Charlotte knew it was probably inappropriate to be making out with Reeve on the steps of his father's house, but she wasn't about to let that stop her. Reeve seemed to override her good manners and common sense.

You are in so much danger.

Charlotte's hands went under the hem of his sweater until she could stroke against the skin of his abs. He was always warm and smelled so damn good, like spice and magic and Reeve. His power rolled against hers in gentle waves that made it fizz in her veins like champagne bubbles.

He pulled back slowly and dropped a small kiss on the tip of her cold nose.

"That wasn't the greeting I was expecting," Charlotte said, her breathing uneven.

His smile would've been bashful if he didn't look so pleased. "Well, you should expect it from now on. In fact, it's the only way I wanted to be greeted by you."

"Reeve, don't you think we..." she began before the door was yanked open.

"What are you two doing out here?" Apollo asked with a big grin. "Your hands got a bit chilly, did they, Charlotte?" He nodded at where they were still buried under Reeve's sweater. She quickly yanked them free.

"Why do you want to ruin everything?" Reeve asked with a sigh.

"We have a general to catch. You two can canoodle once he's dead. Eyes on the prize." Apollo clapped his hands. "To the library with you, saucy deviants!"

"Who the fuck says *canoodle*?" Reeve mocked.

Charlotte coughed to cover her embarrassment. "Sure thing. You're right, Apollo. We should get to work."

"Don't tell him that. It'll make him even more full of himself," Reeve complained.

"Hard not to be when you're right all the time. Isn't that so, Charlotte?" Apollo said.

Charlotte only shook her head at them. Her sisters were just as bad with their continual goading. Her lips tingled at the feel of Reeve's stubble still on them. His hand rested on the small of her back as they went upstairs, and her whole body seemed hyper-aware of him.

Charlotte almost groaned. She really was in so much danger, and Aneirin was starting to rank second to her falling for Reeve harder than before.

She thought morning kisses were probably moving too fast, but once she had made her mind up about something, not a lot could change it. And her mind very much enjoyed Reeve's lazy smile that was so at odds with the single-minded intensity he had when kissing her...or doing other things.

Don't think about the other things, she scolded herself as a warm ache built between her thighs.

Apollo opened the doors to the library, and Charlotte breathed a happy sigh. Books were her first and truest love for good reason. They never disappointed her when people so often did.

"I see you got through my wards again," Valentine said from one of the study desks. From the pile of books and papers scattered everywhere, he seemed to have been there for a while.

"They were really good this time, I swear. I was stumped," Charlotte said, patting him on the shoulder. "At least for a little while."

"You really have to show me how you keep doing that."

Charlotte smiled sweetly. "Do I, though?"

"Yes," Valentine said sternly. "Your magic is unlike anything I've seen, and it's fascinating. Reeve said you did sigil magic, but it's so much more than that."

"As I keep telling her. She wouldn't even need to write the sigil out, just hold it in her mind, and magic would do the rest," Reeve replied.

Charlotte crossed her arms. "Not this again! I have to write it out, or how will it be released?"

"Through intention," Valentine answered as if it was the most basic thing in the world.

"See? I told you," Reeve said, poking Charlotte in the shoulder. "You thought I was full of shit."

"You are," Valentine and Apollo answered at the same time.

They instantly fell into a debate about magic, and despite being frustrated with all three of them, Charlotte was enjoying herself too. She suddenly felt an odd sense of belonging that she had never experienced with anyone.

She loved her family, but they didn't understand most of what she said. The Greatdrakes boys not only understood, but they also knew enough to challenge her with solid arguments. She lost what remained of her social anxiety in the intensity of the conversation. They spoke her language, and for the first time, she didn't feel alone or like an outsider.

"Okay, Val, we are hunting for a way to stop a body from being possessed against its will," Reeve said, trying to bring the argument back on point. "Where should we start looking?"

"Try the third level. All of the darker magics are up there."

Charlotte thought for a moment. "I wonder if we should look at how to possess someone and then work backward. Figure out how they could do it, and reverse engineer it somehow."

Valentine grinned at her. "I do like the way you think, Ironwood."

"That's because you are both maniacs," Apollo replied, shooting Charlotte a wink to take the edge off the insult. "Maybe start with something to stop a possession, and if you exhaust all options, *then* look into reversing a possession spell. You know, like normal people."

"Who the fuck wants to be normal?" Charlotte replied, flicking her ponytail over one shoulder and heading for the stairs.

"She's way, way too good for you," she heard Valentine say to Reeve, and she hid her smile. She liked impressing his brothers and that they approved of...of whatever she and Reeve were doing.

Probably do some good to find out, don't you think?

Charlotte shook the thought out of the way; magic first, emotions second. They had a possession to stop because she had no intention of sharing her body with the goddess of war.

17

Reeve and Charlotte worked their way through the section on dark magic for the next few hours. It was a slower progress than expected because Reeve kept getting distracted by Charlotte's perfume and the way she bit her full bottom lip when she was thinking. On the other hand, she kept getting distracted by exciting books and spells, gasping and appalled one minute or thoroughly engrossed the next.

"This might be something," Charlotte said from the table opposite him. She tapped to the page of a yellowing old tome that Reeve was sure was bound in human skin.

"What is it?"

"An account of a sorcerer in the thirteenth century. He tried to use his servant as a vessel for the fallen angel, Azazel. The possession worked right up until the point that the servant exploded," Charlotte said, sounding way too fascinated.

Reeve rubbed his eyes. "Okay, and why is that something?"

"Because it means that a more powerful being can't just be shoved into a normal human because our physical bodies can't contain it."

Reeve's stomach twisted. "So if Aneirin tries to shove a goddess's shade into a human body, it will explode. They want *you* for that body. You would be the one exploding."

Charlotte's foot found him under the table, and she ran it along his calf. "Calm down, Reeve. I have no intention of exploding. Aneirin would have to perform some other magic on me, or any other human, to contain Morrigan. They would be better off trying it with a fae or a shifter because their bodies are already immortal. They want mine out of revenge."

"And also so they can use your magic," Reeve added darkly.

"The revenge side will make them have to work harder, and if he's furious enough, then he's bound to make mistakes. Look at the attack on the club and leaving that acolyte behind. It's sloppy."

"Or he's leaving breadcrumbs in the hope we walk right into his goddamn trap." Reeve was never going to sleep well again until Aneirin was buried. "I swear to all the gods, I'm going to get gray hairs over this shit."

Charlotte smiled above the book. "Is that meant to be a bad thing? I think you would look rather good with a bit of gray."

Her foot was still against his calf, so Reeve trapped it between his legs. "Is that so? I'm only twenty-seven, but I'm sure dating you will add some gray hairs before long."

"Dating me? Is that what we are doing?" She looked back at the writing on the page, but she wasn't reading it. Reeve slid his hand under the table, pulled off her ankle boot, and stroked her foot. He had to touch her before he went crazy.

"I don't really care what we call it. As long as it's with you, I'm in," he said and hung onto her slender ankle so she couldn't pull away from him. His thumb brushed over the warm, bare skin above her sock, and she bit her lip.

"I don't work like that, Reeve. I need to know in black and white terms what's happening. I don't do casual fling things like you probably do," Charlotte replied with a wave of her hand. "It's not how I am built."

Reeve's eyes narrowed. "Casual. Fling. Thing. You think that's all I want with you?"

"I don't *know* what you want, Reeve. You've never spelled it out. We went from being attacked to kissing, to..." she flushed and looked away.

"To my fingers being buried inside of you as you came with my name on your lips," Reeve finished. The blush on her cheeks went from pink to crimson. "Are you embarrassed about what happened last night?"

"No. I'm embarrassed by this conversation. I didn't expect to be having it today when we are meant to be working," Charlotte said. Her tone was slipping back into a coldness that he hadn't heard in days. Her walls were going up before his eyes.

"No. I'm not having that." Reeve let go of her foot and was around the other side of the table before she could say another word. She glared at him, blue eyes full of annoyance and challenge. Anything was better than that coldness.

"What?" she demanded.

"We are having this conversation right now because I don't want to have you confused about my intentions." Reeve knelt beside her chair and took a patient breath. "I didn't pine over you for the last five years because I want a fucking casual fling. I want you any way I can have you. You can decide what that means. You're absolutely calling all the shots, Charlotte."

"You pined for me?" Charlotte said slowly like that was the only bit she had heard. Reeve ran his fingers over the loose ponytail hanging over her shoulder.

"Yeah, Charlie. I really fucking did. I'm still pining, I think. I know everything is crazy at the moment with the generals and shit. I just don't care. I don't want to waste any more time, letting you think that I don't want you."

Charlotte brushed her fingers along his left cheekbone. "Maybe we can trial date for a bit and see how it goes? I've never really dated. I don't think some casual hookups count. I don't really know how it's done, so you're going to have to show me."

Reeve smiled, her uncertainty making his heart soften even as his dragon side went a little feral, thinking about all the things it wanted to show her. He wrapped her ponytail around his wrist, so her head went back and exposed her pale, pretty neck to him.

"It's done exactly like this," he said and put his mouth over her fluttering pulse.

Charlotte breathed in sharply, and he nipped and sucked his way up to her ear. Her fingernails dug into his hair, and he almost groaned. Every time she touched him, it was like his body went into overdrive.

"Reeve, maybe we shouldn't make out in your family library?"

"Hmm, who's going to stop us exactly?" he mused and ran his tongue over her lips. She opened automatically for him, and he pressed the tip of his tongue along hers. Her grip on his hair tightened, and some final resistance seemed to snap in her. Charlotte kissed him hard, her mouth devouring his like she couldn't get enough.

Fuck, he couldn't wait to get her naked. Once she got out of her own head, she was going to go off in the best way. Reeve was determined to do whatever he could to make her totally lose control.

"Trial dating it is," he said when they finally came up for air. Her lips were flushed with color and so glossy, his cock was getting harder the more he looked at them.

Charlotte's fingers slowly let his hair go. "We need to do the thing. Study."

Reeve kissed her ink-stained fingers and stood up again. Her blue eyes dropped to the bulge in his pants, and the most mischievous smile he had seen twisted her lips.

"Don't look at it like that, or it will cause me even more problems," he complained.

Charlotte hummed. "Well, you did say it was your day today. If you and it are very good, I might give it some attention later."

All the blood left in his body went straight to his cock. He almost hobbled back to his chair. "That didn't help."

"It wasn't meant to," Charlotte replied primly and straightened her glasses. She pushed another book towards him. "On the plus side, you now have a good incentive to find the answers we need, don't you?"

Reeve smiled across at her. "Challenge accepted, Charlie Belle."

∼

Hours later, Reeve's eyes were burning, and his concentration was lagging. He shut the book he was reading and looked down at his scribbled notes and references. Charlotte wrote in a notebook and took photos of a page on her phone.

"This might be worth something, but I want Kian to have a look at it first," she said, noticing him staring.

"Why? We have a houseful of magicians we can ask," Reeve replied, doing his best not to sound jealous. It was stupid, but he couldn't help it.

"Because the writer says that the sigil was created by one of the fae and a priest that had been dealing with Norse demons that were coming with Viking raiders. I want another fae mage to look at it, and Kian is the only one I know," Charlotte said, tapping on her phone before putting it down.

Reeve tied his hair back into a knot and tried not to grin when he saw her following his movements hungrily.

"While we wait for Kian to get back to you, let's have a break. I'm going cross-eyed. Do you want to stretch your legs? Have a look at the rest of the house, maybe?"

"Sure. That sounds like a good idea. I don't know how long Kian will be, and we should try and find something as a backup if this sigil is a bust," Charlotte replied, slipping her phone into her back pocket.

Reeve found himself taking a girl to his bedroom for the first time in his life. The Greatdrakes mansion tended to change with every generation living in it. Magicians loved towers as some unspoken rule, and every one of the brothers had their own.

It was a good thing because if Reeve had to constantly smell whatever noxious thing Apollo was brewing, he would have tried moving out at ten. They all had the space to practice their gifts without their magic hurting each other or the rest of the house.

Reeve had always done his best not to fall prey to the weakness of all scholars by becoming a pack rat. Despite his best efforts, his tower was full of books and magical objects that he had collected from his travels or that he'd received as gifts from other magicians and sorcerers in the family.

"This place looks like you," Charlotte said, looking through a glass bowl of small and interesting objects that Reeve liked to stuff his pockets with, in case he needed to use them for magic. He especially liked mundane things like paper clips, stickers, and rubber bands that would look completely normal to other humans but could be transformed into all sorts of useful things.

"Actually, I expected it to be a lot messier," Charlotte continued, casting an eye around at the posters on the stone walls and overflowing bookshelves.

"Miss Ironwood, I'm wounded. What about me says I would be a slob?" he mocked.

She gave the hole in his sweater a tug. "You don't seem to own any clothes without holes in them for a start."

"It's called bohemian or shabby chic. Thrift shop connoisseur," he protested. "I do have posh clothes, but I only bust them out for very special occasions."

"And what do you classify as a very special occasion?" Charlotte tried not to smile. "You wore jeans with holes in them to Bron's mating party with actual princes in attendance."

"How would you know? Were you checking me out?" he teased.

"And why would I do that?"

Reeve moved to hug her from behind, marveling that she would allow him to do it at all. "Because you might tease me about my clothes, but you still like the way I look in them."

"It's anyone's guess why." Charlotte turned in his arms and placed her own around him. "One of life's true mysteries." She stood on her tiptoes and kissed him. She had never instigated anything before, and it sent a thrill straight through him.

Reeve's hands tightened on her, drawing her closer so he could deepen the embrace. She fit so perfectly in his arms, her tall, lean body aligning with his in all the right ways. Her magic was prickly static against him, and it made his skin tingle all over.

Charlotte moved up against him, her full lips smiling against his when she felt how hard he was.

"In case you wanted to know, no, that's not a magic wand in my pocket," he said, and she laughed softly.

"Your jokes are terrible."

"If that were true, you wouldn't be laughing every time I make one." Reeve jumped as her hand brushed over his groin, and she smiled like a sphinx. "W-What are you doing, Charlie?"

A perfect brow rose. "I should think it was obvious. Isn't that why you brought me up here? Because it was your day?"

Reeve's whole body went hard and hot. "It wasn't the reason why I wanted to show you the tower, but I'm never going to say no to you touching me wherever the hell you want."

"Then let me touch you." Charlotte kissed him again, slow and seductive, and Reeve's heart went into overdrive. This is what he loved about Charlotte; she was unpredictable and never backed down when she had set her mind on something. And at that moment, that something was him.

Charlotte's fingers curled into the waistband of his jeans and popped the buttons. Reeve's breath caught as her hand slipped inside and palmed his cock.

"No underwear. Why am I not surprised?" she chuckled huskily.

Reeve couldn't reply; his brain wasn't working anymore. All of his attention was on her touching him.

Charlotte, who he had wanted forever, was finally in his room, with her hand in his pants. She freed his dick, and then Reeve almost passed out as she dropped to her knees before him.

"Let me know if I do something you don't like," was the only warning she gave him before she opened her glossy full lips and swallowed him down. Reeve took a shaky breath, trying his best not to blow straight away.

"Fucking hell, your mouth, Charlotte," he panted. It was hot, moist suction and pure fucking heaven. She flicked her tongue over his tip before she pulled back.

"Put your hands in my hair, or I'm going to think you're not into this," she said, and Reeve let out a helpless laugh.

"I'm very much into it. I'm just letting you call the shots remember?"

Charlotte's big blue eyes blinked up at him with a mocking innocence. "And if I want you to use me the way you want to? Will I have to beg for it?"

"Fuck, Charlotte," he groaned, his dragon side coming roaring to the surface. It had no issue using every hole she had for whatever the hell it wanted.

Reeve wrangled back his self-control and pulled out her hair tie, so her thick curls spilled out over her shoulders. He gripped a handful of it and held on. "Well, then?"

Charlotte's pupils blew out at the growl in his voice. She gripped his ass and sucked him hard. Reeve tugged on her hair tighter, and she groaned around his shaft, sending waves of pleasure through him.

They found a mind-breaking rhythm, Reeve fucking into her

mouth, using her the way she wanted. She was taking him deep enough to gag on him, and he couldn't hold back any longer.

"Charlotte, I'm going to..." he tried to warn her, but she just sucked harder until he was filling her throat and mouth, and she was swallowing him down. Her mouth finally came off him, and she stared up at him with a smug little smile. Reeve wiped a drop of cum from the side of her lip and into her mouth. She sucked on his finger, and his dick tried to rally.

Reeve grabbed her under the arms, picked her up, and pinned her down onto his bed. "You aren't going anywhere tonight, Miss Ironwood."

"Is that so?"

Reeve squeezed her breast hard, and she arched up into him with the sweetest moan he'd ever heard. "You said I could use you the way I wanted to, and I'm planning on it."

They both jumped as Charlotte's phone started ringing loudly. She fumbled to turn it off but froze when she saw the messages. She hit the contact call button. "Imogen, what's wrong?"

"911, Charlotte! I fucked up. I fucked up so bad!" Imogen's voice said over a car engine.

"Where are you? Are you hurt?" Charlotte had gone white.

"Meet me at home. I need you. Whatever you are doing, it can wait. Just get the fuck home!"

Reeve rolled off her, and Charlotte got to her feet. "I'm coming. Just drive slowly, okay?"

Imogen only laughed wildly. "I can't do that. I'm fading fast." The phone went dead, and Charlotte cursed.

"I'm so sorry. I have to go," she said, turning to Reeve. He was already grabbing his coat.

"No, love, *we* have to go. If it's an emergency, I want to help."

Charlotte pressed a quick, hard kiss to his lips and took his hand. "Thank you. Now, let's see what the fuck she's done to herself this time."

18

Imogen knew she had fucked up royally. Her hand pressed tightly to the wound on her side. Hot, sticky blood oozed between her fingers, and the spare shirt she had wadded against it was already soaked through.

This is just fucking perfect. How do you even get yourself into these situations?

A gorgeous black-haired guy flashed in her mind's eye. Oh, that was how. Her ovaries—the source of all her problems.

Imogen had been wound up, and she had decided that she needed to go out for a drink. Layla had gone north with Kenna on a two-day hunt, and Charlotte was in nerd mode with Reeve.

Her father was on babysitting duty with Moira, and Imogen had been left with a night off. She had become bored as shit in about an hour. She had grabbed her car keys and had headed into the city to go to a heavy metal bar she had begun to favor. It was usually full of loud music, guys with eye liner, and good booze.

In recent months, Imogen had developed a taste for goth boys and knew deep down that meeting the Welsh god of the dead was to blame. She had seen that bastard for a whole ten seconds; it was mental.

Hello, darling, he had said, and Imogen would never get that cursed voice out of her head.

Not that she would admit that to anyone. Kill had already been weirded out that the god had acknowledged her at all, and to calm them down, she had pretended it didn't matter. So she had developed a liking for goth boys—that was totally normal. Natural even. Totally, totally, natural.

Everything at the bar had been going fine. Imogen had started chatting with a lovely guy with long straight black hair, beefy, tattooed arms, and a promising tongue piercing. Then he had started telling her a wild story of seeing a monster swimming in Dublin Bay toward North Bull Island earlier that night.

Imogen had tried to turn off her hunter's instincts and ignore the niggling feeling eating away at her. Aneirin's body collage in the estuary had flashed graphically in her mind. She had gotten Mr. Tongue Piercing's number and bailed.

If Imogen hadn't been a dumbass, she would've called Bron to help check out the island with her. But no. She had thought big sis deserved a date night with her sickeningly hot mate.

Imogen had gone by herself without telling anyone. The most enormous no-no in the books.

It didn't take her long to find the monster that her hot new friend had told her about. In fact, she had found a whole delightful family of the half prey mantis, half Kraken fuckers. She had killed three, chopped off the tentacle that had skewered itself into her side, and had run like hell.

Hot, spiky pain shot through her stomach, and Imogen swore loudly through gritted teeth. She just had to hold on. Charlotte would fix her up like she had so many other times.

By the time Imogen pulled into the driveway leading to the Ironwood manor, her vision was going black around the edges.

Charlotte and Reeve were waiting for her outside, her sister looking pissed. Whatever Imogen had interrupted must've been good.

Her vision swam, and she put on the brakes. The door opened, and Charlotte was there.

"What did..." Charlotte's eyes went instantly to Imogen's wound. "What the fuck, Gen!"

"D-Don't shout at me. My head is splitting," she stammered. A cold chill was seeping through her, which probably wasn't a good sign.

"Reeve! She's hurt."

"Out of the way, Charlie." Reeve's arm came around Imogen, and she was half lifted out of the car. She gripped tightly to him with one hand and her Kraken tentacle with the other. She passed the sticky thing to Charlotte.

"This is what's got me. It had h-hooks and..." Imogen began before pitching over and vomiting all over the ground. Her vision swam, their voices blurring around her.

"We need to get her to the lab."

"Don't... Don't wake Dad," Imogen mumbled. The last thing she wanted was to upset David. It was good Kenna wasn't there, or she would be tearing more shreds off her than the fucking horde creatures.

Together Reeve and Charlotte got Imogen to the lab and onto the hospital chair. Imogen had been stitched up more than once in the chair and trusted Charlotte with tweezers and a needle and thread.

"Go to that cupboard, Reeve. I need the green box of patches," Charlotte said. She placed the tentacle in a plastic tub for safekeeping and washed her hands. She pulled on a pair of latex gloves.

"What the hell happened, Imogen?" she asked in a brisk tone. As Charlotte got saline and swabs and fuck knew what else, Imogen tried to get the story out.

"There was this really hot guy. Black hair, tongue piercing, *amazing* arms, and lips like..."

"I don't care about some guy, Gen! Focus!" Charlotte opened the green container that Reeve gave her, and she took a patch from it with a silver glyph drawn on it. She pulled up Imogen's bloody shirt and placed the patch on the non-busted side of her stomach.

Imogen sighed in relief as numbness shot through her side. Charlotte cleaned off the wound, and Imogen told her and Reeve about going out to North Bull Island and finding the new kind of creatures.

"These fuckers were swimming in the bay. We need to tell someone," Imogen said through gritted teeth.

"We will, Gen. Just..." Charlotte broke off and pulled back sharply.

Reeve put his hands on her shoulders. "What is it?"

"There's something in the wound."

Imogen looked down, but her vision was blurring again. "Then get it the fuck out! What is it?"

"I don't know." Charlotte grabbed a pair of tweezers and leaned in closer. Reeve's magic sparked, and a ball of light appeared and hovered above them.

Imogen could taste metal in her mouth. She focused ahead of her at the drawings covering Charlotte's blackboards.

"Oh fuck," Charlotte murmured. She pulled something out. It was pale blue and gelatinous.

"Is that an egg?" Reeve demanded.

"It impregnated me? The...bastard." Imogen wanted to throw up but didn't have enough control over her body. Black smoke was filling her vision.

"L-Love you," she murmured to her sister. Charlotte started yelling something, but Imogen was too far away to answer her.

∽

BLACK AND GRAY mist wrapped tightly around Imogen. The lab was gone, and she was standing in front of two monoliths of glossy onyx. Silver and gold symbols were carved into them and glowed softly in the gloom.

"Hello?" she called, her voice coming out as a whisper. Through the gloom in-between the monoliths, she thought she could make out green fields. She moved towards them, transfixed at the shifting light and shadows on the other side.

"Hello, darling," a deep voice said, and Imogen froze. She knew that voice.

Imogen turned slowly and stared up at the massive figure standing behind her. He was tall enough that she had to tilt her head back in order to look into his black eyes. His long, black hair moved around him on a breeze she couldn't feel, and on top of his head was a spiky black crown.

Arawan, God of the dead, was looking at her like she was a puzzle he couldn't quite figure out.

"What are you doing here?" he demanded.

"A horde creature got me in a fight. I think I might be dying,"

Imogen replied, wondering why she wasn't more afraid of that thought. It wasn't the first time she had almost died, after all. She looked down at her bloody side but couldn't feel any pain at all.

Arawan frowned, looking her over. "It's not time for you to die. This isn't right."

"No, what isn't right is that the fucking bastard laid eggs in me with its tentacle," Imogen said and wanted to slap a hand over her mouth.

"It tried to put its young in you?" The god's nostrils flared, and he closed in on her. He placed a hand over her side, where her wound was still gaping open.

"What are you doing?" Imogen demanded. She could feel the searing hot warmth of his palm.

"I'm not about to let you die, darling, and I'm certainly not going to let someone impregnate you," he snarled, stepping closer. Imogen stared up at him and realized his crown was growing straight out of his head.

"You're a god of the dead. You aren't meant to heal," she said, her tongue too heavy in her mouth.

"You have no idea what I can do," Arawan replied. His face was only inches from her, his sensuous mouth curled in a smile. "This is going to hurt, so scream pretty for me, darling."

Imogen didn't have time to argue with him. His power slammed into her like he shoved a lump of hot coal into her side. She screamed loudly, collapsing against him until it was only his strength holding her up.

"That should be enough," he said close to her ear, and the pain and power moved out of her again.

Imogen tried to straighten, her legs not holding her upright. She could feel herself slipping away, the mist rolling over them.

"Aneirin is trying to release Hafgan," she said, not knowing how much time she had.

"What did you say?" Arawan demanded, but she was already slipping away.

BURNING, sharp pain blasted through Imogen's chest, and her shade slammed into her body. She blinked her eyes open. The light was burning too bright above her. Charlotte was standing over with a defibrillator, and Imogen groaned.

"S-Stop," she managed.

Tears of relief were flooding Charlotte's cheeks. She pushed Imogen's hair back from her damp face.

"Don't you ever fucking do that to me again," she growled.

"Charlotte, look!" Reeve said, moving her out of the way. "Her wound is closing."

Imogen peered down to see the sides of the gash heal together, leaving an ashen scar in its place. She swallowed hard.

"Damn, sis, your healing patches are unreal," she said, knowing it wasn't Charlotte's magic. They would freak out more if she told them the truth.

"That's not possible," Charlotte replied, shaking her head.

"It wasn't possible that those eggs suddenly burned up either, and we watched it happen," Reeve pointed out. He helped Imogen sit up, and she pulled the defibrillator patches off her with a wince.

"I'm going for a hot shower, and I suggest you do the same, little sis. You look like hell covered in my blood," Imogen said, hopping down out of the chair and onto wobbly feet.

"Fuck you, Imogen," Charlotte replied without any real venom.

"I love you too. Good seeing you, Reeve."

Imogen shuffled down the halls to her wing of the house and bolted the door behind her. She needed to get so fucking drunk.

19

Charlotte let Reeve lead her out of the lab, through her adjoining bedroom, and into her bathroom.

"That couldn't have been possible, Reeve. You felt the magic in that room. It wasn't me," she babbled. Charlotte went to wipe at her face and stopped when she saw all of Imogen's blood on her hands.

"It's okay. Let me help," Reeve said. He unbuttoned her ruined shirt and undid her boots so she could slip them off. He turned the taps of the shower on warm for her. "I can wait outside..."

"Come with me, don't leave alone," Charlotte replied too quickly. She didn't know why she was so scared all of a sudden. It was like her body sensed a threat she couldn't see.

Reeve searched her face for a moment, and with a nod, he kicked off his boots and took off his clothes.

Charlotte tried not to be shy about being naked with Reeve as she shimmied out of her jeans and underwear. She needed him more than she needed to be self-conscious about her body. She stepped into the shower without looking at him and began to rinse the blood off her hands and arms.

"That whole thing wasn't right, Reeve. She had creature eggs in her.

You saw that," Charlotte muttered as she scratched and rubbed at her arms. Large, gentle hands came over hers to stop her from tearing at her skin.

"She's okay, baby. Just breathe with me," Reeve said, pulling her back against him and wrapping his arms around her. Charlotte forced herself to inhale with him and exhale slowly. Once, twice, and the third time, the panic loosened its grip on her.

"I don't understand what happened," she admitted, her voice cracking. Imogen's heart had stopped beating, and then the weirdness started to happen.

"I felt the power too, Charlie." Reeve grabbed a bar of lavender soap and ran it over her skin. "Those eggs just combusted into nothing. It was the grossest thing I've ever seen."

Charlotte bit her lip. "I've felt that magic before, but you are going to think I'm crazy."

Reeve lifted her chin with his finger. "I would *never* think that. You are sensitive to other people's power, so I'd trust whatever you said about it. More than that, I trust *you*, okay?"

Charlotte swallowed the sudden ball of emotion in her throat. "I think it was Arawan's magic. The night Morrigan attacked, I was in the square when Arawan appeared to take her to Annwn. It was like..." She struggled for the right words. "Cool night air and smoke. Ancient, depthless power. Older than Morrigan's and utterly ruthless. That's what the impressions I got that night. It's also what I felt tonight when the eggs burned up and the wound closed over. His power touched her somehow, protected her, all the way from Annwn."

Reeve ran soapy hands over her shoulders and down her back. "I believe you. I can't understand why a god of the dead would give Imogen protection like that, though. Death gods aren't usually the kind that interferes with mortals. They are the ones who only have to wait to get what they want. Everyone pays them homage eventually."

Charlotte turned it over in her mind. "Arawan spoke to her that night. Killian and Kian have mentioned that it was strange that the god noticed her. Maybe he blessed her?"

"It's certainly possible. How else can we explain what we saw?" Reeve replied. "I think Imogen knows more than she's saying."

"We should ask her."

Reeve's hand curled around her hip. "Tomorrow. Give her the night to process. She's had a rough night, and I doubt she will be willing to say anything right now. If she was, she would've hung about in the lab."

Charlotte nodded and turned around to thank him for being there. Words didn't come out as she got her first look at Reeve naked. She knew he was well-muscled from feeling him up, but she had never seen all of his light brown skin, tattoos, and nipple piercings before.

"What? Are you okay?" he asked, looking concerned.

"You're beautiful," she blurted out. She traced the large red dragon that lounged over his broad chest, and he made a humming sound in the back of his throat. "This must've hurt."

"Like hell, but I love it," Reeve admitted. He pulled her closer to him and trailed his fingers down her back. "You have a beautiful body yourself, Charlotte. I'm trying not to get any inappropriate erections right now, but you're not making it easy on me."

"And why would it be inappropriate?" she asked, a thrill racing over her breasts and making her nipples peak.

"Because it will want to finish what it started before all the blood and death gods, and I don't know if that's what you want right now," Reeve replied.

Charlotte took his hand and placed it over her breast. "What if I do?"

Reeve's fingers tightened, and he ran the tip of his thumb over her hard nipple. "Then I'll give you whatever you want, just like I always will."

Charlotte pushed him up against the tiled wall and kissed him hard. Reeve didn't hesitate, only kissed her back and dragged her closer. He was already hard, and Charlotte moved her hand between them to touch and stroke. She pulled away from his mouth and licked the water over the gold bar through his nipple. Reeve groaned with pleasure as she sucked it hard.

"We need to get out of this shower," he said, pulling free from her roaming hands and switching the water off. He ran a towel roughly over them, making her laugh at his haste before being pulled into her room and laid out on her bed.

"Wait one second," she said and activated the wards all over her doors. "Now we won't be disturbed."

Reeve gave her a look so heated that a warm ache sparked between her thighs. "God help anyone that interrupts us again tonight," he said, taking her lips in a deep kiss.

He worked his way down her throat, over her collarbone, and down to her breasts. Charlotte had never thought her nipples that sensitive, but Reeve was proving her wrong with every scrape of his teeth and lap of his tongue. One hand drifted down between her legs and stroked her. She could already feel how wet she was. His fingers sliding over her were heaven.

"Fuck, Charlotte," Reeve whispered against her bare skin. He lifted his fingers to his mouth to taste her, and his eyes flared gold. "I need more."

Reeve began to shift down, and Charlotte quickly grabbed him by the shoulders. "Um, I've never had someone..." she stammered, unable to get the words out. Instead of laughing or freezing like she expected, Reeve's eyes went hot, and a small smile curved his lips.

"Good. I don't want anyone knowing how you taste except me," he replied. His warm tongue brushed over her, and she whimpered.

"Oh...fuck," she managed before she was overwhelmed by sensation. Her fingers tightened in his hair as his mouth kissed and sucked, sending waves of pleasure through her. He tongued her clit, and a cry caught in her throat. She had been missing out on this? It seemed like a travesty.

"Reeve..." Lights danced over her vision, and she was coming hard, back arching and hands almost tearing his hair out.

"That's my girl," Reeve chuckled softly. He kissed the inside of her trembling legs as she came back down. He kissed his way back up her body until he was above her. Charlotte cupped his cheek. He was so gorgeous, it hurt.

Without her having to ask, he lifted her hips and slid inside of her. Charlotte groaned as he filled her completely. She wrapped her legs around his waist and thrust up, trying to get more.

"Damn, Charlie, you really are perfect everywhere," Reeve said, bending down to kiss her.

"So are you. I always knew you would feel like this," Charlotte replied, moving her hips up to meet his. "It's like you're my missing piece."

Reeve's eyes filled with emotion, but he only kissed her again, his powerful body moving against hers and stealing the words from her mind and breath from her lungs. She could feel another orgasm starting again, and she gripped him hard to her, chasing it until he was undoing her all over again. He fucked her all the way through it, dragging it out until she was almost sobbing.

"Fuck, the sounds you make, Charlie. I want them all," Reeve said, kissing her. "You did say I could use you how I wanted, didn't you?"

"Yes," she replied, her body thrumming with aftershocks.

Reeve gave her bottom lip a hard nip. "Good, because I'm not nearly done with you and this sweet pussy of yours."

Charlotte gasped as Reeve pulled out of her, flipped her over onto her forearms and knees, and drove back into her.

She cried out, the force and feel of him inside of her sending her mad. She could lose her mind from this much pleasure. He did exactly what she asked and used her, making her feel more wanted than she had ever had before.

Reeve licked her spine, his teeth sinking into the back of her neck and making her buck harder backward. She fucked back on his cock until they were both crying out expletives.

Magic was burning in the air around them, but she didn't stop to question it. She just needed more. Needed him so deep inside of her that there was no separating them.

Reeve gripped her hair tightly, pulling her head back so he could give her a dirty kiss, his tongue fucking into her mouth in sync with his cock.

Charlotte exploded, her soft inner walls gripping Reeve tight and milking him. His hand tightened on her hip, keeping them from sliding forward as he pounded into her mercilessly until he was spilling inside her with a shout. He hung tightly to her like he was afraid she would disappear. Her heart was pounding in her ears, her chest, her pussy, her whole body beating with him.

"Are you okay?" he whispered, smoothing the hair back from her face.

"Y-Yes, just...don't go anywhere," Charlotte said. He eased off her and onto the bed beside her. He pulled her up against his chest and pressed soft kisses on her face.

"I'm here for as long as you want me," he replied. Charlotte wrapped an arm and leg over him, exhaustion already pulling her under.

"Stay with me, Reeve," she whispered before her eyes slid shut.

20

Charlotte knew she was dreaming by the way the air felt. The misty grove that she stood in pulsed with magic, the earth and trees around her vibrating with it. Gray stone monoliths carved with silver sigils stood in a circle around the grove, and in its center sat a man with glossy chestnut hair. He had woad smeared on his sharp, handsome face and his amber eyes burned with magic. Power thrummed from him, and Charlotte knew him even with the ancient clothes he wore.

"Aneirin," she whispered.

He inclined his head in greeting. "Hello, Charlotte. I do apologize for breaking into your dreams like this, but I thought it past time we talked without any interference," he said in his unique, smooth voice.

"What do you want with me?" she asked. She drew closer to him but not close enough that he could touch her.

"I want a peace treaty. You have been told malicious things about me that just aren't true."

Charlotte hummed. "I saw what you and Morrigan did to Dublin, and that was enough to know that peace is the last thing you want."

"An unfortunate business but necessary. Humans need a certain amount of violence to get their attention these days when there are no more gods or magic to infuse their lives with wonder. They needed to remember who has the real power in this world," Aneirin said unapologetically.

Charlotte crossed her arms, trying to channel her mother's merciless expression that she was so well known for.

"You killed my people and let a war goddess nearly kill my sister and her mate. Your creatures stole my fellow magicians for your spells. I don't see any of your actions being different from what I already know about you."

Aneirin laughed softly. "Those magicians are not your peers, Charlotte. You are a once-in-a-generation magician like I was. Come to me, let me teach you about your power and the strength you really have coursing through your veins."

"So you can try and use my body as a vessel for Morrigan? Yeah, thanks, but I'll pass." Charlotte took small satisfaction in seeing his eye twitch. He probably hoped that his acolyte would've been stronger to hold out against torture. He obviously didn't know who he was dealing with. Cosimo and Valentine were the once-in-a-generation magicians, not her.

"Trust me, Charlotte. If you come to me, hear my proposal, and see what I can truly offer you, you will give yourself willingly to temporarily hold Morrigan's spirit."

"Not interested. Now, let me out of this dream, or I'll make you," Charlotte snapped.

Aneirin's amber eyes sparkled in amusement. "I think I'm going to have to get you to make me."

∼

REEVE WOKE from his doze to Charlotte jerking in his arms. He sat bolt upright in the dark and fumbled for the light switch.

"Charlotte? Charlotte, wake up. I think you're having a nightmare," he said, shaking her shoulder gently. Magic pulsed around her, shoving him backward. "What the fuck? Charlotte!"

White froth appeared on her lips, and he pushed against the power battering him to roll her onto her side. For the second time that night, he could feel an alien presence in the room. His mouth tasted of blood. The thrumming beat of battle drums filled his ears. *Aneirin.*

"Fuck. Charlotte! Wake up!" he shouted. When she didn't move, Reeve leaped off the bed and found his phone. It was past midnight, but he didn't care.

Cosimo answered in two rings. "Reeve? What's wrong?"

"Dad, it's Charlotte. Something is happening, and she won't wake up," he replied, loud and panicked.

"What do you mean?" his father sounded instantly alert.

"It's like she's caught in a dream, but she's pulsing with magic. Something is happening. I can feel... I think I feel Aneirin," Reeve replied, running his hands through this hair as he stared helplessly at his love. "Dad, you need to come and fix this."

"Fucking hell, he's caught her in the dream. You need to wake her up, Reeve. You're the only one who can," Cosimo replied.

"How? I don't understand. You have more magic than me—"

"But she is your mate, not mine."

Reeve sucked in a sharp breath. "H-How do you know that?"

"You think I'm blind? That your brothers are? From the moment I saw her with you, I knew. I wish you would've warned me beforehand, but now is not the time to have that conversation," Cosimo said.

Charlotte moaned softly, her magic starting to make her shimmer with hot, golden light.

"Dad, she's getting worse. Tell me what to do," Reeve shouted.

"You need to get close to her, tell her how you feel, let your power mix with hers, and summon her to you. It's the only way to break through whatever hold Aneirin has on her."

"I don't know if that will work."

"It will. Nothing is stronger than a mating bond, whether she knows it or not. Just try it. Call me back if it doesn't work, and I'll come to you." Cosimo paused for a moment before adding. "Be honest, Reeve. She will feel it, even if she can't hear it."

Reeve hung up the phone. He took a deep breath, focused his power, and pressed his way into the golden light that pulsed from Charlotte. After a moment's resistance, it was like it recognized him and let him in close.

That's a good sign.

Reeve climbed into the bed beside her and gently stroked the hair back from her face.

"Charlotte, please feel me here. Please come back to me from where you are wandering. I need to..." His voice cracked, and he struggled to get his emotions under control. "I need you to come back. I haven't told you about the Greatdrakes curses we inherited from the dragon. One of them is that we always know who our mates are."

Charlotte frowned in her sleep, her head shifting towards him. Hope sparked in his chest that she could sense him after all.

"When we met, I felt an instant connection with you. You shone so fucking brightly. It was like I couldn't look away from you," he continued, his hand stroking her hair. "I'm certain I fell in love with you the first time I saw you smile at me. It only got worse as time went on. I was young and stupid and too fucking frightened to acknowledge the truth back then. I let you walk away, thinking that it was better for the both of us. It was the biggest mistake of my life."

Charlotte's hand reached out and clenched at the air. Reeve caught it and brought it to his pounding heart. He focused his magic and let it reach out to touch hers. He gasped at the incredible feeling of their combined power.

"I'm not afraid to admit it anymore, Charlotte. I know you were destined for me. You are, without a doubt in my mind, my true mate. I fucking love you so damn much." Reeve leaned over her until their lips touched. "Now, wake the fuck up, Charlie. I need you, so fight the son of a bitch and come back to me."

Reeve kissed her hard, forcing his magic into her mouth until it filled her. Charlotte's whole body jerked. Magic pulsed out of her like a shock wave. She started against him, dragging air into her lungs with a loud gasp.

"Reeve," she said, her eyes opening. They widened and gripped him tight. "He had me. Oh fuck, he had me."

Reeve dragged her into his lap and held her tight. "Fuck, Charlotte. You scared the shit out of me." He breathed her in, needing her closer to him.

"Aneirin wanted me to join him. He held me in the dream, trying to convince me to join him. Fuck. I didn't know he could do that!" Charlotte pulled back from him, her face deathly white. "He got through all the wards around us, Reeve."

"It's okay. We'll change them and keep him out. You gave me a goddamn heart attack. How did you get away from him?" he asked.

"I heard your voice calling to me. It's like your magic wrapped itself around me until you were all I could feel, and it yanked me out of it." Charlotte pressed her forehead to his and let out a shaky breath. "I don't know how you did it, but thank you."

"I told you, I'm never letting you go again." Reeve reached for his phone. "I need to text Dad and let him know you are okay. I might have called him up, freaking out."

Reeve shot off the text and received an instant thumbs up. He knew that Cosimo would give him the rest of the night and then be cornering him about everything that happened.

Charlotte stayed in his lap until he tossed the phone aside. She was studying his face carefully.

"What is it?" he asked.

She stroked his cheekbones, eyes scanning him. "I don't know. I could feel your magic in me. I still can feel echoes of it."

"It won't hurt you," he reassured her quickly.

"I know it won't. I just feel...different. What did you say to me when I was in the dream?"

Reeve knew she would freak out if he told her the whole truth, but his streak of dragon was riled up now that the panic was easing off.

He nipped at her jawline. "I reminded you of who you belong to, and it's certainly not that fucking bard."

"That's awfully possessive of you. I belong to myself first," Charlotte said with a bite of stubbornness.

Reeve chuckled. "Sure you do. But you also belong to me, and I'm not fucking letting you go. If you keep arguing with me, I'm going to prove it."

He caught her bottom lip between his teeth and lightly scraped them over it. Her hands gripped his bare skin, a little gasp escaping her mouth.

"I don't know if I'm okay with moving from dating to I belong to you. There's a finality in that that makes me uncomfortable," she said, her body arching against his.

Reeve stroked up her thigh and ran his fingers over her pussy, making her whimper. "Yeah, you feel really upset over the idea."

"Fuck," Charlotte whispered. She was on him in a blink, pressing him back onto her covers and climbing on top of him. Her slender fingers found his cock, jerking him hard.

Reeve let out a husky chuckle. "It's yours if you want it, just like the rest of me."

Charlotte didn't hesitate. She guided him to her entrance and slid over him. Her tight wet heat gripped him as she eased him inside of her inch by inch. When she had him fully in, she let out a sigh of relief.

Oh yeah, she definitely felt the mating bond even if she didn't understand what it was. Reeve rocked his hips, grinding tight against her.

"Still think we don't belong together? We are the perfect fucking fit," he growled, his hands grabbing her firm ass and dragging her up and down his cock. Charlotte braced her hands on his chest, her sharp nails digging into him.

"I know," she panted as she rode him hard. "Doesn't mean I have to like it."

Reeve laughed at her anger. Charlotte snarled wordlessly back at him, Reeve gasping as her grip tightened on him. His chest was going to be clawed up, and he fucking *loved* it. He wanted her to mark him all over.

Reeve sat up, his hand bunching tight in her hair so he could cover her mouth in a bruising kiss. "Fight it all you want, baby, just don't stop fucking me."

"I hate you so much," she complained and came all over him in a body-shaking orgasm.

"Stop lying to yourself." Reeve rolled her onto her back, dragged one of her legs over his shoulder, and fucked her harder.

Charlotte screamed his name, and his release slammed into him so hard, he saw colors. He came back to himself, gripping her tight to him, still buried deep inside of her, their hearts thrumming next to each other.

"I fucking love you, Charlotte Ironwood." Reeve smoothed her damp hair back from her surprised, beautiful face. He brushed his lips over hers. "I don't care how long it takes for you to love me back. I'm not going to stop until you say that you are mine."

21

Charlotte woke well after sunrise, her body sprawled out over Reeve where she had passed out from her second sex coma of the night. She was surprised she slept at all after dreaming of Aneirin. Reeve fucking her senseless and telling her that he loved her had wiped out every piece of resistance she had.

Long, red lines and teeth marks covered his torso from where she clawed him up. Charlotte had never minded sex, enjoyed it for the most part, but it had never been so urgent and desperate like that. Something pulsed inside of her, a glowing remnant of Reeve's magic that had lodged itself in her chest. She stared down at his sleeping face and swallowed hard.

I fucking love you, Charlotte Ironwood.

Reeve hadn't expected her to say it back, and she didn't, but that was only because she was so overwhelmed that her mouth wouldn't work. She was still too overwhelmed.

She needed a dark room and a glass of wine to think things through. She wasn't going to have the luxury of that. There was too much to do.

Charlotte pressed a kiss to the head of the dragon tattooed on his chest and slipped out of bed. Her body ached pleasantly all over, and she grinned to herself. She turned on the shower and tried to sort out her head and immediate to-do list.

First, she needed to touch base with Kian about the sigil she had sent him to stop a possession. Was there a way to modify it to prevent any more nighttime visits from Aneirin?

Second, she needed to find where and how the bastard had gotten through her wards. She knew he was powerful, but there was no gap that she had left that he could've slipped through without it alerting her in some way.

Charlotte's stomach grumbled. She needed food first.

"Now, that is a sight that makes waking up worth it," Reeve said from the bathroom door.

"Don't get any ideas," Charlotte replied over her shoulder.

"Oh, I have several."

Charlotte switched off the taps and wrapped a towel around herself. "File them away for later. I need to eat, and we need to get to work."

Reeve caught her and pressed a kiss to her lips. "Good morning to you too."

Charlotte patted him on the ass. "Have a shower and come downstairs. I'll make you something to eat as a thank you for the orgasms."

"Damn, Charlie, you are romantic in the morning," he teased, letting her go.

"I'll be romantic when we stop a psycho wizard from breaking into my dreams," Charlotte replied, freeing herself from his too-comfortable embrace. Reeve only sighed and stepped into the shower.

∼

Charlotte dressed quickly, making sure any random love bites were covered up, and headed downstairs to the kitchen. Imogen was standing by the coffee pot, staring into space. Her hair was a lavender rat's nest, and she had dark circles under her eyes.

"Hey, you okay?" Charlotte asked softly.

Imogen shook herself back to reality. "Yeah, just a bit out of it. Probably blood loss."

"Most definitely blood loss." Charlotte gently moved her out of the way. "Sit down before you fall down, sis. I'll make you some food."

Imogen nodded and collapsed into a chair. "Don't tell Mom what happened."

"Why not? You found a whole aquatic species of horde creatures last night. You can't keep that knowledge to yourself," Charlotte said. She poured them both coffee and then pulled out a third cup for Reeve. She wondered if he still took two sugars? It had been a long time since she had been inclined to make him anything. Charlotte topped up Imogen's cup with milk and passed it over to her.

"Thanks, sis. I know you're right. Maybe we can say that I found the creatures but not that I got hurt? You *know* Mom and Bron will both rip me to shreds if they find out I went hunting by myself and got hurt because of it."

"And so they should. You know better, Imogen. You can't keep putting yourself at risk like this," Charlotte said, pulling eggs and bacon from the fridge. She was usually a porridge girl in the morning, but she was hungry enough to eat a horde creature.

"I didn't mean to stumble into a whole nest of the fuckers. I couldn't let some random aquatic creature prey on people in the bay, could I?" Imogen argued.

"You still know better."

Imogen scowled. "Are you going to tell on me or not?"

"All depends. Are you going to tell me what happened when you passed out?" Charlotte couldn't say the word *died* without getting heart palpitations.

"I can't remember," Imogen murmured into her coffee cup.

Charlotte was going to argue when Reeve came in, still damp from the shower and smelling like her soap.

Imogen's face went bright with impish glee. "Oh ho, good morning, Mister Greatdrakes. Having sleepovers, are we?"

Charlotte's cheeks flamed, and she quickly passed Reeve his coffee.

Reeve's smile widened. "Yes. You got a problem with that Miss Blessed by Arawan?"

Imogen choked on her coffee. "I don't think blessed is the right word."

"Than what word would you use? Because from where I was sitting last night, the fucking God of the dead's power touched you, and you were suddenly healed," Reeve replied and took a sip of his coffee.

Charlotte knew better than to push Imogen, but Reeve didn't. She quickly got out a skillet and a bowl and started making more noise than necessary.

"I. Don't. Know," Imogen replied slowly like she was speaking to a child.

Reeve's smile threw down a challenge. "And I think you're lying. What I can't figure out is why."

"Because it's none of your goddamn fucking business what happened between Arawan and me!" Imogen shouted. She froze, knowing she had said too much. She swore angrily and banged her head against the table. "I don't know why he helped me. Okay?"

Charlotte dropped some bacon in the pan and slowly beat some eggs. She wanted to scold Reeve, but she was too curious to do it.

"Is that something you should be worried about? I mean, our brothers were all kind of concerned you had gotten his attention," she said gently. "Did he make a bargain or ask for anything in return for his help?"

"No. He just...helped me. I told him about Aneirin wanting to release Hafgan. I mean, if he's successful, then Arawan should be warned, right? He might be the only guy out there badass enough to take on a Lord of the Underworld who can constantly regenerate," Imogen mumbled against the scratched pine tabletop.

"True, but I don't think he's ever been interested in living mortals, so I don't know why he would start now. He might let Hafgan rampage through the human world and not bother him unless he goes after Annwn," Reeve said, sitting down opposite her. "Which brings us right back to why he's interested in you."

"You think I fucking know? Why do gods do anything? Because they *can*." Imogen lifted her head long enough to have another large mouthful of coffee before putting her head down again. "It doesn't matter anyway. He healed my wound because he said it wasn't my time to die yet. Just don't tell Mom or Dad, or I'll tell them you've been letting Reeve sleep over."

Charlotte rolled her eyes and put a plate of food down before her.

She patted Imogen on her head. "Here, eat something and stop being such a grumpy bitch," she said gently.

"He started it," Imogen said, lifting her head and grabbing a fork.

"I know. He doesn't know any better. Get your story straight about the horde creature, and then tell me. I won't say anything about Arawan healing you until you do, okay?"

"Fine. Thanks for the food," Imogen grumbled.

Charlotte put a plate down in front of Reeve. "Don't pick fights before food. It's not the Ironwood way. Kitchen is neutral, got it?"

"Got it. Sorry, Gen," he said, looking chastised.

"It's fine. I'd be freaked out, too, if I had the energy. What are you two up to today?"

"Trying to figure out something that will protect Charlie from getting possessed by Morrigan," Reeve replied between a mouthful of bacon. "Same thing as yesterday."

"But hopefully, Kian will come good with some answers for us," Charlotte said. She took her seat between them and pulled out her phone to text Kian.

Aneirin busted into my dreams last night with a truce proposal. Please tell me you have something to keep him out.

Charlotte didn't know when he usually woke up or looked at his phone. She had a niggly feeling in her gut that they were running out of time, and she didn't like it one damn bit.

They were on their second round of coffees when Charlotte's phone started ringing.

"Hey, Kian, what did you find?" she asked, getting up from the table where Reeve and Imogen were talking about a mutual acquaintance of theirs. She placed her empty dish onto Reeve's and pointed at the sink. Reeve blew her a kiss as she stepped out into the quiet hallway.

"I received word from the fae mages this morning right after your message. The good news is they seem to think that the protection sigil you found acts as a living ward and that it will be safe for you to use," Kian explained.

Charlotte chewed her lip thoughtfully. "Okay, so what's the bad news?"

"The ward will move with you, but only if it's tattooed onto your skin. There's no way around it. Something about it having a blood link to you to be one with your flesh," Kian replied.

"Just don't make it a tramp stamp," Elise called from the background.

Charlotte laughed. "I'd be way classier than that. It'll go straight on my ass."

"What will?" Reeve asked, coming out of the kitchen with too much dragon in his eyes. Charlotte ignored him.

"Do you think it will stop Aneirin from making another stop in my dreams?"

"I'm not sure, Charlotte. Check your warding for loose ends and ask Killian to look over them. Of all of us, he is the most proficient in dreams magic. He might be able to give you insight. In the meantime, whatever you used to pull yourself out of it last night, keep it close at hand," Kian replied.

"I don't think that is going to be a problem." Charlotte looked over at Reeve. "Thanks, Kian."

"Anytime, little sister."

Charlotte hung up and let out a frustrated groan. Reeve looped an arm about her waist. "Tell me the bad news."

"I need to find someone who can do magical tattoos."

Reeve smiled slyly. "I got you covered, Charlie."

∽

CHARLOTTE DIDN'T KNOW how to feel about Reeve hanging onto her hand all the way back to the Greatdrakes. He seemed totally at ease with casual intimacy, and she found it hard to not ask him what he was doing. It didn't matter that her heart sped up a little every time his fingers brushed over hers.

"You sure this is a good idea?" Charlotte asked, shaking their hands before they stepped into the central part of the mansion.

Reeve smiled and kissed the back of her hand. "They know all about this, Charlie. Trust me. They aren't half as dumb as they act."

They didn't need to worry about the brothers because Cosimo was waiting for them with his arms crossed.

"Hello, children. Rough night?" he asked.

"It turned out okay. Sorry for the wake-up, Dad," Reeve said, his hand gripping Charlotte's even tighter.

"I'm just glad that you are alright, Charlotte. What did you learn?" Cosimo asked.

"Kian confirmed that the design we found to stop a possession is viable, but it needs to be tattooed on," Charlotte replied, trying not to sound nervous. She didn't know why, but she was scared of disappointing Cosimo even a little.

Cosimo hummed. "You better do it, Reeve. Unless you want Valentine to do it."

"Wait, *you* can do magical tattoos?" Charlotte demanded. "Why didn't you say that at the house?"

"Because all my stuff to do it is here, and I wanted someone other than me to confirm I have the ability, so you'd let me do it," Reeve argued.

Charlotte didn't like surprises. She knew it was petty, but she still said, "Valentine can do it too, though, right?"

"Yes, he's excellent at tattooing and did Reeve's dragon," Cosimo replied, ignoring the tense glare Reeve was shooting in his direction.

"He's not doing it," Reeve said stubbornly. "The magic will be more powerful if I do it." The men seemed to be having a silent argument that Charlotte couldn't follow.

"Reeve is right. His magic will fuse better with yours because he's intimately aware of you and your power," Cosimo said at last. "Get Val to supervise anyway. He has more experience with it if anything starts to go wrong. This is ancient spell work, and we don't know how unpredictable it is going to be."

Reeve didn't look pleased, but he still muttered, "Fine, I'll get him involved."

Cosimo's attention swiveled back to her. "Did you learn anything else from your dream with Aneirin, Charlotte?"

"Only that he wanted me to join him and didn't want to take no for an answer. He said that I was a once-in-a-generation magician and that he was the only one that could teach me to reach my fullest potential," Charlotte replied, with a roll of her eyes. "The ego on him is astounding. He seemed to think I would fall all over myself from a bit of flattery."

Charlotte sounded a lot braver than what she had felt at the time. She had panicked when she had been unable to wake herself up. Never again. Next time, she would be ready for him no matter what it took.

Cosimo had a fantastic glare when he wanted to use it. He rubbed at his chin thoughtfully.

"Get the tattoo done as soon as possible. I don't like the arrogance of this bastard one bit. He either doesn't take us seriously as a threat, or he's planning something."

"We are onto it, Dad," Reeve said, and he gently tugged Charlotte away

In his tower, Reeve sat Charlotte down on a reclining chair and dragged over a lamp. She pulled out the drawing of the circular sigil and studied it carefully one last time, looking for any way to strengthen or improve it. There was a sharp knock at the door, and Valentine strolled in with a black case.

"Dad told me you were going to do some tattooing, and I needed to make sure you didn't fuck it up," he said by way of greeting and put the case down on one of Reeve's workbenches.

"I don't need the help," Reeve replied coolly.

Valentine sat down on a swivel chair and spun around to face Charlotte. "I don't care what you think you need, baby boy. I've brought some magic-infused inks with me for you to use. They will be more effective. Can I look at the sigil?"

Charlotte passed it over to him. "Here. I can't see any way to make it better. I have to say, Valentine, you didn't strike me as a man interested in tattoos."

"Looks can be deceiving," Valentine replied. He unbuttoned the cuffs of his black button-down shirt and started rolling them up. Beautiful, intricate tattoos covered his arms.

Charlotte leaned forward to study the dense collage of ink on his light brown skin. "Holy shit. Are these for decoration or something else?"

"Each one is magical in nature. I wouldn't put any old symbol onto my body. Tattoos and symbols can give you power if you know how to use them," Valentine explained. His eyes flicked back to the sigil. "Wow, this is a beauty. Where are you thinking of putting it?"

Charlotte swallowed back her sudden nerves. "I'm not sure. I've never had a tattoo done before."

"Can I make a suggestion?"

"Please do."

Valentine pointed. "Do it right there over your solar plexus, above your Manipura chakra. Its energy will help strengthen the sigil and make it more effective."

"It's going to hurt the most there, too, isn't it?" Charlotte complained, making Valentine smile.

"Pain is part of the process. I could numb you, but it would take some of the power away from it. If the spell needs blood to bind it to you, the pain is a tithe. It's important."

Reeve opened the black case and took out a vial of black ink. He shook it, and the light caught swirls of silver in it. "What do you think, Val?"

"Good choice. That ink was a pain in the ass to get right, and it will definitely look the prettiest once it's on skin."

"Just as long as it works." Charlotte tried to put aside any embarrassment as she put the chair right back and unbuttoned her shirt. Reeve glared at Valentine.

"Are you sure you need to be here?"

"Relax, Reeve, I'm not going to look at your girlfriend's lovely tits," Valentine sneered. "I'm here as a professional. Really, Charlotte, I don't know how you put up with him being so moody all the time."

Reeve pulled on a pair of black latex gloves and took out a cordless tattoo gun from a plastic box. Charlotte tried not to be nervous as he set the gun up.

"Are you happy to get it over your solar plexus still?" Reeve asked.

Charlotte nodded and took a breath. Reeve's eyes lightened in amusement.

"Relax, Charlie. It's not going to hurt as much as you think. Take some more of those deep breaths because, unlike normal tattoos, once I start this, I can't stop."

"You should let me do it," Valentine said, rolling his chair to the other side of Charlotte so he could watch better.

"Not in a million fucking years," Reeve said without much malice.

Charlotte took a deep breath, shut her eyes, and tried to focus her magic into her core. "Okay, I'm ready, Reeve."

Reeve pressed a kiss to the spot he was going to work on before wiping the area down with some antiseptic wipes. Valentine wisely said nothing about the kiss.

"You are going to free-hand this, so make sure your magic is in one continuous flow between you, the gun, and Charlotte," he said once Reeve was ready.

Charlotte felt the second that Reeve's power rose. It was like a warm caress against hers, and the part that still seemed to be inside of her from the night before glowed in happy greeting.

Charlotte smiled and tried to focus on their mixed magics as the needles finally touched her skin. It stung but not in an intolerably painful way. Reeve worked quickly and steadily, and with every line, she felt the movement of the ancient spell.

"I can feel it coming together," she whispered without opening her eyes. She didn't want to jerk away or mess with his concentration. There was something unexpectedly intimate about letting him mark her skin. It was like he was becoming a part of her on a whole other level. She expected the fear or worry to bombard her, but it didn't.

I fucking love you, Charlotte Ironwood.

She could feel it in his magic, bolstering the connection between them, enhancing the spell that at its core was about protection. Tears filled her eyes, and she quickly swallowed them down before letting them spill. She didn't want Reeve to think he was hurting her.

"Are you okay?" Reeve asked over the low buzz of the tattoo gun.

"I'm fine, just focusing on the magic," she replied. He placed his spare hand on her shoulder, and she drew on his warmth to calm her the rest of the way down.

"Fuck, the old ones sure knew what they were doing," Valentine said reverently as the building power of the sigil filled the room.

Charlotte could see the tattoo on her skin in her mind's eye, its looping curves thrumming with ancient power. Her heart was beating faster, and a fine sheen of sweat broke out on her forehead.

"Almost finished, baby, I swear," Reeve murmured. Hot, seething magic struck her just as Reeve closed the final line of power. Charlotte moaned and grabbed for Reeve. Their energy was mixed with the ancient ones' intent, and she was vibrating with it.

"I think I'm done here," Valentine said and all but bolted from the room. Reeve put the gun down and carefully wiped the excess ink away. Charlotte looked down at the dark, shimmering lines over her pale skin and back up to Reeve. He was breathing hard, the magic pulling on him as much as on her.

Charlotte dragged him down so she could capture his mouth in a burning kiss of power and lust. Reeve groaned against her lips before he lifted her off the chair and up onto his work counter.

The magic was still thrumming hot between them, and she needed him. God, she needed him.

She undid her pants and kicked them off with her underwear without a word. Reeve dropped his jeans enough to get his dick free, and she was suddenly up in his arms. Reeve lowered her down on his cock, and their kisses grew desperate.

Charlotte clung to him, needing him closer. Her tender, inked skin burned with every brush against it, mingling the pleasure with an edge of pain.

"Fuck, Reeve," she cried, clutching his thick hair and pulling it free from its tie. "What is this?"

"This is love," he breathed against her lips and thrust deeper. Charlotte kissed him hard, and her orgasm streaked through her and smashed into the magic that was still linking them.

"Holy fucking shit, I can feel you coming..." Reeve dragged her off the counter and lowered her backward onto his bed. He didn't stop fucking her until he was coming, and then all the sensations he was feeling hit back into Charlotte. She cried out, a wordless moaning babble that she couldn't hold in. What the fuck was happening? This wasn't natural, but it felt too damn good to stop. Reeve kissed her over and over like he couldn't get enough of her.

"How did that happen?" Charlotte asked when she could finally form a sentence again.

Reeve pulled her closer to him. He hovered his hand over her raw, inked skin. "I don't know, but that sigil caught all of that orgasm energy too."

Charlotte looked down at it and back to him. "It's beautiful. I'm glad you were the one to do it."

Reeve kissed the center of her chest. "Me too. I've never felt anything like that before."

Charlotte ran her fingers over Reeve's cheeks, a smile teasing her lips. "We should definitely do more magic together."

Reeve chuckled. "Anytime, anywhere you want, Ironwood."

22

It was Charlotte's turn to look after Moira that afternoon with Imogen, so she kissed Reeve goodbye and headed home. It was a good thing. She needed the space to think over...well, everything. Her mind was racing with thoughts of Reeve, Aneirin, and magic. She needed a solid to-do list to get her mind straight again.

Imogen looked a lot better than she had that morning. The color was back in her cheeks, and she had managed to get her lavender hair into a neat braid. Moira had her small crossbow with her and looked far too cocky.

"Where are you two off to?" Charlotte asked.

"Crossbow practice. We both need to shoot at things to help us feel better. You want to join?" Imogen replied.

"If it's okay with you, I kind of need some alone time to dissect that horde tentacle you brought back for me."

Moira screwed up her face. "Eww, Charlotte. You can do that, but I'm not going to."

Imogen pulled an almost identical face. "I'm with her." They both turned and headed out into the grounds, and Charlotte breathed a sigh of relief. She stepped inside and almost ran into her father coming down the hall in his chair.

"Shit, sorry, Dad."

David smiled up at her. "It's okay. You are the person I wanted to see."

"Oh no, what did I do this time?" Charlotte replied. She actually had been up to a lot for once.

"And why would you automatically assume you're in trouble? Guilty conscience?" David's eyes sparkled in amusement. "I wanted to see if Kian had set a date for you to go and study with the fae mages."

"Nothing yet. I assumed we were going to decide once Aneirin is dealt with. Why?"

David shifted in his chair, looking awkward. "I have a standing invite to go and see the fae healers as well as the mages. Kenna will stay in Ireland to look after Moira, and I don't want to go alone."

"Dad, that's awesome news. Of course, I'll go with you," Charlotte said, hugging him around his broad shoulders. "Why aren't you happier about this?"

"I am happy, just nervous. I don't want to get my hopes up," he said, rubbing at his numb legs. "I'd love to be able to walk and hunt again. I thought I had accepted this state of things, but when Kian offered, I realized I hadn't. I hate..." He broke off and gave a helpless huff of a laugh. "I shouldn't be burdening you with this."

"Don't say that. If Kian made the offer, it's because he believes they have a good shot at fixing your back. You'll never know what is possible until you go and see them," Charlotte replied and hugged him again. He gave her back a pat.

"What's going on with you? You aren't the kind to give anyone two hugs in one day," he chuckled. "Not even to your dear old dad."

"I just felt like it," Charlotte replied, pulling away. "You want to dissect a horde creature tentacle with me?"

"Absolutely not. I'm going to float about in a physical therapy pool and try and get some peace and quiet."

"You used to be fun," Charlotte called after him.

"Not that much fun."

Charlotte made tea and went up to her blissfully quiet lab. She touched the tattoo on her sternum and felt the answering pulse of power in it. She could still smell Reeve on her skin, feel his magic writhing... Charlotte gave herself a hard shake.

No, she was going to have an afternoon to herself. No thoughts of Reeve in his naked state allowed.

Imogen had placed the tentacle leg in a container of formalin to preserve it, and it now floated about ominously. The egg Charlotte had pulled from Imogen's side had also been placed into it.

"The last thing we need is for you bastards to be breeding," Charlotte told the little floating mass. She put on gloves, an apron, and safety glasses before taking out the tentacle and placing it on a metal tray.

This was something Charlotte was good at. Working on her own, taking things apart, and studying in silence was what she lived for. She took notes as she went, including what Imogen had said about the nest what the creatures looked like when they were whole.

The tentacle itself was a deep blue and black color that would make it almost invisible in the water, especially at night. Had Aneirin made it using magic, or had it somehow come through with Morrigan?

"What secrets are you hiding?" Charlotte used a scalpel to study the suckers and found a sharp black barb in the center of each one. "So that's how you tore Imogen open. What on earth..." She moved the barb back further, and underneath it was a small pouch of eggs. "You're killing creatures and humans and putting your eggs in them to incubate in the warmth? I don't know if that's genius or downright disgusting."

Charlotte lost track of time as she worked, and as the sun faded outside, she switched on her lights and kept going. She had cut the tentacle in half lengthways and found a total of six egg pouches, all crammed full. It worried her just how many of these creatures were out in Dublin Bay at that moment, ready to impregnate whoever they came across. Depending on how long it took for them to get a full size, they could end up with an infestation of the bastards. They couldn't fight them underwater.

A tentative tap interrupted her thoughts, and she saw Reeve in her doorway. It was offensive how good he looked while she was covered in horde creature and probably looked like a mad scientist.

"Are you hungry yet? Thought you could use a dinner break." He lifted a bag, and she saw it was from her favorite burger joint. It was a small, family-owned place that only locals knew about, and they had found it one night in their college days.

Charlotte's whole body filled with affection. "All depends. What did you get me?"

"Chicken, cheese, and avocado burger with sweet potato fries," Reeve said, placing the bag on a clean worktable away from the mess she had created on the other one.

"It should disturb me that you still remember my order," Charlotte said, taking off her safety glasses. She peeled off her gloves and dumped them before washing her hands.

"Why should it disturb you? You remembered how I had my coffee this morning," he replied.

"Good point." Charlotte went for the bag, but he blocked her path. He tapped his cheek expectantly. Charlotte rolled her eyes but kissed his cheek, the corner of his mouth, his lips. "Thank you for bringing me my favorite burger."

"Why, you're welcome, Charlie Belle," Reeve said, passing the bag to her. "How's the tentacle?"

"Gross, but fascinating." Charlotte caught him up on all her small discoveries since they had been apart. It felt good and easy like it always was with Reeve. Except when it came to messy emotions, she had always found him the easiest person to speak her mind to.

"I wonder if there's a way to figure outgrowth cycles," Reeve said, chewing on some fries. "If Aneirin used magic to create them, purposely designed them to breed as quickly as possible, it's not because he wants the world overrun with them. He's breeding an army."

Charlotte nodded. "I know, and that terrifies me. I'm hoping that if we kill him, some of his spells will die with him, including the new horde creatures."

"We'll figure it out. He might be powerful, but there is more of us with one goal to stop him." Reeve squeezed her hand. "And we have you."

"You think far too much of my abilities. I couldn't even keep him out of my dreams," she said with a shake of her head.

Reeve gently brushed his fingers over her shirt where her tattoo lay.

"This will help. Something *you* found and dared to put on your skin. I don't overestimate your abilities, Charlotte. I know what you're capable of."

"You're biased because we are sleeping together."

"We are doing a bit more than that," he said, the intensity back into his tone.

Charlotte swallowed down her mouthful of burger that was in danger of getting caught in her throat. "Yeah, shouldn't we talk about that?"

"I love you. What's more to talk about?" he replied, entirely at ease with such an epic declaration.

"Don't you think that's moving a bit fast?"

Reeve shrugged. "I've loved you for ages. I'm just in a position to tell you now. I don't expect you to say it back until you're ready too, but I'm not going to pretend I feel any different."

Charlotte didn't know how to react when she was put on the spot in such a way. She knew what she felt for him—what she had *always* felt for him. She had never said the words out loud to anyone that wasn't her family.

He was giving her one of his infinitely patient looks like he knew she was scared and understood

She reached for her Coke to soothe her dry mouth. She could say it back; she knew she could.

Before she could open her mouth, a wave of dark power rippled through the mansion.

"Did you feel that?" she asked, leaping to her feet.

"You bet your ass I did." Reeve followed her out into the main part of the mansion. The dark energy was pulling from downstairs beneath them.

"The prisoner," she hissed, and they raced to the dungeons.

Aneirin's acolyte had stripped naked in the cells. He hadn't washed since he was caught, and Charlotte now knew why. His whole body was covered in sigils painted in black and red blood.

"I told you, you are all fucking prey," he shouted and began to glow as the spell on his skin activated.

Charlotte tried to ready a counterspell, but Reeve pulled her down the second the acolyte exploded with magic. Blood and gore covered the cell, and the spell rolled out onto the grounds.

Reeve dragged her to her feet. Charlotte froze, clutching him. She could feel exactly what the spell did.

"Reeve, he's shredded the wards. He *was* the fucking trap! Aneirin is here."

23

Charlotte leaped into action. She ran out of the dungeons into the main foyer of the house.

Ever since they were children, Kenna had made sure they knew all the protocols in case of an attack on the mansion itself.

Charlotte opened a small box on the far wall and pulled the small red lever. Instantly, a high-pitched alarm rang through the house.

"I'm calling in the boys, but it'll take them a bit to get here," Reeve shouted to her and held a phone to his ear.

Charlotte pulled out her own phone and sent a 911 HOMEFRONT message to the family group and the code that meant the mansion was under attack.

David and Moira came into the foyer with the dogs enclosed around them. David already had a massive automatic shotgun, and Moira had her crossbow.

"Up in the battlements with the dogs, Moira." Charlotte passed her an earpiece. "I need you to be my eyes up high." Her little sister didn't argue, just fitted the device into her ear and whistled to her pack of dogs.

"What the fuck is going on?" Imogen demanded, coming downstairs with a double-bladed ax and her handgun holster. Layla followed with a compound bow and knives strapped all over her.

"The prisoner was a plant. I need to get the wards on the grounds back up, but I need cover," Charlotte replied.

She went into the ancient arms display and pulled out a sword. Like her sisters, she had been trained to use various weapons. While she preferred magic, she couldn't risk relying solely on it. That particular sword was a favorite that she had already engraved sigils into.

"The Greatdrakes are on their way," Reeve said, hurrying to join them.

"You any good with a weapon, Reevey?" Imogen asked.

"Of course I am. My favorite is a rifle."

"Excellent, grab one out of that cabinet over there and bring a box of ammo while you are at it," David instructed, pointing to the other side of the room.

"Where's Mom?" Layla asked, looking around.

"She went into the city for a night of shopping. She's going to be pissed that she's missing out," David replied with a fond smile.

"I'm pretty sure she's going to be breaking every traffic law to get back too," Imogen laughed and balanced the ax against her shoulder. "Come on, Charlotte. Let's see what's out on the grounds."

Reeve joined them with a rifle ready and was crackling with suppressed magic. He smiled crookedly at Charlotte. "Gotta say, that sword is doing things for me."

Charlotte's eyes narrowed. "I swear if you make one joke about me being able to handle a big weapon, I'll stab you with it."

"Focus, kiddies, we have things to kill," Layla teased and shoved open the front doors.

Outside, the security lights were blaring on high alert. It wasn't long past sundown, but the grounds were winter black on the stormy night.

"Charlotte, I can see stuff," Moira whispered through the earpiece.

"What can you see?"

"Big shapes moving around just out of the lights."

"Back or front?"

"Back."

"Thanks, Moira. Keep your head down so no one sees you." Charlotte gestured at Layla and Imogen. "Round the back."

Imogen grinned like a fiend and hefted the ax. "Excellent. You get those wards back up. We'll sort out whatever comes at you."

As a group, they headed around the side of the house, with Layla and Imogen going first. One hybrid creature let out a cry, and Layla loosed two arrows, hitting it in both eyes.

"Great shots," Reeve said approvingly.

"Cover me." Charlotte reached for her power and pulled out a woven patch of silver. The revealing spell lit up the wards in gold and orange light.

"Holy gods, Charlotte, they are intense," Reeve said.

"They were, which is why I never thought about an inside attack." Charlotte could kick her ass about it later. Blocking out the sounds of her sisters fighting, she felt out the holes in the wards where the acolyte's spell had torn them to shreds.

Guns were firing; creatures were roaring, and she felt the sharp pulses of power as Reeve threw spells at the horde creatures. There were other traces of magic on the property, which told her that more than one magician had sided with Aneirin.

If they were dumb enough to do that and then attack the Ironwoods, Charlotte had no pity for their fates.

Charlotte fell deep into her magic, weaving, mending, and connecting the magical filaments. The warding around the front of the mansion came back up, and the howling cries of dying creatures split the air as the magic tore any intruder apart.

"Good one, Charlie," Reeve called. She risked glancing at him and saw the blood on his face. Her magic wavered, and he shook his head at her. "It's nothing. I'm fine, keep going."

Pushing down the sudden fear, Charlotte grabbed hold of her anger instead. Someone or something had dared to touch her property, and she wasn't impressed. Reeve was hers, and she would tear apart anyone who harmed him.

Because you love him.

Charlotte hissed, pushing the thought away. She couldn't think about that. Not in the middle of a fight. Two magicians she didn't recognize came running out of the tree line towards her. Charlotte's magic vibrated through the sword, the sigil on its blade glowing with power.

The first rogue magician came at her with two daggers, realizing his mistake too late as Charlotte charged him with zero fear. Swift as a cat, she dodged around his lunge, the sharp tip of her magic-infused blade cutting through the protection spells he wore and sliced across his knees. The man screamed in surprise and agony as he hit the dirt. Charlotte swung again, taking off his head in one powerful stroke.

The second rogue was fighting Reeve and foolishly had put his back to Charlotte. She grabbed the fallen magician's daggers and threw them at his companion. Both hit his back, and he fell mid-swing with Reeve's dagger in his throat.

Reeve's eyes were wide, staring at her gripping the glowing sword. "Do the wards, Charlotte! I got this."

Charlotte lowered the sword and tried to refocus. Dark power was moving fast towards them, but it wasn't Aneirin. This power felt like blazing starlight and shadows.

"Cavalry is here," she shouted.

She jumped out of the way as two large figures dive-bombed the oncoming hybrids. Killian lifted one up and tore it apart mid-air. Bron landed on another, her large black sword cutting it in two and spraying herself in blood.

Charlotte tore her eyes away from the carnage and reached for the wards again. She got the second side up faster than the first, the edges knitting together with the other restored warding.

More magic was moving towards the house, this time tearing down their driveway. Charlotte felt their magic and grinned. The Greatdrakes had arrived too, and not a minute too soon.

Valentine found her first. "Let me help, Charlotte."

"Thanks. Do the western side for me and make sure you throw in something nasty for our enemies," Charlotte said.

"It would be my pleasure, Miss Ironwood," he replied with a deadly smile.

A few weeks ago, she never would've trusted another magician to touch her family's wards. After breaking in through Valentine's wards twice, she knew he could handle them and had plenty of nasty tricks to make them hazardous to the invaders.

Charlotte was working on the northern side when she felt the air stir around them. She faltered, her concentration snapping. A glowing aurora of pale blue light appeared before her, making her magic shake and her ears pop.

"What in hell..." The light burst into a portal, and Morrigan's Battle Bard stepped through. He spotted Charlotte, grinned maliciously, and threw so much power at her, she couldn't move. Charlotte sensed the secondary trap following it but couldn't unlock her body to get out of its path.

A heavy body thudded into hers, pushing her out of the way. Aneirin's magic caught Reeve in its sharp hooks, and he was dragged back into the portal. It disappeared with a quick flash of light, Aneirin and Reeve vanishing with it.

Charlotte stumbled as the freezing magic released her. She scrambled over the wet grass to where Reeve had disappeared.

"Charlotte! What happened?" Bas and Apollo rushed to help her back to her feet.

"He took him! Aneirin took Reeve," she shouted, pushing her hands through her hair. No, no, no. She knew what Aneirin did to magicians. She had seen the bodies in the estuary.

Please, please, not Reeve. That spell was meant for her.

A scream was building up in her chest, her magic electrifying the air around her.

"Charlotte, stop," Bas shouted. Apollo dragged him backward as Charlotte screamed and screamed.

Bolts of crackling magic scorched the air around her in a blast of power. The remaining horde hybrids and rogue magicians tried to run, but the lightning chased them in vicious bolts that scorched everything in their path.

"Charlotte! You need to let the magic go, or you'll burn yourself to pieces!" Valentine shouted in the distance.

Charlotte couldn't stop, couldn't breathe, the vision of Reeve being dragged into the portal with Aneirin seared into her eyes. Cold, dark night wrapped around her like a cloak, smothering her power.

"Reeve..." she whimpered.

"I have you, sister," Killian said, catching her as the darkness swallowed her whole.

24

Reeve was sure the portal was going to kill him. Magic gripped him tight and sliced him down to the bone. The power around him held the screams of dying men and the thrum of battle drums. He didn't know how long he had been stuck suspended in-between space and time before it spat him out again.

Reeve hit cold stone, and air rushed back into his aching lungs. He caught a glimpse of shiny black boots before he was kicked in the face.

"I'm growing tired of people getting in my goddamn way," Aneirin growled. He leaned down over Reeve, eyes blazing.

"Maybe if you weren't such a prick, people would be more obliging," Reeve said, spitting blood out onto the floor. "You really think I was going to sit back and let you take her?"

Aneirin's pissed-off expression shifted. "Ah, you love Charlotte. Interesting. This will make it so much easier. She will come to me now."

A lumbering hybrid grabbed Reeve by the wrist and dragged him across the floor where shackles were hammered into the stone. Without ceremony, he cleared out everything from Reeve's pockets, so he didn't have so much as a paperclip.

"You are madder than we all think if you believe Charlotte will come just because you have me," Reeve laughed at him.

Aneirin's smile grew cold. "Is that so?"

"Goes to show how little you know about her. Charlotte will leave me to rot because I was dumb enough to get caught. Don't think for a second that she's going to make my stupid mistakes," Reeve replied.

It was true too. Charlotte was going to be a pissed-off firecracker. Hell, Aneirin almost seemed like a good choice compared to an angry Charlotte.

Aneirin merely shrugged. "I suppose we will find out, won't we? It's hardly going to matter because after tomorrow, I'll have enough power to walk in and take her, no matter if all three of the fae princes are guarding her."

Reeve didn't like the sound of that. What was happening tomorrow night? He was smart enough to hold his tongue as he thought about it. A cold chill swept through his bones, and then it hit him—the winter solstice. It was a night that was perfect for the darkest of magics. It was the anniversary of the fae returning.

"You will be of service to me whether she comes for you or not." Aneirin stretched his hand out towards Reeve and hummed softly. "Oh, what a strange little magician you are. You have the magic of beasts and man beating inside of you. How delicious your power is going to be when I swallow it down."

"You're really not all there, are you, friend? Your crazy ass acolyte is making a lot more sense now," Reeve replied.

"He had one purpose, and that was to get captured and taken through the Ironwood wards. He knew what it meant and went willingly because that is what being one of the faithful means." Aneirin crouched down and stared Reeve in the eyes. "Perhaps you would be better as a servant than food. You must have a family that is brimming with similar power. How perfect. No wonder Charlotte kept you around. She is going to be a magnificent vessel. Morrigan might even let her go once she has a body of her own."

Laughter threatened to explode out of Reeve again. "She's not going to fall for anything you say or promise. She's an Ironwood. They are all about dying for their cause. There's no way in hell she's going to set Morrigan loose in the world."

"Not even to save the man she loves?" Aneirin asked sweetly.

Reeve's chest tightened. "Charlotte doesn't love me. That you can believe."

"I saw her face when you went into the portal. I know what love lost looks like Reeve Greatdrakes. She loves you, and that is why I am going to get everything that I want." With that, Aneirin turned and walked away.

Reeve cursed under his breath and tugged at his manacles. They had symbols carved in them to dampen his power. Of course they did.

Reeve closed his eyes and tried to reach out telepathically to Basset. Not even a trickle of connection.

"Fuck," he muttered.

Now that his eyes were adjusting to the dim light, Reeve could make out the circular structure he was in. Ancient pictographs were carved into the stones, and he could smell earth and blood.

Other manacles were bolted into the walls around him, with dark rust stains scattered over the musty straw. Reeve's skin crawled, knowing he wasn't the first prisoner Aneirin had kept there.

Would Charlotte figure out where he was before Aneirin had one of his horde creatures tear him apart? He could only hope.

I know what love lost looks like, Aneirin had said. Reeve swallowed, his throat too dry. Charlotte hadn't said it back to him, but he had felt such an emotional connection when they had made love after the tattoo. He hoped that whatever she felt for him was enough for her to try and get him back.

My mate. At least she was safe. As soon as he saw that portal, he knew Aneirin was coming for her, and he couldn't stand there and let it happen.

She was his whole world, and he would happily give his life if it meant keeping her out of the Battle Bard's hands.

Reeve took three deep breaths, trying to loosen the pain in his chest. If he did die, she knew that he loved her. He had said the words more than once. That had to be enough for him.

Charlotte might be bound as an Ironwood not to risk her safety and that of others to try and find him, but he knew Cosimo and his brothers would do their best to track Aneirin down.

With any luck at all, Charlotte and Valentine would do their spell so they could put a magical trace on Aneirin and get to him in time.

The winter solstice was a night when ancient power was at its strongest. The Ironwoods and the princes would know to watch any sacred sites. They might find him that way.

Reeve pulled his jacket around himself tighter and settled into a meditation. There wasn't anything he could do now, so he would conserve his energy, and if the opportunity arose, he would do his best to ruin all of Aneirin's well-laid plans.

∼

CHARLOTTE DIDN'T KNOW what time it was or where she was. She was floating in a sky of darkness and starlight.

Reeve. Where are you?

Charlotte sat bolt upright, her heart pounding and hands lashing out. She was in her own bed, but Killian was seated on a chair beside her.

"What happened?" she croaked. Her whole body ached like she had been pounded with meat mallets.

"You lost your shit, and your magic reacted accordingly, little sister. I had to stop you before you hurt yourself," Killian replied. "I bet you feel like hell."

Hot tears filled her eyes. "Aneirin took Reeve, Kill. How was I supposed to react?"

"I thought you said nothing was going on between you and trash magic," he replied, folding his arms.

Charlotte sniffed. "I lied. There's always been something between us. I was just too naive and hurt to acknowledge it. I was a fucking coward and never told him how I felt. Now he's going to die because of me."

"If he dies, it's not going to be because of you, Charlotte," Apollo said, coming into the room with Valentine. "Sorry, we were eavesdropping. We couldn't go home without knowing you were okay."

Charlotte didn't know what to say to that. They had been so accepting of her, and she had no idea what she had done to deserve it.

"I'll let everyone know you're okay," Killian said, eyeing the two magicians. Valentine only smirked in a challenge that seemed to amuse the hell out of Killian.

Apollo sat down on the bed beside her, clearly not having any idea about personal space.

"Drink this down, Charlotte. It'll make you feel better." He passed her a vial of pink liquid. It tasted sweet like crushed rose petals and strawberries.

"Thanks, Apollo. And thank you both for staying," she said. She looked up at Valentine, who had sat in Kill's vacated chair. "Did you get the rest of the wards up?"

"I did though it took a little while to figure out how you had tied them together. No wonder you get through mine so easily. I've never seen anything like it," Valentine replied.

"I'll take that as a compliment."

Apollo snorted. "You should. He rarely has a nice thing to say about anyone."

Charlotte pulled her knees up to her chest. "I really am sorry about Reeve. If I knew what he was going to do, I would've stopped him, you know that." Tears were starting to fall again, and she hated that she couldn't stop them. "We can't track Aneirin without him sensing us. I don't know how to find him."

"We will figure it out, Charlotte, but not tonight. Reeve is tough. He'll be able to survive the night with Aneirin," Valentine said.

"That's not reassuring at all, asshole," Apollo snapped at him.

Valentine rolled his eyes. "It's the truth, though. Aneirin wanted Charlotte but got Reeve. He'll figure out how to use that to his advantage. You have to think like him, remember? He knows Charlotte has a noble streak that he will want to use against her."

"Val's right. Aneirin might try to reach out, but I want to find him before he does that. We need a plan and to take the fight to him. No more of this wait around and see bullshit," Charlotte snapped. She tried to get up, but Apollo put a hand on her shoulder to stop her from moving.

"We are going to need you at full strength if we are going to find Reeve *and* fight Aneirin," he said.

"I'm sorry, but I'm not the type of person to just lie about while the man I love is in the hands of my fucking enemy," Charlotte snapped.

Apollo and Valentine gave her the same patient smile.

"We know," Apollo said. "That's why you're going to have to forgive me for the sleeping potion I just gave you. Reeve would kill us if we didn't protect you, and that includes from yourself."

"You...bastards..." Charlotte started to slump. Valentine caught her before she slipped off the side of the bed.

"Yes, we know. Come by the house tomorrow when you wake up. We will have a plan by then, sister," Valentine said, tucking her blanket around her.

Charlotte fought between fury and fatigue as the potion hit, and she was once again swept under a wave of darkness.

25

Charlotte was all kinds of worried and furious when she woke up the following day. She couldn't believe that they had drugged her. Charlotte was showered and out the door before any of her sisters could stop her.

Charlotte was fully prepared to tear the Greatdrakes wards to shreds when she got there and was completely taken aback to find that she had been built into them. They recognized her as soon as she stepped up to the gates, and all of her fury seemed to loosen and disappear inside of her until all she had left was worry.

Cosimo opened the door for her and brought her in for an unexpected hug. Charlotte's eyes moistened, but she swallowed back her tears.

"It's going to be okay, Charlotte. We will find him," Cosimo murmured softly.

"I know. It's just..." she struggled to find the words to start. Cosimo understood anyway and led her into the kitchen. The boys were nowhere to be seen, which was a relief as she still didn't trust herself not to want to smite Val and Apollo.

"Take a seat. I'll make you some tea," Cosimo said, moving about the kitchen. Charlotte slumped on one of the stools at the breakfast bar and put her head in her hands.

"I don't know where to start. What if Aneirin killed him because his magic took Reeve by accident?" she groaned.

"You can't think like that. On this particular point, I agree with Valentine. He will use Reeve as leverage to get to you. He still wants you to be Morrigan's vessel, and now he has the perfect bargaining chip," Cosimo replied, placing the steaming mug down in front of her. "You know that Reeve wouldn't want you to do anything that's going to put you in danger."

"I don't care what he fucking wants. He was stupid enough to jump in the way. He can damn well deal with being rescued," she grumbled, and to her surprise, Cosimo laughed.

"He knows that about you too, don't worry."

"What about the trap we were going to put in place around the spell Aneirin has to block tracking magic? I haven't had a chance to look into that with everything else going on, but it's still a good idea," Charlotte said, cradling the mug in her hands. She felt so damn cold on the inside. Reeve was always so warm, and she loved curling into him. She swallowed back her treacherous tears once more.

Please, please be okay, or I am going to kick your ass.

The kitchen door swung open, and Basset came in, looking alert and full of energy. Charlotte wished she was that ready and focused.

"Excellent, you're here. Have you told her yet?" he said briskly. Cosimo threw an irritated glare in his direction.

Charlotte looked between them. "Told me what?"

"Wait, we want to be here for this. Is there more tea, Dad?" Apollo said, rushing in.

"When we get Reeve back, you and I are going to have a long discussion on drugging people, Apollonius Greatdrakes," Charlotte growled.

Apollo looked slightly chastised, which was more than what she could say for Valentine when he came in after him. He only let out an amused grunt.

"Get over it, Ironwood. We did it for your own good. You are no use to Reeve burned out on magic and exhausted," he said. "He let himself get caught because he trusted you would be smart enough to save him. You don't want to let him down, do you?"

"I'm going to turn you into a snake," she threatened with a scowl.

Valentine perked up at that. "You can do transfiguration with live subjects? Fascinating. Have you told her about being Reeve's mate yet?"

Charlotte spat her hot tea out over the counter. "What did you just say?"

Basset did a slow clap at Valentine. "Oh, well done, dick for brains."

"Boys, that's enough," Cosimo snapped, and they all piped down. He wiped up the tea and placed a gentle hand on Charlotte's shoulder. "I know it might be a lot to process."

"It's impossible, though! He's not fae," she spluttered.

Cosimo slid onto the stool beside her. "He doesn't need to be. Our family was gifted the magic and life force of a dragon. That included some...unexpected side effects."

"That included mating?" Charlotte looked around at the others to see if they were trying to play some kind of a joke on her. They were all unusually serious.

"I don't understand."

"It's a phenomenon since Darragh first bonded with the dragon. None of the Greatdrakes have really bothered to wonder why it happened," Valentine said a little bitterly. "It was lazy of them."

"It is because the dragon inside of us is never wrong. Trust me, Charlotte. I found my mate, and it was..." Cosimo's voice broke, and he hurried to clear it. "It was unlike anything I can explain. We fit perfectly together in every way, and when I lost her, it was like my whole world imploded. I won't let you and Reeve suffer through that."

Charlotte let out a strangled laugh. "But what makes you think I'm his mate? He's never said a word to me about it or even implied that such a thing was possible."

"He kept it to himself, right up until you walked through our door. I knew instantly because I could see the change in him. Just like I saw the change in him five years ago when you two had your falling out. I didn't know what happened, but it was like a light went out in him for a while."

"He became a sullen bastard," Apollo said with a shake of his head. "The dumbass should have figured out that you were his mate then."

"But if he knows now, why wouldn't he say anything to me about it?" Charlotte knew herself well enough that she probably would have laughed in his face at the mere suggestion of it. He did say that he loved her, and maybe it was the same thing.

"Reeve has his reasons for everything. He probably didn't want to freak the hell out of you," Basset said, leaning against the kitchen counter. "He started shielding his mind twice as aggressively as soon as you came back into his life, and I knew then something was up with him."

"Charlotte, I don't know if you realize how intimidating you can be. It took Reeve five years to get the courage to try and be your friend again. Maybe you can use that big brain of yours and come to your own conclusions about why he hasn't told you yet," Valentine said, his frustration starting to come through.

"Doesn't matter if I am or not. He's gone, and we need to stop talking about stupid mates and start talking about how we are going to find him," Charlotte snapped. She needed Reeve back so she could yell at him herself.

"That you are his mate is the point, Charlotte. He jumped in front of that spell because his whole base instinct is to protect you no matter the cost to himself," Basset replied patiently. "Mates also have a connection to each other. Reeve might be hidden behind some wards or Aneirin's power, but even those are not strong enough to mess with a mating bond. There might be a way that you can connect with him, and we can use it to find him."

Charlotte rubbed the bridge of her nose. "Explain to me how? And will our time be better suited to this over the other magic to track Aneirin?"

"We can do both. Bas can work with you on making a psychic connection with Reeve. Valentine and I can work on bypassing the protection Aneirin has to block a tracking spell. Apollo can make us some magical bombs for when we attack Aneirin," Cosimo instructed. He gave Charlotte a stern look. "Have you eaten?"

"How is that relevant?" Charlotte asked, straightening.

"You can't work on telepathic connections on an empty stomach. Bas, make her a sandwich," Cosimo said, and the brothers all got going.

"You really don't have to," Charlotte said as Basset began slicing bread.

"Yes, I do. Besides, I make the best sandwiches out of all of us. You'll love it." He began pulling ingredients out of the fridge.

"Thanks, it's... It's really nice of you," she replied, knowing when she was defeated.

Basset gave her the charming Greatdrakes smile over his shoulder. "You're most welcome. Seriously. We are all loving having a woman back in the house. It's been far too long. Reeve would murder us if we didn't take care of you while you were in distress. Really, you're doing me a favor by letting me take care of you."

Charlotte smiled weakly. "Can I ask what happened to your mother?"

"She was in a car accident. Nearly broke my father completely. It's probably the real reason Reeve didn't say anything about you being his mate," Basset replied as he sliced tomatoes. "None of us would want to upset Cosimo about it if we can avoid it."

"He lost a mate, but you guys lost a mother. Do you not talk about her at all?" she asked. It didn't matter how tough Kenna was on them. She couldn't imagine not having her there.

"We talk about her. We just don't talk about mates often, if ever. To be honest, we all kind of thought it was bullshit but now with Reeve... Well, we could all see it when you turned up. Val is pissed because he can't imagine a greater hell than being beholden to anyone." Basset put a stacked ham and salad sandwich in front of her. "Eat that, and we'll get started."

"Thanks, Bas. I appreciate it," Charlotte murmured.

"My pleasure, darling." Basset watched her eat the whole thing before he attempted to talk about magic with her.

"Okay, how do we do this?" Charlotte asked.

"I think our best chance is to try in Reeve's tower. You will feel his presence the closest there, and it will help with the connection."

Charlotte thought it was a great idea, right up until the moment she stepped inside the tower and could smell Reeve's aftershave in the air.

A heavy weight settled on her chest, and for a moment, she struggled to get enough air into her lungs.

"It's okay, Charlotte. Reeve is fine," Basset tried to soothe her.

"How do you know that?"

Basset took her hand and led her further into the tower. "Because you would feel it if he wasn't alive, Charlotte. Cosimo said that he knew the second my mother died. It was like someone had ripped his heart out. He thought he was literally having a heart attack. He sensed the second the mating bond broke."

Charlotte swallowed hard. "But we haven't even mated. Wouldn't I know if we had?"

Basset frowned. "I don't know how a bond is formed, but I'm hoping that because you two have had sex that it will be a strong enough connection."

Charlotte flushed and tried her best not to show it. She thought back to the absolute earth-shattering sex they had after Reeve had finished her tattoo.

They had somehow felt each other's orgasms...maybe it hadn't been a part of the tattoo magic at all like she suspected. Could she have mated with him without even realizing it? God, it was too much of a trip to even consider properly.

"You okay?" Bas asked gently.

"Not really. Just tell me what I need to do."

Bas ran both his hands through his cropped curls. "Alright. Do you have any experience with telepathy or astral travel?"

"Not telepathy, but I went through a stage of trying to astral travel. I would meditate for hours. Never did figure it out, though," she replied.

"Not many people do, even magicians. It doesn't matter that you didn't make it. What matters is that you understand the concept of it. The ability to push your spirit or consciousness to another place in the etheric realms." Bas looked around at Reeve's room. "We need to find something that makes you feel close to him. Something that can enhance your association with him."

Charlotte spotted the maroon knit sweater with holes in the hem. Reeve had been wearing it when she had gone to her knees in front of him. She shut the thought down before Bas could see the red on her cheeks. She picked up the sweater from the coat rack, and her heart ached. She lifted it to her nose and breathed in his smell.

Why did you have to jump in front of that spell, you crazy man?

Bas had said that Reeve did it because he had a mating instinct to protect her, but that wasn't all it was. He loved her and would never let

Aneirin touch her. Charlotte was raised to be the one to do the protecting, not to be protected.

She swallowed the lump in her throat. "This will work."

"Okay, then sit down on the bed with it and get into meditation," Bas instructed, taking a seat on a swivel chair. Charlotte pulled the sweater on over her head and enclosed herself in the warmth and scent of Reeve.

My mate.

Could it really be the answer to why she had never been able to let him go? Why she wanted him all the time? It was too much for her to think about.

Charlotte got herself comfortable on Reeve's bed and shut her eyes. Her breathing hadn't been right since she woke up that morning.

"Okay, Bas, I need to know what to do here."

"Deep breaths, Charlotte. Let's bring you down into the right headspace. Remember, Reeve is your focal point. Focus on him. Everything you love about him," Basset said, his voice dropping to a calm timbre.

Charlotte tried to push all other thoughts but Reeve from her mind as she followed Basset's guiding voice. What did she love about Reeve? Everything. That had always been the problem in her mind. Things she found so irritating, like his easy, almost lazy approach to magic, she also liked about him. He was always teasing, and she would never have tolerated it from anyone else. If he was there, what would he say right then?

What's up, Charlie Belle? Why are you so stressed?

Yeah, that would be Reeve. He would be clueless while she was having a mental breakdown. Or if he had the dragon sheen in his eyes, he would be growling filthy things in her ear while she lay on his bed. She felt for the connection that had bound them after the tattoo session. It had been like they had shared each other's bodies for those few brief moments. She fell into the memory of the sensation and pushed her magic towards it.

Where are you, Reeve?

Images bombard her mind's eye—spiral carvings, dark tunnels lit by candles, cold earth, diamond shapes on the walls, straw against her hands, war drums getting louder, a stone bowl, an altar.

Charlotte gasped, her whole body jolting awake in a disorientating spasm. Bas was beside her in an instant, rubbing warmth back into her hands and helping to ground her back into the present.

"What did you see, Charlotte? Where is he?" Bas asked.

"Spiral carvings, a corridor of stone walls... I know that altar," Charlotte murmured, rubbing her eyes. "Give me a second. My brain is on fire." She stumbled into Reeve's bathroom and splashed warm water on her face. She replayed the images through her head. Steam from the water had fogged up the mirror, and she idly traced the three spirals she had seen onto it.

The answer hit her hard. The stone altar, the corridor of stone, and the winter solstice...

Charlotte ran into the bedroom. "Bas, I know where Aneirin is. He's at fucking Newgrange."

Basset's face shifted in realization. "Of course! The sun aligns with it once a year on the winter solstice. Aneirin is going to use the magic it generates for whatever he's planning."

"Exactly. And he's going to summon every follower he has there to protect him while he does it. Time to call in the family." Charlotte pulled out her phone and smiled viciously. "And I'm going to need Val to help me with a present for Aneirin."

26

Reeve knew that time was running out. Rogue magicians and humanoid hybrid creatures had been busy for hours. They were preparing something out of his eyesight, and it was driving him crazy. Whatever it was, he could feel the deep thrum of power it was already generating.

He had been given a bottle of water to drink and a bucket to piss in, but for the most part, he had been left alone. He had expected some torture, at least. Not that he *wanted* to be tortured. It just seemed a little off-brand for Aneirin to leave him alone.

It's because he knows Charlotte wouldn't want you harmed. It told Reeve that Aneirin still held out hope that she would join him willingly. The thought made him smile. Charlotte Ironwood didn't willingly *do* anything she didn't want.

He had hoped that she would've found him by now. Night had fallen again, and the bone-chilling cold had settled over his prison. Torches had been lit and cast the other rooms in a warm glow.

Where are you, Charlie? Reeve needed to get out of the fucking manacles so he could get some kind of signal to her. Basset could hear him with a telepathic range of fifty kilometers. Were they still in Dublin? He didn't think so. He would hear the traffic, at least. All he heard was the guttural growls of horde creatures.

Reeve shifted in his manacles, doing his best to relieve the cramps in his legs and arms. It didn't work, so he shut his eyes and tried to block out the pain.

Reeve was dozing when someone kicked his foot. Aneirin was standing in front of him. He only wore a pair of leather pants and was covered in painted spirals... Not paint. Blood. Reeve swallowed the bile creeping up his throat. Woad had been streaked over the bard's face and through his hair. He was vibrating with power, his amber eyes lit with magic and a whole lot of crazy.

"Get up, Greatdrakes. You will be a witness to the birth of change," Aneirin said, his unearthly voice drawing him in and repelling him at the same time. A hybrid came forward, unlocked the chain in the wall, and dragged Reeve to his feet.

"What are you doing? What is this magic I'm feeling?" Reeve asked, unable to help himself.

"The ancients built this mound where all the magical creatures, humans, and gods lived in harmony. It is one of the few places left that still has its power intact," Aneirin replied. He led them down the corridor, and the air grew colder and fresher.

Reeve finally recognized where they were. "We are at Newgrange?"

"Indeed. The few of the fae prince's guards that were watching over it were easy enough to dispatch," Aneirin replied, and they stepped out of the tunnels.

Reeve's knees went weak when he saw the crowd of horde creatures, rogue magicians, and followers that had gathered on the green fields around the circular structure.

Vast sections of earth had been torn from the hills to get them all on the same lower levels. Torches lit the crowd; drums began to pound, and they all cheered when they saw Aneirin.

Reeve was cuffed to the metal handrails that had been built for tourists. He had a front-row seat to the huge carved stones at the entranceway Aneirin was using for an altar.

Reeve couldn't see what was on the altar properly, but he could smell the blood and gore. The ground around the stones was covered in it, and he could feel the horrible power vibrating from them. He made out the rune of Teiwaz on the rocks, like the spell at the estuary, and his blood chilled in recognition. Aneirin was summoning the generals.

Fuck, Charlotte, where are you? Reeve pulled at his manacles, and the nearest hybrid hit him hard across the face. Blood spurted out of his nose, and black spots danced in his vision. His head was ringing, and he could barely make out Aneirin beginning his chant. The Bard shone with magic, soaking the air around him. Something slithery and dark crept into the spell, and the hair on Reeve's body stood on end in horror. The crowd of worshippers was chanting in a frenzy, their energy and magic being drawn into the spell.

Reeve's whole body locked up as the first rays of dawn hit the top of the structure. Light filled it, raced through the corridors, and directed straight into Aneirin and the spell he was casting.

Backlit with sun and power, Aneirin lifted slowly off his feet, the strength of his magic flooding the world. The blood painted on the stones began to smoke and burn.

Reeve wanted to throw up, the horrible spell in the air ripping all the hope clean out of him. He slumped against the wall, sweating heavily and struggling to get air into his constricted lungs.

Hot, incredible power sparked in the distance, and Reeve's head shot up, looking through the crowd for its source. He knew that magic.

Cries of rage and roars of horde creatures filled the air, not in ecstasy but in battle fury. Magic pierced the sky, and an invisible hand punched a path through the crowd.

Looking like the pissed-off goddesses they were, the Ironwood sisters appeared in the bright dawn sun, then the princes of the fae and the Greatdrakes.

Reeve choked down a sob. They had all come for him. At their center, glowing with power and wielding the Greatdrakes family sword, was Charlotte.

~

CHARLOTTE WAS FUELLED with magic and rage. The sword in her hand glowed with power, and she silently thanked Cosimo all over again for letting her use it. They had been arming up to leave when he had offered it to her. It had been forged to absorb and conduct the magic running through it, and it was unlike any weapon she had used before.

The battle was a blur of horde creatures, rogue magicians, and frenzied followers. A cold blast shot past her left, and creatures fell with blades of ice pierced through their tough hides.

"Go, Charlotte," Bayn shouted from behind her. "Get your man, and I'll cover you." She didn't thank him, just pushed more power into the sword and cut and slashed. She could see Reeve, bound to a metal railing near the altar.

Still alive.

Relief and love flooded through her. He was all right, which was good because it meant she could kick his ass herself.

"Charlotte Ironwood! You are here at last," Aneirin called over the din. "Come to me, little magician."

Hot power gripped her tight, lifted her over the battle, and carried her to where Aneirin stood beside blood-covered stones. She could see the smoking lines of the spell he had performed at dawn from the sky. It was still charged with energy.

Fuck, it's already started. We are too late.

Charlotte knew it was something to do with the generals, but she couldn't decide what. Aneirin held her in the air, ensuring that her sword was out of range.

"I knew you would find us. I'll admit you worked a lot quicker than what was expected, but I will take what I can get," he said in his impossibly smooth voice.

"Let Reeve go. I'm the one that you want," Charlotte replied. She didn't fight the power holding her. She didn't want him to think that she was lying.

"No! Don't help him, Charlotte. My freedom isn't worth it," Reeve begged.

Charlotte smiled at him. "It is to me, Reeve. I love you, and I'm not going to let you die. Not for me."

Aneirin looked between them and laughed. "I told you, Greatdrakes. I know what love and loss look like. I believe you are a woman of honor, Charlotte Ironwood, but I won't be releasing him until I get what I need."

Charlotte did her best to look like she was defeated. Aneirin's smile became triumphant, and he turned back to his altar. A murmur started from his lips, the beginnings of a song so beautiful that tears sprung in her eyes.

She couldn't move her hands just yet, but she didn't need to. Deep in her mind's eye, a sigil began to form like flames carving into the darkness. She blocked out all the sounds of battle, the spell song, Reeve screaming at her. She held onto the sigil inside of her until it was all she could see.

Strange, ancient magic pulsed through the sword in her hand, and Charlotte could feel all the remnants of the Greatdrakes magic that had been fed into the blade over the centuries.

We are here with you, the voices in the sword called to her.

Tears streaming down her face, Charlotte pulled the power from the sword and everything she had deep inside of her and fed it into the sigil. With a cry, it tore free from her, and the glowing power wrapped tight around Aneirin's throat.

The song was choked off, and he fell forward, gasping for air. He clawed at his throat, trying desperately to speak, but the sigil gripping him robbed him of every part of his voice.

The spell holding her let go, and Charlotte fell to the ground. She managed to keep her feet, and gripping the sword tight, she walked towards the struggling bard.

"You really should have known better than to think I'd ever willingly walk into a trap without a plan," Charlotte said to him. Magic roared in her veins, filling her with light and power. Aneirin's eyes went wide as Charlotte shouted with fury and brought the Greatdrakes sword down on his head, cleaving it in two. The power around Aneirin broke, and horde creatures started dying and screaming as the spells animating them unraveled.

Charlotte put her boot on Aneirin's shoulder and, with a hard tug, yanked the sword free of what remained of his skull. Her whole body felt like it was on fire as she walked over to Reeve.

"My hero," he said, eyes shining with love and adoration. "You came for me."

Charlotte swung the sword at the chain holding him. Magic seared through it and cut it clean in half.

"Well, I couldn't let my mate die, even if he got himself captured," she said, pulling him to his feet.

Reeve wiped some blood from her face with his sleeve. "Thanks for coming, baby."

It didn't matter they were covered in blood and mud. Charlotte kissed Reeve with all the love and magic she had in her. There, in the middle of a battlefield, on the shattered remains of a dark magician's power, the mating bond between them locked into place, and Charlotte had never been happier in her life.

"You really do love me," Reeve said, feeling every emotion she had for him.

"I really do." Charlotte pulled back and glared up at him. "But that doesn't mean you're not in serious trouble, mister."

Reeve's smile was all Greatdrakes charm and devilry. "I look forward to you punishing me later, Charlie Belle."

27

What remained of the fighting died not long after Aneirin did. The surviving rouge magicians were rounded up by fae warriors and would go into one of Kian's dungeons.

Kian and Killian studied what was left of Aneirin's body and the spell he was performing.

"We were too late," Charlotte said, her hand still gripping Reeve's, unable to let him go.

"Only for the first part of the spell," Kian replied, crouching down to study the ashy remains. He looked like the Blood Prince in his full golden armor and red hair shining in battle braids. He was her brother, but every now and again, Charlotte got a sharp reminder of his violent, fear-inducing past.

"This was for a portal and a big one," Killian commented from a few meters away. "If we had been any later, we would have been dealing with Vili and Hafgan too."

"Fuck," Kian hissed, standing up again. "Aneirin has set them loose from Tir Na Nog. He would've had to break their ties before he summoned them."

Killian's wings ruffled in irritation. "Just what we fucking need. We are going to need to have a war council, little brother."

Kian looked at Charlotte and Reeve, and the fierceness in his expression softened. "Go home, you two. You've done enough for now."

"But I can help..." Charlotte began.

"We know you can, but you don't need to. Go the fuck home and look after your mate," Killian said with a mocking stern expression. "We have plenty of hands to clean up. Trash magic looks dead on his feet."

Reeve flipped him off with a grin. "Come on, Charlie. Let's go home."

Charlotte fought an internal war within herself. The Greatdrakes sword felt heavy now that the battle was over, and the magic and adrenaline faded.

"Fine, but no war councils without us," Charlotte told her brothers.

"You bet your ass you're going to be there," Bayn said as he joined them. "If I have to suffer through the boring fucking thing, you do too."

Charlotte smiled at them. "Okay, I'm going."

The Greatdrakes were waiting for them near a group of cars. Valentine was bitching about a wound on his shoulder, but apart from that, they all looked okay.

Cosimo pulled Reeve into a hug. "Good to see you in one piece, son."

"Thanks for coming, Dad."

Apollo snorted. "Always the troublemaker. It wasn't like we were going to let Charlotte come alone."

Charlotte's hand gripped the hilt of the Greatdrakes sword and held it out to Cosimo. "Thank you for letting me use this. It was...incredible."

"You were incredible using it. If you ever came at me like you charged Aneirin, I think I would pee my pants," Basset said with a wide smile. He was covered in flecks of blood and looked nothing like his usual neat self.

"And she used a sigil without drawing it, just like I said she could," Reeve said proudly and kissed her temple.

Valentine rolled his eyes. "We all said she could, but it was me that helped her practice to do it before the battle, so Aneirin couldn't stop her."

Charlotte beamed at them. "You all helped, and I'm grateful for all of you believing in me."

"You are very easy to believe in, Charlotte," Cosimo replied with a fatherly smile that hit her right in the heart.

"Still alive, baby sis?" Imogen called out to her, bloody ax resting on her shoulder.

"I'm surprised to see you in one piece. I'm going home with Reeve. Tell Mom," Charlotte called back. Imogen waved and headed towards the group of fae warriors.

"Greatdrakes and Ironwoods fighting together on a battlefield alongside the fae. What strange times we live in," Cosimo mused.

"One big happy family," Valentine mused and then winced in pain. "Can we go home now? This wound is fucking killing me."

"I have some healing patches that will help," Charlotte offered.

Valentine managed a smile. "I'd appreciate that, sister."

∼

STANDING in the hot shower was the best thing Charlotte had ever experienced. For all the stories of epic battles in the world, none ever talked about how exhausted everyone was afterward. Reeve's arms slipped around her and held her to him.

"I wasn't sure I'd ever be able to get you naked with me ever again," he said and kissed her bare shoulder. Charlotte soaped up a washcloth and turned.

"Come here, you troublesome magician," she teased and ran the cloth over the red dragon on his chest.

"I thought you would be getting angry at me by now. Who is this sweetheart that is taking care of me?" he teased.

"I'm definitely going to yell at you about not telling me I'm your mate—that you could *have* a mate—but I am too relieved to have you in one piece right now."

Reeve pressed a kiss to her forehead. "I was going to tell you once you said you loved me. I didn't want to scare you off."

"I know now. Do I look scared to you?" Charlotte asked.

Reeve looked her over, and his expression went hot. "No. You look delicious."

"Careful, Greatdrakes, you might not have the strength to do all the things that look is promising."

Reeve chuckled. "Apollo made me drink like five of his potions. I know exactly what I have the strength for." He pressed her gently against the tiled wall and dropped down to his knees in front of her.

"What are you doing?" Charlotte asked, her voice breathy.

"Thanking you for rescuing me." Reeve grinned wickedly, slipped one of her wet legs over his shoulder, and spread her. His hot tongue stroked her, making Charlotte gasp and grab onto his wet hair.

Reeve growled. "Hold on tight. I wouldn't want you to slip, baby." His tongue flicked over her sensitive flesh again, and Charlotte was bombarded with sensation. Having Reeve's tongue between her thighs was going to become her new favorite thing. She looked down and almost came at the sight of the water streaming down his muscled back. His dick was hard from pleasuring her, and she trembled at the sight of it.

"Touch yourself," she begged.

Reeve grinned up at her. "You want to watch while I eat you?"

Charlotte nodded, her head getting dizzy from heat and need. Reeve wrapped a hand around his cock and bent his mouth back to her. Charlotte couldn't look away, the sight of him pleasuring them both overloading all of her senses.

Reeve slipped two fingers inside of her, making Charlotte rise up then lower down on them. Reeve worked her until she was sobbing. He twisted his fingers hard, and she cried out, her orgasm catching her off guard. Reeve sucked on her clit, dragging out the sensation. His own release had him spilling over his fist and groaning against her.

Charlotte loosened her grip on his hair, smoothing his wet hair back from his forehead.

Reeve rested his head against her hip. "I'm never going to get enough of you. The more I have you, the more I want you."

Charlotte lifted his face. "You better because I'm not going anywhere, lover."

"You really are okay with being my mate? A Greatdrakes?" Reeve asked, his arms wrapping around her legs.

"I wouldn't be here if I wasn't. I don't know if I'm quite ready to be called a Greatdrakes yet," Charlotte said, suddenly overwhelmed by the idea.

Reeve grinned. "We can call you whatever you like, Charlie. Still doesn't change the fact that you are a Greatdrakes. That sword you used today? It can only be wielded by a Greatdrakes family member. It's why Cosimo offered it to you."

Charlotte swayed at the revelation, but Reeve's strong hands steadied her as he rose to his feet. He kissed her, firm and deep.

Charlotte melted into him, the thought of being so accepted by his family filling her with a sense of homecoming and belonging she never could have imagined. She would no longer feel like the odd one out. The one that didn't fit right.

In the Greatdrakes family, she would never have to hide how powerful she was or pretend she wasn't only ever thinking about magic. They would all be thinking of it too.

"You really think that we can make this work?" Charlotte whispered, her arms going around him.

"We can, and we will. You are everything I have ever dreamed of," Reeve whispered, resting her forehead against hers.

"I dreamed of you too, Reeve," Charlotte replied and brushed her lips against his. "And I would be honored to be a Greatdrakes."

28

Charlotte wasn't summoned home until the following evening. Kian had called everyone together for a war council and a dinner. Kenna had gathered her in a surprisingly tight hug and grumbled something about losing all of her daughters too soon but otherwise seemed happy for her.

Charlotte sat with Reeve, her fingers wrapped tightly around his. She couldn't help how different it was compared to the last council they'd attended.

"You guys are so cute," Layla whispered from her place beside her. "And to think you were getting ready to hex him."

"You were what?" Reeve demanded. Charlotte didn't get a chance to reply because the conferencing screens turned on, and Arne Steelsinger appeared. Layla had a sharp intake of breath that Charlotte wisely didn't comment on.

"Thank you for joining us, Arne," Kian greeted with a grim smile.

"I wish it were under better circumstances, prince," the elf replied. He looked tense and ready for a fight.

"So do I, but the generals being loose is a concern for everyone."

Arne's brows tightened. "My people have put the word out that any sign of Vili needs to be reported back to the queen as soon as possible. Morrigan was a monster, but she kept him on a tight leash. He is not going to remain hidden for long. It's not in his nature," he explained, his worry palpable even from the other side of Europe.

"We are allies now, Arne," Bayn told him. "Your fight is our fight. If Vili comes for your people, he'll have to contend with all of us too."

Arne inclined his head. "Thank you, brother. Vili caused my people a lot of pain when he last roamed free, so I will appreciate any willing blades should his power rise again."

Charlotte listened as Kenna, Kian, and Cosimo laid out possible battle plans. She marveled at all of them listening to each other and offering their expertise. These were indeed strange times, but watching them all work together filled Charlotte with a strange kind of hope. It didn't matter what trouble the generals caused, they had each other, and together there wasn't anything they could defeat.

∼

Two hours later, everything was talked out, and everyone was ready for dinner. Kian stopped Reeve and Charlotte from exiting the board room as everyone filed out and went downstairs for dinner.

"I would like a word, you two," he said, still wearing his serious face.

"What's wrong, Kian?"

The prince crossed his arms. "We need to discuss the terms of our agreement. You found and stopped Aneirin, Charlotte, which means I owe you a trip to the fae mages."

Charlotte's hand gripped Reeve's tighter. "Can Reeve come?"

"Of course he can. I would never dream about separating mates. I was going to request you don't hold off on coming to England. Imogen has asked to come to England to check that the aquatic horde creatures haven't reached our shores, and David is due for a trip to the healers," Kian explained. "I want both of you to help Elise scour my libraries and those of the fae mages for any information on Vili and Hafgan. Just because they are yet to show themselves doesn't mean we should be idle."

Charlotte brightened. "I would love to come, Kian. The Greatdrakes and Ironwoods will keep an eye on things here in Ireland. They won't need us. Besides, how could I ever say no to a trip to some of the oldest libraries in existence?"

"I'll help any way I can. Bas is already reaching out to other magicians to check their libraries for stories of the generals," Reeve added.

"Thank you, the both of you." Kian gave them a smile, his stern countenance finally easing. "I'm glad I didn't have to kill you, Reeve."

"Ah, me too?" he replied, and Charlotte bit down a smile as Kian left the room. "I think he's warming up to me."

Charlotte snickered. "You keep thinking that."

Reeve pressed her up against the table and bit his bottom lip. "Want to skip dinner and ravish me in the greenhouse instead?"

Charlotte sketched a sigil in her mind's eye and sent it in the direction of the conference room doors. They shut with a bang and locked. Reeve raised a brow.

"What? You were the one that gave me the idea to use my sigil magic more instinctively."

"And your instincts say you want me to bend you over and fuck you blind on this conference room table?" Reeve asked, gripping her hips tight against his. "Damn, this mating bond is sharing out thoughts already."

"Oh gods, that could be dangerous." Charlotte laughed and kissed him.

"I love you so fucking much, Charlie Belle."

Charlotte pulled him closer, her heart brimming with how much she loved him in return. Not that she was going to give him the satisfaction of admitting it.

"So you should, Greatdrakes. Now, what was it you said about bending me over this table?" Her heart began pounding in excitement at the thought of it.

Reeve's eyes flashed gold, and he wrapped her braid around his wrist. "Well, I did say you could call the shots."

29

Imogen Ironwood was tired of family gatherings. There had been more dinners and parties at the manor in the last few months than she remembered there being in the last ten years. Not that it was a bad thing to have the house full of life again. Live, laugh, love, and all that bullshit. It was just that it was exhausting.

Life used to be simpler, broken down to hunting and training and fun. Now the Ironwoods were political again, and being political wasn't something she was great at.

All the people in the house did give her the distraction she needed to sneak away. She simply used her excellent hunting skills to vanish into the background and slip silently up the stairs to her bedroom.

Usually, it was a riot of thrown about clothes and weapons. Now it was a riot of books and papers. Ever since the day in the library with Killian and Charlotte, she had been acting like a bit of a dumbass.

She knew it was crazy, maybe bordering on obsession, but the god of the dead had done something to fuck with her the night of Morrigan's invasion. She had put it down to the fascination she had always had with death. And then there he was.

I mean, how often did any living being meet a god of the dead? Exactly. She would've been crazy *not* to be curious. So what if she had told him to go fuck himself when they met? That had just been stress and surprise.

Arawan clearly hadn't taken it personally when he had turned up to heal her from the wound—and impregnation—that the horde Kraken had inflicted on her.

The dark gray scar on her side still hummed a little. She hadn't told Charlotte about it because she would freak out, but sometimes she could feel a tiny thread of Arawan's power still inside of it. That little connection made her think that just *maybe* she could somehow get him a message.

Her new big brothers were fucking awesome and all that, but were they vicious enough to take on Hafgan, an actual lord of hell? She had her doubts. Especially because from all the books she had been reading up on the myths about him, the fucker could literally regenerate from any fucking wound they gave him.

Imogen knew for a fact that only a bigger badass could beat a badass, and the only badass bad enough to ever have defeated Hafgan had been Arawan. Defeated, not killed, because clearly the fucker didn't know how to stay dead.

The original feud was started because Hafgan tried to take over and become the god of Annwn, and Arawan sure as shit wasn't going to let him have it. Imogen could only hope that Arawan still hated the general enough to want to go after him and settle things once and for all.

The real problem was unless Hafgan turned up in Annwn, how was Arawan going to know that his nemesis was walking around free again?

Killian had warned her that summoning a death god was a really bad idea. Imogen loved bad ideas; it was her toxic trait and the reason why she had technically died two times already. After Arawan had healed her from the Kraken, she had instantly started researching a way to summon him if an emergency ever arose. Having Hafgan loose in the world definitely counted as an emergency.

Imogen sat down crossed-legged amongst the piles of books and let out a sigh of annoyance. She had exhausted her resources; there simply was no way to summon Arawan. Either no one had been dumb enough to try, or no one had survived long enough to brag or write about it.

There was *one* other way that she could think of.

Imogen reached under her bed and pulled out her favorite bowie knife. It was a matte black with a non-slip grip for when things got wet. She tossed it up in the air and caught it again.

"What's one more time in the scheme of things?" she asked out loud. Hafgan would slaughter and maim and conquer. She could protect her whole rambling family of Ironwoods, Greatdrakes, and Fae all in one selfless act. Imogen sucked on a tooth.

"Fuck it," she muttered. Then she flipped her knife the right way up and slit her wrists.

~

IMOGEN MUST'VE CUT DEEP BECAUSE AS soon as the blackness crept over her, she was suddenly standing back at the onyx monoliths that were the gates of Annwn.

"Arawan? Are you here?" she whispered. The hazy mist swirled around her legs as she walked towards the gates. In between them, she once again saw the lands of Annwn, and it didn't look half bad. It certainly was a way to get out of any more family gatherings.

"What the fuck are you doing here again?" a voice hissed in the shadows. Arawan appeared before her, blocking her path. His black eyes were like coals of pure fury. Damn, he was so pissed.

"It was an emergency. I needed to talk to you, and this was the only way," Imogen said, straightening her shoulders and glaring right back at him.

Arawan's hands gripped her wrists. "So you cut yourself? Are you insane? Do you want to die so badly?"

"No. But it's not like you have a phone or a summoning spell," Imogen shouted back. "Hafgan is back. He's free from whatever was holding him in Tir Na Nog. I thought you would want to know and maybe want to do something about it."

Arawan's eyes narrowed into slits. "Like *what* exactly? If Hafgan is free, it's because you stupid humans found a way to set him loose."

Imogen tugged at her arms, but she couldn't free them from his grip. "Aneirin set him loose, not us. Hafgan has been locked up a long time, so watch your back because you know he's going to try and finish what he started and destroy you."

Arawan looked her over, his head tilting in curiosity. "You killed yourself to warn me?"

Imogen knew her shade couldn't blush, but it could still feel a full-body cringe. "No. I came to tell you so you would stop lurking here and do something about it."

Hot, heady power seeped into her arms where he gripped her. Imogen gasped in pain, but she held back the scream she knew he was waiting for.

Arawan laughed, and it was cold as an abyss. "Foolish, foolish human. This is the second time I've had to heal you. You know what that means?"

"I'm sure you're going to tell me." Imogen tugged her arms free, and he let them go. Instantly, she felt her body calling her back.

"It means you owe not one but two life debts. You will repay them at a time and place of my choosing. Now, give me your name, human, so I can find you again," Arawan demanded.

Imogen was fading fast and had another brilliantly bad idea. "I told you last time. It's Miss Go Fuck Yourself." She held up both of her middle fingers at his outraged face. "Thanks for healing me again, Daddy."

Arawan snarled and tried to snatch her back, but she was already slamming back into her body. She sat upright with a sudden gasp. She was covered in blood, but her wrists were completely healed.

"Well, shit," she muttered, and then she began to laugh because she had made her near-death experience tally reach number three.

Imogen had a feeling the next time, she wasn't going to be so lucky.

EPILOGUE

Across the Irish Sea, deep in northern Wales, a portal opened from a place none of the fae princes had ever trodden. Black and gray mist boiled out of the portal, and a tall, ancient god stepped through from the isle of Annwn and into the human realm.

Arawan breathed the cold night air, black eyes drinking in the sight of the stars above him. His long, black hair rustled in the cold breeze, and the sacred sigil on his forehead disappeared with his whispered command.

Two white hounds, the size of small ponies, stepped through the portal beside him, their red ears high and alert. Ready to hunt their prey.

Arawan had felt the moment that his old enemy had been released back into the world. Hafgan had always been the worst kind of monster, and there had to be a way to end the bastard once and for all before he tore the world apart.

Usually, the God of the dead didn't care about humans until they were crossing his black gates and into his realm as shades.

Times had changed.

Arawan might not have cared about the living as a whole, but one had caught his attention. He had delivered what remained of Morrigan to Annwn before he went to check that Hafgan hadn't been released with her demise. Satisfied Hafgan hadn't left Tir Na Nog, Arawan had gone back to his realms of shadows.

He thought he would forget about the human woman, her strangely colored hair covered in blood and eyes shining with battle fury. He had forgotten so many women over the eternity.

But not her. Her shining image had branded itself in his mind's eye.

She had been like some feral flower, with bright petals and hidden sharp thorns. The kind of dangerous flower that lured its prey in and delightfully killed it with her seductive poison.

One glance from her all those months ago had been enough to draw him from his dark realm and back into the human once again, all for a chance to touch her bright petals and die on her thorns.

He had been thinking about how to find her again, and then as if he had conjured her, she had shown up at his gates, dying. It had shocked him so much, he had healed her and sent her back to the lands of the living.

Now that very evening, she had appeared again to him in Annwn to say that Hafgan, his ancient enemy, was now free from the confines of Tir Na Nog.

Arawan had made up his mind then and there. He would find his dangerous flower again, and he would tear Hafgan apart so he would never get the chance to harm her. If anyone got in his way, they wouldn't live long enough to regret it.

As for the woman, she owed him two life debts and had pissed him off enough that he was going to be calling them in early.

"Your time is up, Miss Go Fuck Yourself," he whispered.

Smiling at the stars, Arawan clicked his tongue at the dogs and strode into the endless night, the portal closing behind him and leaving only dead grass to show it was ever there.

GOD TOUCHED

IRONWOOD SERIES BOOK 2

ALESSA THORN

PROLOGUE

Hir yw'r dydd a hir yw'r nos, a hir yw aros Arawan

"Long is the day and long is the night, and long is the waiting of Arawan"
-Traditional Cardigan Folk Saying-

Gods from above and gods from below, they walk amongst us. They were once more subtle about it. Since the fight with Morrigan, the fae returning and all the other monsters and magicians coming out, why was anyone surprised about the gods?

No one noticed when a castle of bone appeared overnight in the north of Wales. Most couldn't find it, and even if they did, they wouldn't have any memory of it.

Arawan, the god of Annwn, hadn't come to the human world to make friends.

He had come to hunt.

Aneirin had released Morrigan's feared generals before he met his end. From what the stories claimed, Hafgan and Vili were worse than the Battle Bard had ever been. Hafgan wasn't going to have a chance to try and hurt humans or take over Annwn.

Arawan wasn't going to allow his old enemy to live that long. When the god of the dead wanted something done, he had no problems getting his hands dirty and doing it himself.

And when he *really* wanted something...nothing would stop him from claiming it.

1

Imogen didn't like flying, small seats, or hoping they didn't crash because her cursed ass was on the plane. She hated it all, but she had endured it to escort David to Kian and the fae healers.

Charlotte and Reeve followed two days later, and Imogen had been relieved of her duty to watch over her father. She had tried to feel bad about it. The truth was two days hanging about had been enough to drive her crazy.

Imogen had been restless enough to pack up her ax, jump on a motorbike, and ride north. It was a miserable time of year to be on the back of the bike. Cold and wet and uncomfortable. Imogen loved it.

Anything was better than being bored. That was when all her thoughts would catch up to her, and she wasn't interested in anything that they had to say.

So she had cut her wrists to pay a call to Arawan, the god of the dead. She had no choice. The *world* had no choice but to trust him to destroy Hafgan because Imogen knew that there was fucking no one else strong enough to take him on.

Arawan had healed her, but the gray scars on her wrists were problematic. She needed an ally, and Charlotte had been it. She had berated her the whole time she had helped Imogen clean up the blood and then marched her over to Reeve's place.

Now, her scars were invisible under a cute skull and flowers tattoo on one arm and a dagger on the other. Written on the dagger blade were the words 'Say No' that were meant to remind her to say no to any more bad decisions. Time would tell if the warning would work.

Imogen was impulsive enough that her turning up with two new tattoos surprised precisely no one.

Only Reeve and Charlotte knew what had happened that night, and Imogen intended to keep it that way.

Aren't you forgetting someone?

Imogen turned the music up louder in her helmet and rode faster. It was exhilarating and an insanely bad idea. She didn't care. It was not like she hadn't already escaped three near-death experiences as it was.

The fourth time might stick, bitch, and then where will you be? Certainly not in Annwn.

She had been eleven years old the first time she had drowned and died. Imogen had cheated the Grim Reaper every day of the eighteen years that had followed. She expected to die every single day. As a result, she loved no one that wasn't her family.

She knew *everyone,* that didn't mean she let them get close. Lovers, friends, fuck buddies, everyone only got so far because they weren't worth the pain. Sooner or later, she would die, and it would finally stick.

Her fascination with death was also problematic, so she never told anyone about that either. Except for Bayn and Freya that one time they got shit-faced together after Killian's mating party, but that hardly counted. They were family, so they were bound to find out anyway.

God, aren't you morbid? Maybe it's Wales, she mused, staring at the bleak stormy afternoon.

Imogen had left Cardiff early that day and followed the coast north. She had told everyone that she was going to visit Bayn and Freya and wanted to see the countryside on her way up there. She had never been to Wales and wanted to stretch her metaphorical legs.

It was only half the truth because Imogen hated to make people worry. Maybe Charlotte suspected she was up to something, but she was wise enough not to mention it.

Imogen had walked into a nest of Kraken hybrids four weeks ago. Even with the Greatdrakes insisting the creatures had probably died when Aneirin did, Imogen didn't trust it. It was that *probably* that bothered the hell out of her.

She knew from Kian's reports that some of Morrigan's horde creatures had crossed through portals the night that she had attacked Dublin. There was no way of telling how far they had gone through the United Kingdom.

Imogen fuelled up in Dolgellau, stretched her back for a bit, and then kept following the coast. She wasn't actively hunting or even *looking* for something to fight. She was only on a nice ride…in the middle of winter…in Wales.

If Imogen saw signs of a crazy horde Kraken, she would do her hunter duty and kill every one of them. If the naturists at Morfa Dyffryn were brave enough to sunbake nude in freaking Wales, they deserved a medal and not to have to deal with stray krakens.

The middle of winter ensured there were no naked bodies about, but still, it was the thought that counted.

Naked bodies had Imogen thinking of the extremely hot guy she had ghosted since dealing with Aneirin. What had been his name again? Mr. Tongue Piercing. Sexy, sexy, goth boy.

She had looked at his number a few times before leaving Ireland, but every time her eyes had strayed to the tattoos that covered her scars.

Say No.

The strange ache in her scars agreed that hot goth boys were the source of all of her problems.

Hot goth gods were even worse.

Imogen hadn't said *no* to Arawan exactly. She had expressed her feelings by lifting both of her middle fingers at him. That meant no in every language.

So what if she had pissed off a powerful being? Hell, it wasn't the first time, and she really doubted it would be the last. All three of her brothers were powerful fae princes, and she loved to annoy them as much as possible.

But you don't owe them two life debts.

Imogen was doing her best to forget all about that.

It wasn't like Arawan knew who she was, and he was probably

kicking back in a fancy palace in Annwn with ten wives to keep him occupied. Guy like him would have *at least* ten.

That thought didn't bother her. Absolutely not one bit. Not. One. Bit.

Fucking Arawan.

The sun was fading fast, and Imogen switched on her headlights and slowed down. It wasn't like she had anywhere to be. She pulled over on the side of the road and checked her phone. Harlech wasn't too far away, and it had a fabulous-looking castle. She could stop there for the night, go out for some pints, and flirt with the locals.

Check the beach, it's why you came. Remember?

Imogen took off her helmet and took a small ax from one of the leather saddlebags. Charlotte had put a nifty charm on it, making it a portable, tomahawk size. If Imogen activated the magic, it would grow into her trusty battle-ax.

Her sister mating Reeve had come with all sorts of excellent perks, thanks to the Greatdrakes library. The ax charm was one, and the one to keep her hair growing out lavender was another. It sure saved on hairdressers.

Imogen tucked the small ax into the back of her leather pants and walked down the wet wooden walkways to the beach. The dunes were empty; the misting rain and disappearing sun had driven everyone inside.

Imogen closed her eyes and let the cold rain fall on her face. She breathed deeply, and a tightness in her chest eased for the first time in weeks.

Of course, the one moment of peace she had was going to be interrupted.

The hair on the back of Imogen's neck rose, and her hand drifted to the ax under her jacket. She turned with a smile, hoping it was another person out for a stroll. No such luck.

The sand dune started to shudder and heave. Imogen dived out of the way as a tentacle shot out and swiped at her.

"Yeah, you're not going to get me pregnant this time, you bastard!" Imogen shouted.

She pulled out her ax and activated the charm. The creature shook off the sand just as her ax slid to its entire length.

The Kraken hybrid was the size of a small van, with octopus tentacles and a hard shell covering its main body.

Imogen knew from experience that each of its suckers had a barbed hook for tearing into flesh and egg pouches underneath them for impregnating their victims. That was how she had died the second time.

Imogen gripped her ax with both hands and laughed. "I knew you fuckers weren't all gone."

They both charged simultaneously, Imogen ducking and weaving, her ax dancing in the dusk light as it cut through two of the tentacles before they could grab her.

She might have been expecting to die every day, but she had no intention of seeing Arawan for the third time in a month. That humiliating thought made her work on the offensive.

The creature roared, its hard black beak appearing. Imogen swiped, hitting it with her ax. The blade glanced off it like the beak was made of stone. Imogen changed tactics and went for the tentacles. If it couldn't run away from her, she could figure out how to penetrate the hard shell and kill it.

Imogen lost herself in the fight, dodging the tentacles that tore through the sand around her. She cut off another three before the creature sounded a different kind of cry.

The sand underneath her shuddered, and Imogen's stomach turned watery. The sea bubbled offshore, and she knew she was about to be outnumbered.

Get out, call for backup.

There was only one small problem. The wounded horde creature was between her and her bike.

Imogen swore and then laughed and adjusted the grip on the ax. "What's death anyway? Fourth time's a charm."

Two more creatures rolled out of the depths and screeched their fury at her. Imogen yelled back and charged the wounded creature.

If she could get through it, she might get to her bike before the other two pulled themselves free. Imogen cut away another tentacle and aimed for what she thought was its head. Her ax bit deep into the fleshy underside of its shell. She pulled free just as she was hit from behind and sent rolling across the sand.

She landed hard on her side, the wet sand hurting like hell. She had managed to keep hold of her ax, and with a winded wheeze, she dragged herself up.

The other two creatures were up on the bank now, their large black eyes blinking at her, beaks clicking in irritation.

This was precisely the reason that they had rules about hunting alone. She hadn't even been hunting! Not really. Trouble just always found her.

"For fuck's sake," she muttered, lifting her ax once more.

Something silver flashed in the dying light, and a sword was suddenly protruding from the black shell of the wounded creature. It shuddered all over before collapsing into the sand.

"How the fuck..."

The sword whipped out like an unseen hand had grabbed the hilt and tore it free.

Imogen didn't have time to question it. Another creature was hurtling towards her. She hacked at the tentacles trying to take off her head. Something gripped her foot, and she went down, her skull smacking against the wet sand and causing black dots to darken her vision.

The tentacle held her firm, dragging her down the beach, kicking and screaming. The black beak appeared, and she knew she was about to be food.

Worst death so far, she thought morbidly. Then her survival instincts pushed adrenaline through her, and she shouted in fury, kicking out with all her might at the creature with her steel toe boots.

Black and silver whipped past her, and Imogen suddenly fell back on the sand. The creature tried to shoot back into the water as it fought the black smoke and shadows that surrounded it. Imogen's ears popped as some kind of magic went off in a silent detonation. The horde creature shriveled up, disintegrated into chunks of ash, and exploded all over the beach.

Imogen groaned, the cloudy sky spinning above her. Her head pounded, and her body felt weirdly light. She wondered if she had another concussion.

A pale face framed by long raven hair appeared above her, and the tip of a silver sword rested against her neck.

"Great, dead again," she muttered.

"Not quite," a deep, husky purr of a voice replied.

Oh, fuck it all to Hell.

The face came into focus, and Imogen suddenly wished she had been eaten by the Kraken. Big black eyes, sharp nose, lips that were way too sensual.

"Hello, darling," said Arawan, the god of the dead. His lips curled into a brilliant smile. "Or is it Miss Go Fuck Yourself?"

2

Arawan had never believed in fate or destiny. Looking down at the lavender-haired woman at his feet made him think he might have been wrong.

Arawan had been in Wales for weeks. He'd been slowly ridding the country of any of Morrigan's infernal creatures that he could find. The whole time, he'd had his spies searching for *her*. The woman who didn't seem to understand that dying twice in a week wasn't a good idea. Pissing him off was an even worse one. And yet...

Kill her. He knew he should end her once and for all. Let her shade fuck off and bother some other death deity. His hand gripped the onyx hilt of his sword tighter.

No. If she was going to an underworld, it was going to be his and no one else's.

"So, um, are you going to kill me or let me up because I'm sandy and wet and in no mood—" she began.

Arawan leaned down and pressed two fingers to her rain-soaked forehead. "Sleep."

"Don't you..."

Her eyes rolled into the back of her head, and she was out. Arawan didn't know what to do with her, but he sure as fuck wouldn't let her go until he did.

Letting out a low whistle, a giant white hound the size of a pony bounded between the hills and down to greet him. Arawan sheathed his sword, picked the woman up, and placed her over the dog's back. He picked up her double-bladed ax, reluctant to leave any trace of her behind. He would send someone for her motorcycle.

Summoning a portal, Arawan and his hound stepped through and onto the grounds of his newest residence. It was hidden deep in the Snowdonia National Park, far enough to keep humans away from him.

The castle was made of onyx and bone, big enough to keep his court and some of his warriors. His power protected the grounds, and none of his lackeys could cross the boundary without him knowing.

The shades that served him couldn't even do that. His power there was absolute, the estate acting like a small extension of Annwn itself.

Arawan didn't want to have his bothersome court with him, but they had insisted on being able to visit. He had been asleep for centuries, and they were all nervous about his sudden return.

Good. They had been complacent for far too long.

He had been slowly getting them back under control. As much as he hated it, he needed them to keep his realm going while he had been hunting horde creatures and *her.*

No one was brave enough to comment on his sudden appearance or the human he was taking down to the dungeon. He gave swift instructions to two warriors to collect her gear from the beach and ensure no other creatures were lingering about.

Careful not to jostle her too much, Arawan lifted the hunter from the back of his hound and onto an oversized wooden chair. He clasped the manacles around her wrists but left her feet clear. He didn't want to hurt her; he just needed to ensure she didn't run away again. He needed answers about Aneirin, Vili, and Hafgan. About this strange new world he had returned to. About her. Especially about her.

Arawan wiped the rain from his face and swore. His spies hadn't been able to find any trace of her at all. He hadn't even planned on hunting that day, and yet, he had a sudden burning need to see the ocean.

Arawan had stepped through a portal, and there she fucking was; lavender braid flying, ax lifted high, and screaming like a banshee at three monsters.

This fucking woman. She was a mystery that he didn't have time to solve.

Arawan brushed the strangely colored hair back from her face. Frowning at the blood in her strands, he sent his power through her. It healed the cracks in her ribs and a minor head wound.

What had she been doing on that beach, fighting all alone? He had known from the night he had collected Morrigan that the woman was a warrior. He just knew nothing else.

Arawan touched her forehead. "Wake up, human."

The woman came to with a jerk, her arms and legs trying to hit out at him and discovering she was locked down.

"What the *fuck*?" she demanded angrily. Arawan hadn't heard anyone use such a furious tone on him...ever. "Where am I?"

"You are safe at my castle," he replied, studying every pinch of her eyebrows and snarl on her full lips. She pulled on her chains once to test them before leaning back into the chair and crossing her legs. Her expression went as haughty as a queen's, and Arawan couldn't help but like the shift in attitude.

"So you've taken me as a prisoner to your forbidding castle and shackled me to a chair. Is this the part where you tell me, *'Surrender to me, Imogen Ironwood,'*" she said in a deep growly voice. She battered her eyelashes at him and added breathily, "And then you'll make all my sexual fantasies come true?"

Arawan raised a dark, confused brow. "Bold little thing, aren't you? I do hate to disappoint, but right now, I only need information from you."

He reached over and lifted her chin. Her eyes filled with some kind of brazen defiance he didn't understand but liked immensely. She was full of fire and venom, and he wanted to taste it.

"And if I was going to make all your sexual fantasies come true, darling, I wouldn't need your surrender...only your consent."

Her cheeks didn't flush like he expected, and she didn't look away. Her lip curled into a sneer that begged him to try.

So fucking bold. She wasn't afraid or impressed by him. He would need to change that.

"It would be in your best interest to let me go before my brothers find out," she said calmly.

"Is that so? And who are your brothers that I should be afraid of them, Imogen Ironwood?" he demanded, crossing his arms. He liked her name. It felt good on his tongue and suited the prickly, dangerous flower in front of him.

"They are the three most powerful living fae princes, and if I don't check in with them soon, they are going to worry about me."

Arawan's frown deepened. His spies had said that the fae and humans were on good terms again, the former being governed by the Blood Prince. Now, *there* was a male who had sent legions of souls to Arawan in his time.

He studied her ears. "You are not fae."

Imogen rolled her pretty gray eyes. "Excellent deduction, Sherlock. They married into the family, but they take their new roles seriously. They aren't going to like that you've taken me prisoner without any reason."

"I saved your life on that beach. I took you because I needed to talk to you."

"And you couldn't just do it without kidnapping me? What the hell is wrong with you, immortals?" Imogen pulled at the manacles again. "What do you want to know? I need to get out of here. Wherever here is."

Arawan didn't like that idea. He wanted to keep her close and figure out what it was about her that bothered him so much.

"Do you know where Hafgan is?" he asked.

Imogen shook her head. "No. We only know that he and Vili have escaped Tir Na Nog. We aren't even sure if they have crossed over yet. Aneirin is dead. My sister killed him."

"Good."

"Is that it? You're going to let me go now?"

Arawan undid one manacle but left the other untouched. She glared up at him, and he realized he liked to tease her. "Why do you keep dying?"

"I live dangerously. Why do you keep healing me?" she threw back at him.

Arawan would have liked to know the answer to that himself. "It's not your time to die."

Imogen laughed, a big, loud sound that had never been heard in his dungeons before. "Oh, honey, it was my time to die eighteen years ago. I've been waiting for it to stick ever since."

3

Imogen had wet sand in all the places wet sand shouldn't be. She was tied to a chair, which should only happen in sexy scenarios, and wondered if today was the day she would die. The god of the dead in front of her made her think it was a good possibility. Damn, he was something, though.

Unlike the past few times she had seen him in Annwn, Arawan wore a mortal guise that didn't do much to hide the supernatural creature within. His epic bone crown was nowhere to be seen either. He was still kick-in-the-ovaries hot, and it messed with her brain and lowered her self-preservation instincts.

"Stop staring at me and let me go. I told you I don't know where Hafgan is," she argued.

His black eyes bored into her like she was a strange thing he couldn't figure out. She supposed she should be flattered, considering the mess she was in from the fight.

"Why were you fighting on the beach alone?" he asked, his voice like deep gravel. It made her back straighten and nerve endings spark.

"I didn't plan it. I was on my way to visit Bayn, the Winter Prince, and I stopped to see the sights. The creatures attacked me, and I was lucky I had my ax... Oh, fuck, my ax! Where is it?"

Arwan smiled. "I have it, don't fret."

"Good. It's a family heirloom, and I'd be showing up in Annwn for a third time if I lost it because my mother would kill me." Imogen leaned back in the chair. God, if Kenna found out where she was right now, she would probably kill her anyway.

"Look, your godliness, if you want more information, ask Kian. He will tell you everything you want to know. He'd probably be thrilled to know that you have set up here in Wales. Hell, if you let me go, I'll call him and let him know," Imogen said quickly. She didn't want to panic, but keeping her locked up was never a good idea. She hated small spaces and too much time to think.

Arawan's eyes narrowed, but he smiled, and his warm fingers unlocked the other manacle. Imogen rubbed at her wrists, but he stood too close for her to get up.

You know what? Fuck him.

She stood up anyway, her chest bumping against his, and his eyes widened. Yeah, she had never been intimidated by a man before and wouldn't start now. She shoved at him, making him step out of her way. Not before she smelled his scent of cedar and dragon's blood. Funeral smells. Under that was male. Pure, hot, horny... Imogen took another step back from him.

"I didn't say you could leave," Arawan commented.

Imogen snorted. "Why keep me here? I don't know what else to tell you."

Arawan's face shifted from confusion to something calculating. He held out a hand to the door. "You're right. Let me show you the way out."

"Thanks. And...and thanks for saving me," she said uncomfortably.

"Which time?"

She shrugged. "All of them, I guess? The beach in particular. I don't know how you turned up there, but I'm grateful."

"You're welcome, Imogen."

"You're not going to tell me why you keep helping me, though, right?"

"Correct. Mind your step."

Arawan led her through a door and up a flight of stairs. They reached a hallway with at least four different doors, and she fought the urge to ask what was behind them. Probably things that would give her nightmares for the rest of forever. The door Arawan opened led outside.

The night was black and stormy, but she wouldn't stay a second longer. Her motorbike was waiting on a stretch of grass, her battle ax resting beside it. She made an involuntary happy sound and lifted it. No damage, thank goodness. She activated the shrinking charm and tucked it into her saddlebags.

"I don't suppose you are going to tell me where I am right now?" Imogen asked Arawan. She found her phone in one of the bags. No reception, big surprise.

"As soon as you cross my borders, you will be able to find out," Arawan said and gave her a charming smile. "You could always stay the night as my guest."

She could? Imogen's mind went fuzzy, staring at him all goth and sexy in the shadows, and she began to wonder if maybe... She looked at her tattoo. *Say No.* For once, she took the advice and shook her head.

"Thanks for the offer," she replied quickly, not wanting to offend him. "I got places to be. Good luck finding Hafgan."

"Stay alive longer than a week, Imogen Ironwood."

"Ha! I'll try."

Imogen waved awkwardly, pulled on her helmet, and started up her bike. She didn't turn around for a last look and didn't have to. She felt his dark eyes burning a hole in the back of her head all the way down the road leading away from the castle.

Imogen's skin tingled, and she knew she had crossed through his wards. Her phone instantly started buzzing, and she pulled her bike over. She found ten messages waiting for her from various family members, two dick pics from guys she had ghosted in the last six months, and five unread emails.

Ignoring them all, Imogen clicked on her Maps app, figured out where she was in Snowdonia National Park, and set the directions to Bayn's castle in Scotland. She wasn't going to stay in fucking Wales a single second longer.

She wasn't worried about falling asleep either. It was only seven p.m., and her blood was buzzing from her monkey brain telling her to get the fuck away from Arawan as fast as possible. Her less reliable woman brain was still wondering how a dead guy looked so fucking hot.

No. No hot goth gods for you. Some ideas were so bad that even Imogen knew better than to go through with them.

∼

Seven hours later, Imogen passed through the town of Braemar and headed into the lands that Bayn had claimed as his own. They were technically a part of the Cairngorms National Park, and while he had allowed the humans access to parts of it, he had areas that he refused to part with.

Imogen was frozen, hungry, and still sandy by the time she pulled up at the front of the ice castle. Fae guards nodded politely to her, recognizing her on sight. She slung her saddlebags over one shoulder and almost swayed on her feet.

"Allow me to take these up to your room," a polite warrior suggested and took them from her.

"Thanks. I don't suppose I could go to the kitchen for some food. I've been riding all day," Imogen said, following them inside.

"Of course you can. I can rouse Prince Bayn for you..."

"No. Don't wake them. I'm going to go to bed. I just need something to munch on." Imogen waved him off and wandered towards the kitchens.

She had been to the castle a few times since Killian had mated Bron. She liked Bayn and Freya, and sometimes it was nice to get away from Ireland and the Ironwoods.

After she had mated Bayn, Freya had made sure that the kitchen in the castle was functional. They didn't have as many staff members as Kian, and Freya liked to cook when the mood took her. That required a modern kitchen she could work in.

Imogen pulled open the fridge door and grabbed a beer. "Thank the gods." She opened it and downed half in one long swig.

"Rough day, *lillesøster*?" a woman asked, making Imogen choke on her beer. "Sorry, I didn't mean to startle you."

"What the fuck are you doing awake, Freya?" Imogen replied. Freya looked like a tousled Viking goddess with her tattooed arms and messy blonde hair.

"I heard the bike and wondered what had happened. I need something with bacon. Are you hungry? I'm thinking French Toast?" Freya said, moving Imogen away and reaching into the fridge.

"I'm starving, and I'd love you forever if you made me French Toast. I'd hug you right now, but I'm covered in crud." Imogen slumped onto a bar stool. "It has been a fucking day."

"You look like hell. What happened? I didn't expect you for days."

Imogen drained her beer, and Freya passed her another. "Promise you won't get mad?"

Freya's one blue eye, and the other brown twinkled with magic and mischief. "Me? Why would I get mad at you?"

"Well, I kind of fucked up."

"I can't wait to fucking hear this," a deep voice said, and the kitchen door opened. Bayn was suddenly there, dressed in loose gunmetal pajama pants and his tattooed torso on full display.

It was a sight that always made Imogen feel better about life. She had a type, which was black-haired, tattooed, and pierced. She wouldn't apologize for it either.

"Why do you smell so bad?" Bayn asked, screwing up his sensitive nose. He paused and sniffed again. "Why do you smell like dragon's blood, and... What is that—cedar? And..."

"It's death, okay? I smell like death!" Imogen exploded. The day's stress was suddenly overwhelming her, and she reached for her drink. There was going to be no way to hide it from them. Damn Bayn's nose. Freya glared at Bayn, and he grabbed himself a beer.

"Okay, Imogen. Start talking, or I'm calling Kenna," Bayn said, sitting beside her.

Imogen's scowl had no effect on him. He only waited, watching as Freya started to mix batter.

Imogen sighed, knowing that Bayn and Freya would be easier on her than her mother. "I want to start by saying none of this was my fault."

4

It took Imogen an hour and four French toast pieces with bacon to get through her entire day. Bayn and Freya were frowning at her, and Imogen did her best not to hunch her shoulders.

"You know this sounds fucking crazy," Bayn said, leaning back in his chair. "Why would Arawan be back and hanging out in the human world? He never did that."

"Maybe he figured out Hafgan had been released?" Imogen said, shifting uncomfortably. She wasn't about to tell them about the recent near-death experiences. Especially killing herself to get Arawan a message.

"Maybe. Time will tell if it's a good thing."

Freya gnawed on her bottom lip. "Why did he take you only for information and immediately let you go again? Why not ask at the beach?"

"Right? That's what I wanted to know. It was weird. He's a great big weirdo."

Bayn's dark brow raised. "Anything you not saying?"

"Nothing important? Look, I don't know what he wants. He's here, though, and that might be a good thing. He's a badass and is invested in finding Hafgan. This fight might not be ours after all," Imogen argued. She yawned, her jaw cracking.

"I need to talk to my brothers about this. Especially Kian. He was worried that Arawan had talked to you the night of Morrigan's attack, and he'll want to know," Bayn said, running a hand through his hair.

"Cool. Let me know how that goes in, oh, eight to ten hours." Imogen got up and kissed the air at both of them. "Thanks for the food, guys. I'm crashing, and I still need to soak my bruised ass."

Bayn looked about to stop her, but Freya put her arms around his shoulders, silencing him. "Get some sleep, Gen. We can talk tomorrow," she said.

"Yeah, no doubt," Imogen replied and went to find where her gear had been placed.

Bayn's castle was made of ice, but it was still warm inside, and Imogen was drowsy by the time she found her guest room. She dragged off her sandy clothes and trudged into the bathroom.

She was so tired, and her ass ached from being on the back of the bike for so long. What wasn't hurting was all the bruises she should have had from the fight on the beach.

Weird. She checked her back in the mirror, and there wasn't even a scrape from when she hit the beach. There was blood in her hair, but she couldn't find a cut.

"Son of a bitch," she muttered. Arawan must have healed her when she had been knocked out. What was his problem?

Imogen took a long shower, stretched her cramped muscles out as best as possible, and climbed into bed naked. She hated pajamas when she slept, and unlike her nosey sisters, Bayn and Freya would never barge in without knocking.

Staring up at the dark blue ceiling in her room, Imogen wondered what Arawan was up to. Was he bored in that castle? Would he hate how the human world had changed? Why had he let her go again... and why had he offered to let her stay?

"Maybe he's lonely," she said aloud. She understood loneliness.

Imogen was a professional at looking like she was the life of the party when in reality, she was just alone around people.

She couldn't tell anyone how much she still thought about the day she died and how good it felt once she stopped struggling against the current.

How she had been chasing that high ever since. How could she say that to anyone and not have them think she was totally mental?

Arawan might get it.

Imogen pulled a pillow over her head. It would be better for her mental health if she stayed far away from the God of the dead. He was in Wales, and if she was very careful, she would never have to hear his raspy voice ever again.

～

IMOGEN WOKE to banging on her door. She sat up, adrenaline coursing through her.

"Gen! Get some clothes on quickly! I need you," Freya said through the door.

"Yeah. Yup. I'm awake," she called back.

Imogen dressed in some clean jeans and an off-the-shoulder Nine Inch Nails shirt. Did she need shoes? Probably not. She washed her face, gargled some mouth wash, and ran her hands through her curly lavender hair. Whatever Freya needed couldn't have been an attack or anything, or she would've told her to bring her ax.

Not like anyone would be dumb enough to attack Bayn in the middle of winter.

God, it better be worth her getting out of bed.

Imogen hurried down the stairs, still yawning. "Bitch, you better have coffee going!" she called.

She reached the main entranceway of the castle and almost fell down the rest of the stairs. Arawan and a group of his warriors stared up at her.

He was dressed impeccably in a black-on-black suit with a few too many buttons undone and had a hand resting on the top of a black cane.

Big black eyes looked from her bare feet up to her mussed hair. "Good morning, darling."

"Nope, not today, Satan." Imogen turned around and almost collided with Freya.

"You are not going anywhere," she hissed, blocking her path. "Bayn needs to go and get Kian and Killian, and you *will* keep him distracted until Bayn is back."

"For fuck's sake," Imogen growled. She walked further down the steps and gave Arawan her fakest smile ever. "And to what do we owe the honor of this visit, your godliness? You missed me so bad already, huh?"

Arawan's lips twitched. "Not exactly, mortal. I thought about what you said, and I have come to talk to the princes as you suggested."

"That's me. Full of good ideas," Imogen replied.

"Indeed. I would've liked to get a few more out of you, but you not only left my castle, but the *entire* country." Arawan sounded a bit pissy about that fact, and Imogen's caffeine-deprived brain hadn't kicked in her self-preservation. Fuck him.

"Well, I saw all I needed to in Wales and was unimpressed. There wasn't any point in hanging about." Imogen stayed a few steps up just so she could look down her nose at him.

"I would've liked to speak with you again before you left."

Imogen shrugged. Arawan's eyes went to her chest. "Something caught your attention?"

"I like your shirt," he replied.

Imogen looked down at the 'I want to fuck you like an animal' emblazoned across her chest. *Fuck.*

"Yeah, NIN is awesome. It might not be your speed. You old guys like lutes and shit, right?"

Freya cleared her throat. "If you would like to come through to the dining room, my lord, I can have some refreshments brought. Would your warriors—"

"They will be fine, Princess Freya. I would love some of the coffee Imogen spoke of," Arawan replied with a polite smile. He held out a hand to Imogen to help her down the rest of the stairs.

"It's okay. I'm not an invalid," she said, breezing past him. "I'll see if the cook has that coffee going."

Imogen waited until the kitchen door had closed behind her before she bit her fist to smother her scream. What the fuck was he *doing* there?

"Can I help you, Miss Ironwood?" a female fae asked from her place in front of the stove.

"Nope. Don't mind me. Just need to..." Imogen opened a cabinet where Bayn kept his booze and downed a mouthful of vodka. "We will need some coffee and shit in the dining room. Coffee first. Anything else can wait."

The fae frowned. "And will miss be taking the vodka with her?"

Imogen let out a strangled laugh, held a finger up as she had another mouthful, and gave the bottle to the servant.

"Okay. Okay. I'm good."

Imogen stepped back into the entranceway when Bayn, Killian, and Kian walked in.

"Oh, thank fuck you're here," Imogen said to Killian and collided with him.

"Woah, you okay, Gen?" he asked, rubbing her back. "Did something happen?"

"Nope. Everything is as fine as it can be when you wake up to the fucking god of the dead before coffee," she mumbled in his chest.

Killian made a tsking sound. "It's all going to be fine, sister. Kian will talk to him and bore him so much he goes away."

"Fuck you. We need to be diplomatic. He's a god. One of *our* gods. The only one I've ever paid respect to," Kian grumbled, straightening the cuffs of his suit. He looked very professional and princely. Even his antlers shone.

"You guys seem to have it under control. I'll just..." Imogen went to step away, but Killian hung onto her and wrapped her hand around his arm.

"Oh no, you're not going anywhere. Arawan is here because of you. Bayn told us all about your encounter yesterday. If I have to suffer through this meeting, you do too," he said.

"I don't even have shoes on," Imogen complained.

Bayn grinned. "I'll keep the floors warm for you."

Imogen huffed, but Killian only pulled her into the dining room. Arawan sat at the end of the table, his cane resting beside him. Fuck, he was intimidating...and way too handsome. Like sickeningly, infuriatingly beautiful.

"Find yourself a seat, Gen," Killian said, letting her go.

Where no one but Imogen could see, Arawan tapped his silver

ringed hand on his knee like he was beckoning her to come and sit on his lap.

Heat flushed up Imogen's back. He did *not* just do that. Surely she misread that...

Arawan's smile widened, and that was when Imogen realized that she wasn't the only one in a mood that morning. He was annoyed she had left Wales, and he was going to fuck with her as much as possible.

That's just great.

Very subtly, she dropped her hand to her thigh and folded her fingers in so she was flipping him off. And then she took a seat as far away from him as possible.

"It is an honor to meet you, Lord of Annwn," Kian said and bowed low.

Arawan's eyes fixed on Imogen. "It's a pleasure to finally make your acquaintance."

5

Imogen hated meetings. Before coffee and food, the world was a place that wasn't worth living in. Thankfully, the servant came in with pots of coffee and placed one in front of Imogen, along with a plate of pastries.

She pulled the plate out of Killian's reach. He could get fucked for forcing her to sit in on the meeting. It was not like she needed to be there. Especially looking like a half-asleep banshee while they all looked so neat and put together.

She was never her most mature before breakfast but didn't have the will to stop herself.

"...is that right, Imogen?" Kian asked.

"Hmm? What?" she replied, swallowing down her mouthful of sugary danish.

"The horde Kraken was the same you spotted in Ireland?"

Imogen nodded. "They looked the same. We thought Aneirin had made them, but if they are still kicking about, maybe they were Morrigan's to begin with."

"My warriors have ensured that any remains were dealt with, and they found no others," Arawan said. "It would be nothing for a creature that big to cross the Irish Sea. Might I suggest some patrols on the beaches, Prince Kian? I'm not sure if the humans would be able to fight them off. Even ones as talented with an ax as Imogen."

Imogen smiled, her cheeks bulging with pastry. Freya looked like she wanted to slide under the table and hide. Bayn and Killian were trying not to laugh.

"I have contacts in the human military. They can assist with the patrols. Hopefully, they were the only ones that made the journey," Kian said, trying to keep the meeting on track. "Imogen has said that you are here looking for Hafgan. Have you had any luck discovering his whereabouts?"

Arawan blew on his coffee, and Imogen quickly looked away. She didn't need to be subjected to that. It was too early.

Get through this meeting, and he'll go away.

"Hafgan has always been a sly bastard. I don't believe he will show his hand until he's ready to make his final moves. He will use spies and allies to try and infiltrate my court and sow as much discord as possible," Arawan said finally. "I haven't heard any whispers of his location, but it's only a matter of time before my own spies flush him out. Without Morrigan's protection, he will want to consolidate as much power as he can."

"And where is Morrigan? Should we be worried about her coming back and trying to get revenge on my sister because you saved her?" Imogen demanded.

Arawan let a sinister chuckle. "You think I *saved* Morrigan?"

"Of course we do! She called to you, and you came to save her because of a debt," Imogen argued.

"Is that so? And you didn't stop for a moment to consider the truth?"

"And what truth is that?"

"That she's currently dying slowly, locked away in the darkest part of Annwn." Arawan rested his chin on a hand. "Because that is where she is. The deal I had with her was to save her, yes, and I did that. She didn't say anything about what I was meant to do with her afterward."

A chill swept over Imogen, and she looked away, unable to hold eye contact with him. She always acted defensively when someone pushed her, but it was so dangerous to forget who she was dealing with.

Killian cleared his throat. "Is that your way of saying that we will never be bothered by Morrigan again? Because we still have that sword, and I have a mate keen to finish what she started."

Arawan poured himself some more coffee. "Believe me, prince, there's no escaping where I put her."

"We thought that about the generals too, and yet, here we are," Bayn grumbled.

"I'm not some lazy witch like Morrigan," Arawan snapped, making every shadow in the room darken. "There is no way for her to escape. She barely has the strength to move, and it is only a matter of time before her essence is permanently gone. I suggest you keep that sword close anyway. It is quite the weapon."

"Hmm, might borrow it sometime," Imogen said under her breath and quickly put more pastry in her mouth. Arawan only laughed, which pissed her off even more.

"We aren't enemies, darling. We are hunting the same prey. Hafgan will strike. It is only a matter of time. When it happens, you might like having me as an ally," he said smoothly.

"And you want an alliance?" Kian asked.

"I wouldn't be here otherwise. It might have been thousands of years since I dwelt amongst the living, but that doesn't mean I'm willing to see Hafgan slaughter everyone."

"What can you tell us about him?" Bayn asked. "If he turns up, what is the best way to deal with him?"

"The best way is to call me and stay out of the way," Arawan replied. "Understand, princeling, you are all impressive and powerful, but you are nothing compared to Hafgan. He might be hidden from my view now, but it won't be for much longer, and you will need my aid."

"And we will be honored to have it, my lord," Kian said with a respectful bow of his head. "If there is anything you require that we can provide to help you in your hunt for Hafgan, you only need to ask."

"Imogen Ironwood," Arawan answered. Imogen's fists clenched around her knife.

"Excuse me?" Bayn said, the temperature in the room dropping a few degrees.

Arawan's face was the picture of civility. "You asked what I need, and I have answered. I require Imogen Ironwood. She can be a liaison between us, and she can assist me in navigating these interesting times I find myself in."

"I don't want to, and you can't make me," Imogen snapped.

Arawan's eyes flared in amusement, and he laughed softly. "Oh, I definitely can."

Kian paled. "My lord, I don't think—"

Arawan's cane cracked against the floor, silencing them. "There is also the small matter of the life debt she owes me. Isn't that right, Imogen?"

Two life debts, actually.

Everyone stared at her in horror, except for Arawan, who looked like a wolf in a room full of rabbits.

"It's true. Charlotte and Reeve can confirm it," she said between clenched teeth. She folded her hands on the table, trying to keep her temper in check. "And what exactly would acting as a liaison for you entail?"

"Come and stay with me. I need my liaisons close at hand to pass messages through to their people," Arawan replied. He smiled at the princes. "If you need the reassurance, I swear she will not come to any physical harm in my care."

Physical. What about psychological or spiritual? Arawan's gaze moved back to her as if reading her mind.

"You will be well tended to under my care and protection."

"Is that so?" Imogen crossed her arms. She was frightened and fascinated in equal measure. She might finally be able to get answers to the questions she had about why dying had felt so good and why she had been obsessed with the afterlife ever since.

Arawan was the personification of all of her unhealthy obsessions —death, sex, and violence. It was what frightened her the most.

"I will swear a blood oath if I need to." Arawan's grip tightened on the top of his cane.

"Yes, thank you, I'd like that, seeing how I will be the one that is going to be left alone with your court full of wolves," Imogen snapped. She held out a hand to Bayn. "Dagger, please, bro."

Bayn passed it over. They knew when they were outmaneuvered, and they *needed* Arawan. Imogen had known it weeks ago and had been willing to die to get a message to him about Hafgan. She wouldn't chicken out now.

Imogen moved over to where Arawan sat, a king on a throne. He widened his legs slightly as she approached. The slight suggestive move made her grip on the dagger tighten. She ran the blade's tip over her thumb before offering the knife to him.

"Swear it," she said, staring him right in the eye. "Swear if I become your liaison that you will protect me until my debt has been repaid."

Arawan cut his thumb until silver ichor welled. "I promise I'll protect you, Imogen Ironwood. I'll care for you like you belong to me."

"What—" she began, but Arawan was already pressing his thumb to hers. His eyes gleamed with triumph as he stared up at her. The bond curled around her hand and up her arm, the feel of his power swamping her. It had all the finality of death, burned like heat and ice, and then it was gone leaving her heart pounding and an ache between her thighs.

What the fuck was that? Imogen was shaking and didn't know how to stop.

"It is done," Arawan said softly. He lifted her still bloody thumb to his mouth and sucked hard before his power healed it. Imogen swallowed, staring at nothing and wondering what she had just done.

"Now, I should be getting back." Arawan stood gracefully and lifted her chin with the silver head of his cane. "I expect you to return to my castle by sundown tomorrow. *Don't* make me come and fetch you, darling."

Imogen pushed his cane away. "I'll be there."

They all stared as Arawan's warriors encircled him. He tilted his head as he stared at Imogen, and then he slowly lifted his hand and flipped her off.

Checkmate. Shadows surrounded them, and they were gone before she could toss Bayn's dagger at him.

Freya squawked angrily in Norwegian and threw a pastry at Imogen. "What the fuck did you do?"

"I owed him a debt." Imogen stared at the fresh gray scar on her thumb. "He saved my life."

Kian let out a sound between a growl and a groan. "The god of the dead doesn't save lives, Imogen!"

Imogen lifted her shirt to show the matching scar on her waist. "He saved mine."

Kian shook his head. "No, Gen, death gods *take* lives. And from where I am sitting, he just took yours."

6

Imogen left all of them arguing and went to call Layla. She knew that Charlotte would only yell at her, and she was over being yelled at for one day. She couldn't deal with Kenna either, and the last thing she wanted to do was stress David out.

"Big sis, what's wrong?" Layla answered.

Imogen sat down on the floor in her room and rested her back against the bed.

"I have kind of fucked up, and I need to tell you that I won't be home in a while," Imogen replied.

"Okay, what happened? You sound all weird. What do you mean fucked up? Stole a motorcycle fucked up? Slept with a married guy fucked up?"

Imogen blew out a tight breath. "I was minding my own business, checking out some Wales beaches, and I got attacked by horde creatures. Don't freak out. I'm fine. I had some help turn up unexpectedly."

"What kind of help, Gen?" Layla always knew when she was lying, so she was careful with how much bullshit she spun her. There was no escaping it this time.

"Arawan?"

"As in the God of the dead?"

"The very one."

"Huh, I wondered when he would turn up again."

Imogen frowned. "I'm sorry, what do you mean by that? Why would a god turn up?"

"Because of how he looked at you that night he took Morrigan. It was like...fascination. I kind of had this feeling he would be back, and after Aneirin released his rival, I thought it was just a matter of time," Layla explained. She was always the most pragmatic of them, and her being so calm about it made Imogen relax a little too. "He turned up in a fight to save you? That's kind of romantic."

Imogen rolled her eyes. "I was about to get eaten by a Kraken. It was very far from romantic."

"Have you met you? Killing the Kraken is probably one of your top ten date ideas."

"Shut up." A graphic image of Arawan and his silver sword flashed in her mind's eye. "Okay, it was pretty cool."

"Ha! As I thought. Tell me what happened next."

Imogen ended up telling Layla everything except her cutting her own wrists. Even laid-back Layla would probably kick her ass for that stupidity.

"Wow. You're going to be like a liaison? An ambassador? Damn, he really has no idea how undiplomatic you can be," Layla said and laughed loudly.

"Me and my ax can be extremely diplomatic."

"Exactly my point, Imogen. Some snooty courtier will piss you off, and you'll go at them. Do you have any dresses or anything with you?"

Imogen picked at her chipped black nail polish. "What the fuck would I need dresses for?"

"Because you'll probably be required to go to formal events? God, you really didn't think it through, did you?" Layla scolded.

"I didn't have a choice! Arawan just demanded it, and it had to happen. I owe him a life debt. If he's dumb enough to waste that on trying to get me to play some meek and mild court suck up, he's got another thing coming!"

"Woah, woah, calm down. I'm sure Freya can send you something if it's super important. You two are about the same size, so she can help in a pinch." Layla hummed thoughtfully. "You know, you're right?"

"About what?"

"Why does Arawan want you as a liaison? Like, you're clearly not fit for that kind of job."

"No shit. Who knows what he wants? I don't even think he knows."

"Want my opinion?"

"Sure, because I have no clue what he's thinking." Imogen really didn't. She was going to be a terrible courtier. What the hell was she even meant to do?

"I think that Arawan wants your company, and this was the easiest way to get it," Layla replied. Imogen laughed loudly.

"Come on! Why the fuck would a god want my company?"

"I didn't say it made sense, sis. You said he asked you to stay the night at the castle, yeah? I think he wants someone to talk to."

Imogen pinched the bridge of her nose. "He's got a whole castle of people to talk to."

"Not really. If he's worried about who is going to betray him to Hafgan, there's probably no one he trusts right now. You're an outsider that he obviously likes, and you owe him. Maybe you could help him find out who the spies are?"

"That is an idea. I mean, I'm not going to be sitting in boring fucking meetings all day. I need to be doing something useful." Imogen thought harder about it and then smiled. "You know what? You're the best. I'm going to find his spy for him, and then he will let me go."

"Wait, he hasn't agreed to that."

"I'll make him agree. Love you, Layla, and thanks for agreeing to tell Mom where I have gone. Okay, bye."

"I never said—" Layla began, but Imogen hung up on her too quickly for her to argue.

Imogen tapped her phone against her palm thoughtfully. If Hafgan had spies hanging around Arawan, she would hunt them down and rat them out. She was good at hunting, and she wasn't going to stay tied up in a bargain with Arawan longer than she needed to.

∼

BY THE TIME Imogen left the following day, she had been lectured so extensively by all three of her brothers and Freya that she was almost regretting not going with Arawan the day before.

"Remember, make no more bargains with Arawan or anyone else," Kian said and hugged her goodbye. "You can't trust anyone."

"Noted."

"Kill anyone that fucks with you," Bayn said and gave her one of his daggers. "This one has a charm on it, so if you get stripped of your weapons, this blade will get overlooked. I'm not about to let you go unarmed."

Imogen grinned at him. "And this is why you're my favorite."

Killian pulled her away. "Don't lie to them, Imogen. Everyone knows I'm your favorite. Now, remember to be your charming, delightful self. Courtiers love nothing more than a new toy, and they will tell you all sorts of things if you keep them talking. Learn everything you can, write none of it down, and use it against them if you need to. Don't use weapons when words will do."

"I'll try to be on my best behavior," she said, crossing her eyes at him.

Killian kissed her forehead. "Dork. Get out of here. Go get some dirt on the God of the dead. No fucking him unless it gets you out of the bargain."

"Don't tell her that, you dick," Freya grumbled. She pointed a finger at Imogen. "No fucking Arawan." She pulled her close and whispered, "Not unless it's consensual on both sides, and you tell me about it later."

Imogen laughed and squeezed her tight. "Will do."

"Be careful, Imogen. Check in with Bayn every day," Kian said.

"And if you need backup, I can be there instantly, I promise," Bayn replied.

Imogen picked up her helmet. "Okay, guys. Let me go. I'll be fine. Arawan promised, remember?"

"Make sure you watch yourself regardless. Fucking gods are so tricky," Bayn grumbled.

Imogen waved them goodbye as she drove away, hoping they wouldn't worry about her too much.

She was Imogen Ironwood, for fucks sake. She wasn't afraid of some stuffy courtiers or the God of the dead.

She grinned at the horizon; they were the ones that should be afraid of her.

7

Imogen wasn't sure how to get back to Arawan's castle, so she aimed for Snowdonia National Park. When she crossed the borders, she felt an indescribable mental tug. She slowed her bike down, wondering if she should call Charlotte to ask about magical influences.

Maybe leave her for a few days and check in when she might not rage at you for this insanity.

Arawan wouldn't have left Bayn's castle without her if he didn't trust Imogen could find her way back. The sensation tugged at her again, and her bike took the next left of its own accord.

That's just creepy.

Which was on point for Arawan. It was confusing to have him wrapped in such an irresistible package.

Maybe she should have stopped in Edinburgh and gotten a 'Don't fuck Arawan' tat on her arm as well.

Did the God of the dead even fuck? He was the first god she had met, so she could always ask. Maybe she would if she was in a scandalous enough mood.

Something told her that acting like a brat and purposely not doing her job wouldn't convince him to release her. If anything, he'd keep her longer just to annoy her.

The mists in front of Imogen cleared, and Arawan's castle came into view. She stopped at the border and tried to steady her heartbeat. She had only been there at night, so she hadn't seen it properly. It was made of bone and onyx, with four tall towers.

"Gothic as fuck," she whispered. It didn't look like it had been constructed in pieces either, but it had grown out of the ground like some demented creature.

From Elise's stories, Kian had grown a castle the same way. Unlike Kian's castle, Arawan's felt more than just otherworldly. It felt like it shouldn't be seen by human eyes.

The mental connection pulled harder at her, and she slowly rode through the wards and pulled up in front of guarded double doors. She had just taken off her helmet when the doors opened, and a very tall, gaunt fae stepped out. He had long dark hair and pale green eyes. It took a moment for Imogen to realize that he wasn't alive.

"Hi! I'm Imogen!" she said, far too brightly.

"I see," the fae replied in a calm voice. "My name is Duncan. I'm in charge of running the household. A room has been prepared for you. If you will follow me, I can show you the way."

"Cool, I'll just grab my stuff." Imogen unbuckled her saddlebags and slung them over her shoulders.

Duncan's brows drew together. "That is all you brought with you?"

"Yeah. I travel light. Why?"

"I must confess I've never seen a representative of another court pack so little."

Imogen winked at him. "I'm not like the others, Duncan."

"I can see that." He offered to take the bags from her, but she waved him off.

"I'm okay. Let's check out this room, shall we?" Imogen smiled wider at his confusion. Clearly, Arawan's decision to invite her had ruffled some courtly feathers. Good.

She didn't want anyone touching her shit either. She didn't want them to find how many weapons she had packed. Bayn's dagger was hidden under her shirt, tucked into the back of her jeans.

Duncan led her on silent feet up a winding staircase and into the northern wing of the castle. His frown deepened with every step he took.

"Something wrong, Duncan?" she asked, unable to stop herself from prodding.

"It is unusual for my lord to wish to have anyone in this part of the castle. He must be very concerned for your well-being," Duncan said, surprising her with his honesty. "But I suppose you are the only mortal here, and he wouldn't want to offend the Fae Court by having anything happen to you by accident or otherwise."

"Don't worry, I can take care of myself."

"I have been told. It would be neglectful of me not to warn you of the dangers. Some of the other residents can be petty and malicious by nature when they are here. My advice is to fulfill your duty quickly and then leave."

"That's the plan, but thanks for the heads up," Imogen replied.

Duncan opened a black and silver door and led her into a suite. She checked that the few windows could lock and that there was only one door in and out. The bed was a monstrosity of ebony wood and white linen. The bathroom had a deep tub and, surprisingly, a flushing toilet.

The God of the dead has been doing some research into modern amenities. Now to convince him to let me have phone reception.

"Everything looks great, thanks, Duncan." Imogen took out her small ax and headed for the door.

"Where are you going?" he asked, confused. He moved subtly to block her path.

"For a walk outside. I've been sitting on that bike for hours, and I like to know the lay of the land wherever I'm staying."

"Lord Arawan said that you were a hunter."

"I am. So, kindly, get out of my way," Imogen replied, giving him too much eye contact. Duncan seemed to struggle for a moment before finally doing as she asked.

"Thanks, champ. Do you have the key to this door?"

Duncan straightened. "As the steward of this castle, I have the keys to all the doors."

"Good. Let me have it." Imogen held out her hand.

Duncan's whole face pinched. "Miss Ironwood, it is *most* unconventional—"

"Yeah, that's me. Pass it over."

Still pulling the face of extreme pain, Duncan retrieved a ring of keys from inside of his robe, removed one, and placed it into her palm.

"I was commanded to provide you with what you asked, but I will be speaking to Lord Arawan about this," he said.

Imogen tucked the key into her bra and straightened her leather jacket. "You do that. Where is the boss, by the way?"

"Out. My lord keeps his own agenda."

"Ah huh. I'll see you around, Duncan. Thanks for the welcome wagon," Imogen replied, locking her door and heading back downstairs before he could stop her.

Imogen had expected staff; she hadn't expected that they would be instructed to give her what she wanted. She thought of a hot bubble bath with servants pouring her wine and delivering her chocolate-covered delicacies.

Maybe this liaison thing won't be so bad.

Outside, the guards looked her over but didn't stop her from wandering out into the grounds. It was afternoon, but the sun was still up enough for her not to worry about falling into a pothole and breaking her neck.

Could she die there at all? If Duncan was a shade and getting about corporeal and completely solid, then Arawan's power made it happen. She filed it away for something to ask him.

Imogen stuffed her hands into the pockets of her jacket and walked to the border where she could feel the edge of Arawan's wards without crossing them.

"Okay, let's see how far we have to work with." Imogen went left, following the border. She tried to keep the castle in sight as much as possible, so she didn't get too lost. The forest was larger than she expected and could hide all sorts of enemies.

Maybe Arawan trusted that his wards would pick up anything that would cross through them. A few months ago, Imogen would've been okay with that. After Aneirin attacked the Ironwood mansion, she would never think they were infallible again.

Something crashed in the undergrowth behind her, and Imogen whirled, her ax already growing to its full size. A large white dog stalked out from behind some rocks, its red ears pricked high and alert.

"Hey there, handsome," Imogen crooned, keeping her voice steady. Her hand tightened on her ax. "You must be one of the Cŵn Annwn."

"Good guess," Arawan said from behind her. She wasn't dumb enough to whirl around and give her back to the hound. Arawan wanted her alive, at least for now, but she didn't know about the beast. "He won't hurt you unless I command him to."

Imogen slowly lowered her ax, all her instincts screaming that it was a bad idea. She finally turned. Arawan was leaning against a tree. He was back in leather pants and a long overcoat with a high collar. His large silver sword hung at his side.

Arawan's eyes ran over her, and she fought not to fidget or sneer at him. Her boots and black jeans were splattered with mud, and her braid was a mess from the ride. She should just give up on ever looking neat, especially in front of him.

"Hello, darling. Nice to see you followed instructions and didn't make me come after you," he said with a small smile.

Imogen rested her ax on the ground, going for casual.

"Well, you did seem rather insistent about it. What are you doing lurking in the woods?"

"It is my land, and I can go wherever I wish. What is your excuse?" he replied, crossing his arms.

"I like to be aware of my surroundings. If I am going to stay with you, I want to know what the borders are like and where they are. Not that I don't think you will honor your vow to protect me. I just don't trust you or anyone else," Imogen replied.

Maybe she should be more cautious about how she spoke to him, but fuck it. She always liked to be honest.

"So you shouldn't. I'm bound by our bond to protect you, but you should protect yourself first."

Imogen picked up her ax. "Good. I'm glad you understand. I'll be on my way." She began to walk away when she heard footsteps behind her. "You don't have to follow me. I'm sure you have things to do."

"The thing I need to do most right now is escort you. Let me take you on a tour." Arawan let out a low whistle, and another huge hound appeared. Imogen watched in fascination as they grew to the size of horses.

"Get on. We can ride," Arawan instructed, and one of the hounds lowered down to the earth beside her.

"I don't think I'm comfortable with the idea. My ass is already sore from the ride here today," Imogen said.

Arawan mounted the other hound. "You can ride him alone or ride with me; those are the choices."

He held a hand out to her, a small, challenging smile on his lips. "And if your ass is still sore by the end of it, I'll rub some healing balm into it myself."

Imogen shrank her ax, tucked it into her leather belt, and climbed onto the other dog's back. It trotted up beside Arawan. He looked weirdly pleased.

"See? Isn't it easier to just obey me?" he said.

Imogen laughed. "I don't know if you've realized this, but I'm not really one for taking orders."

Arawan hummed. "We'll see about that."

8

Arawan had known the minute that Imogen had crossed the borders into his lands. She was the only one that was breathing on it for a start.

He had announced to his court that they would be getting a new living ambassador residing amongst them and had delighted in their scandalized faces.

It was recklessly out of character for him. He knew it and didn't care. Keeping them guessing would help him flush out the disloyal ones. He had slept too long, and now he would have to find inventive ways to get them back in line.

Imogen's appearance would make them uneasy.

Arawan was genuinely surprised that she hadn't forced him to chase her down. Looking at the sway of her lavender braid and how she kept one hand on her ax told him that she was no coward. It was one of the things he liked about her.

Watching her hips move as she rode was too distracting to keep a straight thought in his head. He moved up beside her.

"I should warn you not to leave the castle at night. I have wraiths and other creatures patrolling that you wouldn't want to meet," Arawan said, trying to find a way to start a conversation with her. His prickly flower wasn't going to make anything easy on him.

"What if I need to go out?" she asked without looking at him.

Arawan frowned. "What would you need to go out for?"

"Apart from the need to use my phone? What about if I have a hot date?" she replied with a shrug.

"I can fix it so your phone works here, and you will be too busy to have dates," he said firmly.

"But I'm a *liaison*. That means I have to have lots of *liaisons* as part of this job you thrust upon me." She fluttered her lashes at him.

"If I had thrust anything upon you, mortal, believe me, you would know," Arawan replied, hating what that eyelash flutter did to him.

"Are you saying I can't leave? Because I'm not your subject or your prisoner." Imogen's hand was tightening on her ax.

"You will be whatever I want you to be until your debt is repaid."

Her blue-gray eyes flashed with annoyance. "And when will that be?"

Arawan leaned down into her space until they were eye to eye. "When I say so."

"I'm not a damn courtier. I *need* to hunt the horde creatures that are roaming about," she hissed.

"Agreed, but you will be hunting with me or not at all."

"Oh yeah? Well, you already suck at it," Imogen said and threw herself at him.

Arawan swore in surprise as they hit the ground hard. Black claws slashed above his head, and the hound he had been sitting out squealed in pain.

Imogen was off him and moving into action. Her ax flashed as it came down onto the creature that had attacked them.

It was unlike anything Arawan had ever seen. It looked like a sluagh wraith had been crossed with some kind of swamp monster. Arawan could control the dead, but this creature felt odd and wrong.

"Are you going to help or just lie there?" Imogen shouted, rolling out of the way of the creature's claws.

Move, she's one of the living!

That reminder had Arawan jumping to his feet. He pulled his sword free and moved to protect her back.

Another two of the creatures pulled free of the underbrush and roared.

"Have you seen anything like these guys before? They look like wet Sasquatches with horns and raptor claws," Imogen said, lifting her ax.

"I don't know what a Sasquatch is, but no, I have never seen them before. They aren't exactly living, but I can't control them."

"Worry about it once they are dead for real." Imogen didn't wait for him but attacked the nearest beast to her with a fierce battle cry.

Arawan whistled at his uninjured hound, and it let out a vicious howl. It attacked one of the creatures while Arawan dealt with the other. It smelled horrible and rotting, its mouth full of serpent's fangs.

What the fuck were those creatures? Arawan's sword dripped with black blood, but the beast refused to go down. Imogen shouted something that he didn't catch over the fight. Silver flashed by his face, and an ax embedded itself between the creature's eyes.

"I said to go for the head," Imogen said, rushing past him and pulling her ax free. She didn't even look twice as she turned to the third creature. All of its attention was on the hound, so it didn't see Imogen come up behind it.

Arawan froze in sudden, unexpected fear as Imogen grabbed one of the spines on its back and used it to haul herself up. It roared, trying to buck her off, and lashed out with its claws.

Imogen was faster and was upon its shoulders in seconds, holding it by one of its horns. Her ax came down hard on the top of its head over and over again.

"That's. For. Killing. The. Dog. You. Fuck," she shouted, each word punctuated by a blow. The creature slumped to the ground, Imogen still on its back. She yanked her ax free from what remained of its head and spat on the corpse.

Arawan blinked. He hadn't seen that kind of brutality in centuries.

Imogen whirled on him, smeared with black blood, her eyes shining with battle fury. She pointed her gory ax at him.

"What the fuck kind of help are you in a fight?" she demanded. "Why are you staring—"

She let out a startled cry as Arawan grabbed her by her filthy face and kissed her.

9

One second, Imogen was shouting, and the next, the God of the dead's tongue was in her mouth. It wasn't a friendly peck either. It was a breathless, hazardous to her health type of kiss that felt like they were trying to climb inside of each other.

A feeling of euphoria and ecstasy rushed through her; this was the exact feeling she had when she died. Except now, she felt a million other things on top of it.

The ax slipped from her hand, and she grabbed Arawan by the lapel of his jacket, dragging him closer. Strong hands pushed her up against the nearest tree before yanking on her braid to tilt her head up.

Fuck, his mouth was magic, and Imogen was too high on him to push him away. One of her hands tangled in his long black hair. It was as silky as it looked, and she gripped it tighter, unsure if she wanted to make him hurt or get him closer. Both.

His hips ground up against hers, and an involuntary moan escaped her throat.

Arawan pulled back from her, eyes filled with fury and lust. "Now, I know why you've died so many times. You are insane."

"Someone had to be because your situational awareness is rubbish," Imogen replied. She expected him to move, but he stayed where he was, pressing her into the tree.

"Never put yourself in danger to protect me like that again," he growled.

Imogen glared up at him. "If I hadn't, you would've been torn apart by those claws."

"I am immortal! I would've recovered!"

Imogen's temper flared. "Right. Let me up. If that's the thanks I get for saving your scrawny ass, you can fuck right off."

Arawan gripped her face so she couldn't move. "No. Not until you promise me."

"I promise to let you get torn apart by the next monsters we meet. I will even push you in front of them like my own fucking shield so that you get horribly clawed to pieces!" she shouted at him.

Arawan didn't even flinch. He moved his lips against hers. "Good. I'd rather get torn apart than watch it happen to you."

Imogen really wanted to shove him off, but her body wasn't getting the message. Her mouth opened to his, and he took the advantage.

His kiss was deep and slow and absolutely controlling. It was the kind of kiss that would've led to something more if he would've been anyone else.

She could feel his restraint, the roar of his power under the human guise he wore. Warm wet heat spread through her with every flick of his tongue and scrape of his teeth over her lips. She ground up against his leg that was pressed between hers, and he hummed against her lips before pulling away.

Imogen cleared her throat and pulled her jacket straight. "Okay. We need to figure out where those creatures came from."

"No. We need to get you back to the safety of the castle," Arawan said. He moved away from her like their mind-blistering kiss and mild dry humping never happened.

He crouched down beside his dead hound and placed a hand on its head. Power filled the clearing, and Imogen's knees trembled. It licked against her skin, and her side ached in memory of its touch. The wounds in the hound's side closed over. It whimpered, its legs kicking out before it sat up.

"What in the..." Imogen hurried over to it and ran her hands through its thick fur.

Arawan's hand covered hers. "Do you understand now? Everything in this place can be revived because it is an extension of Annwn. You are the only thing that is truly alive and irreplaceable."

Imogen looked down at their hands and back up to his face. Realization smacked her in the back of the head. She had scared him; that was why he had been stunned into inaction. The last of Imogen's temper slipped away.

"I get it, but it's not in my nature to run from a fight. Do *you* understand that? I won't just sit there and do nothing if we are attacked."

"It won't happen again. I'll find out how these creatures got in undetected once you are safe." Arawan climbed up on the back of the hound, and before she could protest, he lifted her up in front of him.

"You know I can ride on my own."

"I am aware." Arawan clicked his tongue, and the hound began to move.

Imogen gripped the fur on the hound's neck and tried not to rub her ass up against Arawan without meaning to. She was still rattled that he had kissed her. Twice.

"Your wards are so strong even I can feel them, and I have fuck all magic," she said, her eyes scanning the darkening forest for anything else ready to jump out and attack them. "If you didn't feel the intrusion of these creatures, then it means someone let them in. Someone who is good enough to fuck with wards without the owner knowing. You got some bold fucking bastards in your court."

She wobbled as the hound leaped over a log, and Arawan's hands went to her hips to steady her.

"I know. They never would've dared, but I left them alone for too long. There is insubordination amongst them, but I don't know who," he replied, breath tickling her ear.

"You think they are working with Hafgan?" she asked.

"They could be. He was always a lot more persuasive than I was. The charming one. He could have made them promises, and they would believe him." Arawan hadn't moved his hands, and she pretended not to notice.

"I've been thinking about this whole liaison thing," she said, reaching for her own charming side. "I think I can help with your rat problem."

"Enlighten me."

"You can't be seen snooping about like you don't trust anyone because it will make you look weak in front of your court. There are no such restrictions on me. They don't even *know* me, and from Duncan's attitude, they are confused as to why I'm here at all. We can use that to our advantage."

"I like how you say we," Arawan said, and Imogen tried really hard not to get turned on by his deep voice rumbling in her ear.

"Yeah, well, we are in this together, right? I'm not posh enough to sit in on meetings and pretend to care about court gossip. I'm a hunter, so let me hunt. I'll find your spies, and we can get out of them where Hafgan is. You can go kill him, and I can get out of your pretty hair," Imogen replied.

"And what if I like you in my pretty hair?" Arawan asked.

Imogen contemplated the merits of falling off the hound and running away. His hands tightened on her as if guessing her thoughts.

"Why would you? As you pointed out, I'm living. What possible reason could you have for keeping me around?"

"My reasons are my own," he replied cryptically. "You find me Hafgan's spies, and I'll try and be open to negotiation."

Imogen snorted. "You will be so sick of me in a week, you're going to boot me out of your castle without an argument."

Arawan laughed softly, the sound sending goosebumps down her body. "I suppose we will find out in a week, darling, won't we?"

Imogen tried to focus on the wildland around her and not on the voice in her head that kept chanting, *Don't fuck, Arawan. Don't fuck, Arawan.*

Imogen almost sighed in relief when the castle's lights came back into view. If the warriors were concerned to see their lord and master riding with a human, none of them were game enough to bat an eyelid.

Arawan slid off the hound and helped her down, lifting her like she was one of those posh skinny chicks in fantasy movies.

Imogen was *not* a skinny chick. She was also soaked in fucking gunk from the swamp Sasquatches and stank like rotting ass.

"Go up to your rooms and stay there. I'll let you know when it's safe to come out again," Arawan said.

Imogen leaned her ax against her shoulder. "Sounds good to me.

You can climb about the freezing woods, and I'll go soak in a tub. Excellent teamwork."

Arawan's lips curved into a smile. "Does said bath have an open invitation for when I'm done?"

"Absolutely fucking not," Imogen said before walking inside.

10

Arawan waited until Imogen was safely inside before turning to his warriors, his grin vanishing.

"Get two patrols together and sweep the entire property. I just had some of Morrigan's horde remnants attack me, and I need to know how the fuck they got in," he snapped. The guards bowed low before hurrying away.

Arawan thought about what Imogen had said. He knew at least four magical adepts that were a part of his court and could manipulate warding. He couldn't ask them about tampering in case they were the ones guilty of it. It would give them too much opportunity to cover their tracks.

The fae princes could assist, but he didn't want them to upset Imogen settling in. The princes got him to thinking of their history, and the answer came to him; the sorceress.

Arawan's more mortal form melted away, and he drew on his power of the God of Annwn. He could feel the otherworld open to him, like a tear in the seam of the world, and cool mist poured through.

"*Aisling, the Lord of Annwn, calls for your aid,*" his voice boomed into the ether.

Within moments, a delicate barefoot woman stepped through the portal and into the mortal world. Her blue eyes were wide as they took the night in. When she spotted him, she bowed low.

"My lord, how may I serve you?" Aisling asked without looking up.

After dealing with Imogen's complete irreverence, her submission was almost strange.

"I wish for you to join my court as my personal sorceress. I also require information from you about your old masters," Arawan said. He shut the gateway to Annwn and resumed his mortal form.

"I didn't have masters, my lord. I served the Blood Prince and his brothers willingly," Aisling answered, raising her head. "What have they done?"

"Nothing, as yet, and they are all living."

Aisling smiled. "Thank the gods. What do you wish to know? They are all very honorable, even Killian—"

"I have their sister," Arawan admitted.

Aisling's blue eyes went wide. "Their sister! But they never had any... Oh, they found their mates!" The sorceress almost danced with impish glee. "This is too perfect. Forgive my exuberance. I'm very pleased to hear that they are thriving."

"They are indeed. I have made an alliance with them while I deal with Hafgan. I need your help, and I feel like I could trust you," Arawan said and explained the matter of the warding. Aisling listened, nodding. She smiled in delight as he told her about Imogen fighting off the horde creatures.

"She sounds fearless. And an Ironwood! Oh, Killian would've *hated* that," she crowed with delight. "I'll see to the wards, my lord, and I would love to be your sorceress. I need to meet this lass."

"She is quite something," Arawan conceded, pushing down the thoughts that had been trying to fight their way free. He whistled, and a hound appeared. "He can take you wherever you need to go. I will have the servants prepare accommodation and clothing for you."

"Thank you, my lord, for the opportunity to be back. Even if for a short time," Aisling said, bowing so low her black hair brushed against the ground.

"Serve me well, Aisling, and I will bring the princes here to see you," he promised.

"Thank you, I would... That would make me very happy." Aisling mounted the hound in one smooth move. "I will return when I have repaired what was broken in the warding. If the magic-user has been lazy, I will find signatures of their power, and I'll be able to trace them that way." With a nod, the sorceress disappeared into the night.

Arawan hoped none of his court would be about to harass him. He needed a bath and some time to think. Probably about Imogen in *her* bath. Fuck.

Duncan was waiting for him as soon as he stepped inside. He looked thoroughly put out, and Arawan could see that Imogen had gone straight through him.

"My lord," he said, bowing.

"Duncan, I trust you put our newest arrival into the rooms I requested?" Arawan asked. He kept walking, and Duncan fell into step beside him.

"I did, my lord. I have concerns that placing someone that could be an enemy so close to where you rest is dangerous," he said.

"What can a mortal woman do to me?" Arawan waved his concern aside. "She isn't anything to worry about."

"She took my key to her room," Duncan complained.

Arawan suppressed a laugh. Of course she did.

"You won't be needing it, and she is entitled to her privacy. We haven't had a liaison from the living fae court for millennia. Make her feel comfortable. She won't be staying forever." Arawan's tongue seemed to trip up on that. He didn't like the idea of her leaving.

She won't be allowed to. Not until I can learn what it is about her that makes me... Arawan didn't have the right word.

"We also have a new sorceress. Give her what she needs, Duncan," Arawan added before dismissing his steward. Duncan knew him well enough to figure out when to drop the subject. At least for the moment.

In the privacy of his own quarters, Arawan unstrapped his sword and stripped off his filthy clothes. The creatures were disgusting, but even covered in their blood, he couldn't stop kissing Imogen.

It had been too much, the fight, the fear that he had felt, the relief when it was over. He ran his hands through his hair. What was it about her?

He couldn't let her die. He had only just gotten her near him and wouldn't lose her because she was so damn reckless. He laughed helplessly. What did he care for one human soul?

Unlike the other gods, Arawan had never paid much attention to the living. Why would he? They had nothing to appeal to him until after they were dead.

But Imogen... There was something about her that made him feel *feral*. Primal. He wanted her to kill her. He wanted to pin her down and fuck every irreverent thought out of her. He wanted her to smile at him and fight with him. He wanted her to worship him.

He *wanted*. It was new and strange. It made him impatient, and that was so out of character that he struggled to know how to process it.

He touched his lips. How long had it been since he had kissed someone? How long had it been since he had fucked someone? He had thought he was too old to have such feelings again. His existence had become so tedious that he had gone deep into the heart of Annwn to sleep the years away.

Nothing felt tedious now. The world he'd woken up to was so loud and fast and immediate.

Imogen was the same—all passion and intensity. She was quick to laugh and quick to anger and quick to kiss him back like she didn't care that she was kissing something unnatural.

It made his chest feel too heavy when she wasn't near and made every part of him burn awake when she was close. It was maddening. It was everything.

Arawan had been in love once. At least, he had thought it was love. He'd had a consort named Brangwen, and Hafgan had stolen her. It was what had started the first war between them. But he hadn't truly taken her ... Brangwen had gone to him.

Once she had betrayed Arawan and told Hafgan everything he needed to know, Hafgan had killed her and left her body in pieces on the borders of Annwn. Her shade had been gone without a trace, so he never got to ask when she started hating him.

It had been so long ago that any love he had once known was gone. All that remained was never-ending, burning hatred.

Arawan couldn't remember ever having this feeling of need and awareness. He could feel the heat of Imogen's living soul moving through her rooms, not far from him.

He would have her, but it would be her choice. He was afraid he would crush her, bruise his deadly flower irreparably if he unleashed himself on her.

She kissed you back.

Arawan considered that thought, relived the moment her body had been pressed up against him. The sensation of her rubbing herself against him.

A smile grew when full realization hit him.

What he was feeling—this twisted connection that had him by the throat—she was feeling it too.

11

Imogen was in the bath when her phone started to beep in the other room. Arawan said that he could fix her reception, and he had. She smiled, weirdly touched that he had done that for her with everything else going on.

"Confusing ass god," she mumbled, blowing at the frothy bubbles around her. The tub was massive, and it was the warmest she had felt all day.

Except for when Arawan kissed you.

Damn it. It was rare for her to ever think she was getting in too deep, but flirting with a god was too deep. If he had been a human guy at a bar and had kissed her like that, she wouldn't have hesitated to drag him to the bathrooms and fuck him blind.

She couldn't do that with Arawan. She *wouldn't* do that. Some things in life were bad for her health, and making out with him had been one of them.

She felt raw and overstimulated from too many days of being wound up, and she knew she would have nightmares that night.

Fucking Arawan.

Imogen rested her head against the lip of the tub, trying to stop her thoughts from racing out of control. She couldn't dismiss his actions as spontaneous either. He had kissed her with purpose because he wanted to. She might confuse the fuck out of him, that much was obvious, but she had felt his desire...it had been pressed up against her.

"Don't think about his dick. You have a spy to catch," she grumbled, and her stomach grumbled back in response. She hadn't eaten since breakfast. No wonder she was grumpy.

∽

IMOGEN SAW no sign of anyone when she left her room twenty minutes later. She probably should've worn something other than flannel PJ bottoms and a Loki sweatshirt, but she couldn't bring herself to get dressed in proper clothes again.

The ache in her muscles reminded her that two long bike rides in less than three days weren't always a good idea. Getting thrown about by swamp monsters straight afterward and then shoved up against a tree had made for one eventful, physically exhausting day.

Imogen knew there had to be a kitchen somewhere, and without Duncan to tell her, she began to explore. She had been in enough old houses and castles recently that she had a good hunch that it would be off a dining room. An empty dining room. Where the fuck was everyone?

If Arawan's court were all dead, did they even consume food? Did they have a chef that prepared fake food to keep an illusion that they were still alive?

Imogen found the kitchen, and like the sudden use of her phone reception, she was surprised to see that it had a fridge, oven, and white goods.

Arawan had known she was coming and had taken care of it. For a guy that hadn't lived in the human world, he had caught up on what humans needed pretty damn quickly.

Imogen pulled open the fridge and found it full of food. *Way* too much food if she was the only one eating it. In her opinion, it was better to have too much than too little. Her stomach grumbled again.

"Yeah, I hear you," she told it and got to work.

Imogen was in the middle of making a stack of sandwiches when the kitchen door opened, and one of the most stunning women she had ever seen walked through the door. She had long black hair and bright blue eyes that lit up in excitement.

"You are the sister!" she said excitedly.

"Ah..."

"Kian's sister!"

"Yeah, that's me. And you are?" Imogen asked, her hand still on the knife she had been using to cut ham.

The woman smiled. "I'm Aisling."

The name rang through Imogen, and she realized where she had heard it before. "You're the sorceress that helped the princes? You told them about their mates being able to break the curses?"

"Yes, that was me. Arawan has summoned me to help you find out who is breaking his wards," Aisling replied. She looked Imogen over. "You are not what I expected. When Arawan said you were a hunter, I imagined leather and scars."

"Don't worry, I have plenty of both. I'm just off duty." Imogen looked down at the extra sandwich she had made and offered it to her. "Can you eat food that way?" It seemed a nicer way of saying *dead*.

"I'm not sure," Aisling said. She had a mouthful and chewed. "It's good."

"We'll take that as a yes." Imogen smiled at her. "Arawan brought you back to help with the magic, did he? That was smart, because he can't trust anyone in his court right now and we need to find out who is behind the tampering. Is there anything else about Hafgan that you can tell me?"

Aisling thought for a while. "I'm assuming you know that he's indestructible? There was more than one prophecy about how he can't be stopped or destroyed by man or beast, so whatever Arawan has planned for him, it won't be to the death. It will be some kind of containment."

Imogen refilled her red wine. "He's probably been thinking about it for centuries too. As long as the fight stays out of the human world, I don't care."

Imogen's phone buzzed in her back pocket, and she giggled at the meme Freya had sent her. "Oh. I've just had the best idea." It was late, but she didn't care. Kian answered the video call on the first ring.

"Imogen? Are you okay? Did you get there on time?" he asked quickly. He looked like he was in his study working on something.

"I did, and I found someone you might know here," Imogen replied and pulled Aisling closer.

"Fucking hell, what are you doing there?" Kian asked, his smile instant.

"My prince, how is this possible? Is this a mirror like yours?" Aisling asked, taking the phone and turning it this way and that.

"No, it is...it is a device for communicating," Kian tried to explain. "I'm so happy to see you, dear sorceress. What are you doing there?"

Aisling explained Arawan summoning her, and Imogen smiled at them catching up while she ate.

"I am happy you are there, Aisling. You can keep an eye on Imogen and ensure she doesn't get into any trouble," Kian said.

"And why would I do that? Trouble is good to get into," Aisling replied, shooting Imogen a wink.

"Imogen gets into more than most, and I don't like that Arawan is too interested in her."

Imogen snorted. "He's only interested in me paying off my debt to him."

"Stop lying to yourself, Gen."

"You can't make me," Imogen replied and stuck her tongue out at him. Aisling roared with laughter. Imogen choked hers down when Arawan appeared in the kitchen doorway.

"Ah, we have to go, Kian. Love you!" Imogen said and hung up quickly. She didn't know why she felt like she had been caught out.

Aisling rallied, giving Arawan a short bow. "My lord."

"Sorceress. What did you find on the borders?" he asked, his eyes not looking away from Imogen. She tried to ignore the stare and his heady dragon blood smell that was twice as strong because he wasn't covered in horde creature.

Arawan wore loose-fitting black pants and a black shirt that crossed over his chest diagonally. Not exactly PJs, but definitely relaxed. It made Imogen feel a little bit less self-conscious about her clothes.

Aisling looked between them curiously before she quickly replied, "The wards were definitely tampered with. One whole section had been removed and patched with another. I couldn't get a read off the magic like I hoped; it was done too well. It felt similar to yours like they had copied it somehow so not to alert you."

Arawan crossed his arms. "So an above average magic-user. Did you see any signs of more creatures?"

"There were three sets of tracks in the mud, so hopefully, that was all of them. The warriors are still checking the grounds. I can build something subtle into the warding tomorrow that will alert us to anyone touching them," Aisling replied.

"That would be helpful. We can do that in the morning, and I can see this remaking for myself," Arawan said. He looked back at Imogen. "You can join us."

Imogen saluted him. "Yes, boss."

Aisling's eyes went wide at her sarcastic tone. "I'll be going to rest so I am prepared for tomorrow's magic. Goodnight, my lord. Imogen." She backed out of the room quickly and disappeared. Traitor.

Arawan leaned against the far end of the table. His eyes glanced down at what remained of her sandwiches and red wine dinner.

"Why have you cooked for yourself?" he asked.

"Why wouldn't I? There was no one around, and food isn't going to magically make itself."

Arawan's frown was instantaneous. "I gave orders that you were to be taken care of."

"Shades don't need to eat even though they can here. They probably didn't even think of it. It's fine," Imogen replied. She washed up her plate and poured herself a nightcap. She needed sleep after that day that wouldn't end.

Arawan was staring at her tits again. She waved a hand in front of them.

"Hey, eyes up here," she snapped.

"Loki. You...pay homage to him?" he asked, frowning. Okay, so *not* looking at her tits specifically.

"Loki is awesome. I think the fandom pays a homage to him by extension," she said. It wasn't the right thing to say. Arawan's whole demeanor shifted. The shadows in the kitchen darkened.

"I'm surprised there is any god that you like with how disrespectful you are to me," he said, stepping closer to her.

Woah, he is fully pissed.

"He's not the real Loki," Imogen tried to explain. "He's a character in modern stories about him. Not the actual Norse God."

Arawan's temper shifted into confusion. Then he stuck his finger in the hole in the shoulder of her shirt and stroked her skin. "Why are all your clothes damaged?"

"It's called having a grunge chic aesthetic. Hey, stop that. You're going to make it bigger," she said when his finger wiggled against her. She battered his hand away, and his confusion turned into amusement.

"Are you attached to this clothing?" he asked sternly.

"Yes?"

Arawan clicked his tongue. "Pity. I feel like tearing it off you. I don't like another god being so close to your breasts."

Imogen's brain went fuzzy, but her mouth had no such problem. "Are you trying to flirt with me right now? Because wanting to wreck my Loki shirt isn't the right way to do it."

Liar. Imogen had never had anyone literally tear her clothes off before. The image had its appeal.

Arawan's smile turned sly. He leaned into her space so she could feel the heat of his body against her. Her traitorous nipples hardened under Loki's face.

"If that were true, darling, why did your breath just catch and your pulse start to race?"

"It's me being offended by your audacity," Imogen lied.

"Do not speak to me about audacity. *You* are the most audacious creature I have ever met in my entire existence," he growled.

Oh, he had no idea. He wanted to play flirty, intimidation games, did he?

Imogen went up on her tiptoes until her mouth was barely an inch from his. Arawan's smile faltered, and his eyes heated.

"I could feel how much you disapproved of my audacity when you had me up against that tree, Lord of the dead," she whispered against his mouth without touching it before moving past him and out of the kitchen.

12

Imogen hated mornings. So much of her hunting adult life had been working at night that anything before ten a.m. wasn't worth getting up to. That's why whoever was banging on her door at seven a.m. was going to get throat punched.

Grumbling, she pulled her Loki shirt, making sure it covered her ass before stumbling to the door. She yanked it open.

"For the love of fuck, *what*?" she demanded.

Duncan held out a tray to her. He looked shocked by her morning banshee appearance for a second before good manners smoothed the surprise away.

"I have your breakfast, Miss Ironwood," he said, moving inside to place it on a small table. "If I had my key, I wouldn't need to wake you every morning."

"If you asked me what time I get up, you wouldn't be waking me up at all." Imogen pinched the bridge of her nose. "Look, I know you're just doing your job. I don't want to bust your balls, but no banging on my door before ten, okay?"

Duncan bowed. "Apologies, my lady. I'll let the kitchen know of your request."

"Thanks. That's nice of you." Imogen opened the door wider for him to leave and saw Arawan the second he came out of his own room.

God, did he ever not look perfect? It was way too early to look at him in leather pants and a black shirt with his laces loose. Imogen might have been a grumpy morning person, but she was also a horny morning person.

Arawan looked at her bare toes and up to her rumpled bed hair in a way that made her lady parts throb. He opened his mouth to say something, but Imogen quickly shut the door before he could get a word out.

Nope. Too early to deal with that voice growling at her.

Imogen lifted the silver lid off the tray and found pancakes, bacon, eggs, fruit, toast, porridge...everything someone would make without knowing what the recipient wanted.

Imogen put some bacon on top of a pancake, rolled it up, and munched it as she climbed back into bed. When she was done, she burrowed under the blankets and put her pillow over her head.

Stupid goth gods and their sexy morning smiles.

Imogen hadn't slept well the night before. Not because she had nightmares; those were regular enough to be mundane, but because of Arawan poking at her shirt.

To Imogen, the only thing worse than being regularly horny over a hot guy was realizing that she also liked them.

And Imogen liked Arawan. He had played bullshit games to try and unnerve her since they met. And strangely enough, she liked that side of him too. She had played horny chicken with him in the kitchen the night before and liked that she could mess with him back without him smiting her.

Had anyone bothered to flirt with the God of the dead? Had they *dared*? It seemed unlikely because he always seemed torn between shocked and intrigued. That only seemed to bring out her shit-stirring scandalous side even more.

Imogen enjoyed flirting and sex and not getting emotionally attached. Maybe she would get away with doing the first with Arawan, but the second and third? That was getting too complicated.

Did Arawan even have sex? There was a thought. A thought she really didn't need when she was trying to go back to sleep.

"Stupid, sexy goth gods," she grumbled out loud. She had a feeling it was going to be another long-ass day.

∽

IMOGEN WAS glad of the heavy black coat that Freya had forced her to pack. It was snowing and way too miserable to be walking around outside. A beanie was pulled down over her braid, but her ears were still cold.

Arawan and Aisling were checking the wards around his borders, and Imogen, who had no idea about magic, was almost praying for something to attack them so she would have something to do. At least the massive hound she was riding kept her butt warm.

"This was where those creatures came through yesterday," Aisling said, bringing Imogen out of her daydreaming.

They had been riding for over an hour. Imogen was happy to let her hound follow the other two. She needed to get proper sleep because she was starting to turn into a zombie.

Imogen slid off her hound and checked over the frozen tracks. There really had only been three of the swamp Sasquatches. But where had they come from? She had taken one step through the wards before a hand closed around her bicep.

"And where are you going?" Arawan asked.

"Those horde creatures came from somewhere. They didn't just appear on your borders out of thin air. There might be more close by."

"They aren't on my property, so they aren't my concern."

"They could be preying on humans hiking in these mountains, which makes it *my* concern." Imogen looked down at his hand. "Remove that, or I will."

Arawan's eyes narrowed, but he let his hand drop. "Aisling? You keep going and make a note of any tampering. I'll fix it on my return."

Aisling looked at Imogen curiously but quickly nodded to Arawan and rode on.

"You don't have to come if you're busy. I can track on my own," Imogen insisted. Being alone with him was starting to feel more and more dangerous.

"What did I say yesterday? You can hunt horde creatures, but you aren't doing it alone. There will be no arguments," Arawan replied.

"Oh, there will be arguments," she muttered under her breath as she walked away.

"I heard that."

"Like I care. I'm not one of your subjects or your prisoner, remember?" Imogen called back without turning around.

Despite the snow falling around them, there was no mistaking the horde creatures' tracks that had chewed up the moss and mud.

"How did you bastards get all the way up here?" Imogen ignored the dark shadow following her. He wanted to trail after her in some misguided need to protect her. That was just fine with her.

The tracks led to a frozen lake and a rank-smelling cave. Imogen put a hand over her nose.

"Yeah, they were definitely here," she said, staring at the black opening of the cave. She took some deep breaths of clean air. "Fuck it, I'm going in."

"Let me go in first." Arawan moved ahead of her before she could argue.

"Fine with me. You can step in horde creature crap and warn me where it is," she said cheerily.

Arawan conjured a torch, lighting it with a snap of his fingers. Okay, maybe he could be helpful after all. Imogen followed him into the damp cave, careful to watch where she was putting her feet.

"Is your life always like this?" he asked, looking at the cave around him.

"Pretty much. I'd still prefer it to castles and courtiers," Imogen replied. "Which reminds me, where is everyone? I thought your castle would be packed with snobby people."

"They are in Annwn. I needed the castle so when I summon them, they have places to stay far from me."

"But you put me across the hall from you," Imogen pointed out and instantly regretted it.

"And that bothers you?"

Yes.

"No. I am only curious as to why you did it."

Arawan glanced over his shoulder at her. "You are mortal. The closer you are to me when my court is about, the safer you are. I didn't want to worry about you."

Why worry about me at all? That was what she should have asked, but she had a brain-to-mouth communication problem again.

"Do you have sex? I mean, you're dead, aren't you?" she blurted out.

Arawan snorted, which could've meant anything. "I'm a god *of* the dead. I'm not living like you, but I'm not dead like them either."

"Is that your way of saying no, you don't have sex?"

His smile was a sharp flash of white in the gloom. "Why do you ask?"

"I thought you would have a bunch of wives or a harem running about."

Arawan slowed his steps and turned slightly. "How do you know I don't?"

"A dude with a harem wouldn't be so pouty. You're grumpy all the time, so I concluded it was because you couldn't have sex."

"My ancient enemy is back and preparing to attack Annwn. I have good reasons to be grumpy that have nothing to do with sex," Arawan argued. He gave her an intense look that had parts of her going tingly. "And some that do."

He turned around and stalked further into the cave, leaving Imogen staring at him like a dumbass.

You had to ask, didn't you?

"I know where they came from," Arawan called, and she hurried to catch up to him. The cave opened up into a vast cavern. It smelled awful and thrummed with leftover magic.

"Do you think they were hiding in here?" she asked.

Arawan knelt to study the splashes of black goo on the sandy floor. The horde creatures had smeared it all to hell with their trampling, but Imogen had been around enough fucked up dark magic in the last month to know a sigil when she saw it.

"I think they were summoned here, and they weren't a part of the original horde of Morrigan's. It's like their maker's mark was different," Arawan replied, standing once more.

"Aneirin could have made them. My sister Charlotte believes he had the power."

Arawan nodded. "Hafgan did too. Like me, he could control all manner of wraiths and ghouls..." He looked around at the cave, eyes going wide. "Get out, Imogen. *Now.*"

"What's—" she began. The ground trembled underneath her feet, and a clawed hand burst through the earth.

Arawan whirled around, his eyes burning a ruby red. "I said *now!*" he shouted, and she bolted back the way she came.

Imogen's heart was pounding, adrenaline and fear making her legs pump faster. The tunnel began to lighten behind her, and she looked over her shoulder.

"Fuck!" she screamed.

The cave was full of fire, coming up hot and fast. Imogen slid around a sharp bend, smacking against the slick wall. Sunlight blinked in front of her, and she ran for the opening and jumped.

Flames licked at her back, and power shoved her forward, sending her sliding across the frozen lake's surface. A fire roared out of the cave for ten seconds before it vanished.

"Arawan..." Imogen scrambled across the ice, her boots finally finding purchase on the bank. The cave's stone walls were still steaming, but she didn't care.

Was the fire his power, or was it a trap? He could still be in there in pain, burned to a crisp and stuck between some horrible life and death place. No, no, no...

"Arawan!" Imogen charged back into the cave, determined to find him. She collided with him hard, coming around the first turn.

"Oh, fuck! Are you okay?" Imogen patted him down, trying to put out the embers that still stuck to him.

"I'm not hurt," he said, putting his hands on her shoulders to steady her. "Look at me." Imogen's panic slowed enough to stare up into his ash-smeared face.

"I'm okay, darling. The fire was of my making. The cave was full of ghouls, and it's the only way to kill them."

Imogen smacked him hard against the chest. And then again. "Don't you ever freak me out like that again!" she shouted at him.

"I didn't have time to explain myself to you, woman!" he shouted back, and then his anger seemed to vanish. "You were worried about me?"

"No!" she said too quickly. Imogen couldn't stop shaking. The whole of her front was soaked down, and her hands were grazed from her slide across the ice. And she had been scared for him; a true moment of blinding panic that he was caught in a fire trap. Imogen hit him again just for that.

Arawan caught her hand and pulled her close. Imogen wasn't a big hugger, especially with people outside her family. She struggled in the embrace for a few seconds, but when he refused to let her go, she melted into him.

"I'm sorry if I scared you. I just needed you to get out before the ghouls could hurt you," he said softly.

"And you thought firebombing them was the only answer?" she mumbled against his chest.

"It's the only way to kill ghouls and ensure they stay dead."

Imogen pulled back a little. "You think they were left as a trap by Hafgan?"

"Yes, or one of his followers." The muscles in Arawan's jaw feathered. "They were to ensure if anyone found the summoning circle, they didn't live to tell anyone about it."

"Has Hafgan always been such a fucking ass hat?" Imogen groaned in annoyance.

Arawan's grim mouth ticked up into a smile. "Yes, actually, he has. Let's get you out of here and back to the castle."

Imogen allowed herself one more inhale of his smoke-tinged scent and stepped back. She wasn't shaking anymore, and the smile he unexpectedly gave her made her forget the cold.

"You really were worried about me. Not such a prickly flower after all," he teased.

Imogen cast her eyes to heaven. "You had to ruin the moment."

"We were having a moment?" he asked, head tilting.

"Nope, my mistake." Imogen went outside, hoping the chilly air would blast some sense into her thick head. Arawan was still wearing the same grin when he came into the light. It only slipped when he saw her wet clothes. The knees on her jeans were soaked and torn, and blood was seeping through them from her scrapes.

"I'm fine too. They are just grazes," she said, pulling her coat closer around her. "Let's get moving before this snow gets any worse."

Arawan pulled off his heavy coat and wrapped it around her. "No freezing to death either, Imogen."

"Spoilsport," she replied, snuggling into his coat. "We need to figure out a way to flush Hafgan's spies out of your court. You said they don't come to your castle here often?"

"They don't, but that doesn't mean they can't turn up when they like. I didn't want them all crowding about when you arrived. They would have had ample time to change my wards in the last couple of weeks," Arawan said as they walked back up the steep hill and away from the lake.

Imogen started to slip, but his hand shot out and caught her. "Thanks." She stared at their clasped hands and then smiled as an idea came to her. "We need to have a party."

"I'm not sure I follow you," Arawan said.

Imogen chewed on her lip thoughtfully as they continued walking. "It would be perfect. Summon the court for a ball or a dinner. I'm sure you can think of something. Get them all here, and I can flush out who the spy is."

"How?" he asked curiously.

Imogen realized she was still holding his hand but didn't let go. And neither did he. Her cheeks went warm, and she smiled up at him.

"I'm a hunter, remember? So I'll hunt."

13

Imogen always expected to have nightmares when she went to bed and shut her eyes. They had been with her for as long as she could remember, and after drowning, they had only gotten worse.

Every time Imogen was in a stressed or emotional situation, she would go to bed and dream of the river. Her sisters would be paddling in the shallower spot, David playing with them and keeping them from wandering off.

Imogen had snuck away and had climbed up on a log to look at the trout swimming in the deeper waters. She had slipped and tumbled face-first into the cold depths.

Panicked thrashing. Weeds around her feet. Rocks smashed into her side. Then euphoria. Peace.

Dying was okay after all...

Imogen woke with firm hands on her shoulders. Someone was talking to her, but her head was still underwater.

"Imogen, wake the fuck up!" Arawan growled. "You dream so fucking *loud*."

"Go 'way," she grumbled.

"I would, but your shade literally spluttered, and I thought someone was killing you."

Imogen opened her eyes. She could barely make him out in the dark room. Arawan was beside her bed and still had a hand on her.

"Just dreaming of when I died. I'm okay," she said, pushing her hand over her damp face. Had she been crying in her sleep?

"When you died? You mean the Kraken?" Arawan asked, voice soft. She should tell him to get out, but her sleep-addled brain didn't want him to go.

"No, when I was little. I drowned," Imogen replied, telling him the story. "I always dream of it when I'm stressed out."

Arawan's hand brushed over her forehead. "You're safe here. You know that, don't you?"

"I know," Imogen admitted. She was still drowsy enough that all of her defenses were down, and his hand stroking her head was so relaxing. "I always dream of drowning because of the feeling I got when I died. I only felt that one other time since."

"When?"

"When you kissed me in the forest," she whispered and then regretted it. She shouldn't have told him anything.

"I see. So it's me that's bothering you?" he said, his hand moving away. Imogen reached out in the darkness and grabbed warm skin. With some mild groping, she realized it was his chest.

"Not in a bad way. You frustrate the hell out of me, but I'm not scared of you."

Arawan's hand closed over hers, trapping it against him. "It would be better for you if you were."

"Why? What am I even doing here, Arawan? What possible use could you have for a mortal?" Imogen asked. She still hadn't been able to figure that out.

"A mortal? Not a damn thing," Arawan admitted. "But you? You existed and were perfection. You were seared into my brain the night I first saw you, and until I figure out why, I can't let you go."

"You know that makes no sense."

Arawan's soft chuckle made goosebumps rise along her arms. "Does it need to? Neither one of us is interested in doing what makes sense. If you had any good sense, you wouldn't provoke me so much."

"Don't pretend you don't like it," Imogen teased. "I'm probably the funniest thing that's ever happened to you in the last millennia."

"You are certainly the most infuriating. Your shade literally fluttered just now when you died in your dream. I thought you were gone, and I'd never be able to..."

"Able to do what? Kill me yourself?" Imogen asked. She was so glad he couldn't see how hot her face was at that minute. Why was talking to him in the dark so much easier?

"Figure you out. I don't know why I need you at the moment. I just know that I feel better when you are close by. You are disobedient and loud and provoke me every chance you get. But still, I feel better," Arawan replied, his long fingers stroking the back of her hand.

"Yeah, I like you too." Imogen's fingers tightened around his. "We will find out who is plotting against you, I promise. You won't have to worry about them for much longer. We will get Hafgan. It's only a matter of time."

"I still like how you say we," he murmured.

Imogen grinned like an idiot. "Yeah, well, I owe you a debt. You're just stuck with me and my disobedience, bad attitude, and clothes with holes in them until we are done."

Warm fingers stroked her cheek. "Oh, little human, you really don't have any self-preservation, do you? Saying such things to me will only make me keep you longer."

Imogen laughed. "I doubt it. You will tire of me soon enough, and..." Imogen's words were cut off by a press of lips against her cheek. Her hands found the curve of his shoulders, and he kissed the edge of her jaw.

"You really don't understand the danger you are in, darling," he whispered in her ear.

"I don't? I mean, I do? You're going to protect me, though?" she babbled, her heart beating too fast.

"From everything but me," Arawan promised and kissed her. Imogen's mouth moved against his, the same feral rush of lust from the forest overpowering her. Her panic while she had been thinking he had been hurt earlier that day blended with her emotions. Imogen tugged him closer, needing to feel him against her.

Arawan's tongue teased against her lips, and she opened for him, moaning at the feel of him invading her mouth.

Arawan's hand slipped around her side and pulled her up to him.

Imogen knew she should stop before things went further, but every one of his touches overwhelmed her. Arawan's hand trailed down her side, and her pussy throbbed, wanting that hand on her.

"Why do I need protecting from you?" Imogen asked breathlessly.

Arawan's teeth scraped against her lip. "Because I shouldn't be this fascinated by anything living. I shouldn't want anything to do with you. And when I look at you, all I feel is want."

Imogen moved against him, the husky purr of his words lighting her up. "What do you want?"

"To fight with you. To kiss you." Arawan's tongue brushed inside her mouth, and Imogen whimpered. "To taste you. To touch you."

"Then touch me," she said, hating how close to begging she sounded. She couldn't see his face in the darkness, but she heard his sharp intake of breath. He hadn't expected her to offer. He didn't hesitate for long. His hand moved to her full breasts, long fingers stroking her already hard nipples.

"Like this?" he whispered in her ear.

"Y-Yes," Imogen replied, groaning when his grip tightened. Arawan kissed her again, his tongue fucking slowly into her mouth.

"Where else do I have permission to touch you?" he asked, voice ragged.

"Fuck. Everywhere. Anywhere you want," Imogen replied. Her nails dragged down his back, and he hissed.

"And you wonder why you need protecting from me," Arawan laughed softly. Imogen jumped as his hand was suddenly cupping her pussy roughly. He palmed her in a slow, hard circle, and she whimpered in pleasurable agony.

"Oh, fuck. That feel's..." She thrust up into his hand, encouraging him to do it again.

Arawan licked and nipped up her neck before his other hand came around it, pinning her to the pillows. The dominance in it made Imogen's whole body shudder.

Arawan's fingers brushed over her slit, growling softly when he slid through her wetness. With one hand holding her down and one circling her clit, Imogen couldn't shift away from the mind-numbing pleasure that was beating against every one of her senses.

Arawan's mouth found hers, kissing her so deep and possessive she felt it with her whole body. Imogen was moaning, her pussy begging for release.

Imogen's grip on her shoulders tightened. "Put your fingers in me."

"Oh no, darling. The first thing I'm going to put into this tight pussy is my tongue, and then my cock."

"Fuck, do it then," she replied, her horny brain not caring how desperate she sounded.

"Not yet. I'm going to take my time to tease you first. You still don't understand what you've done to me," Arawan growled against her lips. "You might not feel it now, but I'm going to burrow so deeply inside of you that you're never going to be able to scratch me out of your skin. No matter how hard you try. No matter how far you run. It will always be my voice you hear whispering to you in the darkness..."

Imogen exploded. Her cry of release was a strangled moan under the pressure around her throat, her orgasm so powerful it felt like he was tearing something out of her. Wetness flooded over his hand as she came all over it, whispering his name like a prayer.

Arawan loosened his grip on her throat, his mouth kissing it tenderly. Imogen was thrumming from her release, unable to think or move. She was trying and failing to steady her heartbeat and ease her breathing. *What the fucking hell was that?*

Arawan kissed her gently. "Sleep now, darling. No more nightmares."

"No, don't go..." she tried to tighten her grip on him.

"Shh, I'm not going anywhere." Arawan's lips pressed to her forehead. "Sleep."

A heavy weight descended over her, and Imogen slipped into a deep slumber. She didn't have a single dream for the rest of the night.

14

Imogen made a point of never being awkward after a hook-up. The God of the dead had gotten her off in the dark; what was there to be awkward about?

Did she make sure her braid was straight and had a bit of makeup on the following day? Yes, but that was only because she wanted to make the most of her post-orgasm glow. It had nothing to do with wanting to look put together for once even though she had been covered in some kind of mud or blood for most of the time she knew Arawan.

Duncan had delivered her breakfast at ten a.m. on the dot and told her that when she was done eating, Arawan and Aisling wanted to meet with her and the princes. She set off a warning group message to her brothers, ate quickly, and went to find Arawan. The sooner she saw him, the sooner any awkwardness would get out of the way.

Fuck, you had one thing to do. Don't fuck Arawan.

Well, she hadn't precisely fucked him. Not yet anyway.

Imogen tried to push all her horny thoughts down into her mind vault because they wouldn't help in the meeting she was about to walk into.

Arawan and Aisling spoke softly in a small dining room lit with bright winter light.

"Good morning, Imogen. How did you sleep?" he asked innocently, eyes glittering with feral amusement.

"Like the dead, my lord," she replied with a sweet smile.

Aisling looked alarmed. "It's nice to see you two getting along better," she said cautiously.

"It took a few days, but I finally found a way to speak Imogen's language," Arawan replied. He gestured to a chair beside him. "Sit down."

Imogen wanted to take a different chair, but that might stir him up even more, and she really didn't need him outing her to her brothers. She sat down and took out her phone.

"Let's hope everyone is ready for us," she said, trying to hide the hitch in her voice. Arawan's hand slipped over her knee, and she almost dropped her phone.

Seriously?

Imogen cleared her throat and dialed Kian. Thankfully, her brother answered straight away.

"Sister, it is good to see you. Are you settling in well? I hope Aisling hasn't told you too many stories," Kian said, giving the sorceress a warning smile.

"Like the time Bayn trapped a wild boar in your tower? No, not at all?" the sorceress replied, making Imogen laugh. She knew that Elise would love Aisling and all the dirt she could dish on Kian.

Underneath the table, Arawan's finger curled into the shredded knee of her jeans to stroke against her bare skin. This wasn't what she expected to be dealing with in a meeting. Fuck. She really should've sat somewhere else.

Bayn and Killian joined the call, and soon they were all catching up with Aisling, too, Arawan and Imogen momentarily forgotten.

"You are glowing with good health this morning, little hunter," he whispered to her.

"Are you serious? We are on a call with my brothers right now," she growled back. "It's inappropriate."

His lips twitched in amusement. He leaned closer and whispered, "No, what would be inappropriate is me telling you how I stroked my cock last night while I licked the taste of you off my fingers."

Imogen turned bright red for the first time in years. She would throw her phone at his head if he didn't shut the fuck up.

"You okay, Gen? You look like you're choking on something," Bayn said.

"Only on Arawan's bullshit," Imogen replied, sounding too stressed out. Arawan went to say something, but she pinched his leg hard. "Okay, let's get this meeting started, shall we?"

"You tracked down the creatures that got through the wards?" Kian asked. Imogen did what she usually did in meetings and let other people talk. Arawan and Aisling were better at explaining the technical aspects of what had happened to the wards anyway.

Arawan still had his hand on her knee, and for all the ways she imagined their meeting going, that wasn't it. Had he really gotten off over her? Fuck, she didn't need that visual burned into her brain.

"Imogen has had an excellent idea of bringing my court together to have a party," Arawan said.

"Yeah, that was me. I remembered what you said, Kill, about courtiers being interested in the newcomers. We can use that to our advantage, see if anyone will spill something," Imogen replied.

"They will be trying to fuck you the whole night, so you better be ready for that too," Killian warned her.

Imogen winked at him. "So it's like every party I go to." Killian laughed with her, but Arawan's grip on her only tightened.

"I doubt you will have to go as far as sleeping with anyone, Imogen. People like to talk to you, and you only need to give them the opportunity," Bayn said. He frowned at Killian. "Don't give her any of your bad ideas."

"I was only going to suggest she carry her dagger and make sure the drinks are strong," Killian replied with mock outrage.

"Let us know how it goes. If there is a spy and more ghouls or horde creatures stationed around the United Kingdom, I want to know about it," Kian said, and they rang off.

"I'll start laying some extra wards in the guest rooms, so if anyone tries to do magic while they are here, we will know," Aisling said, bowing low to Arawan before she stepped out of the room.

"I have organized the gathering for tomorrow evening. We will have people arriving between now and then, so be on your guard and don't go wandering. It will be better to keep your presence as a surprise, and I can introduce you," Arawan said thoughtfully. Imogen got out of the chair, his hand finally letting her go. It was like she could finally think straight again.

"Introduce me as what? They will know I'm new," she said.

"I'll announce you as a liaison to the princes so they will think twice about disrespecting you. Or I could introduce you as my companion for the evening," Arawan replied, resting his chin in his hand. "It would keep the vultures well away from you."

"Just as a liaison, thanks. Can I bring a date?" she asked.

Arawan's eyes narrowed. "You need to be my eyes and ears at this party. You will have no time for a date."

Imogen huffed. "Doesn't sound like a fun party at all."

"Come with me as my companion, and I'll make it a night you never forget," he replied, voice full of promise that had her standing up straighter.

"Thanks, but no thanks. I'll pass."

Arawan let out a huff of irritation. "Why must you be so difficult?"

"Because you like it," she said with a sweet smile. "Also, if I turn up as your fucking date, no one will talk to me because they are going to think we are boning. Do you want to find out who the spy is or not? Now, if you'll excuse me, your godliness, I need to go and see about a dress."

"I can have one sent to your rooms if you want," he offered.

"I'm sure you could, but I got it covered."

Arawan gave her a long look that made her toes curl in her motorcycle boots. "You could wear your hunting gear for all I cared. I'd still want you by my side."

"Charming, but it's not going to happen. I have hunting to do, remember? I can't be good bait if I look like a big, scary hunter that will gut them any chance I get."

"Nothing too revealing. I will have a hard enough job keeping them off you as it is," Arawan complained.

Imogen threw him a sly wink. "Trust me. I know how to pick a party dress."

It was a total fucking lie. Imogen couldn't remember the last time she had worn a dress, let alone bought one. Luckily, she had backup.

Imogen waited until she was back in her room and had a locked door between her and Arawan before she rang Freya.

"I thought I would be hearing from you," Freya answered instantly. "What did I tell you about not fucking Arawan?"

"I haven't fucked him!"

"Imogen, Bayn said that Arawan was looking at you that whole meeting."

"And how is it my fault that I'm so attractive?"

Freya laughed. "What's going on? Really. Spit it out."

"I like him! Are you happy now?" Imogen huffed out. "I don't need any fucking attitude from you either. Out of everyone, you should understand what it's like being around a sexy immortal with a bulldozer of a personality."

Freya started laughing. "Oh, honey. You got a crush on a god. That's worse than a fae prince."

"Not from where I'm sitting. All immortals are fucking crazy." Imogen sat down on a window seat and looked at the snow falling. "I can't help it, okay? Don't bust my tits about it. I feel awkward enough."

"Okay, okay. No tit busting. I just want you to be careful and not your reckless self. Arawan isn't someone you can casually fuck and ghost the next day."

"I know. I'm trying not to think that far ahead." Imogen rested her head against the cool glass. Maybe she should put the whole crush down to sexy chemistry and leave it at that. She had been attracted to plenty of people she had walked away from.

"So what do you need? Come on, little sister, spit it out," Freya coaxed.

Imogen pulled a face. "I need…a dress. For this thing tomorrow night."

"Wow, a dress. You really do like him," Freya teased gently. "Tell me, what do you have in mind?"

Imogen thought for a moment. "Something that will fit my massive tits properly without tape but is so hot it will make every idiot in the room blab all their secrets to me."

Freya was giggling again, and it was so deviant that Imogen grinned. "I have the perfect dress. I'll have it couriered with supplies."

"Thanks, Freya, you're the best," Imogen replied.

"Yeah, I am. Make sure you are careful with Arawan too. You don't want to push him too far with all your flirting. He is a god after all."

Imogen laughed, thinking about his smutty whispering during the meeting. "Something tells me he can handle it."

15

Arawan was starting to think allowing all of his court back to the castle was the worst fucking idea. He had spent the whole day in meetings with various disgruntled parties, all clambering for his attention. It was tedious. And worse, he hadn't seen one purple hair of Imogen.

Arawan had asked her to stay hidden, and she had obeyed him for once. He hated it. He had hoped she would get bored, set his room on fire, cause a scene, something, *anything*. And there was nothing. It was intolerable.

Arawan knew she was still in the castle and on the grounds. He could feel the intensity of her living soul burning away like a bright light in his mind. He had been tempted to go to her like he had two nights ago.

Don't think of it, he chastised himself.

Fuck, it was the only thing he'd been thinking about. He had been taking himself in hand every night just imagining it. He was too old to be acting that way, but he couldn't stop.

If Arawan thought her screams were pretty, it was nothing compared to her moans and whimpers of pleasure. He wanted to fuck her until she went hoarse from making those maddening little sounds.

The ballroom glittered with the shades and wraiths that made up his court. He had told them that he wanted an event to celebrate his rising from his sleep, and they had believed it. If it wasn't for Morrigan summoning him, he would probably still be hidden in the darkness.

Arawan shifted on his throne uncomfortably. He never would've met Imogen if it wasn't for that meddlesome war witch. Maybe it was all for a purpose, a design he couldn't see. The world had changed so much. Perhaps, it had been time for him to rise. As beautiful as all the smiling creatures, fae and humans, in front of him were, he was so utterly bored.

And they are bold to try and betray me and think I'm oblivious to it.

They had all been at the castle since he had created it, which meant they had all had the chance to tamper with his warding and summon the creatures that attacked him. He would find them and then...

A susurrus of unease went through the crowd, and Arawan looked towards the double doors.

"May I present Lady Imogen of clan Ironwood, here representing the Blood Prince of the fae and his court," a herald called.

Arawan couldn't breathe as the lavender hair moved through the crowd. His hands gripped his cane hard enough to break it. Everyone finally got out of the way, and he got his first look at her.

Imogen had assured him she could get herself a dress, and fuck, she'd followed through with the threat. Shimmering black fabric clung to every sensuous curve, with a deep V-neck to show off the tops of her breasts and strong shoulders. Her lavender hair was curling over one shoulder with a black slide over one ear. Full plum-colored lips smiled at the faces in the crowd like she had done this a hundred times.

By the time Imogen made it to the throne, Arawan was so hard, his whole body hurt. What had happened to his dirty hunter? He noticed all the hungry glances on her and knew she was still hunting. The fools just didn't know it. This was his feral flower, showing a whole new set of hidden thorns. And he would make sure everyone knew that she was his.

Imogen came before him and bowed elegantly and low enough that he had a view straight down the front of her dress.

"Lord of Annwn, it is an honor and pleasure to be your guest this evening," Imogen purred, fluttering her long black lashes at him. He realized too late that he hadn't replied. He cleared his throat awkwardly.

"The pleasure is mine, Lady Ironwood. I hope you enjoy yourself, but please save a dance for me," Arawan managed to choke out. Imogen's smile only widened with glee that she had turned him into a speechless idiot. Fuck, she would never let him live it down.

"Find me whenever you wish to spin me around the dance floor, my lord," she said, bowing again and winking slyly at him.

It was the wink that sealed her fate. Arawan tried to steady himself as he watched her wide, delicious hips sway as she glided back into the crowd. He suddenly didn't care if they found Hafgan's spy or not. By the end of the night, he vowed that Imogen Ironwood would be his.

"My Lord Arawan, where have you been hiding that mortal?" a male's voice said, dragging his attention away from Imogen's ass.

One of his three under lords, Aeron, stood in front of him with a slight smile on his handsome face.

"I haven't been hiding anyone. Since I have been staying in the human realm, I felt it necessary to form some connections with the living courts," Arawan replied. It wasn't exactly a lie. He thought it very important to have Imogen stay within his eyesight at all times.

Fuck, he was so ruined over the girl. He wanted to hate it and found he couldn't do that either. Arawan would let her tread all over him and thank her for the privilege.

16

Imogen tried her best to fall into the role she was playing for the night, but goddamn, was it hard when Arawan looked...like that. He was in a black three-piece suit, his hair tied back at the nape of his neck to show off every stark, gorgeous inch of his face. The only color on him was an elegant ruby tie pin and the ruby topped cane that rested next to him.

He sat on a high back black throne on a dais with a table in front of him, piled high with food and wine that looked untouched. From his high vantage point, he could look down his nose at everyone dancing, drinking, and conspiring.

His dark eyes had devoured her, and it had taken all of Imogen's self-control not to say something downright scandalous. She wanted to be scandalized all over him on that throne. She wanted to get on her knees in front of him and go down on him like the king he was. He was simply devastating, and she knew whatever happened between them, she was already ruined.

As if she wasn't already obsessed with him. Imogen had developed a goth boy obsession from meeting him once; she would be beyond repair by the time she left the deal with him. Her stomach clenched horribly at the thought.

You're just hungry and nervous. It's all it is, she reassured herself. The dress that Freya had sent her was intimidating to look at, but as soon as she slipped it on, Imogen felt like a queen. Freya knew her well enough not to send stilettos. Instead, Imogen was wearing knee-high velvet boots. They were the kind of boots that would look great slung over Arawan's broad, pale shoulders.

Imogen grabbed a glass of ruby-red wine from a servant and had a large mouthful. She needed to get her head back in the game.

Everyone in the room was looking at her and pretending they weren't. Good. I meant that whoever she talked to would have people wanting to compete with them and seek her out.

"Lady Imogen, what an unexpected pleasure to see one of the living at this event," a tall fae said, moving in front of her and bowing low. He had curling red hair and piercing green eyes. Beauty and masculinity all rolled into one in a way that only the fae could pull off. "I'm Owain, one of Arawan's lords."

"My lord," Imogen replied with a smile. The fae pressed a kiss to her hand, and she tried not to giggle. "It's nice to meet you."

"I have not had the pleasure of speaking with the living for a long time. Arawan has woken from his sleep in the most usual of moods," Owain said, looking her over. "Although, you are a welcome addition to the proceedings."

"I'm glad you think so. I must say I was surprised when Arawan came to the fae court and asked me to be a liaison. It's an honor to be serving him however I can, wouldn't you agree?" she asked. There was the slightest shift in Owain's expression before it disappeared under the intensity of his smile.

"Indeed. I'd be interested to know exactly how you are serving him," he replied with a touch of innuendo.

What a perve. It didn't surprise her. It was usually the most entitled assholes that would bail up a woman before anyone else could. To the people around her and the lord in front of her, she was fresh meat.

"Lady Ironwood is helping me coordinate our efforts to find Hafgan in the human world," Arawan said from behind her. She felt the slightest brush of fingers on her lower back as he moved to join them.

"How wonderful. What a great opportunity to connect to my fae brethren," Owain replied, a wall instantly going up in his green eyes. "My lady, allow me to go and fetch you another drink."

"Thank you, Owain, that would be lovely," Imogen said, smiling at him.

Arawan moved a little closer to her. "I see you are wasting no time bringing the males in my court to their knees."

"You mean where males belong?" Imogen said sweetly. "Do you like my dress?"

Arawan's gaze darkened. To anyone else, he might have seemed furious, but Imogen had seen him horny and knew the difference.

"Yes," he said through gritted teeth. "I do like the dress."

"What about my boots?" Imogen moved the slit of her dress to show him.

"Why are you like this?" he complained.

Imogen's answering laughter died on her lips as a woman's graceful arm trailed over Arawan's shoulder. The dark-haired beauty was dressed in a revealing red dress that showed her slim form. Red eyes looked Imogen over like she was prey.

"Sorry I'm late, my lord. Who is the fat breather?" the woman asked, continuing to appraise Imogen with a sneer.

Imogen's lip curled. She knew who she was in a way the woman in front of her couldn't imagine. She was scars and cellulite, ripped jeans and attitude, and she had long stopped giving two fucks about anyone's opinion about her.

She had put on a fucking *dress* that night. She looked hot as shit, and she wasn't going to put up with anyone trying to make her feel otherwise.

Imogen glanced at Arawan, a silent plea that clearly said, *"Please let me go get my battle-ax, and I'll show her exactly who I am.*

Arawan's lips twitched in a reply, *We need her to get information about Hafgan...then you may kill her.*

"I'm Imogen. It's *so* nice to meet you. What's your name?" she asked enthusiastically. She plucked the woman's hand off Arawan's shoulder and gave it a vigorous shake that made the woman stumble slightly in her shoes.

"I'm Caitrin," she said, now confused.

"Awesome. You want to be my new friend? I'm new around here and would love..."

"If you'll excuse me," Caitrin said and quickly walked away. Arawan covered his laughter with a cough.

"Wow, she seems nice," Imogen commented.

Arawan's mouth twitched again. "She's a wraith. They are all like that. You probably made an enemy for life with that display."

"I'll add her to my growing list." Imogen allowed herself a moment to just look at him.

"What's wrong?"

"Nothing at all. Now, you really need to fuck off and let me get to work," Imogen said.

"Are you trying to tell me what to do?"

"Yes, because you will ruin this plan if you hover over me all night."

Arawan lifted his glass to his lips. "You didn't seem to mind me hovering all over you the other night."

Imogen went hot all over. She wouldn't give him the satisfaction of showing him how he affected her. "Hmm, you've been thinking about that ever since, haven't you?"

"Perhaps," he replied, leaning closer. Imogen had to get away, or she would be the one ruining their plans. She wasn't going to be the only one flustered if she had anything to do about it.

"In that case, I'll give you something new to think about." Imogen looked around before whispering conspiratorially. "This dress you like so much? I couldn't wear underwear with it."

While Arawan looked like his brain was short-circuiting, Imogen slipped back into the crowd.

She was sure Caitrin would be hovering about, ready to swoop back in to keep him company. Imogen tried not to let the proprietary way the wraith had touched Arawan get to her.

She wouldn't be able to feel him up quite so well if she had a broken hand.

With that thought warming her, Imogen worked the crowd. She had learned many awesome skills over the years, and pickpocketing was a favorite.

While Imogen laughed and flirted with every courtier that crossed her path, she searched pockets, stealing notes and small trinkets easily. She learned many things, and within an hour, she knew who was sleeping with whom, which wife hated what lord, and how they all longed to see more of the modern times if Arawan would allow it.

"Lady Ironwood, I seemed to have lost you in all of the excitement," Owain said, appearing from behind one of the nearest pillars.

"I wondered where you had gotten to. I apologize for not waiting for you. I just had so many new friends to make," Imogen replied. Owain passed her a glass of wine, but she nursed it without drinking. There was something about him that made her hunter instincts twitch.

"New friends is one way of describing them," Owain said, looking about the room. "These parties are all the same. Inane chatter, the same scandals, the same old nonsense. At least when Arawan was sleeping, we could do more with our time than dance to his will."

Is that so? I wonder what you were doing unsupervised, Imogen mused. He was clearly comfortable in his authority to bitch about Arawan to a stranger.

"Now, that sounds like a male jaded by the times. You have a great opportunity to glimpse into the human realm again. Things have changed so much. I doubt you would be very jaded for long," Imogen replied, trying her best to sound enthusiastic.

Owain looked her over slowly. "You know, you are the best thing about this castle. How lucky for Lord Arawan to have you so close and willing to do his bidding."

Imogen looked up at him from under her lashes. "I'm here to foster good relations between our courts and serve any way I can."

Owain's expression heated. He took her hand and kissed her wrist. "Is that right? Perhaps you could come to my suite in the southern tower later, and we can discuss that further."

"This castle has so many suites. How will I know which one is yours?" Imogen asked, biting her bottom lip.

"There is a painting of the Wild Hunt hanging beside the door. You can't miss it," Owain replied.

Imogen placed a hand on his chest and leaned in closer. "How about I go and powder my nose, and when I come back, we can have a dance? You can tell a lot by how a male dances if he's going to be good at other...sports."

Owain smirked. "Is that a fact? In that case, you had better hurry back so I can start to convince you of my prowess, and if my dancing doesn't convince you, maybe the size of my cock will."

Imogen giggled like a scandalized virgin and stepped away from him. "I'll find you soon, my lord."

She slipped out the doors and past the guards. Duncan would never give her the key to a guest's room, so she would just have to do things the Ironwood way.

Imogen had no problem finding which rooms were Owain's. Even if he was forward as hell, the lord was charming enough, but she couldn't dismiss the niggling feeling in her hunter's gut. Her instincts were flashing big red flags at her, and she had learned the hard way to never overlook a red flag.

Imogen checked that the hall was clear before she pulled two picks out of the small clutch hanging from her wrist. It also held lipstick and Bayn's charmed knife, which was everything Imogen needed. There was no way she would step into a snake pit without a weapon on her.

Using the picks, Imogen made quick work of the lock and stepped inside Owain's suite. Growing up in a house of female hunters, Imogen had become an expert in hiding spots. She checked the obvious places, in the drawers of clothing, behind paintings, and tucked into bathroom cupboards.

"Come on, Owain, where are you hiding your dirty little secrets?" Imogen murmured to herself. Then she remembered some of Layla's elite hiding places. Of all the Ironwood sisters, Layla was always the sneakiest because she could play the most innocent. She was also incredibly good at keeping all of her treasures away from her too curious sisters.

Imogen crossed the room and checked the mattress on the bed. There was no tampering and nothing tucked under the bed itself. Imogen lay back on the pillow and something pressed into her neck.

"Sneaky son of a bitch," she laughed, sitting up again. She pulled the pillow out of its case and found a small hole in the stitching. She stuck a finger inside it and dug about in the feathers until she found something cold and smooth. It was a piece of quartz the size of her thumb and carved with runes she had never seen before. It pulsed softly in her hand like a tiny heart. *Magic.*

"I don't know what you are, but I'm sure Arawan will."

It could be something innocent like a charm to help him sleep at night, but she really fucking doubted it.

17

Imogen rejoined the party downstairs, disappearing into the crowd as seamlessly as she had left it. Arawan was back on his throne and looked bored. Well, she was more than ready to spice up his evening.

She wove her way through the press of people, carefully avoiding Owain until she was before Arawan's high table. Interest sparked in his eyes, and a warm feeling bloomed in her chest. She liked that she could have that effect on him, even if for a moment.

"My lord, might I be so bold as to have that dance you offered?" Imogen asked politely. Arawan frowned a little as if sensing something was off about her.

"I could never deny such a beautiful woman anything," he said, stepping down from his throne and taking her hand. He led her to the dance floor and pulled her close.

"Is something the matter?" he asked.

"Just smile and dance with me. People are watching," Imogen replied. He led her out into a waltz.

Kenna had insisted on all of them having dance classes growing up, and Imogen found her feet after a few turns.

"And how are you enjoying your evening, darling?" he asked.

"I can see why you asked them all to stay in Annwn," she replied, and he laughed.

"Are you that bored already?"

Imogen smiled up at him. "You know me, I'm not exactly pretty court lady material. Having to play one is exhausting."

Arawan spun her and brought her close. "And have you found anything interesting on your rounds tonight? I have watched your hands all over people, and I'm not impressed."

"I was hunting for information," Imogen replied. He had been watching her that closely?

"I hope you have found something worth keeping my temper all night." Arawan's hand on her lower back flexed, and she leaned closer to him.

"And you think I enjoyed watching Caitrin rub her skinny ass all over you?" Imogen huffed before she could check herself.

"Was my little flower jealous?" he purred in her ear.

"I don't know about jealous...more like murderous," she admitted.

Arawan chuckled softly. "Good. I like you murderous, as well as jealous."

"Don't tease me about it, or I'll teach this whole court the Macarena to torture you with for all eternity," she threatened him.

"And what is that?"

"Only the most infernally irritating dance ever created. You will be cursing my name for the rest of your existence," Imogen replied, unable to keep in her mischievous snicker.

Arawan grinned. "No teasing. I promise. What else have you found out?"

"Pull me closer and act like I'm whispering something dirty in your ear," Imogen said.

"I don't think I can. You might need to give me some inspiration," Arawan replied, twisting her out and pulling her close so her back was to his chest.

Imogen knew it was probably a bad idea, but she loved those more than any other kind. "How about I tell you how hot you look sitting on that big throne. Did you build it big enough for two on purpose?"

Arawan's pupils dilated. "Why? Would you like to get on it with me?"

"Maybe," she said before he spun her back to face him. Arawan enclosed her in his warmth and sexy cologne, and Imogen slipped the stone she found into the small pocket of his waistcoat.

"I found this in Lord Owain's suite," she whispered.

Arawan's grip tightened on her. "And what the fuck were you doing in his suite?"

"Calm down, or people will notice," Imogen warned him. "And if you must know, I broke into his suite after he make a snide remark about you. I don't know what the stone is, but I didn't like the feel of it."

She looked up into his deep black eyes. "I wasn't in there with him or because I'm interested in him. The only person here that I'm interested in touching me is you."

Some of the anger seeped out of Arawan's expression. "Good, because if anyone but me touches you, I will cut their hands off."

"I will cut them before you even know about it," Imogen snorted.

Arawan brushed his lips over the top of her ear. "It's always a competition with you, my violent little flower."

"Stop pretending you don't love that about me," Imogen replied with a grin.

Arawan's eyes slipped over her shoulder, and his smile froze. Owain joined them, oozing charm.

"My lord, would you mind if I stole your lovely liaison? The lady owed me a dance," he said, looking possessively at Imogen.

The air around them charged like right before lightning struck. The hair on the back of Imogen's neck and arms rose. She stepped out of Arawan's embrace, feeling his power building dangerously.

"Of course you can dance with Imogen, Owain," he said, his voice dropping even deeper in his anger. "As soon as you explain this to me."

Arawan opened his palm where the rune-carved crystal sat. Imogen and the rest of the courtiers backed away from the two men, locked in a stare-off. Owain looked at the crystal, fury etched across his face.

Arawan didn't wait for an explanation as magic crackled in the air and the crystal glowed, the runes activating.

"The warding will need to be disabled in order to let my warriors through into the Undying Lands. You will need to find a sheltered area to create the correct summoning portal..." a stranger's voice filled the air.

Imogen's pulse raced, and adrenaline spiked, trying to warn her of the danger. Arawan's face was twisted in disgust as the stranger continued to give instructions to the horrified court.

Owain snarled and snatched the crystal back. "What the fuck did you expect? You disappeared for *centuries,* leaving us to govern Annwn alone. You abandoned us, and you can't expect to return and have everything be the same!" he shouted at Arawan.

"And you think Hafgan would be a better king? Is that it?" Arawan asked, voice whisper soft. "I allowed you to govern, *trusted* you to serve me faithfully. And this is how you repay me? You let fucking Hafgan give you orders that would put us all at risk?"

Owain hissed and pointed at Imogen. "Not us. The only person at risk is the human whore you chose to bring here!"

Arawan moved so quickly that Imogen could barely track him. He pulled a blade from his cane and cut off Owain's hand in one swift stroke. The lord screamed, the pain and shock driving him to his knees. Not a single courtier moved to save him.

Imogen didn't even know that a shade could be hurt like a human, but whatever Arawan's blade was made from clearly could do damage the same way.

"That is for calling her a whore," Arawan snarled softly. With two quick flicks of the blade, Arawan blinded a screaming Owain. "And that was for coveting what is mine. Guards! Take his fucking traitor to the cells." Three guards in black armor appeared and dragged a sobbing Owain away.

All the courtiers were frozen, too afraid to move. Arawan's power whipped around the room.

"The party is over! All of you get the fuck out!" he shouted, his voice reverberating around them and making the castle shake. The courtiers fled, not a single one daring to linger. Imogen was heading for a door, but it slammed before she got through it. "Not you, Imogen Ironwood. You stay where you fucking are."

Imogen's whole body stilled like her monkey brain knew that running would only make the predator in the room chase her down.

Every door slammed and locked one after the other until only Imogen remained with a furious god of the dead.

Imogen had never been afraid of Arawan. Standing on the other side of the dance floor, the god had removed any mask of humanity or civility. Power boiled in his black eyes, terrifying, merciless violence and fury burning right through her.

Imogen should've been afraid of him when he first noticed her in Dublin. She should've never risked getting his attention again. She should bow, prostrate herself in front of this ancient being that was so far beyond her comprehension that she shouldn't dare to look at him. She should've done everything she could to run away from the storm before her, not try and approach it.

Imogen had never been good at doing what she *should*. She always did what she wanted, and at that moment, all she wanted was him.

Imogen strode across the dance floor as if she owned it and launched herself into his arms. Arawan caught her, hauling her up and kissing her. Imogen tore the tie from his hair, and all of its glossy night spilled over into her hands.

Arawan carried her over to the high table, his power sending everything to the ground. He placed Imogen down on it in front of his black throne.

"So beautiful, my dangerous flower," he murmured, pulling back from her. He looked down at her, his eyes gleaming with ruby red power. "I'm going to enjoy taking you apart." Imogen grabbed him by his tie and pulled him between her thighs.

"I only wore this fucking dress in the hopes you would want to tear it off me," she snarled, dragging him back to her mouth. Imogen's sharp teeth closed over his bottom lip, making him hiss.

"Last chance to walk away, darling," Arawan said, his hand resting over the bare skin of her chest. Her heart pounded hard enough that he had to feel it, to know what he did to her.

"Is that what everyone else has done? Walk away when you lost your temper or became too much for them? I'm not them, Arawan," Imogen snapped. Her boot came up between them, and she kicked him back into his throne. His eyes glowed in feral hunger, hands gripping the arms of the throne like he would tear them off.

Oh, he was wild now, and she loved that she had made him that way. She couldn't stop, her own instincts to push back overriding her.

"You don't frighten me, God of the dead, so snarl and growl as much as you want. Fuck me if you're going to or fuck off and leave me alone!" she shouted.

Arawan's hands grabbed her thighs hard and dragged her ass to the table's edge. Dark ribbons of power tied around her legs and tightened around the arms of the throne. Imogen refused to give him the satisfaction of struggling.

Arawan's lips curled into a snarl as he stood between her thighs. "You have destroyed the last of my patience, woman. You aren't fucking going anywhere until I command it."

Arawan's hand gripped the front of her dress, and he shoved her back on the table. Imogen gasped as he took the edge of the skirt and tore it clean up the middle, exposing her bare pussy to him.

"So you weren't lying about wearing no underwear," he growled, staring down at her, mesmerized.

"I've never lied to you," Imogen said, her voice shaky.

"I didn't lie to you either." Arawan's fingers trailed up one bare thigh. "Do you remember what I told you in the darkness? When I come inside of you for the first time, it'll be my tongue and then my cock?"

Fuck, Imogen could barely stand to look at him, let alone reply. He was a beautiful monster, and he was staring at her like a starving wolf stared at a lost lamb.

His sharp smile was his only warning before his mouth dropped between her thighs and devoured her. Imogen's leg strained against the bonds, but they held her in place. Arawan's strong hand grabbed her by one breast, pinning her to the table with his powerful strength.

Imogen couldn't hold in the sounds being torn from her. His tongue circled the tiny nub of her clit, and her hips lifted clean off the table. Arawan's hand went underneath her, gripping her ass tight and holding her hips so she couldn't pull back from his ravaging mouth. His tongue thrust inside of her, and she cried out.

Imogen felt out of control and entirely at his mercy. And he was nothing if not fucking merciless. He didn't stop eating her, didn't give her a moment to catch her breath. When she was about to lose her mind, her orgasm slammed into her, sending bright lights sparking in her vision.

Arawan's tongue dipped back into her, lapping at her cum and sending her spiraling. Her inner walls clenched around his tongue, and he hummed in pleasure against her.

"Fucking gorgeous," he murmured, looking at her swollen, glistening flesh.

Imogen felt the bonds around her legs loosen half a second before he picked her up and flipped her over. He tore the rest of her dress away before his leg went between hers, kicking them out wider.

Arawan's hand stroked over the curve of her ass before gliding up her spine. His fingers gripped her hair, bunching it in his hand and pulling her head back. He kissed her, his tongue pushing against hers.

"Now, this is the only feast I wanted tonight," he growled, staring at her naked body. "Fuck, you are beautiful like this, my flower. Naked, needy, and ready for my cock. You are even more perfect than I imagined you would be."

Imogen pushed back against him and groaned when she felt his bare skin against her. She didn't know when he got naked and didn't care. She wanted to feel his strong body pressed tight against her.

"Tell me that you want me," Arawan commanded, his voice like dark magic in her ear. Imogen groaned in frustration, her whole body aching for him and oversensitive like an exposed nerve.

"I want you. Fuck, I've wanted you since the first second I saw you. I have tried to want anyone and anything else since, but it's all fucking useless because it's always been you!" she shouted her confession, furious at him for ruining her for all others.

Arawan kissed her cheek; his laugh was infuriating and triumphant. "Good," he whispered and thrust the head of his dick inside of her.

Imogen moaned, trying to shift to push him in further, but he held her tight, easing his way inside her inch by glorious inch. When he was fully seated inside her, he kissed her bare shoulders and held her to him.

"Fuck, you are so tight I could come right now," he groaned.

"Don't you dare," she threatened, making him laugh.

Arawan nipped her neck. "Never fear, darling. I will make sure you enjoy yourself before I fill this sweet cunt."

Imogen went to sass him again, but he pulled back and thrust so hard into her, the air left her lungs. He was so fucking big that she felt him hit her limit with every firm glide.

She tried to use the table for leverage, her nails scoring the wood as she tried to find purchase. The edge was digging into her hips, but she didn't care. Nothing should feel this good. She was almost weeping; she was so blissed out. Arawan shifted, dragging her off the table and into his lap.

"You did say this throne was meant for two," he said, his teeth closing over her earlobe. He spread her, dragging each leg over the arms of the throne. She felt so exposed and decadent and loved every second of it.

Arawan's hand moved down to stroke where they were joined before circling her clit. His other hand cupped her breast. Imogen tipped her face to the side so she could catch his lips in a biting, demanding kiss. He pinched her nipple hard enough to make her groan. His hips rose up, his cock rocking deeper into her.

"Go on, little hunter, make me feel like a king," he growled in challenge.

Imogen *loved* a challenge. She rolled her hips in a slow circle, making a curse escape his lips. That was all the encouragement she needed. She was beyond caring, beyond any kind of self-consciousness or self-preservation. She rode his cock like it was the cure for everything that ailed her.

Arawan growled something in Ancient Welsh and held her tight to him to keep her from sliding too far away. His fingers looped around her aching clit with every hard thrust of his dick.

When Imogen's orgasm hit her, she screamed his name like a curse. Arawan lifted her up and dumped her on the table onto her back. He dragged her heel boots over his shoulders and slammed back into her.

Imogen clutched at her breasts to keep them from bouncing. Arawan leaned over her to kiss her, groaning into her mouth as he came hard inside her.

Imogen's hands shook as she brushed them through his sweat-damp hair. He was staring at her in awe that she had never seen before. She looked at her boots wrapped around him and stifled a grin.

"What?" he asked, smiling back at her.

"I always knew these boots would match your shoulders, that's all," she admitted.

"Deviant woman," he mocked and kissed her velvet-clad ankle before lowering her feet down. She squeaked in surprise as he pulled her upright and slung her over his shoulder.

"You better not be planning to carry me bare ass through your damn castle," she warned him.

"And how exactly would you stop me, darling?" he asked, thoroughly amused. Dark shadows and magic covered them, and suddenly they were in a bedchamber. Arawan placed her on the edge of a bed and unzipped her boots, tugging them off one at a time.

"Stay there," he said, lifting her chin and kissing her once. Imogen tried to pull him down on top of her, but he laughed softly. "I'm not going anywhere, and neither are you."

He released her and disappeared into a bathroom, giving her an excellent view of his lean muscular back and goddamn perfect ass.

Totally tapped that, Imogen thought and giggled like a cum drunk fiend. The water turned on in the bathroom, and she realized he was filling the deep tub. Arawan appeared again, leaning against the door.

Imogen didn't have words for how good he looked, all mussed. A delighted male smile crept over his face.

"What?" she asked, patting at her messy nest of hair.

"You look like you've been fucked hard and well," he replied.

Imogen flopped back on the bed. "My memory is hazy. You might have to do it again to remind me how good it was."

Arawan lay down on top of her, pinning her hands above her head. "Oh, I'll definitely be fucking you again. Unfortunately, I have to go and deal with Owain first. If I leave it until tomorrow, it gives him too much time to bribe guards and any supporters of his to try and help him escape."

Imogen tucked his hair behind his ear. "If you're going to torture him, start with his dick."

"Brutal." Arawan frowned. "Why?"

"Because he seemed really proud when he told me all about his prowess," she replied. "He struck me as someone who wouldn't take no for an answer."

"I see," he said, eyes narrowing dangerously. "Would you like to join me?"

Imogen kissed the tip of his nose. "No, thanks. I've never been much interested in fighting anything that can't fight back."

"Stay here until I return. If Owain does have supporters in the castle, I want you to be safe. Have a bath and relax. I'll be back soon," Arawan said and started to rise.

Imogen's legs locked around his hips. "That's not how you leave after my magnificent pussy just blew your brains out."

Arawan laughed and kissed her so thoroughly that she started to grind up against him, already turned on enough to fuck him senseless again.

"That's better," she said breathlessly. She gave his ass a pat. "Now go torture me a courtier, you gorgeous fuck."

Arawan shook his head at her. "We really need to do something about how filthy your mouth is," he said, pulling himself upright.

Imogen put her hands behind her head and smiled up at him. "Trust me, your godliness, when the time comes, you will love how filthy this mouth can get."

18

Imogen woke the following day wrapped in a thick black velvet comforter. She was also alone. Unease curled in her stomach. She didn't think Arawan was the kiss and avoid kind of guy, but clearly, she was wrong.

Time to leave while you still have some dignity, Ironwood, she told herself sternly and got out of bed.

She didn't know what had happened to the scraps of fabric that remained of her dress, so she grabbed one of Arawan's black shirts.

Making sure the hall outside the room was empty, Imogen walked quickly back to her own suite. It wasn't a moment too soon because she had only managed to get a robe wrapped around herself when Duncan arrived with her breakfast.

"My lady, I'm surprised to see you awake after last night's festivities," he said, placing the tray down.

"I was hungry. Thanks, Duncan," she said with a smile and shut the door.

Fuck, that was close. Imogen poured herself a coffee and checked her phone. She had three messages waiting from Freya. She dialed her number and waited.

"Good morning!" Freya answered brightly.

"Woah, why are you shouting at me?" Imogen grumbled.

"I wanted to let you know that Bayn and I are staying at Wrexham," Freya said, her voice dropping to a normal volume.

"You're in Wales? Why?"

"You sound guilty. What did *you* get up to last night, Imogen Ironwood?"

Had my last brain cell fucked out?

Imogen cleared her throat. "I found a spy of Hafgan's and watched Arawan eye gouge him," she replied.

"Gross. And this was at a party? What is wrong with immortals?" Freya said and, after a beat, added. "Did he like the dress?"

"Ah, yeah. Thank you. And for all the other stuff you sent."

Freya made a concerned humming sound. "You sound weird still. Are you okay?"

No. I'm catching feelings, and it's freaking me the fuck out.

"No, I'm not okay, but I can't talk about it here. Wrexham is only an hour away. How about I meet you somewhere? I need to get out of here for a bit," Imogen replied. She needed her bike and the cold air to blast out all the weirdness that was suddenly sitting heavy in her chest.

"Of course I can meet you. I'll text you a location. Drive safe, okay?" Freya said.

"Will do. I'll see you before lunch." Imogen hung up and hurried to get ready. A ride was exactly what she needed.

Imogen dressed in her warmer leather riding gear, braided her hair, and tucked Bayn's knife into her boot. Feeling more like herself and less like a stressed-out girl, she headed downstairs.

The rest of the court must have been sleeping off their night of revelry because the halls were all empty except for Arawan's usual warriors. It wasn't until Imogen was almost at the bottom of the main staircase when she spotted Caitrin leaning against the banister.

"Morning!" Imogen greeted, walking past her.

"What are you doing here?" Caitrin said, bringing Imogen up short.

"What do you mean?"

"I mean, what use would Arawan have with a living, breathing girl? You are not a courtier even if you dressed like one last night." Caitrin looked her over, her beautiful face twisting in disgust. "You aren't really his whore like Owain claimed, are you?"

Imogen swallowed the urge to smack her in her pretty face. "What business is that of yours?"

"It would be a disgrace for Lord Arawan to lower himself to fuck a human like you. You are shit beneath his shoes, yet he dismissed everyone but you last night, and I want to know why! What did you do to get him to turn on Owain?" Caitrin demanded, poking Imogen hard in the shoulder.

That did it. Imogen knocked her hand away, slammed her up against the stone railing, and pressed her knife to her throat.

"You want to know who I am, bitch? You're right. I'm not a fucking courtier. I am from the greatest hunting clan, living or dead, and if you poke me, call me a whore, or otherwise say anything I don't like again, I'll slit your fucking throat," Imogen snarled in her face. "As for Owain, you heard his orders from Hafgan. He betrayed Arawan and deserves everything he gets. If I were you, I'd stop with your mean girl bullshit and focus on the war coming."

Caitrin's eyes were wide with fear as Imogen shoved her away.

Imogen shouldered the front doors open and took a breath of cold air. Two warriors had seen the whole exchange and had wisely not interfered.

"Keep an eye on her. I don't like how she overlooked Owain's betrayal," Imogen told them. "And make sure she stays the fuck away from Arawan."

"Yes, Lady Ironwood," they replied with small bows.

Imogen nodded and headed to the stables, where she had garaged her bike. She needed to get the fuck out of there.

It wasn't until she was roaring through Arawan's wards that she thought that maybe she should have left him a note telling him where she had gone.

Fuck it. It wasn't like he had hung around after their night together. Imogen had curled up in his bed after her bath and had fallen asleep waiting for him. Whatever was going on, he hadn't returned to tell her about it and had slept somewhere else.

This was precisely why she didn't fuck people she had any feelings for. She might not be able to quantify *what* she was feeling for Arawan, but it was definitely something.

Imogen opened up her bike's throttle and let the engine's roaring drown out all her thoughts.

It was a little over an hour ride from the castle to Wrexham. After spending days living with Arawan, it was almost jarring to be back in the modern world with all of the cars, people and noise. She suddenly wanted to find a pub and get roaring drunk.

Imogen spotted Freya sitting in the window seat of a warm, cozy-looking cafe and had never been so pleased to see a familiar face.

Freya's smile lit up when she stepped through the door and hurried over to give her a hug. Imogen wasn't super touchy-feely, but she hugged Freya back hard.

"Hey, hey, what's wrong? What's happened?" Freya said when Imogen still hadn't let her go.

"I'm fine. It's just really good to see you. It makes me feel grounded," Imogen admitted, and they sat down at their wooden table.

It was a cute and kitschy cafe with warm wood furniture, a roaring fire, and pretty landscape paintings on the wall. It was the kind of spot that tourists would squeal at and put photos on their Instagram.

"I hope the food here is good. I could eat a fucking horse," Imogen said, grabbing one of the menus. "Where's Bayn?"

"Who knows? I told him you sounded like you needed some girl time."

"Good call. I've had my fill of moody immortals. What are you guys doing here anyway?"

Freya rested her chin on her hand and stared across the table at her. "He's worried about you. We all are. He wanted to be close in case something went sideways."

"He's such an old woman, but shit did go down last night," Imogen said and stopped talking as a waitress came to take their orders. She had only drunk coffee all morning, and her stomach growled angrily at her. Maybe she just needed some food to settle her down.

"Don't leave a girl hanging. What happened at the ball? Did you find out who is working for Hafgan?" Freya pressed as soon as they were alone again. Imogen caught her up on her hunting efforts and outing Owain to Arawan. Their food arrived, and Imogen all but fell on her eggs and bacon.

"He's probably still in Arawan's dungeons spilling his guts literally and figuratively," Imogen said, cradling her coffee mug in her hand.

"It's a horrible business, but it needs to be done if he's got his own people working against him," Freya replied. She gave Imogen a long look. "What happened with you and Arawan? I know some courtier getting tortured isn't enough to get you, so..."

"So what, Freya?" Imogen asked, her temper rising.

"Emotional." Freya let out a sigh. "Gen, seriously. Tell me what happened that has upset you?"

"I fucked him, okay? Is that what you want to know? I fucked him, and he left after and didn't come back, and I'm furious with myself because I actually like the fucking fucker!" Imogen snapped, making people at the next table stop talking.

"Oh," Freya said, stirring her cappuccino. "You're freaking out because you have feelings. You should have just said so earlier so I didn't poke you."

"I don't know what to do. I don't like feeling this way."

"What way?"

Imogen reached for more bacon. "Out of control."

Freya laughed softly. "Yeah, I definitely know what you mean. These immortals know how to fuck with a girl's thinking, that's for sure. You were dumb enough to fall for a god, so you can't expect him to act like any other man you've ever met."

"I don't usually stick around long enough to get feelings. I can't escape my agreement with him, so I can't ghost him. Now that we have fucked, he might lose this weird curiosity he has with me and let me go," Imogen replied. She didn't like that idea much either. What was wrong with her? She wanted him to let her out of their bargain, didn't she? She was so confused.

"You need to go back and actually talk to him, you know that, right?" Freya said gently. "You literally can't run from him. You don't know why he didn't return to you last night. He said he was going to interrogate Owain? Maybe he was still in the dungeons. You just don't know, Gen."

"Yeah, I know. I just needed to get out, remind myself that his world isn't...my world. Eventually, he'll go back to Annwn, so it really doesn't matter what feelings I have."

Freya reached across the table and patted her hand. "Arawan has never lived in the human world before, but he's doing it now, and I think we both know Hafgan isn't the only reason. You two have a connection, and such a thing is so rare, Imogen."

"I know," she groaned. "But I'm an Ironwood, Freya. We don't do feelings. We go and get a tattoo and move the fuck on."

Freya rolled her eyes. "Then maybe you should hold off on the tattoo this time and allow yourself to be vulnerable for once."

"Yeah, not going to happen," Imogen said with a shake of her head.

"Whatever you have to say to convince yourself that it's not a good idea. I hope the sex was worth all of this drama."

"Yeah, it was." Imogen was grinning before she could stop. "Want details?"

Freya's laugh was big and bawdy. "What do you think?"

～

IMOGEN ENDED up spending most of the day with Freya. She didn't really have female friends outside of her sisters, and she didn't realize how much she needed to talk to someone like Freya. She had been faced with an impossible romance too, and somehow, she had made it work with Bayn.

Fuck, if Bron could end up happy with a fae, there was hope that Imogen could figure out whatever the fuck was going on with her and Arawan.

Aren't you jumping ahead of yourself? She was and couldn't stop.

She didn't have a word for what was between them. It wasn't something as simple as a crush. She couldn't get enough, which was the complete opposite of every one of her interactions with the opposite sex. She enjoyed men and then lost interest. Something told her she could fight with Arawan for the next thousand years and not get bored.

A few decent orgasms and you're pathetic, Ironwood, Imogen lectured herself. She had been having so many fake arguments in her head that, at first, she didn't notice the dark mist stretching out over Snowdonia.

A cold, creeping feeling of the dead slithered along her skin, and she slowed the bike down. She had to be getting close to Arawan's borders. Had she missed a turn?

The wards closed around her, and she felt the spiky snap of them over her skin. The castle was shrouded entirely in a black gloom.

Imogen didn't bother to take her bike to the stables. If they were under attack, there was no time. She leaped off the bike, grabbed her ax from her saddlebag, and ran to find Arawan.

19

Imogen was gone. Arawan was both furious and devastated. He had left her to sleep the night before, not wanting to disturb her. He had been too agitated from his interrogation of Owain and had gone up into his private library. He had fallen asleep in the chair, a book still open on his lap.

When Arawan woke and checked on Imogen again, there was no sign of her. Confused that she would just disappear, he had gone to her room and found her untouched breakfast. When he questioned the guards, they had said she had gotten on her bike and ridden away. He had been so deep asleep in the library that he hadn't even felt her go.

Lost her again. No. Not lost. She had *left*. Just like Brangwen had.

Arawan had spent the rest of the day not preparing for the night raid that they were planning but tearing himself apart, thinking about what he could have done to upset Imogen. The fucking woman was going to ruin him.

Arawan was pacing his chambers when his door was suddenly kicked in, and Imogen charged through, her ax raised.

"What's happening? Are we under attack?" she demanded, wild-eyed and ready to fight.

"Do we look under attack?" Arawan said. He stamped down his urge to smile at her, to show how relieved he was to see her.

"Ah, yes, actually. The whole castle is shrouded in darkness!" Imogen lowered her ax a little. "You're doing it? Why?"

"Where the fuck have you been all day?" he demanded, his temper rising.

Imogen's eyes narrowed at his tone. "Out."

"You could've had the decency to tell me you planned on leaving."

Imogen pinched the bridge of her nose. "Are you fucking serious right now? This whole black mist is you having a fucking pity party? I thought you were being attacked, asshole!"

"And you were what? Rushing in to protect me with your little ax like I fucking needed the help?" Arawan sneered.

"Yeah, what was I thinking?" Imogen's eyes lit with fury, and her grip on her ax tightened. "And for your information, I went to see Freya and update her as part of being a liaison. The job you are forcing me to do!"

Arawan crossed his arm. "Was fucking me a part of your job too? Did you think I would release you from your debt?"

"No! That was for other reasons," Imogen said quickly. Anger was etched into every line of her. "I don't know why you are so pissed. You were the one that fucked me and never came back!"

"I did. I was in the library upstairs because I didn't want to wake you," he snapped.

"How was I supposed to know? Argh. This is why I don't fuck people I like!" Imogen shouted at him.

"You...like me? I'm death. No one likes me," Arawan said slowly, his brain not processing her words.

"Yes, I like you! When you're not being a raging dick and driving me crazy," she replied. "And sometimes even then."

Arawan frowned. "And you were racing in here thinking I was getting attacked because you like me?"

"You want to rub it in a bit more? You really are the worst."

"Yes, I am. That's why I don't understand."

Imogen shrugged. "That's not my problem. I don't understand why the fuck you're hanging out in the realm of the living, but here you are—"

Arawan wrestled with himself and spat out, "I'm here to protect this world from Hafgan because you live in it! Is that what you need to hear? I'm here because of *you*. The woman who's fucked with me so much, all I've done is fret all day instead of planning the attack on my enemy tonight!"

"You have a lead on Hafgan? Good, I could use the exercise so I don't kick your ass for being a grumpy dickhead," Imogen asked, her moods swinging so quickly, it made Arawan dizzy. She hefted her ax. "Come on, let's go."

Arawan snatched the ax out of her hands and buried it into the door behind her. "You aren't going anywhere until we sort this out."

Imogen rose up on her tiptoes, so she could get in his face. "I don't have anything more to say to you."

"Good because I didn't plan on talking," he replied and pulled her into a violent kiss. Arawan gave her the space to pull away, but mercifully, she didn't. Imogen wrapped her arms around his neck and pulled him closer.

Kissing Imogen made the stress of the day ease out of him and set him on fire at the same time. He was terrible with words, so he poured all his frustration and the fear she had run from him into the embrace. He had never thought much of kissing until he had found her lips, and now he couldn't get enough of them. Kissing her was a revelation.

After a few desperate moments, Imogen pulled back. "You can't just kiss me like that whenever I'm angry at you."

"Can't I?" Arawan teased softly. He rested his forehead against hers. "I'm sorry I made you think that I would use you for a fuck and nothing more. I really didn't want to wake you up."

"You should've done it anyway. I wanted you to come back, and you might not realize this, but wanting to see someone after I've fucked them is a *big* deal for me."

Arawan's eyes narrowed. "Well, if that's true, they can't have fucked you very well."

"I guess not." Imogen's smile was lightning in his veins before she went serious again. "I'm sorry for taking off without saying anything, but I came back. I don't run away from a fight, and I promised I won't leave until my debt is paid. No matter what extra things happen between us, understood?"

"Understood." Arawan nipped at her lips, making her breath hitch.

Imogen raised a brow at him. "A-Aren't we meant to be attacking Hafgan's people tonight?"

"It can wait," he said, picking her up and carrying her over to his bed. "The whole fucking world can wait."

Imogen didn't need any other encouragement. She was already pulling off his shirt in between kisses.

Arawan straddled her and yanked her own shirt above her head. Her breasts looked so full and delicious in the pink lace that cupped them. Before he could suspect her, she wriggled further down so her head was between his thighs. She caught one of the laces of his pants between her teeth and pulled it loose.

"You want my cock that badly?" Arawan pulled himself free, and she stared at him with such heat that he almost came on her face.

"I want to show how filthy my mouth can be," Imogen said with a wicked grin and quickly licked the end of his cock.

Arawan hissed and gripped the bed head to steady himself. He brushed his cock over her full wet lips. "Go on then."

All of his confidence vanished the second she took him in her hot mouth. Fuck. Nothing should feel so good. His flower was more dangerous than he'd thought. She sucked him further down her throat, and he let out a shaky whimper. She pulled back slowly and swirled her tongue on his tip.

"Good?" she asked softly and licked some pre-cum off her swollen lips.

"Don't you dare stop," he said, her answering suck shredding his self-control. Imogen's hands grabbed him by the ass and pulled him further and faster down her throat.

Arawan's restraint snapped, and he fucked her mouth until she was gagging on him and making the prettiest sounds he'd ever heard. If he could've died, he would've right then and there.

As good as it felt, he needed to be inside her after the day he'd had. Arawan pulled back from her, and she made a noise of surprise.

"I didn't do something wrong, did I?" she asked, and he could've wept.

"Absolutely not, and I promise you, one day, I'll paint your pretty mouth with my cum," Arawan swore. He pulled off her boots and pants. "But I need to be inside you tonight to remind you that leaving my bed is a bad idea."

Imogen wrapped her legs around his waist and threw his words back at him. "Go on then."

Arawan spread her so he could look at her deliciously wet cunt before he slid himself inside of her. Imogen swore, her back arching.

"Fuck *me*," she groaned, her breath coming out in a rush.

"I plan to. Every way you can possibly imagine," Arawan replied, lifting her hips to slam harder into her. He felt like he was going to lose his fucking mind when the soft walls clamped down on him. Fuck, he would never forget the sensation of being inside of her. Imogen gripped his back, her nails clawing him up.

"Fuck, that's it. Mark me up, show everyone that I'm yours," he growled, kissing her panting mouth.

Imogen bit his lip hard enough to draw ichor. "You fucking are and don't you forget it. While I'm in your bed, no one else is, or I'll fucking kill you and them."

"Don't threaten me like that, or I'll blow," he warned her.

"You blow before you make me come, and I'll never fuck you again."

Arawan let out a strangled sound and slammed into her. Imogen rolled her hips, meeting every one of his thrusts with an intensity that made him dizzy.

Nothing mattered beyond making her pant and finally scream, his name as she came in full-body trembles. This was the only worship he wanted from her—his name on her tongue and her pussy clenching him hard enough to see stars.

Imogen pulled him down for a breathless kiss. "Come for me."

Fuck, it was all it took, and his orgasm rushed through him like liquid light, filling her until he was empty and shaking on top of her.

Imogen stroked his face in a surprising moment of tenderness, her gray eyes heavy with emotion. "Feel better?"

Better? He felt like she had rearranged every part of him and taken the rest. He rolled his hips, making her moan softly. "Do you?"

"I feel less like murdering you. Does that count?" she replied, screwing up her nose. Arawan bit her breast, making her laugh. He wanted to stay in her soft, luscious body for the rest of the night but knew that he couldn't.

"Do you feel like coming with me on the raid tonight?" he asked, stroking her flushed cheek. "We got a meeting place out of Owain, and I would feel better having you by my side."

Imogen pinched his ass. "You mean my ax is useful after all?"

"Of course it is, just not against me." Imogen's pussy clenched around his sensitive cock again, making him hiss in surprise. "Don't you use *that* against me either, woman."

Her laughter was like sunshine rushing over him. "Would I do that?"

20

Imogen had never been shagged silly and then gone straight into a hunt. She felt so damn good and energized that she wondered why she had never done it before.

She risked looking sideways at Arawan sitting on top of the large black horse beside her.

Oh, that was why.

She had never been interested in fucking anyone twice before, and there was also the small matter of all her hookups never knowing what her actual job was. That the fae and other creatures had come out to the world didn't matter; work was work, and play was play, and those things never mixed.

Beyond that reason, Imogen never hung about because she knew that no matter how great the guy was, she was going to be way too much for them to handle long term. She was, she had learned early, too much for most people after one encounter. She was too weird, too loud, too dirty-mouthed, too obsessed with death. At least the latter was making a lot more sense. If she wasn't obsessed with death beforehand, Arawan's ridiculously gorgeous body would've done it.

And now you have the hots for a guy from a different world altogether. A guy who left that world for this one because he thought you would be in danger... Imogen's entire body went hot, and her insides turned to mush whenever she thought of his angry confession.

She knew then and there she would do stupid fucking things for him. The fact she was on a damn horse at the moment was proof enough of that. Not just any horse; a war stallion of Annwn that could travel literally between the worlds of the living and the dead. As a bonus, all of her weapons now hummed with the new charms Arawan placed on them.

"I'm not taking you into a fight with weapons that are useless against the dead," he had said gruffly before they had left. He had pulled a face at her taking guns with her, but she had slid on a holster with two of her favorite handguns just in case. Without arguing, he had charmed them too.

Arawan had also made her change into her proper hunting gear, which was lightweight body armor. It was all in black, and a tight fit, with reinforced kevlar panels in all the important bits.

Arawan's face was priceless when she walked out in it. He looked like he would cancel the raid and fuck her all over again. It had made squeezing into the damn thing worth it.

Arawan had placed magical protective shields over her before wrapping her in a black, fur-lined riding coat. With her ax strapped to her back, she looked damn badass, if she did say so herself.

Imogen didn't know where they were heading, only that it was vaguely south. Arawan was using magic to find the location and followed some kind of inner beacon. The horses seemed to instinctively follow his lead.

"It won't let you fall, no matter how fast we ride," Arawan reassured her. "If you want, you can always ride with me."

It was an argument they had already had before they left. Twice.

"I'm not going to let your warriors think I'm some dumb bitch fair maiden that's coming along for the fun of it," Imogen replied sternly.

Arawan gave her a knowing look. "You don't think fighting is fun?"

"Shut up."

Arawan laughed, making some of his warriors around them give him funny looks. He mustn't have laughed very often, which was a shame because his laugh was a wicked thing that made Imogen want to jump him whenever he did it.

Arawan drew his horse closer to her. "You should know that this might not be like a normal fight you've been in. The creatures that Hafgan can control are unpredictable and can dematerialize at will. Keep close to me. Don't let anything get behind you."

"I promise," she said with a firm nod. There were times to argue with him for fun, but this wasn't one of them. He trusted her abilities enough to be willing to let her come with them, and Imogen was determined to prove to him it was the right choice.

You want to impress him? You are so gone on him, it's disturbing, Imogen snapped at herself. She didn't really care, though.

"That's the estate," Arawan said, slowing his pace. They were on top of a small ridge, and lights were glowing in the middle of a sloping valley. Imogen could barely see a thing in the darkness, but it didn't matter. The horses were bred in darkness and wouldn't put a hoof wrong.

"Shouldn't there be some guards or something? Scouts at least?" Imogen asked, not liking how quiet it was.

"There's no reason for anyone to suspect us. Owain said this was the night and place Hafgan agreed to a meeting for new orders. It's not a regular base for them to need to protect," Arawan replied.

"I suppose if we are wrong, we could always kick Owain about for it."

Arawan shook his head. "Not exactly. He was executed."

"How does one execute someone already dead?" Imogen asked and then bit her tongue. It really did have a mind of its own.

"You shred their shade and scatter them to the four winds so that they may never join together again or find peace," Arawan replied, his voice so cold that Imogen flinched. She forced herself to look at him.

"He betrayed you, so I can't say I'm sorry to hear it," she replied.

"You really should be more disturbed by what I am, Imogen Ironwood," Arawan said, his dark eyes filled with something she couldn't place. Despite his words, he looked...relieved.

"You are what you are, Arawan. I'd have no interest in changing it, even if I could." Imogen turned back to the valley, trying to push down the soft, squishy feelings that threatened to choke her. "So how are we going to do this? Sneaky or loud?"

"We will encircle the property and work our way in. I don't want anyone to escape us to warn Hafgan."

Imogen pulled her ax from its holster. "You don't think he is here."

Arawan shook his head. "I would feel him. He wouldn't ever expose himself for a meeting so low level either. Owain was an ambitious little rat, and Hafgan exploited that. He wouldn't lower himself to deal with him in person."

Imogen gripped her ax with one hand and the reins with the other. "Then let's go rat hunting, shall we?"

Arawan pulled his silver and onyx sword from its sheath, his grin violent and devastating. "Try and keep up, Ironwood." With that, his horse leaped straight off the ridge.

"Show off," she muttered. Imogen tried not to scream as her horse followed him. They had been going easy on the ride there compared to this. Imogen loved speed, so it took her from being airborne to hitting the ground again for her to start loving it. The warriors were all following like silent death closing in on the house.

Imogen couldn't make out Arawan in the distance but trusted the horse to catch up. He was shouting something back at them. Imogen didn't catch it as the whole world around her exploded in flying earth, claws, and the screeching of horde creatures.

Imogen didn't think. She reacted with all the training the Ironwoods and the fae princes had drilled into her. She pulled one of her guns out and started shooting with one hand and swiping her ax with the other.

The warriors were fighting on either side of her with the ease of the well-trained. They had walked into a shit storm with three times as many creatures as they had been led to believe. That wouldn't stop them from doing what they had come to do.

Something hard and heavy hit Imogen in the back, and she was sent toppling off the side of the horse. She managed to roll when she hit the ground, only narrowly missing the claws of a demented horde creature.

Like the Sasquatch hybrids that had attacked her in the forest, these creatures were slimy and earthy, like they had been made from rotting parts of different creatures and fused together with dark magic. She didn't have time to try and figure out what they were. They were death in the gloom, and she lost herself in battle mode, a dance of screaming, slashing, and shooting. A flash of silver caught her eye, and Arawan appeared beside her.

"There are too many of them. We are outnumbered," he said, his sword decapitating the creature trying to turn her into dinner.

"Tell me something I don't know!" Imogen shouted at him.

Arawan killed another creature and moved to her side. "I can strip off this damn form and fight them on my own terms."

"Then why haven't you already done it?" she demanded.

Arawan grabbed her arm and pulled her close, his eyes turning ruby red. "Because you will never look at me the same way afterward," he said, his voice strained.

Imogen pressed a short kiss to his lips. "Idiot male! Just do what you have to do to get us out of his cluster fuck, or you're going to be burning my body by morning!"

"You will *not* die. Do you hear me? I forbid it!" he snarled, his power rolling out of him.

She let him go, pushing him away from her. "Then go and show them who they've fucked with."

Imogen turned back to the enemy around them, so she didn't see Arawan's transformation. The air went hot behind her, and suddenly a winged black monster rushed past her, picked up the horde creature she had been fighting, and tore it in two.

"Holy fucking shit," Imogen babbled as the massive monster turned.

She knew it was Arawan by the black bone crown rising from his head and the long black hair streaming around him. Huge ruby and black feathered wings with wicked curved talons had grown out of his back, and black claws stretched out of his fingers.

His eyes glowed ruby, and he screeched out a warning call to all the enemy forces that remained, showing every one of his sharp fangs. He spared Imogen one last look before he threw himself into the fight.

Imogen ran after him, taking out anything that still breathed in his wake. In the moonlight, she could make out his powerful wings and arms slashing anything before him. He was a stunning creature of pure violence and savagery.

"That's my Death Daddy," Imogen said, mouth open and

completely in awe. She was also high on battle lust that skyrocketed while watching him be the baddest of badasses. He had been worried she wouldn't want him after seeing him like this? She had never wanted to make out with him more.

Fuck, you are damaged. Imogen grinned; she was okay with it.

"Lady Imogen, don't get too close to him," one tall warrior warned her. "I haven't seen him take this form for over a millennium. The beast might not recognize you and hurt you by accident. He would want me to caution you."

"Okay, noted, but I'm not going to let him fight alone. Are you with me?" Imogen asked. She was out of bullets, so she took Bayn's long dagger from her thigh sheath.

"If I left you go alone, I'd fear what Arawan would do to me far more than what any spawn of Hafgan could do," the warrior replied. She took that as a yes, and they went after Arawan, plunging into the fray.

21

Imogen's arms were aching by the time they reached Arawan. He had left what remained of Hafgan's horde creatures in pulpy hunks all over the valley. The house that had sat in its middle was in burning piles of debris.

The monster that was Arawan watched the flames burn. He scented the air and whirled sharply to face Imogen and the few that remained of the warriors.

Holy God of Death, Imogen stared and stared. His pale muscled torso and arms were covered in slashing gray marks.

It took her a second to recognize them as scars. Her hand went to her side where her own scar was. He was covered in them, and yet this was the first time she had seen them. He had been hiding them from her. His worried words came back to her. *You will never look at me the same way afterward.* He thought that she wouldn't want him? Even in this hulking battle mode, he wasn't remotely ugly. He was...epic.

Arawan turned and looked down at her, a soft growl on his lips. Fuck, he was massive. His glowing ruby eyes looked her over like she was dinner, and the thought made her hot all over.

"Hey handsome, you get them all?" she asked, her mouth dry. She didn't think he would hurt her, but the warrior's warning was still fresh in her mind. She lowered her ax to show that she wasn't a threat. "You know who I am, right?"

Arawan stepped closer, wings out and glistening with menace in the firelight. A clawed hand touched her braid.

"My flower," his voice rumbled like thunder.

It was all the reassurance Imogen needed. She dropped her ax and flew into him, wrapping her arms around his neck.

"You saved all of us," she whispered into his ear. His big arms went around her, lifting her up as if she weighed nothing.

Imogen moved to place her hands on his cheeks, leaning back to study him. He was bigger all over, but he was still Arawan. He might have had fangs, but so did Kian and many of the fae.

Very slowly, so not to freak him out, Imogen kissed him. Arawan made another deeply satisfied rumble in his chest and kissed her back. Even in this form, his touch was electric, filling her with longing and desire.

He held her carefully like she was fragile. Imogen had never been fragile in her life. She wrapped her legs around his torso and held on.

A warrior cleared his throat. "Ah, my lady, what should we do now?"

"Are they all dead?" Imogen asked without looking away from Arawan.

"Yes, my lady. There were only creatures here, no informants of Hafgan's."

Imogen touched Arawan's cheeks. "Then you guys are dismissed or whatever."

"I'm not sure what you mean," the warrior replied. Imogen looked over her shoulder at the small group that still remained upright.

"It means you can bugger off home. Check the area around the castle and make sure it's secure and there are no other creatures on the move. The boss and I will follow after we...work some stuff out," she snapped in the bossiest big sister voice she could muster. The warriors all straightened in attention before riding away.

Arawan nuzzled at her neck. "They respect you," he said.

"They know better than to mess with a woman with an ax," she replied. She threaded her hands through his thick hair and touched the black spike of his crown.

"You're not afraid or repulsed, are you?" he asked, voice full of wonder. Imogen shook her head. She reached around and touched the curve of a wing.

"You look fucking badass," she said honestly. She kissed him slowly, gasping against his mouth when his grip tightened on her ass. "Is everything bigger in this form?"

Arawan laughed softly. "Why? Is the little hunter suffering from some post-battle lust?" Imogen rolled her hips against the leather of his pants. She smiled when she felt the hard outline of his erection.

"It would seem I'm not the only one," she replied and licked his top lip.

Arawan groaned. "I can change back..."

"Don't you fucking dare. You're hot as fuck in beast mode, and I want you. Just like this," Imogen replied, her tongue flicking into his mouth.

"I don't deserve..." he began again, but she put a hand over his mouth.

"Stop talking and fuck me. We can do the feelings part later," Imogen said.

Arawan's eyes heated and, in a blink, had her pressed up against the nearest tree. Imogen managed to get her pants to her knees before he was lifting her up again, her legs folded up against his chest. Imogen grabbed onto one of the spikes of his crown to steady herself. Arawan's kisses were crazed as he guided her down onto his dick.

"Fuck, you are so tight and wet," he ground out between his teeth. His hands cupped her ass and lowered her down further onto him. A breathy gasp escaped her. He was so big that he was filling up every part of her, and she thought she would die from how good it felt.

"Don't stop," she begged.

"I couldn't even if I wanted to." Arawan kissed her again, a wicked smile on his lips. "You wanted to be fucked, little hunter, so you are going to take everything I give you until you're fucking dripping with me."

Arawan pinned her harder to the tree so she couldn't move and then began to fuck her hard. It wasn't even remotely gentle, and it was exactly what Imogen needed after such a battle.

She had lived again, and this was every way she wanted to celebrate it. Her brain was whiting out from the intensity of him, and she didn't want it to end. Arawan fucked her until she was screaming incoherently, her hands tearing out feathers as she grabbed for his wings.

"You're so fucking perfect," she ground out, right before she clenched him tight, and her orgasm roared through her.

Arawan bit into the base of her neck with his sharp fangs and filled her up just as he had promised.

"More," he growled out, dragging her away from the tree to the soft moss at their feet. Imogen was pulled off his cock long enough to be rolled onto her hands and knees, and he was sliding into her again.

Her hands tore at the earth. It almost hurt to breathe as he slammed his hips against her ass. She was reduced to a gasping, screaming mess as he changed position and hit her G-spot with enough force that she momentarily blacked out. It was fucking at its most primal and animalistic. It was the best fuck of Imogen's life.

She hadn't even realized she had vocalized that thought until Arawan's huge body came over and caged her in, his clawed hands covering hers in the dirt.

"That's because your soul is like mine. This is who we really are when all the masks are stripped back. We were born to slaughter our enemies. Fucking in the middle of a battlefield is our truest selves. This is why death always feels so good to you. It is because we are the same beast inside," Arawan said in her ear. "We are death."

Imogen's eyes filled with tears. This was the darkest truth in her heart that she couldn't even acknowledge herself. This *was* who she really was.

"Yes, my love. We are," she gasped out. Her orgasm screamed out of her. It was so intense it hurt, but the edge of pain made it even better.

Arawan held onto her as he came with her, chanting her name like she was the one who deserved to be worshipped.

After he was done, he turned her head so he could look into her tear-streaked, ruined face. Whatever he saw on it made him smile, and Imogen knew she had just had her heart torn out.

22

Imogen rested her head in the groove of Arawan's neck for the entire flight home. She was in a daze. Exhausted by the battle, drained of adrenaline, and fucked without mercy. She was wrecked, and even though she was never one to act like a pampered princess, she allowed Arawan to take care of her.

The sky was starting to lighten when they landed in front of the castle. None of the warriors looked at them or questioned them for returning so much later than the others. Arawan shifted to his normal form, the wings and crown and claws disappearing. He still didn't let her go.

Imogen didn't fight him as he carried her up to his quarters and set her down only long enough to strip off her filthy clothes. She couldn't find the words to protest, so she let him lower her into a bath with him. Arawan didn't seem in a talkative mood either; he only seemed to want to hold onto her and gently wash all the mud, blood, and cum from her body.

Imogen had never had anyone take care of her after a fight. The battle had been nothing compared to what had come after. She felt hollowed out, her body weirdly light like she wasn't in it.

Something had been cracked wide open inside of her, and she didn't know how to push the pieces back together. She thought when someone realized they were in love, that it was all heart eyes, and rainbows. This felt like she'd had her vital pieces removed and her insides rearranged.

This is why every story of a human falling in love with a god is a tragedy, she thought bleakly.

"I didn't hurt you, did I?" Arawan asked from behind her.

"No. I'm just...overwhelmed," she replied, her voice shaky.

Arawan didn't push her, only drew her to him until her head rested on his chest. He hadn't glamoured away the scars on his body, and Imogen knew it was a sign that he trusted her. She had seen his worst and had accepted it. In return, he had ripped her soul and heart open.

Imogen closed her eyes. The hot water and the gentle swipes of Arawan washing her sent her into a doze. She was half asleep when he lifted her out, dried her off, and carried her to bed.

"Don't leave me," she murmured sleepily.

Arawan wrapped his body around her under the thick, soft blankets. He kissed her softly behind her ear. "Never again, darling."

∼

IMOGEN WAS DISORIENTATED and had no idea what the time was when she woke again. Someone was knocking on the chamber door. Arawan pressed a kiss to the back of her head and slipped out of bed. Imogen opened her eyes as Arawan opened the door.

"I'm sorry to disturb you, my lord, but there is an envoy on the borders requesting an audience," Duncan whispered. "They are carrying Hafgan's standard."

"For fuck's sake. Let them through the wards but keep them surrounded. I will meet them in the hall when I'm ready for them and not a second before. After last night, the fuckers can wait," Arawan replied.

Duncan inclined his head. "I'll see that Miss Ironwood is attended to in your absence."

"No, she'll be coming with me. I'm not meeting with them without her and one of the princes. As I said, the envoy can wait. Summon the court but keep them separated from Hafgan's people," Arawan instructed and closed the door again. He sat on the bed beside her and brushed his thumb over her cheek. "Sorry to wake you, but we have trouble."

"I heard." Imogen stretched, her body aching and tired. "How long have we been asleep?"

"About five hours."

Imogen groaned but still sat up. "Better than nothing, I suppose. I'll go and get dressed. If Duncan comes back, tell him to bring me about a liter of coffee. I'll get a hold of Bayn and get him and Freya here. They are closest."

"A good plan." Arawan wrapped her in a thick fur robe. "I'm sorry we didn't get more time."

Imogen gave him her best devil-may-care smile. "You don't need much sleep when you're this fine."

"Go on before I change my mind and keep you here," Arawan said. Imogen didn't like the worry in his eyes when he looked at her, so she kissed his cheek.

"Come by when you're ready to meet with these losers," she said and walked back to her own rooms. Duncan was coming up the stairs with her breakfast tray. He raised his brows at her.

"Don't judge me, Dunk," Imogen groaned, opening her bedroom door and holding it out for him.

"It's not my place to judge you, Miss Ironwood," he replied, placing the tray down for her.

"Says you in the judgiest voice ever." Imogen almost dived on the coffee pot.

Duncan paused by the door. "I have served Lord Arawan for a long time. Despite being human, you make him happy, and all of Annwn can feel it. His mood affects us all. Perhaps that is something to consider if your affections are not...sincere."

Imogen knew she didn't owe him shit, but she still looked him dead in the eye and said, "They are."

Duncan inclined his head, and with the first smile she had ever seen him display, he closed the door.

Imogen found her phone and dialed Bayn. She hoped they weren't busy because she was about to drop a shit storm in their lap.

"What's wrong, Gen?" Bayn answered, not fucking about with any kind of pleasantries. Another reason he was her favorite.

"We followed up on some intel from Owain last night and walked into a cluster fuck. Yes, I'm okay, but Hafgan has sent an envoy. Can you and Freya come? Arawan wants you here, and so do I," Imogen explained in one long breath.

Bayn made a grumbly sound. "We can be there in twenty minutes. I don't like that they turned up so quickly."

"Me neither, but I'm not surprised. I think the horde creature army we took out last night was a backup force Hafgan was saving."

"You took out an army?" Bayn demanded. "What the hell, Imogen! You didn't think to call us?"

"We didn't know it was going to be an army. We had warriors, and to be honest, it felt like an army, but it was dark as shit, and I have no idea how many they were."

"And you are completely unscathed? How is that possible?"

Imogen swallowed a mouthful of coffee. "I don't know. Arawan put some pretty hefty shields on me and badass charms on my weapons. He's an army all on his own."

Bayn was silent for a long moment. "He must care about you to do that."

Imogen's stomach fluttered. "I don't know. Do you think a god is capable of caring for a mortal? He might have done it because he wanted to torment me with this deal we made. Who knows why gods do what they do?"

"Ah huh, whatever you say, sis. We will be outside the borders in twenty, so make sure you're there to let us in," Bayn replied, and they said their goodbyes.

Imogen went through her clean clothes, wondering what she should wear when meeting an envoy.

Fuck them. They don't get special treatment for waking me up.

Imogen grabbed her usual jeans and a T-shirt. She did put on some makeup to cover her sleep deprivation because she didn't want to appear the weakest person in the room.

Imogen found her ax that a helpful warrior had brought back to the castle for her. She felt guilty for forgetting all about it in lieu of getting railed by Arawan.

"Fuck, don't think about it," she told herself and hastily braided her hair. If she started examining her emotions from the night before, she would spiral.

She wanted to talk to someone about it, but it wasn't something she felt she could open up about. There was no good way to say, 'so I got fucked by a monster death god in the middle of a burning battlefield, and he not only ripped out a dark truth from the depths of my heart, but I also realized I'm in love with him.'

"You are going to need so much therapy after this," Imogen told her reflection. She didn't have time for it, so she did what she did best and shoved all of her emotions into a box and tossed it into the dark ether of her mind.

Imogen pulled on her leather jacket and ax holster, keeping it full-sized and strapped to her back. She wasn't going to be dumb enough to not look like a threat.

Imogen's phone buzzed to tell her Bayn and Freya had arrived. Imogen looked at herself in the mirror one last time. She looked like a hunter.

"This is who you are. Not someone who falls in love with someone you can't be with," she told her reflection. The Imogen in the mirror didn't look like she believed her for a second.

23

Bayn and Freya were both a combination of pissed off and concerned. Imogen had sent warriors to let them in through the wards and was waiting by the front entrance for them.

Freya looked amazing, dressed in a suit and a dark blue satin top. Bayn, being Bayn, was dressed like Imogen in jeans and a leather jacket.

"You look ready to put your ax in someone's head," he said with a sharp grin.

"That's what happens when I get woken up too early," Imogen replied, bumping fists with him. "I'll leave looking pretty to Freya."

Freya laughed. "Well, one of us has to look professional. I must say you look positively glowing today."

"It's called the post-battle high," Imogen replied, ignoring the insinuation.

Bayn rolled his eyes. "Come on, let's get this over with."

Arawan was coming down the stairs when they stepped back inside. Damn, he looked *so* fine in a black suit. Imogen wanted to giggle with glee and rub herself all over him.

"Try to look less obvious," Freya murmured.

Imogen grinned. "Not possible."

"Thank you for coming on such short notice," Arawan greeted them.

"We are happy to be here, my lord," Bayn replied. He and Freya bowed politely, which made Imogen snicker. Arawan only shook his head at her.

"Do try and act like I'm the boss in front of Hafgan's people, darling," he said, pinching her chin on the way past.

"I'll behave," she replied, not sounding the least bit sincere. "Unless they deserve an ax to the face."

"Envoy's usually come under a peace agreement, so no axes unless they break the convention first," Arawan replied.

Imogen let out a pained sigh. "You used to be cool."

Arawan made a scoffing sound. "Obey me, mortal, or suffer the consequences."

"Yeah, okay." Imogen waggled her eyebrows at him.

Arawan's expression heated. "Keep back chatting me and see what it gets you. Come along." He walked away, leaving Imogen staring at his fine, fine ass.

Bayn and Freya had their mouths open, looking concerned and amused at the same time.

"For fucks sake, Imogen. Really?" Bayn grumbled at her.

"What did I do?" she asked.

Bayn only shook his head at her and took Freya's hand. "Killian is never going to shut up when he hears about this."

"I think it's adorable in a terrifying kind of way," Freya said.

"I don't know what either of you are talking about."

All teasing and flirting stopped as soon as they walked into the hall. Arawan was already on his throne, with Aisling close to the dais. Arawan gave Imogen a pointed look and indicated the spot on his right.

Imogen ignored every pair of judgmental eyes following her and went to stand in the place just a little behind his throne. Let them all think that she was his bodyguard. Bayn and Freya joined her and looked suitably menacing and aloof.

Hafgan's envoy was a tall man with silver hair and cold blue eyes. A group of ten people surrounded him, one carrying a banner on a pole.

There was the symbol of a tree stitched into it with swords for branches.

Imogen remembered the sigil that Aneirin had created in the estuary with the same mark. She tried to hide her anger and disgust.

"Dafydd, it has been a long time," Arawan said finally, and the gray-haired man inclined his head. It wasn't a bow, and it pissed Imogen off. She might not bow to him, but it was for completely different reasons, and she would never disrespect him in front of his court.

"Lord Arawan, you have been asleep for centuries. Some of us didn't have that luxury," Dafydd replied and looked around at his court.

"I trusted my court to govern in my stead, and they did so admirably." Arawan only smiled at him, completely unbothered. Imogen reminded herself they were under a peace agreement. It didn't stop her from looking Dafydd over and drawing mental targets on every one of his vital points.

The envoy looked at her just as keenly, like he couldn't quite figure out her presence. *Good. Let him wonder,* she thought.

"If you have a message, I suggest you spit it out," Arawan said.

Dafydd didn't break eye contact with Imogen. "My lord, shouldn't we take this audience somewhere more privately. This matter hardly concerns the living."

"Hafgan trying to make war in this land makes it their concern. Prince Bayn, Princess Freya, and Lady Imogen have a right to be here as much as any," Arawan said, a thread of warning in his voice.

"Hafgan isn't trying to make war here," Dafydd replied with a smug little smile.

"Really? Having an army of horde creatures stationed not far from my borders suggests otherwise." Arawan looked sideways at Imogen and grinned. "Well, he *did* have an army."

"Not much of one," she replied.

Dafydd was looking between them suspiciously. "And can I ask what your role is in Arawan's court, Lady Imogen?"

She smiled sweetly at him. "I'm a liaison. Diplomacy is my main area of expertise."

Bayn coughed, trying to hide his laughter.

Dafydd smoothed over his confusion and schooled his features back to neutrality. "My Lord Hafgan sends me with the following message—there is no need for a war between us, Lord of Annwn. It has been centuries since the unfortunate business with Lady Brangwen. Let the past die, and let there be peace between us."

Arawan went still, the shadows in the room darkening. His entire court looked disgusted at Dafydd. Imogen had no idea who Brangwen was, but it was as if Dafydd saying her name was some horrible taboo.

"Hafgan says he wants peace, but his actions are far from it. Bringing up my wife that Hafgan seduced and then killed will not earn you any favors," Arawan said finally.

Imogen swallowed the hard lump in her throat. She had no idea and tried to keep the shock from her face. He hadn't trusted her enough, so he kept that important information from her. Fuck, it hurt like a kick between the legs.

She was already feeling like an emotional wreck from the night before, and this had just made it a hundred times worse. Arawan was happy to toy her along with his bargain, fuck her, but not share strategic information?

You sure know how to pick them, she mentally kicked herself.

The voices blurred around her, and she tuned them out. Let them talk. Arawan clearly wasn't interested in sharing with her anyway, so why should she pay attention to this boring shit.

Hafgan killing his wife was a massive red flag because it made the fight with him more than just a rivalry. It was about revenge. The kind that would have Arawan acting emotionally in retaliation and not like a general.

If this war with Hafgan didn't affect her sisters and family, maybe Imogen wouldn't have cared so much about Arawan not sharing his past with her. But Arawan fucking up the fight meant that all of them were in danger. If he didn't stop Hafgan from whatever shit he was planning, it would be up to her family to do it.

"You have said your piece, Dafydd. Please stay the night as my guest while I consider the reply I should send to Hafgan," Arawan was saying, pulling Imogen back to the room full of faces. She needed this shit to be over with. She needed to clear her head before doing something reckless because she was pissed.

Dafydd finally bowed. "Thank you, my lord. It would be an honor."

Arawan made a gesture that the meeting was over, and Imogen tried not to bolt from the room.

"Gen..." Freya reached for her, but Imogen kept walking. She didn't want Freya to see that she was hurt and pissed off. Imogen needed time to sort out why she felt like an emotional mess and get that shit under control.

Imogen reached her bedroom and was packing a bag when Arawan appeared suddenly in the center of the room.

"Imogen—"

"Don't talk. I need to go for a ride, and if you know what's good for you, you'll stay out of my way," she said, pulling on a warmer jacket.

Arawan crossed his arms, looking confused. It was the clueless frown that made her want to stab him. "What's wrong? At least tell me that."

"What's wrong? Hafgan seduced and murdered your wife! You didn't think that was something I should know? That my brothers should know?" she said, rounding on him. She hadn't even known he'd *had* a wife. She didn't know why it made her so mad, and she was too much of a raw, emotional nerve to figure it out.

"I didn't think the information was relevant," he said.

"Of course it is! This is about revenge for you. Hafgan is going to use that against you every chance he gets. It's going to be a weak spot that will fuck all of us if you can't keep your shit together," she replied, trying to keep her voice steady.

"I wasn't keeping it from you on purpose. It happened a long time ago, and it isn't the only reason I hate Hafgan," Arawan said, taking a step towards her. Imogen moved back from him. "Talk to me. I don't understand why you are so angry about this."

"You didn't trust me enough to tell me about it, which puts me in danger. He will use your own anger and emotions against you with this, and you will walk into every trap he sets. Just like last night. He probably set that whole thing up with Owain because he knew you would charge straight in without thinking." Imogen tossed a bag over her shoulder.

"I will *never* let Hafgan hurt you," Arawan growled through his teeth.

"And you think that's all I'm worried about if he defeats you? You will be dead, and it'll be up to my family and me to stop him." Imogen headed for the door, fighting the images of him dead on the battlefield. Panic and fear fluttered in her chest.

Fuck you for making me care for you so much, she wanted to yell.

"I don't know why you decided not to trust me enough to tell me about this, and I don't give a shit," she lied through her teeth. "But if you are keeping anything else strategically important from us, you can tell Bayn. I'm out of here."

Arawan didn't stop her from leaving, and Imogen didn't know why that pissed her off even more.

Fuck it. Ride, find a party, kiss a boy you don't give a shit about. Let the world burn for the night.

Imogen gritted her teeth and forced her lips in her fuck-the-devil smile. She was Imogen Ironwood, and she didn't have time to deal with clueless fucking gods and all the messy emotions they dredged up inside of her.

24

Arawan still didn't fully understand what he had done. He waited all day for Imogen to return to the castle so he could try and make some sense out of her. He hoped she would come and fight it out with him so he could get to the bottom of what had upset her so much.

Imogen had been withdrawn since the previous night, and he had assumed it was from the battle and their intense fucking afterward. He had been shaken after that himself. How could she go from accepting him in that monstrous form to storming out because she found out Hafgan had killed Brangwen?

He was a god and was not used to having to explain himself or his personal history to anyone. What had happened with his wife was known through all the court. It wasn't like it was a secret, so why did she care about it so much?

He needed someone to help him unravel the mystery of Imogen, and luckily for him, Bayn and Freya were still in the castle.

The fae prince and his mate were chatting and drinking with Aisling in their guest suite. They seemed to be having a good time when he walked in, and he almost felt bad for breaking it up. All three of them rose in surprise to greet him.

"Apologies, sorceress, but I need to have a private word with Bayn and Freya," Arawan said.

Aisling frowned but still bowed. "Of course, my lord."

"What's wrong?" Bayn asked once they were alone.

"I need to talk to you...about Imogen," Arawan replied, suddenly more nervous than he had ever been. Freya tried to hide her smile as she poured him a glass of wine.

"You look like you need this," she said kindly.

Arawan took the glass. "I do?"

Bayn leaned back in his chair and draped an arm around Freya's shoulders. For some reason, the easy affection felt like Arawan had been kicked in the balls. He wanted that for the first time in his long existence.

"Okay, tell us how hard she went through you?" Bayn asked. "Out with it. I knew she was out for someone's blood after she stormed out of the hall."

"She yelled at me for not telling her that Hafgan had seduced and killed my wife." Arawan took a mouthful of the wine, wishing it was stronger. "She said that not knowing about that put her and our alliance in jeopardy because I'd act emotionally to any threats that Hafgan makes."

Bayn chewed on his lip thoughtfully. "Is she right? Because if you're going to do something dumb every time Hafgan starts shit, that will make it easy for him to bait you."

"No," Arawan said firmly. "I haven't reacted emotionally to anything concerning Brangwen for over a millennium. It is very ancient history. Yes, she was my consort. She betrayed me to Hafgan, and when he realized he couldn't use her as a bargaining chip with me to get control of Annwn, he killed her. I don't know why me having a dead wife would concern Imogen or upset her."

Freya snorted. "Men."

"Care to elaborate on that comment?"

"You men are so thick," Freya said slowly like she was talking to an idiot. "Imogen has feelings for you. It's probably the first time she's had deep emotions for someone outside of her family. Anyone paying attention today could see that she had no idea about your wife."

"Imogen has feelings for me," Arawan said, his own heart suddenly feeling too big for his chest.

"Yes, and by not telling her about your wife and Hafgan, you made her feel like she was the last person to know. She also was made to look like a fool in front of the court because you are obviously sleeping together but haven't told her vital information. You downgraded her from important liaison to your fuck buddy," Freya explained.

"I..." Arawan was speechless. "Fuck."

"Exactly." Bayn leaned forward and rested his elbows on his knees. "I know you are a god and could probably smite me easily, but seriously what the fuck are you doing with my sister? Is this a curiosity thing to know what it's like to fuck a mortal? Because I would think a god as old as you would have gotten that out of your system by now."

Arawan didn't feel like a god at that moment. He felt like an asshole, and he really didn't like it. He held out his glass to Freya, and she refilled it.

"When I first saw Imogen, she was like a slap in the face. It was a strange kind of shock that I still haven't recovered from. I brought her here to try and figure out what it was about her that rattled me so much. She is the complete opposite of any woman I've courted. Brangwen was a docile, compliant creature that Hafgan too easily manipulated." Arawan took a shaky breath, and the previous night's revelation on the battlefield rocked through him again. There was a moment when he had looked into her face and known deep in the core of his being that she belonged by his side.

"Imogen is like me," he said finally, refusing to elaborate. He would never share that moment with anyone but her, and he doubted anyone would understand.

Bayn grunted. "Makes a lot of sense that you're the one that has managed to get through to her heart. She's always been obsessed with death."

"What do you mean by that?" Arawan asked.

Bayn told him about Imogen dying when she was a child and how she admitted one night when she was very drunk that she was obsessed with death because of it. And what was worse, she had thought she *should* have died in the river, and every moment since had been stolen time.

Arawan thought back to the day he had strapped her to the chair in the dungeons. Imogen had tossed that glorious braid back and had said, *Oh, honey, it was my time to die eighteen years ago. I've been waiting for it to stick ever since.*

"Imogen has never let anyone get close to her because she knew that death would find her one day." Bayn drained his glass, his eyes dark when they fixed on Arawan. "I guess Death finally has."

"She was always meant to be mine," Arawan said to himself, more certain of that than he had been of anything in his entire life. He put his glass down and got to his feet. "Do you have any idea where she would've gone?"

"Anywhere there's loud music and heavy metal goth boys," Bayn said. He looked Arawan over and snorted. "She does have a type, after all."

"Or you two could leave her be to sort things out on her own?" Freya suggested.

"No. This is too important to wait. She will only keep coming to wrong conclusions without me talking to her," Arawan said.

"Yeah, and knowing Gen, she will be hooking up with the first guy…" Bayn trailed off quickly under the intensity of Arawan's glare.

Freya made an impatient sound and pulled out her phone. "Fine, if you are going to be an idiot about it, who am I to stop you? I have an app that tracks her phone. Let me see where she is."

"If you made a bargain with her, Arawan, I'm surprised you can't find her with that," Bayn pointed out.

"I didn't weave that into the magic. I wanted her to stay with me, but if she really wanted to leave, I wasn't going to stop her," Arawan admitted softly. "I won't be her jailer."

Bayn's eyebrows rose. "But you never told her that?"

Arawan smiled. "I'm not an idiot. If I told her I couldn't find her, she would've left out of spite and forced me to chase her just for the fun of it."

"Yeah, that sounds like her," Bayn said and chuckled.

"She's in Liverpool. It's about two hours away. I'll write the address down for you, but only if you promise not to upset her more," Freya said, her mismatched eyes flickering with power and overprotective instincts.

"It's not my intention, but if she pushes me, I will make her see sense even if I have to fight her every step of the way," Arawan replied.

Freya gave him the address. "Then I hope she doesn't go easy on you for a second."

Arawan's smile was sharp as a blade. "That makes two of us."

25

Imogen couldn't remember the club's name or the name of the hot redhead she had been dancing with. He had a neck tattoo, and that seemed more important. She was four drinks in and feeling better about life. At least, that's what she was telling herself.

She had berated herself the whole ride to Liverpool. Had she picked a fight for no reason? Maybe? She knew she had good reasons to be pissed. He could've told her he had been married.

Was he *still* married to someone else? Fuck, she hadn't even asked him that before she had jumped his bones.

You are a garbage fire of a woman, Imogen Ironwood, and goth gods are not for you.

Every mile she put in between her and Arawan made her feel unsure about everything. Imogen had never been indecisive in her life, so all it did was make her turn her throttle on harder, like if she got enough space between them, maybe she wouldn't feel like she was losing her mind.

"You are the hottest woman in this place," Neck Tattoo said, wrapping his arms around her from behind. He had a brogue so purring and deep it could vibrate a girl's panties right off. "You want to get out of here?"

"Not just yet. I need to dance for a bit longer," she replied.

"How about another drink?" He had a great smile in the dark gloom of the dance floor. A few weeks ago, if a guy that hot had smiled at her, she would've dragged him off to a secluded spot and had her wicked way with him. Now, she just felt strangely nauseous and hollow at the thought of it.

"Another drink sounds perfect," Imogen said, and he de-tangled himself from around her. She didn't want to think about deranged generals, horde creatures, or hunting for a night. She didn't want to be pining for someone she couldn't have. She didn't want to be thinking at all.

Warm arms came around her again, and her whole body melted, recognizing the embrace before her mind did. Tears burned in the back of her eyes, and she swallowed them down.

"How did you find me?" she asked. She spoke too low to be heard over the beat, but it didn't matter; he heard every word.

"Bayn and Freya," Arawan replied in her ear.

"Traitorous assholes," she grumbled. She wanted to shove him off and press closer at the same time. Kiss him and rip his throat out. She wanted him and hated it.

"I needed to talk to you, and maybe in this place, you might actually listen to me." Arawan pulled her close, his height keeping her surrounded and protected in his arms. "I'm sorry I didn't tell you about Brangwen. I wasn't trying to keep it a secret from you. I just felt like it didn't matter."

Imogen tried to move away, but his grip tightened like a vice. He wouldn't let her go until he had said his bit, and there wasn't a damn thing she could do about it.

"It was a long, long time ago, Imogen. It was an arranged marriage that I tried to make the most of. She betrayed me to Hafgan, and when he realized I wouldn't give up my kingdom to get her back, he killed her. It started a war between us that had been brewing for eons." Arawan brushed his lips over the curve of her ear, and a shiver swept over her body. "I haven't had a consort since. I hadn't been interested in anyone for centuries until I stepped through the portal and saw you."

Imogen's hands tightened over his, her heart in her throat. If he kept talking, she wasn't going to survive him.

"You are the complete opposite of anything I thought I would be interested in. You are a stubborn, uncompromising, violent, passionate pain in my ass, and I've never wanted someone more." Arawan tipped her head back and laid a barely-there kiss on her lips. "Tell me it's not just me that feels so twisted up inside."

"N-No, I'm not going to tell you shit," Imogen replied shakily. "If I don't say it, it won't make it real, and I can still feel like I can walk away with some of my dignity intact."

Arawan's dark eyes flashed ruby. "You have three choices, darling. You can tell me the truth right now and make it easy on yourself. We can fight it out, and you tell me with my blade to your throat. Or I can fuck you so hard that you will scream it out."

Imogen's whole body ignited. She forced herself to pull free and face him. He was in a tight black shirt and jeans and looked so fucking good. *Fuck him.*

"I'm going to have to go with option four, where I give you one of these," she said and lifted her middle finger at him. "And I walk away."

Arawan grabbed her wrist and sucked the offensive finger into his mouth. Imogen went wet, and her whole body shook.

"No. You don't get to use those tricks," she snarled, and his tongue flicked over her finger again. She pulled a knife and angled it over his heart. No one seemed to notice, the low lights of the club hiding the blade. "Let my finger go."

Arawan dropped her hand, his smile widening. "Option two and three it is." He moved so quickly that Imogen had no chance to retaliate. He disarmed her and had her knife to her throat in a blink.

"Tell me you love me too, or you know what happens next," he growled.

Imogen swallowed hard, refusing to back down. "You can't love me. I'm mortal. It's never going to work."

"I can love you. I don't care that you're mortal. We can make anything work," he replied.

"Not if Hafgan kills you for being a dumbass," she snapped back.

"Hafgan couldn't use Brangwen against me when she was alive. You really think he'll be able to do it now that she's dead? This isn't about my past. This is about you being a coward and trying to find something to fight with me about because you can't handle that you love me back."

Imogen's eyes narrowed, and she raised her chin. "Fuck you."

"Fuck me? I thought you'd never ask." The dagger vanished from Arawan's hand, and she was suddenly up in his arms. The crowd parted for him as he carried her, swearing and cursing from the dance floor. He kicked open the door to the private staff bathroom and locked it. Imogen's heart was pounding hard, her whole body wrapped around him and unwilling to let him go.

"Tell me you love me, Imogen," he demanded, pressing her against the tiled wall.

"No," she whispered.

Arawan's hand gripped one side of her throat, and he nipped and sucked up the other side.

"Tell me you love me, Imogen. Make me your slave and your fool, just tell me you want me too."

Imogen couldn't fight him anymore. Tears of frustration and longing built in her eyes. "I'm scared if I do, I won't ever get my soul back."

Arawan drew back so he could look her in the eyes. "Give it to me, darling, and I'll take such good care of it, you won't ever want it back."

Imogen's teeth were locked together, but she still ground out the words. "I. Love. You."

Arawan's thumb brushed over her cheek. "There, now, that wasn't so bad, was it?"

"Fuck you—" Imogen started to swear, but his mouth crashed down on hers, devouring and biting and taking until her hand was bunched in his hair, trying to bring him closer. Imogen undid his belt and plunged her hand into his jeans, stroking his already hard dick.

"Option three. I want option three right fucking now," she panted, making him groan. Her jeans were down and off one leg in an instant. Arawan picked her up and pressed her tight against the wall before sinking his cock into her. Imogen's whole body clenched and burned, trying to make room for him, but it felt so damn good she could've started crying again.

"This is where you belong, my love," Arawan said, biting her throat as he pounded into her. "In my arms, my dick inside of you, filling you up until it's only me you can think about."

"Yes. Fuck, don't stop," Imogen begged, her pussy clenching

around him.

"Never." Arawan's hand grabbed her ass tight enough to bruise. "Touch your pretty pussy for me. Let me see you come apart."

Imogen's hand obeyed, first running her fingers through the wetness where they were joined and dragging it over her clit. Lights danced in her vision with every caress. Arawan's gaze was so fixated on each stroke, so hot and devouring, that Imogen was coming within two more strokes of his dick.

"That's it, my flower, come for me," Arawan purred, kissing her cries as she obeyed him. Her body went soft with release, all the tension in the last hours seeping out of her.

Arawan wasn't nearly done. He pulled off the wall, spinning her about and bending her over the sink. She gripped the hard sides of it, trying to keep her legs from shaking. In the mirror, her mascara and eyeliner were smeared, and her eyes were hazy from her sex high.

"Look how perfect you are, how fucking undone," Arawan said from behind her. He pulled down the front of her tank to expose the gray lace of her bra. "Fucking gorgeous and all mine."

"Yes," she managed to pant out.

Arawan stroked the curves of her ass before spreading her and driving his cock back into her. Imogen cried out, and his face flashed with pure, dark satisfaction in the mirror. He moved her hips, thrusting into her in a different angle that had her rising up on the balls of her feet.

"Oh fucking fuck," she groaned.

"That's the spot, is it, beloved?" Arawan chuckled like the sinful fucker he was. One hand went under her, toying with her soaked pussy and over her clit before sliding up to stroke her back hole.

Imogen swore and squirmed as heat rushed to her face and her whole body tightened over his cock. Arawan leaned over her to kiss and nibble at her neck and shoulder.

"My fierce little hunter, you're so greedy for me that I bet I could get you to admit just about anything right now," he teased, grinding his hips against hers and making a choked cry break free from her. "Tell me you're mine and no one else's."

"I'm yours and no one else's. Fuck, I'm yours!" she shouted, pushing back against him.

"Tell me you love me," he demanded, his voice getting ragged. Arawan's cock hit her G-spot harder, and she swore viciously. "*Tell me, Imogen.*"

"I love you, I love you, I love you," she babbled helplessly as his cock and finger worked her mercilessly. She would tell him anything, give him anything. She didn't care. Nothing mattered except for this feeling.

"Fuck, Imogen, you're going to ruin me," Arawan moaned.

"Good. Then you'll know how it feels," she snarled, loving that he was as unraveled as she was. She fucked herself back on his cock. "Come for me, God of the dead. Fill me until I taste you."

Arawan exploded, his thrusts so hard that her nails broke trying to hold onto the sink. Imogen screamed, her orgasm violent and vicious as it tore through her. Arawan pulled her back tight to him and came hard inside her, his body shaking. He wrapped arms around her waist and rested her head against her back.

"Fuck, I love you," he gasped against her. "Never leave me again."

"Never make me leave you again," Imogen replied, her breath coming in hard pants.

Arawan chuckled softly. "Fuck, you can't give a man a break even when he's still inside of you."

"You wouldn't want me if I did," she said. He pulled free of her with a hiss and eased off her. She was a total mess, but he looked at her like she was the most beautiful thing in the world.

"You love me," he said softly, with a dazed expression.

Imogen gave him a crooked smile. "Yeah, I do. Now, get the fuck out of here, so I can clean myself up."

Arawan kissed her possessively. "I like knowing I'm going to be dripping out of you all the way home."

"Perve. Get out." Imogen shoved him toward the door. Arawan looked her over and bit his bottom lip. Imogen shivered and locked the door behind him before things got out of hand all over again.

Love confessions and sex didn't fix everything, but they helped settle a part of herself that had been eating away at her all day.

I can love you. I don't care that you're mortal. We can make anything work. Arawan's words felt burned into her. For the first time, Imogen allowed herself to hope that they could be true.

26

"There is no way I'm letting you drive home," Imogen complained ten minutes later. Arawan held out his hand for the key to her bike.

"You've been drinking, and I'm not letting you drive." He wasn't going to budge on this argument.

"But you don't even know *how* to drive," she said, hands on her hips. Arawan dragged her to him, kissing her as his magic enclosed her. Imogen let out a small gasp as he plucked the knowledge from her mind.

"Now I do," he replied, taking the key from her hand while she was still kiss struck.

"That's a dirty fucking trick," she muttered.

"It's a useful one," he said, tying his hair back. Imogen climbed on the bike behind him and put her arms around him. His heart hurt with how much he was feeling. She was coming home with him, and that was all that mattered. Everything else they could figure out as long as they were together.

Arawan knew why Imogen loved to ride. It had more speed than a horse and there was a wild freedom to it.

They were only thirty minutes away from the castle when sharp agonising pain ripped through Arawan. He screamed, trying to keep control of the bike as his connection to Annwn was torn out of him. They started to crash, and Arawan pulled a terrified Imogen to him as they fell.

They hit the road hard, the bike flipping and shattering ahead of them. Arawan groaned as his back and legs were ripped up against the bitumen, and they rolled to a stop.

"Are you okay? Please tell me you're not hurt!" Arawan gasped out, pulling Imogen's helmet from her head. She was so mortal, so breakable.

"I'm okay. What the fuck happened? Oh, gods, you're bleeding everywhere," she said, cradling his pounding head.

"I'll live. I can't...I can't feel Annwn. Something has happened," he stammered. He reached for his power and only felt a tiny spark in his core.

"Okay, we'll sort it out. Just let me help you stand. We need to get you off the road," she babbled. She looped his arm over her shoulders and dragged him to his feet. A musical jangle echoed in the night, and Imogen fumbled in her jacket pocket for her phone.

"Bayn! Something's happened to Arawan," she said.

"Yeah, that's not all. The castle just spat Freya and me out onto the road and fucking *vanished*. Where are you?" Bayn replied, shouting loud enough that Arawan heard every word.

Arawan swayed, and Imogen helped him sit down on a nearby rock. She was still talking to Bayn when the ground beside them iced over, and the fae prince and his mate appeared through it.

"Fucking hell, did you crash?" Freya demanded, racing to Imogen.

"I'm fine. Arawan protected me."

Bayn placed a hand on Arawan's shoulder to steady him. "You look like shit. What the fuck happened?"

"I...don't know. I can't feel Annwn," Arawan said, staring at the silver ichor covering his hands and clothes. "My wounds aren't healing as quickly as they should."

"It's okay. We'll get you out of here," Bayn assured him. Imogen and Freya were coming back with the saddlebags from the bike. Imogen pulled out a shirt and pressed it to a wound in Arawan's side.

"No dying on me, Daddy," she teased half-heartedly. She was shaking, and Arawan hated it.

"I'm okay, Imogen," he tried to reassure her.

"Bayn, we need to get them out of here," Freya said, eyes scanning the road around them. "I felt strange magic right before the castle vanished. If this is an attack, there will be people hunting them."

"Okay, okay, we're taking you two home," Bayn grumbled, hauling Arawan to his feet.

"Careful, Bayn!" Imogen shouted.

"He's a fucking god, Gen! He will be fine. Tell her," Bayn said, giving him a shake that made Arawan's teeth clench.

"She knows I will be."

"Take him first, Bayn. I'll watch out if someone appears," Imogen said, pulling out her ax.

"And I'll watch her," Freya added, magic crackling over her.

"I'll be quick," Bayn promised and dragged Arawan through the ice. They popped out again in the main hall of a castle. Bayn helped Arawan into a nearby chair. "Don't go anywhere."

Arawan could barely stay upright, but he managed to nod. What had happened to Annwn? How could his castle be gone? Arawan placed a hand over his still bleeding side. He could feel it healing, but it was too slow. His power was stripped entirely.

Imogen appeared with Bayn and Freya, and she was beside him instantly, her face drawn.

"Are you worried about me?" Arawan asked.

"Of course I am, you big idiot!" Imogen exclaimed.

"I've never had someone worry about me before."

"Aw," Freya said before she stopped herself. "Help him get cleaned up, Imogen, and meet us in the kitchen when you're ready. I'm starving after all this excitement."

Arawan couldn't stop Imogen from supporting him all the way to the guest room she usually stayed in. She stripped him off and sat him down on a bench in the bathroom before turning on the water taps.

"I like this," Arawan said, staring at the silver head the water was pouring from.

"It's called a shower. Something we both need," she replied, pulling off her clothes and joining him.

"That's definitely making me feel better," Arawan said, mesmerized by the water glistening over her large breasts.

"Wounded and still a perve," she replied with a shake of her head. "Let me have a look at your back." Arawan turned a little, and she swore.

"Fuck, lover, you're a mess," Imogen whispered, her voice cracking. She took a washcloth and cleaned all the scrapes, so they were clear of dirt and gravel.

"I can't believe you took all of this for me."

Arawan took her hand and kissed the tattooed scar on the inside of her arm.

"I love you, so you might be horrified to know how far I'll go to protect you," he said, pressing her palm to his cheek. "You are mortal, and I'm never going to take that risk. I will heal. It's just taking longer than I imagined. We need to find out why I am disconnected from my power."

"We will, I promise," she said and kissed him softly. "And we will murder the bastards responsible for this fuckery. Every single mark on you right now is their fault, and they are going to fucking regret it."

Arawan put his arms around her and stared into her beautiful, violent face. "What did I do to deserve you after all this time?"

"Something bad, I bet. Or I did something bad." Imogen grinned. His smile widened automatically. "And you're not allowed to look at me like that until you're healed."

"Like what?" he asked innocently, hand dropping to grab her ass.

"Don't make me turn this shower on cold," she warned, tugging on his hair in a way that went straight to his dick. She kissed him deeply. "I...love you too. Don't make me regret it, okay? I'm not good at any of this, and I'm feeling way too vulnerable right now."

"I've never been in love either," Arawan admitted, and her eyes went wide. "It makes me vulnerable too, and I hate it. We can figure it out together."

"Let's figure out our enemy's plans and deal with them first," Imogen said and placed her forehead against his. "Just so we are clear, I'm not some pampered pillow princess. Your battles are my battles. If we are going to do this, know that I won't be left behind, and I won't let you wrap me in cotton wool for fear of me breaking."

"Darling, you being a warrior is one of the things I love most about you." Arawan kissed her. "You are the only one I trust by my side."

"Good. Because my hunter instincts tell me we are in for a fight," Imogen replied, and Arawan could only agree.

27

Freya was true to her word and had a stir fry cooked by the time Arawan and Imogen made it to the kitchen. Imogen gratefully accepted a cold beer from Bayn on the way in.

"How are your wounds?" the fae prince asked Arawan.

"They have been cleaned thanks to Imogen and have closed over," he replied, shooting Imogen a heated look from across the kitchen.

Imogen tried to ignore the spark of electricity that sizzled through her. When he looked at her like that, she would do anything he asked.

"You two have worked things out, I see," Freya whispered to Imogen as she plated up the food. They were on the other side of the kitchen, and Freya was almost bursting with the need to gossip with her.

"Yeah, we did. You know they can hear you, right?" Imogen said, glancing in the direction of the two males.

"They will be polite and mind their own business if they know what's good for them," Freya replied, and conversation on the other side of the room faltered. Imogen snickered. "So are you going to tell me what's going on between you two?"

"I love him, and I proved that by shagging him stupid in the club bathroom."

Freya laughed. "Well, I suppose that's one way to go about things."

"What? I find it easier than talking about feelings," Imogen said, lifting the beer back to her mouth.

They all sat down around the table, and it was almost bizarre to see Arawan acting like a regular guy, talking to Bayn in only a black shirt and a pair of loose black pajama pants. Damn, he looked fine in anything.

Or nothing, her brain added, unhelpful as ever.

Imogen did her best to rein that side of her in. Doing that was hard work when he pulled out the chair beside him and gave her one of his devastating smiles. She thought about sitting somewhere else just to mess with him, but after seeing him torn to shreds for her, she wanted him as close as possible.

"You said you felt strange magic before the castle disappeared," Arawan began, his hand slipping over Imogen's knee under the table. "Can I ask you to elaborate on that?"

Freya sat down next to Bayn. "Aisling and I were still up drinking wine, and it was like she shimmered. It was as if she started to fade, and she whispered something about a call...and then the whole castle seemed to be ripped away and tossed us out onto the road."

"I was about to have a bath, so it was a good thing I hadn't undressed yet," Bayn added. "I didn't feel the presence of magic so much as a rush of heat through the castle, and then it was gone."

Arawan frowned. "The castle was powered through my connection to Annwn. The whole area was a literal extension of the land of the dead. Whoever has done this somehow managed to sever it."

"You think Hafgan is behind it?" Imogen asked.

"He would have the power, but I would have felt the presence of his magic in the castle."

"Maybe Aisling would know. Kian has some of her blood and has used it to summon and speak with her while she was in Annwn," Bayn replied thoughtfully.

Arawan nodded. "That would be helpful. She's a sorceress. She will be more sensitive to the magic that managed to achieve it. I will need to find a way back to Annwn to stop whatever is happening, but I don't know how to get there if I'm not connected to it."

Imogen waggled her eyebrows at him. "I could always kill you, and that will send you straight home."

"Oh, very funny. I bet you would love that," Arawan said, rolling his eyes at her.

"No one is killing anyone, you psychos," Freya snapped at them. She dared to give Arawan a stern look. "Don't encourage her."

Arawan only gave Imogen a smile that said he was going to encourage her to do all *kinds* of reckless things. Loving him might actually be the most dangerous thing she had ever done.

After Bayn had finished eating, he went to collect Kian, Elise, Killian, and Bron. Imogen crashed into her sister, holding her close.

"I'm sorry for waking you up and dragging you into this on such short notice," Imogen said into Bron's dark hair.

"To be honest, we expected something to happen and were ready for it," Bron replied.

Killian pulled Imogen into a hug. "So you didn't take our advice to not shag the god of the dead."

Imogen laughed. "Come on, bro, don't act like you didn't have a bet going. Did you win at least?"

Killian's smile said it all. "Of course I did. Arawan is quite literally all of your weaknesses tied up into one sexy package. You both looked ready to tear each other apart or fuck each other stupid from the day he turned up."

It was so accurate, Imogen didn't even bother to try and deny it. Bayn appeared with Kian and Elise, the latter a bundle of bright eyes and dark hair.

"I haven't been out in ages! This is way too exciting," Elise said by way of greeting and hugged Imogen.

"Don't say that like there's any other place you'd rather be than Kian's library," Imogen replied.

"Not true! I'm very partial to being in between his thighs as well. But really, have you seen Kian's library? I'm going to need years to go through it all. Charlotte is having a blast studying all the magic books I have no idea about." Elise looked across the room to where Arawan was standing. He watched them all curiously like he had never seen a family before. "Damn, Imogen, I can see why you're willing to risk it all."

"He can grow a crown made of bone and has wings too. Just putting it out there," Imogen replied, shooting him a salacious look. His eyes flashed ruby and her lady parts clenched.

Fuck, look away! Look away!

It was too late; she was caught in his spell and was walking toward him before she could stop herself.

"What are you doing hiding over here," she asked. Arawan draped an arm around her waist. He looked uncertain of the gesture, so she leaned into him.

"I'm not hiding. I'm observing," he replied.

"We are all a bit loud when we are together. Don't let it intimidate you." Imogen slipped a hand underneath the back of his shirt. "How are you feeling?"

"I'm healed, Imogen. I told you I would." Arawan's mouth twitched a little. "I'm surprised you're concerned at all, considering you offered to kill me in order for me to get back to Annwn."

Imogen's hand dropped to pat his ass. "I was teasing. I'm not going to give you up without a fight."

"I promise when Hafgan is dealt with, I will let the court run itself again, and I will devote a year to making you scream in pleasure," Arawan whispered in her ear.

Imogen bit the inside of her cheek. "Is that a promise or a threat?"

"Both."

"Are you two interested in summoning Aisling or not?" Bayn called out to them, and Imogen had to force her eyes away from Arawan.

The fae princes and their mates were all staring at them. Bron gave her a look that said some kind of big sister lecture was bound to happen in her future. Imogen didn't care what anyone said; she wouldn't walk away from the only person who ever really understood and accepted her. *All* of her.

Surely Bron would understand that. She had never gotten close to anyone before Killian either.

Kian pulled out a small vial. "I only have half of Aisling's blood left, so let's hope this works. Where have you put your mirror, Bayn?"

"This way." Bayn waved at them to follow him. "Haven't had much use since we started using phones, so I put it where I place everything else I don't need."

Imogen's hand drifted to take Arawan's. His long fingers around hers felt like the most natural thing in the world. She had never thought she would be happier just from holding a hand, but clearly, Arawan had fucked out the last of her cynicism.

"Are you serious, Bayn? In here?" Killian complained when Bayn opened a set of double doors.

"Why not?"

"Because it's weird and creepy," Elise replied, stepping closer to Kian.

Inside, the hall was filled with frozen bodies, and propped against a huge fae was a silver mirror with runes carved around the edges.

"What else am I supposed to do with them? It's not like I can just throw them out," Bayn replied and looked at Freya. "Do you think it's weird and creepy?"

"Yes," she said and kissed his cheek. "But I like that about you."

They all knew that Bayn would always be the fae prince executioner, and these were the enemies they had defeated. Imogen had heard about the hall of frozen bodies from Freya but had never actually seen it.

"Bro, this is the coolest, weirdest trophy room I've ever seen," Imogen said, looking closely at the twisted, frozen face of a warrior. "Madame Tussauds got nothing on this."

Bayn shot her wink. He lifted the mirror and placed it upright on a throne. Kian stepped forward, muttering under his breath at the scratches on the frame.

"If I knew you were going to throw out an enchanted mirror, I wouldn't have given it to you," he muttered, tossing his long red mane behind him.

"Don't be so dramatic. It will work perfectly fine," Bayn argued.

Arawan's warm body pressed in behind Imogen. "Are they always this argumentative?"

"Yes, they are actually behaving because you are here," she replied. "Why?"

"I'm starting to understand why you've always been so disobedient."

Bron snorted. "Imogen didn't need the influence of three brothers to be disobedient."

"Don't you tell him a damn thing, Bronagh Ironwood, or I'll make you regret it," Imogen warned, hands on her hips. Bron mimed buttoning her lips, and Arawan chuckled softly. Bron's eyes went wide in surprise.

Imogen crossed her arms. "Yes, Bron, he can smile and laugh. He's not that impressive even if he is a god."

"I'll show you how impressive I can be," Arawan growled, and goosebumps broke out along Imogen's neck and shoulders.

"It's working," Kian called, interrupting them. Bloody runes had been scrawled over the mirror's surface and were glowing softly. They moved around the mirror, and Aisling appeared through the mist and gloom.

"Thank the gods you're okay! I thought the castle disappearing had killed you," Aisling said to Bayn and Freya.

"Aisling, what is happening?" Arawan demanded.

"I'm not sure, but I am searching for the answers. The castle and Annwn are intact here, and from what I have seen, the courtiers are unharmed," Aisling replied. She looked about her nervously. "You should know, I think that Hafgan's envoy did something to break your connection to Annwn. My lord, you have to get back before he arrives. Dafydd has been strutting about like a squawking rooster, saying that he's coming to take your throne."

Arawan laughed. It was cold and vicious. "He can try. I will find a way home, Aisling. Tell the court. Don't let Dafydd worry them too much."

"I will, my lord, but hurry," the sorceress said as she began to fade away.

"I swear, Hafgan's days are fucking numbered," Arawan promised, gripping the mirror frame tight. "You tell them I'm coming, and any traitors will answer to my blade."

"Hurry..." Aisling whispered and was gone.

"What now?" Killian asked softly. Arawan let the mirror go, and Imogen saw the cracks he'd made in it.

"Now, we find a way to get to Annwn without dying," Imogen said, keeping her voice steady. "There has to be a way. What about the obsidian gates, Arawan?"

"What obsidian gates?" Killian asked, his black brows drawing together.

"Um. When I died recently, I kept finding myself at these two black obelisk things. I could see Annwn through them like they were a portal or a doorway," Imogen tried to explain. Both times had faded like a weird dream. The only thing she really remembered was Arawan.

Freya yawned loudly. "We can figure it out tomorrow. A few hours of sleep will do us all good. Don't forget you were in a bike accident tonight."

"You were fucking what?" Bron demanded, rounding on Imogen. She grabbed Arawan by the hand and yawned dramatically.

"Oh, so tired, sis. Good night. Love you all!" she said quickly and tugged him toward the door.

"You are in so much trouble, Imogen Ironwood!" Bron shouted behind her.

"What else is new?" Imogen shouted back. Oh yeah, that big sister lecture was going to be a doozy.

28

As a rule, Imogen didn't sleep with her hookups. She preferred to keep actual sleeping as a solo affair. She really hated the idea of sleeping without Arawan after the night they'd had.

Arawan looked tired for the first time, and Imogen wondered if he was lying about being as fine as he claimed. She snuggled up in bed beside him, her body fitting perfectly into the curve of his. Arawan's arm went around her and pulled her tighter up against him.

"Why aren't you angrier right now?" she asked him in the darkness. "You've lost your home and most of your power. You should be furious."

"I *am* furious, but I'm trying to save my energy for the fight again. I don't want to frighten you, but I'm not much more powerful than your brothers right now," Arawan replied, his fingers stroking her hair.

"But my brothers are ridiculously powerful, Arawan. Being stronger than them still makes you the biggest badass around."

"Not compared to what I usually am. I keep things contained while I'm in this realm." Arawan kissed her temple. "I am angry, Imogen, but you also told me you love me tonight. Everything comes second to that."

"Who would've thought the god of the dead was such a softie deep down?" she teased, turning a little in his arms so she could look at his heartbreakingly beautiful face.

"Certainly not me. It still doesn't change the fact I'm in awe that you've chosen me," Arawan replied, fingers tracing her cheek, her jaw, her lips. "I have fought in many battles. Defeated Hafgan more times than I can count. I've only felt like this once, and it feels like the biggest threat to my sanity right now, not whatever the hell Hafgan is up to."

Imogen kissed him, not knowing how to reassure him or tell him what he needed to hear. She was always terrible about talking about her feelings. Arawan made her feel so many things at once it was like her body wasn't big enough to contain them.

"You make me crazy too," she said when they finally pulled back. Arawan's eyes glowed a soft ruby in the shadows. "But I'm not going anywhere, understand? You go running back to Annwn to take down Hafgan's bullshit rebellion. I'm coming. I won't be left behind."

"It will be so dangerous for a mortal, my love," he said, voice straining like he had to force the words out. "But I need you by my side. You remind me what's worth fighting for."

"Yeah, my ass is pretty great, it's true," Imogen teased, trying desperately to ease the worry in his voice. Arawan's hand slid from where it was draped over her stomach and glided around to cup her generous curves.

"It's not just pretty great. It's perfect, and it's mine, and I'm going to protect it no matter what happens," Arawan said, his teeth dragged over her ear. "I have too many filthy, filthy plans to let it come to any harm."

"Keep talking like that, and we aren't going to get any sleep at all." Imogen shifted, so her butt pressed up against him.

"You keep rubbing it on me like that, and I'm going to fuck you again." Arawan kissed her, his tongue doing a slow and sexy exploration of her mouth in a way that made her whole body shiver. "Go to sleep, darling."

Imogen wanted to argue and say that she needed more orgasms than sleep, but her eyes were already closing, and she had drifted off before saying another word.

∽

IMOGEN WOKE, and the first thing she noticed was the god sprawled out on the pillows beside her, his long black hair spilling like ink on the white linen.

Well, damn, if that's not the best thing I've ever woken up to. With all that had been happening, she hadn't had a moment of slow exploration of him. Something she planned to correct immediately.

His whole torso was covered in ashy scars in all shapes and sizes. It was the body of a warrior, and Imogen's was similarly marked up from various scrapes she had been in over the years.

Imogen bent her head down and kissed a jagged scar over his pec. She sucked his nipple, and he murmured something in his sleep.

Imogen grinned and pulled the sheet down to expose more of his lean, sexy body. Her fingers traced down the dark trail of hair from his navel. He was already hard, and she wouldn't miss the opportunity to wake him up in the nicest way possible.

She moved down the bed, careful not to disturb him, and tongued the head of his dick. Arawan shuddered in his sleep, his back arching. Fuck, it was the sexiest thing she had ever seen. She wanted him unraveled, entirely at her mercy and making more of those sexy helpless sounds. The predator in her wanted to play, to torment. Imogen felt him stir and quickly lowered her mouth over him and sucked hard.

"Fuck! What..." Arawan glanced down at her, his pupils blowing out.

"Good morning," Imogen purred, digging her nails into his thighs to stop him from moving. She sucked up the side of his dick, making him whimper. "You want me to stop?"

"Don't you fucking dare," Arawan snarled. He thrust his hips up a little. "You started it, so you better fucking finish it."

Imogen went wet at the bossy tone. It did it to her every time. She went back to work, licking and sucking. She slowed down when she tasted pre-cum and gently pulled away.

"Wait, don't stop," he begged in a tone she had never heard from him.

Desperation.

"I'm not stopping. I'm getting on," Imogen said, pushing him back down and straddling him. "Hands above your head, and I'll give you a treat." His eyes burned hot; pupils were blown out with desire. He slowly lifted his arms to clasp behind his head, his biceps flexing. He looked like the dark and decadent god he was.

"Don't leave me in suspense, darling," he warned. Imogen didn't break eye contact as she stroked her pussy, smearing her fingers with her own wetness. She held them out to him.

"Suck," she commanded. Arawan whimpered and sucked her fingers into his mouth. Imogen lowered herself down onto his dick at the same time, and the sound that came out of him... She didn't have words for how sexy it was. She took a steady breath, forcing her aching body to make space for him. He was big, but he was perfect. Imogen rolled her hips, her hand toying with one of his nipples as she sucked and bit his other one.

"Imogen... Fuck, let me see you," Arawan said, lifting his hips to meet every thrust of hers. Imogen sat up, nails scraping along his torso and leaving red scratch marks. She stared at the marks, and something snapped inside of her. She didn't want to play with her food anymore; she wanted to feast. Imogen rode him so hard she could feel him deep in her core. She grabbed him around the throat.

"Tell me you love me," she groaned, her orgasm starting to overtake her.

"I do love you, Imogen Ironwood. I love your ferocity and your smile and how good your sweet pussy feels clamped around me," Arawan growled out. "I love how you fight, how vicious you are. I love that your shade sings to mine."

Imogen screamed, and lights danced over her vision as she came hard on him. Her body was shaking with the violence of the emotions and the release burning her alive.

Arawan took advantage of her weakened state, dropped his hands, and rolled her onto her back. He grabbed her by her hips and slammed his dick into her so hard, she cried out like a porn star. She felt him in every part of her, invading her soul and heart, taking and giving.

His black eyes locked on her. "I love you so much I feel like it's going to destroy me. I'm never going to let you go. I'm never going to want anything as much as I want you. I could have all of you forever, and it wouldn't be enough time. I love you."

Arawan licked at the tears running down her face. He kissed her, and she could taste their salty sweetness as he came, filling her up with him and sending her spiraling into another orgasm.

"I love you too," she sobbed. Arawan rested his head on her chest, his heart pounding against hers. Imogen threaded her fingers through his hair and over his broad shoulders.

"You are the only thing I want to wake up to from now on," he murmured against her skin. "I wish I could keep you here all day."

With uncanny timing, there was a hard knock at the door. Imogen wondered who would dare.

"Fuck off or I'll throat punch you!" she shouted, making Arawan shake with laughter on top of her.

"Like to see you try, bitch! Get your asses up," Bron shouted back. "We might have an idea on how to get to Annwn."

29

Imogen was still walking on shaky legs when she made it downstairs with Arawan. He was smirking like he knew exactly what he had done to her. Imogen was too full of endorphins to want to be dirty about it.

Everyone was in the dining room, eating piles of waffles, fresh fruit, and coffee.

"Jesus, Freya, have you been possessed by Nigella Lawson or something?" Imogen asked, looking at the massive spread.

"Ha! No. Bayn went and got Kian's cook this morning," Freya laughed. "I'm too pretty to be slaving away in a kitchen for you lot."

"Good idea. I'm starving," Imogen said, sitting down and going straight for the coffee pot.

"I can't imagine why," Elise replied with an innocent flutter of her lashes. Imogen flipped her off, making her gasp in outrage and Kian grin.

"You said you have found a way into Annwn?" Arawan asked, jumping straight to it. Imogen had started filling his plate without even realizing it. She scowled in confusion. She was fussing over him.

Goddamn it.

Bron was staring at her with an infuriating smile on her face. The others might not realize how out of character Imogen was acting, but her older sister did.

"Imogen mentioned obsidian gates last night, and it bugged me because I felt like I had seen something similar before," Killian said, leaning back in his chair. "When the fae were first cursed, I spent years tracking down every set of gates and weak points in Faerie, trying to find a way back into the human world. I found a weak spot that had two black obsidian monoliths. They were carved with glyphs I had never seen before. The whole place gave me the creeps so badly, I left and never dared attempt to see where they led."

"It sounds similar to the ones I kept finding myself at," Imogen replied, trying to recall more details. "I wasn't creeped out, though. I wanted to go through them."

"All the same, it's still worth investigating to confirm whether or not they lead to Annwn." Arawan steepled his fingers. "I will have to figure out a way to get to my weapons once I get into Annwn. I can't face Hafgan without protection. He's too skilled and too vicious. If I confront him with nothing on, he'll just strike me down."

Imogen's whole body filled with ice, but before she could snap, Kian put down his coffee.

"My brothers and I discussed that this morning too. We might not be able to follow you into Annwn to assist you in battle, but we can offer you something that can help," Kian said, and Bayn and Killian both nodded at him. "Our father had magical armor that we would like you to use. It is in Killian's castle in Faerie, so you will need to collect it before going to the black gate."

"What kind of magical armor?" Imogen asked.

"The unbreakable, impervious to damage kind," Killian replied. "Don't forget our parents were strong enough to keep Morrigan out of Faerie. The sword Bron carries was Father's too. His armor was made from the same meteorite metal the sword is."

"I would be honored to defeat our enemies wearing it," Arawan replied, with a bow of his head.

"So it looks like we are going to Faerie," Imogen said, shooting Arawan a wink. "I've never been, but it sounds fun."

"You still want to do this despite the danger?" Arawan asked, taking her hand.

Imogen's smile widened. "Death himself couldn't stop me."

"Smartass."

"You love my ass."

Arawan raised a brow at her. "Indeed. I'll be punishing it too once this is done."

"If you keep trying to stop me from coming with you, I'm going to fuck you so hard that you—"

"Hey! We are right here," Bron complained, tapping her fork loudly on her plate.

"So?" Imogen and Arawan said at the same time and then snickered.

"Fucking hell, there's two of them now," Killian said and laughed.

∽

IMOGEN LEFT the others to work out the logistics of a trip into Faerie and went and called Layla. Her sister picked up after five rings with a mumbled grunt.

"Still asleep, little sis?" Imogen teased.

"Went on a hunt last night. Where the fuck have you been? You think you could call me occasionally."

"Bron didn't tell you? We've had shit going on," Imogen replied. She gave a sleepy Layla a rundown of the last twenty-four hours.

"Goddamn it. You and Bron are the worst with keeping people in the loop." Layla muttered something, and there was a rustle of blankets. "Going into Faerie! For fuck's sake. I feel like you guys get to have all the fun projects."

"I dunno about that. I know how much you like regular camping, let alone a trek into Faerie. You'd hate it."

"Yeah, probably. I'm still feeling stuck at home. How's it going with tall, dark and dangerous?"

"Arawan? Ah, good?"

Layla laughed. "You're so fucking obvious, Gen. You jumped his godly bones yet?"

"Yep. And I'm going to do it again."

"Fuck yeah, that's my sister." Layla yawned dramatically. "Okay, so what's the purpose of this call? You need love advice?"

"Ha! No. I just..."

I'm going into Faerie and Annwn, hunting a general who can't die, and I just wanted to say goodbye if I didn't get a chance to. Imogen cleared her throat.

"I just don't know how long I'll be away for. Time moves differently in Faerie, and I wanted to make sure I got to talk to you before I went."

"Don't talk like you're not coming back. You're the baddest bitch I know. If you're brave enough to fuck the god of the dead, you're brave enough and strong enough to survive whatever happens next," Layla replied, her tone so confident, Imogen got a lump in her throat.

"Thanks, Layla. I love you, you know that, right?"

"Jesus, you must be worried you're not coming back if you are saying that," Layla retorted. "I love you too, Gen. Go kick some ass and come home and tell me about it. Bring Arawan with you. I want to see Mom's face when you introduce him."

"Mom would probably try and kick him in the nuts for trapping me into a bargain," Imogen said with a fond smile. "Tell the others I love them too. And for God's sake, if something does happen to me, make sure you get rid of all my sex toys before anyone clears out my room."

"I must really love you to agree to that."

"You can take your pick of all my clothes and weapons as a thank you."

"Fuck, don't be morbid. You're coming home, sis, or I will get an ouija board to summon you and then abuse you."

"I gotta run. Goodbye, Lay Lay," Imogen said.

"I'll see you soon, shit head," Layla replied and hung up on her.

Imogen took a picture of her flipping her off and sent it to her before she grabbed her bag and got ready to follow the man she loved on a suicide mission.

"Piece of cake," Imogen said aloud and went to find Arawan.

30

It was decided that they would go through the Stonehenge gates to get into Faerie. Not only was the place powerful enough not to need any particular phases of the moon or day to use it, but it also led to the same place every time.

Imogen wondered how much power Bayn had pent up to be able to portal them about as much as he was. After kissing Freya goodbye, Bayn took Arawan and Imogen through the ice to Kian's castle. He had brought Elise, Kian, Killian, and Bron back earlier and didn't seem tired in the slightest.

And Arawan still has more magic than that. Imogen had no real concept of magic and refused to let Charlotte explain it to her. She was determined to treat her brothers as she treated her sisters and Lachie and not be impressed with them in the slightest. It was probably why she wasn't intimidated by the God of the dead currently holding her hand.

"Is Dad still here?" Imogen asked, looking towards Kian's castle and the fae busily working and training on its grounds.

"No, he's in Faerie with the healing mages. Did you want to see Charlotte?" Bayn replied.

Imogen shook her head. "No. She'll lecture me, and probably

Arawan too, and I don't want to disturb her happy time with Reeve and a new library. I'll let Bron tell her what I've been up to."

"Great, throw me in the shit as usual," Bron said, riding up on a black stallion and leading another. "Kill's castle is a half a day's ride when we cross over into Faerie. You okay on a horse still?"

"Sure am. I have been riding all kinds of beasts lately," Imogen replied.

Arawan clarified, "She has been riding the Cŵn Annwn."

"Ah huh. I don't need to know," Bron said with a shake of her head.

Arawan fixed Imogen with a loaded look. "You can always ride with me if you like, darling. I like keeping you close."

"Riding with you got me into this mess," Imogen huffed, flicking her braid over one shoulder.

"Don't worry, my lord, your horse is on its way." Bron looked over her shoulder like she sensed the second Killian was coming closer. He rode up, leading another horse.

"Okay, let's get going if you two want to get to the castle by nightfall," he said and checked Imogen over. "You got enough weapons on you?"

"You can never have enough, in my opinion," Imogen said, pulling herself up into the saddle of the giant Faerie mount. "Besides, I couldn't say no to Bayn when he offered me some of his collection."

It was true she might have overdone it a bit, but she knew enough stories about Faerie to want to be prepared. She had her ax strapped to her back, a dagger on each thigh, and another two on her belt.

Bayn had also given her a bandolier of throwing daggers carved in runes that did gods knew what. She figured if accepting them made Bayn feel better, she wouldn't say no and had strapped them across her chest.

Killian clicked his tongue. "Sounds like the little icicle is worried about you."

"And you're not?"

"Not in the slightest. Hafgan should be more concerned about you coming for him than Arawan, in my opinion," he replied.

Bron laughed. "I can agree with that. I've seen you in a rage, after all, little sis. Hafgan should be running if he knows what's good for him."

"Aw, guys, that's the sweetest thing you've ever said to me," Imogen crooned at them. Arawan was giving them another one of his pleased looks, like seeing them interacting together made him happy.

"Imogen will make the whole of Annwn tremble, I have no doubt," he said, his gaze heating as it fixed on her.

"You've got it so bad, my lord," Killian said with a shake of his head.

"How can I not? It's not every day you meet a woman with a tongue as sharp as her blades," Arawan replied.

Kill's emerald eyes glittered with mischief. "Clearly, you need to hang out with the Ironwoods more."

∽

THEY CROSSED into Faerie with little effort, and Imogen did her best not to feel like a dumb tourist excited by everything she saw. Even the air felt different in Faerie, lighter and cleaner and infused with magic.

"Now that I'm not on my own, hunting, I really like it over here," Bron said beside her. The two males talked ahead of them, and Imogen knew she was about to get the big sister lecture she had been waiting on.

"Is it because it's quieter?" Imogen could hear the birds in the trees and running streams. It seemed so much more peaceful than the stories had led her to believe.

"Partly. The fae still gets nervous and excited when they see Killian, but they are used to me now. It's nice to get him all to myself, too," Bron replied. A slight frown appeared between her brows. "Are you serious about this relationship with Arawan?"

Imogen pulled up short. "What do you mean by that?"

"Try and see it from my point of view, Imogen. You have never really dated or had a relationship. You've never been interested in anyone for more than a night. You've never seen men as a serious pursuit," Bron replied. She looked back towards Arawan's tall back. "If this is a curiosity thing for you..."

"Fuck you, Bron," Imogen snapped before she could stop herself. Bron pulled on the reins of her horse and turned in her saddle. "Yeah, you heard me, fuck you."

"I'm just asking, Gen. Help me understand because he is *god*."

"And Kill is the Night Prince! Our family's generational enemy! You came home with him, and I never fucking judged you over it."

"It is not the same thing, and you know it. He isn't like anyone else, even the fae," Bron said, drawing her horse over so they were side by side.

"I know that, and it still doesn't change how I feel about him. It's not curiosity, it's...cosmic." Imogen took some deep breaths and tried to calm her temper down.

"I never got close to someone because I always accepted the fact I was overdue to die. I didn't want to waste anyone's time, especially my own. I'm sure I would've changed my mind if I had met someone I felt half of what I do for Arawan. But I never did, Bron. I was waiting to die my entire life because I was waiting for *him*. I was obsessed with the Afterlife because I didn't know I was searching for Arawan. I thought you would understand what that is like more than anyone."

Bron reached over and patted Imogen's arm. "I'm sorry, I didn't realize. You have been so quiet about everything that has been happening. I wanted to hear it from you."

"Yeah, okay, I get that, but if I had told you that I got obsessed with him after the fight with Morrigan, you all would've worried. We all had enough going on for me to want to add to it," Imogen replied.

Bron's expression softened. "I understand, but Gen, he's going to have to return to Annwn sometime. You are mortal and won't be able to follow."

"We will figure it out after Hafgan is dealt with," Imogen said stubbornly. She couldn't think of a future beyond that.

"Are you even going to be able to cross through the gates into Annwn without dying first?"

Imogen shrugged. "I suppose we will find out, won't we? I know you're grilling me right now because you care, but stop it. We are Ironwoods. We are made to fight and to die. I'm not afraid of either."

"I know, Imogen. I love you, that's all, and I want you to be happy. Is he going to make you happy in the long run?"

Imogen stared at the god in the distance. "Yes. I can't explain how I know this. I just know that he will."

Bron sighed. "You never could do things the easy way."

Imogen smiled. "Where is the fun in that?"

By dusk, the forest had started to thin, and Imogen got her first look at Killian's castle, which sat at the base of a mountain range.

"Why is there no one around?" she asked.

"It only has a small staff to maintain things. A lot of the fae decided to cross back into England with Kian. We keep the castle here as a base now more than anything. When our festivals are on, fae come from all over to gather here," Killian replied, staring up at the black stone towers. On one side, it was covered in vines and blooming roses.

"This was my parent's castle before I inherited it. Bayn and Kian took theirs to England, as you know. They were made with magic and could be shifted. This was made with sweat and love," Killian said, his eyes lost in some memory. Bron's wing stretched out to touch his leg, and he came back to himself. "You see that tower there? That's the one Fergus Ironwood scaled in order to shoot me in the ass."

Imogen threw her head back and laughed. "Prove it."

"Funnily enough, your sister asked the same thing when we first met."

Bron's feathers ruffled. "I was trying to identify who you were, not look at you naked."

"Sure you weren't," Imogen replied, sharing a teasing grin with Killian.

"This land sits on a wellspring of power," Arawan said softly, staring around him like he could see the magic no one else could.

"It's true. My parents built it here because it was a crossroads of magic." Killian looked back towards the castle. "Let's see if the kitchens have anything good to eat, and we'll go down to the crypts at nightfall."

"Just to be creepy?" Imogen asked.

"No, they only open when the stars are out," Killian replied like it was the most logical reason. Maybe for the fae, it was.

They left the horses with a surprised stable hand, and Imogen spotted the other running off to warn the other occupants that the Night Prince and his mate had returned.

It was strange to see the fae calling Bron a princess and bowing to her. Bron was almost as rough around the edges as Imogen was. None of them seemed to notice or care. The doors to the castle opened for them, and they stepped into the warmth and beauty of the halls.

"It might be best not to tell anyone who you are," Imogen said to Arawan. "We wouldn't want to cause a riot."

"And who am I supposed to be?" he asked with a small smile.

"You can be my hot boyfriend that has magic."

His smile grew wider. "Is that what I am now? Your boyfriend?"

"You're a pain in my ass."

"Not yet, I'm not," he purred.

Imogen went hot all over. "Stop that."

Arawan, being the bastard he was, only laughed huskily at her and ran his hand over her braid and let the tail slip between his fingers. It was a very possessive gesture that every fae nearby noticed.

Imogen's eyes narrowed. "What are you doing?"

"Making sure all of those hungry eyes know who you belong to," he replied.

Imogen grabbed him by the front of his shirt and kissed him. She felt like she hadn't kissed him in days, so it was more thorough than she had planned.

Imogen pulled back from him. "Now they know who *you* belong to."

"I love you," Arawan said breathlessly.

She patted his cheek. "So you should."

31

Imogen had decided that if she ever needed a getaway castle to hide in, this was the place she wanted to be. Everywhere she went were beautiful carvings and strange and lovely murals. It was like strolling about a gothic Rivendell cross Beauty and the Beast castle, and she loved it. She didn't care that she had no phone reception; in fact, she liked not being on call for every Ironwood emergency.

After a quick meal, Killian led them through the stone corridors and out into a large interior garden filled with blooming luminescent flowers. Even the trees seemed to glow with magic.

"This is so cool, Kill. Why don't you stay here more often?" Imogen asked.

"After being trapped here for so long, it's been nice to go back to the noise and business of the human world. Faerie has been the same for centuries and can become stagnant." Killian looked around at the gardens, and a small smile appeared on his face. "After the generals are dealt with, we will come back more often, but I don't like not being close to my brothers if something should happen. Until things settle down, it's better to only make short trips."

"This garden feels like your power," Bron said, her fingers brushing against a dark purple bloom.

"No, it feels like Kynan, my father. He had the same power I did and was a creature of the night. My mother, Rhiannon, was the opposite. He created this garden for her so that she would have light and flowers even at night," Killian said, his voice cracking. He cleared it quickly. "Their tomb is... It's this way."

For the first time, Imogen wondered if the princes giving Arawan their father's special armor was a good idea. It was clear that Killian especially missed their parents, and offering up their family's heirlooms was a big deal.

The entrance to the tomb looked like a small building from the outside and was made of black and gold stone. A large clear stone was placed in the archway above the door.

"It shouldn't be long now," Killian said, looking at the sky.

"What do you—" Imogen began, her words falling short as a bright star winked to life where Killian was looking.

Instantly, the gem above the door started to shine, and the stone doors opened to reveal a set of stairs.

"That's the coolest thing I've ever seen," Imogen said, eyes wide. "You guys have to bring Layla here. She would be losing her little nerd mind right now."

"Don't worry, we will," Bron said, following Killian inside.

Killian reached up and placed a hand on a polished stone. It lit beneath his hand, and instantly other stones lining the passageway burned to life.

"This way, watch your step. I haven't been down here in a while," he said softly. Bron took his hand, their eyes passing silent messages. Imogen followed, with Arawan coming in last, his hand resting gently on the small of her back. Even in the clean black hunting suit she had squeezed into, she could feel the heat of his palm through the Kevlar reinforcements.

"This is a beautiful place to honor your dead," Arawan said to Killian.

"I had it built after their deaths. Rhiannon would've hated being buried in the darkness, so these crystals ensure that she never is."

They stepped down into a wide circular room surrounded by soft light. A single wide sarcophagus stood in the center of the room. One side of it was made of a golden stone and the other black. On top, a carved golden woman and onyx man lay entwined in each other's arms. A lump formed in Imogen's throat as she stared at them. She wasn't a sappy romantic person, but something about resting eternally in the arms of your lover made her heart hurt.

"Maybe we shouldn't disturb them for some armor," Imogen said softly.

"You thought I was going to rob my parents grave?" Killian asked, biting back a laugh. "No, love. Their bodies are in amber, and they weren't in their armor when they died." Killian went to a far wall that was carved with a mural of his parents in a forest. He pressed on one of the star carvings, and two panels slid back from the wall. Inside were two stone statues of Kynan and Rhiannon. Kynan's was dressed in matte black armor with a silver star on the chest plate. Rhiannon's was silver and had a golden sun in the center of hers.

"As we said, my father's armor was made from the meteorite stone and can't be damaged by any forged weapon, no matter if god or man is wielding it," Killian explained. Imogen's hands burned to touch the silver armor in front of her.

"And Rhiannon's?"

"No one really knew except for her. It was an heirloom of her house. She said it had been made by..."

"Gofannon," Arawan finished, staring at the armor.

"Yes, how did you know?"

"The smith god's work is unmistakable. It is humming with his power too. He created his own mixtures of metals and infused them with magic, so there's no way to know what that's made of." Arawan looked it over again. "Gofannon could make a sword out of a widow's tears and a butterflies wing if he wanted to. It is something to be treasured, prince."

"I know it is. They both are, but you are both family, and the fight you are walking into will affect all of us," Killian replied. He looked at Imogen. "You will wear my mother's armor."

"Kill, I can't—"

"No arguments. You really think I'm going to send my baby sister into Annwn with only Kevlar and some daggers?" Killian said, putting his hands on his hips. "Rhiannon would come back from the dead just to box my ears if I even thought about it."

Imogen hugged him tightly. "Thanks, Kill. Are you sure Kian and Bayn will be okay with it too?"

"Are you kidding me? Bayn has given you some of his favorite daggers, and Kian was the one that suggested offering you the armor to begin with."

"You guys are then best fae brothers a girl could ask for," Imogen said against his chest. She pulled back and studied the armor. "Now, show me how to get it on."

Imogen had never worn plate armor before, but it molded perfectly to her body over the top of her hunting suit. It had to be magic because there was no way Rhiannon had been a plus-size woman.

"You look like a total badass," Bron said to Imogen, looking her over.

"She *is* a total badass," Arawan corrected. He was looking at her in a very different way.

"Aren't you putting yours on?" Imogen asked him, ignoring the horny gleam in his eyes.

"I will when we get to the gates. Killian said the quickest way to get there is to fly, so I will need to shift."

"Really? Where are these gates?"

Killian led them out of the crypt and back out into the garden. He turned and pointed at the highest mountain behind them.

"It's there, in a cave close to the summit. I found it by pure accident. No one crosses that part of the mountain because the legends say it's cursed," he explained. "I was coming back from a journey in the north when I was flying over them and felt the gates' magic. It surprised me so much I went to investigate. And once I found them, I flew home as fast as I fucking could because I was so freaked out."

"Awesome. They sound cool," Imogen said, eyes going wide with excitement. "Can we go now?"

Killian shook his head. "You are crazy to want to go at night, but I suppose with Arawan with you, it will keep all the monsters away."

Imogen turned to Bron. "Are you going to fly up with us?"

"Absolutely not," Kill answered before Bron could.

"What Killian means is that my wings aren't strong enough yet to get to that altitude. Not because I'm afraid to go," Bron corrected.

"I'm afraid to go. Just because Imogen is crazy enough not to be scared doesn't mean I'm going to risk taking you there," Killian argued.

Imogen shook her head at them before hugging Bron. "Wish me luck, big sis."

"You don't need it, but you *do* need this." Bron pulled out a long, black knife that was big enough to be a short sword from the inside of her coat. "This was Kynan's dagger. It was made at the same time as the god killing sword. I'm hoping it will be just as effective as the sword was on Morrigan."

"I don't know what to say," Imogen pulled the dagger from its sheath and whistled. "Oh yeah, I'm going to do so much damage to someone with this."

"I hope so. We'll keep the sword close in case Hafgan decides to cross over to the human world," Killian said. He didn't need to add that if Arawan and Imogen failed, the black sword on Bron's back was probably the only weapon in existence that could stop Hafgan.

"I feel like it's an early Christmas," Imogen said, buckling the weapon onto her belt. "Let's get going. I'm pumped for a fight."

"That's my fierce flower," Arawan replied.

His dark power rose, and Killian swore, taking a step back from him. Arawan grew larger, his ruby and black wings unfurling from his back and the bone crown rising from his head. Like the last time he took on that form, Imogen's heart began to pound with excitement.

Fuck, he really is awe-inspiring.

"There's my magnificent monster," Imogen purred. Bron and Killian were staring in horror and surprise. Imogen didn't want Arawan to feel self-conscious, so she wrapped her arms around his neck. "Hey, Death Daddy, ready to take me for a ride?"

"Don't make me tear that armor off you when we've just got it on," Arawan replied. One large, clawed hand cupped her ass and lifted her up into his arms. "We are ready. Lead the way, prince."

Killian kissed Bron before unfurling his wings and launching into the sky.

"I'll see you soon, big sister," Imogen said as brightly as she could. Arawan's grip tightened, and Imogen screamed as they were suddenly airborne.

Arawan chuckled. "You should be used to flying by now."

"Why, because we did it once when I was almost unconscious?" Imogen said, her arms and legs locking around him tighter.

"I will never drop you, my love." Arawan nuzzled at her neck, and Imogen's body softened. "There we go. Look at how beautiful the night is."

Imogen wriggled so she could look at the moonlight shimmering over the valley below. Like the first time, her fear eased, and she stared about in wonder.

"You doing okay, Gen?" Killian called to her. He was grinning like a fiend. "I don't think I've heard you scream so loud before."

"I have," Arawan growled in her ear.

"Are you trying to make me horny before going into battle? Seriously, head in the game, mister."

Arawan only laughed, and they followed Killian up the mountain until he was pointing to a black opening near the summit. Arawan made a rumbling sound in his chest.

"I can feel the power Killian was talking about. This is a strong gate," he said.

Imogen's legs were wobbly when she slid down off Arawan and onto a rocky outcrop outside the cave mouth.

"Yeah, this is as far as I'm going," Killian said, staring at the darkness. "It creeps me out far too much."

"Thanks for everything, bro. I promise I'll return the armor as soon as we are back," Imogen said.

Killian pressed a kiss to her forehead. "Just make sure *you* come back, okay?"

"Don't get sappy on me. Off you go," Imogen replied, giving him a playful push.

"Protect my sister, God of the dead," Killian said to Arawan before leaping off the ledge and disappearing.

"Everyone seems to think that you are the one that needs protecting. They really don't know you at all," Arawan said. His whole body began to shiver and shrink as he took on his normal form again.

"They know, they just think I'm super reckless, and I need watching. I mean, they are right, but being reckless is my superpower," Imogen replied. Arawan put on his borrowed armor with such efficient movements, Imogen couldn't help being a bit turned on.

"You look hot as fuck in that," she said before she could stop herself.

Arawan kissed her. "Now you know how it feels. Let's find this gate." He summoned a ball of light, and they stepped down into the darkness.

32

Arawan could feel the dead all around him. Shades and wraiths were roaming the cave, restless and anxious.

"Something strange is happening here," he murmured.

"Strange as in interesting, or strange as we are about to get fucked by a pack of goblins or a Balrog?" Imogen whispered behind him. "Every hair on my body is standing on end right now."

"It's only the dead, Imogen. They can't hurt you, only mess with your perception a little." Arawan took her hand in the darkness to reassure her. He would never let any harm come to her.

Arawan knew that letting her go with him into Annwn was dangerous. He could hope that the gates wouldn't let her go through as a mortal. The problem with Imogen was that normal rules never seemed to apply. He only knew that she was meant to be at his side from now on.

The cave tunnel curved, and Arawan felt the pulse of the gates growing with every step.

"We are getting close."

"We better be. I really don't think anyone should be down here. What is a gate to the underworld doing in here anyway?"

Arawan would like to know the answer to that too. "All the worlds touch at different weak places, this you know. Those weak places can also exist in the dark realms. If I had to make a guess, I believe that this is one of the weak places, and a legend grew up around it that the mountain was haunted to keep anyone from wanting to come in here. What I don't understand is why there are so many restless shades here."

"What if they tried to go through and couldn't?" Imogen asked.

"You mean as living beings?"

"Sure. If I found a portal in a cave, I'd probably try and go through it too."

Arawan sighed. "Of course you would. You have no sense of self-preservation."

"My lack of self-preservation led me to you, didn't it?" she replied.

Arawan lifted her hand and kissed it. "It did, but I wish you never had to go to such extreme methods."

"Sometimes it takes being brave enough to use extreme methods to find what you're really looking for in life."

"Or the Afterlife," Arawan replied. They walked for another few minutes until the tunnel suddenly ended. Two onyx obelisks rose out of the center of a small cavern. As soon as Arawan approached, they lit up with golden runes in the language of the dead.

"So Killian was right after all. These definitely lead to Annwn, but I'm unsure of which part," Arawan said, running his fingers over them.

"Does that matter? When we get there, won't your power rush back to you?" Imogen asked.

"It all depends on how they cut me off from it. I will be stronger through the weak connection I still maintain to it."

Imogen studied the gates and let out a long breath. "Only one way to find out." And before he could stop her, she walked through the center of them and disappeared.

"Fuck, Imogen!" Ice-cold fear shot through Arawan's veins. She hadn't fallen dead at his feet, which was a miracle. Cursing, Arawan hurried after her.

The darkness clung to Arawan's skin, pulling and tearing at him in a way that it had never done before.

"I am your master, take me home," he commanded it in the tongue of the gods. The sides of the portal thinned at the command and spat him out into a field of green grass.

"You took long enough. I've been waiting here for like an hour," Imogen complained and hurried over to him.

Arawan grabbed her by the shoulders. "What the fuck, Imogen? Why would you walk straight through a portal you had no idea where it went?"

"It felt like you! The same way your power does when it rises. I knew exactly where it was going to take me!"

Arawan clutched her face with shaking hands. "But you didn't know if it was going to kill you in the process."

"I don't care! I told you, I'm not going to be left behind! Get that through your thick head," Imogen growled at him.

Arawan wanted to shake her for such idiotic logic that put her at risk. He kissed her instead. They were the only two options when it came to her; fight or make love.

"I thought you weren't coming," she said between panicked kisses.

"There's nowhere you can go where I won't be able to find you," he promised her. An awareness prickled at the back of his neck, and he turned. "My babies."

"Your what now?" Imogen demanded.

Arawan laughed as a pack of hounds bounded over the green hills. They were yipping and howling in excitement as they circled Arawan, red tails wagging and pushing at each other to get pats.

"Now, this is the welcome home I was looking for. How are you?" he crooned at them. Imogen was giggling at him, but he didn't care. He had missed his pack of mongrels.

"Don't let their wagging tails fool you. They are vicious hunting dogs," he warned her.

"Yeah, they really look it." Imogen raised a brow. "Where do we go now?"

Arawan closed his eyes and orientated himself. He was close to where he had last fought with Hafgan, and he didn't think that was a coincidence.

The ring of stones had been a meeting point on the borders of Annwn since the dawn of time. He had fought Hafgan there many times. The last time had been right before Morrigan had turned up and convinced Hafgan to go and be her general. She had approached Arawan first with her silky lies and promises.

Arawan had told her that if she managed to convince Hafgan to stop bothering him, he would owe her a single favor. He had said it half-heartedly, but the goddess had taken him seriously. Arawan had no idea what she had promised Hafgan in return for serving her.

Arawan looked at the jagged white stone rising out of the green earth. It didn't matter how much time had passed; he would always see Brangwen's broken body lying in the middle of the circle. Now, he had brought the woman he loved to the same horrible place. Imogen's hand tightened in his as if she was sensing his unease.

"What is it?" she asked.

"Only ghosts, my love." Arawan pulled her closer. He could feel Hafgan in the distance and knew it wouldn't be long until he sensed him. "You are everything I have always searched for and never thought I would find. I don't deserve you, but I'm so happy you're mine."

"You're starting to freak me out, so stop talking like that," she said, her fingers tangling in his hair. "Don't do anything stupid, okay? We are in this together, and I'm not going to leave you no matter what happens."

"I'm a *god*, Imogen. If I fall to Hafgan, you will get on a hound and get the fuck out of here," he said, cupping her cheeks. Her eyes were gray and filled with storms. She wanted to fight him, he could see it, but she nodded.

"I never thought I would see the day that you would stoop to get attached to one of the living, God of Annwn," a rumbling brogue said from behind him.

Arawan turned slowly to face his ancient enemy. Hafgan hadn't changed in all the centuries he had been in Morrigan's service. His red and gold hair was braided back from his face, and his chest and arms were covered in woad and tattoos.

"Hey, I know you," Imogen said, stepping around Arawan. "You're Neck Tattoo guy. You were at the club."

"What?" Arawan hissed.

Hafgan laughed, a rich, happy sound that had no place in the psychopath's mouth. "I was at the club, lass. I went there to grab you and use you as bait to lure out Arawan from his castle. Turns out I didn't need to because he followed you as dopey as one of his hounds."

Imogen threw a knife at him. It thudded into Hafgan's shoulder and only made him laugh more. "I was planning on fucking you before I killed you. I think we could have some fun."

"I'll have lots of fun carving you up with my knife, dick," Imogen replied.

"It might surprise you how much I would enjoy that too."

Arawan swallowed down his rage, refusing to let Hafgan get under his skin. He pulled out his sword. "Are you going to leave Annwn peacefully, or are we going to have to do the same old dance."

"It's been a while since I've had a challenge. I could use a fight to warm me up for my war against the humans."

"You should ask Aneirin how well that turned out for him," Imogen said, looking Hafgan over with an unimpressed expression.

"Aneirin thought too much of his abilities without Morrigan's aid to support him. I'm not going to make that mistake. Tell me where Morrigan is, Arawan, and I might let your little human live."

Imogen laughed and pulled her ax from its holster. "I'm not a little anything. I'm a fucking Ironwood, and I'm really going to enjoy watching Arawan fuck you up."

Arawan had never loved her more. He gave her a hard kiss. "It would be my pleasure to make him scream for you, darling."

"Make me proud, lover," Imogen said, with a parting smack on the ass. He couldn't stop smiling. The audacity of her never ceased to shock and amuse him.

Hafgan looked between them with narrowed eyes before letting out an amused bark of laughter. "So that's why you still maintained a thread of connection to Annwn. You always were a sly fucker."

"I don't know what you mean," Arawan replied innocently.

"You're tied body, heart, and soul to Annwn, but you've given part of your heart away to the mortal. We couldn't cut your connection completely because she was safeguarding it. Now, I know why you're keeping her around."

It wasn't the reason at all, but he didn't owe Hafgan an explanation. He stepped into the ring of stones.

"We don't have to be enemies, Arawan. Just give me Morrigan, and don't interfere with the humans. We will leave Annwn be. Things can go back to the way they have always been," Hafgan tried to negotiate with him. Like it would work. Imogen was still living, and the human world was hers.

"Morrigan is as good as dead." Arawan raised his sword. "And soon, you will join her."

Hafgan's face flushed. "She is *not* dead. I would feel it. My goddess will rise and live again."

"Not fucking likely after the stabbing my sister gave her," Imogen snorted.

Hafgan bellowed a war cry and charged her. Arawan moved, stepping between them, and stopped Hafgan's ax with his sword. Hafgan snarled out an ancient curse as Arawan knocked him back.

Hafgan's face twisted into a mask of fury. "I hope she fucks harder than Brangwen did."

Arawan pushed all thoughts of Imogen and her safety out of his mind and attacked with everything he had.

33

Imogen stumbled back from the ring of stones as Arawan and Hafgan began to duel. She had never seen anything like it. They moved so fast that her human eyes could barely follow them. Silver and gold ichor splashed on the ground around them as every blow connected.

Imogen thought of herself as a brave person, but watching two gods tear each other apart inspired a kind of awe and terror that was indescribable.

She was trembling. The hand she had clutching the hilt of Bron's long dagger was slick with sweat. She tried to steady her breaths to stop herself from hyperventilating. It was worse than watching wolves fight, or horde creatures, or anything in her realm of understanding.

One of Arawan's hounds came to lean into her, a comforting gesture that made her hand drop to its soft white fur.

"It's okay, boy, it's okay," she told it, her voice shaky.

The gods kept the fight within the stone circle like there was a rule she didn't know preventing them from stepping out of it. They clashed and clashed again, their speed and ferocity not slowing. She didn't know how long it had been going for. Time itself seemed to be holding its breath.

Bile crept up Imogen's throat as she realized where all of the scars on Arawan's body had come from. She had wondered what could scar a god like that; now she knew. Arawan's black armor was smeared with ichor, Hafgan finding the gaps in it to wear him down.

Imogen's blood went cold as Hafgan's ax slammed into the back of Arawan's knee, and he stumbled, rolling to the ground. Hafgan kicked his sword away and pulled Arawan's head back by his hair.

"Tell me where Morrigan is, or I will slaughter you in front of the girl," Hafgan shouted in his face.

"F-Fuck you. You kill me, and all of Annwn vanishes and Morrigan with it," Arawan replied.

"You can live without all kinds of things—your eyes, your hands, your cock," Hafgan taunted. "How about I start cutting and see how quickly you change your mind."

He lowered the tip of his ax down to Arawan's eye, and Imogen roared. She threw her ax with all of her strength, and it buried itself into Hafgan's back with a meaty thud.

The god shouted in fury, dropping Arawan in surprise and anger. His arms flailed behind him to try and reach the ax, but Imogen was already closing in on him. She threw Bayn's runic knives at the struggling god, burying them into his thighs and arms.

"You fucking cunt! I am going to cut you to pieces and fuck your corpse," Hafgan shouted. He tried to pull one of the daggers free and was too busy focusing on Imogen to see that Arawan had picked up his sword.

"Come and get me, you fire crotch piece of shit!" Imogen taunted him. Hafgan stumbled towards her and suddenly fell to the ground, both of his legs cut out from under him.

"You fucking dumb bastard. How many times must we do this? Cut me to ribbons, and I will always regenerate," Hafgan snarled, crawling across the churned-up grass towards Imogen. "No man or god can kill me!"

Imogen pulled the black dagger from its sheath. "Then it's a good thing I'm neither."

Imogen kicked his reaching arm out of the way, moving around him and slamming her knees into his shoulders to pin him down. She grabbed him by his hair and hacked Hafgan's screaming head from his body.

Power exploded out of the god, and Imogen was hurled backward. Her body crashed into one of the standing stones, her skull cracking hard against it. Pain reverberated through her body, and she hit the dirt.

"Imogen!" Arawan was screaming, but everything sounded like it was underwater again. It felt worse than the concussion on the beach all those weeks ago.

Arawan's pale face hovered above her, and he gathered her in his arms. "Just breathe, love. Oh fuck, Imogen."

"Is 'kay," she gasped, blood bubbling out of her lips. "Told you I'd die...for you." His face started to blur, and the pain moved away from her. She wanted to touch his face one last time, but her arms refused to move.

"You are not going to die, Imogen Ironwood." Arawan gathered her close, his warm tears falling on her face.

"*I* control life and death, not you. You will live because you belong to me, and I won't allow you to leave me."

Arawan's mouth pressed to hers as her last breath slipped out of her.

Imogen's body went weightless, a soft tingling sensation racing through her. This was the death she had always known was coming for her...

Imogen screamed as power slammed into her. Her whole body was burning like it had been hit with a lightning bolt. Ice and fire split her apart, and she screamed again and again.

Arawan's hands clutched her tight to him. "Breathe, Imogen! Breathe!"

Imogen sucked air into her lungs, and the burning sensation in her body eased. Arawan kissed her cheeks. "That's it, my love. In and out, let the power settle."

"What did you do to me?" she croaked, her voice raw.

"I saved you, my love. Just keep breathing. Don't ever stop." Arawan was rocking her gently. "Everything is going to be okay now."

Imogen didn't know how long they lay on the grass, but the pain in her head and body finally disappeared, and she felt okay to move.

"We need to get back to your court," she said, sitting up. "Fuck, Hafgan. Is he dead? Did I do it?"

"Well, yes and no," Arawan replied, helping her to her feet. Hafgan's head was lying a few feet from her, his eyes still blinking at her.

"You fucking idiot. Do you have any idea what you've just done?" Hafgan snarled.

"Fuck, that's just creepy." Imogen picked up the head just before his still twitching arm could grab it. Arawan pulled off his black helm and held it out to her.

"Put it in here. We need to keep it separated from the rest of his body. With any luck, the properties of this metal will stop any of his remaining magic from trying to regrow his body from the neck down," Arawan replied.

"You think this will contain me? I am truly immortal! It might not happen now or in the next five hundred years, but my body will find me!" Hafgan's head snarled at them.

"Hold him." Imogen passed the helm to Arawan before walking over to the legless torso. Her body felt strange, like she wasn't entirely in control of her limbs. She could still feel echoes of Arawan's power in her, burning away.

Future Imogen's problem, she thought and pulled her ax from Hafgan's back.

"Let's see you regenerate this," she muttered and began to hack the god into pieces. All the fear, the rage, and terror she had felt in the moment he had knocked Arawan to the ground came out of her in a massive, violent rush. The weeks of stress waiting for the generals to attack, Aneirin kidnapping Reeve and trying to hurt Charlotte. The worry that Hafgan and Vili were free and planning to plunge the world into war...

By the time Imogen finished, her arms ached so much that she could barely lift them. She was covered in sweat and ichor, and fuck knew what else. Arawan was staring at her with wide eyes.

"Seeing you in a rage never fails to take my breath away," he said.

"Yeah? Let it be a warning to never be on the receiving end of it," Imogen replied. She whistled at the dogs. "Supper time!"

"I..." Arawan began and stopped as the white hunting hounds obeyed her, tearing apart and eating all that remained of Hafgan's body.

"Let's see him try and pull himself together when it's spread between a pack of dogs," she said.

"You will pay for this, whore!" Hafgan shouted from the helm Arawan still held. Arawan and Imogen stared down into the ranting god's face.

A devilish idea hit Imogen, and she grinned. "You want to pee on him?"

Arawan's smile was as merciless as a blade in the dark. "I have a better idea."

34

Imogen was still exhausted from the fight with Hafgan by the time Arawan restored the castle back in Snowdonia.

They had secured Hafgan's head in the same dark cells that Morrigan was dying in. He had cursed right up until Arawan had sewed his mouth shut before locking his head in an obsidian box and sealing it with magic.

Arawan had gathered up a tired, swaying Imogen and flown to where Hafgan's spell had dumped the castle.

Imogen had quickly left Arawan to sort out the details and calm down his court. She would happily step in and help him fight against every enemy...except a frantic courtier. He was on his own.

She had climbed into his massive bathtub and passed out shortly after. She woke long enough for Arawan to pull her out of it, dry her off and place her into bed.

Imogen knew something had happened to her. It hadn't been the usual pain of when Arawan had healed her the other times. Something was wrong. She was just too tired to figure out what.

When Imogen woke again, it was to Arawan kissing up her bare shoulder. His long body was wrapped around her, enclosing her in warmth and safety.

"Hey, how long have I been asleep?" she murmured, reaching for him and snuggling into his chest and dragon blood scent.

"Not long, about two days," he whispered.

Imogen jolted in wakefulness. "Two days?"

"Shh, it's fine. You were exhausted, and we did two world crossovers in the time span of a few days," Arawan said, stroking her hair to try and calm her down.

Imogen wriggled out of his arms. "I need a second."

She grabbed the robe that someone had laid for her and went into the bathroom. She washed her face and was brushing her teeth when she actually looked at herself for the first time since the fight.

"What the hell..." Imogen leaned closer to the mirror. She looked remarkably refreshed and good. She *never* looked that good in the morning. It took her a moment to realize what was wrong; her gray eyes now had black flecks in them. Imogen spat out her toothpaste and charged back into the bedroom.

"What the fuck did you do to me?" she demanded.

Arawan was lying back on the pillows with his arm tucked under his head. It was like he knew she was going to be in a mood and had arranged himself to look as hot as possible.

"I healed you," he replied.

"What *else*? Don't make me beat it out of you."

Arawan stretched a little, making all the muscles in his chest ripple. "Come and try if you're so confident."

"Yeah, if memory serves, it was me that defeated Hafgan, so I think I can take you."

Arawan snorted. "I had that fight completely under control. I needed to get close to him to finish him off, and before I could, you charged in. Reckless as ever."

"You were taking too long, and I'm sorry I wasn't okay with him carving up your pretty face."

Arawan crooked a finger at her. "My pretty face wants to thank you, so come and sit on it."

Imogen flushed hot all over. "Talking dirty to me won't work this time. Tell me what you did to me."

"Come here, Imogen, and I will tell you," he purred.

Imogen moved closer to the bed with the intention of staying out of it. It didn't work. As soon as she was close enough, Arawan moved god quick, dragging her back onto the black linens and pinning her underneath him.

Imogen hated that she wasn't strong enough to shove him off. Instead, her legs parted to make room for his muscular body.

"Tell me, I need to know," she said softly.

"I shared my power with you." Arawan brushed her hair from her face. "You were dying, the back of your skull smashed in. I couldn't live without you, and I refused to let you go. So I gave you part of my essence and...and immortality."

"Are you fucking serious?" Imogen's body tried to move, but he kept her pinned. "Let me up."

"No, not until you accept this." Arawan grabbed her arms and pressed them into the mattress above her head. "I don't know why you are mad."

"I'm not mad that you saved me, idiot. I'm mad because you giving me a part of your power is going to make you weaker!" Imogen replied.

Arawan rubbed his nose against hers. "No, my darling. With you by my side, I've never been stronger."

Imogen swallowed back her sudden tears. "Don't say stuff like that to me when I'm trying to be angry with you."

"You can be angry all you want. I'm still going to love you and never regret sharing myself with you. I want you by my side, Imogen, wherever I am. You couldn't do that as a mortal. You died, and I gave you new life." Arawan's hand cupped her cheek. "Maybe it was selfish of me to rob you of your Afterlife, but I couldn't let you go."

Sharing a part of his power wasn't a terrifying prospect, but being without him was. Imogen knew exactly why he had done what he did because she would've done the same thing. They were the same, after all. Imogen stared up into the face she loved more than anything.

"Being with you is the only Afterlife I've ever wanted anyway. I'm just...scared. What am I now?"

"You are a goddess. *My* goddess. You will be able to maintain your normal life for a time. Like me, you can leave this place and walk in the world. You'll just be stronger and less breakable. Sooner or later, people will realize you're not aging, though, and you'll have to tell them. For now, they can be none the wiser."

Imogen's heart hurt at the thought of lying to her family, but then she would cause them more pain by telling them she had died.

"We still need to help take down Vili, so I'll tell them after," Imogen replied.

"We will, I promise." Arawan loosened the grip on her arms but didn't let her go. "Are you still mad, or can I kiss you now?"

"You better," she said. Arawan smiled and pressed his mouth to hers. She bit down hard on his bottom lip, making a bead of ichor well up. His eyes shone with ruby light. "*That* is for not telling me straight away."

"Vicious little flower," he growled and crushed his mouth to hers in a brutal kiss. Imogen was powerless under the intensity of it, his tongue and lips taking her sanity. Arawan pulled the tie on her robe and pulled back the sides to expose her naked body.

"All mine, forever," he said with a devilish smile.

"Prove it," Imogen replied breathlessly, unable to stop herself from provoking him. Arawan quickly complied, his mouth ravaging her down her neck to her breasts, leaving red marks in his wake and turning Imogen into a trembling mess. His hand dipped between her legs, stroking her and teasing her clit until she was aching for him.

"Get inside of me," she begged, her body desperate for his.

"Yes, my goddess," he purred, and she almost came. "Oh, you like that title, don't you, *my goddess*."

"I always knew I was one. I just like that it's finally official," Imogen replied and then gasped as the tip of his hard dick pressed into her.

"You might be my true immortal consort now, but you were always my equal, my other half," Arawan said, pushing in and out of her with short, maddening thrusts.

Imogen was losing her mind. "Oh, god, stop talking and fuck me." Arawan laughed and did just that. He slid home until he was at both of their limits. He bent down to kiss her.

"Now, my love, do as I say, and scream pretty," he commanded, voice like dark sin.

Imogen's nails dragged down his back, making him groan. "We'll see who screams first, God of the dead."

Neither one could back down from a challenge, and Imogen had never been fucked so deeply and completely in her life. Arawan was always going to be her everything. She still didn't have words to describe everything she felt for him and didn't need to. He knew what she felt, knew every dark and vicious part of her soul.

In the end, they both ended up screaming.

Imogen's body, which had felt so strange since her death, now aligned as she exploded in pleasure. Arawan was and always would be her missing piece.

"I love you so fucking much," she said, catching his mouth in a desperate kiss.

Above her, Arawan smiled her favorite, teasing smile. "So you should."

35

It took another day before Imogen was ready to deal with her family. Arawan decided it would be better to go to Kian instead of everyone coming to them. His court was still too uneasy about everything that had happened, and having a whole family of living hunters and fae arrive at the castle would do nothing to settle them.

"You're looking suspiciously good for a journey to the underworld," Elise said, hugging Imogen as soon as she stepped into the library.

"It's the endorphins from all the sex I've been having," Imogen replied, glib as ever.

"Not something I need to hear from my sister," Layla said, appearing from around the stacks. She was wearing a T-shirt that said, "Tolkien is Daddy" in bright pink letters.

"I didn't know you were coming!" Imogen said, letting Elise go so she could grab her sister in a crushing bear hug.

"You went on an adventure to the fucking underworld, Imogen. Of course I came. I needed to see you were okay for myself." Layla pulled back and studied her. "What happened to your eyes?"

"I got hurt, and they changed when Arawan healed me." It wasn't a lie. It just wasn't the whole truth. Layla, the human lie detector, narrowed her green eyes but didn't push it.

"Where is your hotter other half?" she asked.

"Talking with Kian in the conference room. Come on, sis, if I have to sit through a meeting, you do too," Imogen replied, linking her arm in hers. "I missed you."

"You did not, and I'm not offended by that. If I was fucking someone as hot as Arawan, I'd never leave his castle again."

Imogen laughed loudly. "Don't tempt me, Lay Lay."

∼

ARAWAN WAS SITTING at the head of the table when Imogen walked into the conference room. He looked like the conquering dark god he was in his black suit, his sword cane resting against the side of his chair. He raised a brow at her and patted his ringed hand against his leg. This time, Imogen took him up on the offer and sat down on his lap.

"You make an excellent chair. I regret not taking you up on this earlier," she said, twisting the end of his black hair around her finger.

"You can sit on any part of me whenever you like, darling," he whispered in her ear.

"Hey, there are other people in this room," Layla snapped, but she was smiling when she said it.

"Are you ready to start, my lord?" Kian asked Arawan. He didn't seem to care that Imogen was using the god of the dead as an armchair. Beside him, Elise was smirking in approval.

With everyone spread out over Europe, they all video called in. Bayn and Freya came online first, and then the tribe of Ironwoods and Greatdrakes. Not a single one of them seemed surprised to see Imogen curled up with Arawan. Not even Kenna.

Arne and Torsten came on last, and Layla sat up a little straighter. Imogen tried not to grin. She always knew when her sister had a crush. Arawan's eyes narrowed slightly when he looked at the handsome elf and the huge Úlfhéðnar beside him. Before Imogen could ask what the matter was, Kian clapped his hands.

"Let's begin now that we are all here," he said over the chatter. "Imogen and Arawan, would you like to tell everyone what happened with Hafgan?"

Arawan let Imogen talk, jumping in only when he told them about the magic used to contain Hafgan.

"There's no way for him to regenerate, and even if he did, there's no way to escape the prison I've placed him in," Arawan assured them.

"Two down, one to go," Bayn said with an approving nod. "We still haven't had any sighting of Vili yet and have no idea if he was working with Hafgan still."

Arawan frowned. "If we are looking for Vili, why don't we ask his son?"

"His son? We didn't know he had one," Killian said.

Arawan was looking pointedly at Arne. "You haven't told them? What game are you playing at, elf?"

Everyone's attention snapped to Arne. He muttered something in elvish under his breath.

"I haven't said anything because it wasn't important," he said.

"The fuck it's not! You're Vili's son? What the hell, man?" Bayn demanded, his hurt evident. They had been friends since he had met Freya, and Arne had kept it from him, from them all.

"It doesn't matter whose seed I came from. I haven't seen Vili for over a millennium, and neither has my mother. I've never had anything to do with the fucking monster," Arne replied, his eyes flashing in anger. "If Vili shows his face in Alfheim or Svartalfheim, the elves will know and report it straight away. None of us want him returning. We are going to have a summit meeting in the next month to discuss the threat of him and how we can work together to hunt him down. My mother, Alruna, would like you to send someone to represent the humans."

"Alruna, as in *Queen* Alruna of the Light Elves?" Layla demanded, her voice rising. "You're a fucking prince too?!"

"It wasn't relevant information to give. It changes nothing. I'm still working with the humans the same as you," Arne replied stubbornly.

"I'm going to kick your ass so hard," Bayn growled at him.

"You're welcome any time, frostling."

"Do you think he would go to Odin for help?" Arawan interrupted the brewing argument.

"Odin?" Layla squeaked.

"Why would he go to Odin?" Imogen asked. They hadn't seen any sign of the old gods apart from Morrigan and himself.

Arawan laughed. "You really have no idea who Vili is, do you?"

"He's the son of Kvasir," Arne began, but Arawan only laughed louder.

"Oh, you idiots, Vili has fooled you all," he said with a shake of his head. "Vili is Odin's brother. One of the three sons of Borr that slew the giant Ymir and made the world. Vili is a primordial god, and you better hope and pray that he's still fighting with Odin. Otherwise together, they will kick off Ragnärok."

Imogen grinned. "And here we go again..."

EPILOGUE

Layla walked through the halls of Kian's castle, wondering if she should have left Ireland. She had agreed to come and keep David company as he continued his healing with the mages and had needed to see that Imogen was okay.

None of the Ironwood women were keen on leaving David alone. It didn't matter that he had told them he was fine on his own; they were all fussing. He drew the line at them sitting in on his actual sessions because if one of the fae did anything to hurt him, they would probably get smacked in the face. Their father had suffered enough.

Fathers... Layla tried to push out the picture of devastation on Arne's face when Arawan had outed him as Vili's son. None of the others knew elvish, but she had caught the words he had muttered in his native tongue. *'He's no father of mine.'*

Layla couldn't imagine hating David like that. She was an absolute daddy's girl; all the Ironwoods were, except for Bron, who had always been the most like Kenna. Bron would still protect David with her life. She never would've spat out words so viciously to him; it didn't matter that there wasn't a drop of blood between them.

But Arne wasn't only Vili's son; he was an elven prince, his mother the current Light Elf queen.

And you knocked him back when he asked you out for a drink.

Layla had regretted that since Bron's mating party. She had liked fighting with Arne when Morrigan attacked. She had never seen an elf fight before, and he had moved like a bloody melody.

At Bron's party, he had asked if she wanted to go into the city and get a drink. Layla had been so shocked and nervous that she had stammered out something about needing to look after Moira. Arne hadn't seemed offended, only smiled and bowed.

And that was the last time Layla had seen him. She had hoped he would come back to Ireland to visit so she could ask him out for that drink, and now she would never get the chance. She had blown it.

Isn't it for the best that you did? Layla would never have the guts to ask him, knowing he was a fucking prince and a demi-god.

Layla was so focused on the patterns in the carpets under her feet that she didn't see a side door open, and she crashed hard into someone.

"Layla," a soft Scandanavian accent said.

"Fuck," she squeaked and stumbled backward.

Arne Steelsinger looked down at her with a confused expression on his face. He was dressed in his traditional black elvish armor, his twin swords strapped to his back. His black hair had been pulled back into a messy knot, highlighting how big his golden eyes were. He would've been teenage Layla's wet dream. Hell, he was twenty-six-year-old Layla's wet dream too.

"What the fuck are you doing here?" she asked when she realized she was staring at him.

"I've come to talk to Kian and Bayn," he replied, straightening to his full height.

"Cool, they are in the library. Hope they kick your ass. Bye," Layla stammered, turning around and hurrying away.

"I came to ask you a favor too," Arne called after her.

Layla froze mid-step. "What kind of favor?"

"I was asked by my mother who the best candidate would be to come to the Light and Dark Elves summit," Arne said, coming up behind her. "I told her it was you."

Layla's shoulders hunched inward, physically holding herself back from turning around. If she looked at him, she knew she would give in.

"Thanks for the recommendation, but I don't do favors for liars," Layla replied.

With a shaky breath, she walked away from him and didn't look back.

ELF SHOT

IRONWOOD SERIES BOOK 3

ALESSA THORN

PROLOGUE

Far above the arctic circle, in the northern reaches of Finnmark, an area that crowned the top of Scandinavia and Finland, wild and mythical creatures still roamed.

If you went there, you could feel the deep magic in the land and knew that it didn't quite sit in the same reality as the rest of the world.

The human shamans and magicians always found themselves in the north, called by the magic, and when they returned to their warmer southern homes, they always carried a touch of that wildness within them.

There the trolls walked; the shapeshifting wolves and bears made their dens, and the elves quietly governed. They moved through their lake and forest portals, visiting the nine worlds of Yggdrasil as quickly as they would any other country in Midgard.

The fae came out in England with brutal purpose and dazzling force. The elves in the far northern wilds watched on, horrified and amused at their fae brothers' lack of tact and open hostility.

They didn't understand the fae's desperation because they had never left their lands and had never been forced by the humans to go. They moved seamlessly from their worlds of Alfheim and Svartalfheim and into ours, much as they had done since the beginning of time.

They never had to make peace treaties with the humans. They had always been there, and the humans knew it. They could feel the magic in those places and respected it without needing to see the proof of the beings that lived there.

When the fae returned, the elves made themselves known more openly, but Finnmark had always been their land and always would be.

They would never negotiate their right to be there, and they certainly wouldn't let a fallen god take it from them.

1

Arne Steelsinger, Prince of the Light Elves of Alfheim, hadn't traveled the dark paths of Yggdrasil for three hundred and twenty-four years. Despite that, his feet and magic still remembered the way, the portals moving him seamlessly to the heart of the World Tree.

The heart was a waypoint, and not everyone could find it. It had a series of portal doorways that accessed all the branches of the Nine Worlds. Then there were the darker paths that led to the underworlds —Niflheim and Urd's Well. The latter was his destination, though he didn't know why.

Arne had woken two days ago, a rune burning on his palm, and he knew he was being summoned by beings too powerful to deny.

The timing couldn't have been more shit for a quest. Arne was still trying to undo the damage to his relationship with the fae princes and the Ironwoods. Well, one Ironwood in particular.

Fucking Arawan and his big mouth, Arne cursed that damn god every day. Not that the Lord of Annwn gave a shit about Arne's world exploding and making him live his greatest fear.

It had taken Bayn a week to take his calls. When Arne finally had a chance to explain, the fae prince had cuffed him in the back of the head and told him not to hide shit like that from them.

Bayn and Freya were his friends again, and Arne was on his way to building a solid alliance with Kian and his fae army.

The summit for the light and dark elves was only a fortnight away, and Arne was still trying to convince their chosen human ambassador to come.

Layla Ironwood. The source of all his misery. He had gone straight to the Ironwood manor to try and fix the damage Arawan had caused. Having Layla call him a liar was like getting knifed in the chest. He had still refused to give up. There was only one small problem.

The woman was *gloriously* stubborn.

Arne had sent emails and text messages and had even tried calling her twice. He hadn't left a voice mail; hearing her voice on the recorded message had gutted him both times, and he had hung up before getting a word out.

Worry about it later, Arne scolded himself. He needed to focus. The paths of Yggdrasil seemed quiet and peaceful, but only fools would believe that. Usually, dead fools.

The rune on Arne's palm pulsed with power, and he opened the doorway it led him to. It revealed a dark staircase. He rested a hand on the hilt of his dagger and stepped through the door.

In the pitch black, he placed his sigil-burned palm on the cold stone wall, and pale crystals hanging from the roof lit up at once. They were mixed with sharp stalagmites that would fall on trespassers who didn't wear the rune of passage.

How he was in a cave and walking a path twisted with the roots of the World Tree was one of Yggdrasil's many mysteries that he refused to think about too hard.

The elves were all born with an innate sense and acceptance of magic around them. They could feel it in the elements and in others. They could bend and twist that magic to shape the world around them.

There was some magic that not even the elves could fight, and as he reached the bottom of the path, he prepared himself to face it.

The power of the Norns hit Arne first. It was a rolling, pulsing thrum like he was standing inside a thunderclap. His palm was burning, but he didn't stop walking. He passed through a carved stone archway and stopped by a deep, black pool.

Twisted roots framed and dipped into the pool, and he didn't dare look into its inky depths in case it looked back. The chamber was lit with more glowing crystals. There were no fires in that place, but it wasn't cold. The air was warm, moist, and laden with so much magic that he could taste it on his tongue.

"The prince finally arrives," an ancient voice crackled. From behind a large root came a crone with a gnarled staff in one hand, carrying an empty bucket. "You took your time, little eagle."

"Apologies for keeping you waiting, Lady Urd," he replied, giving her a deep bow.

"All we have is time in this place, where it doesn't exist at all." Urd pressed the wooden bucket into his hands. "Here, fill this for an old woman."

Arne took the bucket and dipped it into the pool. He shut his eyes as he did it, refusing to look even for this.

Urd cackled. "Still smarter than you look, prince."

Arne pulled the full bucket free from the pool and only opened his eyes again when he had straightened. "What would you like me to do now?" he asked.

"Carry it and follow me." Urd leaned heavily on her staff and hobbled off. Arne swallowed his nerves and hurried after her, knowing better than to dawdle.

Threads of light curved down and around the roots, all tangling together. Arne was careful to step only where Urd stepped and kept his mouth shut. There were few beings in all the Nine Worlds that Arne was afraid of, and he was about to be in the presence of three of them.

A straight-backed, middle-aged female with silver in her black hair sat on cushions in a circle of roots. She had the threads of light twining through her long fingers before they fell to a twisting spindle.

"Ah, a visitor," Verðandi said and smiled in greeting. "And a prince of the Ljosalfr no less."

"One with strong enough muscles to carry a full bucket from Urðanbrunnr without spilling it," Urd added, waggling her thin eyebrows at Arne.

"Where shall you have me place it, Lady Urd?" he asked.

"You will water the roots, and we will see what we see," a new voice called. Arne glanced up higher in the roots, and amongst the glowing stalagmites was Skuld. She sat in a nest of light threads, her flaxen hair tangled with them. Despite that, when she grabbed the nearest root and slid down it like rope, the threads released her.

Skuld glowed softly. She was the future, always shining with the brightness of possibility. She was the one who Arne feared the most. She stared up at him with pale gray eyes.

"Tall. I approve of that. This way, eaglet." Skuld looped her arm through his, and Arne's magic pulsed inside him. She took him through another doorway and into a chamber that was only roots. These ones were pale and tender shoots.

Skuld gestured to them. "Pour, but spread it wide and do it gently, prince."

Arne gripped the bucket and slowly began to water Yggdrasil. He did his best to not disturb the frail roots. Skuld walked behind him, watching the black waterfall.

"Why is it always Daddy issues?" she muttered, and Arne almost dropped the bucket in surprise. He didn't answer her, only kept up his task until the bucket was empty.

Skuld stared at the gleaming wet roots, her light pulsing around them. Finally, she let out a long sigh.

"Vili being loose is going to be problematic," she said.

Arne nodded; this he knew. "How can I kill him?"

"He's a primordial god, eaglet. You can't kill him. You don't want to add patricide to the weight of your soul anyway. Nasty business."

"So Vili wins." Arne gripped the bucket tight enough that the wood creaked.

"No. I said you can't kill him, not that you can't defeat him," Skuld corrected him. "Very different things."

Arne's despair eased, and his breath steadied once more. "Do you see how we can defeat him before he kicks off Ragnarök?"

Skuld's smile went feline. "Oh yes, but as handsome and valiant as you are, you aren't going to be able to defeat him alone. You need to become more than what you are, eaglet."

Arne knew better than to snap at her in frustration, but he wanted to. He had never met a seer who could give him a straight answer. "Can you tell me how?"

"You seem a bit slow and impatient today, so I will spell it out for you, hmm?" Skuld patted his cheek. "You need your mate, Arne. Unless you have her by your side, Midgard will burn and become ashes under Vili's feet."

Arne started to laugh, long and broken and desperate.

"What did you do to him?" Urd asked, appearing through the roots.

"Told him the truth."

Urd poked Arne hard in the chest. "I think you broke him."

"I didn't!"

"Prince, if you don't stop braying like a donkey, I will hit you with my staff," Urd threatened.

"I'm sorry, my ladies, it is a stress response so I don't cry." Arne tried to stop laughing and cleared his throat. "If I don't have my mate fighting by my side, Vili will burn the world. Do I understand that correctly?"

Skuld's eyes narrowed. "That's what I said. What are you having trouble understanding, eaglet?"

"Better prepare for Ragnarök, ladies," Arne said, helplessness threatening to choke him. "Because my mate wants nothing to do with me."

Urd hit him, a sharp rap on the top of his head. "Knock any sense into you? Hmm? If your mate wants nothing to do with you, it's because you fucked up, my boy."

"I didn't mean to." Arne rubbed at the bump on his head. "I don't suppose I can get another bucket of water, and you can tell me what to do to fix it?"

"You don't need more water." Urd grabbed him by the chin, forcing him to stoop to her level. "You stop being a coward. That's how you fix it, Arne Steelsinger. And you better, because if Ragnarök is unleashed because you didn't know how to apologize, I will feed you to Fenris myself."

Arne valued his life, so he only nodded.

"Good! Now, get to it," Urd said, letting him go. Before Arne could stop her, Urd twisted her staff and hit him in the center of the chest. He stumbled and fell backward...and landed hard on the forest floor.

Arne stared dazed at the birch and pine leaves above him. He knew without looking that he was home in Finnmark. He rubbed at his eyes, the journey already going hazy. The message was clear—he needed to win his mate over before Vili made his move.

Arne lay where he was, letting the sounds of the forest settle him, and he tried to think of a plan. He knew without a doubt who his mate was. The problem was Layla wouldn't answer any of his calls so he could apologize or explain himself.

When Arne had asked the fae princes to mediate for him with Layla, all three of them had politely told him to go fuck himself.

Actually, Killian hadn't been polite. He had looked him dead in the eye and told him to go fuck himself. He knew better than to get into a fight with an Ironwood.

Arne needed to petition an authority higher than the princes and only one step down from the gods. He smiled up at the sky as a name formed on his tongue. "Kenna."

⁓

A FORTNIGHT LATER, Arne stood in front of Kenna Ironwood's desk, wondering how a stocky human female could make him feel so intimidated. Her graying red hair was tied back in a braid, and she was wearing her hunting gear, just like always. He had seen her fight the night Morrigan attacked Dublin and knew that the matriarch of the Ironwood clan was more than formidable.

She looked him over slowly before reaching into a drawer and taking out a packet of nicotine gum.

"How do I know I'm going to need at least three pieces to deal with whatever is about to come out of your mouth?" she said, unwrapping the gum and putting them in her mouth. "You going to start talking or just gawk at me, elf? What do you want?"

"Layla. I mean, I want Layla to represent the human and fae alliance at a summit the elves are having in two days," he said, straightening his shoulders.

"So ask her."

"I did. She said no."

"That's surprising because she's obsessed with you lot." Kenna shrugged. "But she said no, so there you have it. Find someone else."

"There *is* no one else!" Arne ran a frustrated hand through his hair.

"The elves are highly secretive, and they don't like outsiders. Layla speaks elvish and knows enough of our customs that the queen has agreed to let her attend."

"The queen as in your mom?" Kenna chewed her gum.

"Yes, my mother is Queen Alruna of the Light Elves." Arne was starting to sweat, and for the life of him, he couldn't figure out why.

Kenna popped her gum and pointed to a chair. "Sit your ass down, prince. You're so wound up, you're giving me a headache."

Arne did as he was told. Sitting didn't help his anxiety, but she wasn't kicking him out, so that was a start.

"Now, I don't know much, but I know when someone isn't telling me everything," she began, folding the gum foil between her fingers and rolling it like a cigarette she was trying to give up. "So...anything you want to add?"

"I went and saw the Norns to learn how we can defeat Vili," Arne replied, leaning his elbows against his knees. "They told me that unless Layla helps us, the world will burn. It's why I need her to attend. The goddesses of fate themselves have decreed it."

Kenna only popped her gum again, her expression not shifting.

"I know you don't really care for supernatural creatures, but you care about this world. If Vili is allowed to reach Midgard, he'll kick off an apocalypse."

Arne desperately tried to think of something he could offer her.

"The elves would pay you an extremely generous fee. I also know that you have more hunters due to turn up and stay at the manor for training and to form a safe base. It's a lot of mouths to feed and many people to discipline. The elves are some of the most elite fighters in the world. I will send you elves to help train the new recruits."

Kenna held up her hand. "If you keep offering me things, I'm going to think you're going to use my Layla for a blood sacrifice. Just...take a breath, lad. There you go. I'll do you up a contract for Layla's services. She'll be pissy about it, but she's a good girl and will do what's right. If she wants to fight about it, she can fight me."

Arne sagged with relief. "Thank you, Kenna. I have a plane to take her to Finnmark. Would it be possible for me to speak to her while I am here? I'd like to give her an itinerary and tell her what meetings she will need to attend."

*And to see her face for a moment. Pin her down and make her listen to my apology. Perhaps just pin her down...*Arne quickly shook those thoughts away.

"Yeah, you can't see her right now, lad. She's busy tonight, but I'll talk to her tomorrow," Kenna said, turning to her laptop and bringing up a contract template.

"What do you mean she's busy? The fate of the world hangs on her getting this done correctly."

Kenna rolled her eyes. "And it can wait until tomorrow. She's got a date tonight and hasn't had one in a while."

"A date," he said flatly. Arne's vision swirled with red.

"The girl needs to have some fun, especially if she's about to be working with the elves for gods know how long," Kenna said.

Arne couldn't be sure, but he thought her eyes gleamed with mischief for a moment. His nervous sweat had turned cold, and his hands were clenching the arms of the chair too tight.

"It is very important I speak with her. Do you know what time she will return?" Arne asked, trying to keep his voice steady.

"If it goes well, I imagine it won't be until tomorrow morning." Kenna raised a brow at him. "Have to admit, I'm kind of jealous. The restaurant she was going to is a new Italian place that just opened up in Temple Bar. *Roberto's*, maybe? It sounded good anyway."

Some of the red cleared from Arne's vision. Had she just told him where to go? Kenna's printer buzzed, and a contract slid out. She passed it over to him.

"Sign on the line, prince."

Arne did so without checking any of the details. He was too busy thinking about another male touching Layla and all the violent things he would do to make it stop.

2

The light buzz of Reeve's tattoo gun was like straight dopamine to Layla's brain. From the first sting of the needle, her anxiety seemed to ease, and it was like she could breathe again. She sat in a chair in the Greatdrakes's laboratory, staring up at suspicious stains on the roof and wondering what spell had backfired to cause them. Anything to take her mind off what she was about to do.

"Remind me again why I thought going on a date was a good idea?" she said, turning her head to watch the blood and ink well on her pale skin.

"Because the world has almost ended like three times in the last six months?" Reeve replied, wiping the ink away. "I don't know why you're nervous. Seamus is a cool guy. Apollo wouldn't set you up with anyone who was a jackass. Trust me, the O'Connells are magicians and good people."

Layla huffed out a breath. "I know. It just seems, I dunno, like a frivolous thing to do with another general walking about."

"Or it's more important *because* another general is walking about," Reeve pointed out. "No one has seen or heard from Vili anyway. Killian thinks he's not even in the human world. We know he won't stay gone forever, so we might as well have fun while we can."

"Yeah, I suppose you're right." Layla stared up at the ceiling, relishing the feeling of the tattoo taking shape. It was a clean pain that was easier than figuring out messy emotions.

"The elves have their summit in a bit. I'm sure if they know anything about Vili, Tor or Arne will say something," Reeve continued.

Just hearing Arne's name was like a stab in her chest. "Or they won't say anything at all, like usual," she said, sounding way too bitter.

"You gotta get over that, Layla. If my dad was a psycho primordial god, I wouldn't want to advertise it either."

"We were hunting a general and looking for information on Vili, and he just said nothing. That's not cool, Reeve. We are meant to be allies."

Reeve lifted the gun from her skin. "Did you ever stop to think that maybe he didn't say anything because he doesn't know either? Vili has been one of Morrigan's generals for centuries. Depending on Arne's age, maybe he knows as little about his father as we do."

"Yeah, maybe." Layla wasn't convinced. She didn't know why it bothered her so much. The princes had gotten over it and were friends with him again.

Arne had tried to send her emails and messages. She had obsessed over every line before doing herself a favor and deleting the lot. The elves could find someone else to be a human advisor at their summit. It wasn't like she was even qualified for such a job.

Sure, she spoke elvish, but she had learned it from an online course and wasn't even sure she would be fluent enough to sit in on meetings or anything.

Apart from that, she didn't have the skills needed for that kind of posh job. She didn't even look the part. She had two sleeves of tattoos and looked like the hunter she was. She didn't have delicate manners and didn't think she could fake them either. If she went, all that would happen was she would make a total ass of herself in front of the elvish leaders and embarrass Arne.

Prince Arne, because let's not forget his mother is the fucking queen, Layla's inner asshole prompted her. That was another reason she hadn't answered any of his messages. Maybe if he was just an average warrior, she wouldn't feel so awkward, but he was a real-life, honest-to-God prince. A prince who had asked her out for a drink, and she had turned him down because she was a dumbass. And now, she felt even more awkward.

I wonder if this is how Frodo felt when he learned that Strider was really a lost king? Was he hurt that he was never told?

Layla's feelings were definitely hurt. More than that, she felt like a total dork at how she had talked to him before she knew. She had anxiously gone over every one of their interactions for all of their cringe content.

"Maybe a date is exactly what you need to take your mind off the broody elf," Reeve said, breaking into her thoughts.

"I don't know what you're talking about. I don't think about him at all," Layla lied.

"Ah huh. Well, you are all done anyway."

Layla looked down her forearm where Reeve had fitted an Evenstar in a patch of bare skin that she'd had between two roses.

"I love it so much. Thanks, bro. You're the best," she said, throwing her arms around him.

"You know I'm always happy to provide spontaneous tattoos and advice whenever you need it," he replied, patting her on the back. "You should get going, or you will be late."

"Yeah, yeah, it's only a short walk."

Ten minutes later, Layla stepped out of the Greatdrakes mansion with her new tattoo wrapped and a grin on her face. She could feel spring in the air, so she had decided to wear a black skater dress with black tights, heeled boots, and a blazer. According to Apollo, the restaurant wasn't overly formal or anything, so she had tried for a mix of what she thought of as classy casual.

"Yeah, a date is a great idea," she said to herself as she checked her red lipstick in the reflection of a shop front. "I look amazing. Fuck handsome elves and their bullshit baggage. I'm going to have fun tonight." She was doing her best to psych herself up, and it was working.

The fresh sting of the Evenstar tattoo made her feel better about life, and she was hoping all the post-tattoo euphoria would carry her through dinner.

Seamus was waiting for her outside of the restaurant. They had met once before at the Monkey Paw, so she knew who to look for. He was lanky and handsome, with a shy smile, auburn curls, and the cutest spray of freckles on one cheek. His blue eyes lit up when he saw her.

"Layla Ironwood, you look outstanding," he said in greeting.

"Thanks. I just want to get out of the way that I haven't been on a date in ages, and I'm super nervous," her mouth said, already running off without her.

Seamus's shy smile widened. "Me too. Also, you are one of the famous Ironwoods, which is intimidating. So I'm thinking, drinks first?"

Layla laughed. "All the drinks. I like the way you think, O'Connell." He held out his arm to her, and she took it.

Inside, the restaurant was already packed. It was all polished timber and black tables and was lit with Edison bulbs tangled in with hanging greenery. It had a fun and funky vibe that suited Layla. She didn't usually like crowds, but the table they were led to was tucked out of the way, so she didn't feel the press of people. They were next to a glass wall that looked out onto a courtyard garden.

"This is a great spot," she commented, sitting down when he pulled the chair out for her.

"Yeah, as soon as it opened, I knew I had to eat here. I remember Apollo saying you don't like too many people, so I requested this table. Besides, I want to be able to hear you over all the noise," Seamus replied.

Layla couldn't help but be weirdly touched. "That was really thoughtful of you."

"Dating is awkward enough without making it worse."

Reeve was right; Seamus was a cool guy. The tips of his ears went a little red when she smiled at him, and she liked it.

"Let me get a waiter's attention so we can get some drinks," he said, looking about. He sent out a small pulse of magic, and a waitress in a white and green dress headed toward them.

"That's a cool trick," Layla commented.

"You felt that? I wouldn't normally use magic for such a small thing, but I will need that drink if you keep smiling at me."

Layla laughed. "I don't think I've made anyone nervous before."

"Not that you've noticed, maybe. You're an Ironwood. People know who you are and are nervous by default."

"Don't be. I'm not one of the important Ironwoods," she said before she could check herself.

Seamus frowned. "I don't understand?"

Shit. She had to say something now.

"I mean, I'm not one of the famous ones. Bron is the best hunter and married a fae prince. Imogen is now a consort to a god, and Charlotte is a magical protégée. I'm just...Layla," she finished lamely.

Before Seamus could reply, the waitress arrived. Layla ordered a double Jameson on the rocks. She was going to need it.

"It's okay, Layla. I get what you're saying. Having that much spotlight on your family must be hard, and you have a massive legacy on top of that. I can't imagine how fucking annoying that all is," Seamus said once they were alone again.

Layla sighed in relief. "It really fucking is. Even before the fae returned and outed the magical world, I was kind of the odd one out anyway. I sound like I'm bitching, but I really don't mind. I hate being the center of attention. It's like ants under my skin. I'm happy to be in the background, doing my own thing."

"I'm kind of the same in my own family," Seamus said, rubbing the back of his neck. "I'm an okay magician, but I still haven't found a specialty. I like too many things, which makes me the odd man out. My brother and sister knew what kind of branch they wanted to pursue from the cradle. And they are overachievers. It's very annoying."

"Siblings are the fucking worst," Layla said, making him laugh.

"Yeah, they really are."

Their drinks arrived, and Layla lifted her glass. "To being the odd man out and hiding from the spotlight."

"Hear! Hear!" Seamus said, tapping his glass of gin and tonic against her whiskey. Jameson caught in her throat as she looked up and saw the elvish warriors in full armor, filing into the courtyard beside them. She swallowed an ice cube in surprise.

"What the hell is going on?" she whispered hoarsely.

"Shit, I hope there hasn't been another horde creature sighting," Seamus replied. The restaurant hushed as six warriors walked through the maze of tables, and at the head, looking like he was about to burn the place to the ground, was Arne.

3

Layla slid down in her chair and was halfway under the table when Arne spotted her and headed straight for them. She glanced at the door leading to the courtyard, but his warriors were already guarding it.

"Save me," she squeaked. It was too late. Arne was there, staring down at her.

"Layla Ironwood, I need you to come with me," he said, his Scandinavian accent making him sound like an angry Viking. The hairs on her arms rose at the sexy growl, and she hated it.

"Go away. I'm on a date," she hissed, pointing to Seamus. "See?"

"Oh, I can see just fine."

"Great. You can see I'm busy. Now, go away," she said through gritted teeth. Everyone in the restaurant was staring at her. Hot horror slid over her entire body. She sure as shit was the center of attention now. "You are making a scene."

"Then come with me, and I will stop," Arne replied, his leather armor creaking when he crossed his arms.

Layla pinched the bridge of her nose. "Are we under attack?"

"No."

"Horde creatures invading?"

Arne shifted his weight. "No."

"Has your father decided to show up, and I need to go immediately to a family meeting?"

"No."

"Then would you fuck off?" Layla squeaked a little too loudly. Arne didn't budge, his golden eyes catching hers in a glare off. "I told you I didn't want to be a stupid ambassador or whatever the fuck you wanted me to do. Take the hint."

Arne gestured to a warrior who handed him a piece of paper. Arne unfolded it and held it up. Layla's stomach plummeted as she spotted the Ironwood crest at the top.

"Your services have been acquired and paid for. You will come with me so we can discuss logistics." Arne leaned down to look her dead in the eye. "I'm not leaving without you."

"I'm not leaving until my date is over," Layla snarled back.

"By all means, continue." Arne's smile was deadly. "I can wait."

"You do that. Like, over there or something." Arne took one step away from the table and crossed his arms again. Layla cringed and looked back to Seamus. His blue eyes were bugging out of his head.

"Family issues. Just ignore them, please," she said sweetly.

Seamus looked at Arne and back to Layla. "Yeah, I'm not getting involved in whatever this—" he gestured at them "—happens to be."

"Please don't go," she whispered, hating that she sounded like she was begging.

Seamus got up from his chair and walked to her side of the table, blocking Arne from view. "We can do this another time, doll. Looks like Ironwood duty calls."

"I really was having a nice time," she said, taking his hand and squeezing it. "I'm sorry."

"Don't be, Layla. This was the best date I've had in a year. Give me a call when the job is over, and we'll try again, yeah?"

"Yeah, I'd like that," she said. Seamus kissed her cheek, and Arne made a feral growling sound.

"Don't let him push you about," Seamus whispered with a wink.

"I won't."

The elves stepped out of his way as he left the restaurant, Layla staring after him and feeling like a total asshole. It was ridiculous because the elf staring daggers at her was the one who was the asshole.

"Happy now that you scared him off? I liked him!"

"My heart weeps for your loss," Arne replied, droll as ever. "Let's go."

"No. I'm not leaving until I've eaten. I never get a night off," she said, the urge to be a brat overwhelming her.

Arne made a small gesture, and the elves behind him fell back and joined the others in the courtyard. He remained where he was like he was waiting for her to ask him to sit down.

Yeah, that wasn't going to happen. Layla opened her menu and ignored him completely. A timid waiter came up to them.

"A-Are you ready to order, miss?" he asked.

"I sure am. Can I please get the creamy garlic prawn pasta? And another double of Jameson? Thanks so much," she said, giving him a big smile.

The waiter looked awkwardly at Arne. "Would sir—"

"Sir is not eating," Layla said quickly. "Just think of him as unwelcome furniture, like I am."

"O-Okay," the waiter replied and hurried away.

"Would you please—" Arne began.

Layla took out her phone and opened her e-book app. "Furniture can't talk."

Arne growled something in elvish that was too low for her to catch. She pretended to be reading, resting her chin on her palm. A trickle of nervous sweat ran down her back. She was never this rude to anyone, but he had started it by crashing her date. She opened her messaging app and opened her chat with Kenna.

What the fuck, Mom? You signed a contract with the elves without even talking to me? She added a line of angry emojis for emphasis.

Sorry, darling, you can't be precious when the fate of the world is at stake. It's an easy job for an eye-watering amount of money that will help the family and the hunters a lot. I'll give you a big bonus.

Layla wanted to hurl her phone at the glass wall. It shouldn't surprise her that Kenna would do something like sign her services away. Layla always did as she was told for 'the good of the family.' She'd never argued even when sent on awful camping trips or when she gave up her free time to look after Moira or help David. She was always on call to help with research or whatever they needed help with.

This is bullshit. I don't care about the bonus. I already told the elves no, she shot back, her nails clicking hard against the glass screen.

The pretty one said that, but he seems to think you're the best person for the job, and so do I. He's pushy, but it'll be good for you. How else will you get invited to see the elves, like in those hobbit books you like so much?

Layla drained her whiskey. Trust her mother to use the only shit that brought her joy against her. 'Those hobbit books' had always been a point of contention because they were Ironwoods; they were meant to hunt and kill magical creatures, not read fantasy books about them. She *had* always wanted to see the elves, the real elves. She just didn't want to do it like this.

Layla wrote out a reply three times and deleted it. She was writing out a fourth when her food arrived.

"Thanks," she said to the waiter, who still looked scared.

Arne was staring at her, his golden eyes shining with intense annoyance.

Good. Layla wasn't hungry, but she was too stubborn to back out. She picked up her fork and went back to her reading app. She tried really hard not to flick any cream on her clothes as she ate and read at the same time. She could feel Arne's eyes boring into her, following every movement.

Her phone buzzed, and she looked down at the message from Apollo.

How's the date going? Didn't I tell you Seamus was the cutest?

Yeah, you did. The date was going well until a big elvish asshole crashed it.

????!!

Layla turned her phone, snapped a photo of Arne obnoxiously, and sent it to Apollo.

Told you. Big. Elvish. Asshole. He scared Seamus away.

Rude! But to be honest, he looks like he's about to pounce on you.

I'm making him wait while I eat pasta. Fuck him.

You are my hero. I'd give him whatever he asked for.

Layla bit down a laugh. *You slut.*

If only he was interested in crashing any of my dates. The pouncing look makes more sense. He probably has blue balls watching your big lips sucking on linguini. Mine are blue just thinking about it.

It's fettuccine, actually.

Work it, girl, suck those cheeks in. You show that elf who's boss. He looks like the type who would love to be dominated. All pent up and princely, he probably needs to hand the control over to someone else, if you know what I mean? Get him on his knees.

Layla went hot all over with that visual of Arne kneeling before her. Naked. And sweaty. She wasn't usually dominant in bed, but the image had its merits.

Jesus fucking Christ, Apollo. I'm trying to eat. Keep your dirty thoughts to yourself, she texted back, angling her phone so there was no way Arne could see it.

They are our dirty thoughts now, Lay Lay. Let me know if you make him cry by the end of the night.

Will do. I really did like Seamus. Layla sighed. Of course, the first okay date had to get ruined.

"Your date messaging you and making you smile like that?" Arne asked.

"None of your business, elf."

When the waiter returned with her drink, Arne took it and growled, "Bring me a vodka on the rocks."

"What brand, sir?"

Arne's eyes narrowed. "Do I look like I give a shit?" The waiter all but ran back to the bar.

"Hey, that's mine," Layla snapped. Arne sat down opposite her and placed her whiskey in front of her. "I didn't ask you to sit."

"I'm not a dog. I can do what I like," he replied. "Looks like we will have that drink together after all."

"You crashed my date so you could try and have another one?" Layla demanded.

"The date looked like it was crashing all on its own," Arne replied. "You looked bored."

"You wouldn't know."

"I know." The waiter appeared and placed a vodka down in front of him. He didn't wait for a thank you before he bolted away.

"I'm never going to be able to come back here. I hope you're happy." She had a mouthful of Jameson. "And I wasn't bored. I was having a nice time with Seamus."

"*Nice*," Arne said snidely. "That's what does it for you, is it?"

"What does it for me is also none of your business." Layla praised herself for getting the words out levelly. Jesus, he was intense.

"It could be."

Layla's whole body tightened. "I don't date liars."

"I never lied to you."

"Bullshit. You're a prince, and what...a demi-god? The fuck you didn't lie."

Arne raised a brow. "I didn't tell you about my parentage. That's not the same as lying. Perhaps I didn't want to tell you because I knew you would act like this."

It could have been the whiskey coursing through her, but Layla thought she heard a tinge of hurt in his voice. Not possible.

"Why would you give a shit about how I would act? You know what? Doesn't matter. I don't care." Layla drained her drink and gestured to the waiter for a cheque. "I honestly can't figure out why you won't take no for an answer. I'm not qualified to be an ambassador."

"You are a human and a sister to the powerful fae princes. You speak elvish, and you are intimately aware of the threat that the generals pose. You are the *only* person qualified for this task," Arne replied.

"Take Bron. She's better suited."

"She doesn't speak elvish."

"She can use a translating app."

The glass Arne was holding cracked. "Bron wasn't chosen by the Norns themselves for this task!"

"The Norns?" she squeaked. "The Norns are real too?"

"Very. And they told me that you need to help the elves, or Vili will start Ragnarök," he replied.

Layla blinked a few times and then burst out laughing. "That makes no sense. I'm no one, Arne. I don't stop the likes of Vili. I stand behind the people that do and make sure they have everything they need."

"The Norns don't lie. They said it was you. That it could be no one else." His golden eyes narrowed. "And you will come and help us even if I have to hurl your very fine and stubborn ass over my shoulder and carry you all the way to Finnmark myself."

"You wouldn't dare." Though Layla suddenly kind of wanted to see if he would.

"Wouldn't I?" Arne's lip curled as he leaned forward and whispered, "Keep fighting me and find out how far I'll go to get what I want, Ironwood."

Layla's breath caught as her body did the whole tight freeze of arousal she got way too often when he was around. Fuck, she shouldn't have had that second double.

"Your bill, miss," the waiter said, making her jump. Arne tapped his phone to the portable machine, paying before she could stop him.

"Gods, you're annoying," she muttered.

"The feeling is mutual."

Layla didn't wait for him as she got up and walked out of the restaurant. The night had gotten cool, so she buttoned her jacket up. A black BMW pulled up next to the sidewalk, and Arne opened the door for her.

"I can get my own ride," she said, rounding on him.

"But now you don't have to. There is a folder on the seat. Please familiarize yourself with its contents. This car will return to Ironwood manor tomorrow at ten a.m. sharp to take you to the airport."

Layla put her hands on her hips. "Anything else, Your Highness?"

"Yes. You have food on your face." Arne reached over and wiped his thumb over the corner of her mouth. Layla wanted to die of shame when she saw the cream on it. When he put his thumb to his mouth and sucked the cream off, she almost fainted instead. She scrambled into the car so fast, she banged her knees on the seat in front of her.

"For the love of God, drive," she begged, but the car didn't move.

Arne closed the door, and the window slid down. "If you want to know why I never told you about Vili, I suggest you be on the plane tomorrow and don't be late."

Layla was still trying to think of something to say when the car pulled away, and Arne disappeared into the night.

"Fucking elves," she grumbled, her head dropping back on the seat behind her. "No offense."

"None taken, Miss Ironwood," the driver said. "Finnmark is still cold this time of year, so I suggest you pack warmly and try not to irritate Steelsinger too much."

"Thank you for your unsolicited advice that I didn't need," she snarked.

The driver chuckled and turned up the radio. "The elves are going to love you."

4

"And *then* Arne was all like '*You have food on your face*' and gave me some cryptic guff about if I want to know about Vili, I will be on the plane today," Layla complained loudly to Charlotte as she paced up and down the labs.

"Guff," Charlotte said with a frown. "Is that even a word? I don't think it is."

"Does it matter? My point is he's—" Layla struggled for the right word. "He's rude!"

Charlotte's brows drew together tight. "He's a prince. Have you met our brothers? They all act like that."

"Don't talk smack about my brothers. They would never force a contract on someone!"

"Ah, what about when Kian took Elise as a slave? And Bayn pretty much turned up in Freya's store and refused to leave until she agreed to work for him?"

"Shut up. You know what I mean."

"No, sis, I don't. You are rambling. How much sleep did you get?"

Layla stopped pacing and slumped down onto a swivel chair. "I don't know, like two hours. Even my trusty vibrator didn't help."

"Ew, Layla," Charlotte complained.

"What? Masturbation is healthy."

"I still don't want to hear about it." Charlotte went about gathering a few items and placing them into a pile. "Your car will be here in an hour, so let's put some supplies together. Although, it is only a summit, they are meant to be peaceful and boring."

"Yay for me," Layla griped, her leg bouncing irritably. "I'm also going to the middle of nowhere by myself so load me up. I'm an Ironwood. We need to be ready for anything."

"Whatever you say, Layla." Charlotte took some blank patches from a drawer and started to sketch on one. "These ones should help you sleep. As for the others, take them, but I doubt you'll need them. Arne and Tor won't let anything happen to you if there is trouble."

"Yeah, sure they won't. Arne would probably throw me at the enemy and run away."

"You don't believe that, so stop pretending you do because you're pissy at him." Charlotte stopped sketching. "Have you even tried to think about things from his point of view? From what we know, his dad is a total monster. He would have to be to get Morrigan's interest. Not to mention his mom is like a queen."

"What's your point?" Layla demanded.

"Being an Ironwood can be bad enough, but can you imagine being the son of a god *and* a prince. He probably hates it. Maybe Arne wanted people to get to know him without all of that hanging over his head."

Layla didn't like how much Charlotte was making sense. "Yeah, maybe. He could've at least told Bayn."

"You know the elves are private. It might be an inbuilt thing."

"Why are you so determined to defend him?"

Charlotte let out a groan of frustration. "Because you liked him, Layla! And he asked you out, so you know he must've liked you too. You have also refused to date anyone since you met him."

"I've been busy! I shouldn't have told you about any of that anyway," Layla grumbled.

"Too bad. You did. You came to me for advice so here it is: it's dumb to fight over stupid shit when we have bigger enemies threatening to destroy us. You don't like him anymore? Fine. But be professional. You have a job to do, so do it, and then you never have to see him again."

Layla didn't know which part of that statement she hated more.

"You know I won't do anything to embarrass the family," she said finally.

"I know." Charlotte handed her the bag of magical tricks. "I think you're overlooking one very important thing right now."

"And that is?"

Charlotte grinned. "There is quite literally going to be hundreds of elves everywhere at this thing. Like really, really hot ones."

"Huh." Layla's head tilted to one side. "You know, that's the advice you should've given me from the start." She got up and pulled Charlotte into a hug. "Thanks, sis. I'll miss you. I mean, I will if I'm not busy being hip deep in some high-quality elf D."

"Yeah, if that happens, and you need to talk about it? Call Imogen," Charlotte said, and they both laughed.

"Deal."

Thirty minutes later, Layla had her small suitcase downstairs and was waiting on the front stoop.

"You taking some weapons with you?" Kenna asked, coming up behind her.

"Yeah." Layla tapped her Doc Marten against the leather case that carried her bow. The fae made recurve bow had been a gift from Killian, and it was gorgeous. Inside each of her boots were thin daggers she never went anywhere without.

"Don't be shitty at me. It will be good for you to do a job on your own for once." Kenna bumped her shoulder against Layla's. "Have fun and don't fuck it up. Ciara is working a job in Sweden, so give her a call if you get in a jam and need some backup."

"Sure. Thanks for throwing me into a situation I didn't want to be in," Layla replied as the BMW pulled up in front of them.

Kenna put her hands on her hips. "Don't act like a brat. We need to take out the third general and ensure that our family, not to mention the world, is safe. This isn't just about you, Layla Brigid Ironwood."

"When is it ever?" Layla muttered, climbing into the car and slamming the door behind her.

∼

It was a twenty-minute drive out to the private airport from the Ironwood Estate. Layla used the time to smooth her sweating palms over her black leather leggings and practiced her calm breathing while listening to her favorite playlist. She couldn't make up her mind if she was anxious or excited or a mixture of both.

It was true she didn't do any hunting jobs on her own, mainly because her family were all better hunters, and she was better at being the backup.

It's not hunting. It's just meetings, remember?

After talking to Charlotte, Layla had decided that she would hear Arne out and then act professional for the rest of the trip.

By nature, she was probably the most forgiving of all of the Ironwoods. She wasn't like Imogen and Charlotte who nursed grudges to a level of a petty that took real commitment. Sure, she was pissed Arne had crashed her date, and he could apologize for that too so they could move forward.

The problem was, Layla was terrible at asking what she wanted, and her tongue struggled to work properly around Arne on a good day.

Just make him say sorry and let it go. If he does it while not wearing a shirt, maybe it will help with the healing process. Gah, shut up brain! Layla argued with herself, her leg starting to bounce again.

They pulled up in front of a hanger, and Layla recognized the tall and brawny blonde Viking waiting for them.

"Tor! I didn't know you were here!" she said excitedly. She pulled him into a hug, and he squeezed her tightly.

"Little Layla, I'm glad to see a smile on your face. Arne told me you were angry at us," Torsten said, his deep voice a grumble in the very ripped chest she was pressed against.

Layla was almost as interested in the Ulfheðnar as she was the elves. Ever since Arawan had announced that Odin was still alive and walking the earth, Layla had wondered if his wolf-shifting warriors knew where the All-Father was. She may have done some digging herself because she was just like that when she got obsessed with something.

"Nah, I'm not angry at you, Tor. You didn't crash my first date in ages," Layla replied.

"He did what now?" Tor pulled back from her, and she wasn't ashamed to say she admired the Norse tattoos on his ridiculously big biceps.

"Leave that part out, did he? He turned up with like fifty warriors, and my date left. And then Arne just *stood* there and watched me eat like a weirdo. You would think a prince would have more manners," Layla huffed.

Tor's gray eyes twinkled. "Yeah, you would think. You should have answered your emails if you didn't want him being dramatic. Elves are real drama queens when they want to be."

"Apologies should be done in person not over an email." Layla crossed her arms.

"I agree. He doesn't think straight when he's stressed out," Tor said and picked up her suitcase. He gestured for her to head up the stairs into their private plane.

"What's he so stressed...about..." Layla's brain stopped working when the elf in question appeared in the doorway of the plane. He was out of his warrior gear and was dressed casually in dark jeans and a cream knit jumper that was tight enough to show off just how fit he was.

Odin's beard. Layla's boot hit the edge of the stair, and she was falling. Strong arms caught her before she face planted.

"Are you okay?" Arne asked, helping her upright. Layla scrambled to get out of his grip and would have gone backward if Tor's hand hadn't steadied her.

"Yeah, fine. Just feet. I mean, I'm not quite awake. Ah, thanks," Layla blabbed, her face burning. *Just feet? What the hell is wrong with you?*

"If you can make it into the plane, there's coffee." Arne smiled down at her. "I don't know if I'm relieved or disappointed you didn't make me come and fetch you."

Layla's mouth popped open. "Ah, what..."

"Maybe you could flirt when we are all on the plane?" Tor suggested from behind her.

"Welcome aboard, Miss Ironwood." Arne stepped back inside and let Layla through the door.

She shouldn't have been surprised that the private plane was fancy as fuck. She pretended not to be impressed and sat down in one of the plush blue leather chairs and dumped her bag on the floor at her feet.

Tor stowed her suitcase and bow case in an overhead locker and instantly went to the bar to pour coffee. Arne was still staring at her. He had his black hair out of its tie, and it brushed the cream of his sweater. It was obscene how good he looked.

Rude. Layla had a weakness for hot men in knitwear. She couldn't stay mad at anyone who looked that good.

"Here you are, Layla. You have it black with one sugar, right?" Tor said, setting the coffee down at the small table beside her.

"I do! Good memory." Layla had a sip and hummed in pleasure. "You're my big Viking hero." She looked Arne over. "You, I'm still mad at."

"Big surprise."

"I am a professional, so I will choose to be civil if you can be," she added and blew on her coffee.

Arne's lips pressed tight together as he nodded. With that, he sat in the chair opposite her, and Tor settled across the aisle.

The plane engines began to purr, and the door was shut. Layla always got nervous when she flew, but she did her best to hide it as she clipped on her seat belt. She was about to put her headphones in when Arne's boot tapped against hers.

"You still want to know why I didn't say anything about Vili?" he asked.

Layla lowered her headphones. "Yeah, of course I do."

They fell into a staring competition as the plane took off so smoothly Layla barely noticed it.

"I didn't say anything because I really don't know anything about him," Arne said. He unclipped his seat belt and rolled his shoulders. "He was gone before I was born, and my mother had no idea who he really was until they were mated, and he finally revealed his true self. The things I do know about him are what everyone knows—that he's Odin's brother, that he ruled in a fortress in Svartalfheim for a time, and that he became Morrigan's general."

"He never, I dunno, tried to reach out to you?" Layla asked.

She got along so well with David that she couldn't imagine how she would've turned out without him raising her. Layla and Imogen would have probably killed each other as soon as they hit puberty for a start.

"No. I'm not even sure he knows I exist. My mother certainly did her best to hide my parentage from the elves too."

Layla frowned. "Why? If she was duped by Vili, she's a victim."

"My mother would never tolerate being a victim." Arne leaned forward and rested his elbows on his knees. "She didn't ever want me to be a target or used as a pawn for anyone wanting revenge on Vili. It was bad enough that I was already a prince. Vili had fooled everyone into thinking he was just another dark elf, and a lot of elves took that poorly. He was a brutal ruler when he did rule. Then one day, Morrigan turned up, and he went with her. He became her general and her monster. At least, that's what my mother was told."

Layla chewed at her bottom lip. "Is she scared Vili will come for you guys now?"

Arne shook his head. "There's no reason for us to be scared. If Vili has known about me, he's never showed the slightest bit of interest. No, whatever his plans are, it doesn't involve making up for lost time with his son."

Arne didn't sound bitter about it, but Layla still heard the faint sting in his words. No one liked the idea that their parent didn't give a shit about them. It didn't matter that Vili was a monster.

"Do you think any of his old enemies will try and hurt you?" she asked, her stomach clenching uneasily at the thought.

"I believe they would have tried by now because my mother couldn't hide my parentage from the elves for long." Arne shifted and cleared his throat. "Apparently, I look like him."

"Oh." Layla hated the sadness in his golden eyes, so she added, "I suppose something good had to come out of it."

Arne smiled a little and then flinched as if in pain. "Shit."

"What? Are you okay?" Layla asked.

"It's nothing. Just a migraine I haven't been able to kick for a few days," he said, rubbing at his brow. "I'm going to lie down. We can continue our talk later if you have questions, okay?"

"Sure. I get migraines all the time, so I understand," Layla replied.

Arne got up and looked at Tor. "Get her whatever she wants."

"Sure thing, *bróðir*," he replied, and Arne walked to the back of the plane.

Layla watched him go with a frown. "Is he going to be okay?"

"Yeah, he'll be fine. He's had a rough few weeks. Trips around Yggdrasil to see the Norns can fuck with a male." Tor raised a brow at her. "So can pretty hunters with sharp tongues."

Layla rolled her eyes. "It's not like I crashed *his* date."

"Still, ever since the Norns, he's been worried. More than I've ever seen in fact." Tor scratched at his blonde stubble. "Look, it's not my place to interfere, but try not to bust his balls too hard. What he won't admit is that he liked pretending he was just a normal elf warrior. The princes and their mates, you Ironwoods, it's the first time he's really had anything that resembled friends."

"Why? He's a prince. I thought he would have loads of them," Layla said, sipping her coffee. "You're a good friend to him."

"He's not good at letting people close, and I am sworn to protect Odin's bloodline, even his nephew. I'm his friend, yes, but I'm also his guard." Tor hesitated and looked where Arne had disappeared to make sure they were still alone. "He won't say it, especially not to you, but he's always been scared that his blood carries Vili's darkness."

"That's crazy. I'll admit he's got a jerk streak, but I've seen darkness in the shit that I've hunted over the years, and he's not dark," Layla argued.

Tor grunted. "Try telling him that. Just go easier on him if you can. I'll admit he went about everything the wrong way, but he wasn't trying to hurt you."

"If he wasn't, then why hasn't he said sorry for lying or crashing my date for that matter? Like saying two words isn't hard."

Tor let out a string of Norwegian curses. "He hasn't even said sorry?"

"Nope. Not in the emails or texts or anything."

"Maybe you need to go and tell him that's all it will take. He's a bit of an idiot when he's stressed out and loves to overcomplicate things. If that's all you want in order to put aside the sniping at each other, maybe you need to make the first move and tell him," Tor suggested. He clasped his hands together dramatically. "Please, Layla, for the love of all the gods, talk to him because I will end up knocking both of your heads together if you force me to put up with your bickering. Be the bigger person."

"But I'm *always* the bigger person," she complained.

"It's because your heart is the biggest."

Layla laughed despite herself. There was something about a Viking shapeshifter being a sweetheart that weakened her resolve.

"That was cheating, but I think I have some migraine tablets that might help him anyway," she grumbled.

"You are as noble and brave as you are beautiful," Tor replied, giving her a big smile.

Layla dug about until she found her emergency stash of pain killers and went to the bar to pour out a glass of Coke.

"Wish me luck?" she said.

Tor smiled at her. "You don't need it. Go on."

5

Layla found Arne lying on a bed in a small room at the back of the plane. She tapped lightly against the door, and his eyes opened. She gripped the glass in her hand harder. She could do this. Like ripping off a Band Aid.

"I'm tired of fighting with you. Say sorry, and I'll give you things to make the migraine go away," she said in a quick breath.

"What kind of things?" Arne asked, flinching as he sat up.

"Say sorry and find out," she replied.

Arne looked up at her, his eyes full of pain and sadness. "I am sorry I didn't tell you about Vili. It was never my intention to hurt you or anyone else."

"Accepted. Now apologize for interrupting my date," she said, doing her best to remain stern.

Arne frowned. "But..."

"No buts. Apologize."

"I'm sorry for interrupting your date," he grumbled. "I should have tracked you down before you got to the restaurant."

"Good enough. I guess. Truce?"

Arne nodded. "Truce. I don't like you being angry at me."

"Well, don't piss me off." Layla showed him the tablets. "Take these.

They are the only things that make any difference when I have a migraine. Drink the Coke. The caffeine will make them work quicker."

Arne smiled and opened his mouth. Layla's pulse jumped as she placed the pills on his tongue and gave him the Coke. He drank it down.

"Thank you, Layla. How long will they take to kick in?" he asked, placing the glass down on a bedside table.

"Twenty minutes. Give me your hands. I'll show you another trick."

Arne held out his hands to her. They were warrior's hands, calloused palms and fingertips from swords and bow work. Layla pinched the skin between his index fingers and thumbs.

"How is this supposed to help?" he asked.

"It's a pressure point. Ciara does it for me. Give it a second." She held on, Arne watching on curiously. She tried not to notice how nice his hands were shaped, or how sharp his cheekbones. The small points of his ears peaked out from his dark hair, and she had the urge to touch them.

"You like my ears?" he whispered.

"Yeah, I do," she replied because she had been busted looking. She released the pressure points. "There."

"I don't feel...ohhh," Arne breathed. "That is amazing. Thank you. What other tricks do you know?"

Layla's mouth went dry. "Permission to touch your face?"

"Always," he replied, and heat streaked up her spine.

Keeping her professional face on, she used her thumbs to slowly massage the point where his jaw met his ears. Arne's eyes rolled back in his head.

"Good, right?" Layla said, adding more pressure. "No wonder you have a headache. You got massive knots from clenching your jaw too much."

"I call one 'Layla' and the other one 'Ironwood,'" Arne replied with a teasing smile.

"Very funny. In future, maybe you should just apologize when you're being a dick, instead of dragging it out like a ridiculous male." Layla moved her fingers to the back of his skull.

"I'm sorry, I'm sorry, I'm sorry. Just don't stop doing that," he groaned. His legs on either side of her closed a little to trap her where she was.

Layla's cheeks were burning, but she didn't stop. She hoped he couldn't hear how fast her heart was racing.

"You must get a lot of migraines to be so good at this," he said drowsily.

"Well, I have a stressful work environment, and I don't always sleep great, so it happens," she replied. She marveled that they had moved from arguments to massages so quickly.

Just me being professional. So, so professional.

"I don't sleep well either," Arne admitted.

"Good to know. I might need an insomnia buddy on this trip. I'm kind of nervous."

"Don't be. I wouldn't have pushed so hard for you to come if I thought you couldn't handle it." Arne opened his eyes. "Thank you for the head rub. It really is helping."

"It's okay. You can do my feet one night and make up for it," she said, her mouth running away on her again.

Arne laughed softly, and her insides went squishy. "It's a deal. You can touch my ears if you want."

"It feels like a trap. Is it a weird elf taboo I'm not aware of?" she asked skeptically.

"No. It was an offer to satisfy your curiosity." He was smiling when he said it in a way that made her think it probably *was* taboo. "Scared?"

"No, but you better not crack an awkward boner or anything. We aren't that friendly," Layla replied, and his laugh deepened.

"Too late for that."

Layla looked down, and he laughed even harder. "Who knew elves were so sassy under their grumpy exteriors?"

"What can I say, you bring out the best in me."

"You're only saying that because I'm helping your migraine."

Arne hummed. "Maybe." She smiled and ran her thumbs behind his ears, and his eyes fluttered closed. He had long inky lashes that made her feel a little envious. "Fuck, that feels amazing."

Layla's fingers moved of their own accord and caressed the silky points of his ears.

"Instant boner," Arne whispered, and Layla cracked up laughing.

"Shut up or I'll stop."

Arne grabbed onto her, making her jump. "No! Don't... This is the best I've felt in weeks."

"Okay, but this is going to be an additional cost on my contract," she replied, trying to keep her voice steady.

"Mercenary."

"Damn straight. Girls shouldn't work for free."

Arne loosened his grip on her legs but didn't let go. She could smell the heady scent of fir trees coming off him, and she wanted to press her nose into it. She shook the image away before it could do any more damage.

"Can I ask you a question? Now that we are friends again?" he said softly.

"I guess?"

"Why didn't you want to come and have a drink with me after Killian's party?"

Shit. Layla didn't want to tell him, but she did. "I panicked."

"Why? We fought together and got along."

"I panicked when you asked because I didn't think someone like you would ask me out."

"Someone like me," Arne said slowly, his golden eyes opening. "You have something against elves?"

"Gods, no. I love elves. I was just sideswiped by the offer. I didn't think you would be interested in me."

Arne frowned. "Because you are human?"

"No. Because I'm Layla."

"That doesn't even make sense."

Layla cringed at the thought of explaining it to him. "Don't worry about it."

"I probably will, but I'm glad you love elves." The flirtatious grin was back, and Layla's head started flashing a red light of warning. She still couldn't help poking him.

"Yeah, I do, and you just invited me to an all-you-can-eat buffet, so thanks, friend," she said, patting both of his shoulders and stepping out of his grip. "Make a mental list of all the hot cousins you can introduce me to."

"Wait, that's not..."

"You should get some sleep. It'll make the tablets work better," Layla said, talking over him. She paused at the door, shooting him a smile. "Feel better!"

6

Arne woke with his head clear and the captain announcing that they would be landing in twenty minutes. He didn't know whether it was the pills or Layla, but his migraine had finally broken. What had Urd said? Something about being fed to Fenris unless he apologized? He could almost hear the old crone cackling with glee because she had been right and saying sorry had been the answer all along.

Of course, she was right. It's her sole purpose.

Arne sat up and rubbed his hands over his face, trying to dislodge the grogginess from his head. To be fair, he'd had every intention of apologizing long and profusely to Layla Ironwood. Except that plan had dissolved in red heat and alpha male bullshit as soon as he had seen her in the restaurant, laughing brightly with a male who wasn't him.

Fuck that guy. Arne had gone from having a cool head to burning with ridiculous mating fury in the blink of an eye. He had wanted to stab his sword into every male who had looked over. And there had been plenty because her curvy body swathed in that tight black dress had looked so fucking good, he wanted to cry.

Gods, those red lips smeared in cream would haunt him until Ragnarök finally wiped them out.

Arne groaned, trying desperately not to get hard thinking about it. It wasn't an easy task because her scent was *everywhere*. It was like chocolate and nectarines and pheromones. It was probably a good thing that his migraine had impaired him because he would have lost his fucking mind if she touched him like that with a clear head.

Having her close was enough to soothe his frayed edges. It was like he could think straight for the first time in weeks. Well, up until she had made the flippant comment about introducing her to eligible cousins. He would blind any one of them who attempted to flirt with her.

Gods, listen to you. You can't let the beast get involved, or she'll never want you. The voice in his head made all his passion cool.

The beast. That's what he called the fucking *thing* that lived in his blood. It was the magic he had inherited from Vili. He had gotten the name *Steelsinger* because when he let it loose in a fight, he slaughtered everything in his path.

It was the side of him that had seen Layla fighting amongst the horde creatures and decided she was his. It had known, and it didn't matter that he had met her earlier and found her beautiful and interesting. The mating roar hadn't kicked in until she was smeared in horde creature and fighting for all she was worth. Her feral side had sung to his, and he had known he was fucked for all others. It was only ever going to be her.

Arne went into the little bathroom, washed his face, and ran his hands through his hair. He looked like a wreck, but that couldn't be helped.

Tor's deep rumble of laughter echoed down the plane. He came across as gruff and serious and stoic until he was comfortable with someone. He had always liked Layla. It was hard not to when she was so warm and funny.

You are ridiculous. She is barely tolerating your existence right now.

Arne could work with that, even if the way she said 'friend' made him want to cry. He was sure he had a charming side somewhere.

When he joined them, Layla had her boots off and feet tucked under her. They had been drinking vodka, and she was laughing so hard, she was red.

"Oh my God, Arne. Did you really eat the wrong mushrooms in the forest and trip balls for like three days?" she asked.

Arne's eye twitched. He was going to fucking murder Torsten.

"I was twelve, and it was a valuable lesson," he said, glaring at the innocent looking shifter.

"It was hilarious is what it was," Tor said.

"I bet." Layla's brown eyes were filled with glee. "Tor is a champion and has agreed to be my wingman for the summit. You're the actual best because Arne is going to be too busy being all princely and shit to have any fun at all."

Arne's head started to ache again. He rubbed at his temple. "I am thinking about redecorating my house with a lovely wolf pelt."

"Aw, don't pout. We want Layla to have a good time on her stay, don't we?" Tor said, his smile as innocent as the driven snow. Arne wanted to throat punch him.

Tor *knew* that Layla was his mate. Arne was forced to admit it when his scent changed, and Tor confronted him about it. There was no hiding shit from a wolf. Nosey fucking creatures that they were.

"I've never been this far north, so I want to see Alta and play tourist if I can," Layla said, staring out the window at the land rapidly rising to meet them.

"If it's what you want, I'm sure we can make time for it to happen," Arne said, sitting down beside her and buckling his seat belt. He ignored Tor's smirk.

"How's the head?" Layla asked.

"A lot better. Thank you for your tablets and the massage. They helped a lot," he said. He fought the urge to take her hand that was resting on the armrest.

You'll have to tell her she is your mate eventually, Urd's voice said in his mind. If she was another elf, she would already know. It would have made so many things easier.

Arne stared at the curl of a tattooed rose petal on her wrist, the colors peeking out from her sweater. He wanted to press his lips to it. Yes, Layla being an elf would have been easier, but where was the fun in easy?

The plane shook with turbulence, and Layla's hand grabbed onto his forearm.

"Oh fuck, we are going to die," she groaned.

"No, we aren't. The winds up here can get wild, but the captain wouldn't be trying to land if it was dangerous," Arne tried to soothe her. The plane rocked again, and Layla swore. He touched her face, turning it towards him. "Look at me, Layla. Just breathe. You're safe."

Layla's eyes fixed on his, and he took a deep a breath. She copied him, flinching as the plane bobbed, but didn't look away. "You're always going to be safe with me," he said softly.

Layla's lips twitched. "Yeah? What about if I piss you off?"

"Are you planning on doing that?"

"Not right this second, but I'm sure it'll happen at some point."

Arne smiled. "You only need to worry if you start trying to date one of my cousins."

"Don't be such a pussy blocker, Arne, or I am going to think you have a thing for crashing dates," she replied.

Arne's brain short-circuited at the word *pussy* coming out of her mouth. The plane touched down, and Layla let go of her death grip.

Outside, the cold snap in the air hit Arne's lungs and some of the tension in him eased. He was home; Layla was with him like the Norns wanted; the council would meet, and everything would be okay.

And that was when he saw his mother waiting for them with two of her bodyguards.

"I didn't know you were going to be here to greet us," Arne said, walking across the hanger to her.

"I was here to meet with another delegation and thought I would wait for you." Alruna pulled him into a hug, her silver-gray braid tickling his nose as he kissed the top of her head. "And you know I'm far too nosey to let you sneak a human in without letting me look at her first."

Layla was laughing at something Torsten was saying as he carried her bags down the stairs. Her expression sobered instantly when she saw who Arne was with. It didn't matter that his mother was dressed casually in dark jeans, boots, and a blazer. Layla knew instantly who she was, and her whole body language shifted.

Arne gestured for her to come over, his heart beating a little erratically when Layla touched her hair self-consciously.

"Layla Ironwood, may I introduce my mother, Alruna," he said.

Layla bowed low and said in perfect elvish, "It is an honor to meet you, my queen, and a privilege to be invited to the summit."

Alruna raised an ashen brow at Arne. "You're welcome, Miss Ironwood. My son has told me a lot about you."

"Only good things I hope," Layla said, shooting a warning look at Arne.

"Why would I say anything else?" he replied sweetly. "She never bows or greets me so nicely."

"Well, your mother hasn't ever crashed one of my dates."

Alruna looked between them and started to laugh. "Oh, dear. Please don't blame his lack of manners on me, Miss Ironwood."

"Please call me Layla. There are so many Miss Ironwoods in my family, I'll never know if you're talking to me or not."

"Then you must call me Alruna. I get enough 'my queens' from everyone else." She turned to Tor, who had stowed the last of their gear into the back of the town car waiting for them. "Where is my kiss, wolf?"

"Hello, Auntie," he said and planted a kiss on her cheek. "It's nice to be home."

"I thought you were going to keep an eye on Arne and stop him from doing anything stupid."

"Well, you know how he gets. There's no stopping the stupid sometimes."

"I'm right here," Arne complained. Layla covered her laugh with a cough. "And what are you giggling at, Ironwood?"

"Nothing, just...families," she replied.

"Are you coming back with us, or do you have your own car?" Arne asked Alruna.

"I have a car. Walk me to it." Alruna turned and smiled at Layla. "It was nice to meet you finally. I will see you at the dinner tonight."

Alruna took Arne's arm, and they walked out of the other side of the hanger and into the parking lot.

"She's not what I expected," Alruna said.

"I know the feeling."

"Did you really crash her date?" When Arne nodded, Alruna frowned. "Is the person she was with still alive?"

Arne rolled his eyes. "Of course, he is. I'm not that out of control."

"You are mating with someone who has no idea that it's happening. You have to tell her and soon. She needs to have a choice in this."

"I know, and she will. Have you seen her? She's not the type to let anyone decide anything for her," he huffed.

Alruna's eyes softened. "Don't forget you have a choice too, my eagle. You don't want to make the wrong decision with something so important. Mating can be beautiful, but it can also be destructive." Arne knew she was speaking concerned out of her own experience with Vili and that it was not a criticism of Layla. Sometimes a mating should never happen.

"I like her, Mother. I think you will too once you get to know her. Besides, the Norns have decreed that this fight cannot be won without her. You don't want to try and defy the Norns, do you?"

Alruna sighed. "Not today."

7

Layla tried not to show how panicked she felt after meeting the Queen of the Light Elves. A part of her had expected someone aloof like Galadriel, but Alruna was down to earth and motherly. She was also the first elf Layla had seen with gray hair. Her face was mature, but she didn't look older than fifty.

She must be older than dirt to have gray hair. Which instantly begged the question of how old Arne was.

"Relax, Layla. She liked you," Tor said from beside her.

"I don't know if I can relax. I didn't expect the queen to be waiting for us."

Tor smirked, gray eyes brimming with amusement. "Neither did Arne. He should've known his mother wouldn't wait to meet the one woman Arne has liked in centuries."

"He has a funny way of showing it," Layla replied, ignoring the butterflies that decided to flutter in her chest.

"Give him a chance to, and he will." Tor poked her. "And you're not half as pissed at him as you like to make out."

"You don't know shit," Layla snapped.

Tor tapped his nose. "It doesn't lie."

"Oh God, the elves can't smell like that too, can they?" Layla asked. The thought alone made her cringe.

"Not as well as a shifter. Arne doesn't have to sniff you to know that you don't hate him. I don't imagine you would give just anyone head massages."

Layla crossed her arms. "I was trying to help. In a professional capacity."

"Ah huh, real professional."

"Has anyone ever told you that you're a sassy ass bitch under all the silence and glowering?" Layla muttered.

"You should know by now that's our front for the world. We don't want hundreds of curious humans wandering about in our lands and damaging our forests. Our silent aloofness keeps people from going where they aren't wanted," Tor explained.

"I'll have to tell Ciara. She seems to think you don't know how to talk properly." It wasn't exactly the truth, but they had the best glare offs when they were together that she couldn't help pushing that button.

"She would learn otherwise if she bothered to have a conversation with me."

"Well, good luck with that. Her silence and stoicism aren't an act. She's just a badass."

"Who hates wolves," Tor grumbled.

"Who has a reason to."

Arne returned and climbed into the front seat of the car. "You two behaving in here?"

"Would we do anything else?" Layla asked. She nudged the back of his chair with her knee. "Thanks for telling me your mom was going to be here. I would have made an effort to look nice."

"I didn't know she was going to be here." Arne dropped the sun visor so he could look at her in the mirror. "And you always look nice."

Layla quickly looked out the window to hide her goofy grin at the compliment. Alta was a picturesque town, skirted by a fjord and a river. Layla knew it had ancient rock carvings and a strong Sami culture that she couldn't wait to learn more about.

"Are we too late to see the Northern Lights?"

"They are usually winding up at this time of year, but you can never predict when they will put on a show," Tor replied. "Have you seen them before?

"No, but I've always wanted to. Are they amazing?"

"The most beautiful things you'll ever see in your life."

They pulled up at a hotel on a fjord. Its walls were all glass to take in the landscape and water. The staff in the lobby didn't even ask Arne to check in, just passed him key cards.

"We have the whole hotel booked for the summit," he explained to Layla. "Apart from a few staff members, you are the only human. I've got you a room between mine and Tor's for safety reasons."

"You think I'm in danger?" she asked. She thought of the bag of magical tricks that Charlotte had prepared for her. Maybe it wouldn't hurt to carry a few surprises with her, just in case.

"No one and nothing would dare attack you or anyone else here. The hotel is warded up, and I'll set the wards on your room myself," Arne replied.

They rode the elevator up in silence, Layla suddenly grateful that she had her daggers in her boots. Arne was doing his best to reassure her, but the hunter in her was suspicious that they needed the wards at all.

Arne opened the door to her room and checked it over. Layla's breath caught at the floor to ceiling windows and incredible view of the fjord and the mountains and the forest surrounding it.

Arne went to another interior door and opened it. "I'm in here if you need anything."

"I thought you said we had rooms next to each other, not the same room with a door," Layla said, tossing her bag on the queen bed.

"I'll see you two at dinner," Tor backed out and disappeared across the hall.

Arne leaned against the door frame. "I won't violate your privacy, Layla. I only want to be close in case something happens."

"Like what? You keep telling me I'm safe, but everything you're doing is indicating that I'm not."

"It's not like that at all. You *are* safe. I'm taking extra precautions because of who you are, that's all."

Layla finally realized what he was getting at. "Because the fae princes are my family and you don't want a fight with them if anything should happen."

"What? No. It's not about the princes. It's because you're Layla Ironwood," Arne said. "The dinner begins at seven. Tor or I will come and get you." He closed the door and locked it, leaving Layla more confused over his behavior than ever.

∽

LAYLA SWIPED MORE dark maroon lipstick on her lips and double checked she hadn't gotten foundation on her neckline. She didn't know how formal the events at the summit were going to be, so she had packed clothing that could be dressed up or down. Being an Ironwood, she also chose functionality. The black velvet jump suit had long split sleeves and a wide enough pant leg to hide the daggers strapped to her shins.

The temperature inside the hotel was warm enough to not need a jacket, so she placed a black fur stole around her shoulders. She had curled her platinum hair and pinned the top half back in a loose style that suited her. She had been going for classy goth rock, and she had nailed it in her humble opinion.

Nerves fluttered along her ribs. It was her first event of this type alone. Well, not totally alone. Torsten would be close by and Arne... Well, she didn't know what was going on with him.

His words on the flight about asking her out and that he was protecting her because she was Layla had shaken her. It had been easier to be angry at him than have her crush rearing its ugly head again. She didn't know if it was incredibly stupid or incredibly hopeful for her to think she had a chance with someone like him.

She brushed the tattoo on the side of her wrist. It said 'I choose me' in Tolkien's elvish, and it had been her first tattoo. She had gotten it as a reminder that she didn't have to be anyone's first choice as long as she was her own.

"Play it by ear, and see what happens," she told her reflection.

There was a knock at the door when Layla was zipping her high heel ankle boots, the same red color as her lipstick.

"Coming!" she called and hurried to open it. Torsten wore a steel gray suit with a black shirt and tie, his hair braided back neatly. Layla fanned herself with her hand. "Gosh, Tor. Don't you clean up handsome."

"As do you, hunter," he teased, gesturing her to spin. "I feel sorry for Arne already."

Layla frowned and looked about for her room key. "Why?"

"No reason. Are you ready?"

Layla grabbed her small velvet clutch bag, checked it had her lipstick and key, and adjusted her fur stole. "Ready. Let's go and be the best-looking people in this place."

∼

INSTEAD OF HEADING for the ballroom like Layla expected, they joined a crowd of elves moving outside to the fjord. Layla looked about curiously; her arm wrapped over Tor's so she wouldn't lose him.

The first thing that Layla noticed, with considerable joy, was how diverse the elves actually were. Subconsciously, she knew they weren't aloof shining beings like Tolkien made them out to be, but it made her heart so happy to see the differences. Brown and black elves, short elves, curvy elves, tall elves. Elves with tattoos and piercings, elves who looked like they had stepped out of a Vogue shoot, elves who looked like modern Viking gods.

"You have a funny look on your face right now," Tor commented. "Are you okay?"

"I'm just...really happy. I got called Fat Galadriel once when I dressed up as an elf for Halloween because everyone thinks they are all tall and willowy and perfect," she tried to explain. She waved her hands at her curvy body. "Which I am not."

Tor's brow lowered in anger. "Do you remember who called you such a name? Arne and I would happily go and teach them some manners."

"Aw. That's nice of you, but I already kicked him in the balls for being an asshole."

Tor chuckled. "Good. I hope that suit is warmer than it looks."

They stepped outside into the cool evening air, and Layla adjusted her fur stole around her shoulders. It was chill but not unbearable. The sun was setting on the fjord, turning the sky pinks and purples.

"This place is so beautiful," she said as they all gathered around the waterfront.

"It is," Tor replied. "You will be the first human to see this in a long time."

Chanting began around her, an earthy, haunting sound. If it was in elvish, it was in a dialect she didn't know, and Layla wondered if it was Sami. Drumming began and the crowd parted to let through a small procession.

Alruna wore a crown of white reindeer antler spikes and a cream dress stitched in designs resembling traditional Sami symbols but were different types of figures.

Primordial elf art? Layla thought but didn't want to interrupt by asking. Alruna also wore a cloak of reindeer fur and carried a wreath of pine, birch, and fir leaves, woven together around the reindeer antler. In its center was a red and white candle.

Arne walked behind Alruna, looking more like a prince than ever in a black suit with a similar reindeer cloak. He had a sword strapped to his side and kept his head high, joining Alruna on the shoreline.

His golden eyes searched and found Layla in the crowd. As soon as they locked with hers, an electric shock of desire and magic sizzled right through her. If she thought her crush had been bad before, the look he was giving her had dialed it up to eleven.

The beating of the drums changed, and a new party arrived. At their head was a dwarf with black hair and a braided black beard.

"That's Brökk, a dwarf king and the elf behind him is Queen Eydís. Between them, they rule most of Svartalfheim," Tor whispered in her ear.

Eydís had long silver and black hair woven in intricate dread locks and had silver runes tattooed across her brown forehead. She wore a black dress with silver patterns that Tor explained was the story of her clan. Over the dress, she wore a ceremonial breastplate with a black jewel at its center.

Brök carried a black candle and Eydís a silver one. They stood with Alruna and Arne on the water's edge and were joined by a Sami shaman. Brök and Eydís added their candles to Alruna's wreath along with a piece of raw silver ore and a shard of obsidian.

The Sami shaman started to sing, and a lump appeared in Layla's throat as the Svartalfheim rulers, Alruna, and Arne lit the candles together. The shaman scooped up a few of the stones from the shore and placed them onto the wreath.

"They are doing a unity ceremony, aren't they?" Layla whispered, and Tor nodded.

"The elves and the Sami have always shared this land, and they are more neutral to perform this instead of getting one of the elvish shamans to do it."

The shaman held the wreath up for all to see and then placed it in the water, the tide moving it out into the fjord as a fiery beacon into the fallen darkness. The singing concluded. Everyone clapped, and those with drinks toasted before they started to head back inside.

"That was so lovely," Layla said, squeezing Tor's arm tightly and looking around her.

"Arne will get rid of his gear and find us soon. Let's get you back in the warmth and find you a nice drink," he replied.

Layla leaned into him. "Thank you for making sure I'm not alone in all of this so I didn't get overwhelmed."

Tor patted her arm with his big hand. "It's my duty and a privilege to look after you when Arne cannot, Layla Ironwood."

8

The ballroom had been set with wide round tables, a full bar, and walls of glass that overlooked the water on one side, and a balcony and garden on the other.

The tables had been decorated with centerpieces much like the wreath used in the ceremony. They were made of burning white candles, freshly cut pine and fir leaves, and clusters of yellow cloud berries and bright red lingonberries. The ceiling above them was made of white panels and shone with small pieces of mirror that had been set into them in swirling designs.

Layla decided she loved Scandinavia, especially when staying in a luxury hotel and having a shifter helper, keen to bring her drinks. She took a quick selfie with the water and the beautiful room and sent it to Ciara.

See? This is how you need to do the wild north, near a fire and with a glass of delicious mead in your hand. The cold on the outside.

Layla could imagine her cousin seeing the picture and scoffing. After the trip to Germany, Ciara knew exactly how much Layla appreciated camping rough. As in not in the slightest and never again even if the apocalypse was happening.

Layla didn't mind the outdoors; she just preferred to be able to get into a warm shower and bed at the end of the day.

Layla sipped her honey mead and watched as elves, dwarves, and shifters all mingled together. There didn't seem to be any other ceremony for the night, just people hanging out and catching up. It wasn't the stuffy vibe she had been expecting at all.

"I'm going to grab another. I'll be right back," Tor said. He grinned at her playfully. "No chatting up any handsome elves while I'm gone."

"No promises. The place is packed with them," Layla replied. She wasn't wrong either. She'd caught the eye of a few, but they had changed their mind about approaching her when they had seen Tor beside her. He was meant to be her wingman, but perhaps she should have chosen someone less intimidating.

A tingle swept down her spine, and Layla knew who was behind her long before his scent of fir trees wrapped around her. A warm hand closed around hers.

"There you are. I have been looking everywhere for you," Arne said, making her turn.

"Hey," she replied, looking up at him and trying not to blush.

"Quick, we have to hurry, or we will miss it," he said and tugged her gently through the crowd. He opened a glass door that led outside and down into a garden.

"God, it's freezing out here," Layla complained.

"Yes, but look up," Arne said excitedly.

Layla glanced up at the sky and almost dropped the glass she was holding. The sky was burning with flames of green and blue and purple.

"What are the chances?" she gasped, unable to tear her eyes away.

"The elves will take it as a good omen for the proceedings," Arne said, drawing her closer and into his warmth. Layla didn't look away from the lights, too awestruck to form words. She was aware of the hand that slid to her waist but didn't object to it being there.

"What do you think? The gods are riding the Bifrost?" she asked. "Just light? Magic dust that links universes?"

"The elves believe the lights are the souls of our ancestors," Arne replied. "I like to think that they are keeping an eye on us."

Layla smiled. "Mine are probably furious with me being here right now, with the enemy, but fuck them. Racist dicks."

"The enemy, am I?" Arne laughed softly.

"Not right now, you aren't." Layla finally turned her gaze to his face. "I don't think I could have stayed mad at you for much longer to be honest."

"No?" Arne's golden eyes glowed softly. "You were doing a pretty good job of it for the past few weeks."

"I can't stay mad for long. It takes too much energy. I especially can't stay mad at someone who's so pretty," she tried to tease. The heat in her cheeks kind of ruined it for her.

"After this summit, would it be okay if I asked you out again?" he said softly.

"You are persistent, but I don't know if that's a good idea."

Arne frowned a little. "Can I ask why?"

"Because you are a prince for a start. Shouldn't you try and date princesses or something?" Layla said, her heart starting to pound.

"No. Elves don't really care about that kind of thing. Tonight's ceremony is about as formal as we get." Arne twisted one of her curls over his finger. "Any other objections?"

Layla threw her hands up in frustration. "I just don't get why you want to. I mean, look at me!" She gestured at all of her tattoos and general Laylaness. "Like there are layers of tattoos and nerdiness here that you are yet to uncover."

Arne traced his fingers over her arms and under the velvet sleeves. "I think your tattoos are beautiful, like the rest of you. Nerdiness included. I want to know what each one of your tattoos mean too because I think they are a puzzle that if I could figure out, I'd know all the secrets you keep hidden away. Any other objections?"

Layla was starting to sweat. She didn't know why she was arguing with him about it when her crush was telling her to just say yes. Especially when he said kind shit like that to her that made her insides melt.

"We probably have bad chemistry?" she blurted out.

Arne gave her such a look of disbelief that she desperately tried to think of something else to add. He huffed in annoyance, pulled her close, and kissed her.

Layla made a small squeak of surprise before she leaned into him. Heat rolled through her body, and her hands gripped his waistcoat before pulling him closer. He was gentle right until the moment she opened her mouth to his, and then he took over, soft mouth devouring her.

Layla had never been kissed like that. It seemed he was trying to use his lips and tongue to suck her soul right out of her body.

She let out an embarrassing groan but didn't pull away. She had wanted to kiss him to pieces since the moment he and Torsten had walked into the Ironwood manor. Just for once, she didn't think of whether or not she should do something and kissed him back.

Arne moaned as her tongue moved into his mouth, taking from him like he had from her. Her body moved of its own accord, her hips rolling against him.

"*Layla,*" he whispered against her lips, the ache in his voice breaking down whatever resistance she had around her heart. Something inside of Layla's chest unlocked, like a door opening.

Finally, it whispered.

Desire and magic and heat rushed through her like burning honey. She didn't have magical abilities like Charlotte, but she could use a little of it, and she certainly felt it when it was about. It was radiating off Arne like sunlight, and she wanted to roll in it.

"Fuck," Arne growled, his hands gripping her tight as he took a step back. His eyes were shining with bright golden magic. "Did I hurt you?"

"Huh? God, no. Do your eyes normally glow like that?" Layla asked. Arne rubbed at his face.

"No. Only when I'm losing control," he admitted and then swore again.

"Hey, it's okay. You weren't losing control in a bad way. I mean, you might have lost your pants if you had kept it up, but you didn't, so you're safe!" Layla babbled, reaching out for him. "Is this a Vili thing?"

Arne still had his eyes closed, but he nodded. "Yes. It's his side of me, the power I inherited. It takes over, and I can lose myself in it. I don't want it to hurt you—"

Layla took his face in her hands. "Hey, just take a breath, okay? I know you would never, ever hurt me, Arne. If I didn't want you to kiss me, trust me, I have two daggers that would've made it known."

She circled her thumbs over his cheekbones. "Open your eyes for me."

Arne slowly did, the shining light fading until they were only their normal gold again. "How did you do that?" he asked in awe.

"Talk you down? Have you seen *any* of my sisters when they are angry? You and your god powers got nothing on them," she teased.

Arne ran his hands up her arms. "I'm sorry it interrupted us. Though I think it proved my point about our chemistry."

"Yeah, you win that round, Steelsinger," Layla said, trying not to laugh awkwardly.

The side door opened, and a dwarf with golden braids appeared. "Apologies for the interruption, my prince. The queen sent me to talk to you about a private and urgent matter."

Arne started to argue, but Layla pressed a kiss to his cheek. "It's fine. Do your prince stuff. We can talk later."

"Count on it," he replied, making Layla grin all the way back inside.

She checked her reflection in the mirrors behind the bar while she waited to be served and thanked all the gods that she had worn her immovable lipstick that night. She was sure it would've been smeared from one side of her face to the other like the Joker if she hadn't.

You just made out with Arne Steelsinger. Layla covered her mouth as a hysterical bubble of laughter threatened to bust free from her. The bartender saved her and took her order for 'all the vodka' with a smile.

She toyed with the candle holder made of a thick piece of pine while she waited, turning it slowly to see the carved runes in it. There wasn't the slightest detail in the room that wasn't perfect.

"Layla, I hope you are having a nice time," Alruna said, appearing beside her with Torsten. Like Arne, she had lost the reindeer fur, but she still wore her bone crown.

"Yes, thank you," Layla replied, hastily taking her vodka from the bar. She tried really hard not to think of Arne's tongue in her mouth. "I'm having a great night. Your ceremony was beautiful and very moving."

"It has been a long time since we were all together like this. It's going to be a good summit; I know it. Have you seen Arne anywhere? I'm surprised he let you out of his sight for long," Alruna replied, a knowing twinkle in her eye.

Tor covered his grin with his glass of mead. He *knew* they had been making out. He could probably smell Arne all over her from where she had ground up against him.

"You know, I think I saw him talking to one of the dwarves outside," Layla replied and drank a big mouthful of vodka. A flicker of light caught her eye, and she looked up at the mirror designs on the roof in time to see a panel slide back.

"That's weird..." she began, freezing when the edges of a cross bow appeared. "Get down!" Layla grabbed a metal serving tray off the bar and threw it up in front of Alruna. Her arms jarred as two bolts pierced the metal tray by her face. Torsten had Alruna tucked underneath him in a blink, shielding her with his body.

"The shooter is in the roof!" Layla shouted, throwing one of her daggers at the hole where the crossbow was being pulled back through. The ballroom erupted into a panic.

"Keep the queen safe and find where the fuck the roof access is!" Tor roared at a group of elven guards. Layla pulled her other dagger free just as Tor's hand grabbed her. "You need to stay out of the way, Layla. We need to keep you safe."

"Let me go!" Layla shook him off. "If they are shooting at Alruna, we need to get to Arne."

Tor's face shifted immediately. "Where did you leave him?"

"Outside in the gardens, near the balcony. Follow me." Layla worked her way through the panicking people to the edge of the glass wall and followed it around to the door. She ignored the fear that was pulsing through her, her hunter training shoving it down so she could focus.

Layla pushed out into the cold air and hurried across the grass and through the trees. Magic hit her, her mouth filling with the taste of blood and iron filings. She stumbled, but Torsten grabbed her before she went down.

"Fuck...that magic. I know it..." he stammered. Layla ran to the circle of trees where she had kissed Arne. The golden hair dwarf and two huge black-haired shifters stood before a portal, Arne's limp body over one of the shifter's shoulders.

"Arne!" Layla shouted. Torsten roared into a shift, racing across the grass toward them in wolf form.

"Too late, little alpha. Vili will have his boy back," one of the shifters taunted as Arne was dragged through the portal.

Layla threw her dagger, hitting the shifter in the shoulder. He only laughed as he disappeared into the light. Torsten leaped for the portal, but it vanished under his paws.

Arne was gone.

9

As a child who had way too much responsibility thrusted upon her shoulders at a young age, Layla had learned to control her temper early. Losing it happened rarely, but when it did, it was something to be feared.

"What do you mean you didn't find the shooter?" she demanded. The elf warrior took a step back in shock at the fury in her tone.

"They got out of the roof through a large air vent. There's a hole in the wall where they pulled the grating off."

"I bet the shooter was one of those big fucking shifters," she said to Tor as she paced the trashed ballroom.

"It was Varg and one of his pack," Tor said to Alruna. "I thought he was dead."

"Clearly, he went to Svartalfheim after the Ulfheðnar exiled him," she replied.

"Or since Vili returned. He would've loved the idea of serving Odin's rival after we kicked him out."

Brök and Eydís were sitting at Alruna's table, both looking tired and pissed off.

"We haven't seen any new Ulfheðnar coming through the portals from Midgard," Brök said. "Vili has always preferred the bear shifters over wolves."

"Varg is one step away from feral. His fury would appeal to someone like Vili," Alruna replied.

Layla stopped pacing. "Wait up. You guys all know where Vili is? Like right at this second?"

"Not for certain, but there's a good chance he's back in his old halls in Svartalfheim," Brök replied. "My scouts have seen smoke rising from the mountains furnaces again after centuries of being abandoned. The forest around there has always been a dangerous place, and four dwarves have gone missing on its borders already."

"We have had seven elves go missing in a village south of there too," Eydís added. "One was a black smith; the rest were women."

"So why hasn't anyone gone to check it out to make sure?" Layla demanded.

"Because we weren't going to risk anyone going near that cursed place without speaking as a council first," Brök replied.

"That Varg guy said that Vili would have his boy back. It's obvious they were working for him or are planning on taking Arne to him for some kind of reward. We need to go after them before the trail is completely gone!"

"Layla, calm yourself," Torsten said, his voice dropping to a soft growl.

"I will not be calm! Arne is *gone*! He's one of the best warriors I've ever seen, and he was taken..." Layla's heart was beating too fast, panic starting to overwhelm her. She started to sway, black tunnelling her vision. Strong hands steadied her, and Torsten lifted her up into his arms.

"I have you, hunter. You'll be alright," he grumbled in her ear.

"Tor? Please take Layla upstairs. We will let you know our verdict on a hunt shortly," Alruna said.

"My queen," Tor replied and carried Layla out before she could fight him.

Hot tears filled her eyes, and she palmed them away, smearing her mascara to hell.

"I don't know what's wrong with me," she said, horrified that she couldn't control her emotions. She always cried after getting angry because it happened so rarely.

"I do. That fucking elf marked you before he was taken, and it's fucking with you," Torsten replied, setting her down so he could open the hotel door.

"Arne did what? What are you talking about?" Layla stammered. She sat down on the bed and kicked off her boots.

Torsten ran his hands through his hair, unraveling his braid. "Arne marked you, like...put a claim on you. It's a way for elves to prove that they are...spoken for?"

"He only kissed me! I didn't give him permission to mark me!" Layla exclaimed.

"He might not have meant to do it, but because of the mating thing perhaps it happened... Oh fuck." Torsten went white. "Shit. Layla, I..."

"What. Did. You. Just. Say?" she demanded, her whole body vibrating with emotion.

Torsten looked at his feet and shifted his weight. "So, um, funny thing about Arne. He could be your...mate?"

Layla's eyes narrowed. "*Could* be?"

"Well. More like, *is* your mate. But still also it's a 'could be' because you both have a choice on whether to act on it?" Torsten stammered.

"I am going to get Arne back, and then I am going to *murder* that elf," Layla snarled before storming into the bathroom and slamming the door.

She tore off her clothes and sat on the floor of the shower, hot water pouring over her. She tried to breathe and shove all her emotions back into her body.

She needed to get help, and if the elves were going to argue over the merits of a rescue party, Layla would go elsewhere. She thought about the file of information that she had gathered on her laptop but quickly shook her head. No, that was going too far, too quick.

She would call Ciara and have her meet her in Oslo at Freya's place. They all had a key to her apartment so they could use it if Freya was in Scotland. She would get her brothers to help her with a portal to Svartalfheim.

My mate, my mate, my mate... a voice chanted underneath her desperate planning. She couldn't think about all the problems with that. She needed to focus on one thing at a time.

Layla dragged her ass out of the shower and dried off, wiping the last of the night's makeup off her face. She packed up all of her cosmetics and went back into her room to find clothes.

Torsten was still standing by the glass wall, nursing a tumbler of whiskey in his hand. "Are you...okay?"

"No. I'm leaving," she said, tossing the cosmetics into her suitcase and finding some clean clothes. "Turn around."

Torsten didn't argue, just faced the other way as she dropped her robe and got dressed.

"The elves will still hold this summit. It's more important than ever. You should remain here and do your job," he said.

"They can get Kian to come like they should have done to begin with. I'm not sitting around here while Arne is fuck knows where." Layla pulled on boots and laced them up. "Did you check his room for any nasty surprises?"

"No. They took him. That's the nasty surprise," Torsten replied.

"I'll check." Layla opened the door to Arne's rooms and was bombarded by his scent. She switched on the lights, but the room was pristine and undisturbed. His famous swords were still crossed in their holsters and sitting on a table. Tears rose hot and horrible in her throat as she picked them up.

"What did you do to me to make me this ridiculous?" she murmured.

The tears were probably better than the cold ball of rage in her chest. She was going to fucking kill Vili for taking him.

The doors to his room opened, and Alruna stepped inside. She saw Layla's tears and her hands on Arne's swords.

"Oh, my dear," she said, her shoulders slumping a little. She didn't look like the calm queen she had been downstairs. She looked like a worried mother.

"When do we go after him?" Layla asked, sniffing hard.

"The council won't send an official contingent of elves after Arne. It's too dangerous, and it might antagonize Vili to attack Eydís and Brök's people in revenge. As the Light Elf queen, I must support this," Alruna replied. Layla opened her mouth to start swearing, but Alruna held up her hand. "As a mother, I would ask you to go and find my son. Tor, you will go with her."

"Auntie, you can't let Layla go. Arne would lose his fucking mind if anything happened to her," Torsten argued.

"Fuck off, Tor. Arne got kidnapped. He gets no say in the matter," Layla snapped. She picked up Arne's swords. "I'm taking these with me."

"Here, you will need these too." Alruna held a small leather pouch. Inside was a carved wooden stave and a block of a silvery white crystal. "The stave will grant you passage to the World Tree Heart. From there, you can take a back path into Svartalfheim. Once you have Arne, smash the crystal, and a portal will instantly appear to bring you back home."

"Thank you," Layla said, taking the pouch. "I won't return without him. I promise."

Alruna smiled. "I know you won't. The Norns don't make mistakes, and they said that the only way we would defeat Vili is with Arne's mate."

"And you think that's me? Because Arne said that the Norns named me personally," Layla replied.

"They said mate, but Arne knew who that was without a doubt. He's stubborn that way," Alruna said, her eyes going damp again. "Don't worry, we will both yell at him when you get him back. He could've warned me before he decided to mark you tonight."

Layla cringed. "Oh, great. So you can see that too?"

"My dear, every elf in Midgard is going to be able to see it. Arne never does things by halves." Alruna embraced her quickly, Layla not knowing how to react before the queen was pulling away. "He's the best of me. Please find him."

"I will."

Alruna nodded at Torsten. "Don't let anything happen to her."

"Easier said than done."

"Don't worry, Tor. I'm calling in the cavalry." Layla pulled out her phone and waved Alruna goodbye as it rang. She shoved the remaining clothes into her suitcase.

"This is Ciara Ironwood. I'm busy, so leave a message."

"Cus, 911. Meet me at Mardøll as soon as possible. Fuck the hunt you're on. We have bigger game," Layla replied and hung up. She called Bayn next and was ready to kill the call when he finally answered.

"Layla, why are you calling me after midnight?" he grumbled.

"I...I..." Layla began and burst into tears at hearing a familiar voice.

"Ah, fuck. Don't cry, baby sis. What's wrong? Who fucking hurt you? Where's Arne?" Bayn demanded, his voice getting louder and angrier.

"They took him, Bayn! Vili took him, and I need to get to Oslo straight away so I can go after him. Please come and get me," she sobbed, unable to hold it in.

Bayn made panicked shushing sounds at her. "Okay, deep breaths. Don't cry. Big brother is coming. I got the hotel's name. Meet me outside in fifteen, okay? You have Tor with you?"

"Yeah, he's coming too," Layla replied. "I'm sorry, I can't stop crying because Arne marked me 'cos I'm his m-mate, Bayn."

There was dead silence on the other end of the line before Bayn exploded, "He did fucking what?! No. Don't say any more. Ten minutes, Layla."

"I'll be there," she said and hung up. She grabbed a tissue and blew her nose before strapping Arne's swords to her back.

Bayn would come and help her sort everything out. She really loved having overprotective brothers.

Tor took five minutes to change his clothes and grab his bag. He left whatever he didn't need in Arne's room, and they headed downstairs and out of the hotel.

Layla stared up at the clear sky where only hours before she had watched bright colors dance. Her lips tingled with the memory of her kiss with Arne, and the cold rage in her chest ached and ached.

"How pissed is he going to be?" Tor asked as a patch of ice started to freeze the ground beside him.

"Not nearly as pissed as Ciara is going to be," Layla replied.

"Ciara! But we are meant..." he began, but Bayn took that second to appear. He took one look at Layla, and his sapphire eyes went wide.

"Infernal gods, that asshole didn't half mark you," he growled. He shook off his surprise and gathered her up into a hug. "You okay?"

"Bit shit, but I'll get there. I need to get to Oslo."

"I know. Ciara texted Freya to tell her because she figured you wouldn't. She's on her way, driving from Karlstad, so she'll be a few hours." Bayn looked over at Torsten and held out his hand. They clasped each other's forearms. "Rough night, wolf?"

"And it's about to get rougher," Torsten grumbled. "Layla saved the queen's life and threw a dagger at Varg."

"Varg was here too? Fucking hell, this keeps getting better." Bayn pulled Layla tighter to him. "Good job on all accounts, sis. Okay, both of you hold on tight."

Layla took a deep breath, shut her eyes, and let the ice pull her under.

10

Layla relaxed a little once she was sitting at the counter in Freya's kitchen and amongst familiar surroundings. Bayn was on the phone with Kian, updating him in a low murmur that she couldn't make out. They needed to get a representative to the summit, and Kian was the best and most diplomatic choice.

Torsten had left to get weapons and other gear, leaving Layla under Bayn's overprotective watch.

Layla held Arne's swords in her lap, unable to put them down for some unfathomable reason.

Wherever you are, Arne, you better be okay, or I really will kill you, she thought. She didn't know of any elvish gods she could petition on his behalf.

She thought of the Norns and their cryptic words that she was the one to help against Vili. She snorted at the ridiculousness of it. No one willingly chose Layla to do the important shit. She was the backup, the researcher, the babysitter. It's why she had always chosen herself. No one else did.

Layla stared at the steam curling up from her tea, and her grip on Arne's swords tightened.

"Did you get a chance to eat anything tonight before shit went down? I can make you something if you like," Bayn said, coming back into the kitchen.

Layla shook her head. "I don't really feel like eating."

"You better because I just had to wait behind two drunk guys for fifteen minutes to get you hot chips," Ciara said, stomping up the stairs. She was in jeans and a black sweater, her blue-black hair in a tight braid and boots still mud splattered from wherever she had been when she got Layla's message.

Layla started crying again when her cousin dropped a bag of Kentucky Fried Chicken in front of her. It was her emotional comfort food, and Ciara knew it. She pulled Ciara into a hug, her dark hair smelling of the cold and apple blossom shampoo.

"You better start talking, Lay Lay, or I'm going to start hunting down whoever is making you cry," Ciara said, sitting down at the counter beside her. "I haven't seen you cry this much since the first time you saw *Return of the King*. What the hell is going on?"

Bayn made coffees, and Layla nibbled on chips as she spilled everything that had happened. She showed them the portal crystal and the small wooden stave that would take them to the heart of Yggdrasil and onto Svartalfheim.

"I didn't know there was an actual heart," Bayn said, studying it. "Magic like this is more Kian's expertise. I didn't tell him about the mating thing, only that Arne was taken and that you need to go after him because of what the Norns said. I don't think he or Killian would act really well to Arne marking you, and they wouldn't be able to hide it from Elise and Bron. We aren't even going to tell Kill you're in Svartalfheim until you're gone because he'll lose his shit."

"You better tell Freya. I don't want to cause any trouble between you two," Layla said.

"Freya can keep a secret, though she's going to bombard you with questions about the mark on you," Bayn said with a fond grin. "I know Kill would try and prevent you, physically if he has to, from going anywhere near Vili."

Layla's hand gripped Arne's swords. "But you won't?"

"As much as we don't like the idea, Kian and I aren't going to even attempt to stop you. Arne is your mate. There's no fucking with that.

And I'm not about to fuck with the Norns or the elves. Or Torsten for that matter."

"Wiser than you look, fae," Tor said, his voice a deep grumble as he came up the stairs with a pack of gear. His gray eyes scanned over the kitchen and landed on the frowning hunter. "Good evening, Ciara Wolf Slayer."

"Torsten," she said flatly.

The Ulfheðnar took a coffee from Bayn and placed a comforting hand on Layla's shoulder. "You feel any better?"

"Not really. What's our next move?" Layla asked.

"We need a day to collect proper supplies if we are going into Svartalfheim. Much of it is wild country, and we don't know how long it will take us to find Arne. The more prepared we are, the better," Tor replied. He held up a hand when Layla started to make protesting sounds. "I know it feels like you're losing your mind, but I'm not going to risk taking you there unprepared, Layla. You are my charge, my blood brother's mate. If I had my way, I wouldn't be taking you at all."

"You better be packing for three because I'm coming too," Ciara said, and Layla turned to her. "What? You really think I'm going to let you go off into another world with a stranger to steal from a god?"

Tor growled, folding his impressive arms and looking more imposing than ever. "I'm not a stranger, and I would never let anything happen to Layla. It's because you don't trust wolves."

"I don't trust anyone. Especially with my baby cousin who was in your care for barely a day and now look at her," Ciara snapped. "Weeping at the drop of a hat and with a fucking mating bond she didn't ask for."

Layla groaned. "You two can play who is the bigger alpha later, okay? Don't fight. I can't handle it."

"Layla is right," Bayn added. "If you two are planning on traveling together into hostile territory, you need to do it as a team, so stop your bullshit."

"Fine with me," Tor said, his eyes still on Ciara. "If you can't handle the company, Wolf Slayer, you'd best stay here."

"I have no problem. I'm here for Layla." Ciara placed a hand on Layla's arm. "Are you going to tell Kenna?"

"Only when I'm about to leave. She will just try and stop me, and

I'm not in the mood to argue." Layla looked up at Tor. "A day. That's all I'm willing to wait and then I'm going after Arne."

Tor nodded. "It'll be done. I'm going to try and get some more detailed directions to Vili's old keep out of Alruna. If she doesn't know, maybe she can find out from Brök and Eydís without alerting them to what we are doing. The council forbade a rescue mission, and we don't want them getting suspicious."

"And if she can't get the information?" Ciara asked.

Tor shrugged. "Then we track them the hard way. Layla is Arne's mate. We can use that bond too if we have to."

Or we ask someone who knows Vili better than anyone, Layla thought. She knew where to go for help. It might be a fool's chance, but she was desperate enough to risk it. To get Arne back, she would risk the wrath of the gods themselves.

11

Layla had often been accused by her sisters of being the sneakiest of them all. It wasn't sneakiness she was good at; it was patience. That's why she waved Ciara and Torsten off in the morning as they went on their separate shopping trips and gave Bayn a hug before he went back to Scotland for the day. He promised he would come back that night and see them off, a frown creasing his brow like he suspected she was up to something.

With a brave smile, Layla had assured them all that she was fine, and she could use the day to sleep and rest and mentally prepare for traveling on the World Tree. Ciara only laughed, knowing exactly how much Layla hated camping on a trail.

Layla waited a full thirty minutes after they had gone before she had grabbed the keys to Freya's Audi, turned on her maps guide, and headed north.

Okay, maybe you didn't think this through as well as you should have, she admitted to herself outside of the town of Otta. It was three and a half hours away from Oslo, and Layla had made it in nearly an hour under that. She was already preparing the apology to Freya for the speeding tickets that would most likely arrive in the mail.

It couldn't be helped. Layla felt every passing second clawing at her. She was regretting not talking to Arne weeks ago, for saying no to being his summit representative, and for being too chicken shit to go for that damn drink with him months ago. She knew she liked him when she had first met him, and it was her own dumb fear and skewed self-worth that had held her back.

"You better be okay, Arne. I don't like being this stupidly emotional for no reason," she muttered under her breath.

Layla didn't know if it was the mating bond or just how she felt about Arne in general that was making her so crazy.

Crazy enough to piss off everyone by running away without telling anyone.

Otta was a pretty town, built where two rivers met. There were a lot of campers and hikers about, tourists taking photos of the picturesque mountains and red and white cottages. There was even a stave church nearby that Layla wished she had the time to see. No sightseeing for her. Only crazy hunch following that was the result of obsessive searching... all because Arawan had mentioned Odin.

Layla drove through the town and along the river, following her maps instructions before they stopped in front of a gate. The small white and blue house was built away from the others with birch trees shielding most of it from view.

"This could end so badly," Layla murmured to herself. She pulled her phone off its charger and rang Kian.

"Layla, are you okay?" he answered almost immediately.

"Um, at this second? Yes. But I'm probably about to do something dumb, so I'm going to text you an address, and if you don't hear from me in an hour, that's where you need to go to find the body."

"Layla, what the fuck have you done?"

"Please, please, just trust me, Kian. You can't tell Bayn or anyone, okay?"

There was a long pause on the other end of the line. "One hour. You had better tell me what this is about when you call me back because right now, you're supposed to be in Oslo."

"I know. I know. Thanks, Kian."

"One hour, Layla."

They hung up, and she messaged him the address. She checked her dagger in her boot and got out of the car.

The metal gate squeaked as Layla lifted the latch and opened it.

She had expected dogs, but there were no warning snarls to greet her. Taking a deep breath, she knocked on the front door. "Hello? Anyone home?"

After there was no reply, Layla walked around the side of the house and spotted a man with his back to her. He was cleaning fish at an outdoor sink and tossing the guts to the wolf-like huskies at his feet. He was tall and broad, gray streaking his braided black hair and trimmed beard.

"You are trespassing," the man said in a deep bass voice.

"I'm sorry, but I needed to talk to you. It's about...it's about Vili," Layla replied. She kept her eyes on the watchful dogs. They hadn't moved, but their whole bodies were tense, waiting for their master's command to rip her throat out.

The man turned, and Layla's mouth turned to dust. He was broader and had lines creasing his sun browned face in a way that could've placed him between fifty and seventy, but the family resemblance to Arne was unmistakable. A golden eye looked her over.

"Who are you?" he demanded.

"My name is Layla Ironwood," she squeaked out and quickly ducked her head respectfully.

"What else are you?"

"I'm Arne Steelsinger's mate, and I'm here on his behalf." Layla straightened her shoulders. "It's an honor to meet you...All-Father."

"Call me Havi. I haven't been the All-Father for quite some time," he muttered and dried off his hands. "How did you find me?"

"It's a long story, but mostly, the internet. It's not important," Layla said, waving it aside. "Vili is back, and he's taken your nephew, Arne. I want your help to get him back."

Havi crossed his arms. "Where has he been taken to?"

"Svartalfheim. There are rumors that Vili has returned to his old keep there."

"Then I can't help. Svartalfheim isn't my concern, and Arne is Vili's by blood," he said gruffly and with a finality that made Layla see red.

"Are you serious? Vili will kill him!"

"You don't know that. He was bound to remember he had a son one day and make a claim on him. It happened, and I won't interfere."

Layla felt like she had been hit in the guts, all the wind knocked out of her. "Do you even care that Vili is loose again? That he was Morrigan's general and all of them have had plans to destroy and rule the human world?" she demanded. She was trying not to scream, the tiredness and worry overwhelming her.

Anger flashed in Havi's golden eye. "Vili chose to be the lap dog of that goddess. It has nothing to do with me. Neither does his return to Svartalfheim. I can see the bond that's hurting you right now, girl, but watch your tone when you talk to me."

Layla's chin rose. "And if Vili comes here and starts burning and pillaging? The Norns said that if we don't defeat him, he will start Ragnarök! Will it be your problem then?"

"Fucking Norns. Those witches do not control my fate," Havi spat, and Layla wanted to shake him. He let out a growl of frustration. "If they are right, and Vili steps one foot into Midgard to try and start Ragnarök, I will intervene. Until he does, I will do nothing. Svartalfheim has always been his domain, and Arne is his son."

"I'll go after him alone then," Layla said and threw up her hands. "Fuck, I can't believe I thought you would give a damn enough to help him."

"This isn't my fate being played out, girl. It's yours." Havi's golden eye shone with power, and magic burned the air. "You want to go and die a hero's death, trying to steal your prince back? That's your business. I won't stop you, but I will warn you. Do not underestimate my brother for a single moment, or you will regret it. His keep is in the Vestri Mountains, and all of the paths in will be watched. That's all the help I can give you."

Layla nodded, and even though she was pissed, she still said, "Thank you for the information."

"Don't waste any more time, girl. My brother will have a reason for trying to claim the prince now, and he has many ways of getting what he wants," Havi replied.

"I'll get him back." Layla began to walk back to the car but was still angry enough to call over her shoulder. "Sharpen your spear, All-Father. You will want to be ready for when your brother comes for what *you* love next."

12

Arne had two distinct thoughts when he finally drifted back to consciousness—'Where the fuck is Layla?' followed closely by, 'Where is the dwarf I'm going to kill?'

He cracked open an eye and held back a yelp of surprise. He was suspended by vines from the roof of the cavern. His eyes grew accustomed to the darkness, and he could make out stone stairs and cells... rows and rows of cells cut into the mountain and sealed with iron.

"Where am I?" he murmured. He shifted, trying to relieve the cramps in his arms and legs. The vines holding him shuddered, and he stilled. He may have had rapid healing powers, but there would be no point getting free if it was to have every bone in his body broken on impact.

Arne looked around him the best he could, searching for Layla just in case they had stolen her too. He remembered the golden-haired dwarf speaking then something heavy hitting him in the back of the head.

The last he saw of Layla was her swaying hips and smiling mouth heading back inside the hotel.

Please, please be safe. Arne had to believe it. He trusted that Torsten would protect Layla when he couldn't. He would make sure she wouldn't do anything too rash when they found him missing.

Despite waking up in whatever dark hell this was, Arne smiled when he thought of Layla kissing him back. It was like everything in his world had suddenly aligned again for the first time since meeting her.

Now that he knew the touch and taste of her, nothing was going to keep him from her. Whoever was keeping him locked up was going to learn that taking him away from her was the biggest mistake of their life.

"Ah, he wakes at last," a deep, melodious voice said in the darkness. Golden magic flashed through the dimness and settled into the vines like stardust. The vines shuddered and began to lower him slowly down to the stone floor.

Arne stopped when he was eye level with the male who had haunted his dreams and nightmares his entire life. It was a face that might be his own in a few hundred years.

Long silver-streaked black hair and a braided beard couldn't hide the similarities between their face shapes, the quirk of their lips, the curve of their jaws.

Vili had runes tattooed on both cheeks and forehead and a scar running down his neck.

"My son, you've grown," Vili said with a small smile. Two gold-flecked green eyes watched for his reaction, but Arne didn't give him the one he wanted.

"I'm not your son," he said as calmly as he could.

Vili chuckled. "Have you not looked in the mirror recently? There's no doubt where you came from, my boy. She tried her best to keep you from me, but here we are at last."

"Kept me from you? You were Morrigan's monster before I took my first steps and you never gave a shit about the mess you had left behind," Arne snarled. He pulled at the vines holding him, hating himself for reacting like the wounded child he was.

Vili raised a brow. "Do I seem the kind of male who wouldn't want to raise his own progeny? The power in our veins shaped the worlds, boy. Alruna knew it and kept you beyond my grasp." He touched Arne's face, making him flinch. "Oh yes, I can feel Frey and his slut sister's magic all over you, shielding you from my gaze."

"Don't touch me," Arne growled, his magic sparking to life.

Vili only laughed. "She never told you and you never thought to ask why you were raised in Midgard? A prince of Alfheim and Vanaheim raised amongst mortals. Gods, what a sorry upbringing. There is going to be so much to correct in your personality. I don't even know where to begin."

"You can start by letting me go?"

"After I went to the trouble to retrieve you? I don't think so."

Arne tried to push his anger down and focus. "You could at least tell me what you want after so long. You have known I existed for centuries, and you still chose to be a slave to Morrigan so you can't want me for my company."

"That's where you're wrong. I made the alliance with Morrigan because she swore to help me get you back. I couldn't touch you on Midgard, and I couldn't find where my darling mate had hidden you because she had the Vanir gods shielding you." Vili pinched Arne's chin, forcing him to look up. "I burned worlds, became the monster, all for this moment."

"You just want to play father and son? Get to know one another?" Arne leaned down as far as he could and snarled, "Don't fucking lie to me. What purpose does all of this serve?"

"Ragnarök. I'm building an army, and I want my son by my side as I crush the Aesir under my boots and take the Nine Worlds," Vili replied and held up a hand. "And save your breath trying to tell me you'll die before you follow me."

The vines lowered Arne closer. Arne struggled as his father's golden power began to pour over him, binding him tighter than the vines.

Vili's breath was warm on his ear. "I don't *need* your compliance, little eagle. I will *take* it, and then as the years pass and you're doing my bidding, there will be no desire in you to return to your old life. You won't be able to anyway because you will be a monster. Just. Like. Me."

Arne screamed and screamed as his world turned gold, his lungs filling with it, the magic dragging the parts of him that made him who he was deep inside and locking them up. The last thing he saw was Layla's teasing smile before she was gone...

When he finally stopped screaming, the vines placed him on the ground and released him. Vili cupped Arne's face affectionately. "My boy. Welcome home."

13

Layla made it back to Oslo thirty minutes before Ciara turned up again, carrying a bag of gear and weapons. They had divided everything in between two packs before heading over to Tor's apartment at sundown.

"You still up for this? I'm sure Torsten would be capable of hunting Arne down for himself," Ciara asked softly. They were standing in the hallway outside of the apartment. Layla knew that Arne also had an apartment somewhere on the same floor, and her heart started to ache again.

"I'm going," she said flatly.

"Okay, then you call Kenna before we leave. Or I will," Ciara replied. Layla knocked on Tor's door without replying.

"Right on time," he greeted, opening up. He was dressed in a dark blue thermal shirt that showed off every bulky muscle on his chest. Layla fought a grin while Ciara's eyes bugged out of her head before she quickly looked away.

"Only a pack each. Good. The lighter we are, the better," Tor said.

Ciara gestured with her head. "Tell that to Layla. She's refusing to leave those damn swords behind."

"Arne will need them when we get him back," she replied stubbornly. She didn't want to tell them that carrying that piece of him with her made her feel better. Tor's gray eyes softened. He knew and understood.

"You call your mother yet?" he asked. Layla shook her head. She didn't want the argument. "I'm not showing you how the stave works until you do, Layla. You want to not waste time in rescuing Arne? You had better hurry up."

Layla's eyes narrowed. "Are you two assholes in this together?"

"We aren't saying it for our own good, Layla," Ciara argued. "Kenna deserves to know that her daughter is about to leave the world."

"Fine! Gah! You both suck," she snapped, pulling her phone out.

Ciara and Tor shared a smile and then quickly looked away when they realized they were in agreement on something.

Layla stepped into the bathroom and shut the door behind her. She wasn't sure of the time zones and couldn't be bothered to look them up. She should've rested that day like she said she was going to, not waste her time with—

"Layla? How are the elves?" Kenna answered.

"Mom. I need you to listen to me and not get mad, okay?"

"Layla..."

"Just listen!" Layla told her quickly of the summit attack and Arne being taken. "I have Ciara and Tor with me, and...and we are going after him. To Svartalfheim."

"No, you are not," Kenna snapped, her brogue going thick. "You need to come home and let the elves deal with this. You don't owe Arne anything. You didn't even want to go with him two days ago, and now you're going to Svartalfheim? No."

Layla's hand gripped her phone tight. "I am not asking for permission. I'm telling you as a courtesy."

"You aren't ready for a hostile planet, Layla. You couldn't even handle a forest in Germany for Christ's sakes! You were only meant to sit in on some meetings because it would've been good representation for the family. You're not built for this kind of infiltration mission, and I could use you back home. It would be best for everyone if you let Ciara handle this if she wants to go, and the elves want to pay her for it—"

"I'm not asking!" Layla shouted, her voice echoing off the tiled walls. There was dead silence on the other end of the line. She squeezed her eyes shut and forced the words out. "All I have done is think of the good of the family. I've done everything you have ever told me to do. I've never complained about it. I've never fought you about it. I'm not doing this for money. I'm doing this because it's Arne, and...and he makes me feel seen, unlike the rest of you. I'm not leaving him in Vili's hands. So no. I'm not coming home because it would be what's best for everyone. This once, the family can go fuck itself."

Layla didn't wait for a reply before she hung up and turned her phone off. She caught her reflection in the mirror, the sadness in her eyes. She washed her face with cold water, fighting the sudden nausea that always came when she spoke up for herself. No. Not this time. She braided back her hair and took a deep breath before stepping back into the lounge room.

Bayn and Tor were talking in the kitchen, and Ciara pretended not to be listening in. Bayn pulled Layla into a hug but didn't mention the screaming that they all would've heard.

"You ready to go?" he asked.

"More than ready," she replied, giving him a fake smile that he saw right through.

"Kian said that he wants you to call him as soon as you get back. Something about a project that you two were talking about earlier today?" he asked.

"Oh that. Yeah, just research stuff. It's fine."

Layla let Bayn go, picked up Arne's swords, and slid her arms through the holsters so they sat on her back. Bayn helped her adjust the leather straps so they sat snugly between her shoulder blades, before helping her put her pack on over the top of them.

"How is it? Too heavy? Because I can look after the swords," he said.

"No, they are fine. I'm used to having a heavy pack."

Ciara scoffed. "It's because she always overpacks and carries all her girly face shit with her."

Layla flipped her off, but she still smiled. Her cousin giving her shit at least felt normal.

"Go get him, sis," Bayn said and kissed her forehead. He looked at Tor. "Watch out for them or I'll kick your fucking ass."

"You really think I'm more afraid of you than Arne?" Tor snorted and slung his pack over one shoulder. "Just be ready for our return, frostling. And maybe take a step back."

Tor took the wooden stave from Layla and held it out in front of him. Layla's skin tingled with magic as he began to chant. The tiny runes on the stave began to glow with a pale blue light, and then the apartment around them fell away.

Layla's knees buckled as they landed on a wooden platform. Soft, silvery lights glowed in the thick branches above them. What she had mistaken for a platform was a wide thick branch.

"Welcome to the Heart of Yggdrasil," Tor said, giving Layla back the wooden stave. "Watch your step because if you fall off the path, fuck knows where you will end up."

"How do you know where to go?" Ciara asked cautiously. There were narrower branches veering off, pathways leading to doors and others into nothing but sky and stardust. Magic hung so heavily in the air, it made Layla feel drowsy.

"I've been here with Arne and Alruna when they have needed to travel fast and secretively. Not many beings can make it here to the heart, and we wouldn't have gotten this far without Alruna's token. The elves and wolves are always watching the portals in Finnmark, so going this way means that we are unseen leaving and returning," Tor explained.

He led them along the path and down to a set of archways made from branches. Runes were carved into the wood unlike anything Layla had ever seen. Each door seemed to pulse with a different kind of energy, and she wished Charlotte were with them. She would know exactly what it all meant.

"These ones will take us through to Svartalfheim," Tor said, pointing to four doors. Wrapped into their branches were small chunks of onyx, silver, gold, and ruby.

"North, south, east, west?" Ciara guessed, studying the doors.

Tor gave her a surprised smile. "That's right. The only question is which to take. Alruna didn't get an opportunity to subtly get out of Brök where the stronghold was."

"Vestri Mountains," Layla said, and they both turned to stare at her. She didn't want to explain her spontaneous trip to yell at the All-Father. "When I was doing Vili research, I went through every myth I could find in Kian's library. I was there to keep David company, so I had a lot of time to read. There was a story that mentioned Vili building a fortress in the Vestri Mountains."

"It's a good enough lead for me. West it is," Tor said, though his eyes were studying her closely. Layla hoped he couldn't smell the lie.

The Ulfheðnar were the All-Father's elite warriors, so telling Tor how she not only had the audacity to track down Havi's holiday house and then yell at him probably wasn't the best of ideas.

Tor walked to one of the archways and placed his palm on a rune. Instantly, the space between it flared with light and a forest glade came into view.

"Ladies first," he said with a wink. "I have to keep my hand on the rune to keep the door open, Wolf Slayer, so stop glaring at me."

Ciara unsheathed one of her daggers. "Me first, Layla." She crossed through before Layla could stop her.

"She's a real charmer, your cousin," Tor grumbled.

"I know. Lucky she's so pretty to make up for it, right?" Layla teased before stepping through the archway.

Magic sucked at her skin, and for a moment she felt like she was suspended in thin air. The ground rose up to meet her, and she stepped into a cool afternoon in Svartalfheim. Ciara was guarding the portal, her eyes scanning the trees and the sky.

"Two moons," she said, pointing. Layla turned to see a crescent moon rising from the east, and a full moon rising up from the west.

"So cool!" she exclaimed. Tor came through the portal, and then it shut with a burst of light.

"The moons are rising, so we have about two hours of light left," he said, studying the sky. "Your choice, Layla. We can stay here, or get ground covered."

"Let's walk. I need to work off some jitters from all the magic. Which way are we heading?"

Tor turned her and pointed at the dark mountain in the distance. It was the highest peak in a range surrounded by thick forest, and at least a three-day walk away.

"That's Vestri, one of the four biggest mountains on Svartalfheim, and named after one of the dwarves Odin commanded to hold up Ymir's skull," he explained.

"The big, dark, ominous mountain because of course it is. Why would I expect anything else?" Layla huffed, trying for bravado and ignoring the twisting that was back in her stomach.

Ciara flicked Layla's braid. "Maybe Smaug will be at the top, eh?" she teased.

Layla laughed, but she shared a knowing look with Tor behind her cousin's back. They both knew that what was waiting for them was a hell of a lot worse than a dragon.

14

It took Layla a whole day before she started thinking she had made a terrible mistake. She was reminded with her first pee behind a tree just how much she hated camping.

If she had thought Ciara was insufferable when she hunted through a forest, reading trails and looking for signs, it was nothing compared to both her *and* Tor doing it at the same time.

Tor was a wolf, so he had an excuse to be weird about touching broken sticks and smelling trees. Ciara was just more interested in what was happening in a forest than she was in anything else. She had a kind of intense hyperfocus when she hunted that Layla only got with a really good book or a bacon sandwich after a night of drinking.

Layla didn't know the names of the trees or wildflowers they passed, and she didn't pay much attention to the different bird songs. It was all just forest to her, and it was good she had them with her because she would have assumed she was walking in circles because it all looked the same.

Just when Layla would start pouting about her feet being sore, she would think about what kind of horrible shit Arne was going through that moment. It was enough for her to keep her mouth shut and keep going.

Would he have done the same for you if you had been the one taken? An annoying as hell voice had been niggling her at the back of her head for two days now. Tor had said she was Arne's mate, but she wasn't sure if she believed it. Yeah, there had always been the buzz of *something* between them, but a mate? Surely, he would have said something to her. It wasn't as if they were strangers.

Maybe he doesn't want to claim you, ever think of that? She kind of wished she hadn't, but she did. Despite his insistence to go on a date with her and have her at the summit, he had given her no indication of something more than seeing where their chemistry took them.

Are you forgetting that magical, mystical fuck off mark he put on you when he kissed you? It sounded like the elf equivalent of a dog pissing on a tree.

Layla's teeth ground together. She was going to rescue Arne, and then when they were back safely on Midgard, she was going to kick his ass. And then she would probably kiss his face off. Or the other way around. She didn't care.

She just wanted the sick feeling in her guts to be gone and to have him safely back where he belonged. Where she could see him. And annoy him as much as she liked.

"Earth to Layla? Are you in there?" Ciara asked, waving a hand by her face.

"Yeah? What?" Layla started.

Ciara passed her an energy bar. They tasted like cardboard and fake flavoring, but Layla still took it. She had to remind herself that it wasn't about the taste; it was about the kick it would give her. She *really* must've been out of it to let Ciara food shop for the trip. It was like she had gone to an army surplus store and got rations. If it wasn't for Tor pointing out edible berries and offering to hunt for them at night, Layla would've probably broken after day one.

"You are spookily quiet, little cousin. I'm worried," Ciara said as they walked and ate.

"We are in enemy territory. It's better if I'm quiet. You taught me that, remember?" Layla replied.

Ciara bumped her shoulder against Layla's. "I did, but you've never actually listened to me before. You're all serious and shit, like you've been hanging around the wolf too long."

"Tor is actually quite hilarious and chatty when you get to know him. You might have found this out if you had bothered to talk to him at all."

"I talk to him."

"You talk *at* him. There's a difference," Layla scoffed.

"Yeah, well, not all of us can forget our past and training so easily. Up until Bron started fucking Killian, they all were our enemy, Layla. You know I don't see the fae like that now. I love my new fae cousins, but the other creatures..." Ciara hesitated, her hand touching the hilt of a dagger strapped to her thigh. "Sometimes being on guard is an automatic reaction. I don't know how it will stop because most of the time, I don't see the nice ones. I see the feral, cruel, psycho ones that need to be put down."

Layla knew Ciara's past and could understand the hate, but Tor was different. He was an ally and a friend they had fought with.

"Maybe you need to have a break from hunting occasionally, and then you would have a chance to hang out with the nice ones," Layla suggested.

Ciara sighed. "Once Kenna has trained up more hunters, then maybe I will. No matter what's going on in the world, I feel like there's always going to be something to hunt."

"There probably will be, but that doesn't mean you have to be the one to do it all the time."

"If not me, then who?" Ciara replied. "We are what we are, Layla. If I'm not hunting, what's my purpose?"

Layla had had this argument with her and Bron more than once over the years. They were the best hunters they had, and because Ciara's parents had also been hunters and Ironwoods, she felt the responsibility to their memory keenly.

Bron had slowed down now that she had Killian, and Layla secretly hoped Ciara would find someone who would do the same for her too.

Layla needed to change the topic. "How much further do you think we have to go? This forest feels never ending."

"We'll know when Torsten returns from his scouting trip. Don't worry, Layla, we will be back to warm showers soon enough."

"Thank God because there are only so many days I can handle dry shampoo and wiping myself down with a cloth as opposed to a real shower." Layla grinned. "Though it's okay when Tor tips a bottle of water over himself at the end of the day."

Ciara rolled her eyes. "Pervert. You're meant to rescue your mate, not ogle his bodyguard."

"You say that like I can't do both. The mate thing is debatable anyway."

Ciara laughed at that. "Whatever you need to do to convince yourself, cousin. I suppose it makes more sense that you would be an elf's mate than Bron being Killian's."

"What you mean by that?" Layla asked.

"Well," Ciara said slowly, "You've loved them and been obsessed with them forever, haven't you? You still have a Legolas pin up poster on the back of your bedroom door."

Layla pulled out her water bottle and had a swig. "So? What's your point?"

"You're twenty-six years old."

"And? I'm supposed to not appreciate Orlando Bloom all of a sudden?"

Ciara tried to hide her smile. "I would think that most twenty-six-year-olds don't have Thranduil jammies either."

"Anything else sounds boring to me. I like fun clothes," Layla said, trying not to be offended.

"You only wear black," Ciara argued.

"They can still be fun if they are black!"

"Ah huh. As long as they have elves on them."

"Exactly!"

Ciara shook her head at her. "And you wonder why I think your elf obsession finally makes sense."

Layla scowled at her. "You know what? Elves happen to be extremely cool. There's plenty of reasons I'm obsessed with them that has nothing to do with some maybe cosmic love destiny that I may or may not have with a certain elf."

"Riiggghht."

"Just for that sarcasm, I'm now going to start listing the reasons that elves are cool," Layla said.

Ciara's smile slipped. "God no, please don't start."

"Oh, I'm starting alright," Layla declared loudly. "Starting right back to the *Silmarillion* and the *Years of the Trees* and the *Awakening of the Elves*..."

∼

AS MUCH AS Layla hated camping in the day, she hated the night more. She couldn't see the bugs coming for her in the darkness, and the forest was full of sounds she didn't recognize.

The one consolation was that the Svartalfheim stars were incredible, the two moons creating different lights that made the sky shine in a haze of blues and purples.

Giving up on getting any rest, Layla got up and placed another log on the fire and sat down beside it.

"Can't sleep?" Tor appeared through the trees, his eyes gleaming with animal light.

"No. I can take over the watch if you like," Layla replied. Tor was sleeping less than even she was.

"I'll be okay." He sat down beside her. "I have always liked Svartalfheim when I've visited, but something feels so off in the land. I don't know if it's because I haven't been to this part before or Vili's return, but the forest feels wrong."

"What do you mean?" Layla asked.

"It's far too quiet for a start. There should be a lot more animals around, but from the tracks I've been seeing, they have been migrating."

Layla frowned. "Away from the mountain?"

"Yes. Animals always know when to leave an area that is hostile to them." Tor rubbed his face. "The sooner we get Arne and go back home, the better."

"That we can agree on. You can tell Ciara loves all of this nature, but I've never been able to relax out in the open like this. Too scared of spiders trying to make a nest in my sleeping bag or laying eggs in my ear or something," Layla replied with a dramatic shiver.

"That sounds horrible," Tor chuckled. His gray eyes drifted to the curled up sleeping ball of Ciara. She was shivering a little, her dreams bothering her like they usually did. Layla knew better than to try and wake her up. "Why does she hate wolves so much? I know you are all hunters, but her hatred is kind of famous. She earned her Wolf Slayer title."

Layla chewed on her lip, debating whether or not she should say anything at all. Ciara never would, and Layla didn't want Tor to take her cold mood personally.

"When Lachie and she were kids, their parents were tasked to hunt down this crazed werewolf. He was a serial killer and had a bunch of copycats that made the whole hunt messy and confusing. They thought they had finally killed the real beast, and they returned home," Layla whispered, not wanting to wake Ciara up by accident.

"But it was another copycat?" Tor guessed.

"Yeah. The actual killer tracked them back to the house and killed them. Ciara woke up with the screaming. She went straight to Lachie's room, woke him up, and then hid him in the back of a linen cupboard. Then she went to confront the wolf in the house."

"Fucking hell. How old was she?"

"Eight." Layla pulled her jacket closer around her. "The wolf cornered her in the kitchen. The place was covered in what remained of her father. He had...he had gone down for a midnight snack when he had been attacked. I don't know all the details, but I do know Ciara killed the crazed wolf by shoving a butter knife through its eye and into its brain. Ciara and Lachie came to live with us after that. Wolves became her specialty."

Tor was staring at the fire, his face racked with sadness. "Those poor kids. No wonder she hates all wolves so much. The Ulfheðnar clean up their own messes when a wolf goes bad. I sometimes forget not every pack is like that."

"Is that what happened with Varg?" Layla asked.

Tor poked the fire with a stick, his expression shifting to anger. "Varg was exiled because he was becoming extreme in his thinking. He had always been a dark soul, but after the fae returned, he got a lot worse. He saw it as a time for the magical kind to rise up and take their place above the humans. He was getting followers that were terrorizing humans when they could. Girls went missing, and though we never found the evidence we needed to execute them, we all knew Varg and his cult were to blame. One of the girls who went missing was...was my sister."

"Fuck, Tor, I'm sorry." Layla placed a hand on his arm. "Did you ever find any of them again?"

Tor shook his head. "Not a sign or a whisper. They were just gone. Linnea was always different. I still don't know why they would have taken her except for revenge on me."

"What do you mean?"

"She is a wolf from a powerful bloodline, but she has never shifted. Not once. She was shunned a lot because of it. She preferred to live in Oslo, amongst the humans. It was easier for her."

Layla didn't want to dredge up anything more painful, but she still asked, "Why do you think Varg took her? If she was living in a city by herself, anything could have happened."

Tor shook his head. "I know it sounds crazy. Trust me, plenty of others have told me the same, but I *know* Varg. He is petty and vicious. I was the one who started speaking against him to the Ulfheðnar council. He took Linnea out of spite. I couldn't find where he and his cult went after we exiled them."

"And now you know they came here to Vili," Layla said, and Tor nodded.

"It makes sense that they would. Varg probably sees Vili as a way to get what he and his cult wants."

"And what's that?"

"The location of Fenris," Tor replied, and a chill swept down Layla's spine. "If Vili wants to start Ragnarök, he'll need the Great Wolf. Varg's cult sees Fenris as the first shifter. Our god. They will do what Vili asks for, just for the chance to find him."

Layla stared at him. "Fuck, Tor, you've been holding this back since we were in Alta? What the hell? How are you not totally wild right now, seeing your sister's killer?"

"Going wild won't help anything. Arne is my brother, and getting him back is my first duty," Tor replied firmly. "And I don't think my sister is dead. I would feel it, Layla. Varg took Arne, so if we find one, we will find the other. Stopping Vili means stopping Varg, and maybe then I'll be able to get some answers about my sister. I didn't have permission to pursue him before because there was no evidence. This shit with Vili will give me leverage to hunt Varg and his followers down."

Layla sighed and stared up at the sky. "What a fucking mess this is turning into."

"We will get to the stronghold tomorrow, so we just need to focus on the next thing and then the next thing," Tor said and patted her on the back. "For you, that's going to sleep with your new spider friends."

"Thanks a lot," Layla scoffed. She moved back to her bedroll. "Maybe don't mention to Ciara that I told you about her family."

"I won't. I value my nuts where they are," Tor replied, making her smother her laugh. "Thanks for telling me anyway."

"No problem. Just don't take any of her bullshit too seriously. It's not you she hates," Layla replied with a yawn.

She curled up on her side and was drifting off when she heard Tor move. She cracked open an eye and watched him stand over a dreaming Ciara, a frown on his face. With a soft growl, he grabbed his blanket and draped it over her before going back to the fire. Layla smiled a little, and finally went to sleep.

15

They reached the mountain the following afternoon. Tor had become increasingly paranoid, so they had stayed off any paths and had crept through the trees like shadows.

"There should be more guards or patrols than this," Ciara whispered.

"Not if you're not afraid of being attacked. No one would be stupid enough to try and fight Vili on his own ground," Tor replied and then winked at Layla. "Except for you maybe."

"I'm not going to fight him. I'm going to steal Arne back and get the hell out of here," she replied.

They were hiding up on a small ridge and could see a group of warriors standing outside of an entrance carved into the rock. Layla lifted her binoculars again and tried to see what was going on.

"There's got to be another way in. A back entrance. Vili wouldn't be dumb enough to only have one way in or out," she said.

Tor let out a soft growl. "I'll go and do a scout. You two stay here until I get back. I'll move faster alone and as a wolf." He started to strip off and Layla got an unexpected eyeful of a ripped chest covered in Viking tattoos and fine dark blonde hair.

"Gods, Torsten, warn us, will you?" Ciara muttered, quickly turning and hitting Layla to do the same.

"If I had known you were shy about nudity, I would have. Who knew a big fierce hunter was afraid of a little skin?" Tor teased.

Ciara's ears went red. "It's common decency."

"I thought it was pretty decent," Layla said and Ciara hit her again.

There was a snapping, growling sound, and Tor's big furry head bumped against Layla. His gray eyes were huge as they stared down at her. He was as big as a bear, and she would have wet herself if she didn't know him.

"Yes, yes, we'll stay here," she said, patting his silvery fur. "Off you go."

Tor pawed the ground once and then bolted off through the trees.

"Here's hoping he doesn't get seen in that form. He's hard to miss," Ciara commented.

"We are in a magical world. Maybe big ass wolves are common enough that people wouldn't look twice." Layla lifted her binoculars again and tried to see anything of interest.

There was a light glowing inside the cavern entrance, torches now being lit to prepare for the coming darkness. The warriors were all as big as Tor, with black leather armor. Vili was already gathering an army to him, that much was for certain. There was no way to tell how many warriors were in the fortress. They would be going in completely blind.

"Having second thoughts?" Ciara asked.

"No," Layla replied stubbornly. "We need Arne back. If Bron could live inside Morrigan's fortress in Tir Na Nog for a month, we can find a way to rescue one prince."

"We aren't Bron, Layla."

"No shit. But we will have to do the best we can." Layla opened her pack and took out the pouch of magical tricks Charlotte had packed for her. Charlotte was so much better with her magic now thanks to the Greatdrakes teaching and library. The magical objects she was making for her sisters were more effective, longer lasting, and convenient.

Layla flicked through the patches, reading the labels on the small plastic bags they were packed in. Charlotte was nothing if not organized with them.

"Ah! Here we are. I knew she would have some glamor patches in here," she said, pulling them out. "We can use these."

"Let's hope they will hold under whatever wards Vili has up," Ciara said.

"If he only has a small group of warriors guarding the entrance, I doubt he's going to waste his magic putting up anything super sophisticated." Layla tapped the patches against her palm. "We are going to have to risk it regardless."

Ciara clicked her tongue. "I hope this elf is worth it, Lay Lay. I mean he's pretty and all, but if we get caught in there, we are never getting out alive."

"Don't come if you are scared," Layla replied, her hand curling around one of the hilts of Arne's sword.

"I'm not scared. I'm just saying, if you go through all of this and he ends up breaking your heart, I'm going to murder him."

Layla tried to laugh, but it came out more of a choking sound. "I will murder him. And I'm not doing it because of hearts."

"Sure, you aren't. You've been smitten with that elf since he first showed up. Anyone with eyes in their heads could see that," Ciara replied.

"Thanks. This whole conversation is making me feel so much more relaxed." Layla didn't want to talk or think about feelings. She wanted to be clear and calm, like she was on a usual job. "I like him. Is that what you want me to admit? I don't understand what the mark and mating bond is doing to me, but I know I will go mad if I don't get him back because they are eating me alive. Once we save him, he can take the damn thing off me, and then I won't care if he's kidnapped again."

Ciara put her hands up in surrender. "Okay, whatever you say."

Layla took a sip of water from her bottle, but it didn't do anything to calm the jitters running under her skin. Whatever the mark he put on her was, it could feel Arne close, and it was setting her off.

Layla would rescue him and then get him to remove it as soon as possible because she couldn't live this wound up all the time. She was the easy-going, go with the flow person, not this highly strung human wreckage she had become.

Layla was starting to pace when Tor appeared through the trees and began to shift. Both Ironwoods turned to give him some privacy to pull his pants on.

"You were right about a back entrance into the caverns. I followed a group of dark elves that were taking some carts up to it," Tor said when he was on two feet again. "I got good news and bad news. Good news, they are having a feast tonight and some of the people going in were girls and entertainers. It means the warriors will be expecting faces they don't know."

"And the bad news?" Layla asked.

"Bad news is the feast is to celebrate the return of the lost prince who has finally taken his rightful place by Vili's side," Tor replied.

Layla's chest tightened. "You think Arne has sided with him?"

"Fuck no," Tor growled defensively. "He's either playing Vili so he can be a spy or to keep himself alive. Or he's under an enchantment."

Layla tried to think through her panic. "Vili is a god. He would be strong enough to fuck with someone's head no matter how strong they were."

"Vili is kind of famous for it too," Tor said, his voice dropping to a growl. "I heard a story growing up that he was once in a battle against an army of dwarves. His magic infected them and stole their will. He made them march back into the city he wanted to conquer and kill their own families. Then he made half of them kill themselves. The other half, he left alive to remember and to tell future generations what would happen if they tried to defy him."

"Fucking hell," Ciara muttered. "This is the guy you are willing to piss off?"

"Yes, because Arne would do the same for any of his friends. And he is one of us."

Ciara crossed her arms. "Would he really do it though? You barely know him!"

"But I do," Tor said taking a step toward her. "And Layla is right. There's no way Arne wouldn't try and get a friend back that had been taken. You add the mating bond into it and how he feels about Layla? He would tear that mountain apart with his bare fucking hands to get her out of there."

"He would?" Layla swallowed the sudden lump in her throat. "W-What kind of feelings? He's never said..."

"How about we go and rescue him, and he can tell you that himself?" Tor said, placing a hand on her shoulder.

Layla nodded and showed him the glamor patches Charlotte had made. "I've got a plan."

∼

CARTS FILLED with casks of wine, mead, and food were still being unpacked at the other entrance of the mountain fortress. It was a square hole leading into a tunnel that was wide enough for carts to move in and out.

Layla's glamor itched against her skin, but as long as no one got too vigorous feeling her up, they wouldn't realize she wasn't wearing a revealing dress, but hunting gear and two swords on her back.

She had tailored the glamors so they looked like dark elf versions of themselves. Tor was looking like the other guards in black and gold armor, his face covered with a helm on the off chance that Varg or any of his followers recognized him.

"Here we go. Hope you're ready for this," Tor murmured. He slung an arm around each of them, and they began a swaying, giggling walk towards the two warriors guarding the entrance way.

"And what have you found?" one asked Tor, looking Layla over.

"Presents for the prince. They were the prettiest in the villages to the south. All the rest looked like the wrong end of a dwarf. You girls are more than happy to come to a real party, right?" Tor asked them. Layla and Ciara giggled.

"Especially if all your friends are as big and strong as you," Ciara said, wrapping her hands around his thick bicep. "Look! They are bigger than my hands!'

"I got something else you won't be able to wrap your hand around," Tor replied, and Layla almost choked on her tongue.

"Go on through. They are already getting rowdy in there," the guard replied, waving them through. "You wouldn't want to keep the prince waiting. If he's got an appetite like his father, he's going to need a fresh stream of girls at all times."

"How promising!" Layla said a little too loudly. The thought of Arne touching another person, let alone *a fresh stream* of them made her vision blur with rage.

Stupid elf mark.

The dark tunnel was lit with torches and was crowded with people dropping off deliveries and warriors carrying fresh casks. Layla could hear the uproar of revelry, and she drew closer to Tor as Ciara and she got looked over like hunks of meat.

"Why are men so gross everywhere?" Ciara muttered under her breath. A rowdy dwarf tried to palm her ass, but Tor's reflexes were lightning quick, knocking the dwarf's hand back.

"These ones belong to the prince, and not your grubby paws," he snapped.

The dwarf only smirked and lifted his ale mug. "That's fine. I'll have 'er after he's done."

"Gross," Layla said, her need for a bath increasing with every step they took. The tunnel led through some kitchens and food storage areas. They followed the roar of noise and picked up some ale mugs so they didn't look out of place in the crowd.

They followed the flow of dwarves, dark elves, and shifters, and Layla suddenly felt she really was about to stumble across Erebor.

The feast was being held in a cavern that was as big as a football stadium. Tables and benches, open cooking fires, musicians, warriors, and revelers—all made the rock shake. The mountain had been carved away for function without any unnecessary designs into the rock. They didn't need it because everywhere they looked were Vili's black and gold banners.

Layla suddenly remembered the sickening photos of the blood magic in the estuary when Aneirin had been contacting the two generals. The rune Teiwaz was what they had thought was Vili's symbol, and Charlotte had been right, as usual. It was a warrior rune that could be used to enhance strength so that the average person could become a berserker. It was stamped in gold nearly everywhere Layla looked.

"He's over doing it a bit, don't you think?" Ciara whispered.

"He's a god. They can't help themselves," Tor replied.

Layla's heart began to pound, and an awareness swept over her, just like the night Arne was taken.

"He's here," she said, grabbing Tor's hand. She looked around but couldn't spot him.

Tor seemed to know exactly what was happening. "Follow the feeling, Layla. There are too many scents in here for me to track him, but maybe you can."

They hung onto each other's hands so they wouldn't get lost in the crowd, and Layla followed the deep tugging feeling in her chest. She might have been pissed off that Arne had marked her, but at least it was being of use.

Layla froze as they made it to where a table was set up on a dais. A giant of a man sat on a throne made of stone and covered in black bear furs. He had his long hair in braids and decorated with gold. He wore a leather breast plate but had his tattooed arms free. A broad sword rested at his side of easy use.

"He doesn't half look like Odin," she murmured.

"What?" Tor demanded.

Layla's heart stopped altogether when the doors behind the dais opened, and Arne walked out. He was dressed in the same armor as Vili, his hair back in braids, and his eyes were smeared with kohl.

Arne placed a hand on Vili's shoulder and said something that made the god throw back his head and laugh. Arne sat by Vili's side, and they knocked ale mugs together like they really were father and son enjoying each other's company. They looked so much alike, Layla's heart hurt in a mixture of longing and horror.

"Tor?" Layla whispered, her voice breaking. "I think we are fucked."

16

Layla's head felt like it was underwater. She could hear Tor telling her over and over again that it wasn't Arne. She was torn between wanting to run away and leave him there and throwing a sword at him for making her worry so much about him. He wasn't locked in some dungeon, getting tortured. He looked like he was right at home.

"We need to get him alone, Layla, and try and break whatever Vili has done to him," Tor said, giving her shoulder a shake.

"What if he's done nothing? What if he's just decided to side with his father?" she replied.

Ciara was keeping an eye on the people around her, waiting for Layla to make a decision on what to do next. Layla was never good at making decisions, especially mid-job. She liked to plan things out, and now her plans were all tangled up in her emotions, and she couldn't think straight.

"Layla, look at me," Tor demanded, and she did, focusing on the gray eyes she could see in the slits of his helm. "That's *not* Arne. He's not even moving the same way. He's under an enchantment, I swear it. We need to get him alone."

"You may have a chance," Ciara said and gestured with her head. "Deep breaths, cousin."

Layla was lucky she obeyed her cousin because when she turned back and saw the girl draped over Arne, whispering in his ear and making him grin, Layla stopped breathing. When they got up together and headed down a dark cleft in the rock behind them, Layla became furious.

"Fuck, prepare yourself, Ciara," Tor growled.

Layla was already moving, not caring if they followed, or if she had to cut her way through every goddamn person in her way.

She had enough sense about her to stay in character, swaying a little as she drank from her mead. Gods knew, she probably needed it to cool the rage coursing through her. Not that it worked. No one stopped her as she moved around the other revelers and slipped down the passageway.

There were torches burning in sconces that lit her path. A pair of dark elves were making out and dry humping in a corner and didn't pay her any attention at all.

As she passed a door, the tugging sensation gripped her hard. She didn't know what she was about to walk in on, and her self-preservation was gone. Layla was pissed. She opened the door without knocking.

In the bedroom, the female had her back to Layla and was giggling while slowly stripping off her dress. Layla moved silent as a shadow behind her, and with one swift hit to the back of the head, the woman dropped. Arne sat on a huge bed, his gold eyes going wide in surprise.

"Was that really necessary? You could have joined us," he said, his smile widening as he looked her over. "Though you are definitely more my type."

"Do you not know who I am?" Layla asked.

Arne tugged her into his lap. "Do I need to?"

"Shit, Tor was right."

"Who is Tor, lovely?" Arne purred.

"Me," the shifter said, coming into the room with Ciara. He shut the door and took off his helm. "Do you know who I am?"

"No. And like I told this one, I don't need to in order to have some fun," Arne replied.

Layla tried to climb out of his lap, but he held onto her. She looked at Tor for help. "Any ideas?"

"Mating bond is stronger than just about any enchantment. Maybe kiss him?"

Arne brushed his nose up the side of her neck. "I agree with him. You should definitely start by kissing me. Gods, why do you smell so good? It's like something from a dream."

Layla tried not to respond to him or his hardening dick pressing into her thigh. She had to snap him the hell out of whatever Vili had done to him and fast. She ran her hands over his braids and gripped them so he lifted his head from her neck.

"Show me how a prince kisses," she said and licked his full bottom lip. Arne's smile was devilish as he leaned in and took her mouth with his.

If his odd behavior wasn't enough to convince Layla he was under a spell, the kiss would have. It didn't feel the same as it had in Alta. His energy and the way he used his tongue were totally different.

"Come back to me, Arne," she whispered against his lips. Golden light shivered to the surface of his skin.

"Layla..." his voice broke, sounding like her Arne, and then the light was sinking back into his skin, and his eyes went cloudy again.

"Arne, you must fight it," she begged. She remembered the magic that had overwhelmed him in Alta. She had been able to calm it then, so she had to be able to break it now. She pulled him closer. Kissed her way up his strong jawline.

"Please, Arne. I'm in danger here. I need your help. Your *mate* needs your help. Come back." She kissed him again, and the golden light started to seep out of him. "Help me, Arne. I'm so scared." His hands tightened on her hips, dragging her closer, but the light didn't vanish. She decided to appeal to another side of him.

Layla looked over her shoulder at Tor. "If this doesn't start to work soon, I say we knock him out and carry him out of here." Tor nodded, and she turned back to a dazed looking Arne.

Layla took his face in both of her hands. "Arne, if you don't pull your shit together right now, I'm going to leave you here, and as soon as I get back to Midgard, I'm going to call Seamus for another date. I want to know what those freckles on his cheek taste like," she said, pulling away from him. Arne let out a snarl so low that the hair on her arms rose.

"*No*," he said, hands tightening around her.

"Why not? You don't know who I am. Why do you care?" she replied.

Arne looked at her, his eyes searching hers. The golden light that had been coming out of his skin was slowly vanishing into the air like mist.

"You are...you are mine," Arne said, confusion making his brow furrow.

"Am I? This is the first I'm hearing about it. Maybe I've wasted my time coming here. Probably for the best we never went for that drink."

Something flickered in his eyes. "The drink. We were going to... Layla."

"What?"

"I kissed you when the sky was burning with souls and stars," he whispered. He pressed his face to her neck and breathed her in. "My mate. My Layla."

"Yeah, we need to talk about the mate thing, but I'm willing to let it slide when you're acting crazy," she said. The last of the golden light vanished in the air, and Arne shuddered all over.

"Layla... *Layla*." Arne pushed back from her. He looked from her to Tor and then Ciara. "What the fuck are you doing here?"

"We are here to save your ass," she said and climbed out of his lap. "Now, get up. We are leaving."

"You brought my mate into this place? Are you fucking insane?" Arne demanded, getting to his feet and closing in on Tor.

"Have you tried to get her to do anything she didn't want to do? Either I came with her, or she was coming alone. Good to see you too," Tor grumbled. Arne looked ready to explode when there was a knock at the door.

"My prince? Are you in there?" a voice called through the door.

"Shit, you need to look debauched," Layla said and ruffled his hair. She lay back on the bed, the swords digging into her back.

Arne opened the door, and Tor grabbed Ciara, pinning her to the wall and hiding his face in her dark hair.

"What? Can't you see I'm busy?" Arne demanded. The warrior looked in and flushed.

"Apologies, my prince. We only wished to know your whereabouts."

Arne let out a frustrated growl. "Well, now you know. Gods help anyone who disturbs me again before dawn!" He slammed the door in the warrior's face. Tor dropped Ciara and took a hasty step back. Layla didn't think she had seen her cousin so red-faced in all her life.

"Shit, we need to find a way out of here," Layla said.

"Portal crystal," Tor replied.

Layla fished around in her pockets for it. She pulled it out, but Arne's hand closed on hers.

"It won't work. Vili's wards in his territory nulls portal magic. He wants to be able to control who is coming in and out. We need to get out of the mountain and through the forest as fast as we can," Arne replied. He pulled off his breast plate, leaving him in a sleeveless tunic. Layla may have admired his arms a little bit in the process.

"Here, I brought these for you," she said, dropping the glamor. His face was unreadable as she slipped off the swords and passed them to him. He gripped them tight.

"You carried them all this way?" he asked.

Heat crept up her neck, but Layla shrugged. "Thought you might need them."

Arne loosened the straps to his size and put them on. "Vili and his warriors will be feasting for the rest of the night. We don't have much time until my absence is noticed."

"So what's the plan?" Tor asked.

Arne went to the back of the room where a heavy woven standard hung. He pulled it aside to reveal a small door. "We go out the back way. Only Vili and I know about this passageway. It's an escape route if the mountain is attacked."

"You and Vili got close enough for him to show you? How nice," Layla said, failing to keep the annoyance out of her voice.

"We can argue about it later, Layla," Arne replied.

"Oh, we are going to argue about it, mister. And the fact that you put a fucking mark on me that has been screwing with me ever since you were taken."

"I didn't..." Arne looked at her closer and flushed. "Fuck."

"Yeah. Fuck. Now get moving before we start having the argument now," Layla replied.

Arne let out a string of curses under his breath, then he opened the door. Tor grabbed one of the torches from the room and stepped in after Arne. Layla took two deep breaths, trying to shove down the sudden bombardment of feelings.

"He's okay, Layla. You got him," Ciara said, reading her far too easily. It was an Ironwood trait to get angry in order to hide what they were really feeling. Layla searched her pockets and found some of the incendiary spells Charlotte had created. She placed one on the back of Arne's bedroom door and another on the headboard. She didn't want to think about the people he had been fucking in it while there. She looked at the woman still on the floor. She couldn't leave her there, no matter how angry she was.

Layla tapped her on the face. "Hey, wake up. You passed out."

"What...where is the prince?"

"He left. Come on, up you get. Let's get you back to the party." Layla led her out the door. There were no guards around. "Go on, have fun now."

The woman mumbled something and walked away. Layla locked the door and activated the patch.

"You're in a particularly vengeful mood," Ciara commented as she activated the one on the headboard.

"It'll slow down anyone coming after us. And fuck Vili and his mind tricks," Layla growled.

Tor stuck his head out of the passageway. "What's the holdup? We need to move."

"Just leaving some presents behind."

Tor grinned and hustled them into the passage before shutting them into darkness.

"So glad I have no issue with claustrophobia or being buried alive," Ciara murmured. The passage was small enough that Tor had to hunch over, and his shoulders almost brushed the sides.

"I won't let you get buried alive down here, Wolf Slayer," Tor promised her. "If you start to panic, I'll knock you out and carry you."

"Thanks? I guess?" Ciara replied.

"Aw, look at you two getting on," Layla crooned because she couldn't help herself.

Arne was waiting for them with another lit torch. He looked Layla over, his expression neutral but his eyes burning with so much emotion she had to look away.

I'm not dealing with whatever the hell that is.

"Lead on, prince. We are wasting time," she said gruffly.

Arne nodded, and they started to jog along the passageway. Layla hated cardio, but she hated that mountain even more. The sooner they got out of there and into the forest, the better.

17

Layla lost time in the tunnels. She was torn between relief and exhaustion and also had the buzz of being close to Arne to distract her. She hadn't been physically this close to him since Alta, and she wanted to kick his ass and climb into his clothes at the same time.

Fucking magic. Maybe Charlotte could figure out a ward that could stop handsome elves from putting claims on unsuspecting people.

Arne slowed his pace. "We are near the end. Keep it quiet. I don't know if Vili has this passage guarded."

They ditched the torches and edged slowly toward the opening. Layla could smell cold, clean air and the rotting greenery of the forest. Arne pulled one of his swords free, ready for a fight. He held a hand up to halt Layla before he checked the opening on all sides and stepped out.

A few moments later, he reappeared. "Looks like we are clear. Tor, I might need you to shift and see if your nose can pick up anyone close by."

"On it," Tor replied. He dropped his glamor, shifted, and disappeared through the trees.

Outside, the moons where falling, and Layla knew it was close to dawn. The mountain loomed in the distance, and everything seemed suspiciously quiet.

"We are going to have to forget about going back for the packs. I hope you didn't have anything too important in yours," Ciara said, taking off her glamor and rolling her neck and shoulders. "Magic always makes me feel weird in my body after."

Layla's skin stopped itching as soon as she tore the patch off her skin. She had to hand it to Charlotte for ingenuity with portable magic.

Arne was watching them carefully, like he was still disorientated from finding them there at all. He looked tired but not hurt in any way from his time with Vili.

Layla pulled out the portal crystal, but it held no hum of power. "Shit. We are still under Vili's dampening magic."

"We have to keep going then. Tor will track us," Arne said and started off through the forest.

Layla rubbed at her face, biting down all the annoyance she felt. Ciara smiled at her, and Layla groaned. "Don't say it."

"I don't know what you're talking about."

Layla started to follow Arne, Ciara falling into step beside her. "The next time I decide to go running off to another world for a male, punch me in the tit, will you?"

"It's a promise, little cousin." Ciara nodded toward Arne. "You still managed to get him out. Take it as a victory even if you want to yell at him, okay?"

Layla nodded. She needed to suck up her bullshit a little bit longer.

"You should go talk to him. He seems upset," Ciara said.

"What does he have to be upset about? He wasn't even a little bit tortured like I thought he was."

"You don't know what the magic made him do, Layla. Go and talk to him. I'll watch our backs until Tor returns."

Layla let out a huff of annoyance and then walked faster to catch up with Arne. He wore a glare, fierce enough to scare most people away, but Layla had seen Kenna's war face and not much frightened her more than that.

"How did you get here?" he demanded before she could say a word.

"Your mother gave us a stave that took us to the Heart of Yggdrasil. Then we walked," she replied. She wasn't ready to tell him about her trip to see the All-Father and his hot tip on where to find his brother.

"You shouldn't have come here. It's too much of a risk."

Layla's hand gripped the portal crystal tighter. "You wanted to keep being Vili's bitch, did you? Because that's what you would have remained if I hadn't come."

Arne flinched. "I'm not ungrateful."

"Really? Because you sure are acting it," Layla snapped. Her temper was getting the better of her, and she didn't have the willpower to stop it from bubbling over. "Do you know how much I hate the outdoors? A fucking lot, Arne. I have been in this fucking forest for days looking for you, and I don't want to hear any of your bullshit about how I've wasted my time."

Arne grabbed her arm to stop her from walking.

"I'm just going to go back a bit and cover our tracks," Ciara said, and walked off again.

"Why did you come after me?" Arne said. He was looming over her, and Layla shoved him out of her space.

"Because no one else was going to! The elves weren't going to send anyone to rescue you, so Tor and I knew we had to," she replied. Her pulse was racing too fast, but she couldn't stop. "I've felt like I've been losing my goddamn mind since you went missing. This mark you put on me has been clawing away at me non-stop. All I have been able to think about is getting you back so you can remove it. In fact, you can remove it right now."

"Layla, I didn't mean..."

"*Now*, Arne. I didn't give you permission to magically piss all over me," she snapped, moving into his space.

"I didn't mean to put it on you at all." Arne placed two fingers on her forehead. "The magic flared up when we kissed and must've done it. I'm...sorry. I've never heard of a mark creating any emotional problems before."

"Well, it did. Now I'd like these fake feelings removed, thanks."

"Fake feelings," Arne said flatly. Layla suddenly felt like crying which was just stupid. She swallowed down the impulse. They didn't have time to waste. He whispered some words in a dialect of elvish she didn't recognize, and tingles of magic swept over her body.

"There. It's removed, so now you don't have to feel anything for me at all," Arne snapped.

He was too close to her, but he didn't move and neither did she. The mark was gone, and she still felt like her skin was hurting from wanting him so badly. Neither looked away. The angry tension left Arne's face, and all that remained was yearning.

"Layla, stop looking at me like that," he whispered.

"I thought you were getting tortured. That we would find you locked in a cage with pieces of you missing," she said, her voice breaking.

Layla had pushed down all the anxiety and worry for him so that they could get the job done. Now he was standing there whole, and she couldn't push it down anymore.

"I'm sorry I put you through that. I'm okay now," he tried to reassure her. He lowered his forehead to hers. "You saved me."

"Don't get all soft on me when I want to be angry at you—" Layla began, but then she was kissing him, unable to stop herself. Her hand went around his neck, pulling him down so she could have more of him.

Arne's hands cupped her face, and his tongue slipped between her lips, tasting her in languid strokes. She knew the enchantment on him was still broken just by the feel of his lips and tongue and teeth.

They had to keep moving; they had to get out of Svartalfheim. Layla couldn't stop; she was breathless with the need for him burning her up.

It wasn't the mark at all, she realized suddenly.

Oh gods, that made everything so much worse. She broke off the kiss and stumbled back from him. He looked shaken and ruffled, but a slow smile appeared on his lips.

Layla pulled her shirt straight. "I'm still angry with you, but we need to move. You first. Ten feet from me at all times. I don't need you smirking at me like that either."

"Whatever you say, *vennen*," he said, trailing his fingers over hers as he walked past her.

"Fucking elves," she muttered.

Tor and Ciara caught up with them not long after. Ciara raised a brow at her, but Layla shook her head. They could talk about love hating on Arne later. She wanted to go home. As soon as she thought it, the portal crystal in her hand grew warm.

"Wait! I think something is happening," Layla called. Arne hurried back to her. "I can feel the magic. It's..." Something snapped in the trees, and Layla turned as Varg and three other shifters appeared around them.

She didn't hesitate. She threw the portal crystal hard at the ground. White silvery power burst around them, and a portal opened.

"You don't want to do this, Arne. Your father can give you more than what—Ah! You bitch!" Varg screamed as Layla's flying dagger sliced off part of his ear.

"Tor, now!" she snapped. He grabbed Arne and tackled him through the portal, Ciara jumping through after him.

"You've made the biggest fucking mistake of your life," Varg snarled at her.

Layla only smiled the famous fuck you Ironwood smile at him. "Tell Vili if he wants Arne, he's going to have to stop being a coward and come to Midgard himself. He can stop sending pups like you to do the work."

"Bold words, little girl. Vili will come to Midgard, and when he does, he'll unleash Ragnarök."

Layla threw another dagger at him, but Varg ducked. "Looking forward to it, asshole."

Varg's men pounced for her, but she was falling through the portal. It snapped shut behind her with searing heat. A second later, she was on the floor of Tor's apartment, Ciara's face hovering over her.

"Did you just start a pissing contest with a primordial god?!" she demanded.

"He shouldn't have touched my things," Layla said. Ciara helped her upright. Tor was still holding onto Arne like he had been stopping him from going back through. They all looked pale and pissed off.

Layla straightened her shoulders. "I'm sure you two have a lot of calls to make. Alruna will want to know you're safe. Come on, Ciara. We are out of here."

"Layla, please..."Arne began.

"No. I'm going back to Freya's to have a hot shower and sleep," she said, refusing to look him in the eye. "You are home safe, and that's what Alruna asked of me. The summit will be over, so whatever contract you had with Kenna is completed. Job. Over."

Layla hurried out of the apartment and got far away from all the feelings she didn't know what to do with.

18

Layla spent the first day back in Oslo curled up in the bed in Freya's guest room. She vaguely registered Ciara coming in to wake her to say goodbye and tell her that she was going back to Sweden to finish her hunt. Layla had hugged her, waited until she had left, and pulled the covers back over her head.

Layla hadn't bothered to turn her phone back on. She wasn't ready to deal with Kenna, her sisters, and Lachie, who would undoubtedly give her shit for not sharing any of her plans with them.

Layla was getting out of her afternoon shower on the second day when she heard voices in the apartment. Three distinct male voices.

Well, you couldn't hide forever, she thought glumly.

Layla pulled on clean sweats and her favorite Legolas shirt. She looked puffy and sad, but a good face moisturizer could only do so much.

Kian, Killian, and Bayn were all in the kitchen. Bayn was fussing about, cleaning up her empty takeout bags and brewing coffee. Killian took one look at her and was beside her in a second, gathering her up into a tight hug.

"Never, ever, *ever,* make me worry like that again," he said, squeezing the life out of her. "And if you assholes ever let her do something so crazy without telling me, I will kick your asses so goddamn hard..." His rant broke off when Layla sobbed into his chest. She loved Kill and his dramatics so much.

"I'm sorry I kept it from you, but I had to go. The magic made me," Layla said, though she didn't know if she believed it anymore.

Killian pulled back and studied her face. He wiped the tears off her cheeks. "You are crying?! What did he *do* to you?" he snarled.

"He put some kind of elf mark on me before he was kidnapped. It's fucked with all my emotions, but he didn't—" Layla tried to explain. Killian wasn't in the mood to listen. His eyes had turned black, and he was gone from the apartment in a burst of shadows and black feathers.

"Fucking balls," Bayn groaned.

"Can you please stop him from killing Arne? I don't have time for a war with the elves," Kian complained.

"Yeah, I'm on it," Bayn replied and was gone in a flurry of ice.

Layla pushed her damp hair out of her face. "He didn't let me finish. Arne didn't mean to put the mark on me, and it's gone now anyway!"

"Killian has always been a bit overprotective, you know that. It'll be okay," Kian replied. He fixed her a coffee and placed it down on the counter for her. "Now, Layla, we are going to have a nice talk like adults before they get back. I have a family of Ironwoods I've managed to convince to give you some space, but I need you to tell me everything. Please, stop crying. I can't handle it."

"I can't help it. It won't stop even with the stupid mark removed. I think it's just been too much stress at once."

Layla cradled her coffee in her hands and told Kian all that had happened since she left Ireland, including her trip to see the All-Father and telling Kenna that the family could go fuck itself. He didn't interrupt, just frowned a lot at her.

"I must say, I am impressed, little sister," Kian said finally. "Kenna is pissed off at you—that's true—but it's coming from a place of worry more than anything."

Layla sniffed. "I don't want to go home yet. I can't. I need some time to think all of this through."

"And you have the mating bond to consider." Kian held up his hand when she started to protest. "Layla, no, don't argue. Listen to me. I don't know how it is with the elves, but a mating bond with the fae is something so powerful, you can't run from it. You have a choice not to explore it, but can I ask what your true objections to the idea are? I thought you liked Arne."

"I do! But he's a prince, and I'm just me, Kian. I can't let him tie himself to someone who isn't going to offer him any value. He needs someone who can be the princess his people deserve. Not a human who doesn't know anything about politics or whatever princesses are meant to know about." Layla put her head in her hands. "This connection, this bond, whatever you want to call it, it's tearing me apart. I can't live like this, Kian."

He placed a hand on her back. "Layla, it's because you are fighting it that it's hurting."

"We don't even know each other!"

"It's not how it works," Kian said gently. "And if you don't spend time with him, how will you ever get to know him?"

"Because it will only hurt more when he realizes that I'm a bad mate and decides to leave me! That's the reason I'm holding back. I'm trying to give him an out, Kian. He doesn't need a mate like me," Layla exclaimed, her heart hurting from the confession. "And I don't need the pressure of never being good enough for him."

"Oh, Layla," Kian sighed and hugged her to him. "You are more than enough for that damn elf. Besides, Fate doesn't lie, and it says that you're perfect for each other. The Norns decreed it for you both."

"The fucking Norns. They are another reason I can't leave Norway. They said I need to stand with the elves to defeat Vili. What if I leave and he attacks and then kicks off Ragnarök? I need to see this through, Kian," Layla replied, resting her head on his shoulder.

"I understand that. I must say you're off to an interesting start," he mused. "First, you somehow managed to track down Odin and pretty much tell him he's a coward to the point he admits he won't do anything about Vili until he steps foot on Midgard. Then you go and steal from Vili, in his own keep, and tell Varg to pass on the message he's a coward as well if he doesn't come to Midgard to get Arne himself." Kian laughed, a deep chuckle that made Layla smile. "And everyone thinks that you're the sweet-natured, compliant one."

"No. I'm the strategic one, Kian," Layla said, lifting her head from his shoulder. "I won't let Vili take Arne again. I mean, there's the whole avoiding Ragnarök thing as well. But mostly, Arne doesn't deserve to be Vili's puppet and have his brain all fucked up."

"I understand entirely." Kian smiled. "Everything becomes secondary when you have a mate. The world ending included."

Layla groaned. "What should I do, Kian? I'm fucking miserable. I feel like my insides are shredding apart, but I can't be responsible for Arne's future unhappiness."

"Layla, you don't know how he feels about the matter because you refuse to talk to him. You don't know you'll make him unhappy. I know you have abysmal self-esteem, but this decision isn't only up to you. It's a choice that both of you need to make together—pursue the mating or separate as far as possible until the bond breaks."

"How far is far enough? He was all the way in Svartalfheim, and I still felt like I was being torn apart," Layla complained.

"Then it wasn't just the mating bond. Or the mark he put on you. Neither thing could cause such pain." Kian squeezed her hand. "It was your own heart in distress, dear one, and you need to admit that to yourself."

"I don't even know him," she repeated helplessly.

"Something that is easily remedied," Kian replied. "You won't ever know if you are too scared to try."

Layla let out a long sigh. She hated being so down, but was it worth it so she didn't get heartbroken in the future? It was a question that she still didn't know the answer to. She was never good at taking what she wanted, but could she live with letting it go?

19

Arne was pouring another whiskey when he felt the dark magic closing in on his apartment. With a sigh, he drained the glass and prepared himself for what was coming.

Killian exploded through his door, shadows filling the apartment with darkness. He tackled Arne to the carpet, and Arne let him.

"What the fuck did you do to my sister, elf?" he snarled, face twisted with feral anger.

"I didn't—" Arne expected the fist. It was almost a relief to have pain exploding through his face, anything to stop feeling so numb and heartbroken.

"Kill! Get off him!" Bayn shouted and yanked his brother off Arne. "Think what you're doing, you dumb shit. He's a prince, for fuck's sake."

Killian snarled in the ancient fae tongue at Bayn but didn't make a move to attack Arne again. Bayn's face hovered above him.

"Still with us, elf?" he asked.

Arne nodded, his mouth full of blood. Bayn helped him to his feet, and he stumbled to the kitchen to spit the blood out in his sink.

"Is Layla okay?" he asked hoarsely.

"No. She's a wreck from that mark you put on her!" Killian

snapped. Arne took a clean kitchen towel and held it to his bleeding nose.

"She doesn't have a mark on her. I removed it. I didn't mean to put it on her, and also, marks don't affect emotions, no matter how strong they are," he clarified.

"Then I don't get it." Killian frowned. "She's a wreck. My Layla is usually the optimistic one, and she's devastated."

Arne rubbed at his chest, the thought of her pain tearing into him further. "It's because she's fighting the mating bond. We both are."

All the anger seeped out of Killian's face. "Oh."

"Yeah."

"Shit." Killian poured himself a drink and then poured one for Arne. "Here."

Arne took the drink and had a mouthful.

"Maybe get all the details next time before you decide to go on a rampage," Bayn said and fixed himself a drink too.

"She was *crying*, Bayn. Over *him*. She went to fucking Vili's fortress without telling me. How the fuck was I meant to react?" Killian replied, slumping down into an armchair.

"I never would have let her go into Svartalfheim. You have to believe that, Killian," Arne said. He ran a hand through his hair. It was sticking up at all weird angles from how many times he had done it in the last two days.

"Sit your ass down, Arne. You're giving me chest pains just by looking at you," Bayn complained. Arne took one of the armchairs and tried to get his own feelings and words in order.

"I hated that she came for me the way she did. I was so fucking angry when I saw her in Vili's mountain. I've never been so scared in my life," he admitted.

Killian pulled a face. "Great. Now I can't be mad at you at all because you're just as sad and pathetic as she is. Of course Layla would go after you! She is an Ironwood, and for better or worse, you are her mate."

"Layla doesn't want to be my mate, and I don't blame her, Killian."

Bayn let out a pained sigh. "And that's why you've stayed away from her the last two days?" Arne nodded. "Then you are both fucking idiots."

"Still doesn't change the fact that she deserves better than me." Arne drained his drink. "I can't remember a lot of what happened when I was under Vili's enchantment, but I know enough. I killed people. Tortured them. I did it for him, and I laughed about it."

Killian and Bayn shared a knowing look. Arne knew enough about their pasts to know they weren't spotless.

"We have both been torturer and executioner in our times. We did it willingly; you did not. Layla will understand that," Bayn said.

"Knowing Layla, she's probably saying she doesn't want to be your mate because she thinks it's for the greater good," Killian added, leaning back into the couch.

"The greater good? How is *any* of this good right now?" Arne demanded. His insides felt like they had been doused in acid.

Killian rubbed at the back of his neck in frustration. "Look, it's not really my place to explain this. I love my sister, but she has a messed-up perception of herself. She thinks she's the lesser Ironwood. The fact that you're a prince will only make her feel that more."

"That...doesn't make any sense. How is she lesser in any way? The girl crossed worlds to save someone she hardly knows!" Arne said.

The very idea of Layla thinking terribly about herself made him want to scream. She had voiced objections about them in Alta because she thought they were mismatched. It was absurd. Every time they touched, it was like some missing piece finally clicked into place.

"Maybe we need to change the subject," Bayn suggested, a worried look in his eyes. "What are the elves doing to prepare for Vili?"

"My mother has told everyone of the threat, and the warriors have been assembled in Finnmark. She wants to have a meeting with all of us to discuss a plan if Vili does turn up. She also wants me to return home...with Layla," Arne explained. His mother was getting more than a little vocal about the latter.

"Why take Layla?" Killian asked, his frown returning.

"One, she's a part of the prophecy by the Norns. She needs to stand with the elves to defeat Vili. Two, she painted a big fucking target on herself by stealing me back. Varg doesn't like losing, not to mention how Vili is going to react to her challenge. Three, she is my mate, and according to elf law, she is already one of us. My mother has summoned all elves to return to Alfheimstod, our village in Finnmark.

That includes Layla," Arne explained. "I won't leave Oslo without her, but I can't force her to come either."

Killian leaned forward and flicked Arne in the forehead. "Go and talk to her, you dickhead."

"She made it clear enough she doesn't want anything to do with me."

"Yeah, well, she's an Ironwood."

Arne frowned. "So? What does that have to do with anything?"

"As someone who has mated with one of the family already, let me try to explain something to you. The Ironwoods are like tanks. Very hard and violent on the outside, and even harder to kill," Killian said. "They are taught to be tough, so when they get emotional, they turn that into anger. Really, they are super soft once you get past the ridiculous rage and the armor. Layla is as downhearted as you are."

Arne chewed his lip. "Doesn't mean she wants to be my mate."

"You're not going to find out until you nut up and go talk to her," Bayn said, nudging Arne with the toe of his boot. His phone buzzed, and he grinned when he saw the message. "Kian also says you need to go and talk to her. Like right now."

"What? Why? Is she okay?" Arne asked, sitting up straighter.

Bayn clicked his tongue as he read the message. "Nope. She told Kian that 'she thinks that if she goes through with the mating bond, you'll regret it in the future and break her heart because she'll never be enough for you.'"

"*What the actual fuck*?" Arne couldn't believe what he was hearing. "She's fucking incredible. Why—"

"We aren't the ones you need to convince," Killian said, getting to his feet. He gave Arne an encouraging pat on the head. "Sorry about breaking your face."

"It's already healed," Arne replied. "And I let you hit me."

"Sure, you did, elfling."

"Good luck," Bayn said and looked him over. "Maybe have a shower before you go."

Arne got up and headed for the bathroom. He wasn't going to stand by and let Layla think she wasn't good enough to be his mate. The absurdity of it rankled him. He was going to set her straight once and for all.

20

After Kian left, Layla put some popcorn in the microwave and finished cleaning the kitchen. Her appetite had been almost non-existent for days, but she was going to watch her comfort movies, and she couldn't do that without popcorn. She felt a bit better from talking with Kian, but she still didn't know what to do with all of her feelings for Arne.

Layla was tipping the popcorn into a bowl when the clawing and burning inside of her suddenly vanished. She rubbed at her chest, wondering what had caused it.

Bang! Bang! Bang! Layla jumped as a heavy hand pounded on the door downstairs. She went down to look through the peephole, expecting to find a client looking for Freya or a lost delivery person. She didn't expect Arne.

Shit. Now she knew why the pain in her chest was feeling better. Layla rested her head against the door, trying to breathe through her sudden dizziness. She looked through the peephole again. Arne had placed his palm on the door.

"Please, Layla, open up," he begged, and her pulse went into overdrive.

Layla didn't want to see him while in baggy sweats and a messy yoga bun, but she still opened the door. Arne was wearing another unfairly sexy knit sweater, in black this time, and the scent of fir trees and man washed over her.

The bond between them stopped its infernal squeezing, and a look of relief swept over Arne's face. He looked tired and sad, and Layla knew the last few days had been hurting him as much as her. He studied her from head to toe, a small smile curving his lips. Layla's resistance broke, and she stepped aside.

"Come in. I've just made popcorn," she said.

Arne stepped inside, and she tried not to lean in to smell him. Really, it had to be a pheromones thing that made her want to stick her face in his inky hair and breathe.

"Is Kian still here?" he asked, walking up the stairs in front of her.

"No, he left not long ago. I thought sisters were pushy, but fae brothers really win awards for their overprotective meddling," she replied, checking out his ass. She was only human. "I hope Killian wasn't too much of a dick."

"I let him get a few hits in, and it seemed to calm him down," Arne replied. "I thought you might have gone home to Ireland."

"Nope. I'm avoiding my family for the foreseeable future." Layla grabbed her bowl of popcorn and curled up on the couch. She pointed to the place beside her, and Arne dutifully sat. She offered him the bowl.

"Me too. Why are you avoiding yours?" he asked, taking some popcorn.

"I might have told Kenna that the family could go fuck itself," Layla admitted, making him choke.

"You didn't. Your mother is terrifying. Why did you do that?"

"She told me I couldn't go to Svartalfheim after you. That I didn't owe you or the elves shit. She actually commanded me to come home." Layla shrugged. "So I told her to get fucked. Now, I don't want to deal with the argument because I won't apologize."

"I would've tried to stop you going too. You really didn't owe anything to me, Layla," he said, his knee brushing against hers.

"I know. Let me ask you this though." Layla looked him dead in his golden eyes. "If Vili had taken me instead, would you have left me in the mountain?"

"No fucking chance," Arne said with a growl.

"Then quit bitching that I did the same for you."

Arne took some more popcorn but didn't eat it. "Are you going to talk about the mating thing, or am I?"

Layla's stomach filled with butterflies. "You could have told me from the start."

"I didn't want to scare you off. You had to be coerced to even talk to me after you learned Vili was my father, and by the time we were friendly again, I was kidnapped," Arne admitted. He turned slightly so he was facing her. "I wanted you to know that you had a choice, that you still do."

"Do I?" she asked, her voice breaking. "Because I've felt like I've been torn apart for days."

"Me too," he admitted, his eyes sad again. "And yes, you still have a choice. I'm not going to force you into it, Layla. If you really don't want to give this a chance, I'll make it so you never have to see me again."

Layla's throat felt like it was filled with broken glass. "I won't force you either. You know that, right? I...I don't know if I'll be good for you, Arne."

"Why do you think that? I want to understand your reasoning behind this," he said, his voice tightening with frustration. "*Please*, Layla. You tell me why you think you would be a bad mate for me... and I will tell you why I think I don't deserve you. Deal?"

"Yeah, okay. Deal." Layla looked at the bowl of popcorn. She wouldn't be able to say the truth if she was staring into his beautiful face. She owed him the truth, and maybe spelling it out for him would force him to understand. She licked her lips and pushed down her nerves.

"I'm not princess material, Arne. You deserve someone who can play that part, and so do your people. I'm human and weird. Like there's so much weirdness about me, you haven't even scratched the surface. I'm not even some great warrior to use that in my favor. I'm an average hunter at best." Layla fiddled with the ratty hem of her shirt and took a shaky breath.

"I've spent my whole like making up for my averageness by being as helpful as I can so that I have some kind of value to my extraordinary family. I feel like I have nothing of value to offer you or the elves.

And...and I'm scared when you realize that for yourself, you'll break my heart in a way that I won't ever recover from."

"Fuck, Layla," Arne whispered.

"Don't argue with me about it. You wanted to know how I felt, and that's the truth." She bumped her knee against his. "Your turn."

Arne leaned back on the couch, resting his head on the back to look up at the ceiling. Layla stared at the curve of his neck and Adam's apple, her fingers tingling with the need to touch him.

"My father is a monster, and my mother didn't know even after she mated with him," he began softly. "He is her true mate, and she still loves him despite everything he's done because that's how strong the bond is. I'm scared that one day the power I have from Vili, the beast that lives inside of me, will take over. I understand how you feel obligated to be the best you can all the time for the good of your family. To have value. I have always tried to be the perfect son and the perfect prince so that no one will think I'm anything like my father. That I'm not tainted or a liability. But what if I am? I can't remember a lot about when Vili enchanted me, but I remember enough to know I did some horrible things. He commanded me to. When he put the magic on me, he said that he would make me a monster so that I could never return to my life because everyone would hate me like they hate him."

"What a fucking asshole," Layla hissed, her temper flaring. "You are nothing like him, and you can't be responsible for whatever he made you do. It wasn't you, Arne."

He turned his head to the side to look at her. "But what if it *is* me? I don't deserve someone as kind and brave and beautiful as you to be my mate, Layla. I could be some fucked up magical time bomb, just waiting for the right moment to go off."

"You aren't Vili, Arne." Layla reached across and laid a hand on his shoulder. "You have an incredible power inside of you, but if I remember anything about Charlotte's long lectures about magic it's this—you inherit *potential*, but it's how you use it and shape it that is individual. Vili might have given you power, but only *you* can decide how to use it. He clearly wanted you to be his weapon because he can shape that potential in you. You haven't learned to use it, so it's like a blank canvas. You can still use it how you choose to, Arne."

Arne was staring at her, wide-eyed. "You really believe that?"

"I wouldn't have gone into Svartalfheim if I thought you were anything like your father or had the capacity to turn into him. I *hate* camping, Arne. Like fucking despise it. I still sucked it up and did it because I thought you were worth the bugs and the lack of showers," Layla said, and Arne began to laugh softly. "That's not even mentioning how fucking annoying Ciara and Tor are when they are all like reading the forest and following animal trails and whatever else they were doing scratching about. It was a nightmare even before we hit the mountain."

"I can imagine," he said, and his laughter eased. "What are we meant to do now?"

"I'm not sure. Wait until Vili turns up and starts a fight?"

"I meant about us, Layla. Fuck Vili."

Layla bit the inside of her cheek. "You don't think the Norns have made a cosmic mistake by making us mates?"

"The Norns don't make mistakes. Besides, even if we weren't mates, I would still want you because you are just so...you." Arne pressed his cheek to her hand that was still on his shoulder. "Please give me a chance. We can be friends first, take things as slow as you want or need. I know you feel this connection between us that goes beyond a possibility of a mating bond."

Layla stroked her thumb over his cheek, wanting him more than she had wanted anything in her life. Her self-preservation refused to let her admit it just yet. "Okay, we can hang out on a trial basis. Get to know each other better before we decide to mate officially."

"You won't regret it." Arne moved and pressed a kiss to her wrist. Her skin tickled when he breathed her in. "Why do you always smell so good? It's like chocolate and nectarines."

"I use coca butter on my skin," she said, her butterflies fluttering as she reached for the remote. "Okay, you want to know me better. We are going to start right here. I hope you got the next six to eight hours free because we are watching *The Lord of the Rings*."

"I've never seen it." Arne pulled her legs up over his lap and grabbed some more popcorn. "And there's nowhere else I'd rather be."

She smiled and pressed play. This was going to be interesting.

LAYLA SPENT a lot of the first movie watching Arne's reactions to it. He seemed to give his entire focus and didn't even try and interrupt to ask questions. She expected him to get offended by the time they hit Rivendell, but he only got a small, pleased smile on his face.

"What's that grin all about? You think Arwen is hot?" Layla asked, unable to help herself.

"It's not that." Arne's thumb stroked over the curve of her ankle, making heat streak up her leg. "You love and admire these movies, yes?"

"Yeah, obviously," she said, pointing to her Legolas shirt.

"I'm smiling because I now have a human and elf relationship you love to point to as an example. If they can make it work, we can," Arne replied.

Layla gasped. "You would use Arwen and Aragorn's love for your own nefarious plans to seduce me?"

"Absolutely." Arne's smile sent warm tingles straight to her lady parts. "And I have so many plans, Layla."

"Stop that," she said, pushing a cushion into his face. "Watch the movie."

Arne pushed the cushion away and leaned over to pause the player. "Can I ask why you love it so much?"

"Honestly?" Layla thought about it. "It's the only thing I've ever felt like it belonged to me. It's kind of hard to explain, but all my siblings have their thing that they excel at. I've never had a special ability, like Charlotte, and I was forced to train and kill even though I'm not all that fussed on hunting, like Bron and Ciara. This fantasy world was a safe place to escape to. To rest in. I have always loved the idea of running away to Rivendell, and when everything feels like it's too much, it's still a comforting place for me to land."

"Does your family know they've made you feel this way?" Arne asked, a small frown starting on his face.

"God no. They are all too caught up in their own shit to remember I exist half the time, unless they need something. It's always been that way because I've always been the quieter, easy-going one. I've never been a priority to any of them," she replied. It still made her feel shit at times, even though she had accepted it. "Going to Svartalfheim and staying here is the most rebellious thing I've ever done. It's probably why they are being so dramatic about it."

"Thank you for telling me. I like hearing why people love the things they do." Arne reached out and took her hand. "And thank you for rebelling for me."

"What can I say? I got a thing for elves," she joked lamely.

Arne kissed her fingers. "I like that about you."

Blushing, Layla pressed play again before she melted into the couch. Or she climbed on top of him. It was going to be a long movie marathon.

21

Layla woke pressed into soft wool, feeling warm and content for the first time in weeks. She mumbled sleepily and slipped her hand under the blanket. Warm skin and soft hair shifted under her.

Something is different. Layla cracked open an eye and found herself curled around Arne like a touch starved koala bear. Her hand was under his sweater on his deliciously warm abs.

A part of her knew she should probably untangle herself and wake him up. That part was smothered by the sleepy part of her that wanted to stay where she was, comfortably tucked into his side.

"What time is it?" he murmured. Layla pretended to be asleep. "I know you're awake, but I'm happy for you to stay where you are."

"Coffee," she grumbled.

"There's a nice café across the street that does excellent espresso and pastry," Arne replied, rubbing her back. "You want a breakfast date?"

Layla wanted to stay where she was, but pastry was a really good argument. She rubbed her face against him, breathing him in. She shifted her leg and felt something hard against her hip.

"Not that I'm complaining, but you might want to stop grinding against me unless you want something else for breakfast," he chuckled sleepily.

Layla had never moved so fast in her life. She leaped off him and banged her knees on the coffee table on the way up.

"Shit, fuck, I'm up," she stammered.

"Breakfast pastry it is," he sighed. Arne tucked an arm behind his tousled head, his sweater riding up enough to show her the lean stomach she was just snuggled into. His grin was decadent, and her sleep-dazed state had her staring blatantly at him.

Layla shook herself. "Shower." Arne's soft laughter followed her all the way to the bathroom.

By the time Layla had a shower, put some light makeup on for vanity's sake, and dressed in 'leaving the house' clothes, Arne had used the other bathroom to clean up and was drinking coffee.

"Morning, *vennen*. Feeling better?" he asked.

"How far did we get in the movies before I fell asleep?" she asked with a wince.

"Paths of the Dead. I kicked on while you tried to climb into my clothes."

Layla stole his coffee and had a mouthful. "Doesn't sound like something I would do. What's your verdict?"

"On the movies or you getting into my clothes? Because I enjoyed both."

Layla laughed and tried not to blush. "There's hope for you yet, Steelsinger. I thought the elves representation would annoy you."

Arne shook his head. "There are clans in Alfheim that they are similar to. I can take you to see them some time if you like."

"You're playing dirty now," she said, grabbing her leather jacket.

"I haven't even begun to play dirty."

"Stop flirting with me, or you might regret it."

Arne grinned. "I really doubt it, *vennen*."

It was way too early to deal with how hot he was when he was in a playful mood. Layla found the apartment keys. "Feed me, then flirt with me."

The cafe that Arne took Layla to was tucked into a small side street she hadn't noticed before. While she was waiting for food to be brought to her, she finally turned on her phone. Ignoring all the messages and missed calls, she brought up her text chain with Freya.

What does *vennen* mean?

Freya's typing bubble appeared almost immediately. *Now she messages back!*

Come on, just tell me. It's Norwegian right? I don't want to have to fuck about by Googling it.

It's an endearment that means like 'darling' or 'love.' Why? Who's using it...oh my gods, is ARNE WITH YOU?

Layla was rescued from answering by the waitress arriving with more coffee and a plate of pastries. Her phone buzzed, but she ignored it for the apricot Danish she tried not to stuff into her mouth all at once.

"Family bothering you?" Arne asked, raising a brow.

"Something like that. Just Freya wanting to know if I'm still in the apartment and alive," Layla said. They looked down where her phone lit up with an all-caps message.

ARE YOU FUCKING HIM?

"Oh my God, please ignore that," Layla groaned and turned her phone screen over.

"I thought Torsten was nosy," Arne replied with a soft smile.

"Try having sisters, their mates and *their* relatives as well. They wonder why I haven't dated since I met you. It's because they are ridiculous."

"I can't say I'm sad about that." Arne lowered his coffee. "Is that the only reason?"

"Hmm maybe? I might make you charm it out of me just for fun," Layla replied. The sugar and caffeine were hitting her system, and she was finally waking up enough not to be dickmatized by him.

"It's been a while since I've had to be charming," Arne said, tearing his pastry into small pieces. "I haven't dated since I met you either."

Layla quickly put food in her mouth so she wouldn't say something ridiculous. Arne opened his mouth to say something else when his phone started to ring. Alruna's picture flashed up, and he swore under his breath.

Almost instantly, Layla's phone started buzzing. It was Kenna.

"Do you think it's an emergency?" she asked, showing him her screen. A cheeky idea popped into her head. "Swap?"

"Happy to," Arne said, taking her phone.

Layla would take Alruna over a pissed off Kenna any day. "Hello, Layla speaking."

"Layla! Should I ask what you are doing with my son's phone?" Alruna replied.

"He told me to answer it. Are you and the elves, okay? Is Vili attacking?" she asked. She looked up at Arne who was smiling as he talked to Kenna.

"No, there is no sign of Vili." Alruna's pause was long and telling. "Has he convinced you to come home to Alfheimstod yet? I want you here with the elves, Layla. You are both too exposed in Oslo."

"Why? Is this about the Norns?"

"Partly, but also because you stole Arne from Vili for me, and I feel responsible for what happens to you as a result of that," Alruna replied.

"I didn't steal him just for you. You don't owe me anything."

Alruna let out a sigh that sounded too much like Arne.

"Layla, you are Arne's mate, whether you two have worked it out between yourselves or not. We need him at home, and he's not going to leave you. Do you understand that? He's chosen you already. He's just doing the courtesy of waiting for you to catch up," Alruna said. "Please come home. Don't make a queen beg."

Layla's insides turned to mush. "I wouldn't dream of it. We will come tomorrow. There are things I need to work out with my family before I run away to the elves." A laugh escaped her. "Really, they shouldn't be surprised."

"Thank you, Layla. I'll see you both tomorrow. *Early*. I will make a portal when you are ready to travel."

"Yes, my queen." Layla hung up at the same time Arne did. He looked thoughtful. "Kenna kick you in the balls?"

"She accused me of bewitching you, so I told her you are my mate, and then she swore at me a lot. She really wants you to go home," he replied.

"I'm sure she does." Layla passed him back his phone. "She's going to go off when she learns I've run away with you."

Arne's brows lifted. "You are running away with me?"

"Well, the Queen of the Light Elves has invited me to the mysterious Alfheimstod. Can't say no to a queen's request now, can I? It would be rude," Layla said, ignoring the butterflies in her stomach.

"It would be very rude," he said. Under the table, his leg brushed up against her. "When do we leave?"

"Tomorrow morning. I have to sort out what to do with Freya's apartment and probably buy some more clothes. How long do you think I'll be there for?" she asked.

"As long as you like," Arne replied with no hesitation.

Layla grinned. "How about we reassess after we deal with Vili?"

"Whatever you wish, *vennen*."

After breakfast, they stood outside, and Layla felt awkward on how to proceed.

"So your mom was insistent that we get to Alfheimstod early. Means you should probably stay with me tonight or vice versa, yeah? For practicality purposes, so you can wipe that smile off your face," she said, toying with the zipper on her jacket.

"We should definitely sleep under the same roof. For the sake of the bond and all of that," Arne said, his smile staying where it was.

"Yeah, we would want to get a good night's sleep. Can't do that with the bond keeping us awake," Layla agreed.

"Very sensible. How about I come and collect you at six?"

"Sounds good."

Arne took a step closer to her, so she had to tilt her head to look up at him. Her butterflies went into overdrive as his gaze traced her lips.

"Can I kiss you goodbye?" he asked, his voice husky.

"Please," Layla replied before she could chicken out. Arne's fingers grasped the edges of her jacket collar, bringing her close before pressing a gentle kiss to her lips. When he made to pull away, she grumbled a noise of complaint and grabbed onto him to stop him from moving.

Arne smiled before kissing her with an intensity that made her knees tremble. He nipped and sucked at her lips with just the right amount of dominance that made her want to agree to anything he asked. She wasn't embarrassed by the thought; she was okay being a power sub, especially when her partner knew what they were doing. And Arne knew *exactly* what he was doing.

He didn't seem to care that they were in public as his tongue fucked into her mouth, using it with enough precision to make Layla's panties wet.

"You keep kissing me like that, we are going to get arrested for public indecency," she murmured, pulling back for her own sanity.

"I wanted to give you something to think about for the rest of the day," Arne said, his expression completely innocent.

Layla rolled her eyes at him. "I'll see you at six, Steelsinger." She looked at him with kiss-swollen lips and ruffled hair. "You better not be late."

Arne inclined his head. "Wouldn't dream of it, *vennen*."

∽

LAYLA WAS certain that Arne wouldn't be early, so she was surprised when she heard the door to the apartment opening at four. She should have expected that she wouldn't get to slink off with the elves without a fight.

"Ah, so you are still here," Freya declared, coming up the stairs. "Is the hot elf around?"

"No. Why would he be?" Layla said.

Freya snorted and wrapped her up in an aggressively tight hug that she was famous for. "Because males are stupid when they are mating, that's why."

"We aren't mating. We are...testing out the waters."

Freya threw her head back and roared with laughter. "Oh, my darling, you actually believe that, and it's *adorable*."

Layla scowled at her. "I'm trying to be responsible here."

Freya's mismatched eyes sparkled. "Sure. Going off to Svartalfheim was *so* responsible, Layla."

And that's not even mentioning going to see Havi. Layla knew better than to mention that. Freya had hunted down the All-Father's dagger to save Bayn from his curse and would no doubt be too curious about his location. Layla still couldn't believe her hunch had been right.

"What are you doing here?" Layla asked.

"Here as in my own house? The cheek of you." Freya opened the fridge and pulled out a beer. "Don't worry. I'm not staging an intervention. I personally think it's about damn time you stood up for yourself and stopped being your family's doormat."

"Wow, Freya, don't hold back."

Freya opened a second beer and passed it to her. "I don't intend to. I love your family, but they are thoughtless on how they treat you sometimes, and it annoys me."

Layla took a mouthful of her beer. "I honestly didn't think anyone noticed."

"It annoys the boys all the time," Freya admitted.

Layla needed to change the subject before she started to get emotional. "Where is your more handsome half anyway?"

"He's gone to see Tor and Arne. They are dragging his moping ass out to Ritual. We are going to join them later," Freya replied.

"How good of you to organize my life for me. I happened to have plans tonight."

"Plans involving the sexy elf?"

"Not that it's any of your business, but yes." Layla turned red the longer Freya smiled knowingly at her. "Shut up."

"I didn't say anything, but she's going to," Freya said, gesturing with her beer. Layla turned around as shadows boiled out of thin air and a portal opened.

Imogen's lavender hair appeared. "Thanks for having us all worried, shithead."

Layla flipped her off. "Eat a dick."

"She will later," Arawan replied, coming out the portal and closing it with a cool burst of magic that didn't ruffle a single strand of his long black hair.

Layla was still a little nervous around the newest member of their family, but he so openly adored Imogen that Layla liked him immensely. He was dressed in a black button up shirt and trousers, which was about as casual as the god ever got.

Imogen in comparison was in her usual jeans, boots, and Led Zeppelin T-shirt. They would seem like a mismatched pair until you got to know them and realized they were spookily perfect for each other.

Imogen punched her arm and then hugged her until she groaned in protest.

"Help," Layla begged Arawan.

"No. She's been upset since you vanished, and I didn't appreciate it," he replied.

"Prick."

Arawan grinned. "You have bits of god power in your aura. What have you been up to?"

"Yeah, Layla, what have you been up to?" Imogen demanded, letting her go and stealing her beer at the same time.

"Nothing. I don't know what you're talking about. I have had no gods up in my aura."

"Don't lie. I can see three separate signatures, Layla," Arawan argued. He folded his arms, and Layla instantly felt like she was in trouble.

"Three! You went to a god orgy or something?" Imogen asked, waggling her brows.

"Not that kind of signature, my love. It's power. You have been around Arne and Vili, but who is the third?" Arawan squinted his dark eyes at the air above her head. He started laughing. "Well, well, you actually found the old bastard. Do we need to be worried?"

"No. It's fine," Layla replied quickly. She gave him a meaningful look. "And it's a private matter."

Arawan's smile widened. "Have you met your sister? You're better off just telling her."

Imogen was looking between them, and her eyes narrowed. "Tell me what, Lay Lay. Arawan? What's going on?"

"Oh, look at the time. I was meant to be meeting Bayn at Ritual. I'll see you there, darling."

"Hey! Don't you—" Imogen began, but Arawan blew her a kiss and vanished. Imogen let out a sound between a growl and a curse and rounded on Layla. Her eyes had gone black, a side effect of whatever power she was now sharing through her bond with Arawan. "Layla Brigid Ironwood, what the fuck have you been doing?"

Layla's ovaries shriveled, and she wet her lips. "Promise you won't tell Mom?"

The sun was down, and the three women were finishing off pizza when Layla finally finished telling Freya and Imogen everything.

"Tomorrow I'm going to stay with the elves until this is all over," she said finally. She raised her chin a little. "And you aren't going to stop me."

"Wouldn't dream of it, Lay Lay," Imogen said, opening another beer.

"Really? I thought you would tell me to use my common sense and go home to Ireland?"

Freya snorted. "Like Imogen would ever recommend using common sense."

Imogen shrugged. "It's boring, that's why. I only wanted to know what's really happening. I'm not here to stop you, sis."

"Really? You're not going to like tell me that I don't know Arne well enough to mate with him or that the Norns were high when they decided to write me into their prophecies?" she asked. Acceptance was the last thing Layla expected.

"Do you love him?" Imogen asked.

Layla turned red. "I don't know."

"Pretty sure you wouldn't have gone on a camping trip into Svartalfheim if you didn't. I know how you feel about spiders."

Layla picked at the label on her beer bottle. "It's way too early for love, right?"

Freya and Imogen shared a look. "When it's the right person, time doesn't really come into it. It takes our brains longer to catch up with what the heart automatically knows," Imogen said. She replaced Layla's empty beer. "The heart wants what the heart wants. I don't blame it wanting the elf. He's fit as fuck."

"And heroic. You should have seen the elves we rescued talk about him," Freya added, fanning herself with the back of her hand. "They got all breathy when saying his name alone. He's a good guy, otherwise his reputation would be very different. You are going to spend some time with the elves, you'll see what I mean."

It felt silly to consider love so soon, but Layla's heart had always been insistent when it came to Arne. Maybe she did just need time for the rest of her to catch up.

"Yeah, she's in love. Look at that face. I've only ever seen Layla make that face over Tolkien shit," Imogen teased. "No shame in feeling those feels, sis. Just don't run from them. We are Ironwoods. We don't run from shit."

Layla nodded. She had tried putting distance between her and Arne, and it had only made her miserable. She wasn't going to do that to herself anymore.

"It makes my heart so happy seeing you smile like that all cute. I just want to squish your cheeks," Freya crooned at her.

Layla looked between them and let out a laugh. "I thought you two would be convincing me to go home, not giving me love advice."

"Nah. This is good for you," Imogen said, putting an arm about her shoulders. "My little Layla is growing up, falling in love, taking what she wants in life. Rebelling against Mom for the first time. This is great."

Layla was still laughing when her phone buzzed. She checked the screen. Butterflies exploded in her stomach when she saw it was from Arne. There was a picture in his contact profile that he must have taken when they were at the cafe and set when she was distracted by Alruna. Sneaky elf.

Please come to Ritual and save me from unsolicited advice from fae males and a god.

Layla laughed and quickly texted back. **What's in it for me?**

Unlimited sexual favors.

Layla's brain fell offline for a few moments. She didn't know if he was joking or not. **I can already get that for myself. I learned long ago to never rely on anyone else for emotional support, money, or orgasms. What else you got?**

The text bubble appeared and vanished a few times, each time making Layla's smile widen.

How about a bow made by the elves with a quiver that magically replenishes?

"Ohhh, he's a sly bastard," Layla murmured. Freya and Imogen were snickering at her, but she ignored them.

I will throw in a massage in my hot tub for free, Arne added.

Layla went warm from her toes to her ears. It seemed like a really good time to start taking what she wanted. She looked up at her smirking sisters. "Looks like I have a pressing need to go to Ritual."

Imogen snorted. "I bet you do, hussy."

22

Arne let the noise of Ritual wash over him and drown out all the voices of doubt in his head. Bayn and Tor had turned up at his apartment two hours beforehand and declared they were in need of drinks before Arne, Layla, and Tor headed back to Finnmark.

They had gotten their first round when the god of the dead turned up.

"Thanks for outing me in front of everyone, asshole," Arne said because he was still dirty about it.

Arawan only smiled a too sharp, unrepentant smile. "Ironwoods don't like lies, little demi-god. I did you a favor. Better to get these things out in the open, trust me on that."

Arne had a mouthful of his vodka so he didn't say something he would regret. He thought of waking up with Layla's arms and legs tangled around him, and it soothed his frayed edges. Despite Arawan's meddling, things had begun to work themselves out. Layla knew his biggest fear about Vili's power inside of him and still had curled up with him, unafraid.

"Have you convinced her to accept the mating bond yet?" Bayn asked.

Tor snorted. "No."

"He wasn't asking you, wolf," Arne said.

"Doesn't matter. The answer is still the same," Tor replied. He tapped his nose like a smug bastard. "Her scent is on you, but it's not sexual."

"Lucky for you," Bayn said, eyes narrowing.

Arne fought not to groan in frustration. Gods save him from overprotective fae brothers. "If you must know Layla and I are taking things slow."

"Hmm better not be too slow or Von is going to beat you to it," Bayn mused and pointed. At the bar beneath them, Freya, Imogen, and Layla were chatting with Ritual's charismatic owner. He put his arm around a smiling Layla, and Arne's vision hazed.

"Deep breaths. He's a friend, remember?" Bayn called after Arne. He barely registered it, his legs already moving through the crowd and down the stairs.

The mating bond pulsed inside of him with every step he got closer to Layla.

Arne's magic tingled in his fingertips, and Von yelped as his arm was telepathically removed from Layla before he floated five feet away from her. She saw Arne and gave him an exasperated smile. Arne lowered Von back to his feet.

"What the Hel, Arne? I was just saying hello," the blonde-haired Viking complained.

Arne bopped him on the nose. "Mine."

"Then how about you bring someone in who's single for once?" Von complained.

Arne ignored him, turning to a still grinning Layla. "You came."

"You were very convincing." Layla sipped her martini. "And I really want an elvish bow for my collection. Will you dress up as Galadriel when you give it to me?"

"All depends. Will you dress up as Legolas?" he replied, moving into her space. Layla bit her bottom lip, her cheeks flushing.

"Wow. This is the nerdiest foreplay I've ever seen," Imogen said, leaning against the bar. "If you start stroking his pointed ears and purring, I'm out."

Layla's brown eyes flicked to the ears in question. "I do like your pointy bits."

"I know," Arne replied. His fingers brushed against hers, the small contact sending a thrill up his arm.

Imogen let out a loud laugh. "You two are gross. I'm going to find Arawan and kiss his face."

"And you say we are gross," Layla replied. Imogen made kissing faces at her and vanished in the crowd. Freya and Von had already gone somewhere.

"Imogen and Freya hounding me for details about us was so damn exhausting. A few weeks away, and I forgot how loud and pushy my family is," Layla said. She surprised Arne by leaning her head against his chest. "I can honestly say I'm ready to run away to the elves just for the peace and quiet."

Arne put his arms around her, his fingers skimming underneath her black lace top to touch her soft skin. "Me too. I like the idea of having you to myself without any fae princes interfering to growl or hiss at me whenever I look at you."

Layla lifted her head, her hand resting on his stomach. "Really? And how are you looking at me that they would feel the need to growl at you?"

"Possessively," Arne admitted. He leaned down to whisper in her ear. "I'm happy to have this go as slow as you need, *vennen*, but make no mistake. I'm not going to give up until I've claimed you."

Layla's hand clenched the fabric of his shirt. "That sounds like a threat."

"A threat, a promise, a vow, take your pick." Arne skimmed his lips over the soft curve of her ear. "It all means the same thing."

"So the emotional confessions and fan girling last night didn't turn you off?" She sounded so vulnerable like she was worried he would reject her over such things.

"There's nothing about you that turns me off," Arne assured her. He could spend all night telling her the ways he admired her. He didn't want to scare her away again, and she seemed to find it hard to take a compliment at the best of times.

Layla tilted her head a little, giving him her throat in a submissive gesture that had his dick hardening and the beast side of him growling with approval.

Arne pressed a kiss to her fluttering pulse and breathed in her warm scent. Layla made a soft whimpering sound, and it made him want to pin her down on the nearest table and see what other sounds he could get her to make. She was going to drive him crazy, and he would happily embrace insanity.

"I'm scared what will happen if I give into this," Layla admitted.

"I know." Arne pressed a line of soft kisses over the curve of her jaw. "I'll give you whatever you need to reassure you that I'm not going to hurt you, Layla. I only need the opportunity."

Layla didn't look at him, but she did curl closer until she was pressed into his chest. "I'm...I'm really bad at asking for things that I want, so you'll just have to be patient with me, okay?" she admitted, her hand drifting under his shirt.

"I will be, *vennen*. If you want anything from me, you don't even have to ask. Just take it if it's easier for you. I'll give it to you."

Layla rose up on her tip toes and kissed him, her full lips maddeningly soft against his. "What if I want you to be in control because I don't want to be?"

"Fuck, Layla. Be careful what you offer me in public," Arne groaned and ground against her so she could feel how hard he was. "This will be problematic if you keep talking."

Layla laughed huskily. "Maybe I just want to give you something to think about, like you did to me today."

"And did you think about me?" he asked with a wicked smile.

"Maybe a little." Layla glanced up at him. "Do you still think it's a good idea to spend the night together? We do have an early start after all."

"Stay with me," Arne said quickly. He looked over at where Freya and Bayn and the others were laughing and drinking. "They are going to need her apartment so there won't be room for us."

"True." Layla's lips twitched. She looked about at the crowded club. "I'm about tapped out with the noise and people. Do you want to get out of here?"

Arne took her hand. "More than anything. Should we tell them?"

"Nah, let them wonder where we've gone. If they get angry about it, I'll just say it was your idea to sneak out," Layla replied, placing her empty glass on the bar. "You're just such a bad influence on me. I was so well behaved until you came along."

Arne laughed. "I think you just needed some good enough excuses to rebel."

"Or one really handsome one," Layla replied and pulled him into the crowd towards the exit.

Happiness bloomed in his chest, and Arne wondered what else he could bring out in her.

23

They detoured past Freya's to grab Layla's bags before they headed back to Arne's apartment. Arne didn't let go of her hand the whole time, and there was an easiness in it that Layla didn't expect.

That feeling vanished as soon as she stepped into his home and anticipation coiled inside of her. Layla shouldn't have been surprised that it was stylish in a way that only Scandinavia could be—lots of warm wood surfaces, and dark maroons and blues that gave everything a masculine feel.

"Nice place," she said, eyes gravitating to the bookshelves.

"You seem surprised," Arne said, taking off his leather jacket and rolling up his sleeves. Layla stared at his masculine forearms a little bit too long.

"Ah, no? Not surprised. Just happy you're a clean person because I don't like a mess," she stammered out. He helped her out of her jacket, and the gesture made her even more flustered. She wished she had one seductive bone in her body instead of saying the first thing in the front of her mind.

Take what you want, Layla. She could totally do this.

"Layla? What's wrong? You've gone adorably red," Arne asked, a slow smile creeping along his face. "Are you having naughty thoughts?"

"I'm allowed to," she replied.

Arne went over to a fireplace and turned it on, the flames leaping to life. He lifted a decanter. "Drink?"

"Yes. Good idea," Layla replied. Maybe some alcohol would make her feel braver.

Arne passed her a glass. "The elves make this vodka. Let me know what you think of it."

"Elves who make vodka. Be still my beating heart," Layla replied and sipped. It was smooth as silk down her throat, leaving a burning taste of berries on her tongue. "Ohh, what is that?"

"Cloud berries," Arne replied. He brushed his thumb over her cheek. "Why don't you tell me what has you so nervous all of a sudden, hmm?"

Layla took another sip. Fuck it. She was a big girl; she could say words. Nope. She had a bigger mouthful of vodka. "Ithinkweshouldhavesex," she said without taking a breath.

Arne's glass paused halfway to his mouth. "Did... Did I just hear you say we should have sex? Layla Ironwood. I'm speechless."

Layla was so red she was sure she was hotter than the fire beside them. "You can say no."

"I'm absolutely not going to say no. Though I'm curious to know what's brought this on."

Layla gestured at him. "All that you're rocking isn't enough? I mean, have you looked at yourself in a mirror lately?"

"Layla," he said, a touch of a command in his tone. Fuck, the way he said her name like that made her melt.

"I want you, okay? I told you at the club, I'm bad at asking for what I want, especially when it comes to sex." Layla tried not to fidget, but she still did anyway. "I did a lot of thinking today, and I do really want to give this—*us*—a chance, and that also means I have to get over certain hang ups, and that includes having sex."

Two fingers slid along her jaw, and Arne tilted her chin up, so she was forced to look at him. His golden eyes were simmering with a desire that made her breath catch.

"In the club, you said you wanted me in control," he said, voice dropping. "Is that what you would like?"

Layla's heart was threatening to burst from her chest. She nodded.

"I like...I like other people taking control in the bedroom. I like not having to think because all I do is fucking *think*."

"How fortuitous. I happen to like being in control, and I can be quite vocal about it." Arne brushed his lips over hers, and her thighs pressed together at the pressure already building between them.

"I know. Your eyes flashed gold in the club when I mentioned it," Layla replied. "That side of you doesn't scare me, Arne. It's a part of you, and I want it."

Arne made a sexy sound in the back of his throat that made Layla kiss him as gently as he had her. "Is there anything you don't like?"

Layla thought about it. "I'm pretty open to anything except water sports, and don't make fun of my body. It took me a long time to accept it, and I don't want to ever go back to that place of being ashamed of it."

"I would never want you to be ashamed of something so fucking beautiful," Arne growled. He cupped her face, and kissed her cheeks, her nose. "Every part of you is so perfect, it drives me mad how much I want you."

"Show me how much," Layla said, leaning into his embrace. She could feel the hard line of his erection, and she brushed against it.

Arne hissed. "Naughty. I thought you wanted me in control?"

"I do." Layla wanted him inside of her more with each passing second. She couldn't believe she had a real chance with this gorgeous elf in front of her.

"Good." Arne stepped back from her and refilled his glass. He sat down on an armchair and studied her from head to toe. The look he was giving her made her want to agree to anything he asked. Layla drained her vodka to try and help with the nervous excitement dancing through her.

Arne leaned back in his chair. "Take your clothes off but leave your underwear on," he said, the commanding prince back in his tone.

Layla wished she had put on nicer lingerie, but she was in her plain black cotton set. Oh well. What was a girl to do?

Layla put her glass down and pulled her lace top off over her head. Arne's eyes flicked over her breasts, and Layla went hot again. She unbuttoned her jeans and shimmied out of them. She ignored the reflex to cover herself, to try and hide the curved softness of her tummy that never went away no matter how much core work she did.

Arne's eyes flickered with power and lust as he took her in. His energy had shifted, and she felt like she was trapped. It probably shouldn't have made her as wet as it did.

Arne drained his vodka and widened his legs. "Come here, my beautiful Layla."

Layla moved in between them but didn't reach out for him. She waited, letting him look at her.

"Turn." Arne's finger made a circling motion. If Layla thought it was nerve-racking having eye contact, not being able to see his expression made her pulse triple. Arne brushed the back of his hand down her spine, sending goosebumps skittering along her skin.

"Bend over," he said, and Layla's face flamed, but she didn't hesitate. "So obedient, my precious mate."

Arne's hands glided up the backs of her legs, his strokes comforting and arousing at once. He squeezed her hips, and Layla jumped as the warm heat of his mouth seeped through her cotton panties.

"Oh, gods," she whimpered, her knees trembling.

Arne's answering growl vibrated through her pussy. His fingers looped around the sides of her panties, and he dragged them slowly down her legs.

"Fuck. Look at that gorgeous cunt." Arne's voice sounded strained. Layla had never felt so exposed or so aroused in her life. His fingers stroked over her skin and spread her. "So wet for me already, and I've barely touched you."

The first lick of Arne's tongue against her had them both moaning. Layla had to grip her shins to stop herself from falling forward. Arne held her hips to keep her steady and buried his face into the heart of her.

Layla couldn't do anything but try and breathe as his tongue, teeth, and lips nipped and sucked. It was too much, pleasure drowning her senses and making her see stars. Her pussy clenched, needing to be filled, begging for the release he was edging her towards.

Arne pressed his tongue inside of her, and Layla cried out, unable to hold it in. His finger circled her clit, the pressure breaking her. Layla moaned, high and keening as her orgasm scorched her insides like lava.

"You taste like heaven, my mate. I could eat you for hours, but I need to be in you before I come untouched," Arne said, his voice a husky purr.

Through her daze, Layla felt the burn of magic against her bare skin and his clothes vanished. He pressed two fingers into her, curling them on the way out.

"I'm going to use all of this delicious wetness to slick myself down, and then I'm going to make you take every inch of me."

Arne's hands gripped her waist and guided her back onto his wet cock. Layla groaned as he stretched her and pulled her into his lap at the same time. Arne's chest was hot against her back as he held her steady and let her adjust to having him filling every part of her. Arne lifted her legs over his and held her tight against him.

He kissed and licked his way over her neck and shoulder. "Okay?"

"Y-Yes." Layla gripped his forearms to steady herself.

Arne cupped her heavy breasts, fingers teasing her nipples and making her gasp as pleasure pain danced through her. One hand turned her face. His pupils were blown out, his expression worshipful.

"Kiss me, Layla."

She did, her hands slipping behind her head to touch his silky hair. He rocked his hips, his dick shifting in her, so she moaned straight into him. Arne's tongue licked and explored her, his kiss bruising in its intensity. He pulled back and kissed her shoulders, the base of her neck.

"Now, show me how well you can fuck," he demanded, leaning back in the chair.

Layla gripped his legs to steady herself and began to roll her hips, pushing herself back and riding his perfect dick. Any nerves she had remaining were obliterated as her body took over, demanding more of him. She needed him hard and deep inside of her.

She could feel the bond between them singing with every slap and pant. Sex had never been this good, this *right*. Arne's hands gripped her hips, dragging her back against him in a maddening rhythm.

"Touch us, Layla," he said raggedly. He widened his legs, spreading her. "Touch that delicious little clit of yours." Layla's hand dropped to her wet pussy, stroking them both as his dick thrust in and out of her. Arne murmured something in elvish, so she added some pressure.

"Fuck," he groaned. He leaned forward so he could see over her shoulder. "Look at how fucking sexy you are, Layla. Look how well you take me, how we fit together."

Layla looked, saw her swaying breasts, the curves of her stomach, her swollen pussy riding him. It was the most erotic thing she had ever seen. Her pussy clenched around him.

"Oh gods, I'm going to come, Arne."

"Did I say you could?" he growled.

Layla wanted to cry, the pressure was too much for her to take. Arne moved her hand out of the way and replaced it with his own. The heat of his palm seeped right through her, making her cry out.

"Please, please, let me come."

"Fuck, you even beg so sweetly. Call me your mate, and you can come," Arne snarled in her ear, his teeth catching on her lobe. "I want to hear you say the words, Layla, and we'll go together."

Layla's nails had scratched up his legs trying to hang on. She felt the magic between them, the bond that was calling to her louder every day. There was a flicker of feral rebellion in her, so she picked up her pace, riding him hard enough that stars danced in her vision. Arne growled, his own self-control getting ragged as his dick swelled even bigger inside of her.

"My beautiful mate, let me come on your cock," she pleaded.

"Oh, fuck, Layla." Arne gripped her pussy tight, his dick driving up into her, and she was gone. Layla exploded with light, her orgasm tearing her apart.

Arne was shaking, his release painting her insides with heat and making her clench around him, holding onto him while he clung to her.

Layla collapsed back against his sweaty chest, unable to form a word let alone a sentence. Arne brushed a damp lock of hair back from her face and kissed her cheek tenderly.

"My precious, precious, Layla," he murmured against her skin. "I'm going to make you so happy that you're never going to want to leave me."

Layla turned her head so she could see the god power in his eyes. He couldn't hide the possessiveness in his gaze. It should have freaked her out, but Layla had never felt so wanted, so cherished.

"I'm going to hold you to that, Steelsinger." She kissed him softly until his eyes changed back to their normal amber.

"Still worried about our chemistry?" he asked with a teasing smile.

Layla laughed. "I'm currently more worried about not being able to walk to the shower on my own."

"I'll help. I want to take care of you," Arne said, both of them moaning when he slipped free from her. With his hands on her hips, he guided her to a black tiled bathroom and turned on the shower.

Layla was floating in post orgasm bliss as Arne soaped up a soft cloth and ran it over her skin. He was as perfect naked as all of her wet dreams had imagined. His long lean muscles were covered in a fine dusting of dark hair. He had elvish runes tattooed on his back in a swirling pattern.

"I love this," she said, licking water off his inked skin. "I was worried that the elves would look down their noses at my tattoos."

"Why? They are beautiful," Arne replied, tracing his fingers over them. "The elves have a deep tattoo tradition. Who do you think taught it to the Vikings and the Nordic tribes? All of Tor's tattoos are elvish done. If you want, I can introduce you to one of the ink shamans in Alfheimstod."

"*Ink shamans*," Layla gasped over the title. "I might never leave."

Arne pulled her close. "That's the plan."

24

Layla woke to a warm kiss on her cheek, and steaming coffee wafted under her nose. She cracked an eye and was greeted with the mouthwatering sight of Arne in a pair of black pajama pants and no shirt.

"Morning, *vennen*. How did you sleep?" he asked, stroking the hair from her face.

"Like the dead. Someone banged me unconscious," Layla mumbled, reaching for her coffee. It was hot and perfect. When she groaned, the tips of Arne's ears went pink in the most adorable way. "What time is it?"

"About eight. We should probably get a move on. We can grab some breakfast when we get there," he said. He looked over her. "I would prefer to stay in bed with you, but my mother has already been sending me insistent messages."

It was Layla's turn to blush. "Ah, responsibility calls."

"Yes. She's going to open a portal for us to get us there sooner. It's a twenty-hour drive otherwise, and she's impatient."

"Portals are so handy," Layla yawned. She sat up and stretched. Arne stared at her bare chest with a hungry eye. "Hey, don't look at me like that, or we will never get anywhere."

Arne shook himself. "You're right. I'm going to go shower in the other bathroom. If I go with you, I'll have to fuck you again." He kissed her forehead and quickly moved out of the room, a telling bulge in his pants. Layla grinned, happy that he had that reaction to her even when she was looking like a tangle-haired witch.

They showered in record time and were getting ready to leave when Tor came in.

"Woah, gods what did you do in here," he complained. His eyes went straight to the armchair. "You're going to have to throw that thing out. It smells like fucking in here."

"Try not to be too jealous," Arne said and grabbed his keys.

Layla giggled at Tor's expression. "What are you doing here?"

"I had Alruna ring me to come and make sure you two were awake. I'm going to come with you through the portal, and then I'll go see the Ulfheðnar. They are getting twitchy now that they know that Varg is working with Vili," Tor replied.

"Try and get them ready for a teleconference this afternoon. We need to get Kian and the Ironwoods online too and make a plan," Arne said, taking Layla's hand.

"Have you heard from Ciara how her hunt went?" Tor asked.

Layla raised a brow. "No, but she tends to fall off the grid when she's working. Why? You're not worried, are you?"

"Not even a little," Tor said, putting his hands in his pockets. "It's just that Varg saw her, and we need to assume that he will target her too."

"Good luck to him if he does. She'll make a great rug for the Ironwood mansion out of his hide," Layla replied and took out her phone. "I'll text you her number. Maybe send her a message. She might be more inclined to answer you because you aren't family."

"I doubt it, but I will anyway." Tor went back to his apartment to grab his gear, leaving Layla smiling after him.

"I suppose you better call your mother. It seems like she's waiting."

"She wants to see if we are mated and is going to be nosy about it," Arne huffed. "Just ignore her if it gets too much."

"Ignore the queen? Never." Layla gasped playfully.

"You have no issues ignoring me, and I'm a prince."

Layla pulled him down for a kiss. His hands moved over the curves of her ass and squeezed in a way that made her brain hazy.

"What was that for?" he asked.

"Just because." Layla stroked the tips of his ears and pressed another kiss to his lips. "We better get going."

Arne let out a tight breath. "The sooner we get there, the sooner I can get in you."

"How confident of you that you will get another shot at all of this," Layla teased, gesturing to herself. "I might make you work for it."

"That is your right, *vennen*, but once you give in, don't think I won't make you pay for it."

Gods. Layla was still blushing when Tor returned.

"I'm glad I'm going back to the wolves if you two are going to be this ridiculous," he snorted.

Arne rang Alruna, and within minutes, a glowing white and silver portal appeared in the middle of the living room.

"Finally," Alruna said on the other side of it. "Lovely to see you again, Layla."

"My queen," Layla replied, steeping out of one of Arne's homes and into another. She moved out of the way to let Arne and Tor through, her eyes trying to take in her new surroundings. She was in a modern style log house, with wide windows to look out at the forest around them. There was a large deck and a small jetty that jutted out into a lake.

"Cool place," she murmured. The inside was much to Arne's taste —wood furniture, jewel tones, and beautiful wrought iron light fittings. A large fireplace was already burning, and an honest-to-God black bearskin rug was in front of it.

The things I could do on that. Layla did her best to keep all the naughty thoughts off her face.

"I'm glad you like it," Arne said from behind her.

Alruna was speaking in low tones to Tor on the other side of the room, so Layla gave Arne's hand a quick squeeze. She didn't know how open he wanted to be around his mother or the other elves, but she was finding it hard not to touch him in some way at all times. Arne's eyes heated, and Layla's mouth went dry.

"Layla, I want you to reach out to your brothers. As soon as we can organize this teleconference the better," Alruna called, making Layla take a hasty step back from Arne.

"Mama, we haven't even eaten yet," he complained.

Alruna put her hands on her hips. "Is it my fault you don't know how to feed yourselves? This can't wait, my eagle. I have been patient enough with you two dancing around each other."

Layla giggled as Arne started muttering something in Norwegian. She pulled out her phone. "It's okay. I'm on it. We can grab some food after."

"See? At least your mate has common sense," Alruna said.

"Potential mate," Layla replied. Arne glared at her in a way that promised all kinds of trouble for that comment. "I better make these calls."

She stepped out of the glass doors and onto the wide deck. The air was cold, but the sun was shining, so it was tolerable.

"Layla, have you made it to the elves safely?" Kian answered on the first ring.

"Just arrived. Alruna wants to have a meeting this afternoon if we can arrange it. She's tense. I think she's really expecting Vili to act soon," Layla replied.

"It will be done. Are you talking with Kenna yet, or would you like me to give her the details?" he asked.

Layla kicked her boot against the railing. "I would like you to because I'm your favorite sister ever."

"Hmm, you all claim that when you want something," Kian replied. "How is everything going with Arne? Have you mated officially yet? Imogen has already been gossiping to Elise about how you two were last night at Ritual."

"Shocking," Layla replied drolly. "As I told them, we are taking our time. There are too many bigger things to worry about right now."

"Layla, this is the biggest thing. It is the most important decision you'll ever make in your life."

"That's why I'm not going to agree to it until we are both ready."

"If you say so. Let's aim for three this afternoon, shall we? It will give me time to track everyone down," Kian said and rang off.

Warm arms slid around Layla. Arne kissed the back of her head. "Everything okay?"

"Yeah, we are on for three."

"Excellent. It will give us some time to show you around. Tor will be back later, and my mother is insisting we go to her place for dinner tonight. It's a short walk that way," Arne said, pointing at a path that led through a grove of birch trees. Layla leaned back into him, enjoying his warmth at her back. "You're trusting me a lot to come here on your own, and I want you to know I appreciate it. I already feel calmer having you behind the elves warding, but I want you to tell me if you start to feel overwhelmed at all. This is a lot, I know, and..."

Layla turned in his arms and kissed the side of his neck where she could reach. "I'm happy to be here, Arne. If I feel like it's getting too much, I am an expert at slipping away for a few moments."

"I still appreciate you taking the chance." Arne kissed the tip of her nose. "Now, let's get you some breakfast."

Layla's stomach growled with uncanny timing. "Sounds like the perfect plan."

∽

ALFHEIMSTOD WAS a large village spread out around a lake. It wasn't on any maps because the borders were impossible for humans to find without the leave of one of the residents.

According to Arne, Ulfheim, the Ulfheðnar village, was ten kilometers away and guarded the main road leading into Alfheimstod.

Layla and Arne had walked together down to a café for breakfast on the lake. They received a lot of curious looks from other elves, but no one seemed to look disgusted that their prince was seen hand in hand with a human. It made Layla relax a little more.

In many ways, it was like many of the other villages Layla had seen in Norway, with picturesque houses and pretty gardens, but with a strong Viking village flair with triangular houses made of wood that had heavily carved decorative beams and awnings. One of things that surprised her the most was that everyone was on foot.

"There are only a few roads, that's why. Everything is so central that most of us walk everywhere," Arne explained. They stopped in front of a blacksmith's workshop. "I need to go in here and check on an order."

"I haven't forgotten that you promised me a bow either," Layla said with a cheeky wink.

"Then you are going to love this." Arne opened the door to the workshop and called out in Elvish. Seconds later, a tall, fair-haired and ash-smudged elf appeared.

"My prince, it's good to have you back. Though now I understand why you have been away for so long," the blacksmith said, giving Layla a smile. "Looks like your measurements for her are going to be spot on."

Layla's eyes narrowed. "What measurements?"

"For the armor," the blacksmith said and waved them through. "Come, I'll show you how it's coming together."

Layla's heart squeezed. "You...you are having elvish armor made for me?"

"Of course I am." Arne smiled bashfully. "It was going to be a courting present, but now it might be getting used sooner than expected. I wanted to give you something that you might want, and you don't strike me as a jewelry person. I want my mate as safe as possible. What's the matter? Why are your eyes filling?"

"Happy tears." Layla threw her arms around him, squeezing him tight. "I honestly think you're the only person who has ever understood me in my entire life."

Arne's arms tightened around her. "You keep saying nice things like that, and I'm going to have to get him to throw in some daggers as well."

Layla laughed and then hurried to follow the blacksmith. It was hot in the forge, Layla's skin pricking with sweat in seconds.

"Now this is your breastplate," the blacksmith said, holding up the piece. "It'll be shiny when it's done, but right now it's still in process. Now that I can get final sizing, it should be finished in the next day or so."

Layla's excitement overpowered her sappy feelings as she touched each piece, admiring the craftsmanship even with unfinished items. Arne watched her chatting, a small indulgent smile on his face that made her insides happy.

I love you, the words had almost escaped her mouth more than once. She hung onto them despite her joy. Arne's steady golden gaze could probably read it anyway.

"Thank you, Arne. Really. I've never had anyone give me such a thoughtful gift," she said once they were back outside in the cool air.

Arne kissed her hand. "I told you I'm going to do everything I can to make you happy, Layla. You only have to give me the chance."

⁓

Hours later, Layla sat beside Arne and Alruna in a brightly lit conference room. Tor came in just as they were dialing in Kian and Kenna.

"I'm not late, am I?" he asked, slipping into the chair beside Layla. He looked windswept and a little sweaty.

"Did you run here?" she whispered.

Tor nodded. "Was faster than driving. Ciara didn't message me back, but she's seen it."

"Then it's up to her," Layla replied and patted his arm. Her stomach tightened when Kenna's face appeared on screen with Imogen beside her.

"Layla, I see you're well despite not knowing how to pick up a phone or obey orders," she said coolly.

"Is this really the time?" Layla sighed, her face starting to burn.

Kenna ignored her. "Queen Alruna, mother to mother, I would ask you to please send my daughter home to Ireland where she will be safe."

"Respectfully, that's Layla's decision. She is a grown woman," Alruna replied steadily and gave Layla a small nod. Layla steeled her nerves and faced her mother.

"I've always put the Ironwood family and your needs first, Mom. I've never done anything for myself. I am *done* feeling like a secondary character in my own life." Layla took a steadying breath. "I'm staying with Arne and will be standing with the elves in this fight like the Norns predicted. That's the only way we will win against Vili, and this is where I want to be."

Kenna turned red and opened her mouth to object, but Arne beat her to it.

"Lady Ironwood, Layla will be safer here than anywhere on the planet," he said, his hand finding hers under the table. "We are also mating, and as my mate, Layla is now a princess of the elves. Her place is right here, beside me, with our people."

Layla's mouth fell open as her heart exploded.

"Oh my God, look at her face. She's never coming home now, Mom. Just accept it," Imogen said, laughing loudly. "Layla has been waiting to be an elvish princess her entire life."

Layla only had eyes for Arne. "I'm going to kiss you so hard later, it's going to get gross," she whispered.

"I hope so." Arne winked at her. He turned back to their audience. "Now, can we please get on with this council?"

25

Layla stood in front of the bathroom mirror and nervously fidgeted with the sleeves of her black sweater. It was only meant to be a casual dinner with Alruna, but she was still nervous as hell.

The council had agreed that everyone would ready their warriors and wherever Vili showed his face first, the others would join as reinforcements. Kian also had informed the human governments of the threat and would pass on any information they had on any of Varg's followers still in Europe.

Layla had let the conversation wash over. She still felt like she had been punched in the chest with Kenna trying to treat her like a child and Arne and Alruna backing her up.

She always felt awful after standing up for herself, but she had meant what she had said. She wouldn't leave Arne and the elves just because Kenna wanted her back under her thumb. Her mother might not believe in the Norns, but Layla had seen the heart of the World Tree. She knew what Vili was brewing in his mountain fortress. She wouldn't run away from the fight or Arne. She wouldn't let Vili touch Arne ever again.

My mate.

Arne had looked her mother in the eye and told her straight. To have Arne openly claim her meant more to her than she realized.

Layla fidgeted with her sweater again and made sure her makeup was perfect. She still didn't know if she was what was good for the elves, but she knew that Arne was good for her, so she had to do her best to win Alruna over. If the queen had no objection to her, then hopefully none of the other elves would.

Arne was drinking a beer when Layla finally came out the bedroom. His eyes widened. "You look amazing."

"Thanks," she said and took his beer. She had a mouthful. "I'm nervous."

"Don't be. It's only my mother," Arne replied. His fingers skimmed over the hem of her top. "Oh gods, this is so soft I want to rub my face on it."

"You're trying to distract me," she said, going hot.

"I was thinking you are trying to distract me."

Layla removed his roaming hand from under her sweater and wrapped her fingers around his. "Please don't make me wet before going to dinner with your mother."

"Is that what's happening in those tight jeans?" Arne grinned and leaned over to whisper in her ear. "I'm thinking of all the things I'm going to make you do tonight with that sinful red mouth."

Layla's whole body shivered. "Help me get through this dinner, and I will give you whatever you want."

"Deal," he said, changing demeanor instantly.

"Jerk. You did that on purpose," she grumbled.

"Of course I did. You're forgetting I'm playing to win, *vennen*." Arne opened the side door and pulled her into the chill air. It helped cool her too hot body and get her brain back onto neutral things that didn't involve licking Arne's sleek muscles.

The sun was setting over the lake, the solar lights along the path of white stones flickering to life. Layla didn't doubt that Arne could find his way in the dark. The trees were birch and others she didn't recognize.

"Seems like a good forest to get lost in. And before you laugh and say it's impossible, I am hopeless with trees and stuff. I get lost on the Ironwood property all the time."

"I'd hunt you down if you did," Arne said with a teasing smile.

"Oh gods, you don't have a weird primal elf hunting kink, do you?"

Arne laughed. "No. Hunting kinks is more Torsten's thing. Why do you think he's so fascinated by Ciara. She is literally so good, she can hunt wolves to ground and then kill them. He hates that it turns him on."

"Holy shit. I've never put that together."

"Please don't tell her. Those two are only just starting to be civil to each other."

Layla snickered. "No way am I going to tell her. It's going to be so much funnier for me to watch it play out." More lights from a house grew through the trees. "What's it like living next door to your mom? Aren't you worried she would randomly drop by when you're getting naked with someone?"

"It's never been an issue because I've never had a sexual partner in my house here," Arne replied.

"What? Why?"

"Because this is my family home. I haven't ever wanted to bring someone here that I wasn't serious about, and until you, I've never been serious about anyone."

"Oh. That makes me feel unexpectedly special," Layla said.

Arne wrapped an arm around her and kissed her temple. "You *are* special. You should know that by now."

"It's one of those things that will take me a while to get used to. I've always been the not special one in the family. I know you don't get it, that's okay, but it's something that I'll have to work through," she said, feeling awkward trying to explain it.

Arne tightened his grip on her. "Don't worry. I'll be here to remind you every day until you do get used to it."

"Gods, you really are perfect, aren't you?"

Arne's smile was a slash of white in the growing shadows. "Perfect for you is very different from being perfect."

Layla hadn't expected Alruna to be in a castle, but she did expect something bigger than the house they came to. It was gorgeous, built in the same design as some of the other houses she had seen in the village. It was a log home with carved wooden arches and beams painted in a dark red. Warm light burned inside, showing Alruna working in the kitchen.

"I don't know why I thought she would be in a bigger place," Layla said.

"What's the point when it's only her now that I've left? She always has friends staying, but she's never wanted a mansion. There are other places in the village that visiting dignitaries can stay in. At the end of the day, she likes her privacy."

"It's her sanctuary," Layla said, understanding that impulse. Living in a big family meant she had to take her quiet moments where she could get them.

Arne made to move for the doors, but Layla pulled him back. "What is it?"

"Can I have a kiss for courage?" she asked.

"You don't need courage. She's going to love you." Arne lifted her chin. "And you never have to ask for a kiss." He embraced her sweetly, the anxiety inside of her loosening at the touch.

When they finally made it inside, Alruna greeted them with cheek kisses.

"Layla, you can come talk to me in the kitchen. Arne, can you please go chop some extra wood?" Alruna asked.

"Sure, Mama." Arne looked at her suspiciously, but his mother only smiled sweetly.

"Are you sure there isn't anything I can help you with?" Layla asked. The kitchen was filled with delicious smells, a pile of salad ingredients beside a chopping board.

"Everything is done really. I only want the company." Alruna pointed at the kitchen counter stools for Layla to sit on. She placed a chilled glass of beer in front of her.

Layla turned with the first hard thud of ax against wood. She peered out of the window and spotted Arne, his shirt off to keep wood chips off it. He had his tattooed back to them, his inked muscles flexing with every swing. Layla's mouth watered.

I get to kiss that whenever I like, she thought, joy running through her.

"I want to thank you again for going to rescue him," Alruna said. Layla jumped and quickly spun about so she wouldn't ogle the hunky man show in front of his mother.

"You're welcome, but thanks really aren't necessary. He's my... Arne," Layla fumbled, not knowing exactly how to classify him.

Alruna raised an ashen brow. "Can I ask why you still haven't agreed to mate with him? You two are very comfortable, and it's obvious your bond is strong."

"Arne is amazing. It's me who's unsure," Layla replied. She sipped her beer, smiling at the honey and herbs taste layered into it.

Alruna began to chop up some fresh red tomatoes. "What are you unsure about?"

"Whether or not I would be a good mate for him. I'm human, and he's an elvish prince. Don't you want him to bind himself to a princess? Or at least one of your people?" Layla asked. She needed an outsider opinion because Arne was too good at arguing how perfect they were for each other.

"Elvish mating is similar to how it is with Ulfheðnar. Only people that are going to strengthen the clan are chosen as mates. Fate has decreed that you are Arne's mate, so it must mean you will strengthen our people," Alruna replied. She stopped chopping. "Although, I think Arne would have argued with the Norns themselves if they had dared suggest someone else is his mate. Whatever force decides such things, he's always known it was you."

"Did you know with...with Vili?" Layla was pushing her luck, but she still had to ask. How someone so noble and kind like Alruna could end up with Vili was a mystery to her.

Alruna started chopping again. "I did love Vili. I think a part of me always will. When we first met, I thought he was one of the dark elves. And when he finally revealed himself and I knew the horror he had inflicted in his never-ending animosity with Asgard, I panicked and attacked. I chose the life growing inside of me. I chose to protect Arne over whatever I was feeling for Vili. I didn't want my son to be another weapon in his war. The day I left...my hair turned white. Leaving him, even though it was the right decision, was the most traumatic experience of my life."

Layla swallowed down the lump in her throat. "And you wonder why I'm scared to mate with Arne. I never want to inflict that kind of pain on anyone."

"Arne isn't his father, and you are a good woman, Layla Ironwood.

Don't let my experiences cloud your judgment in this." Alruna tipped the chopped vegetables in a bowl. "I don't regret mating with Vili because I got Arne. He is the best of both of us. He has Vili's power and beauty and none of his malice."

Love and protectiveness surged, and Layla's hand clenched into a fist. "I won't let Vili take him again. Arne deserves better than to have his memories and free will stolen from him."

"You know, the best way you can protect Arne is to mate with him," Alruna commented.

"What do you mean?"

"Arne is a man grown, but Vili is his father and has a claim over him. There is a magical power in that. It's why he could overcome Arne's mind so easily," Alruna explained. "The only bond stronger than blood is a mating bond. He would belong to you and no one else."

Layla sipped her beer and thought over her words. She wanted Arne to belong to her and vice versa. "I don't think I deserve him," she admitted, barely more than a whisper. Alruna wiped her hands before coming around Layla's side of the counter. She placed her hands on Layla's cheeks, a cool and gentle touch.

"Sweet girl, we all feel undeserving of love, but that's why we must take hold of it with both hands when we know it's true. Yes, my marriage and bond failed, but I would still do it again, knowing what I do now. The moments we had together are still precious to me. There is nothing more pure and powerful in the world than this kind of love." Layla's eyes filled with tears, but Alruna wasn't done. "I have seen more than once your strength and bravery, your clever wit and how happy you make my son. You are *everything* I prayed to Freya that my son's mate would be. You deserve the world, and you certainly deserve him. Mate him, Layla. Make our family feel complete again."

Tears fell down Layla's cheeks, her heart too full to handle the acceptance that Alruna was offering her. She gathered Layla into a hug that smelled of sweet berries and something maternal that she couldn't identify. Layla couldn't remember the last time Kenna had hugged her.

"Now," Alruna said, pulling back. She wiped the tears off Layla's cheeks. "Let's get some places set and food dished up, hmm?"

26

Arne never thought something as simple as eating dinner with his mother and Layla would cause so much joy. He loved watching them together, the way Layla would light up when she learned something new about the elves, or the way his mother would give him a pleased and fond smile when Layla wasn't watching. He had hoped that they would get along, but now he had hope they would one day become friends.

Layla had been fascinated with Alruna's loom when she showed her how to use it and had admired the paintings she had done. His mother may have been a queen, but she was a creative soul, and every part of her house reflected that. Layla loved it all.

The darkness in you will crush her light one day, Vili's voice whispered insidious poison in his ears.

Arne's power thrummed in his fingers. No, he had believed Layla when she had said his god magic was potential... and he could do whatever the fuck he wanted with it. He would ask Kian about how he could learn how to use it the next time they were together. Maybe then Arne would stop feeling like it was Vili's magic and start believing that it was his own.

Layla's hand hung onto Arne as they walked through the dark forest and back to his house.

"It's so quiet here. There's no roaring of cars in the distance or shouting sisters or training hunters," Layla said, pausing by the lake and closing her eyes. "I don't think my head has ever been this peaceful."

"You might learn to miss the noise after a time," Arne replied, unsure if the elves lifestyle would suit such a modern woman.

"If that happens, we can always go and visit Oslo or something," she replied. "That's why you keep the apartment there, right?"

Arne nodded. "When you have such a long lifespan, it's important to stay connected to the world and its changes."

Arne opened the door to the house for her before turning on the fireplace. It was a cool night, and he always loved to have a fire burning.

"Drink?" he asked.

"Sure," Layla replied, holding out her hands to warm.

"I'll give you a nip of a liquor that we distill here. It's quite herby and aniseed heavy, but I think you'll like it," Arne said, reaching for a black bottle on his side table.

"You'll have to take me to all of these distilleries. I might have to get you to carry me home afterward."

"Happily. They aren't big. The elf I know who makes this does it in a shed in his backyard."

Layla smiled and accepted the small glass. "So this is like elvish moonshine?"

"More or less," Arne replied, tapping his glass against hers.

Layla sipped, and her eyes lit up. "Oh, I like this. It's like the longer it sits in my mouth the more the flavor changes."

Arne took another sip to help him with his sudden nerves. "You do like it here, don't you?"

Layla's brown eyes softened. "Yeah, I do. The town, the lake, your mother. It's surprising how much I'm enjoying myself and how relaxed I feel here. But more importantly, I really like *you*."

"You do?"

"Especially when you're cutting wood with no shirt on. That was great," she said, her lips lifting in a naughty grin.

Arne laughed. "Is that so? I'll have to remember that next time we argue, and I need you to warm up to me again."

"Take a seat." Layla pushed him gently back onto the couch.

Arne sat, his smile disappearing. "Why do I feel like I'm in trouble?"

"You aren't." Layla drained her glass and put it down. She fidgeted a little like she always did when she was about to say something serious. She blew out a breath. "Arne Steelsinger, will you be my mate?"

Arne's heart stopped beating. He forced his mouth to work. "What happened to taking it slow?"

"I don't think more time will change how I'm feeling right now. I know it's soon, and I still have hang ups about us that stem from my own self esteem stuff. But despite all that, I want you," Layla replied. She stopped fidgeting and finally looked him in the eye.

"Recently Reeve reminded me that the world has almost ended like three times in the last six months, and let's face it, when Vili gets his shit together, it could happen again. I don't want to face the possibility of another apocalypse not having been brave enough to take what I want. I'm scared shitless that I'm going to fuck this all up, but I'm choosing love over fear because I love you. So please, Arne, be my mate."

Arne leaped out of his seat and tackled her to the bear skin rug on the floor.

"Is that a *yes*?" Layla laughed underneath him, her hands snaking under his shirt.

"Yes, yes, yes," Arne said and kissed her deeply. "I need to get you naked."

Layla brushed his dark hair behind his ear, her brown eyes heating. "You're in charge, remember?"

Arne's dick hardened. Fuck. This woman. "Then take your sweater off."

Layla's pupils blew out, and she pulled the soft dark fabric over her head. Her skin shone like pale gold in the firelight, her hair gleaming like silver on the blackness of the bear fur. She was a goddess. *His* goddess. To cherish and defile and cherish again.

Arne pulled off his shirt and leaned down over Layla. Her cool fingers stroked against his muscles in a shy exploration.

"You're so hot, it hurts to look at you," she murmured.

"Look and touch all you want, my mate," Arne said, lowering his head so he could suck her hard nipple through the satin of her bra.

Layla whimpered, her back arching a little, offering herself up to him. He needed to see her bare and writhing with pleasure. Arne licked the curve of her breast, his teeth digging in.

"I need you naked, so forgive the magic," he growled.

"What—" Layla jumped as his magic surged and their clothes were suddenly gone. "I wondered how you did that last night. Hmm handy." Her eyes looked down, staring at his dick with a satisfied smile.

"Like what you see?" he couldn't resist asking.

"I'd like to know what it tastes like," she replied, and then her cheeks went red. "Shit, I said that out loud didn't I?"

"Yes, you did, and I think it's an excellent idea. " Arne chuckled. He lifted off her and sat down with his back against the couch. Layla sat up, a gorgeous queen on the fur. Gods, what did he do to deserve such a mate?

Arne spread his legs and beckoned at her with the crook of his finger. "Come on then, *vennen*, come and taste me."

Layla licked her lips, wetting them as she moved between his thighs. Arne didn't hurry her. He wanted to see what she would do. Layla kissed the center of his chest, licking and nipping her way down his stomach. She kissed the crease of his hip before shifting his leg wider to accommodate her.

Arne hissed an ancient curse with the first hot suck on the crown of his cock. She licked him down to his base, making him wet all over. She swallowed him down, and Arne groaned at the hot heaven of her mouth.

"Fuck, Layla. So good." He fisted her hair, and she pulled back off him.

"Grip it harder," she said, before taking him in her mouth again.

"Harder?" Arne's fingers tightened in her hair. "Does my sweet mate want to be used a little, does she?" Her answering moan sent vibrations through his cock. He was going to lose his mind if she kept that up. Arne pulled her down harder.

"That's it. Take it as far as it will go. I want to feel the back of your throat until you're gagging on me. Until I fill that fucking pretty mouth of yours with my come and make you swallow it down."

Arne's whole body trembled when she took his words as a challenge, sucking him hard enough to see stars. She gagged a few times but didn't stop. The sight of his cock disappearing between her full lips made him feel wild, the beast in him roaring in triumph over her submission, her willingness to please him.

"You're doing so good, Layla. Don't stop."

Heat and static built at the base of his spine, and when he hit the back of her soft throat again, his control shattered, and he came with a surprised cry. He loosened his grip on Layla's hair but didn't let her go, pleasure surging through him as she swallowed him down and then licked his cock clean.

He lifted her off, wiping a bit of come off her chin and putting it on her swollen lips to suck off.

"You are perfection, my gorgeous girl," he said, kissing a tear off her cheek. His teeth scraped at the curve of her ear. "I'm going to fuck you tonight until you think you can't take anymore. I'm going to ingrain my scent so deeply into you that no one will ever doubt who you belong to."

Arne slid his hand between her thighs, finding the wetness dripping out of her. Layla made a helpless sound as he ran his fingers through it, circling her clit before lifting his glistening fingers to his mouth. His dick was hardening again, unable to relieve the ache that the sweet musky flavor of her conjured.

"Do it, Arne. I'm yours. Claim me," Layla begged. Arne kissed her, tasting the both of them, sucking her tongue into his mouth until her arms and legs were wrapping around him. She ground her wet pussy up against his dick, trying to find relief.

Arne pushed her back down onto the rug, breaking the kiss so he could place her feet down and open her legs. She was exposed fully to him, her gorgeous pussy gleaming. Layla traced her hands over her breasts, squeezing her nipples until they were pink.

"Look at you being a little tease?" Arne said, pressing his finger inside of her. Layla made a helpless sound that made him want to drive himself into her. He wanted her needy, begging for him to fill her.

"Don't stop touching those beautiful tits. I want us both to give you the pleasure you deserve. Gods, you are fucking perfect."

"Arne...get inside of me," she said, hands tightening on her pale flesh.

"What if I want to keep you just like this?" Arne pushed another finger inside of her, widening her, thrusting hard until her hips were rocking against him.

"More. I need more." Layla fucked herself faster on his fingers, her cheeks flushing as her release drew closer. Arne pulled his fingers free before she could, and she cried out in frustration.

Arne grabbed her hands, pulling them away from her breasts and pinning them to her stomach with one hand. He lifted her hips with the other and drove his cock into her, forcing her to take him in one deep thrust.

"Oh, fuck Arne," she gasped, tilting her hips higher to adjust to him, to take more. "That's what I need."

Arne chuckled darkly. "I know, love. It's what we both need. What we will *always* need. You are my mate. You belong in my care now, body and soul and heart. I will have all of you."

Layla's eyes filled with tears. "Do you promise?"

"It's more than a promise." Arne released her hands and leaned down so their noses touched. Their eyes locked on each other. "You are never going to be free of me, Layla Ironwood. I claim you as my mate, and I'm going to keep you, treasure you, and worship you until Ragnarök fucks the world to ashes, and then I'll love you in whatever is left."

"I want it. I want all of it. I fucking love you so damn much," Layla said, pressing her lips to his. Arne rolled his hips, driving his cock into her, their eyes locked on each other.

Golden magic unspooled inside of him, and ribbons of light unfurled out of his chest and wrapped around her. The ancient elvish words of mating fell from his lips, Layla's sharp nails digging into his back as she clung to him. The bond between them burned, both of them crying out in sudden pain-pleasure as parts of their souls fused like molten metal.

Black lines started to rise up on Layla's skin, Arne pulling back to watch as his mating mark appeared like a tattoo over her heart. The runes were so primordial, no one living knew what they meant, but he knew it was the shape of their bond written down.

Layla stared in wonder at it, her hands clasping onto Arne's biceps like she was scared to let him go. "Fuck, Arne, it burns," she whimpered.

"Just breathe, love," Arne fucked gently into her, and her eyes rolled back in pleasure. "Let it roll over you and mix with the feel of me inside of you."

"Yes, more. God, that feels..." her words trailed off, and Arne went deeper and slower, his body filling her until she could take no more. He circled her clit with his thumb, and Layla cried out, her whole beautiful body shining with sweat and shaking. The last of the marks appeared, and she was coming, her pussy squeezing him tight enough that he momentarily blacked out, and still he pushed her further.

"Yes, Layla. Come on me, mark me, claim me," he groaned. Her nails dug into his side, and with a sudden move, she had him on his back, her hand gripping the base of his throat. Arne laughed in feral joy.

"I'll fucking claim you alright. I will fuck you so hard that you forget your own name," Layla snarled.

The black bond under her breast was so dark against her pale skin. Finally, he had her. He would have her forever. Arne gripped her hips as she rode him, her face set in furious determination.

Her body was a thing of wonder to watch under normal circumstances. When it was lowering itself down on his cock, he lost all fucking reason. Her hand tightened around his throat, and Arne came on a cry, his release so intense, it hurt. Layla's thighs clamped around him, and she was coming again too, her head thrown back in a gasping cry of victory and sheer fucking joy. She smiled down at him, and then her expression slipped, and she placed a hand over his heart.

"It...you don't have one. Did it not work for you?" she asked.

"Fuck yes it worked." Arne sat up and kissed her. "Elvish males have never had them, but a lot of them will go to the ink shamans and get identical ones done. We can go tomorrow."

Layla traced his cheekbones. "And what makes you think I'm going to let you leave this house tomorrow, mate?"

Arne nipped her bottom lip. "Good point."

27

Layla rested her head against the curve of Arne's shoulder with a happy sigh. Her whole body was pulsing with aftershocks, and she never wanted it to stop.

"Now, if I remember correctly, you promised me a massage in a hot tub," she said.

Arne kissed the top of her head. "If my mate wants a massage, she can have one."

"Excellent answer."

Arne lifted her off and laid her back on the destroyed bear skin. "Stay here in the warmth, and I'll get it ready."

"Happy to," she murmured, feeling drowsy and content with her post orgasm bliss. She ran her fingers through the soft dark fur.

Fucked senseless on a fur rug in front of a fire. It's off my bucket list, she thought and laughed softly. How had this become her life? She wasn't about to complain. Arne came back with a towel slung around his hips. He held a soft, thick robe.

"Here we are. This will keep you warm," he said, helping her up and wrapping it around her.

"I think we ruined your rug," she giggled.

"It'll survive," Arne assured her.

Out the back, on a deck was a steaming hot tub that looked out over the lake. There was a small building next to it that Arne said was a sauna and bathroom.

"Yeah, I'm never going to leave now you told me that," Layla said and jumped when he caught her up in his arms.

"Like I would let you leave," Arne growled and placed her on the top step leading into the tub.

"I could always use my feminine wiles to convince you it was a good idea." Layla undid her robe and let it drop. She threw a coy look over her shoulder. Arne was staring at her ass like he was about to sink his teeth into it. A part of her hoped that he would.

Layla shivered as she stepped down into the steaming water. It was a delicious contrast to the cool air. She bundled her snarled hair up in a bun on the top of her head and lowered herself down to her shoulders. Arne was still wearing a dazed expression.

Layla grinned. "You are looking a bit pussy struck there, my dear."

"I am trying not to let the mating frenzy steal all my reason," Arne admitted.

"Wait, mating frenzy is a real thing?" she asked, brows shooting up.

Arne dropped his towel and gestured at his already hard dick. "What do you think?"

"Gosh," was all she could say in wonder.

Arne lowered himself into the water and ran his hands over her wet shoulders. "It's a leftover thing from our more primal days. The mating frenzy was to try and get a female pregnant as soon as possible."

"Thank gods for modern birth control. I can enjoy all the orgasms with none of the risk," Layla said, putting her arms around his neck.

"An excellent idea. Most mated couples are left alone by the clan for a few weeks, but I don't think we are going to get that luxury. The wolves have it worse. When their mating occurs, they get ultra-territorial. Usually, they are sent to a literal cabin in the woods until it passes," Arne explained. He began to massage her shoulders and a little moan escaped from Layla. Her shoulders were always so damn tight. "Gods, Layla, you have knots everywhere. Turn around so I can do this properly." With a happy laugh, Layla did, and Arne pulled her back into his lap. His big hands knew exactly where to press.

"That feels so damn good," she said, her eyes fluttering closed.

"You keep making those sounds, and I'm going to have to fuck you again," Arne warned her. His hands slid down her spine to cup her ass and squeezed.

Layla did moan then. "You aren't making it easier not to make a sound."

"I love all of your little sounds," Arne whispered in her ear, his hands curving around her lower back to brush against her stomach and up to her tender breasts. "Especially when you make them on my dick."

Layla rubbed her ass over the erection pressing into it. "You mean this dick?"

"I'm warning you..." he hissed.

"Oh no, not a warning," Layla mocked. She yelped in surprise as Arne surged forward. He lifted her over the side of the pool so only her legs were still in the water and her ass on display in the cold air.

"You are going to learn to watch that sassy mouth of yours," he said, spreading her. Arne made a helpless sound that made Layla smirk. She bit her lip as his fingers explored her, dipping inside where she was still wet and slippery from his release. "Are you just going to stare at it all night?"

Arne's hand came down on her ass, making her cry out in surprise. "I'll take my time to enjoy you as I wish, mate."

His hand smoothed over the mark, making heat and wetness run through her. She had never thought she would be into spanking, but nothing would surprise her if he was the one doing it to her.

The tip of Arne's dick pressed against her, and she tried to push back against it. "So needy already. I was worried about the mating frenzy being too much for a human, but look at you, pussy weeping for me already."

"Gods, Arne, please," Layla begged. She didn't care she was as desperate as she sounded. She wanted him to be in her, claiming her. She had never felt so wanted in her life, and she was greedy for him to use her the way he needed. The way they *both* needed.

Arne ran a soothing hand down her wet spine and slid his cock into her a little bit at a time before pulling back. Layla was losing her mind by the time he finally got in her. His teeth dragged against her shoulder, making her cry out.

"Does my mate want to be fucked gently this time? Or does she want me to pull her hair and ride her as rough as I like?" he growled, lips licking the water off her neck. Layla gasped as he rocked into her. "Speak, little mate."

"Fuck me rough. Do what you like with me. I'm yours," she said, cheeks flaming as she forced the words out.

Arne pressed a gentle kiss to her cheek. "There's my perfect mate."

He grabbed her messy bun, pulling her hair hard enough to make her scalp tingle, and slammed his dick into her. Layla was glad they didn't have neighbors because Arne was making her shout like a porn star. No one had ever been more attuned with her body, giving her what she needed to send her mad with desire. Arne really was all of her wet dreams rolled in one.

Layla screamed his name as her orgasm took her. Arne pinned her trembling body to the wood beneath her, their wet skin slapping hard as he fucked her through it without mercy before coming hard inside of her. Arne's arms held her tight up against him so she could feel his rapid heartbeat against her back.

"So fucking perfect," he murmured, kissing any piece of her that he could get his hands on.

"You read my mind," she panted.

Arne carefully lowered her back into the steaming water, holding her on his lap. His hand splayed against the mating brand over her heart.

"Thank you for choosing me, Layla. For taking the chance when I know it scared you, when I have a monster's blood in my veins," he said. Layla slipped around so she could straddle him. He looked so emotional, his eyes soft. She cupped his cheeks and pressed gentle kisses to his lips.

"You are worth all the love I can give you, Arne. Your blood doesn't make you who you are. By all the laws, I have the first claim on you now," Layla said, remembering Alruna's words. "You are *my* love. You belong to me and no other. No one is going to take you from me."

Arne pressed his forehead to hers. "No one will dare get between us, my fierce beloved." Layla pressed a kiss to his lips and rested against his chest. For the first time in her life, she finally felt like she was where she belonged.

28

Layla should have known that the moment she had been happiest in her entire life was also the moment a wayward army would arrive to crap on her day.

Waking up in Arne's plush bed, her limbs all tangled about with his, was rudely interrupted by a massive wolf landing heavily on the deck outside and crashing through a door.

"Arne! Layla! Get your asses up!" Tor hollered, making them both startle awake.

Layla wrapped a robe around herself as Arne dragged on some clothes and hurried out to find Tor.

"What's going on?" Arne asked, his hair sticking up at odd angles.

Layla squinted at the pink sky. "What time is it?"

"Sorry to interrupt, but at dawn, four portals opened on the northern border, and warriors are already filing through," Tor said, his gray eyes wild and shining with a wolf's bright sheen.

"Has Vili been spotted yet?" Arne asked, grabbing his phone off the kitchen counter.

"No, but Varg has. The scout who reported to me knew him on site. That fucker!" Tor's pacing stopped, and his eyes shot to the bearskin on the floor. "Seriously? Can't you two fuck in a bed like normal people?"

Layla smirked. "What? I chased him through the house. That's where he landed, so that's where he was fucked."

"Don't tell him that. He'll believe anything," Arne said, fingers dancing on his phone screen. "Tor, go wake my mother up. She will need to reach out to Brök and Eydís to let them know what's happening and activate the extra wards around the city. Do you have wolves watching the army now?"

"Of course I do," Tor growled. "They are going to get back to me with head counts and any movements they make further inland. What are you going to do?"

"Rally the warriors." Arne looked at Layla. "Sorry, *vennen,* the ink shamans will have to wait."

"Ink shamans! Have you two..." Tor looked between them and then inhaled. "Well, fuck. Congratulations."

"Thanks," Layla said, trying not to go red.

Tor's smile slipped. "Shit, Arne, you sure you two are going to be okay with the fight while in the frenzy?"

"I think it's going to make me kick Vili's ass twice as hard for interrupting my shagging marathon," Layla said with bite in her voice. She kissed Arne. "Go wake the warriors. I'll get a hold of my brothers and let them know what's going on."

Arne brushed a thumb over her cheek. A look of longing in his eyes. Layla gave him a gentle shove. "I know. Just go. We need to get to the borders and surprise them before they expect us."

"I'll be back soon," he promised, and he and Tor headed out the door.

Layla found her phone and sent an SOS message to the family group chat before calling Bayn.

"What..." he answered on the fifth ring.

"Vili's army has turned up," Layla answered, jumping right in. "I've sent an alert but need you to go wake up Kian and Killian."

"On it. Have you got some decent gear with you, or should I bring you something?" he asked, his voice already alert.

"I'm good for gear, but I'd like to see your face if you're up for a fight today," Layla replied hopefully. It wasn't that she didn't think the elves would be able to seriously kick ass, but having three fae princes wouldn't hurt their odds either.

"You don't even need to ask, little sis. We will come. Keep us updated, and Layla? Make sure you eat something. It's easy to forget in a crisis, but you need it for energy."

Layla couldn't help but laugh at his mother hen instincts. "I will see you soon."

Layla dug about in her bags and pulled out her black hunting suit. When she had originally packed it for the elf summit, she thought that she was being over cautious. It was a pain in the ass to get in and out of, but at least the reinforcements over her vital spots would give her a bit more protection.

Shame you don't have your fancy elf armor ready, she lamented while dragging on the tight-fitting material. Her phone buzzed, and she hurried to look at her message from Kian.

I hope your back up plan works.

I suppose we will find out. Coming for the fight? Layla bit her lip. The backup plan she still hadn't told Arne about. Fuck. She didn't want to make him mad or get his hopes up. He had too many other things to think about.

Wouldn't miss it. I've been itching for one for a while.

Layla grinned. Vili didn't stand a chance.

∽

ARMED AND READY FOR A FIGHT, Layla walked up the path from Arne's house to Alruna's. She had gotten a message to meet him and Tor there. What he hadn't mentioned was the pack of warriors and wolves that encircled the place.

They didn't stop her from heading inside, but all of them stared at her curiously.

Could they somehow see the mating mark? Layla didn't want to think about it. The wolves could probably smell the all-night fuck fest she'd had anyway.

Arne, Alruna, Tor, Brök, and Eydís were all around the dining room table with a map spread out before them. They were all dressed in magnificent armor, and Eydís had a sword almost as tall as Layla resting against her chair.

"Ah Layla, good you're here. Have you spoken to your people?" Alruna asked, wasting no time with pleasantries.

"Kian and Bayn are coming. I'm waiting to hear from the others."

"Only two?" Brök grumbled. "Much good that will do us."

Layla's eyes narrowed. "Only two? My brothers are the Blood Prince and Winter Prince of the Fae. They could probably annihilate Vili's army on their own with the power they wield."

"Now, now, there's no time for arguments," Eydís said, resting a hand on Brök's shoulder. "Keep your beard on, dwarf. I have heard of these mighty warriors, and we will be happy to have them at our side." Brök grumbled something in dwarfish but didn't argue further. Eydís rolled her eyes at Layla over the top of his head, and Layla bit down a grin.

"I have gathered some armor that should fit you, Layla. Let me show you," Arne said, getting up from the table.

"Hell yeah," she said. She was probably way too excited about armor but couldn't help herself.

Arne showed Layla to a room where armor pieces had been arranged on a bed. As soon as she was through the door, he closed it and Arne's hot, hungry mouth was on hers. Layla buried her hands in his hair and gave into the embrace. There was too much armor and gear in between them.

"Gods, I've wanted to do that all day," Arne said, his breath warm on her face.

"All day? I saw you thirty minutes ago," Layla pointed out playfully. Arne's hands slid over the tight fabric of her suit and cupped her, making them both groan.

"We need…armor…army," she stammered, her eyes rolling back in her head.

"They have it under control, but I do not," Arne replied. He undid the zip and button on her pants and slid his hand inside. "Fuck, baby, are you ever not wet?"

"Around you? No." Layla clawed at the shoulders of his hard armor, her heart racing. Arne's fingers slid inside of her, and Layla bit down onto his neck to muffle the sounds coming out of her.

"Can't get enough," Arne growled. He pulled down her pants to her boots and dropped to his knees. He dragged her to the floor, spread her, and had his hot mouth on her in a blink. Layla bit her lip to hold in her cries. Arne's big hand went over her mouth to silence her.

"Shhh, no sounds but keep your eyes on me," he said. He had his leather pants open, his dick in his hand. He put his mouth back over her pussy, his golden eyes never leaving hers as he pleasured them both. Layla squirmed, her body on fire with the intensity and the secret naughtiness of it all.

"Put your fingers inside you," Arne commanded, pulling back from her. Layla obeyed, masturbating in front of him, chasing the orgasm he had already edged her towards. Arne was stroking his cock harder, his eyes burning as they stared at her.

"That's it, my mate. Let me see you come," he said. Layla bit the skin of his palm as she circled her clit a few more times and her vision whited out, her orgasm rushing through her. Arne groaned and came hot over her bare pussy and stomach.

Arne slowly removed his hand from her mouth and kissed her, their breaths ragged.

"What the fuck was that?" she whispered.

"Me needing you and also needing to think straight today. Let me get a cloth," Arne said and kissed her again. He got up, fixing his pants and went into an adjoining bathroom. Layla lay in a blissed-out daze, staring at the ceiling, and listened to the water running. Arne came back with a cloth and stared down at her.

"Gods, that's hot," he growled. He shook himself and kneeled beside her. The cloth was wet and warm as he tenderly cleaned up the mess he had made on her.

Layla grinned up at him. "I don't know how you expect me to concentrate now."

Arne laughed and helped her up. He pulled her pants up and pressed a kiss to her soft belly. "We just need to get through today, and we can go back to what we are meant to be doing. Fucking. Lots and lots of fucking."

Layla blushed and quickly started to rebraid her now snarled hair. She needed to focus and fast. "How about you show me how to put some of this armor on?"

Arne helped strap on the leather and steel chest piece, vambraces, and spaulders. With each piece, he made sure she still had a full range of motion.

"I thought it would be a lot heavier to wear than this," Layla commented.

"It's the way it's made. Extra strong, extra light. Your custom armor will be a lot better than this and a lot lighter," Arne commented. He reached under the bed and pulled out a long wooden case and offered it to her. "This, however, was ready for you on time."

Layla's heart raced as she opened the metal clasps. Inside was a recurve bow, made of golden wood, and carved with silver runes. She could feel the magic pulsing off it.

"This...this is for me?" she hesitated to even touch such a beautiful thing.

Arne smiled. "I'm sorry I didn't have time to dress up as Galadriel. You can touch it. It won't bite."

Layla swallowed down her unexpected tears as she lifted it out of the box. She pulled the string back and hummed at the feel of it.

"The length, the tension... It's like it was made perfectly for me," Layla marveled.

"It was, beloved," Arne admitted. The tips of his ears went pink. "After the fight with Morrigan, I asked the bowyer to make it for you. I didn't know when I would get a chance to give it to you, but I knew that I would one day."

Layla lowered the bow. *This bloody elf.* She wrapped her arms around him and kissed him. "You are the best mate a girl could ever ask for, and I love you so much I can't even express it right now. Thank you so much for such a thoughtful and perfect gift."

Arne kissed the tip of her nose. "You are welcome, my Layla. Now, let's go and stop a war."

29

The air was cold, and clouds had gathered over Finnmark. Layla walked through the war camp with Arne, their hands clasped together. She had never seen so many elves in one place. Rows upon rows of warriors assembled and patiently waited. There was a tent set up for the queens and Brök. The Svartalfheim rulers and a small party of their people would fight, and if Vili brought in more reinforcements, Eydís and Alruna would open portals and bring through more of their warriors.

Vili's army was gathered through the pine and birch trees in the distance. It was hard to tell where they were, but the Midgard elves and wolves knew the land and forests better than the enemy ever could. Vili's army was a mixed group of elves, dwarves, berserker bear shifters, and wolves led by Varg.

"If we can stop all the traitors to Svartalfheim here, it will solve a lot of headaches later," Brök grunted beside them. He spat. "Bastards the lot of them. Vili seems to have gotten the loyalty of every discontent fucker he could find."

Familiar chill magic had Layla turning in time to see Bayn and Kian appear through a patch of fresh ice. She let Arne's hand go and hurried over to them. They were in full armor, their hair braided back. Gold and black paint was smeared on Kian's antlers, his famous golden armor provoking a thrill of terror in her. Last time she had seen it was in footage of him terrorizing London. From the looks on the elves' faces, they remembered it.

"Wow, you guys look badass," Layla said, hugging them both. "Thank you for coming."

"Can't let you have all the fun now, can we? Kill and Bron send their apologies. They wanted to remain in Ireland in case Vili kicks our asses and they need to rally the humans," Bayn explained. He paused and looked her over. "Well, well. Someone's mated already. So much for holding out on the elf."

Layla laughed. "Have you seen him? How good do you think my self-control is?"

"Congratulations," Kian said with a wide smile. "And to you too, Arne."

"Thank you," he replied, coming up behind Layla with Tor.

"You don't want to cover up a bit more?" Bayn asked, lifting a brow at Tor who was only in a pair of leather pants. His chest and arms were covered in war paint, a thick band of black over his face. All of the other wolves still in human form were dressed the same way.

"Ulfheðnar don't fight with armor." Tor had a touch of crazy already in his eyes that Layla had never seen before. "We don't need it."

"Easy, Tor. It will start soon," Arne murmured. Tor nodded and walked away. "Ignore him. He's already been into the war mead that the Ulfheðnar take ceremonially before a fight."

Layla's face lit up. "There's war mead!"

"Not for you, beloved," Arne said, pressing a kiss to her temple.

Layla wanted to argue that she could use a drink when a deep horn sounded from Vili's camp.

"Do you think he's finally here?" Layla asked.

Arne shook his head. "I haven't seen any other portals open."

"Looks like they want to talk," Kian said, pointing where Vili's ranks had parted and a group carrying Vili's standard was coming across the battlefield towards them.

"Varg, that piece of shit," Arne growled when he saw who was leading them.

The elvish warriors parted to let Alruna, Brök, and Eydís through. Tor, Arne, Layla, Kian, and Bayn fell into step behind them.

"I don't see him," Alruna muttered. "I would know if he was here."

Layla wouldn't have been half as calm as the queen if her deranged ex was about to face her in battle. She wanted to take Arne's hand but didn't. She didn't want to appear like the needy, weak woman of the group, because Eydís, dressed in full battle gear, her dreadlocks braided back and decorated with spikes, looked fucking terrifying. And that was without the huge sword hanging from her back.

How is this my life? Layla thought for the hundredth time in the past few days. Her ruined date felt like a million years ago. She looked up at Arne, and the uneasiness in her settled. As long as he was there, she wouldn't worry about the craziness her world had become. The cawing of a crow made her look up. The branches of the trees were filling with carrion birds as if they instinctively knew that blood and carnage was about to be wrought.

Layla fought back a shiver and focused on the group of Vili's people waiting for them. Varg sneered when he spotted Layla. He was missing a large chunk of his ear, and she smirked back at him.

"Queen Alruna and Prince Arne, you will lay down your arms and submit yourself to the will of the Dark King," Varg said, wasting no time in being a twat.

"And where is your master, dog?" Alruna demanded, looking as imperious as Layla had ever seen her.

"He will be here soon enough. He is offering you this one chance to live and to join him, to be a family and stand by his side as he takes what is rightfully his," Varg replied. "I suggest you take his offer and be grateful, woman."

"Be grateful," Alruna said, a soft snarl in her voice that had the hair on Layla's neck rising. "Do you know how many times I've been told to take the shit deal and *be grateful*? More times than the days you've been breathing, dog. I've never bowed to Vili when I was married to him, and I would rather slit my own throat than stand by his side as he starts Ragnarök for his own ego. If you have nothing more to say, we are done here."

Layla had to bite her tongue not to cheer. *That's my mother-in-law.*

"I hope that you remember those words as my king crushes you under his boots. I hope your pride comforts you as we slaughter your men and rape your women before burning your precious Alfheimstod to the ground," Varg replied.

Darkness bloomed in the air behind him. Golden power flickered at its center, and Vili stepped out of Svartalfheim and into Midgard. He towered over everyone, his presence making Layla feel like ducking her head. She refused to do it even if she had to grit her teeth against the compulsion.

"My mate," he said, staring at Alruna. "You still look as beautiful as the day I first saw you."

Alruna looked up at him, her eyes flashing. "Don't do this, Vili. You know that causing Ragnarök won't give you peace, and it won't heal the past."

"My past had peace. It even had happiness, and then you stole my boy from me. You didn't think I would ever find out?" he snarled.

"He is *my* son, not yours. I don't regret leaving. I knew you would twist him for your own purpose and design." Alruna's whole body shimmered with rage and magic. "The first thing you did when you stole him back was rob him of his will. What kind of father does that?"

"One who has no time to undo the weakness you have put in him," Vili replied. He looked over at Arne and then at Layla. "You mated with a fucking human? How you continue to disappoint me."

"I'm long past needing my father's approval for anything," Arne replied coolly. "She may be a human, but she was strong enough and brave enough to break into your own house, shatter your enchantment, and steal me back."

Layla smiled the fuck you smile her family was so well known for. "That's got to be embarrassing for you."

Vili began to laugh, and before any of them could move, golden power shot out of him, blanketing the Midgard army in a wave.

Layla clutched at her head as voices started shouting at her, telling her how weak and pathetic she was. Cold fear dripped down her spine. She rubbed at her stinging eyes and saw warriors dropping their weapons, their eyes clouded with Vili's power. Kian and Bayn were on their knees screaming out for the slaughtered kin.

"Don't die without me, Layla, "Arne begged, clutching at the dirt.

Vili was looking about and smiling as his magic pulled everyone's darkest fears and horrors to the surface.

Layla pushed the voices away and unslung her bow from her back and nocked an arrow. Vili was too busy looking at the destruction around him to notice her. Layla breathed out and sent the arrow flying. It cut through the haze of magic and struck Vili in the leg. He roared in fury, rounding on her as his spell began to crack. He started to hobble towards her.

"How? How are you fighting this, human?" he demanded.

"Because there isn't a single thing that your fucking fear magic can say to me that I haven't said to myself a million times. I've had to fight those voices every single day of my life, and guess what? I always win!" Layla shouted at him.

She didn't hesitate, sending arrow after arrow shooting towards him. Vili knocked two aside with his sword, but one got through and struck his other thigh. He stumbled as blood seeped out of his wounds and stained his clothes.

With a sound of pure fury, Vili raised his sword high and charged her. Layla pulled one of Arne's swords free from the holster on his back. She whirled to meet him, blade for blade.

Magic exploded around them, an invisible force detonating between them and throwing them backward. Layla managed to stay upright on one knee, Arne's sword digging into the dirt to stop her slide.

Lighting struck the ground in thunderous cracks, and from a cloud of screaming ravens, stepped the gods of Asgard.

30

Layla struggled to breathe as Havi appeared on the field, his shining spear in hand. Power and light exploded around them, and a goddess with golden braids and a god with one hand and dark hair pinned a thrashing Vili to the ground.

The All-Father hadn't just kept his promise to come if Vili stepped foot on Midgard. He had brought his war gods with him.

Layla got back to her feet, her hand gripping Arne's sword. Vili's enchantment had broken, and all around her, groans echoed as warriors regained their reality. She hurried to Arne's side.

"Are you okay? Talk to me," she begged, clutching at his face.

"You're alive," he sobbed.

"I'm alive. On your feet, love, this isn't over." Layla helped him up. Bayn and Kian were already up and staring wide-eyed at the gods in front of them. Layla froze as Havi held out a hand and assisted Alruna back to her feet.

"Havi, I..." Alruna stammered before finally settling on, "It's good to see you."

"And you. Are you hurt?"

Alruna shook her head. "No, I'm fine. What are you going to do with him?" she asked, looking over at where Vili was hogtied with shimmering ropes. They were unlike anything Layla had ever seen.

"I will take him back to Asgard and put him where he will cause no more trouble," Havi replied.

"You think binding me in these dwarf fetters will hold me?" Vili shouted in fury.

Tyr dragged him to his knees, and Freya took up a position behind him, the tip of her sword resting on the back of his neck.

"You may speak to him if you wish to," Havi said, placing a hand on Alruna's shoulder.

Vili saw the touch and pure hate clouded his features. "Don't you fucking dare touch my mate, Havi!"

Layla held her breath as she watched Alruna move to stand in front of Vili. His expression cracked under the weight of her gaze, the anger and energy that had been animating seeping away.

"Don't do this, Runa. Please," he begged.

Alruna placed her hands on his cheeks, tears rolling down her face. "You brought this on yourself because you were never satisfied with all that you had. You lost everything because I was never enough."

"It was never about you. I loved you in all the ways I knew how," Vili replied. He smiled sadly at her. "Come and visit me in my new prison?"

"Perhaps." Alruna placed a soft kiss to the rune mark on his brow and went to stand by Arne. She looked like her soul had been ripped out of her body, but she still kept her head up high.

Havi raised a brow at Layla. "Niece, I trust you can clean up this rabble?"

"With pleasure, Havi. Thanks for keeping your word," Layla replied.

Havi shook his head, but she still caught his grin. "Keep an eye on your mate, Arne. She's a dangerous one."

"I will?" Arne replied, his brows knotting in confusion. "Layla?"

"Shh, I'll tell you later," she said.

Havi walked back towards where the gods waited for him. Vili started to laugh, a sad, broken thing. "You think you can stop Ragnarök by binding me? Even now the world conspires to awaken the Great Wolf! Nothing will stop him, and in the end, you will release me, begging for my help."

Layla didn't hear Havi's reply. There was a bright strike of lightning, a roar of wind, and the gods were gone, leaving nothing behind but raven feathers.

Arne pressed a hard kiss to Layla's lips. "We need to have a talk, Layla Brigid Ironwood."

"Sorry, love, no can do. You heard the All-Father. We have to clean up the rabble," Layla said, passing Arne back his sword before drawing out her daggers.

Varg was shouting orders, horns blew, and Vili's army came surging towards them. Layla fell in beside Arne as the Midgardian army shouted, and as one, they raced to meet them.

∼

IN THE END, the battle barely lasted twenty minutes in a tangle of blood and screams. Most of Vili's army refused to fight after seeing the gods of Asgard drag their king away. Part of the army had seen the Midgardian's winning and had surrendered or fled. The worse part was that when the dust had settled, Varg wasn't amongst the living or dead.

"He can't run from me forever," Tor snarled as he shifted out of his wolf form. He was naked and covered in blood and gashes. "I have sent a group of wolves to try and pick up his trail. Without Vili to make him a portal, he's grounded in Midgard."

"We'll get him, Tor," Arne said, passing him a cloak to cover himself.

"We need to get home to our mates and tell them that it's over," Bayn said. His armor was scratched to hell from taking on a bear shifter, but other than that, he looked fine. Kian's golden armor was soaked in blood, and he had a feral grin on his face.

"I worry about you, bro," Layla said with a shake of her head.

"You worry about me? I wasn't the one who tracked down one of the old gods, yelled at him, and then provoked *another* old god to come to Midgard," Kian replied. He looked around at the astonished faces of the queens, Brök, Arne, and Tor. "You don't know? Layla, who you all think is such a sweet human, provoked two gods to a pissing match!"

"It worked, didn't it? We couldn't take Vili by ourselves. Only Havi could. You can all pout as much as you want, but I won't apologize,"

Layla stated and crossed her arms stubbornly. She squeaked as Arne gathered her up in his arms.

"And you don't think you're good enough to be my mate," he said with pure exasperation. He kissed all the arguments from her mouth.

When they finally pulled apart, Arne looked at her with the kind of love in his eyes that could change worlds. "You are so much more than I could have ever dreamed of, Layla Ironwood, but don't you dare provoke any more old gods."

Layla grinned and placed a quick feisty kiss to his lips. "You're not the boss of me, prince."

Arne's golden eyes heated in a way that promised retribution when they would be alone. Layla couldn't wait.

31

Layla lay back on the tattoo bed, relishing the sting of a sharp piece of carved reindeer bone being tapped into her skin. Every now and again, Layla would feel a spike of magic coming from the shamans. Arne hissed beside her as the ink shaman worked.

"What's the matter, my mate? Did they hit an ouchy bit?" Layla teased. Arne narrowed his eyes at her.

"It surprised me, that's all."

"Sure it did," she said. Both of the ink shamans working on them snickered but didn't stop working.

They had been in the chairs for hours, Layla deciding that she needed a tattoo in a hurry. In another hour, their entire family was going to arrive at Alruna's for a dinner to celebrate Arne and Layla's mating. She needed something to calm her ramped up nerves, and nothing made her calm like a fresh tattoo.

"Your mating mark is finished, my prince," the elf working on Arne announced, wiping off the excess blood and ink. Arne's eyes went soft as he looked from his mark to the one over Layla's heart.

"Don't get all mushy on me," she said, her heart beating faster like it always did when he smiled at her.

"I'll save it for later," he replied.

Layla's tattoo was of a twisting stylized tree done in a Viking knot style. It fit perfectly in the remaining space on her inner left arm. It seemed fitting that Arne and the elves were the missing piece. She had slotted easily in with them, feeling more comfortable every day that she lived amongst them. She still hadn't been home to Ireland to see her family, so her family was coming to her.

"It looks perfect," Arne commented a short while later, studying the tattoo as they walked to Alruna's house.

"I know, right? I thought it would hurt way more than that," Layla said excitedly, swinging their clasped hands, the post tattoo euphoria still riding her.

Arne twirled her, laughing at her enthusiasm. "Who would have thought pain and ink would make you smile so much." He spun her into him and kissed her. "You ready to do this?"

"No, but that's not going to stop our mothers from doing it," Layla said.

"Good point. Better we are there to make sure no one starts any fights," Arne replied.

Alruna had set up the party in her pretty garden beside the lake. Wooden tables were covered in red linen cloths and decorated with centerpieces of candles and the wildflowers that were growing like crazy in the warmer months.

"There you are! I was about to send out a search party," Alruna said, striding across the grass. She was barefoot and dressed in a pretty white linen and lace dress.

"I wouldn't leave you to suffer alone," Layla said, and Alruna smiled fondly at her. They had struck an easy friendship since the battle. Layla had been more than happy to get to know her better. Despite Alruna reassuring her and Arne that she was fine, they knew that seeing Vili had affected her greatly.

"*I thought after so much time, I would feel different,*" Alruna had admitted one night to Layla.

"But you didn't?"

Alruna had shaken her head and squeezed Layla's hand. "*The heart is a strange and mysterious thing. The pain will pass as it did last time.*"

The queen was lying, but Layla was polite enough not to point it out.

"I hope you're ready for this," Layla said to Alruna. "My family are a rowdy bunch."

"Hush, we are going to have a lovely time," she replied and opened a portal.

Arne placed an arm around Layla's shoulders as the Ironwoods and the Greatdrakes came through.

"Laaaayyyylllaaa." Moira barreled into her legs. "Look at my dress! Killian got it for me!"

Killian and Bron waved at her from across the garden.

"Well, turn around and show me," Layla laughed.

Moira spun about to show off the pink and purple princess dress. For a child that slept with a cross bow and a German Shepherd, Moira had a ridiculously strong girly streak. She took off at a run down the lake, leaving Layla shaking her head after her.

"You are looking well," Kenna said, coming to stand beside her. "Are you happy here?"

"Yeah, Mom, I am." Layla couldn't stay mad anymore. She hugged Kenna. "Sorry for yelling at you and stressing you out."

Kenna patted her back. "Well, maybe I deserved it. Just don't make a habit of it."

"Out of the way, Mama Bear. I want a hug!" Apollo cried and caught Layla up. She laughed as Basset hugged them from the other side.

"Guys, you're squishing me," she complained.

"You deserve an ass kicking. Hunting down gods and running away to other worlds. I swear you'll give me wrinkles," Apollo complained. He looked over at Arne. "Though I can't blame you. Are all the elvish boys and girls as pretty? Because I could use a holiday." He waggled his golden eyebrows at her.

"I missed you, whore bag."

"Don't encourage him," Charlotte said. "You'll have to tell me about how my patches went."

"I will but..." Layla turned as another portal opened to England. She expected to see Kian first. Instead, her father came through. And he was walking. "Oh my God."

"We wanted to surprise you," Charlotte said, but Layla was already running towards him. He was leaning heavily on a cane, but he was upright.

"How is this possible?" Layla cried, throwing her arms around him.

"Careful, baby. I'm still a little wobbly," David said, rubbing her back.

Lachie's black hair and brilliant blue eyes appeared beside them. "Those fae know what they are doing after all."

"Of course we do," Kian said, coming through the portal with Elise. Bayn, Freya, Arawan, and Imogen followed them through. There was one face she was missing.

"Where's Ciara?" she asked Lachie.

Her cousin shrugged. "Fuck knows. She requested some personal time a week ago and said if she wasn't back by tonight to let you know she's proud as hell of you. You know what she's like. Probably for the best she has a break somewhere. She's had a bee in her bonnet since she came back from Svartalfheim."

Apollo appeared with a large mug of mead. "Layla! Come and taste... Oh. Hello Lachlan."

"Apollonius. I didn't know you were coming," Lachie said, frowning at the golden-haired magician.

"And miss my Layla's party? Not for the world. Excuse me, I need to be over there," Apollo said, striding away with a sassy flick of his golden curls.

Layla raised a questioning brow at Lachlan. "What's up there?"

"Don't know what you're talking about. Oh look, there's Tor. I need to talk to him," Lachlan said and went off in the opposite direction.

"Weird boys." Layla shook her head. The whole garden was packed with people, and a burst of anxiety rushed through her. They all seemed to be getting along fine for once, but there was a tingle starting in her stomach that told her she was close to getting overwhelmed.

A warm hand slipped into hers, and the tightening inside of her eased. Arne tucked her under his arm. "Want to get out of here for a moment?"

"Please," she whispered. They weren't noticed as they slipped through the garden and down to the lake. The sun was setting over it, and Layla sighed at the beauty around her. By winter it would be freezing cold and frozen solid, so she would enjoy it while she could. They slipped out of their shoes to paddle in the cool shallows.

"I have been thinking about my magic," Arne said. There was something in his tone that made her stop.

"What about it?" she asked.

"You once told me that I could use it any way I wanted. Do you still believe that?"

Layla rested a hand on his chest. "Yes, it's your power to do with as you want. I'll support you in whatever you decide. You know, as long as it's not to start Ragnarök."

"Not even a little funny," he huffed.

"Kind of funny." Layla tugged on his shirt. "Out with it, Arne. Tell me."

"I want to use it to make you immortal," he said in a rush.

"What?!" Layla would have gone over into the lake in surprise if he didn't grab her.

Arne cupped her cheeks. "I want you by my side forever, Layla Ironwood. When Vili's magic hit me, I felt what it was like to have you die in my arms. I won't go through that again."

Layla's heart ached, remembering the anguish and terror that had been on his face that day. "Arne, it was just Vili fucking with you. We will *all* die at some point, my love. You can't change that no matter how much magic you have."

"I know that, but I want your life to be at least as long mine. Please Layla, let me use it for something good," he begged.

Layla looked over at her messy family, all drinking and talking together. They were chaos, but she loved them. She knew Bron and Imogen would live a long time because of their partners, so it wasn't as if she would be alone. She looked back at Arne, at the love shining in his eyes. No, alone was the last thing she would be.

"Okay, Arne," she whispered.

"Really? You'll do it?"

"Yes, I'll do it. But if you change your mind in like fifty years, we are *not* allowed to take it back," she said. She laughed as he lifted her up in his arms and kissed her. Loud wolf whistles and jeers started up almost instantly from her rowdy family.

"Just ignore them," Layla said, giggling at their antics.

Arne kissed her sweetly. "I've only ever seen you anyway, *vennen.*"

EPILOGUE

Sweat poured down Ciara's back and ran into her eyes. The cars on the streets of Oslo blurred in front of her, but she managed to park.

"Almost there. Keep it together," she whispered. Her mouth was so damn dry. Warm, wet blood seeped through the bandages on her shoulder, her arm hanging uselessly at her side. She checked her mirrors for anyone that could be following her. She wiped at her sweaty face and zipped up her leather jacket to hide her wounds.

Ciara climbed out of the car, and her vision started tunneling. Fuck. Fuck. Fuck.

Have to get to safety, her father's voice said in her head. *You're almost there.*

Ciara took a deep breath, and the blackness cleared. Her legs were like jelly as she shuffled across the road and into the apartment lobby. The receptionist was too busy on the phone to notice the blood Ciara was dripping on the polished floors and all the way into the elevator. She pushed the button quickly, so no one could get in after her.

Ciara looked like a pale, blood-flecked corpse in the mirrored sides of the elevator. She looked like she was about to die. Maybe she was. The thought didn't scare her as much as it probably should.

Got to pass on the message, and then you can die, Ciara.

The door binged open, and she shuffled down the hallway. With the last of her strength, she banged on a familiar door, leaving bloody handprints on its pristine surface.

"Please be here..." she croaked. The door opened, and Torsten caught her as she toppled forward.

"Ciara! What the fuck! You're bleeding," he said, carrying her inside and putting her on the couch. He pulled back the corner of her jacket and swore at the bandages. "Gods, Ciara."

"Torst..." she tried to get the words out. She caught at his hand to halt him. "*Listen* to me."

Torsten crouched down beside her. "Okay, I'm here. What happened?"

"Tor. I found..." Ciara swayed, and his strong hands steadied her. Her vision was growing black again. She was out of time. "I found where Varg was hiding. W-We fought. I got away but he b-bit..."

Tor's eyes went fully wolf. "He bit you? Ciara, you need—"

"Shhhh not important bit."

"The fuck it isn't," he snarled.

Ciara shook her head and put her bloody hand over his mouth. It was such a nice mouth. Ciara's eyes blurred as the blackness took her. "Tor...I found your sister."

Luna Cursed

Ironwood Series Book 4

Alessa Thorn

PROLOGUE

There were many stories about how the Ulfheðnar first came into being. Some said they had been called to life at the time of creation and had always been walking the earth.

Others claimed that Odin All-Father had gathered nine of his best warriors before a battle and blessed them with power and strength, imbuing them with the spirit and form of wolves. Those berserkers had sworn their loyalty to Odin for the gift and pledged their allegiance and that of their bloodline for all time.

This was the story that the Ulfheðnar were telling now. That they were the blessed warriors of Odin and would always be loyal to the All-Father and those of his family until Ragnarök ended them all. On that day, they would fight by the sides of the Aesir and meet their end as the Norns decreed. Until then, whenever the All-Father called, they met him on the battlefield. They were always prepared for the call, honing themselves into an elite warrior society, ready to serve the gods.

There was one other story that had always been whispered far from pious ears. It told of a third creation of the Ulfheðnar. They came into being not as a blessing from Odin, but from a curse.

In the beginning, there was Fenris—a mighty wolf, the first shape changer godchild. Born of Loki, the god of change and tricks, and the powerful giantess Angrbothr.

Fenris was the first wolf shapeshifter, and he had posed no threat to the Aesir. Fenris lived, and Odin hated that he was more powerful than his own children. He fretted that Fenris would one day rise and take his rule and cause trouble like his father so often did.

Fenris loved, and when his mate became pregnant, Odin acted. He couldn't allow such beings to be born stronger and more powerful than man. He swore to bind Fenris for the safety of the realms and set about laying his plans, gathering support from the gods. None of them dared to tell Loki.

For all of his great wisdom, Odin overlooked Fate. And Fate did not like to be forgotten.

So the Norns made plans of their own.

They told Fenris that there was only one way for his family to live. He had to send his mate and children far away, hiding them in Midgard until the All-Father's temper cooled. Fenris himself had to submit to the All-Father's binding as the price of keeping his family safe. He had to become the monster that all would fear.

Fenris did. He let the gods tie him down with Gleipnir, magical bindings created with the sound of a cat's footfall, the beard of a woman, roots of a mountain, the breath of a fish, the spit of a bird, and the sinews of a bear.

Mighty Fenris submitted for love and swore his vengeance on the All-Father.

After a time, Odin learned of the wolf shifters living and thriving in Midgard. They had forgotten Fenris, their father, and they didn't know the story of where they had come from.

Generous Odin blessed them with a new story. And they were thankful and oh, so loyal. The chaotic power in their blood had been tamed. And Odin slept easier at night.

Deep in the darkness, Fenris waited, and he dreamed.

1

Tor was tired, and at the same time, he was wound up tighter than he had been in years. He had turned down Alruna's offer to portal him back to Oslo after Arne and Layla's mating party. He craved the drive, the still cool spring air streaking through his hair as he drove too fast. He needed to get away from Finnmark.

It wasn't that he wasn't happy for his blood brother; it was a joy to see Arne with Layla. Tor loved her like she was his own blood and only wanted happiness for both of them.

Tor just needed to get away and get his head together. To not think about the one person who hadn't been there to share the couple's joy. Lachlan had said that Ciara had requested leave and had fallen off the grid. They didn't seem to worry about it, as if Ciara did that kind of thing all the time.

Tor instantly got a twinge of unease between his shoulder blades, like his wolf side sensed the trouble brewing. He didn't think that Ciara was lying on a beach in a bikini, though he did take a moment to think about how it would look on her.

What was she doing that she was off-grid? Tor didn't like worrying about someone who didn't like him. He didn't want to think about how she spent her holiday...and with whom. Especially not with whom.

Tor hated that he cared most of all. He hated that he had picked her up in Svartalfheim, buried his face in her neck, and breathed in her apple blossom scent. He had known he would live to regret it.

And gods, did he regret it. Ciara was the Wolf Slayer. She would never let a wolf touch her again. His wolf didn't like that one damn bit. Luckily, it didn't have a say in the matter. Ciara Ironwood would never trust a wolf to hold her or keep her safe.

Tor had gotten back to Oslo and had slept for two days. He had only dragged himself out of bed when someone had decided to bang on his door. The scent of blood hit him halfway across the apartment.

"Fuck, what has happened now?" Tor yanked open the door, and Ciara Ironwood collapsed into his arms. "Ciara! What the fuck! You're bleeding." Her clothes were soaked in it, her scent tainted by sharp fear. Tor picked her up and carried her inside. "Gods, Ciara."

He had fucking *known* she wasn't on some beach getting a fucking tan. He placed her on his couch, not caring that the blood would stain it.

"Torst... Listen to me," she croaked.

Tor went down, so they were at eye level. "Okay, I'm here. What happened?"

"Tor. I found... I found where Varg was hiding. W-We fought. I got away, but he b-bit..." Ciara stammered, her skin going paler.

The wolf inside Tor roared in fury. "He bit you? Ciara, you need—"

"Shhhh, not the important bit."

"The fuck it isn't," he snarled. The infection would already be in her bloodstream. The touch of her hand over his mouth made him go still. Her eyes were sliding out of focus.

"Tor...I found your sister," she whispered. Her eyes rolled in the back of her head, and Tor caught her before she face-planted the carpet. He pushed down the fear and panic that suddenly roared through him. He pulled her jacket off and laid her down. She was passed out, not dead, but if he didn't help her, she would wish that she was. Tor grabbed a medical kit from his bathroom and crouched beside her.

"Sorry about this," he murmured.

Gripping the collar of her T-shirt, he tore it to expose her neck and shoulder. A low growl emanated from him as he pulled off the sodden fabric she had over the weeping wounds. He could see the pattern of the teeth that had tried to tear through her. He was going to kill so many people for this.

"The fuck you were doing hunting Varg on your own?" he muttered.

He washed the wounds out with saline and put fresh bandages over them. He only needed to slow the bleeding until he could get her the help she needed. He fished his phone out of his pocket and rang Alruna.

"Tor, darling, did you get to—" she began.

"Auntie, I need you to make a portal to my apartment right now."

Alruna didn't hesitate. The air burned with magic, and she stepped from her kitchen and beside Tor. Her eyes went wide at the blood all over his hands and the broken woman on his couch.

"Varg bit her. We need to get her to Gudrun before the infection takes hold," Tor said, picking Ciara up in his arms.

"Tor, she is the Wolf Slayer," Alruna said softly. "You know that Gudrun might not want to help her."

"Ciara is Layla's family. Layla is now Odin's family. Ciara *is* Odin's family. Gudrun will help," Tor replied, his mouth filling with fangs.

"I hope you know what you are doing."

Alruna opened a portal, and a hut appeared in front of them. Tor held Ciara tighter to him, and she whimpered softly.

"I got you, little one. It's going to be okay now," he promised her. He just hoped that the Völva was in a good mood.

2

There had been a Völva in Ulfheim since they had been a village. She lived in a wooden hut outside the main village with a forest and a stream nearby. No matter how many times the wolves offered electricity to the hut, the Völva refused. The old one chose one of the pack's women with the seeing gift and trained them to take the helm. It had been the way for hundreds of years, a piece of tradition that couldn't be altered.

The current Völva was Gudrun, a sharp-eyed, sharper-tongued wolf with brilliant red hair. She opened the door to her wooden hut as soon as Alruna's magic had stirred the air.

"And what brings you to my hut tonight, little alpha? And with the queen of the elves no less," she demanded.

"Please, Gudrun, she's been bit by Varg," Tor said, carrying Ciara up the steps to the Völva.

She shrugged. "So she becomes a wolf on the next full moon."

"She is Ciara Ironwood," Alruna replied. "Help her, and I will owe you a favor."

"A favor from the elf queen. How delicious." Gudrun looked down at Ciara's face. "I thought the Wolf Slayer would be bigger. Bring her inside before someone sees and decides to cut her throat instead."

Tor's eyes whipped around the night-time forest around them, a low, threatening growl rising in his chest. No one would touch Ciara.

"Like that, is it?" Gudrun huffed to Alruna.

Alruna smiled. "Come on, Tor, get her inside. There's no one here but us."

Inside was hot with a fire burning even in summer. Gudrun gestured them to a bare wooden table, and Tor placed Ciara down. Her skin was clammy with sweat, and the color had leeched out of her lips until they were gray.

"She's lost a lot of blood," Gudrun said. She placed a hand on Ciara's brow and closed her eyes. She whispered under her breath, and Tor's nose tingled with the earthy scent of her magic. "Her soul is drifting. She's going to need an anchor and power to heal her."

"I'll do it," Tor said with no hesitation. The thought of losing her was unacceptable. He couldn't stop the clawing in his chest at the thought of letting her die.

"Torsten, you do this, and it will be the beginning of a true bond. She will share some of your strength and power. She *hunts* our kind."

"Only the ones who deserve it, Gudrun. She's just better at it than everyone else." The power inside of him that made him an alpha stirred to life. "Don't make me force you."

Gudrun growled low. "Don't you fucking dare. I'll do it, but the consequences will be on *your* head. If you bond with her, you will make her Ulfheðnar, and she will be bound to return at the next full moon in case she turns. You will not leave her side until she either turns or she doesn't. Understand?"

"Yes, Völva. I swear it." Tor glanced down at Ciara's face. "Though she's not going to like it."

Alruna placed a hand on his arm. "But she will live to be angry, Tor. That's what matters. Gudrun? Can we draw the infection out?"

"We can try. Tor, sit your ass down. You are going to need your strength for what happens next."

Tor sat at the table and dared do something he would never do while Ciara was awake. He took her small, calloused hand in his own and held it. She had split knuckles and bruises on her forearms from a recent fight. Tor swallowed down his anger at not reaching Varg when he had been on the battlefield. If he had focused on getting him, none of this would be happening.

The women moved around him, crushing herbs and gods knew what with a pestle into a small mortar. They got rid of Ciara's ruined shirt and the bandages Tor had put over the fang wounds. She would wear Varg's marks on her skin forever. His wolf bristled inside of him, making Gudrun whimper.

"Stop it, Torsten. I'm working as fast as I can," she snapped, smearing the mixture over Ciara's wounds. She placed a small dish in front of him and poured a sweet-smelling oil into it. A small knife appeared beside it. "I need blood, freely offered."

Tor took the knife and opened his palm. The burning sting of pain was worth it if Ciara was well enough to fight him again. He dripped the blood into the oil until Gudrun declared it was enough and tossed him a cloth to stop the bleeding.

Chanting an ancient healing song, Gudrun used the blood and oil to paint runes along Tor's arm, down to the hand that still held Ciara's. She continued the marks up Ciara's arm and to her heart. Tor's skin rippled as the magic struck him. He gritted his teeth, burning pain racing through him and setting the runes alight.

Please, gods of my ancestors, make this work.

The burning increased, and he felt the second the bond with Ciara was made. A piece of him left him and attached itself to her. The burning eased, and he swayed, suddenly dizzy and exhausted.

"Easy, Tor. Breathe through it," Alruna said, her hands resting on his shoulders to steady him.

Gudrun's chant eased off, and she opened her eyes. They all looked down at Ciara. Her skin was flush again, the sweating had stopped, and she breathed deeply.

"I didn't think that was going to work," the Völva said and let out a surprised laugh. She poured them all small cups of black liquor. Tor downed his and felt better. "I hope she's worth all the trouble this will cause."

"Nobody gives a shit what I do, and this is my business. If they have a problem with it, they know where to find me," Tor grunted.

Gudrun sipped her drink thoughtfully. "You say that now. Keep her on Ulfheðnar lands until her wounds are healed. I can't help if I'm not close. She's one of the clan now."

"The bond really worked?" Alruna asked.

Gudrun laughed. "Oh, it worked. Probably too well. Take her home, Tor. Don't forget that she can leave once her wounds are closed, but she has to return for the full moon. That's two weeks away."

"Thank you, Gudrun. I won't ever forget this," Tor said, getting to his feet. He picked Ciara up and cradled her close.

"I won't ever let you. Bring her by again when she's up. I want to see what the fuss is all about."

Tor nodded but didn't make any promises. He had no doubt that when Ciara woke, she would be angry enough that the gods would feel it.

Alruna opened a portal to Tor's cabin. It was between the wolf and elves settlement, next to the lake and surrounded by forest. He didn't like being around the wolves too much but needed to be close to Arne. It was the best compromise he could come up with.

"You did a good thing tonight, Tor," Alruna said, opening the front door with the key he kept hidden under a plant pot.

"She's not going to see it that way," he replied. He placed Ciara down on his bed. "Thank you for coming when I called."

"Of course, Torsten. You are my family," Alruna said, placing her hands on his cheeks. "You are the best man to help a woman in such need. Try and get some rest. I'll tell Arne and Layla what has happened. Message us when Ciara's awake so Layla can visit her."

"She's going to fight me about it. Layla might be needed sooner."

Alruna smiled. "I'm sure you can handle it." She placed a kiss on his cheek before disappearing.

Tor looked down at the woman in his bed in dirty jeans and a plain black bra. She was going to be furious when she woke up and found out they had a bond. Tor still couldn't find it in him to regret it. He could see the healing abilities he had given her through the bond already working. He unlaced her boots and slid them off her feet before drawing a blanket over her. He stumbled to the couch and was asleep as soon as his head hit the cushions.

3

Ciara woke with her body on fire and her mouth dry as dust. She cracked an eye open and tried to lift her head from the soft pillow under her head.

"Where the fuck am I?" she mumbled.

It had been a long time since she had woken up in a strange place and missing her shirt. Her vision cleared, and she tried to take in the neat bedroom. The walls and ceiling were pine, and her bed was made of repurposed timber. Out of the windows, she saw a lake and trees.

Ciara tried to sit up, wincing at the pain burning through her neck and shoulder. She tried to think, but her head didn't seem to want to clear.

"You might want to go slow," a deep voice said. Torsten was standing in the doorway, his hair a long golden tumble around his broad shoulders. With his gray eyes, clipped golden beard, and wide chest, he was a Viking god wet dream. Ciara would know because she'd had more than one.

He was wearing a red and black flannel shirt with a few too many buttons undone and faded jeans, a combination that did weird things to Ciara's libido that she didn't understand.

Am I still dreaming? Ciara frowned up at him.

"Hey, don't glare at me like that, Wolf Slayer. You came to me, remember?" he said with a grin.

"No, I don't remember," she croaked. She struggled to sit up again, and two big hands were suddenly helping her upright.

"Here, drink some water before you try snarling at me," Tor suggested, holding a cup out to her.

Ciara gripped it, but it felt like she didn't have a drop of strength in her entire body. She managed to get it to her mouth without it sloshing everywhere. It was the best thing she had ever tasted. She drained it, and some of the fog began to clear. She had been driving around Oslo and had been truly scared for the first time since she was a girl.

"Where am I?" she said once the glass was empty. Tor took it from her and placed it on the nightstand.

"Ulfheim. Well, just outside of it. You came to my apartment in Oslo and said Varg had bitten you. You were..." Tor's eyes gleamed with a feral wolf light for a moment before it vanished. "You were bleeding out. I got Alruna to come and get us. I took you to the Ulfheðnar Völva to heal you."

Ciara touched the bandages that were covering her neck and shoulder. There was a strange herbal smell rising from them. "I was bit."

The room swirled around her with all that it implied. Lachie was going to kill her. Literally. They had a pact from when they were kids that if either of them turned, the other one would put them down with a silver bullet to the brain. Tears filled her eyes.

"I'm going to be sick," she said, struggling to get out of bed.

Tor was beside her in a second. She couldn't fight him as he plucked her out of bed and carried her into the adjoining bathroom. He placed her on her feet, and she gripped the basin with one hand and pushed him away with the other.

"Get out. I don't need an audience."

"Don't worry, I wasn't going to help you wipe anything," Tor teased, closing the door behind him. "Try not to fall over and bash your head."

Ciara sank to her knees in front of the toilet bowl, getting the lid open before vomiting. She clung to her pounding head, and her memories started to come back thick and fast.

Ciara had been hunting Varg. He had escaped the battlefield and still had followers in Norway. She had been awake in Svartalfheim and had overheard Tor telling Layla how Varg had stolen his sister. It had churned around her head for days afterward. She couldn't help but think how if it had been Lachlan, she wouldn't have been half as calm. She had gone to work, investigating Linnea's disappearance for herself. She had looked through all of Varg's last known locations and had done what she did best.

Then Ciara had found Varg and a group of his followers in Onsøy, and everything became a blur of claws and blades and searing pain. She had gotten one dagger in him and sprayed him with wolfsbane; it had been enough to get the shifter off her. She had made it to her car and driven with only one goal—to get to safety and tell Tor that his sister was still alive. She had thought she was going to die.

No such luck. The wolf couldn't help being a hero and saving your ass. Fuck, it was embarrassing. She didn't even want to think about why her painfilled, panicked body had associated him with safety, either.

Ciara flushed the toilet, and with considerable effort, she wriggled out of her dirty clothes and climbed into the bathtub. She was starting to shiver, the shock hitting her hard enough to make her teeth chatter. Hot water rushed over her legs, and she groaned in relief.

"Are you okay in there?" Tor asked through the door. Ciara pulled her knees up to her chest as the door cracked open. "I'm not looking, just putting a fresh towel here and something for you to wear."

"Thanks," she said, knowing he was just trying to help.

"Do you want something to drink?"

Ciara sniffed, horrified that tears were building up in her eyes. "Don't suppose you have anything alcoholic?"

"I'm Scandinavian. Of course I have something alcoholic." Tor disappeared for a moment before returning with a small glass of black liquid. "You covered? I remember how shy you are about nudity."

Ciara's knees were still tucked up to her chest. "Covered enough. And I'm not shy about nudity. I only liked to be warned."

Tor removed his hand from over his gray eyes. His gaze skimmed over her back, and he froze. "Gods below, you are covered in bruises."

"It's a hunter's life for me," Ciara replied and held her hand out for the drink. "What is it?"

"Something the elves make. It's alcoholic, but it's good for you. It'll help with your healing." Tor passed her the glass. "You want help taking the bandages off? Gudrun's ointment should have healed up your wounds by now."

Ciara sipped the herby drink. It burned on her tongue and throat, and something in her relaxed. "Go ahead."

With gentle movements, Tor helped unwind the bandages over her shoulder and neck. Goosebumps spread over her skin with every brush of his fingers against her skin.

"They are closed, but I bet they are hurting like a bitch," Tor said, examining them.

"Closed already? That's some ointment."

Tor took a clean flannel from the small cupboard under the basin. "Gudrun knows her business," he said, but there was a slight hesitation in his voice that Ciara couldn't interpret. Tor soaked the flannel under the hot water and placed it over her shoulder.

"Are you seriously going to wash my back for me?" Ciara asked, sounding far more annoyed than she meant.

"Well, you can't do it just yet. Besides, Layla would kick my ass if I didn't help you," Tor replied, unfazed by her. Just like always. "You came to me for help, remember? So let me help."

Ciara swallowed hard and then tilted her head so he could wipe over the back of her neck. She couldn't remember when someone else had helped in such a way. Probably not since her mother... Ciara shut that thought down.

"Does Layla know I'm here?" she asked instead.

"Alruna told her. I can get her to come if you want, but due to the circumstances, it's better if you give it another day," Tor replied.

"What circumstances?" Ciara's eyes drifted shut against her will as the warm cloth swiped over her back.

"You were bit, Ciara. I don't need to tell you what that means. Gudrun did her best to try and stop the infection from spreading, but until the full moon, we aren't going to know if you will...if you..." Tor struggled.

"If I'm going to turn into a wolf," Ciara said to him. Ice was running through her again, and she sipped her drink, washing her tears back.

"Yes." Tor resumed the gentle strokes of the cloth like he was doing his best to soothe her. There was no soothing the turmoil rolling through her. She wanted to run and scream but only had the strength to sit there. "There's something else."

Ciara sniffed back her tears. "There always is. Out with it."

Tor placed the cloth over her shoulder and took a step back from the bathtub so he could look her in the eyes.

"You were dying, Ciara, and didn't have enough strength to pull yourself back from it." Tor crossed his arms. "I...gave you my strength."

Ciara frowned. "I don't understand."

"Ulfheðnar can create bonds with other people. I created a bond with you and shared some of my strength and healing abilities with you to help you survive."

"A bond." Ciara glared up at him. There was only one such bond she knew of. "Like a mating bond?"

"Fuck no. We aren't mated," Tor hurried to explain. "It's just a bond. A power share. Some warriors are fighting pairs. They use a bond to share each other's strengths and abilities. It's not mating. The last thing I want is to be mated to you."

Ciara flinched by that unexpected stab but did her best to hide it. "I have some of your strength."

"Yes, and some healing abilities."

"And nothing else? Nothing like the crazy mark thing Arne put on Layla?"

"Nothing like that." Tor shook his head. "If you turn, you will be more powerful than most. I'm an alpha, so you will be too."

"We won't know if I will turn until the full moon?" Ciara asked. There was still a slim chance she hadn't totally fucked her life. "When is it?"

"About a fortnight?"

Ciara drained her glass. "Anything else I should know?"

"You will need to come back for it. First turnings can be rough. You'll be volatile, and it's better if you're near other wolves. I'm to watch over you until then because even though Varg bit you, I took responsibility for your life. You are...Ulfheðnar."

The fuck she was. "So you're going to babysit me until then?" she demanded.

"Yes, and you can be pissed off about it all you want," he growled, making the hair on her arms rise. "You came to me for help, and you're going to get it, whether you want it or not."

Ciara's eyes narrowed at his tone, and she turned away from him. "Get out."

"Be shitty about it all you want. What's done is done, and you have no one to blame but yourself. You should've thought about the consequences of hunting a monster like Varg on your own," Tor said and shut the door behind him.

Ciara drained her drink and made a decision. As soon as she was strong enough, she was out of there, and one wolf wasn't going to be able to stop her.

"Guardian, my ass," she hissed and slid under the hot water.

4

The next time Ciara woke, it was afternoon. She was wearing the soft cotton shirt Tor had left for her, and there was a travel mug of soup on the bedside table that was still warm. Her head was clearer than the day before, and all her bones seemed to crack when she stretched. It was probably the most she had slept in years.

Ciara sipped the vegetable soup, and her brain came back online. She needed to find a phone and get Layla to bring her some clothes and get the fuck out of there. She couldn't let Varg's trail go cold. That fucker had bit her, and she wasn't going to stop until she had cut his damn head off.

Ciara got out of bed with ease and used the bathroom. She examined her injuries and found none. Tor's bond had given her some of his healing after all.

"Holy crap." There wasn't a single bruise on her, and the bite was nothing but a circle of small pink scars. She would wear that fucker's marks for the rest of her life.

"He has to die," she said, and it came out as a growl. Her eyes went wide at the sound. Fuck. "No. Don't think about it. You need to focus on getting out of here."

Ciara walked out of the room and looked around the small house for Tor's phone. The rest of the place was neat, with comfortable-looking furniture and an incredible view of the lake. A thumping sound had her stepping outside into the cool afternoon. Tor's shirt was big enough to brush her knees, but she still felt too naked. She needed Layla, and that meant dealing with her wolf babysitter.

Ciara almost tripped over when she went around the side of the house and found Tor shirtless and standing next to a massive wood pile. His broad back was covered in dark blue Viking tattoos and scars that looked like they had been made by claws.

She had done her best not to look at him when he decided to be shirtless in Svartalfheim, but now she found herself staring. Maybe she had gotten so used to him being around that she forgot how massive he was.

"Awake again. Come to yell at me?" he asked, lifting the ax and splitting the block of wood with one perfect strike.

"I need..." Ciara cleared her throat and dragged her eyes off him. "I need clothes." That made him turn. Tor raised an ashen brow.

"You're wearing some," he said.

"Real clothes. I need your phone so I can ring Layla and get out of here."

Tor's ax came down hard on the block and stayed there. "How are you feeling?"

"Fine. No bruises. Nothing. I'm good to go," Ciara said. Tor walked over to her, and she felt a wave of masculine heat and power hit her. She had always been aware of the BDE he seemed to exude, but now it hit her like a truck and made her take a step back. All her hunter senses were suddenly telling her to run, and she had to physically stop herself from doing just that. Ironwoods didn't run.

"Go where?" he asked.

"Anywhere I want. You can't keep me here, Tor. I don't care what your guardian bullshit is," she replied, lifting her chin.

"I could, you know, keep you here," he said, eyes flashing wolf.

Ciara didn't like that tone one fucking bit. "I'll fucking walk to Layla if I have to. Call her right now."

"Or what? You'll run?" Tor smiled, showing way too many teeth. "Please do, *kanin*."

An unexpected thrill ran down Ciara's spine at the thought. She had always wondered who would win if they went head-to-head. She smiled back at him and let the Wolf Slayer come into her eyes.

Tor chuckled. "Ah, there she is. Some fight left in you after all."

"A fight you're going to get intimately acquainted with if you don't give me your phone," she replied, not backing down.

Tor's head tilted in curiosity. He shook himself. "Yeah, you're not ready to take me on just yet. Here." He took his phone from his back pocket and unlocked it. "Just remember, wherever you go, I'm following whether you like it or not."

"We'll see about that," Ciara said, snatching the phone out of his hand. Layla's number was already ringing. Her instincts were screaming not to do it, but she still turned her back on the dangerous wolf in front of her and walked back towards the house.

"Tor? Is everything okay? How's Ciara?" Layla answered.

"Ciara is pissed and needs some clothes and for you to come and get her straight away," she replied.

"Cus! I'm so happy to hear your voice. Of course I can bring you clothes. Tor invited us around for dinner anyway."

He had? Why didn't he say anything? "Oh. Good."

Layla was quiet for a beat and then asked, "If you need clothes, what are you wearing?"

"One of Tor's shirts. Just bring me something. I can't bare ass it around any longer."

Layla cracked up laughing. "Yeah, okay. I'll be there soon. I hope you are feeling better because I will give you the lecture of your life when I get there. Okay, bye!"

Ciara let out a sigh. No one had issues with her hunting by herself before. She didn't know why it was an issue now.

Probably because you got hurt, unlike all the other times, she thought and flinched. She had reacted emotionally on a hunt for the first time ever, and it had almost gotten her killed.

"Get a hold of her?" Tor said from behind her. He was carrying an armload of wood like it weighed nothing.

Ciara opened the back door for him. "Yeah, she'll be here soon, and I'll be out of your hair."

Tor began stacking the wood into a neat triangle next to the fireplace. "Just because you keep saying it doesn't mean it's going to happen. I'm responsible for you until the full moon, and you need to accept it."

"I'm a grown-ass woman, Tor. I don't need a babysitter." Ciara put her hands on her hips, making her shirt ride higher up her thighs. "I can take care of myself."

"I can tell by the way you turned up at my apartment, bleeding and afraid." Tor's eyes skimmed over her legs, and a hot flush crept over her. "You need to tell us where you found Varg, and if we get some suitable answers, then we make a plan. Those ideas you have about going back after him alone? Forget them. It's not going to happen."

"I'm getting really tired of you trying to tell me what to do, wolf," Ciara said, eyes narrowing.

"You should've thought of that before you decided to come to me for help."

"Maybe you should've let me die instead." The words were out of her mouth before she could stop them. Tor growled so deeply that goosebumps broke out on her skin. She held her ground as he closed in on her.

"I'm never going to let that happen. It doesn't matter that you've hated me since the second we met. You came for help, and I gave it. Resent me as much as you like, Wolf Slayer. I'm never going to regret saving you." Tor leaned down until they were nose to nose. "You're stuck with me until the full moon, and there's not a damn thing you can do about it."

Ciara's heart was beating hard, and she knew he could hear it. She glared into his gray eyes, unable to think of a single thing to say. When Tor focused on you, it was as if nothing else in the world existed, and to be the center of that kind of attention was terrifying and thrilling at the same time. It made all thoughts stop working.

Words had never been Ciara's strong suit anyway. She didn't want to talk; she wanted to fight him. Throw him to the ground and show him just who he thought he could boss about. The anger in Tor's eyes shifted to a different kind of heat, and Ciara's mouth dried out. Her body must've been telling him something because a slight grin appeared on his full lips. Shit.

"Knock knock!" Layla called, making Ciara jump back from him. Her cousin all but bounced inside with a bag of gear swinging in one hand. She was happier than Ciara had ever seen her. "Look who is up and about." Layla caught Ciara up in a hug. "Don't you ever scare me like that again, or I'll get Tor to kick your ass."

Ciara snorted. "As if he stands a chance."

Layla handed her the bag. "Here, take these. Maybe once you're wearing underwear again, you won't be so grumpy."

Tor's grin turned into a full-blown smirk. Ciara snatched the bag and hurried back to the bedroom before he saw how red her face was. These were going to be the worst two weeks of her life.

5

Tor pulled on a shirt and went to the fridge for beers. He wanted to stick his head in the freezer or throw himself into the lake.

"Everything okay in here?" Arne asked from behind him. "How's your guest?"

"Fine." Tor passed him a beer before opening his own and downing half of it. "She's delightful." Arne's lips twitched. The bastard.

"You knew who and what she was when you decided to save her. How's the bond?" Arne asked. Of course Alruna told him about that as well.

"Itchy," Tor replied. He dragged his hair back in frustration and tied it into a knot. "It's fine, Arne. You don't need to look at me like that. Wolves make bonds all the time, and it's totally fine. It's not a thing like it is with elves. Fuck, if she doesn't turn on the full moon, I'm sure Gudrun can undo it. There are ways. It'll be completely fi..."

"Fine?" Arne sipped his beer, golden eyes shining. "I'm sure there is a way to undo it if you want it."

"What are you two talking about in here?" Layla asked, coming into the kitchen. Arne immediately pulled her to him, so her back was against his chest and he held onto her. Layla didn't seem to care. She only took his beer and had a sip. Their happiness radiated off them, and Tor could feel the intensity of it. It was like standing in the middle of a summer day.

"How delightful and grateful your cousin is that I saved her life," Tor replied.

Layla giggled. "Doesn't sound like Ciara. You okay? She can be savage when she's in a mood."

"He's fine. He told me three times," Arne said, and Tor wanted to punch him.

"Ciara doesn't want to accept that I need to watch over her until the full moon. There's no way around it. I can't let her go off on her own. If a change starts to happen early, then she'll freak out and could hurt someone. I'm going to ensure it doesn't happen. Can you talk to her, Layla? Make her see reason?" Tor asked.

If she didn't, he would do it his way, which would involve throwing his alpha power at Ciara and making her submit. She would *really* hate him then, and not just...whatever they had between them now.

"I can say something, but I don't know if she'll listen to me." Layla chewed her bottom lip thoughtfully. "She will want to kill Varg for biting her, so frame your guardianship as backup to hunt him down instead of babysitting, and she might calm down. She got hurt badly. You saw her at her most vulnerable, Tor. She's going to hate that you saw her so weak."

"We all need to be taken care of sometimes, no matter how strong we are," Tor grumbled. "I don't think she's less of a hunter because I had to wash her back for her."

Layla choked on her beer. "She let you wash her back?"

"Well, she couldn't do it. She couldn't even lift her arm yesterday," Tor replied. Layla looked genuinely shocked. "What?"

"She doesn't let anyone help her, even when hurt. If she let you do that, she doesn't hate you half as much as she makes out."

Tor knew that but for an entirely different reason. Before Layla interrupted them arguing, Tor had caught something in Ciara's scent that wasn't anger. The only other time he had smelled that sweet arousal was in Svartalfheim when he had pinned her to the wall.

He had grabbed her to trick the guards, but when he had buried his face into Ciara's neck, his senses had been overwhelmed with the scent of apple blossoms and woman. It had been so delicious that his tongue had licked her skin just to see if it tasted as good. It tasted better. Her scent had altered in a split second, arousal mingling with the apple. He had thought he had imagined it until just now in his living room. He had been one step off licking her again when Layla had busted in on them.

Fuck. Being horny over a woman who would never touch him in a million years was a new low. The wolf in him loved the challenge. It wanted to hunt and harass and wear her down until she gave up the chase and submitted to him. Now, there was an idea...

"Tor?" Layla waved a hand in front of his face.

"Sorry, what did you say?" he asked.

"I said do you know where she was when she found Varg?"

Tor shook his head. "She's only just healed enough to be in a talkative mood. I knew I wouldn't get anything out of her, so I want you to."

The door to the bedroom opened, and Ciara came out in dark blue jeans and a purple top that slid off one shoulder. Varg's marks were pink against her light brown skin. Tor bit back the snarl in his throat. He hated that she would wear them forever.

Unless you mark her over the top of them, his wolf side prompted unhelpfully.

"Would you like a beer?" he asked, dragging his eyes away from the scars.

Ciara nodded and slid onto a stool at the breakfast bar. "Okay, Layla, you might as well start your lecture now."

"Why didn't you tell anyone where you were going?" Layla asked. "You know how dangerous Varg is, and to think you could take him and a whole cult out on your own is actually insane."

"Firstly, I didn't know Varg was there. I had been hunting a different wolf in Sweden, and it turned out that he was a part of the cult," Ciara explained. Tor passed her a beer, and she shot him a small smile. Well, wonders never cease. "Secondly, when I *did* spot Varg, it was your mating party, and I didn't want to interrupt...all of that." She gestured at Arne, still holding Layla in the cradle of his body.

"So you decided to take them on all on your own?" Tor asked.

Ciara shook her head. "I was only meant to be spying on them. I was going to wait until after your party to call it in. I was getting a lay of the land, figuring out how far the camp stretched, and getting numbers of how many wolves there were. I saw your sister."

Something ripped inside of Tor. "How did you know it was her?"

"She looks exactly like you."

"No, she doesn't." Tor gripped the bench in front of her. "How did you know?"

"I looked up her disappearance. There was a picture. Happy?" Ciara replied.

No, he wasn't fucking happy. How did she know that Linnea had even disappeared? Layla wouldn't have told her...which meant she had been awake that night in Svartalfheim and had heard them talking. It still didn't explain why she took it on herself to look into it.

"Was she okay?" he asked.

"From what I could see, she wasn't injured. There was a group of women that seemed to be helpers or servants for Varg and the few wolves that looked like leaders. They weren't wearing manacles or anything."

Tor's teeth ground so hard together that his jaw ached. Varg had turned his sweet sister into a slave? He was so fucking dead.

"They wouldn't need to wear manacles. There's no way they could escape and outrun a full pack of male wolves," Arne said because Tor couldn't seem to open his mouth. He took a few deep breaths.

"How did you get hurt?" he asked when the rage had been pushed back down.

Ciara picked at the label on her beer. "I must have been spotted or smelled no matter how careful I was. Varg and two others jumped me from behind. When I wounded his men, he decided to get in on the action. He got me on the ground and thought he had me. He had just clamped his teeth when I sprayed a full can of wolfsbane in his face. It was enough to get him to let go and blind him as I ran to my car and got out of there."

Tor felt sick. That much wolfsbane would have melted half of Varg's face off. If he fully healed from that, he would kill Ciara in the most painful way possible.

"So why didn't you call us? Why did you go straight to Tor?" Layla asked and fluttered her long lashes innocently.

Ciara scowled at her and drank her beer. "I thought he'd want to know that I saw his sister. Figured he would be home. He was also closest to where I was."

"And where was that exactly?" Arne asked.

Ciara didn't fall for it. "At a camp."

"You're going to have to tell us. We need to go after Varg. He's probably not even there anymore," Tor said irritably.

"Which is why I'm not going to sit around here being babysat by you. That fucker did this to me." Ciara pointed at her ring of scars. "That's before I even get to the fact I might turn into a fucking wolf at the full moon."

"And going wolf would be a fate worse than death, wouldn't it?" Tor said and then hated himself.

Ciara's eyes narrowed. "I want Varg dead. I want to cut off his head and put it on my fucking wall, and no one will stop me."

"We wouldn't try, Ciara," Layla said, trying to soothe her. "Hey, we are still family, aren't we? Which means we fight together. We want you to go after Varg. We just don't want you trying to do it alone again."

"You're too busy with the elves, and you're mating, Layla. You're not going on a hunt," Ciara said stubbornly.

Arne laughed softly. "On that, we can agree. Layla is staying with me. Tor is going with you. I release you from bodyguarding duties. I don't plan on leaving Alfheimstod until the mating is over. You're free to hunt Varg with Ciara."

"Well, now that I have your permission," Tor said and rolled his eyes.

"That's not necessary. There are other hunters I can call in for backup," Ciara began to argue.

Tor turned on her. "You don't get a say. You already had your ass handed to you by Varg once. He'll just slaughter other hunters. You need a wolf with you to track him faster and have enough muscle to take him down. You're an Ironwood for fuck's sake. You should think more strategically than this."

A low growl rolled out of Ciara, and the whole kitchen froze. Tor's insides lit up with the challenge in the noise, the pure wolf in it.

"Ciara, what the actual fuck?" Layla whispered. Arne had pulled her behind him. He knew Ciara had just thrown a challenge right into an alpha's face, in his home, no less.

"It's nothing," Ciara snapped and walked out of the house.

Oh no, she wasn't walking away after that.

"Tor, don't—" Arne began.

Tor was done listening. He strode after Ciara, kicking the door outside open. Her scent went into the woods. Yeah, she wasn't getting away that easily. Tor followed her apple blossom and anger until he spotted her swaying dark hair.

"Go away!" she shouted.

"Stop, Ciara. I'm fucking warning you," Tor replied. She kept walking. That did it.

Tor moved so fast, he barely rustled a leaf and tackled her to the moss. Ciara's elbow went up, smashing him in the ribs. He absorbed the blow and pinned her wriggling and furious underneath him.

"I said *stop*," he snarled. He grabbed her hands and held them tight.

Ciara's blue eyes were so full of fury, they turned electric. "Let me go."

"No. You need to listen to reason, or I'll make you," Tor said, his alpha power begging to unleash on her. "*Don't* make me, Ciara."

She went still underneath him, something finally clicking in her brain that made her realize how much shit she was in. "Get off me."

"No. You will lie still until I can get some sense into that stubborn head of yours." Tor didn't loosen his grip. He wasn't that stupid. "You need help to take down Varg. I'm coming with you, and that's it. You're only fighting the help because it's me, but it doesn't matter. We are bonded until the full moon, so it means I can't let you out of my sight. I physically *can't*."

Ciara's anger faded into confusion. "It's a part of the magic?"

"Yes. I'm not trying to be an asshole. I gave you a part of myself to heal, and until we can undo it, it will damage both of us to be apart. Do you remember what Layla was like when she tried to fight a bond? It will be that but worse."

"I thought you said it wasn't like a mating bond."

"It's not, but it's still a new bond. It needs time to settle, and it can't be removed until we know whether you are going to wolf out." Tor wasn't exactly sure that was true, but if she did turn into a wolf, she would need the extra strength he gave her for the transition. Ciara didn't need to know that. "Please, just stop fighting me about this. Let's work together for the next fortnight, kill Varg, and then it will be over."

Ciara looked like she still wanted to argue with him. Then she went soft underneath him with a sigh. "Okay."

"Okay?" Tor raised a brow. It felt like a trap.

"We can work together. Just don't use your bossy alpha shit on me. I like my free will, and if you try and use your power to take my choices away, I *will* kill you," she replied. She would do it too. There wasn't a flicker of hesitation or bluff in her. Tor hated that he liked that about her.

"Agreed. Now, will you try and hit me in the balls if I move? Otherwise, we are going to be here a while," he asked.

Ciara smiled up at him, and it was so sweet, he felt like he'd been hit in the head. "Would I do something like that?"

"Yes. You absolutely would." Tor tried not to think about how good she felt between his thighs. His dick wasn't listening. He needed to stop this and get off her. "Truce?"

"Truce. No ball hitting, I promise."

Tor slid off her and tugged her to her feet. "It's going to be a pleasure working with you, Ironwood."

"Hmm, we'll see about that," she said and flicked her long dark hair over her shoulder as she turned away from him. Tor's senses were hit by a wave of her silky scent, and he stood paralyzed as she walked back towards the house.

Tor changed his mind; the next two weeks would be pure hell.

6

Layla grabbed Ciara as soon as she walked back into the house. Tor came in a minute later, the knees of his jeans stained with the green moss he had pinned her to. For some insane reason, it made Ciara want to grin. Maybe she really did need to fight it out with him. She wasn't strong enough yet, but the small tussle had released some of the energy inside of her.

"You should know wolves better than to growl at one like that. What the fuck, Ciara?" Layla asked, sitting her down on a couch. Arne and Tor busied themselves in the kitchen before going outside to where Tor had a barbecue set up on the deck.

"It kind of slipped out. I don't know why I did it," Ciara admitted. She looked up at Layla's brown eyes and voiced her deepest fear. "What if I do turn into one because of this bite? Tor said their Völva tried to draw the poison out, but what if it didn't work?"

Layla's expression softened. "It wouldn't matter, Ciara. No one would care but you. You're the one with feelings about wolves. Totally justified feelings. It won't change how any of us look at you."

"You don't think Kenna would try and shoot me?" That wasn't even mentioning Lachie. How was he going to react?

Layla shook her head. "Her son-in-law is the actual Night Prince. The family enemy. If Mom can accept Kill, she can accept anyone. You were bit when fighting for your life. I won't say it's not your fault because you were dumb enough to scout Varg on your own."

"I'm never going to live that down, am I?" Ciara complained, flopping back into the cushions. "It's not like Imogen hasn't done a million dumb things like hunt on her own."

"And I busted her ass about it too. You're usually the smart one, the responsible one! What triggered this insanity?"

"I didn't want him to lose her, okay?" Ciara snapped.

Layla frowned, and her eyes darted to Tor outside. "You were awake in Svartalfheim."

"Yes. I was. He helped us get Arne back. I felt like I owed him to look into his sister's disappearance. All I could think about was, what if it was Lachie and no one helped or believed me? I would lose my fucking mind," Ciara tried to explain. She ran her hands through her hair. "I was going to investigate more as soon as the current hunt was over. It was just my luck that they were connected."

"Oh, Ciara." Layla put an arm around her shoulders. "You have poor Tor thinking that you hate him."

Ciara wasn't sure how true that was. Her body told him secrets she never would. "Probably better that he does think that. He'll remove the bond after the full moon, and he won't have to be worried about being connected to the 'Wolf Slayer' anymore."

"Yeah, the Ulfheðnar aren't going to be happy about that. I'm just warning you now. He's pretending it's not a big deal, but wolves don't bond with people outside the pack, especially not an alpha as powerful as Tor. That he shared that strength with you will cause problems," Layla replied, holding Ciara closer.

"All the more reason we need to get through the next two weeks, and he can have it back," she said.

Ciara wasn't an idiot. She knew that no one would want her to be a wolf or to be connected with Tor. She was the Wolf Slayer, whether she liked it or not. No one would care that every kill she had done were monsters. Her vendetta wasn't only about them being wolves. It was about ensuring that there wasn't another little girl waking up to her parents being massacred by a supernatural serial killer.

Ciara pulled herself away from the memory before it was triggered too badly. She needed to focus, and she would wallow if she thought about her parents for too long. She didn't have the time.

"Tor was doing what he had to in order to save your life. Don't hate him for it," Layla said softly. "You both aren't as tough as you like to make out. He's my friend, and you are my family. Don't put me in a position where I have to choose between you."

"You don't have to worry. We made a truce outside. We will find and kill Varg and be back for the full moon. Just another job. I can be professional if he can be," Ciara said.

Layla laughed. "Yeah, I gave myself the same speech. Just know that backup is around if you need it. We all want another run at Varg."

Ciara looked around at the polished timber floors. "This place needs a rug, and Varg's hide might do nicely."

"Well, if it's too taboo for the wolves, I'll take it. I could use another fur rug," Layla replied with a smirk.

Ciara chewed her lip. "Any tips on dealing with this bond thing? What if I start crying non-stop like you did?"

"That was a different bond, and I was fighting it. You're not. I'm sure it's going to be fine." Layla's smile widened. "Why? Are you feeling any different?"

"Different how?"

Layla waggled her brows. "You feeling lusty after Tor?"

No more than usual.

"No," she said. Ciara risked glancing out the window where he was cooking with Arne. It really was obscene how someone could look so good in dirty jeans and a T-shirt. "He's hot and all, but I know better than to go down the lust road. As you pointed out, he's a family friend, and I won't risk it. I feel stronger physically, and the growling thing happened, but that's it."

"So far." Layla saw her horrified stare. "I'm sure that's it! It's like a warrior bond or something. It's not a mating bond where you always want to climb him like a tree. If it changes, you can talk to me, you know that, right?"

"Yeah, I know. It's going to be fine," Ciara replied. If she said it enough times, she might actually start believing it.

THEY ENDED up watching the sunset over the lake, eating grilled lamb and fresh salad, and talking about things that weren't Varg.

Layla recapped their mating party for Ciara and how there were no fights, surprisingly enough, except Apollo was pissed off at Lachie about something. That didn't surprise Ciara. Her brother could piss off even the most amiable person when he wanted to.

Ciara let the easiness wash over her. A part of her had needed Layla to reassure her that if she did turn wolf, no one would care about it. She needed to talk to Lachie, to tell him everything that had happened. No doubt he would lecture her too.

"We can get Alruna to portal us to Oslo tonight," Tor said. "That way, we can start the hunt fresh tomorrow."

"Good. I have some gear at Mardøll still. I don't know what happened to the car I was in," Ciara said, frowning. It was probably towed by now.

"I had it taken care of," Tor replied. Just like that.

"Oh. Um, thanks," she said.

Layla was watching them, her brown eyes full of mischief. "You two are going to make a great team. All your alpha aggression will be directed at other people instead of each other. You never know. You might realize how much you're alike and finally be friends."

Tor and Ciara shared a look. He knew what Layla was doing too.

"Nah, we like our hostility. It keeps things interesting," Tor said.

Ciara bit back her smile. "I still think we need to have a proper fight. Get the 'who is the bigger alpha' question solved once and for all. See who ends up on top." She said it casually, but the word choice put her straight back into the forest again, Tor's big body pinning her down.

"You have a short memory, *kanin*," Tor said, the slow smirk returning. There was a touch of feral in his eyes that had Ciara going hyperaware of him, her hunter senses alert.

Arne choked on his beer. "Did you just call her rabbit?"

"She tried to run," Tor replied before turning to Ciara. "That's what bunnies do. Don't they, bunny?"

Ciara glared at him. Tor could play host as much as he liked, make dinner, joke with Layla, and fool everyone into thinking what a good tame wolf he was. Ciara knew the truth. She'd felt that hot alpha power he kept bottled up. It had been a split second, and that had been enough. She smiled the Ironwood smile at him, and the wolf flickered in his eyes. It knew a challenge when it was thrown down.

"Just wait until I'm healed up. You are going to regret sharing your strength with me when I'm kicking your ass," she said sweetly, not dropping his stare.

Tor hummed, leaning into Ciara's space. "Joke's on you, bunny. I'm into that."

Layla tapped Arne. "Is this actually happening?"

Tor's energy suddenly shifted, his eyes darting at something in the tree line. "We have company. Let me do the talking."

Two wolves, one gray and one brown, appeared and trotted across Tor's yard. A woman followed them, and Ciara instantly thought, 'Valkyrie.' She was tall, built, and blonde, with stunning green eyes. She was gorgeous, and she was looking at Tor like she wanted to eat him alive.

Arne whispered a curse under his breath as Tor stood and walked to the patio's edge.

"Petra. What brings you out here?" Tor asked, his tone casual.

"Tell me the rumor isn't true, Torsten," the blonde said.

"What rumor is that?"

Petra pointed a finger in Ciara's direction. "That you put a bond on that wolf murdering bitch!"

Ciara raised a brow. Well, this was interesting.

"I don't think that's any concern of yours or your brothers'," Tor replied, looking at the wolves flanking her.

"The hell it's not! You are my fiancé, for Odin's sake!" Petra shouted, her eyes flashing golden with the wolf under her skin.

Ciara's whole body went cold like she had plunged into the lake. Tor didn't move, only angled his body between the wolves and Ciara.

"We aren't engaged, Petra," he said, his voice deepening in anger. "Whatever agreements stood between your father and mine died when he did. I've told you this more than once."

Petra didn't look like someone who got told no often, and the snarl on her face was vicious. "You just need time to get used to the idea. Our mating would produce a powerful bloodline. Something that will strengthen the clan. Are you really going to pass that up for what? This skinny human bitch who hunts wolves for sport? Fuck no. I won't allow it. We are fated, and there's no changing that."

Layla's hand closed around Ciara's wrist. "Don't even think about it."

Ciara was gripping one of the steak knives, but she didn't remember even going for the blade. Something about the woman's possessive staring at Tor set her teeth on edge, and it had been an automatic reaction.

"Petra, we aren't fated. I don't know what lies your father told you over the years, but I'm not changing my mind. Who I bond with is my fucking business, mating bond or otherwise," Tor said, his voice dropping to a growl.

Petra's eyes were fixed on Ciara. "I don't know what spell you've put on him, but I will break it and the bond between you, one way or another. You're dead."

Ciara smiled but said nothing. She didn't need to. Tor's snarl had enough alpha in it to send the two wolves scampering off into the forest. Petra shot one more baleful glare at Ciara before shifting and vanishing after her brothers.

"Well, she's as delightful as I remember," Arne said. He pulled out his phone and started texting. "I'll let my mother know we are on our way. Probably a good idea for you to go to Oslo and let this blow over?"

Tor was still watching the trees. He shook himself before turning. His eyes were fixed on Ciara and the knife she was holding. He smiled a little.

"Planning on being my backup?"

Ciara shrugged. "I didn't like her tone. You should have told her you'll remove the bond at full moon."

Tor's eyes darkened and locked her down. "That's between us and none of their business. If she threatens you again, I'll deal with it."

"No, *I* will deal with it," Ciara replied. Something told her Petra wouldn't stop with threats. "Are you two really fated?"

"No fucking chance," Tor replied.

"How do you know? She seemed pretty sure just now." Ciara didn't know why she felt compelled to ask.

Tor gave her a pointed look. "Trust me. I fucking know. I'm going to pack a bag. The sooner we leave, the better."

Arne waited until Tor had disappeared inside before turning to Ciara. "I hope you are ready for the storm that's about to hit you," he said.

Ciara gathered up the empty plates. "I'm not scared of Petra. If she wants a fight, I'll be happy to oblige."

Arne looked like he was about to say something, changed his mind, and shut his mouth again. Layla got up and helped Ciara clear the table.

"Well, at least dinner was good. Do you want a cool elvish dagger to take on the hunt?" she asked. Layla was going for normality, but Ciara was too tense for that.

Ciara's eyes drifted to the dark trees around her, and protective instincts rushed through her. She really hadn't liked the possessive way Petra had looked at Tor, like he was a hunk of meat to be fought over.

Ciara wouldn't let Tor step in for her like that again, either. The next time a wolf came to pick a fight, Ciara would give it to them.

7

Tor was a tensed-up ball of frustration and fury. He had only begun to unwind when Petra decided to crash their dinner. He thought it would take longer for the word to get around about Ciara, but he should have known better.

Tor tossed some things into a bag that he thought he might need and didn't have at his apartment. He didn't really want anything extra; he needed the excuse to walk away and try and think straight again. Easier said than done.

Ciara had looked ready to take her steak knife and skin Petra. He could smell the aggression and over-protectiveness that he never would have expected from her. It was a hit he hadn't seen coming, just like her insistence that he remove the mark on her after the full moon. He had known she would want it gone, but it still got under his skin.

Tor messaged Bayn about opening a portal to Mardøll and received a thumbs up. Tor didn't want to leave. He wanted to keep Ciara to himself and ensure she didn't get hurt again. The wolves wouldn't give him that option. Not now that Petra had probably run off to the council to complain. He ran his hands over his face.

"Fuckkkk," he groaned. He took three deep breaths to steady himself before grabbing his bag and heading for the door. He didn't have time for a pity party.

Ciara was in the kitchen with Layla, chatting and turning the dishwasher on. It was a strangely domestic moment that made something hurt in Tor's chest.

His childhood home had never had laughing women in the kitchen. His mother had walked out after one beating too many and had left Tor and Linnea behind. Tor knew his father would have hunted her to the ends of the earth if she had tried to take them. It still didn't make him feel less abandoned.

Ciara's gaze flicked to him, and her brows drew together. She was picking up his moods through the bond already. "You okay?"

"Yes. Thank you for cleaning up, ladies," Tor said quickly, giving them a relaxed smile.

"Thank you for cooking," Layla replied, flicking him with the dish towel. "You ready to go? Alruna is waiting for us."

"More than ready."

Outside, Arne was standing near his SUV and watching the trees and lake. He was standing guard.

"Anything?" Tor asked, keeping his voice low so the women wouldn't hear them.

"If there's anyone out there, they are too far out for me to detect. You okay?" Arne replied. He could always tell when Tor was upset.

"I will be as soon as Ciara is out of here. I don't trust Petra not to stir up a mob. Maybe keep Layla in Alfheimstod and don't venture too far near wolf lands while I'm gone. I don't want any of this to blow back on her."

Arne's smile was vicious. "They wouldn't dare."

"You never know with Petra. Her whole family is crazy, and they are proud, which is worse. They might also try and cause trouble with your mother and the council," Tor replied.

"They can try. She'll take care of it. You just focus on getting Varg and sorting out whatever is between you and Ciara."

Tor snorted. "There's nothing between us except this bond I foolishly put on her."

"You're sticking with that? Really?" Arne said with a shake of his head.

"No point in imagining anything else," Tor replied, tossing his bag into the car. Ciara and Layla joined them, and they drove to Alruna's without Tor spotting any other wolves.

Alruna greeted them with a smile and looked Ciara over. "It's nice to see you healed and looking so well. Tor, doesn't she look well?"

"Compared to two days ago? Yeah," he said, trying not to blush. Ciara looked like fucking dinner in that purple top.

"Thank you for your help," Ciara replied politely.

"You're family now, darling. It was my pleasure. Now, Mardøll, is it?" Alruna opened a portal that showed Bayn and Freya already waiting for them. "Please keep me updated on your hunt for Varg. If you need backup, the elves are at your disposal."

"Thanks, Auntie." Tor dropped a kiss on her cheek before stepping through the portal. He watched Ciara hug Layla goodbye before following him through. It closed with a snap of bright light.

"You look good for a dead woman," Freya said to Ciara. "You are in so much trouble, missy!"

Ciara groaned. "So everyone keeps telling me."

Bayn raised a brow at Tor. "How is everything?"

"About as good as it can be. Can I get you to watch over Ciara while I go and grab some things from my apartment?" Tor asked. "We want to start hunting tomorrow, and she won't stay with me. Not when she can be here."

Bayn nodded. "Sure thing. I know what it's like with a new bond."

"It's not a mating bond," Tor grumbled. It only made Bayn smile. "Just watch her so she doesn't run off again. She still hasn't told me where she was when she spotted Varg as if I'd leave her behind and go without her."

"Give Freya ten minutes, and I'm sure she'll know," Bayn said with a grin. "How is Ciara feeling about being bonded to you? Just so I don't step my foot into it accidentally."

"Not impressed but not as furious as I thought." Tor fidgeted a little. "She wants it gone."

"Ooff. I'm sorry."

Tor tried to shrug it off and pretend he didn't care. "To be expected. It was only meant to be a temporary thing to save her life anyway. Watch her. I'll be back later. I need...I need to breathe a bit."

Bayn nodded. "Take your time. I promise she's not going anywhere."

"Thanks," Tor replied and headed out into the cool night air. He felt the bond give a strange tug in his chest like it was trying to warn him he was getting too far away from Ciara. He gritted his teeth and struggled past it.

It was going to be a good thing when the bond was removed, Tor tried to tell himself. He would go back to pretending Ciara didn't exist, and he wouldn't ever have to worry about her being just another woman that left him.

8

Ciara found Bayn's backup burner phone collection and helped herself to one. She needed to talk to Lachie, and if she sat up with Freya and Bayn, she would have to endure another lecture. It was good to be back in a familiar place with some of her gear to ground her.

Ciara had known the second Tor left the apartment and flinched as something yanked on her insides. He was back in his own city. It made sense he would want his own bed and space now that he had Bayn and Freya to keep an eye on her. She didn't know why it made panic tickle up her spine.

Has to be the stupid bond, she told herself. She should be relieved he put some distance between them. She wouldn't have any once they started hunting Varg.

Ciara sat on the guest room bed and dialed her brother's number. It was probably the longest they had ever gone without talking to each other.

Lachie's phone rang out. Ciara messaged him: **It's your sister, not a one-night stand you are trying to ghost.**

Ciara huffed out a laugh as her phone instantly started ringing. "You're unbelievable."

"I don't answer numbers I don't know! Where the fuck are you?" Lachie answered.

"At Freya's place. Can you talk? I'm... I'm not okay," she replied.

Lachie was the only one she let know when she was having a bad day. She couldn't handle a certain level of vulnerability, even with her cousins. Lachie and Ciara were two years apart, and losing their parents had made them band tighter together than twins.

"Yeah, I got time. I've just finished up with the new recruits for the day. We had another four people turn up, wanting to be hunters. Kenna is getting overwhelmed, so she asked me to hang about a bit and help," Lachie explained. "There're even a few cute ones."

Ciara laughed. "Just don't seduce anyone that you're training. We need all the hunters we can get, so don't shit where you eat."

"I said they were cute, not that I wanted to seduce them. Like I have time for that shit anyway."

"Doesn't sound like you."

Lachlan *always* had time to charm the pants off everyone who crossed his path—sometimes literally. It was Ciara who had the problem getting close to anyone. Attachment and relationships always meant opening up and allowing yourself to be vulnerable to another person. The thought of doing that made her feel like her whole body was turning to acid. Ciara just couldn't do it.

She remembered what Layla had said about Apollo and him at the party. "Is this sudden celibacy something to do with whatever Apollo Greatdrakes is pissed off at you about?"

"Gods no. Goldie is angry at me because I stopped him from going home with trash a few weeks ago. We were out at Monkey Paw, and this guy who is always sleazing around there tried to pick him up. I sent the fucker on his way, and Apollo decided to be offended over it."

"You cock blocked him! No wonder he's pissed off at you."

"Did you not hear what I said about the guy being total trash? He's repellent, and if he ever touched Apollo, I would have to break all the asshole's fingers on principal alone," Lachie complained.

"Not really your call to make, is it? I mean, how would you feel if Apollo did that to you?"

Lachie made a frustrated noise. "The Greatdrakes are practically family. We protect our family from nasty sleazebags with god knows how many gross STDs. Apollo can be pissed about it as much as he wants. I won't apologize for looking out for him. He needs someone watching him because his brothers don't seem to care."

"Ah, huh. Well, good luck with protecting his virtue in the future. Just remember he's a magician, and if you act like too much of a dick, he'll turn you into a frog or some shit," Ciara teased him.

"Oh please, like he would dare."

"You know Apollo. He's going to get revenge. Be prepared for him to cock block you every chance he gets now," Ciara said, fighting back a giggle.

"He won't get the chance. Like I said, I'm too busy to fuck about at the moment anyway. I'm *extra* busy because someone tried to be a hero and ended up getting fucked up. You better spit out what really happened, sis, before I come over there and throttle you for making me worry so much."

Ciara chewed on her lip. "Promise you won't get mad?"

"Absolutely not."

Ciara sighed and told him everything anyway. Unlike when she was talking with Layla, she let Lachlan know how scared she had been, how she had thought she was going to die, and how now she was possibly going to turn into a wolf. She didn't have to explain herself to Lachie. He knew precisely what turning into a wolf would mean to her.

"Fuck, Ciara," Lachie murmured once she was done. "Fuck."

"Yeah. I have about two weeks until I know for sure. I want to focus on catching Varg until then...just in case I'm not the same after," Ciara replied. At least hunting would stop her mind from running about in circles non-stop.

"I'm sure you're going to be fine. Tor got you to help super quick, and a wolf shaman will know their shit." Lachie was silent for a long moment before continuing. "If you do turn, what do you want me to do? I know what you used to say, but times have changed. All the creatures are out, and Tor won't let you go through the transition alone. He'll help you. I'll still love you if you can shapeshift."

Ciara's chest ached. "I know, I'm just... What if I turn and I'm no longer me? What if I lose who I am and can't control it? What if I accidentally hurt people?"

What if I become like the monsters we've spent our lives hunting? She didn't need to say it. Lachie knew.

"You won't, Ciara. If anything, it will make you an extra strong badass. If you turn, and for whatever reason, you do lose yourself, I'll... I'll go through with it. I'll put you down," Lachie replied, his voice cracking.

"You promise?"

"Yeah, I promise. Just don't expect me to do it under any other circumstances. You're still going to be my sister." Lachie sighed. "Fuck, I need a drink now."

"Sorry to dump it on you. No one else will do it for me. No one will understand," she said, tucking her knees up to her chest.

"I know, but it's a last resort thing, okay? Don't start acting like you're terminal. Not unless it's going to lighten you up a bit and make you live for more than hunting. Actually, I changed my mind. Pretend like you're terminal. Go get drunk and fuck some hot people. Blow off some steam," Lachie suggested, making her laugh.

"Yeah, because meaningless hookups is how I blow off steam."

"You could try it and see what you think."

Ciara *had* tried it. When she did feel the urge for company, she always picked up a stranger and left straight afterward. It was better not to get familiar or too attached. It never bothered Lachie, but it always left her feeling even emptier later.

"I'll be fine as soon as my blade is sawing through Varg's neck," Ciara replied.

Lachlan laughed. "Yeah, that sounds more like you. Be careful, okay? Don't take on any more crazy wolves unless you have Tor with you."

"He is a crazy wolf, too," Ciara pointed out.

"Crazy hot. Maybe you should—"

"Nope. Good night, Lachlan," she said quickly.

"Think about it, is all I'm saying. Tor is fucking hot," Lachie replied.

"Yeah, he is, and that's just another good reason not to go there."

"Whatever. Keep me updated on the hunt. Don't do anything dumb and get yourself hurt."

"I promise. Be good and stop harassing Apollo. He's a grown-ass man and can make his own decisions," she replied.

"Yeah, not going to happen until he learns to make good ones," Lachlan said, stubborn as ever. "Text me tomorrow so I know you're okay."

"I will. Night, little brother. Love you."

"Love you too. Be safe." He hung up, and Ciara felt a little lighter just from talking to him. If Varg wasn't really out to kill her, she would have asked Lachie to join her. Varg had wanted her dead since Svartalfheim, and the face full of wolfsbane would have made him even more eager for revenge. No, it was better that Lachie was far away from her entire mess.

Ciara's chest hummed and a door shut outside her room. She knew Bayn and Freya had already gone to bed, so she tip-toed out in her pajamas to see what was happening.

Tor was pulling the couch apart and making a bed on the floor.

"I thought you were gone," she said, sounding dumb. She tried again. "I mean, I thought you were staying at your own apartment tonight."

Tor's eyes glowed in the low light, and a thrill went through her. "It's funny you think that I would be able to sleep without you near."

Ciara rubbed at her chest absently. "You felt that too? I thought it might have just been me."

"Yeah, I can feel it," Tor replied irritably, tossing a pillow onto his makeshift bed.

"I'm sorry," she said.

Tor looked over at her. "Don't be. It saved your life."

"I shouldn't have put you in that position. I should never have gone to you." Ciara didn't know why she was admitting it at all. Maybe it was easier to say what she was thinking in the darkness. She stared at the carpet under her feet so she didn't have to look at him. "The wolves are going to start shit with you over it, and I'm sorry about that too."

Ciara didn't hear him move, but warm fingers slid under her chin and lifted it. Tor's gray eyes were silver when they fixed on hers. "Stop saying sorry. I knew exactly what I was doing when I put the bond on you. You came to me when you were scared and hurt because you know deep down that we might snip and snarl at each other, but I'm always going to look out for you. You're safe with me, Ciara, and you know it."

She swallowed hard, unable to look away as his words sank in. She made a sound like a sob mixed with a laugh. "I must be crazy, right? I was half dead, and all I could think about was telling you about Linnea being alive. I thought I was going to die, and I didn't care as long as you knew you hadn't lost her completely," she rambled. The stress and confusion of the last few days had finally cracked her. "I've been hunting wolves my whole life. Who would've thought I'd go to one when I needed to feel safe?"

"Not just a wolf. Me. You came to *me*, Ciara." There was a touch of proud alpha in his voice, the wolf coming through and making the hair on the back of her neck rise. His thumb ran over her cheek, and her pulse leaped to her throat. "You don't have to worry, little bunny. I will protect you and keep you safe, just like you need me to."

A part of Ciara wanted to climb into his arms and accept what he was offering. She couldn't let that part of her win. She hadn't felt safe since her parents had died and had fought to create her own way to protect herself. *She* kept people safe, not the other way around.

Ciara took a careful step back from him, making his fingers drop from her face. Her legs were wobbly as she went back to her room. Tor was watching her retreat with a predator's eyes.

"Goodnight, Tor. I'm... I'm glad you came back," Ciara said and quietly closed her door. She half expected him to come in after her. When he didn't, she climbed into bed and put a pillow over her burning face. She was such an idiot.

∼

IT TOOK Ciara ages to fall asleep, and when she did, she was caught up in nightmares. She hadn't dreamed the whole time she had been recovering, and now they hit her with fever intensity. She was back on the wet ground, Varg's heavy body on top of her, jaws clamped tight.

"Stop struggling, little hunter," he said, turning into Tor. When he bit her, it wasn't a cry of alarm; it was ecstasy. Then he was Varg again, ripping her throat clean out, blood smearing his muzzle and fangs as he laughed and laughed.

A warm hand touched her shoulder, and Ciara roared into wakefulness, lashing out at the big figure in the darkness.

"Woah, Ciara, it's just me," Tor said. He grabbed her hands so she would stop trying to hit him in her roiling fear and panic. She was covered in sweat and shaking. "Are you awake?"

"Y-Yes. What are you doing in here?" she asked.

"The bond woke me up, and when I smelled your fear, I came in to see if you were being attacked," Tor explained, his eyes shining in the darkness.

"No, just...just nightmares," Ciara replied, kicking off her blanket and sitting up.

"Varg?" Tor guessed.

"Yeah. He got my throat out this time," she admitted. Tor hissed softly but said nothing. "What do you mean, the bond woke you up? I thought we didn't have that kind of connection like a mating bond?"

"We don't, but I still felt it." Tor sat down on the edge of her bed. "I know you're freaked out about it, but unless we create the mating bond intentionally while we have sex, it's never, ever going to be a mating bond. Although I hear sex when you're bonded is something else."

Ciara pushed her hair out of her face and huffed out a laugh. "I bet they all say that. Just keep your little wolf in your pants. We don't need any more trouble than what we already have."

"Bunny, you wouldn't be able to handle my little wolf without the bond, let alone with one," Tor replied. Ciara went hot all over, and a tingle went straight to her lady parts. In Svartalfheim, he had joked that she wouldn't be able to wrap one hand all the way around it... Nope, nope, nope, she wasn't going to think about it.

"Get out of my room." Ciara hit him with a pillow. Tor caught it and yanked it out of her hand.

"Stop having nightmares, and I will."

"Yeah, that's not going to happen. All I have is nightmares," she replied.

"The bond will stop them if I'm close." Tor dropped the stolen pillow onto the carpet beside the bed and lay down.

Ciara stuck her head over the side. "What are you doing?"

"Making sure we both get some sleep tonight. Trust me, it will work. It's a pack thing. It would work better if we were touching, but I know my little wolf frightens you."

"So do your manners."

"Shh, I'm trying to sleep."

Ciara bit back a laugh. It was beyond ridiculous, but she was too tired to fight him. She pulled her top blanket off and dropped it on him.

"I knew you liked me," Tor whispered.

"Do not," Ciara replied, smiling into her pillow as she drifted back to sleep.

She didn't dream.

9

Ciara didn't wake up again until the following morning when the smell of coffee was wafting through her door, and she could hear Freya and Tor chatting in the kitchen. The pillow and blanket were back on her bed, and she had a moment of wondering if their midnight talk had been a dream. She picked up the spare pillow, pressed it to her nose, and inhaled. She could smell the forest and something warm and masculine that screamed Tor. No, it wasn't a dream. There was a tap on the door, and she quickly tossed the pillow aside before Freya opened it.

"Wake up, sleepyhead, or I'm going to get Tor to come in and jump on you," she said, a naughty gleam in her eye.

"I'm awake!" Ciara replied, dragging herself out of bed. She went through the clothes she'd left behind and headed for the bathroom. Outside her room, Bayn and Freya were cooking eggs, and Tor offered her a mug of coffee.

"For the shower," he said, passing it to her.

"How did you know... Thanks," she replied, taking the mug and hurrying for the bathroom. She always had a coffee while having her morning shower, but how Tor had known was a mystery.

Surely the bond wouldn't share that kind of information with him, would it? Ciara shook herself. She was becoming paranoid. She sipped her coffee. It had milk and half a sugar, just like she liked it. She scowled. It wasn't possible; bonds didn't give coffee orders.

Freya might have remembered, she thought, stripping off and climbing under the steaming spray. Of course, Freya would have told him. She really *was* getting paranoid.

Fifteen minutes later, she was dressed in her familiar black jeans and felt almost normal again. She tied her hair back in a braid, marveling that there wasn't the slightest twinge of pain remaining in her shoulder. Shifter healing was something else. Maybe being bound to a wolf would have perks after all.

～

"Okay, Ciara, where were you attacked?" Freya asked as soon as Ciara made it to the kitchen.

"Come on, can't I eat something first?" she complained.

Bayn held a plate of bacon, eggs, and fried mushrooms out to her. "You can have this if you give me a name."

Ciara let out a pained sigh. "Onsøy."

"That wasn't so hard. Tor, you should've just bribed her with food," Bayn said, shooting Ciara a wink before passing the plate over.

"Don't tell him that," Ciara said, sitting at the counter.

Freya placed a knife and fork down in front of her. "Onsøy is named after Odin."

"So is half of Scandinavia. How is it relevant?" Ciara said and chewed on a bit of bacon.

Tor sat down beside her, his knee brushing against hers. She knew it wasn't intentional, but she felt the touch run up the entire length of her body.

"It's relevant because when I was hunting Varg, the last known sightings were also at places named after Odin," he explained.

Ciara swallowed her bacon. "I thought he was obsessed with Fenris. Why hunt places named after Odin, who was his enemy?"

"Let's ask an expert," Freya said, pulling out her phone. She put it to her ear. Someone answered, and the background music was so loud Ciara could hear it from the other side of the room. Freya shouted something in Norwegian, and the music vanished. Freya put the phone on speaker. "Von? You there?"

"What are you calling me for about at this time of the morning? Please tell me it's a booty call. I'm about to close up the club," Von answered.

"I can hear you, asshole," Bayn replied.

"Good. Is this a booty call? Because Daddy needs his bed and beauty sleep."

Freya rolled her eyes. "It's got to do with Odin."

"What about Odin?" Von demanded, the party boy vanishing from his voice almost instantly.

"If I was obsessed with the Fenris legend, why would I lurk at sites named after Odin?" Tor asked.

"Torsten! Is that you, my big handsome wolf?" Von's tone changed again to be sugary sweet.

"Yeah, it is. Now, why don't you help me out and answer my question? You *are* the best Odin expert I know," Tor replied. Freya flipped him off.

"I think this question deserves to be answered in person. I'll be there in fifteen minutes."

"Get here in ten, and I'll take my shirt off."

Von, the biggest flirt that Ciara had ever met, actually giggled. "You got a deal," he said and hung up.

"Well, that was easy," Tor commented.

Bayn chuckled. "He's going to make you take your shirt off before he gives us anything, you know that, right?"

"Small price to pay if he can answer our questions."

Ciara's eyes rolled at him. "Is there anyone that doesn't want your dick?"

"Only you, bunny," Tor said, snatching some bacon off her plate and only just avoiding the fork she tried to stab him with. He laughed, and she wanted to push him off his chair.

Freya and Bayn were grinning at them, and Ciara turned back to her plate so she wouldn't have to look at them.

Von arrived nine minutes and thirteen seconds later. The downstairs door opened with a bang, and he called, "That shirt better be off by the time I get up there!" His long blonde hair was a wild snarl that matched his dark eyeliner, leather pants, and tight pink tank. His eyes found Tor, and his smile went wide. "Now, you are definitely a welcome sight in the morning. A little too clothed for my tastes. Come on, off with it."

Ciara almost choked as Tor very slowly unbuttoned the top of his dark gray Henley and dragged it off. Von pretended to swoon.

"Quick, give me coffee before I pass out," he said to Bayn. "Feel free to take your shirt off too."

"Nice try," Bayn replied and filled a mug for him.

Von collapsed on the couch. "Now, Freya, my love, what glorious mess have you gotten into?"

"No mess. Not yet anyway. Ciara? Why don't you take the lead on this one?" Freya suggested.

"I'm looking for Varg. He and his cult are hunting Fenris because they think he is their true god. Why would they lurk around towns and sites named after Odin if that's the case? I'm sure they were actually trying to excavate at the last place I saw them," Ciara explained.

Von's eyebrows shot up. "Well, fuck. They are really trying to find Fenris, aren't they?"

"Yes, I just told you that," she pointed out.

"You don't understand, my pet. You would have to be insane to worship Fenris because you're defying Odin. *Odin*, who rumor has it, has come out of hiding and was seen with the elves," Von said, crossing his arms. "I don't suppose you know anything about that?"

"We could if you have any useful information to exchange for it," Tor said.

Von's smile turned delighted. "You have a deal. If they are digging at sites named after Odin, they might be buying into a mostly unknown legend about where Fenris was bound. Most of the stories imply it was in Asgard, but there is no way Odin would allow his enemy to be that close. There's another collector I know. He's mad on Fenris legends. I can reach out to him to see if any of the old tales has an exact location where Odin imprisoned him. Where else was Varg spotted?"

Tor rattled off a list, and Von nodded. "Definitely all named after Odin. They will end up digging up half of Scandinavia if that's their only lead. How quickly do you need the information?"

"The quicker, the better. Ciara and I will head to Onsøy this afternoon to see if Varg is still there. Doubtful, now that Ciara blew his hiding place, but there still might be something left behind," Tor replied. He draped his shirt over one wide shoulder, and Ciara couldn't stop staring at it. Better that than all of the mythical creatures from Viking legend tattooed over his chest.

"I'll leave a message with my contact, but he is a bit of a crazy recluse, so it might take him a day or so to get back to me. He tends to forget to charge his phone and then ignores it for days," Von said. "Keep me updated if you find anything interesting at these digs. I'll be able to move them for you."

Ciara's eyes narrowed. She knew what collectors were like, but she still didn't like the idea of her aiding the black market antiquities trade. If it meant finding Varg, then that was the only thing that mattered.

Von left not long after, dropping more than one hint to Tor that he was welcome to come with him. Ciara had always liked Von, but at that moment, she had the sudden urge to push the pretty Viking down the stairs. Once he was gone, she pointed at Tor's shirt.

"Can you put that back on now?" she asked.

"Why, does my bare chest bother you?" Tor replied, getting into her space and forcing her to take a step back.

"No, but we are leaving, so maybe you should cover up for public decency." Ciara ignored the way Bayn and Freya watched them spar. She needed to get to Onsøy, find Varg, and kill him. Then she would worry about her bond with Tor and focus on getting it removed. She had a plan and would stick to it, even if it killed her. With the way he was smiling at her, it probably would.

10

Onsøy was a peninsula located roughly an hour's drive south of Oslo. Ciara could barely remember the last time she drove there, poison and pain and blood loss robbing her of the smaller details. That night she'd had only one focus—getting to Tor. It seemed strange to be doing the drive again with him beside her.

It was afternoon by the time they drove through the town and out towards the forest and water. A spring storm was rolling in, the sky getting darker by the minute.

Ciara directed Tor down a small side road that led out to the site. She strapped a knife to her thigh. The chances of Varg being dumb enough to wait around for people to turn up were slim, but he might have left a guard or two.

"There's a small side road behind those trees," Ciara said, pointing at the track in the growing darkness. "This is where I parked. It's a short walk from here."

The muscles in Tor's jaw tightened. "I can't believe you came out here all by yourself."

"It's what I was trained for, Tor, whether you can accept it or not. I'm not an idiot. I knew what I was doing," Ciara argued. She jumped out of the car as soon as he pulled up.

The forest smelled clean and damp. She shut her eyes for a

moment and breathed in. It was like everything was opening up, readying for the rain that was due to start falling. She could never explain the sensation to anyone, the way the trees seemed to be breathing around her. It calmed her and energized her at the same time.

"Which way, Ciara?" Tor asked, bringing her back to herself.

"Through here. Watch your step. Varg had someone lay bear traps on the perimeter, and they might still be there," she said and took the lead through the undergrowth. She had spent two days crawling around, hiding her scent and footprints in and out.

Behind her, Tor was a bundle of energy. She could feel it building; his alpha power was starting to leak with the tension of going into his enemy's territory. There was no sign of anyone, but the ground was trampled and wrecked from booted feet.

Tor let out a low, deep growl. "I can smell Linnea's scent." Without another word, he shifted and sprinted off through the trees, a giant silver wolf on the hunt. Ciara jogged behind him, careful of where she was placing her feet.

What had been a bustling camp by the water only days before was a churned-up mess of mud, cold fire pits, and squashed grass from where tents had been pegged. Tor was sniffing around a large muddy patch of ground that had been a pit the last time Ciara had seen it. Whatever they had been looking for must have been a dead end.

Count that as a blessing, Ciara thought. The last thing anyone needed was Fenris being free to go on a rampage. The sky opened up, and rain started to fall down through the branches of the pine and birch trees in a soft hushing sound.

The air went hot around Tor, and he shifted back. His jeans were in tatters but still mostly covered him. His shirt was gone.

"She was here not a day ago," he snarled, pacing the forest floor. His eyes were shining with wild anger. "I can smell her *everywhere* and Varg too. He must have shamans working with him because I can feel dark magic all over this place. It's seeped into the ground and trees. There's blood too. Lots of it. Whatever they did, it was a fucking vile thing."

Ciara couldn't sense the magic, but his words made her blood go cold. Tor's alpha power was rolling out of him in thick waves. He whirled on her.

"If you hadn't been so fucking stubborn, we could have had them by now!" he shouted. Ciara stepped back from him. He had never raised his voice at her, and paired with the power coming off him, it made her want to bare her neck to him and submit. Fuck that.

"I was following my training and intuition, so I had enough information to ask for help with," she said, trying to keep her voice steady.

"You should have called us as soon as you found out that your target was working for Varg," Tor said, taking a step towards her. He looked like he would go full berserker, his whole body coiled with violent power. She should have run or been readying for a fight.

"I don't answer to you. I did what I thought was right at the time and got *this* for my trouble!" she said, pulling the collar of her T-shirt back to flash the scars on her neck. The sight of them seemed to enrage him more. A low snarl rolled out of Tor, eyes glowing as they fixed on her.

"I know you want your sister back, but you better back the fuck off me. You wouldn't even know she was still alive if it wasn't for me." Ciara went to go back to the car, but Tor mirrored her moves, blocking her path. "Get out of my way. This is a dead end."

"You could have been a dead end for your recklessness," Tor hissed. "You really think I'm only annoyed about Linnea? You came out here, telling no one, and you stayed even when you found out Varg was involved. You're a good hunter but no match for a pack of wolves. You could've died. You almost did. Was your pride really worth your life?"

Ciara's hands clenched into fists. "You're looking for a fight right now, I understand, but you better back off me, Torsten."

"Or what?" Tor demanded, prowling right up to her so he could get in her face. Her heart was hammering too fast. The heat radiating from his body hit her like a brick. Water was trickling down his bare skin, and his eyes were still glowing with fury and challenge.

Ciara should've been scared, but she wasn't because she *did* know that he would never hurt her no matter how angry he got. He was so tall that he loomed over her, making her feel small. Still, she didn't run.

Tor leaned down and whispered in her face, "What are you going to do, Wolf Slayer? You going to try and stab me with that little knife of yours?"

"Fuck you, Tor," Ciara snarled and kissed him. It was like a bomb going off inside of her. Tor's lips were hot and angry on hers, his large hands pulling her up into his arms. Ciara wrapped her legs around him, her hands bunching in his wet hair as her mouth plundered his. Tor gripped her ass tight enough to bruise; his tongue invaded her mouth, and she melted into him. Alpha heat rolled out of him and over her, making her whimper as it hit her core. Fuck, she needed to stop but couldn't.

She clung to him, her nails scratching up his slippery wet shoulders. A growl rolled through him and into her, and Ciara's pussy pulsed. Fuck. Fuck. Fuck. She couldn't stop.

Thunder boomed overhead loud enough to rattle the trees and knock some sense into Ciara, making her aware of her surroundings. They were soaked, their breath pluming in heavy mist as the temperature dropped.

"We need to get out of here," Tor said.

"I know a place we can stay for the night if they have the room," Ciara replied. They were both wide-eyed and staring at each other. She swallowed hard. "Um, maybe you should put me down?"

Tor's grip tightened like he would argue, but he shook himself and lowered her to her feet. "I..."

"Don't. Let's just go," Ciara said quickly and almost ran back through the trees. Her skin felt too tight, and the cold rain wasn't helping relieve the heat burning through her. The kiss had stopped their fighting, but she was suddenly worried that it had awoken something far worse in its place.

11

Tor didn't argue when Ciara got into the driver's seat. He was covered in mud, and his jeans were utterly ruined. He should have had more control or had enough sense to strip before the shift. He had smelled Linnea after so long, and he hadn't even thought about what he was barrelling into. The camp was abandoned, but if it hadn't been, he would have walked into every damn trap that Varg had left behind.

Varg was gone. Linnea was gone. Everything had smelled of blood and darkness and magic, and he had nothing to take his frustration out on. He hadn't been able to save Linnea; he hadn't been able to find her, and now she was gone again.

He had wanted to provoke Ciara to hit him, so he could feel anything but the total helplessness and failure that was eating away at him. He hadn't expected her to kiss him, especially not like that. It was like she was poisoned, and his tongue was the antidote. It had been desperate and hot and had ripped all his anger out of him and replaced it with horrible, gnawing desire.

He wanted her. It wasn't news to him. He had wanted her since the fight with Morrigan. He had wanted her at every encounter since. He had gotten really good at convincing himself that he didn't. Finally, tasting her skin in Svartalfheim had been the last nail in his coffin.

Whatever *that* had been in the rain was the equivalent of throwing said coffin into the sea. Now, all he could do was drown.

Ciara didn't say a word until they pulled up in front of a quaint-looking red and white painted bed and breakfast, the kind that sent tourists giddy with Instagram opportunities.

"Stay here," she said and got out of the car without looking at him. Like he was going to go anywhere in half a pair of muddy jeans, the wolf inside of him raging. He watched her disappear inside and his wolf scratched in his chest when he could no longer see her.

"No, no, no," Tor growled and tried to breathe in and out, pushing his wolf side down so that it didn't force him to go after her.

Ciara appeared again minutes later. "We are in luck. They had a cancellation at the last minute," she said and slowly drove down to a small red cabin.

Tor all but jumped out of the car, grabbing their bags from the back and following her inside. It was a tiny one-room space with one large double bed, a bathroom, and a kitchenette for making coffee. One bed. Looks like he was getting the floor again.

"Going for a shower," he said and locked himself in the bathroom. He heard Ciara sigh, but he turned the taps on in the shower, so he didn't hear anymore. He was losing his goddamn mind. He needed to get himself together.

Tor stripped off what was left of his ruined jeans and climbed under the hot, steaming water. He leaned his forehead against the cold tiles and let the mud and leaf litter wash off him. He could still smell apple blossoms and arousal in his nose, the scent imprinted on his mind.

Fuck, he had to stop this. He would never have her, and if he could, he would never keep her. Ciara had been clear on what she thought of wolves and was keen to have the bond gone. Tor was soaping down when he felt the pull in his chest that told him she had left.

Just like they always do. Tor gritted his teeth. No, he was just feeling emotional and irrational now. He wrapped his arms around himself and squeezed tight, fighting the urge to go after her. When it calmed, he tipped some shampoo into his hand and washed his long hair. It didn't matter that Ciara left. At this point, it would be better for his emotional and mental health if she did.

The memory of arousal and apple blossoms hit his senses again, and he groaned. His hand was on his dick before he could think too much about it. He just needed to get off, and he wouldn't think about her lithe body wrapped around him, her nipples going hard under the wet fabric of her shirt. Her lips had been so soft and eager and perfect. She had been as desperate for him as he had been for her.

Tor had wanted to strip her and fuck her like an animal right on the forest floor, hold her down, and sink his teeth into her soft skin. His orgasm punched through him, quick and hot enough to make him stagger and grip the tiled walls for balance.

"Fuck," he moaned under his breath. When his heartbeat evened out, he could feel that some of his spiky edges had softened. Thank fuck. He might be able to control himself to think straight.

Varg and his cultists had moved, but they had at least identified without question that he was searching Odin sites. With any luck, Von would find something they could follow up on. Ciara had found Linnea once, and he was sure they could do it again. That was if he could keep his shit together around her.

Tor got out of the shower, dried himself off, and tied a towel around his waist. He was hunting through his duffel of clothes when the door opened, and Ciara returned, carrying a plastic shopping bag.

"I thought you'd left," he blurted out before he could check himself. Ciara put the bag down on the small table.

"I went to get you some food in case you needed it after the shift. Good to know you think I'm going to run off any chance I get," she said testily. Her eyes dropped to the towel around his waist and darkened. Tor was getting hard again and was back to the raging beast in seconds.

"Stop staring at me, bunny, or I'm going to think you want something," he growled.

"If you don't want me staring, maybe you should put some pants on," she snapped, her cheeks flushing.

Tor put his hands on his hips. "What if I don't want to? What are you going to do about it, Wolf Slayer?" he said, his voice dropping.

Ciara snarled wordlessly at him, throwing down a challenge like she had the day before. Oh no, she didn't. Tor was not putting up with that shit. Not again.

"You think your fangs are sharp enough to take me on?" he asked, firming his stance in case she attacked.

"Stop picking a fight with me, or you're going to find out, wolf." Ciara's lip lifted in a slight sneer. "Maybe we should finally get it out of the way. I think I'll have you stuffed when I'm done. You would look good mounted on my wall."

"Yeah? I think you would look good mounted on my dick," Tor snapped back before his common sense could think it through.

"You did not just say that," she said, her face turning even redder. He could smell her arousal again, and he was done for.

"I did. Maybe you need a good fucking to get that stick out of your ass," Tor teased.

Ciara exploded, moving faster than a human should, and swung a fist at him. Tor grabbed her hand, but she twisted, breaking his grip as she swiped out a leg and tried to trip him up. He grunted as the blow connected, but he didn't fall, only staggered backward. She was up and out of his reach in a flash.

"Looks like you got a bit of strength with the healing abilities I gave you," he chuckled. She had her hands up, ready to go again.

"You keep pushing me, and I'll make you regret ever saving my life," she panted with a feral grin that hit him straight in the dick.

"Back down, bunny, I'm warning you. I'm trying to be a good wolf right now, and you're not making it easy," he growled.

"Oh, a warning. My knees are trembling."

"You're only going to get one, so listen closely. You play Viking games, you're going to win Viking prizes," Tor said and smiled viciously. "Come at me again, and the next time I get you pinned, Ciara, I'll pull those tight jeans down and fuck you so hard you scream. Understand?"

Ciara's mouth had dropped open, and her pupils blew out. Tor was about to ask if she got the message when she attacked him again.

12

All of Ciara's common sense had fled. She had registered Tor's threat, and her body had responded by striking first. Her fist whipped out and slammed him in the sternum.

Tor groaned, and then it was a struggle of feet, fists, and flesh, and Ciara was dragged to the carpet. She snarled and swore, but Tor was bigger and stronger. He had her on her stomach, his hand around the back of her neck, pinning her down.

"You had to push me, didn't you?" he snarled by her ear. Ciara's whole body broke out in goosebumps as he held her firm. "I told you what would happen, and you still did it." His hand slid under the back of her shirt, the touch of his skin against hers overwhelming her. The bond between them throbbed, and she could have cried with how good it felt.

"You knew what you were doing. Does that mean you *want* me to follow through with my threat?" he asked, his body caging her in. "Better squeak, bunny. I'm losing my remaining shred of restraint."

"Yes," she admitted into the carpet, her face burning.

Tor emitted a feral sound right before his hands tore open her jeans and dragged them down to her knees. He didn't let her kick them off the rest of the way, the fabric keeping her legs tied up.

Tor muttered something in Norwegian and then tore the back of her shirt in two, her bra popping open and exposing her back. Ciara couldn't move, couldn't participate; she could do nothing but lie there and take whatever he wanted to do to her. It was so hot, her pussy grew wet, and he'd barely touched her.

Warm breath tickled the back of her exposed neck, and a hot kiss was pressed into her spine. Ciara trembled but stayed still as Tor kissed and licked all the way down the curve of her spine.

"Fuck, your skin tastes so good," he groaned against her lower back. Ciara didn't have time to tell him how weird that was when he pulled her hips up and licked her pussy. The heat of his mouth made her gasp, her body trying to lurch forward. Tor only pulled back and held her in place, his mouth returning to her to taste and lick.

"Oh god, I don't think I can take this," she panted.

"You can and you will," he replied, sliding a finger into her. "You're so hot and tight. I'll have to get you good and wet before I can get inside you, bunny."

Ciara cried out as his mouth joined his hand, teasing and pleasuring her until her hands gripped the carpet, desperate to hang onto something.

The tip of his tongue swirled over her clit as he added a second finger and thrust into her. She could die from the feelings bombarding her, parts of her held down tight as others were spread and worked open.

"I knew you would be like this, fighting every step of the way, needing to be pushed into giving in to what you want. I can smell this sweet pussy in my dreams. It haunts me every time you get wet in my presence," Tor said, his words curling around her and making her squirm. She knew she should be horrified that she would never be able to hide it from him, but it just made her hotter.

Tor's stubble grazed roughly over her sensitive clit, making her brain haze in a mix of pleasure and pain. His fingers curled inside her, his tongue flicking over her, and she came with a surprised cry. Hot, wet heat flooded her. She was shaking when he moved his fingers from her.

"Look at you, so soaked, you're dripping with it," he said, deep voice tinged with awe.

The only warning Ciara got was a brush of the broad tip of his dick against her pussy, and then he pressed inside her. Ciara gasped, the air knocking out of her lungs. She tried to widen her legs, but her jeans prevented it. He was so big, she felt like she couldn't possibly take all of him.

Tor ran a hand down her back. "Breathe, bunny, and I'll get you there," he said, his voice dropping and alpha power burning the air between them. "I'm going to make it so good for you. Just be a good girl and let me in."

Ciara melted under him, the tension vanishing from her as he moved inside her with shallow thrusts until he bottomed out. He held her hips tight, just holding her and letting her body relax around him. Tor was trembling; she could feel it against the back of her thighs and ass. She shifted back against him, and he groaned. Her body wanted more, needed him to take and conquer. The bond shivered between them, and Tor chuckled breathlessly.

"Oh, is that what you want?" he said, answering her without realizing she hadn't said a word. Tor took it as a challenge and began to thrust into her.

"Holy shit," Ciara gasped, rising up onto her forearms. The carpet burned against her skin, but she didn't care. She wouldn't have stopped for the world. Tor's hand dipped under her to squeeze and tease her breasts, rolling and pinching her nipples. Ciara's pussy clamped around him, making him laugh again.

"Like that, do you?" Tor dragged her upright, holding her back against his chest, his knees on either side of hers. His lips dragged over her neck and shoulder, both hands running over her breasts and pussy, his dick moving faster inside her. His warm alpha power was pouring into her, urging her to bare her throat, surrender, and give him whatever he wanted. And gods, did she want to.

"Yes," she managed to whimper before she began to shatter. It was too much sensation for her body to handle. Tears leaked from her eyes as she came, screaming in ecstasy.

"Fucking hell, Ciara. I'm going to destroy you," Tor growled. He bent her over the bed and unleashed himself on her.

Ciara cried out into the mattress. Tor's big hand was on the middle of her back, holding her down as he pounded relentlessly into her. The bond shivered between them, and for a split second, she felt the mind-blowing bliss that he was drowning in before he was coming hard, and she was thrown back in her own body, heat flooding her. Tor hung onto her, shaking. They slid to the carpet beside the bed, panting hard and dazed.

A giggle bubbled up inside Ciara, and she couldn't hold it in. Tor started to shake next to her until they were both laughing uncontrollably. She turned to look at him, trying and failing to hold her smile back.

"Just don't expect me to cuddle you now," she said, fingers trailing over his abs because she could get away with it.

Tor raised a brow at her. "You'll do as you're told."

"Sure I will," she said with a roll of her eyes. Ciara yelped as he picked her up and tossed her onto the bed. It was almost too soft after the carpet. Tor grinned down at her naked body, showing fangs as he pulled off her boots and jeans and placed a blanket over her.

"Just stay there where I can keep an eye on you," he said, heading over to see what food she had brought.

"Okay, but just this once..." she replied as her eyes shut, and she fell asleep.

13

Tor woke the following morning with Ciara curled up into him, her arm and her leg flung over his body to get as much of herself touching him as possible.

So much for not wanting a cuddle, Tor thought and smiled sleepily. He should probably move her to save her the embarrassment later. He couldn't go through with it. He liked having her exactly where she was. And wasn't that the problem?

Tor stared at the ceiling and wondered if he had made a massive mistake. Whether they liked it or not, sleeping together would change things. He hoped for the better, but knowing Ciara, she was going to fight him every step of the way. He was up for the challenge if she was the prize. It wouldn't be any fun at all if she gave in straight away.

Last night had been a revelation; she loved the fight, but she loved the fuck too. She did both with an equal intensity that matched his. The bond between them had made it go to another level.

He'd never experienced anything like her before and would do what he had to do to keep her.

Tor kissed the top of her head and breathed in the smell of her hair. He didn't know when he would have the chance to do it again.

His phone started to ring, and he cursed, fumbling for it on the bedside table. It was Von. He shouldn't ignore it.

"What?" he answered, trying to keep his voice low.

"Good morning to you too," Von all but shouted. Someone had clearly not gone to sleep yet. "How is Onsøy?"

"Dead end. All trace of them is gone," Tor replied. Ciara stirred in his arms, her body stretching against his. Tor's hand twitched to pull her closer, to stop her from fleeing.

"I don't think they found anything there. It might be named after Odin, but there's nothing to support that he spent a lot of time in Onsøy," Von replied.

Ciara woke up enough to realize she was curled into Tor. She went stiff and then slowly started to edge away. Tor tried his best to ignore the quick stab of hurt it caused him. She slipped out of bed, and he got a lovely view of her scarred back and perky ass as she disappeared into the bathroom.

"Have you found anything useful for us?" Tor asked, sitting up. "Or is this a social chat?"

"Touchy wolf. I wanted to let you know that I heard a reply from my Fenris expert. He's going to go through some rarer copies of the Binding of Fenris stories and see if anything shakes loose."

"Thanks. Hopefully, Varg won't have access to the same versions."

Von hummed. "Doubtful. Siegfried is an absolute recluse. He wouldn't deal with anyone, and if someone as obsessive as him was out there, he would know about them. My guess is that whatever path Varg is following, it's magic that's leading him."

Tor thought about the dark magic he'd felt at the campsite, and his hackles rose. "You might be right there."

"I think you should check out Uppsala. It was one of the places where Odin was known to have an estate," Von continued.

"I already have. Uppsala was a dead end too."

"Did you get out to Old Sigtun on Maelare Lake?"

Tor frowned. "No? Why would I?"

"Because Uppsala was technically Frey's estate, not Odin's," Von replied.

"I've never heard that. Explain."

"In the *Heimskringla* by Snorri Sturluson, he set down all the estates that the Aesir established in Midgard. Frey was given Uppsala; Njörðr took Nóatún; Thor had Thrudvang, etc. Odin had Old Sigtun outside of Uppsala and even had a temple built so the people of the area could pay homage to him," Von explained, his voice rising in excitement. "If Varg has done any decent research at all, he would've bypassed Uppsala and gone further out."

"Shit, you're right. We are about five hours from Uppsala, but if we leave soon, we should get there at a reasonable time," Tor replied. He wanted to kick himself for not digging deeper into Uppsala months ago.

"And how is the lovely Ciara? Still glaringly in love with you?" Von asked sweetly.

Tor snorted. "You thinking of the right Ciara? Doesn't sound like the one I know."

"Then you are not looking closely enough. You haven't seen how she looks at you when she thinks no one notices."

"Oh yeah? And how's that?" Tor knew he probably shouldn't ask for his emotional well-being. Clearly, he was a sucker for punishment.

"Yearning. Longing. Angst." Von sighed. "I always enjoy watching when people think their love is unrequited. Anyway, I must run, but I'll let you know if I find anything else."

"Thanks, Von, I appreciate it." Tor hung up, and the door to the bathroom opened. Ciara came out dressed, hair braided, and looking like she was ready to punch the day in the face. Her cheeks turned pink when she caught Tor staring at her. Gods, it was adorable.

"How is Von?" she asked.

"He had a lead. Looks like we are heading to Uppsala if you are keen for a drive?" Tor said and got out of bed. Her eyes raked over him before she quickly turned away. It was a little too late for her to be getting shy.

"Sounds good. Better than waiting around doing nothing," Ciara replied, pulling on her boots. Tor bit his tongue to prevent him from giving her a list of options of what he thought she could do instead... like sit on his face.

Fuck, get out of the room before you get an awkward boner, he chastised himself.

"About last night..." he began.

Ciara held up her hand. "No, don't. We have a hunt to get on with, and that takes priority. I'm going to grab some coffee. I'll be back," Ciara said and headed for the door.

Tor tried to think of something to say, but she was gone before he could get his mind to work properly. With a sigh, he headed for the shower. He had known she would shut him down, and it still stung like a fucking bitch.

It was going to be a long day.

14

Ciara walked through the parking lot and tried to breathe in the crisp morning air. She needed to cool down and clear her head. Waking up entangled with so much man was unexpectedly pleasant.

Get it together. You're on a hunt and know better.

Ciara reached the café that was already busy with people grabbing breakfast. She ordered coffees and some bacon and egg muffins before pulling out her phone.

Uppsala was a five-hour drive away. Five hours of being in a small space with the hottest man she had ever seen. *Great.*

She had known he would be good in bed but *fuck*. She should have had better self-control. She thought she would be sore after the absolute thorough shagging, but she wasn't. She felt great. Too great.

Wolf healing strikes again, she realized. Now that was a thought she didn't need.

Ciara needed advice. Bron was in Faerie with Killian, and Lachie would only tease her mercilessly. She sent an update of where they were heading in the family chat before she rang Imogen.

"Fuck you calling at this time for?" she mumbled in answer. Imogen was a 'no talking before ten a.m.' person.

"So, um, I slept with Tor and need to talk to someone."

"What?" Imogen now sounded wide awake. "I'm sorry, did I just hear correctly?"

Ciara stared at her boots. "I rang you because I thought you would be the least likely to judge me."

"I'm not judging, just surprised." Imogen laughed, and it was utterly filthy. "You have to tell me about his dick."

Ciara went bright red. "Monster."

"I fucking bet because that lad is huge. Well, well, you little slut. It's about time."

"What do you mean by that?"

"Oh, come *on*, Ciara. You two have looked like you've wanted to tear each other's clothes off since the moment he walked into Ironwood manor. I'm surprised it took this long."

Ciara grabbed her order off the waitress and went back outside. "It kind of just happened. Heat of the moment thing. I shouldn't think too much about it. I mean, he's a wolf."

"And you might be too. Just saying. Also, who actually gives a fuck? Literally no one."

"Lachie might."

"*Please*. He wouldn't have passed up an opportunity to fuck Tor either," Imogen replied. "This is a good thing for you."

"How? I feel like a total moron."

"Why? Was it bad?"

"No, it was..." Ciara trailed off, her mind drifting to tearing clothes, demanding hands, and the burn of the carpet.

"Haha, that good, huh? I don't think you have anything to be worried about. Tor is a good guy. He's not going to be bothered by some fun while you are out hunting together. You don't have to overthink everything, you know?"

Ciara chewed the inside of her cheek. "Yeah, but I'm still going to. I mean, what would my parents say if they were alive?"

"Who gives a fuck? They are dead, cousin. I'm sorry, but they are. You aren't. You've put enough of your life and happiness on hold getting revenge for them. Maybe you should think about what's going to make you happy. That's all they would want for you anyway," Imogen replied with her usual sucker punch style of love.

"I suppose you're right. Doesn't matter. We are on a hunt, and it will be dangerous to be distracted. After Varg is stopped, maybe then I can consider it?"

Imogen made a frustrated sound. "Yeah, you consider it some more, like you haven't been for the last few months."

"Wow, I shouldn't have called you. You're way too bitchy in the morning."

"You know this. It's why you called me. You want someone to tell you it's okay. It is. Tor is awesome. You need to pull your head out of your ass and see that for yourself. Maybe give his monster dick another go and see if that helps your decision-making process."

Ciara couldn't help it; she cracked up laughing right in the middle of the parking lot. "I hate your advice sometimes."

"And yet you still ask for it because you know I'm right." Imogen made a groaning sound. "You're on a hunt. Sure. Whatever. Try and have fun occasionally too. You're not dead yet, so maybe live a little. You're on the trail of a psycho with a smoking hot guy as your backup. Really, what more do you want in life?"

"Good point. I'm so bad at this," Ciara admitted. She walked back to the cabin. There was no sign of Tor outside. She tried not to think of him in a steaming shower.

"So is everyone. Dating is weird. Focus when you need to focus, but maybe be open to the fun stuff when you don't have to be on duty."

"I'll try. I don't know if it was just a one-night thing to him or not. I kind of walked out when he tried to talk about it."

"Oh my god. You are unbelievable. Poor Tor. Good luck to him," Imogen replied. There was a deep grumble in the background, and Imogen snickered. "I have to go. Arawan has just come in, and I have to talk to him about something very serious."

Ciara laughed. "Ah, huh. Sure you do."

"Happy hunting, bitch!" Imogen said cheerily and hung up on her.

Ciara stared at the cabin door and exhaled slowly. "You can do this." She straightened her shoulders and opened the door. Tor had managed to get a pair of low-slung jeans on, his hair a tangled wet mess. Her tongue stuck to the roof of her mouth, and everything she wanted to say seemed to vanish from her brain.

"Here. Breakfast," she managed to squeak out and thrust a paper bag at him. "I got you two muffins because I figured you would need them."

"I do. Some gorgeous hunter fucked my brains out last night," he said, making her choke on her own tongue. "One of those coffees for me too?"

Ciara passed it to him. "Um, about that..."

"Thought you didn't want to talk about it," he said, sipping his coffee.

"I don't want to. It doesn't mean we shouldn't," she huffed. "I think we need to focus on finding Varg, and whatever is between us will distract us too much."

Tor put his coffee down and started to pull his hair back into a knot. "I distract you?"

"Oh my god, stop," Ciara begged and slumped down at the small table.

"Stop what?"

"Everything."

Tor chuckled softly and pulled on a black T-shirt. "You don't make a lot of sense in the morning. I get what you are saying. I could be wrong, but it's not a no to us; it's a not now?"

Ciara forced herself to nod. "If it's something you also want to...consider."

Tor sat down at the table beside her. "I have considered it, and I want you. Deal with that how you will."

"Are you sure?" Ciara said before she could stop herself.

Tor raised a brow at her. "Of course I'm sure. Fucking you was about as close to a divine revelation I've ever had."

"Huh. That's not a compliment I've ever had before," she said, flattered and a little dazed. She wasn't the only one who felt like it was something that went beyond a casual hookup.

"I get that you've had a lot thrown at you in the last week, and I don't want to add to that," Tor said, going serious. "I'm happy to wait until you're ready for something more, but don't expect me to roll over and not fight for you."

Ciara swallowed hard. No one had ever fought for her. *She* did the fighting.

"Annddd, I've freaked you out," Tor said with a sigh.

"No, I mean, yes, you have, but it's going to take me a little bit to wrap my head around."

Tor leaned back in his chair, a satisfied smile on his face. "I can be patient while you figure out I'm going to be the best thing that ever happened to you."

Ciara's eyes narrowed. "You might be waiting a while, and I could turn around and decide not to bother with you. I wouldn't get too smug about it."

"Too late. I've already been inside of you, and I know it's worth the fight you're going to give me for it."

"Oh my god, stop." Ciara screwed up her paper bag and threw it at his head. It bounced off, and Tor's smile only widened.

"I hope you think about fucking me all damn day. It will put us on even ground."

"Dream on. All I'm going to be thinking about is the hunt. As soon as we leave this room, I will be professional and not think about you at all except as a hunting partner." Ciara stood up to go and got her bag. Tor grabbed her and pulled her into his lap so she was straddling him.

"As soon as you walk out that door, huh?" he said, brushing his nose against hers. Ciara's hands went to his chest, fingers twisting in the fabric of his shirt.

"Back to being professional," she said, swallowing.

"One for the road." Tor brushed his lips against hers, and she opened for him. He was gentle as he savored her. Ciara's legs tightened around him, and a tingle rushed down her spine straight to her pussy. She leaned into the kiss, her tongue stroking against his, and all the tension rolled out of her. Kissing him felt like coming home.

Fuck. This was precisely why she needed boundaries with him. Nothing would get done because she would kiss him and not be able to stop.

Tor growled low, his chest vibrating against her hand. He pulled back from her. "We need to go."

"Where? Oh. Uppsala. Right. Yes," Ciara said. She climbed off him and onto unsteady feet. He looked way too pleased with himself. God help her. "Anywhere in particular in Uppsala? Or are you winging it off some random thought of Von's?"

"A bit of both, actually." Tor filled her in on the details of the conversation. She took out her phone and tried to find Old Sigtun on a map and came up blank. "It doesn't exist."

"I went to Google, and it's now called Signhildsberg. It's got an estate and not much else. Do you want to drive first? You know, so you aren't distracted," Tor said with an innocent smile. Ciara flipped him off and snatched the keys off the table on the way out.

15

Tor only made it through the trip without reaching for Ciara by falling asleep in the first hour of the drive and not waking up until they were almost there.

"You should have woken me," he said, rubbing a hand over his face.

"And miss all the gossip you were telling me in your sleep? Why would I do that?" Ciara asked. She still looked perky. They must have stopped at some point because she had a small bottle of Coke in the cup holder and a Mars bar wrapper in the console.

"I don't talk in my sleep." At least, he hoped not.

"You do, but the problem is you also talk in Norwegian. Don't worry. Your secrets are safe for now, Torsten." Ciara was smiling, and damn if it didn't light up her whole gorgeous face.

"Look at that. You can joke after all," he teased.

"Of course I can."

"Not with me."

Ciara was silent for a long minute. "I didn't know you."

"And now you do?"

She raised a brow at him. "Biblically."

Tor tipped his head back and laughed. "Pretty sure I missed that part, or I would've taken some notes."

"Need some ideas, do you?"

Tor looked her over. "No, I have plenty. I would love to hear any you wish to share."

"Stick around, and I just might, wolf."

If Tor had been shifted then, he was sure his tail would have been wagging. He liked this non-defensive, almost flirty version of Ciara.

As they took the signs into Uppsala, Ciara turned on her navigation and found a café next to a park close to the university.

"Why are you stopping?" Tor asked.

"Pee. Food. Walk. In that order. I'm starving, and I never hunt without something in my stomach," she said and jumped out of the car. "And I really need to stretch my legs."

They used the public toilets at the park before drifting into the café. It was afternoon, but there was still a decent crowd waiting for coffee, cake, and sandwiches.

Tor got a few curious looks, and a group of teenage boys stared at Ciara like she was their wet dreams come true.

Get in line, kids, Tor thought. She was his wet dream too. He shot them a warning glare, and they quickly returned to their food.

They were sitting outside in the sunshine, eating, when Tor felt the first sticky wave of dark magic.

"Did you feel that?" he asked, looking around. Ciara immediately went on guard, her eyes scanning the families, university students, and pensioners walking through the park.

"What is it, Tor? What am I not seeing?"

"I feel magic."

"The same as Onsøy?" Ciara guessed.

"If not the same, then similar. It's dark and oily." Tor's head whipped around in time to see a tall, broad figure walk into the café. "There. That's a wolf. He was a friend of Varg. Fuck, what was his name?"

Ciara scanned the crowd. "There are too many people around to confront him, so what's the plan?"

Tor was flattered she would defer to him at all. It showed a trust he didn't know she had in him. "We stay out of sight and follow him. When he's alone, we'll take him."

Ciara nodded. "If he's here, there are bound to be others. How many followers does Varg have? Could he have more than one dig happening at one time?"

"Fuck, I hope not. There's always a possibility that he recruited the last of Vili's followers. They seemed determined to follow through with starting Ragnarök that they would follow someone willing to take the lead," Tor replied. The name came to him like a smack in the face. "Askel. The guy's name is Askel. He tried to get Gudrun to take him as an apprentice, but she refused."

"Why?" Ciara asked.

"Because he was a man. Völva are always women. He left not long after that, determined to follow his own path to magic."

Ciara clicked her tongue. "Followed it all the way to Varg and his fucked-up plans."

"He does attract a type. Makes me sick thinking about Linnea caught up with them, forced to serve them," he growled. He was doing his best not to let the guilt eat away at him; it wouldn't help them find her any faster.

"She didn't seem physically harmed. When I saw her, she was carrying around a large wooden bowl in a procession. Perhaps they were making her perform some ritual to Fenris? I'm sorry, I'm not good at recognizing magic. It's more Charlotte's thing," Ciara replied. She placed a hand on his forearm. "We'll get her, Tor, I promise."

"Can I ask why did you go looking for her after Svartalfheim?"

Ciara shrugged. "I couldn't stop thinking about what if it was Lachlan and no one would help me. I couldn't handle the thought of anything ever happening to him. I know what it's like to lose people, and I thought if I could give you back your sister, it might help repay all the help you've given us."

"I didn't fight Morrigan or any of the rest with the hope of payment, Ciara. It was the right thing to do, and you guys are my friends. Or *they* are. I'm not sure about you," he said, shooting her a smile.

"I'll keep you guessing a little while longer. It makes life interesting," Ciara replied, smiling back at him.

Askel came out of the café with a coffee and headed down one of the pathways.

"Fun time is over," Tor said, and they got up to follow him.

Ciara slipped her arm through his. "Try not to look like you're sneaking up on someone to tear their throat out. We are just a happy couple strolling through the park."

"Are we? Pretty sure there would be more kissing involved," Tor said.

"Nice try, but we both know if we start, we won't stop, and we will lose Askel."

Tor squeezed her arm. "I'm glad you recognize our chemistry."

"Animal magnetism?"

Tor raised a brow. "Was that an attempt at a joke? Who are you, and what have you done with Ciara Ironwood?"

"Shut up. And stop looking at me like that. We are working, remember?" she said, cheeks flushing.

"You were the one who said we were meant to be playing a happy couple."

"Something tells me our version of a happy couple isn't going to be the mushy-eyed mess that others are," Ciara replied.

Tor was going to ask what she thought they would be like, but then Askel turned down another path. One that was secluded enough to present an opportunity.

"You go left; I go right," Ciara said, letting him go and starting to move off. She moved as silent as a wolf across the grass towards Askel.

Tor did as she asked and went left. Askel slowed his pace, his nose lifting in the air. His head whipped around to Tor, spotting him, and instantly jumped into action. He turned to bolt and found Ciara with a baton that she had pulled from her left boot and flicked out. She went low, cracked Askel hard on the knees, and as he went forward, she sidestepped and hit him in the back of the head. He was out before he hit the ground.

"Holy shit," Tor said, jogging up to her. "Those were some smooth moves."

"Ones that Lachie and I practiced a lot." Ciara looked down at Askel. "We need a quiet place to question him."

Tor thought about it. They couldn't risk doing it in a hotel room. A lightbulb went on in his head. "The forest around the lake should have some unused cabins. It's not summer yet, so we might find an empty one with a woodshed."

Ciara nodded. "Okay, you watch him. I'll go get the car."

Tor crouched down beside Askel and started going through his pockets. "Now, let's see what secrets you are hiding."

16

Ciara and Tor found an empty cabin after their third try. It looked like it had been locked up since the previous summer. A fine layer of dust blanketed everything, and leaves covered the small patio and a boat shed.

Ciara pulled out some lock picks and made quick work of the boat shed door. It had a dock inside that opened directly out onto the water. Handy for a clean-up, and it would've been perfect if they needed to waterboard Askel. Unfortunately, it wasn't the most ideal way to get information out of a wolf.

Tor dragged Askel into the shed and used zip ties to fasten him to a chair.

"They aren't going to hold him," Ciara said and pulled out a black box from the bag. She swallowed hard, wondering if she should let Tor beat the crap out of Askel instead of revealing what she had in it.

"Have you ever tortured someone?" she asked.

"No," Tor replied. "I've kicked their asses, and I've killed. None of it involved torture."

Ciara straightened her shoulders. "Maybe you should wait outside."

Tor frowned. "Why?"

Because you're not going to want me after you see this side of me, Ciara almost said. She gripped the black box tighter.

"I have tortured people before. Wolves. I...I don't think you're going to want to witness this, and I'm trying to protect you from the reality of it," she replied instead. It was still the truth.

Tor crossed his arms. "This asshole knows where my sister is and has supported Varg in doing fuck knows what to her. I'm not going anywhere."

Ciara nodded. "Don't say I didn't warn you."

She put the box down on a wooden counter covered in paint stains. She flicked the locks and opened them. She took out a pair of silver cuffs engraved with sigils that nulled a wolf's strength and magic, and locked them around Askel's wrists. Almost instantly, the burning on his skin began, and he came to with a startled cry.

"What the fuck!" he demanded. His eyes glowed with blue fire when they landed on Tor. "You fucking traitor. You're going to let the Wolf Slayer carve me up?"

Tor's face was cold. "Depends on whether or not you tell me where Varg is. Make it easy on yourself, Askel. Tell us what we need to know, and I'll take you back to be judged by the elders."

Askel spat. "Fucking elders have no authority over me. A bunch of long-in-the-tooth wolves that should have been put down years ago. Makes sense that you would throw your lot in with this bitch. You are both wolf slayers, after all."

What? Ciara kept the surprise off her face. Tor let out a feral sound, and his fangs dropped. He looked ready to tear Askel's throat out.

"I take it that's a no to telling us where Varg is?" Ciara asked, pulling out a vial of wolfsbane. Charlotte had made it herself and mixed it with silver nitrate. Ciara usually coated her knives and bullets with it on a hunt.

"It's a fuck no. Varg is my king, the true king of the wolves. I'm his shaman and..." Askel's fingers had been moving in a pattern. He paused and tried again.

"I hope you're not trying to do magic because the cuffs will prevent it. Clever, aren't they?" Ciara said cheerily. She held up the bottle. "This is the hard way, Askel. Don't make me do it."

"Go right ahead, bitch. I know you get off on killing wolves. Never thought I'd see the likes of you with Mr. Straight Laced over here." Askel snarled wordlessly at Tor. "Fucking waste of a wolf you are.

Strongest alpha in centuries and you refuse to use any of your power like a pussy."

Tor nodded to Ciara. She stepped forward, pulled the dropper from the bottle, and drizzled some of the solution onto Askel's cheek. He shrieked, a high-pitched, panicked sound of pure agony.

"Tell me where Varg and my sister are!" Tor shouted over the noise.

Askel breathed heavily through his teeth. "Your sister is the key to finding Fenris. He'll never give her up even if you find him."

Tor looked more confused than ever. "What does she have to do with any of this madness?"

Askel laughed, a pain-filled maniacal sound. "She's the key to it all, and she's going to help Varg whether any of you like it. She'll bow before Fenris just like the rest of you. You fucking Ulfheðnar disgust me. Serving a god that wants nothing to do with you. He only turned up at that battle with Vili because he couldn't handle the thought of his blood getting more powerful than him. Odin hasn't appeared in centuries and doesn't give a fuck about the wolves."

"And what? Fenris is going to be a better god to serve? He's destined to destroy the world, you idiot. Do you really think he will grant you dumbasses wishes like a djinn? He'll kill *all* of you," Tor argued.

"Lies. He's our true god, and you are all too blind to see it."

Ciara stepped forward with a small silver knife and pressed it to his unmarred cheek below his eye. "You're going to go blind in a minute if you don't give us the information we can use."

"Killing me won't do any good. There's no way for you to stop what's happening. Others in the Ulfheðnar know this. Do you think you're being noble hunting Varg down for your precious council? They won't be in power much longer, you father killing, toothless alpha!" Askel screamed as Ciara stuck the blade into his eye.

Tor looked pale, but she didn't know if it was from the poisonous rant or the torture. She didn't think about it.

"I don't care about any of your political propaganda. Tell us where Linnea is, and I'll make your death quick," she hissed.

Askel bit his lip hard enough to draw blood. He started to chant, and before she could stop, he spat out a mouth full of blood. The curse sizzled the air like a lightning strike.

Tor snatched Ciara, ran towards the opening of the shed, and tossed her into the freezing cold lake. Above her, a large boom shook the sky, turning it orange and sending vibrations through the water.

Ciara breached the surface of the lake with a loud gasp. The shed was a fiery ball of rubble.

"Tor!" she shouted, scanning the water. "Tor!"

Ciara dived back down, searching the gloom. Something gold flickered, and she swam toward it, the bond pulsing. The gold was Tor's long hair. Ciara grabbed him by the shirt and heaved him upwards, kicking hard to drag him to the surface.

"Tor! Wake up!" she shouted. He didn't move. Ciara got him into a rescue position and started to swim him back to the rocky bank. "I swear to God, you better wake up, or I'm going to get so mad."

Ciara bent down and breathed into him. She started compressions when he came to and vomited up lake water. She rolled him onto his side and then saw the blood.

"Fuck, Tor," she gasped. His back was a ruined bloody mess of bits of wood chips from the shed. He must've still been above the surface when it exploded. He had protected her, getting her out of the way.

"Oh, gods, I hate that asshole," he groaned. "How bad is it?"

"They don't look too deep, but I'll need to pick the wood out with some tweezers. You crazy bastard, you could have gotten killed!" She didn't want to yell at him but couldn't seem to stop.

"But I didn't. We are both okay," he tried to soothe her. It only made her madder.

"Can you walk? We need to get out of here," she said.

There was nothing left of the boat shed or her special wolf hurting kit. The car was covered in debris but still started fine. Ciara got Tor into the passenger seat and leaned on the dash, blood staining what remained of his shirt and trickling over the seat. Ciara found her phone and quickly called Arne.

"Ciara? What's happened?" Arne answered.

"Do you still have that fancy plane?"

"Yes, why?"

"I'm going to need you to send it to Uppsala. We got one of Varg's supporters, but Tor... Tor's hurt," she said, her voice cracking. She sniffed hard. "He's okay. Just banged up, and we need to get back to Oslo fast."

"All right, I'll make it happen. Do you have somewhere safe to wait for an hour or two while I get the plane to you?" Arne asked.

"I can sort something out while we wait at the private airport. And Arne? Don't trust the Ulfheðnar."

The elf swore impressively for a prince. "Let me guess? Varg has rats."

"Apparently so."

"Fuck. I'll go and take care of the plane. You look after Tor," Arne said and rang off.

Ciara put down the phone and looked at Tor. "I need you to hang in there a bit longer. He's sending the plane. I'll find us somewhere safe."

Tor didn't reply. She brushed his hair back and saw that he'd passed out. It was probably for the best. Ciara took a deep, steady breath and drove away, the sound of sirens already in the distance.

17

Arne was true to his word, and Ciara's phone buzzed within an hour with a message saying the plane had landed. She had used some of their T-shirts to stop Tor's back from bleeding everywhere, but she hoped the plane would have at least one first aid kit. The bond throbbed between them like it knew one of them was hurt.

Ciara pulled up outside the hangar Arne directed her to, and two tall elf guards appeared.

"Miss Ironwood, let us assist in getting Tor onto the plane," they said in greeting. She waved them on, too tired to want to argue with them. Tor grumbled but still let them put him on a stretcher and carry him aboard.

Ciara grabbed everything out of the car and walked to the plane. She was cold, and her wet jeans were chafing like crazy.

"I don't know what to do with Tor's car," she said, just remembering about it. She was so damn tired.

"Not to worry. We have one of the guards going to drive it back to Oslo," one of the elves replied. They had placed Tor face down on a dark blue couch. "Do you require anything from us before we take off?"

"The first aid kit and a bottle of whiskey," she said, pulling out some dry clothes and heading into the tiny bathroom. She was pale, splattered with blood and ash.

Tor's blood... Ciara leaned over and threw up in the toilet. The cuffs should have stopped the shifter from doing any magic at all. How was it possible? Tor could have died because her equipment was faulty. Charlotte was going to be so mad that her cuffs didn't work either.

Ciara washed her face and used a travel kit toothbrush to clean her mouth. She scrubbed as best as she could and got into some dry clothes. Not wearing wet boots was a relief.

Tor hadn't moved from the couch, but someone had placed a bottle of whiskey and some glasses on the small table beside him. On the floor was a large first aid kit. The captain announced they were taking off, and Ciara sat down and buckled in. Tor didn't move with the plane, just lay facing the back of the couch.

Ciara waited until they were horizontal again before getting up and going to his side.

"Looks like I'm the one who gets to play nurse," she said, trying to lighten the mood. Tor turned his head so he could look at her.

"You're wearing too many clothes. Take a few off, and I'll start feeling better," he said.

"Yeah, you're in no shape to give me the fucking I deserve," Ciara replied. She went through the kit and pulled out all the things she needed.

"Do I get a whiskey before you start digging into me?" Tor asked.

Ciara poured out two glasses and offered him one. "If you need the courage."

"I saw you gouge a man's eye out today, bunny. There's nothing wrong with my courage," Tor replied, taking the drink.

Ciara didn't look at him. She only took a pair of scissors and started cutting up the back of his ruined shirt. The guards had placed white towels under him, so at least the couch didn't end up too bloody.

Tor finished the whiskey and passed it back to her. "Let's get on with it. I don't need my wounds to start healing the wood inside of it."

Ciara used saline to wash the cuts and abrasions. Luckily only a few had dark bits of wood still lodged into them. The bond between them ached again.

"Tell me, do people sharing a bond feel each other's pain?" she asked, picking up the tweezers.

"Not usually? Why...ow, fuccckkk," Tor groaned as her tweezers dug into the first cut.

"I didn't feel a thing," Ciara hummed, dropping the splinter into his empty whiskey glass.

Tor shot her a baleful glare before his face cracked, and he started laughing. "You're the worst, you know that?"

"I do. It's why you find me so interesting," Ciara replied. "How about you tell me a story while I do this?"

"Sure," he hissed while she dug about in another cut. "What do you want to know?"

Ciara inspected the end of her tweezers for the splinter. "Hmm. Missed it. I would like to know what Askel meant when he said you were a wolf slayer too."

It bothered her more than anything else the fanatic shaman had ranted about. She thought she knew Tor. The more time she spent with him, she realized not only how much she didn't know, but how much she had misjudged him.

Layla had tried to tell her that he had layers that he didn't show anyone, and Ciara had thought she meant his fun side.

"I don't want to tell you that story," Tor said, his gray eyes cold. "You won't want me after."

"Come on, Tor. You saw me torture one of your own kind today. You didn't think I had the exact same worry?"

His ashen brows rose. "You did? I didn't think you cared what anyone thought about you."

"I don't," Ciara huffed. "But you aren't anyone, are you? I didn't want you looking at me like the other wolves do. Like, I'm the fucking bogeyman. Which is ironic considering that it's you fuckers that were *my* bogeyman."

Tor was silent, even when she dug out three more splinters. He seemed to weigh up her words. "I'd never look at you like that. That's not to say you aren't the source of all my dreams and nightmares, but you are not my bogeyman. My father, Skari, was my bogeyman."

Ciara pretended not to notice the hitch in his voice like he hated saying the name. "Was?"

"Yeah, I killed him," Tor replied. Ciara placed a hand on the part of his back that wasn't wounded.

"Did he deserve it?" she asked softly.

"Many, many times over."

"So what finally broke you?"

Tor turned his head straight. "He wanted to banish my sister from the clan. She couldn't shift, so he saw her as less than useless. Wolves breed for strength, and it's not uncommon to have an arranged marriage. My father saw us as ways for him to climb in status. My mother left after one beating too many, and he never got over the shame of her walking out on him."

"Not the shame of beating her until the point she left?" Ciara grumbled. "Sorry. Go on."

"No, you're right. He didn't care. My mother knew if she took us, he would follow her to the ends of the earth, so she left us behind." Tor didn't sound mad about it, just matter-of-fact. Ciara's teeth ground together, but she kept her opinions to herself.

"After she left, Skari turned his anger on us, especially Linnea. She looked so much like my mother, and he hated the sight of her. I was in between them all the time. He berated her any chance he got because he was a prick."

"And how did he treat you?" Ciara asked softly, knowing she would hate the answer.

"He wanted me to be the strongest, most powerful wolf of the clan, so I was raised to fight and train and fight some more. It wasn't until I met Arne by pure chance in the forest one day that I realized there was another way that kids spent their time," Tor replied, his fingers toying with the corner of the towel underneath him.

"Alruna took me under her wings, tried to make things better for me. It only worked so much. Arne wanted to rescue me because that's just how he is. I wasn't going to leave Linnea with Skari. Not for a second. Alruna would've taken us both, but even the elf queen can't take children away from their awful parent. Elves aren't allowed to meddle in wolf business."

Ciara swallowed a lump in her throat. She thought about Lachie and how she would do anything to protect him. If she had been in Tor's position, she would have done the same thing and stayed.

"Anyway, when I was about eighteen, my father decided that my sister should be banished. She wasn't a real wolf. She had never shifted and showed no signs of it ever happening. He would have killed her if he could've gotten away with it. I walked in after a day of hunting, and he was laying into her, trying to make her survival instincts kick in and force the shift."

"Jesus," Ciara whispered, feeling sick. She wanted to hug him so badly. She just kept working, her fingers shaking.

"I ripped him off her, and I did the only thing I could do legally and called a *holmgang* on him. Do you know what that is?" Tor asked.

Ciara searched her memory. "It's like a duel?"

"Kind of. The wolves still honor it. Basically, you can call anyone out over a grievance to fight it out legally. Depending on the terms agreed upon at the beginning of the fight, it can be until surrender, incapacitation, or death. After the fight, the losing family can't take any action against the other. It's sorted." Tor shifted uncomfortably. "I called him out to the death. He was a good fighter, but I had something worth fighting for. If he was dead, we would be free from all the bullshit. He wanted to force me into an arranged marriage and become the wolves' leader because of my alpha strength. I didn't want any of that. It was a short and messy fight, and when I tore his throat out, all I felt was relief, not shame."

"You saved yourself and your sister. There was nothing to be ashamed of," Ciara said, squeezing his shoulder.

"Yeah, I thought that too. It still didn't stop Linnea from being shunned until she left the way my mother did, and it didn't stop the wolves gossiping about how I walked away from my destiny," he replied.

"Well, it was a crap destiny. I met Petra, and I wouldn't want to be married to her either," Ciara said, trying to make him laugh. He managed a smile.

"She's a lot, but then I dashed her dream that her parents had fed her too about being the queen of the wolves. Don't expect to make a friend there even if you do turn. The fact we are bonded will make her hate you forever."

Ciara laughed. "That's okay. I'm not friends with sore losers."

"You don't think I'm a terrible person for killing my father?" Tor asked.

"No. I would kill anyone that hurt Lachlan; I don't care who they are. He's my brother, and it doesn't matter that he can be a clueless asshole sometimes. I would defend him until the end. You did the right thing, Torsten," she said honestly. "We will get your sister back too. Never doubt it."

When his large hand curled around her calf a moment later, she didn't shove him off. She could feel how upset he was through the bond, and if hanging onto her leg comforted him, she wasn't going to deny him.

Ciara pulled out the last splinters, put antibiotic cream on the cuts, and covered the bigger ones with bandages. Tor watched her clean up and drank the bottle of water she gave him.

"Is there anything else I can do to speed up the healing?" she asked.

Tor tugged her to the couch and put his head on her lap. "Just stay here. We'll land soon. Touch helps when a wolf is hurt, especially with those that are bonded."

Somehow, Ciara knew he wasn't talking about the scratches on his back. Talking about his father cost him like it cost Ciara to ever talk about her own parent's death.

She didn't know how to do affection well, so she did what she used to do when Lachie was little; she gently stroked his hair and hummed 'Who wants to live forever' from *Highlander*. Lachie had been obsessed with it, and it had been the only thing to calm him down when he was distraught.

She missed her brother. He would know what to say and do to make Tor feel better because he was the opposite of her—open, affectionate, and charming. People loved it when he walked into a room, and they looked the other way when Ciara did.

Ciara knew she would probably be embarrassed about it later, but Tor didn't seem to be worried about it. He only smiled and went to sleep.

∼

CIARA WAS DOZING when the plane touched down in Oslo. Tor grumbled and wrapped his arms around her to stop her from getting up.

"Hey, wake up. We are here," she said, giving him a shake.

"Don't want to move. I like it here," he complained.

Ciara laughed softly and poked him in the side. "Come on. As soon as we get off the plane, the sooner we can have a hot shower."

Tor lifted his head. "Together?"

"You won't find out if you don't move."

"Hmm, you should come to my apartment. I have a bathroom I can actually fit in," he said. She helped him sit up and put a hoodie on with a zippered front. He looked like he had been through a grinder, and she doubted she looked much better. Which was a shame because as soon as the plane door opened, she was met with Bayn, Freya, Arne, and Layla. They all looked worried.

Ciara tried not to groan; she didn't want an interrogation. She wanted a shower and twelve hours of sleep.

"Brace yourself," Tor murmured behind her.

"I can't believe you didn't call me to come and help back you up in a fight," Bayn complained.

"I can't call on you whenever I get into a scuffle, cousin," Ciara replied.

"Yes, you can. He needs the exercise," Freya said, looking Ciara over with her mismatched eyes. "Any of the blood yours?"

"No, it's Tor's."

"You two look like hell," a new voice said. A tall man appeared from behind Bayn. His black curly hair and bright eyes were the mirror image of Ciara's. She dropped her bags and launched herself at her brother.

"Lachie, what are you doing here?" she demanded. She suddenly felt like crying and didn't know why.

Lachie patted her back. "You sounded weird on the phone, and I was worried. Kenna thought you might need some backup."

"Hey, what am I?" Layla complained.

"You're dick struck over your new mate, who won't let you go waltzing off to hunt a feral pack of wolves," Lachie retorted.

Arne grinned. "He's right. What the fuck happened, Tor?"

"I'm fine. I just need a meal and sleep." Tor took the arm that his blood brother offered him. "And you need to talk to your mother about calling a council with the wolves."

18

In the end, Ciara and Lachie ended up going to stay at Arne's apartment instead of Freya's.

Arne was smart enough to know that Tor wouldn't let Ciara get too far from him because of the bond, and Freya's place couldn't hold them all.

Ciara left Tor to update them on what happened and headed straight for the shower. The hot water felt like heaven pouring over her cold skin.

She stared at the orange water at her feet and tried not to let the horror of seeing Tor hurt overwhelm her. She was a hunter; people got injured. Why did she feel so terrible about it all of a sudden? He was alive. That's what mattered.

Damn bond is messing with your head, she told herself and soaped herself down again.

By the time she got out and into clean pajamas, Tor was gone, and pizzas had arrived.

"I ordered you a vegetarian one," Lachie said, passing the box to her. "I know how you're not up for meat after an interrogation."

"Thanks, bro," she replied, a lump in her throat. Her brother always surprised her with the small things he remembered. She sat down on the carpet in the lounge room and pulled out a piece. Cheesy carbs were the answer.

Layla came out of the bedroom, and she and Lachie joined Ciara for a picnic on the carpet.

"Where are the boys?" Ciara asked.

Layla waved a hand. "Sorting out logistics. We need to go home to Finnmark tomorrow and talk to the wolves. I can't believe Charlotte's cuffs failed on you."

"She's going to be so mad. Especially 'cause the dude is dead, and there's no way she can find out what he did," Lachie replied, stacking two pieces of pepperoni pizza on top of the other before having a big bite. "What's going on with you and Tor?"

"Nothing," Ciara replied. Both Layla and Lachie rolled their eyes. "He put a bond on me, and after this fight with Varg and the full moon, he will remove it. In the meantime, I have some of his strength and healing abilities. It's a pretty good deal."

"What about his monster dick?" Lachie asked.

Ciara choked on pizza. "Excuse me?"

"Don't act all offended. Imogen told me. She was worried about you too and called me. It kind of slipped out."

"I'm going to fucking *kill* her."

Layla laughed. "It's your fault for telling her. You know she sucks at keeping a secret. Don't worry, I'm sure only we know."

"Great. I've never given you a hard time about your hookups," Ciara said. She didn't want to deal with teasing after the day she'd had.

"We aren't giving you a hard time. It was bound to happen. You two were either going to have a proper fight or fuck it out. It's good that you went with the latter," Lachie replied. He bumped into her. "You guys talk about it, or are you doing a Ciara and refusing to acknowledge it happened?"

Ciara picked at the cheese on her pizza. "We talked about it and decided it's not a good idea to have distractions on a hunt. So there's nothing to tell. We should probably go back to Uppsala and check things out properly. He was just bleeding everywhere, and I..."

"You panicked?" Lachie guessed, and Ciara nodded.

"He got hurt because he shielded me from the blast. He could have died. I couldn't live with myself if that happened."

Layla put a hand on Ciara's arm. "You did the right thing to bring him back to a safe place to heal. You guys didn't know how many of Varg's cult were around, and if they ambushed you, there would be no way to survive it. We can always go back, but it's more important we tell the wolves they have a spy."

"I'm sure they will love hearing it from the Wolf Slayer," Ciara grunted. Her appetite was gone, but she forced herself to eat another piece of pizza.

"They'll listen to Tor, don't worry. Alruna and Arne will be there to back him."

"But elves can't meddle in wolf affairs," Ciara replied, thinking back on Tor's story.

"Varg is everyone's affair. Until he is stopped, an early Ragnarök is still a possibility. No one wants that," Layla argued. She got up to get them all fresh beers, and Lachie leaned his head on Ciara's shoulder.

"I'm happy you and Tor are finally recognizing there's something there," he said softly. "He gets you, Ciara. He sees past all your grumpy bullshit. You'd never have to hide who you are from him."

"Yeah, I know. I can't think of it and deal with Varg and maybe turning into a wolf as well. It's too much for my brain," Ciara replied. She rested her cheek against his hair. "It scares me a bit."

"I know, but it's okay for you to give a shit about a man that's not me. You've taken such good care of me over the years, sis. It's time you let someone take care of *you*," Lachie replied.

Ciara's chest ached. "I don't think I know how."

"You'll figure it out. You wouldn't be working with him, and you certainly wouldn't have slept with him if he didn't make you feel safe."

"A wolf making me feel safe. Who would've thought?" Ciara said.

Layla came back and passed them their beers. "Tor isn't just any wolf. He's special, just like you. Honestly, if you do turn into a wolf, it would give you a good excuse to get all weird about the forest and sleeping under the stars."

"Are you saying I'm weird now because I can appreciate how fascinating a forest ecosystem is?"

"Yes," they both answered.

"This is from the woman obsessed with fake elves and a guy with a framed *Highlander* poster in his room."

"We are all weird in our unique ways, and I don't see any need to change it," Lachie replied. "Anyway, we were talking about you and Tor."

"Nothing more to tell. I want to know if you have apologized to Apollo yet," Ciara said, wanting the subject far away from her.

"I have nothing to apologize for."

Layla looked at them both confused, so Ciara added, "Lachie cock blocked him, which is why Apollo was pissed at your party."

"And why would you feel the need to cock block him?" Layla asked innocently.

Lachie scowled. "It's not what you think. I was trying to protect him because none of his brothers give a shit."

"Maybe because they are all grown-ups. If it was Valentine in the same position, would you have cock blocked him?" Layla asked.

"Val is the scariest motherfucker in Ireland! He doesn't need protection. He needs a leash. Apollo is too nice, and people will use him," Lachie huffed and crossed his arms. "Someone needs to make sure he doesn't become a statistic."

"How noble of you to take up the cause," Layla snickered.

Ciara looked at the door to the apartment. "Any idea when they are coming back?"

Layla shook her head "Nope. You might as well get some sleep while you can. Big day tomorrow."

"Yeah, good idea." Ciara hugged them both before retreating to one of the guest rooms. She tried not to prod at the bond to see if Tor was okay. He was with Arne; he was totally fine. Ciara flopped face down on the bed and let the day finally catch up with her.

∼

HOURS LATER, Ciara was still staring at the wall in the guest room, unable to sleep but too tired to be awake. She always had problems sleeping after torturing someone, which she thought proved that she was still human enough to not enjoy it.

That night felt different. It wasn't guilt keeping her awake but a sickening feeling of how close she and Tor had been to dying. It was the bruised feeling in her heart every time she thought about how rough his childhood had been and how they needed Linnea back as soon as possible.

She got up and paced the room before running her hands through her snarled hair and cursing.

You need a drink of water, and you'll be fine, she told herself and tiptoed out of the guest room.

Arne must have come back because Layla was gone, and Lachie had crashed in the other guest room.

Instead of going to the fridge, Ciara walked out of the door and down the hall. She lifted her hand to tap on Tor's door when it opened. He looked tired and tousled. He didn't say anything, just made a small gesture with his head for her to come in.

"How are you feeling?" she asked.

"Better now," he replied. "Come on, bedtime. Don't make me carry you."

"I...okay."

There was no point arguing when she was the one who showed up on his doorstep. Again.

Tor lay down on his massive king-size bed and pulled her down beside him.

"Don't worry, I won't count this as cuddling either," he said.

Ciara smiled in the dark and wriggled into his side. "Good. This is purely to help you heal up. Can't have you going into battle hurt."

"Sure, bunny. Whatever you need to tell yourself to sleep better."

Ciara curled her leg over his and heard his breath catch. "Sweet dreams," she whispered.

Tor leaned down and kissed her. "Stop teasing me, you terror."

Ciara chuckled softly, placed her head on his chest, and was asleep in minutes.

19

"I think you should stay in Oslo," Tor told Ciara the next day. They were drinking coffee in his kitchen after the best night's sleep Ciara had had in ages.

"I'm sorry, I don't think I heard you right. You want me, your only witness, to stay behind in Oslo and let you go and face a bunch of surly wolves by yourself? When we know Varg has supporters there? And you are hurt?" Ciara lowered her cup and stared directly into his gray eyes. "Over my dead body."

Tor let out a frustrated growl. "It might come to that. Wolves hate outsiders."

"You really think I care? We need to stop Varg. I don't care if I make them uncomfortable." Ciara put her empty cup in his sink. Tor was behind her in a blink, his arms coming around her.

"What if I ask you to stay really nicely?" he purred into her ear.

Goosebumps broke out along her arms. "Answer is still no. I'm not letting you go alone."

"Worried about me?"

"You wish," she replied and jumped when he nipped at the side of her neck. "Careful playing those games, wolf. You are still recovering from yesterday and are in no condition to give me what I need."

Tor ran a hand under her shirt and stroked her stomach. "All depends on what you need?"

"Patience. No matter how much you feel me up, I will not change my mind. I'm going to get ready. I suggest you do the same," Ciara replied. She tried to slip out of his grasp, but he held on. His other hand snaked around her throat and made her head tip back.

"Just one taste," he said, leaning over her to press his mouth against hers. He was coffee and pine-scented warmth, and Ciara melted back into him. She didn't know how stressful the day was going to be, and being kissed was an excellent way to take her mind off things.

Tor's hand stroked down her stomach and under the hem of her sleep shorts. She should stop things before they got too out of hand. Tor cupped her pussy with his big hand, and she trembled against him. All thoughts of stopping vanished.

Ciara pressed back into him and moaned into his mouth as his fingers slipped through her arousal and toyed with her clit. Oh, gods, it wasn't fair how quickly he could undo her. He pressed a finger inside of her, and she thrust against him.

"Fuck, Ciara, you're going to ruin me. You're so hot and wet," Tor growled. "I'm never going to resist."

Ciara's vision hazed, and she clung to his arm, hard enough to leave nail marks. "Tor, don't stop, please I'm..."

"I know, sweet bunny. I have you. Come for me, let me watch," Tor replied, adding another finger. He did something with his thumb, and Ciara's orgasm hit her like a slap, an embarrassing gasp escaping her lips as sparks danced in front of her eyes.

Tor kissed her deeply, stealing her breath and what remained of her common sense. She wanted him inside of her. Needed him filling her up until she couldn't take it anymore.

"If only we had time," Tor said, pulling back from her. He untangled his hand from her shorts, and Ciara burned red as he licked her come off his fingers. His eyes flashed with a wolf sheen, and a growl rumbled through his chest. "I promised myself only a taste."

"Fuck me," Ciara groaned, not caring how pathetic she sounded.

"I will later. It'll give you something to look forward to because I can guarantee today will suck for all of us." Tor grinned and nodded towards the door. "Run, bunny. Alruna is opening a portal in thirty minutes."

Ciara covered her face with her hands, a frustrated groan escaping her. "You did that on purpose."

Tor laughed, a full deep laugh that chased the last of the shadows from his eyes. "Guilty. Now go."

Ciara muttered obscenities all the way down the hall to Arne's apartment. Layla answered after the second knock.

"Well, well, the hussy herself," she crooned.

Ciara flipped her off. "Shut up. Nothing happened. It's a bond thing. I couldn't sleep."

"Sure, okay, and that glow in your cheeks is a new serum you've been using. Portal is opening in thirty minutes."

"I'm painfully aware," Ciara said darkly and headed for her room.

So much for keeping things professional. Her epic self-control was completely gone. She dug through what remained of her clean clothes and produced tight black jeans and a plain navy T-shirt. She didn't know how strict about dress code wolf councils were, but she was out of options. She put on a little makeup for formalities' stake and braided her hair. It would have to do.

Ciara stepped into the lounge as Tor came through the door, wearing dark jeans and a white button-up shirt with the sleeves rolled to his elbows to show off tattoos and golden skin. All her thoughts plummeted straight to the gutter. The grin on his face said Tor knew it too.

"How's that going for you?" Lachie whispered from behind her, and she turned to whack him. "As I thought."

"Shut up."

His eyes went serious. "You okay going back to Ulfheim today?"

"Yeah, it'll be fine."

"I'm glad you think so because I'm coming too."

"What? Why?" Ciara asked. Putting herself in danger was one thing. Letting her baby brother do it was something else entirely.

"I trust Tor. That doesn't mean I trust any other wolves who are thinking of making a name for themselves by taking out the Wolf Slayer." Lachlan had set his jaw, and Ciara knew there wasn't any point in trying to argue.

"Okay, but if shit kicks off, you don't get involved."

"Sure thing, big sister," he said, but his smile told her she could go fuck herself.

Just great.

~

THE COUNCIL HALL of the Ulfheðnar was a long Viking hall carved with wolves, world trees, and everything associated with Odin. Ciara had never seen anything like it. It looked like it had been there since the dark ages and probably had.

"So cool," Lachie said, staring up at it.

Ciara's head turned as a beautiful red-haired woman came walking down a path towards them. She wore a dark green and black dress and had dark blue runes tattooed on her face. She hummed with magic and could have been anywhere between thirty and fifty.

"It's nice to see you healed and whole, Ciara Ironwood," the woman greeted.

"Have we met?"

The woman smiled, her bright green eyes shining. "Not while you were awake. I'm Gudrun."

"The Völva," Ciara guessed, putting it together. "Thank you for your help."

"I almost didn't do it, but Tor can be convincing when he's determined. I see the bond is strong between you. It's a good thing. You might need it today," Gudrun replied and headed into the hall.

"That's the one you need to be afraid of," Lachie whispered to her, and Ciara nodded. Gudrun had power in the bucketloads, and if she was the only Völva in the village, she would have influence.

Layla's head appeared out of the wide wooden doors. "Are you two coming in or not?"

Ciara and Lachie walked in together. They had trained as hunting partners their entire lives and fell naturally into formation, ready for an attack.

Inside the hall was one long feast table and a fire pit at its center. The three elders, wolves aged between fifty and seventy, sat across the table from Arne, Layla, and Alruna.

Ciara's eyes adjusted to the low light of the hall, and she realized wolves were sitting at other small tables behind their elders, some in wolf form and others human. They had all come to hear what Tor and the elves had to say. A murmur and more than a few low growls echoed around the hall when the wolves spotted Ciara.

Ciara didn't care. She kept her head high and went and stood with Tor behind Layla. She didn't doubt that if there was any trouble, Arne would protect Layla, but Ciara wanted to make sure she had her back guarded.

"You have called us together under such urgency, Torsten Skarison. I hope for a good reason," a grizzled elder asked. He looked like the oldest of the three.

"The reason is that the hunt for Varg has produced disturbing revelations," Tor replied respectfully. He was hunched over, his energy drawn in to not appear threatening or challenging. It made Ciara's teeth clench. She kept her mouth shut as Tor relayed their hunt for Varg, finding Askel and the information they had gotten from him before he exploded.

Gudrun hissed at the mention of Askel and the magic he had used to kill himself. Tor did his best to explain the feeling of the dark spell, but the wolves weren't interested.

"You are claiming we have traitors in the pack, Tor. Do you know who? If you don't, what do you expect us to do about it?" the female elder asked.

"I think it's all bullshit," a female voice announced. Ciara's eyes narrowed as Petra strode into the hall like she owned it.

"Let me guess? Tor's ex?" Lachie whispered to her. Ciara nodded.

"Bold of you to interrupt a council," Alruna said coolly.

"Bold of *you* and your pampered prince to interfere in wolf business, elf," Petra snapped.

Oh no, she didn't. Ciara placed a hand on Layla's shoulder, pushing her back in her seat.

"Watch your tongue, girl. You will respect this council or get the fuck out," the grizzled one snarled.

"It's the respect I have for the council that I open my mouth at all. Torsten has been bewitched by the Wolf Slayer. I highly doubt Askel was captured at all! As for Varg, there's been no sign of him since the battle with Vili," Petra charged on.

Tor crossed his arms. "And how would you know? You weren't at the battle. You need to stop making this personal, Petra. Varg is the enemy, not Ciara," Tor snapped.

"Unless she's the one working for Varg," Layla said, somehow looking down her nose at Petra while sitting in a chair. Ciara tried not to grin, but her cousin wasn't done. "That's the only reason I can see why an Ulfheðnar wouldn't have turned up to fight an enemy of Odin's."

"I was out of the country, or I would have been," Petra replied, lifting her chin.

Layla raised a brow. "You have a way to verify that, do you? Because I can't understand why you would object to stopping Varg from waking Fenris unless you were working for him."

"We don't even have proof that Varg didn't go back to Svartalfheim!" Petra snarled at her. "You shouldn't even be allowed to talk—"

"I've seen Varg since the battle. At a camp at Onsøy," Ciara interrupted.

Petra looked at Ciara, her face twisting in utter disgust. "Like any of us should believe the words of the Wolf Slayer. You have done enough damage by enchanting Tor and forcing him to put a bond on you."

"She didn't force him. I witnessed the bond," Gudrun replied. "There was no enchantment. Tor offered it willingly."

Petra's face flushed. "I don't trust the words of a witch either! Why else would a wolf want to bond with a woman who has slaughtered our kind? It makes no sense!"

"You make no sense. I haven't enchanted Tor. I wouldn't even know how. I've never killed a wolf that didn't need to be put down for the safety of others," Ciara replied steadily.

"No! I won't accept this." Petra turned to Tor, her eyes full of proud fire. "I will save you from whatever they have done to you. We will be together as promised."

"Petra, she has done nothing to me. She's my friend and a part of Odin's family through marriage. We are sworn to protect *all* in the All-Father's family," Tor replied. There was a flicker of alpha in his voice despite how much he was trying to hold it in.

Petra snarled, her eyes turning wolf. "I call a *holmgang* on Ciara Ironwood, the Wolf Slayer."

"For fuck's sake," Tor muttered. Everyone was looking at Ciara to respond to the challenge.

"What are the terms?" she asked, feigning boredom.

"To the death. That's the only way to remove a bond for certain," Petra declared.

"And if I refuse to fight you?" Ciara asked.

"Then you will be forced to relinquish the bond with Torsten of your own free will and never step foot into wolf lands again."

Ciara growled low, an utterly wolf sound that had the other wolves suddenly on guard. "Looks like you'll have to try and kill me because I will never give up my bond with Tor. You'll have to tear it from my soul, bitch."

Tor's expression shifted to surprise before his gray eyes heated and Ciara had to look away. She couldn't go into a fight being emotional, and what was hammering at her through the bond wasn't something she could acknowledge just yet.

The female elder cleared her throat. "Is that your official acceptance of the *holmgang*, Miss Ironwood? It *is* to the death."

Ciara smiled the cold bitch Ironwood smile and let the Wolf Slayer flood her eyes. "Let's do this. I don't have all day."

20

"You don't have to go through with this, sis," Lachie said ten minutes later.

The whole village was in an uproar over the challenge. They were all gathering at a stone circle on the edge of the village that was the traditional place for *holmgang* challenges. Ciara and Petra would each be given a sword and a single wooden shield to battle it out. A few wolves had jeered at Ciara, telling her to back down and save herself.

Ciara was in no mood to back down. "I do have to do this, or she'll never stop."

"You aren't a wolf. Petra had no right to challenge you at all," Layla hissed.

"If it was Arne, would you walk away from it? Give your bond up?" Ciara demanded.

Layla drew back as if she'd been struck. "That's different, and you know it. Arne is my *mate*. A few days ago, you couldn't wait to get rid of the bond with Tor, and now you're going to fight to the death over it?"

"A lot has happened in the last few days," Ciara admitted. Realization seemed to hit Layla and Lachie at the same time. Ciara had finally caught feelings.

Lachie exhaled loudly. "Fuck."

"Don't...don't say anything to anyone, okay? Especially not Tor. I need to figure myself out, but Varg has to come first. Petra needs to be dealt with so the wolves will take the threat seriously," Ciara hurried to explain.

"Somehow, I think Tor already knows, especially now that you're going to fight his ex for him," Lachie replied.

Tor hadn't been allowed to speak with Ciara since the challenge had been accepted. Only family was allowed to talk with the challengers, so they could work out final wills and other arrangements in case of death. Ciara could feel Tor watching her. She refused to look at him. She needed to be calm and focused.

"If you die, I get all your stuff, right?" Lachie asked. He was trying to be cheeky, but his deep blue eyes betrayed how worried he was.

"Sure, if you want it. It's going to be okay, little brother." Ciara pressed her forehead to his. "I'm so proud of the man you've become, and I know our parents would have been too. I love you."

"I love you too," Lachie whispered, his voice breaking. "Now go kick that bitch's ass."

"I will." Ciara stepped back from him. She winked at Layla before picking up her sword and shield and walking into the stone circle.

Petra was standing with her family across the other side of the ring. Her parents looked furious at her. She noticed Ciara was ready and picked up her weapons. She strode into the ring, haughty as a queen.

Ciara cracked her neck. "You ready?"

"I'm more than ready. I'm going to enjoy killing the famous Wolf Slayer," Petra snapped, circling Ciara. "I will free Tor and mate with him on your grave."

"You are one crazy stalker, you know that, right?" Ciara sidestepped as Petra swung her sword. She was fast, but Ciara had fought wolves before. She attacked low, aiming for Petra's knees. Petra dropped her shield, and Ciara's blade cut deep into the wood. Petra immediately brought her sword down, aiming for Ciara's head before her blade was free. Ciara dodged it and felt the air of the blade on her shoulder.

Too close. She used Petra's forward momentum to drive the edge of her shield up and smashed the wolf in her pretty nose.

Ciara pulled her sword loose, yanking Petra's ruined shield off. The wolf backed up, trying to keep her feet as blood poured down her nose.

"You fucking bitch!" Petra screamed.

Ciara blocked out the sounds of the crowd, the beating of her own heart, and the smell of dirt and blood. She dropped down into her killing space, where there was nothing but her blade and her target.

They clashed, steel against steel, again and again until sweat was running down Ciara's back. Petra demolished her shield with one massive blow that would have pulverized Ciara's skull. She threw it off, ignoring the cut on her forearm that was bleeding freely.

She would never give up, never give in. The bond opened between Tor and Ciara, and new strength rushed through her body. Ciara didn't waste it, and she would never let anyone else have it.

"You had to come and interfere and ruin everything," Petra snapped. "Even Odin, who has ignored us for centuries, turned up because your slut cousin called."

"It's all a part of the Ironwood charm," Ciara replied, blinking sweat out of her eyes. "You think Fenris will be immune? I doubt it."

"Fenris will ensure wolves have their rightful place above the fae, the fucking elves, and the weak humans," Petra snarled. Her eyes went wide, realizing what she had said.

"Isn't that interesting?" Ciara mocked her.

Petra screamed and charged at her in a fury. Ciara ducked at the last second, her leg coming around and kicking Petra in the lower back with all of the strength Tor had given her. Petra went sprawling to the ground face down, her sword clattering outside the ring of stones.

Ciara raised her sword. "Yield. You don't have to die today."

"I will never yield," Petra snarled, rolling onto her side. She got to her feet and raised her fists.

"The fight's over. You lost," Ciara said.

She didn't want to kill Petra, even if she deserved it. If Ciara did, the wolves would never accept her. They would always blame her for killing one of their own. She didn't care what they thought, but it would matter to Tor.

"If you don't fight me, I will hunt every member of your family down before I kill you last," Petra declared. She spat blood and dirt at Ciara.

"You have no weapon to fight, and there's no honor for me fighting an unarmed opponent," Ciara said, trying not to let her temper overrule her.

"I don't need a weapon. I *am* one." Petra's eyes glowed, the air shimmering around her. "I want you to know that once you're dead, I'll be killing your pretty brother next."

Ciara went still; all remaining compassion she had was gone. Petra shifted into a wolf with a roar and launched herself at Ciara. Ciara dropped to her knees; Petra soared over the top of her, and Ciara lifted her blade, cutting the wolf's belly open and spraying herself with blood. Petra went down, collapsing into the dirt beside her.

"Never threaten my brother," Ciara snarled and cut the wolf's head off. No one moved for a full ten seconds.

"Wolf Slayer," someone hissed. "Wolf Slayer, Wolf Slayer, Wolf Slayer." The name echoed around her.

Ciara's body was sticky with blood and boiling hot with fury.

"That's right! I *am* the fucking Wolf Slayer!" she shouted back at them. She pointed at the crowd with her sword. "You want to know about the wolves I've killed? Sigmund Wagner! He broke into my home when I was a child and killed my parents. He was about to rape and kill me when I took the knife from my dead father's hand and drove it into his eye!"

The crowd went quiet, but Ciara was too far gone in her anger. She started to list her kills, one at a time, with all the crimes they had committed before they got on her list. She stopped at her tenth, but gods, did she have more.

"Every wolf I killed had it coming! They were allowed to roam free, slaughtering humans and other beings because the wolves didn't do a fucking thing about it," she said, breathing heavily. "You think you are a clan of ancient and mighty warriors, but you hide here in your forest while one of your own tries to start Ragnarök. You have no responsibility. You have *no* honor. It's no wonder Odin abandoned you all. If *any* of you try and get between Tor and me or threaten my family again, you will end up like her!"

Ciara tossed her sword to the ground beside Petra's head and strode out of the stone circle. She needed to leave before she killed them all.

"Take her home. I'll deal with the rest," Tor said, his alpha power rolling out of him. Ciara's shoulders hunched inwards, fighting not to go to him. That would make everything worse.

Lachie took her by one arm, Layla by the other just as Alruna opened a portal, and they marched Ciara through it before anyone said another word.

21

The portal closed with a rush of heat and magic. They were back at Tor's cabin next to the lake. Ciara sagged, her knees going squishy.

"Breathe, Ciara, breathe," Lachie said urgently. He hugged her tightly to him, and she began to sob. She was so angry, it was choking her.

"I didn't want to kill her," Ciara said.

"I know. They all know. She forced it, and she paid the price."

Ciara looked about. "Where's Tor and Arne?"

"They'll sort out the wolves," Alruna said. "You need to get cleaned up because when Tor comes back, you're going to have to deal with the consequences of your actions."

"Consequences? I was pressured into a fight to the death."

Alruna let out a tired sigh. "Not those consequences. You claimed him in front of the whole clan, Ciara, and threatened to kill anyone who touched him. You killed your rival for him. All of that *means* things to the wolves."

"It should mean that they need to keep their fucking noses out of my business and stop picking fights when we have bigger enemies to fight," Ciara snapped.

"That as well. As soon as Tor arrives, the rest of us will be getting out of here for our own well-being. That includes you too, Lachlan," Layla replied. She looked shaken. They had seen a lot of battles together, but there was something so wasteful about the fight that had just happened. It didn't matter that Petra could've been working for Varg. It shouldn't have escalated to that point.

Ciara still didn't feel bad about it. She was furious that Petra thought she could bully Tor into loving her. Tor had been bullied enough in his life, and if he wouldn't stand up for himself, Ciara would.

Alruna opened the front door and pointed to the bathroom.

"Wash the blood off. We'll find you something clean," she said. Her eyes snagged on Ciara's arm. "I'll find something to patch that up too."

Ciara looked at the bloody, sweaty fright that she was in the mirror. She looked feral, a dangerous light in her eyes that she had never seen before. She didn't know if it was the wolf in her through the bond or her own violence.

"Fucking wolves," she growled. She stripped off her clothes and got into the shower. The gash on her arm needed stitches and was bleeding freely again.

She had an overwhelming urge to cry, but she held it in. She had screamed her personal history at a pack of wolves who were probably all planning to kill her. She pressed a hand to her aching chest and hoped Tor and Arne were okay. They had left them in the middle of a shit storm. She didn't dare touch the bond.

Ciara got out of the shower, and there was a tap at the door.

"I have some clean clothes for you," Layla said and passed them over. "Alruna opened a portal home so I could grab you some of mine. Pretty sure yours need to be cleansed with fire."

"Thanks," Ciara said, grateful she didn't have to put the filthy jeans back on.

In the kitchen, Alruna had set up a first aid kit and made a pot of tea.

"Drink some water first. With all the adrenaline and sweating, you're going to crash if you're not careful," she said, sounding like a mom.

Ciara sat down at the counter and placed her arm on the towel

Alruna had set up. Ciara drank her water and tea in silence while Alruna fixed up the gash on her arm.

"Tor gave you some of his healing, so I'll only use some zip stitches," she said.

"Thank you," Ciara replied. The numbness was creeping in, and she was fast becoming incapable of being social. She never thought she would have an elvish queen patching her up either. "How pissed is Tor going to be at me?"

Alruna fixed another stitch in place. "You scared him today, in more ways than one. He won't be pissed, but he'll be grumpy about it."

"I scared him?"

"My gods, you really don't know why? He cares about you, Ciara, and you walked into a *holmgang* ready to die, and he could do nothing about it. How do you think you would have felt in the same position?" Alruna asked. She finished the last stitch and started cleaning up all the bloody gauze.

Ciara said nothing. She couldn't because all she could think about was if their positions *were* reversed, she would've probably killed Petra before Tor could've walked into the ring.

"Are wolves always so fucking ridiculous?" she asked instead.

Alruna laughed softly. "They are stubborn as hell and just as loyal. You shamed them all today, so well done. They are still going to be afraid of you, but take it as a compliment. They respect that."

Layla got up and went to the door like she could sense the moment Arne and Tor returned. Layla checked Arne all over, and he gave her a reassuring smile that he was okay. That they both were.

Ciara's stomach exploded into butterflies as Tor filled the doorway. She had never had that reaction before. Tor had never made her nervous. Now she felt like she was in trouble and didn't like it.

Lachlan kissed Ciara on the forehead. "Good luck, sis. I'll give you a call tomorrow."

"You might see me sooner than that," she murmured.

Tor wasn't smiling; he looked like he was about to go to war. Everyone vanished, leaving her behind to deal with a pissed-off wolf.

"I can smell your blood," he said in a low growl.

"It was a scratch," Ciara replied, lifting her arm. "How much shit am I in?"

"With the wolves? None." Tor stalked into the kitchen, a bag of food in his hands that he placed in the fridge.

"Don't lie to me, Tor. Petra was one of theirs, and I'm the Wolf Slayer," Ciara said. She wanted him to give her the bad news and not leave her stewing over it.

"Petra called a *holmgang*. She got what she deserved. The elders had her place searched, and she was definitely reporting back to Varg. Her family is horrified and dishonored."

"Shit." Ciara ran a hand through her hair. "Is she the only one?"

"They will look for more. At least they believe us now."

"It shouldn't have come to that. She was a raging bitch, but I didn't want to kill her."

Tor let out a sigh. "I know. Everyone saw you try and get her to yield. She shifted in the fight, and that was forbidden, which would have meant exile for her at the least if she had killed you. She dishonored herself from start to finish. The wolves don't blame you for any of it."

"Then why do you look so mad?" she demanded, unable to take it anymore. "What happened to make you so angry at me?"

"I'm not angry at you, Ciara. I'm trying to find a way to talk to you about us."

Ciara swallowed hard. "Us? What about us?"

The muscles in Tor's jaw feathered. "In the eyes of the wolves, you killed your rival and shamed them all as cowards. You swore blood vengeance on anyone who comes near me. You claimed me in front of the wolves, and we already have a bond."

"They think we are mating?" she squeaked, finally catching up to what they had all been trying to tell her.

Tor nodded. His expression shifted, and she saw the rawness underneath. "And they aren't the only ones, Ciara."

"No. No. No. You are only thinking that because you think I'm going to turn into a wolf, and I'm the only one who's ever stood up for you."

"Ciara, please just listen."

"No." Ciara was on her feet faster than if someone stuck her with a hot poker. Her day had been too fucked up as it was. She was not dealing with the idea of mating on top of it. She stuffed her feet into her boots and headed for the door.

"You can't run from this. If you do, I'll hunt you down," Tor said, his voice all growl and threat. "I'm not letting you go. Maybe before I could have, but not anymore."

Ciara stared him down. "I'm not afraid of you."

"You should be." Tor moved slowly around the counter, his eyes glowing. He stopped just out of her reach. He knew she would attack if he corned her like he had at the hotel.

His smile went feral. "I knew you were mine since Svartalfheim, and for such a great hunter, you had no idea that you were being stalked all this time."

A flicker of excitement danced inside of Ciara, all her instincts letting her know she was trapped with a predator.

Tor nodded at the open door. "You want to run from us? From me? Do you know what will happen when I catch you? The same thing as last time you tried to push my patience. Do it. Run. I fucking *dare* you."

Ciara's breath caught, her heart pounding too hard in her chest. Her body tensed, and the strength he'd given her through the bond coiled hot inside her. She loosed her breath and bolted.

22

Tor's body burned. He pulled his shirt off and dropped his jeans. He *knew* she would run. It was like she couldn't help herself and had to make everything a fight. It was one of the things he liked about her.

Tor grinned, his mouth filling with fangs, and the wolf burst free from his skin. She might want to play games, but he wasn't in the mood to play fair. The day had been one long anxiety-fuelled nightmare, and he needed the release.

Ciara's trail headed straight into the forest. He followed it, not hurrying, wanting her to think she was getting a head start. He could have followed the trail of her arousal alone. She knew exactly what was going to happen when she got caught.

Tor began to trot, weaving through the trees and picking up his pace. He was eager for her. Had been *burning* for her all damn day.

After she had fought for him, he was almost mad because of his need for her. The fierce and feared Wolf Slayer had claimed him. *Him.*

Tor couldn't get over it. He wouldn't. It didn't matter that she would need to be convinced. He would have her because no one else would ever be able to satisfy him. He wanted her vicious heart, and he would fight to get it.

Ciara was headed for Alfheimstod. Maybe she was thinking if she made it to Layla, that she would be safe. Nowhere was going to be safe for her. He would hunt her to the ends of the earth until she submitted to him.

Ciara was standing in a glade, glancing around like she could sense him coming. Tor circled her, sticking to the shadows. Her face went alert. She knew she was being stalked. Tor shifted and pounced on her from behind.

Ciara was lightning quick, ducking and throwing him over her shoulder and to the ground. Tor stared up at her. She looked wild in the moonlight, her inky hair a tangle of shadows, blue eyes glowing.

"Is that all you got, Wolf Slayer?" he asked, grinning up at her. "Why do you always want to fight me instead of just asking me to fuck you?"

Tor expected her to take advantage of him being down to throw some kicks in and take off again.

"Where's the fun in that?" she replied. She launched herself at him, wrapped her arms around his neck, and kissed him.

"I'm going to fuck you, but I'm not going to mate you," she growled against his lips.

"Not tonight, but you will. It's inevitable, bunny. We belong together, and you fucking know it," Tor replied. He pulled her shirt and bra over her head, rolled her, and dragged off her boots and jeans. She was stunning. Every part of her.

"I can wait until you're begging to be my mate, Ciara Ironwood. I will hunt you and fuck you and hunt you again until you finally submit to me. I won't stop until you accept what you are."

Ciara snarled wordlessly at him. Her legs locked around his waist, and she rolled him until she was back on top.

Tor laughed softly and bit her bottom lip. "You take what you want, just like an alpha should."

"Compliment me all you want. I'm still not mating you," Ciara replied. She grabbed his dick and pressed it to her wet entrance. "This is all I want from you right now."

Tor took a handful of hair and pulled her head back. His teeth dragged down her neck. "Be mean all you want. I like that about you too."

Ciara whimpered and lowered herself onto his dick. Tor grabbed her hip with his other hand and pulled her down fast enough to make her gasp. Her nails were tearing into his chest and shoulders, and it felt so damn good. Everything with her always did.

Ciara rocked her hips, riding him, taking what she wanted. Tor let her. He kissed her, teeth and tongues locked in their own kind of battle. She was just as feral as he was. She was everything.

Tor bent his head so he could lick and bite at her perfect, perky breasts. Ciara's hands were buried in his hair, holding him to her and crying out when he bit down. Her whole body trembled with power, and Tor opened the bond between them.

They both gasped, swamped with feeling the other's pleasure. If this was what it was like with a normal bond, he couldn't imagine what an actual mating bond would do to him.

"Fuck, Tor," Ciara panted, and she shook with release, her inner walls gripping him tight and flooding him with warmth. Tor didn't give her a second to catch her breath. He pressed her back into the soft moss, lifted her gorgeous hips, and drove into her.

Tor would never forget her blissed-out expression, the moonlight pouring over her as he took her. It was primal. Nothing would ever be so right as that moment.

Fuck, I'm so in love with you, he thought and bit his tongue so he wouldn't say it out loud. The wolf in him roared to mark and mate her. He released her hips and put his hands on either side of her head, caging her in.

Ciara kissed him, her legs locking around his lower back and hanging on. She looked up at him and very deliberately bared her neck to him. *Surrender.*

Tor came at the sight, unable to hold it back. He buried his face in her shoulder, his fangs begging to sink into her.

Ciara's fingers buried in his hair, her lips pressing into the crown of his head. He dragged her into his arms, sitting back to get her off the cold ground. He brushed the hair from her face and kissed her swollen lips.

"You look good like this. Like a wild god of the forest," she whispered, brushing her nose against his in a small affectionate gesture. "I like it."

"Then I'll make a note to fuck you under the stars more often." Tor kissed her sweet smile. "Let me take you home, Ciara."

If she demanded to go to Layla's, he would take her. He didn't really care where they were as long as they were together.

Ciara put her arms around him and placed her head on his shoulder. She breathed him in and made a little growl of contentment.

"Okay, but you're going to have to carry me," she murmured.

"I planned on it," Tor replied, standing up and cradling her close. "You have had a big day. Let me take care of you for once."

"Because I'm so great at letting other people do that," she said bitterly.

Tor kissed the top of her head and held her closer. "You'll get used to it, bunny."

23

Ciara was feeling a million things at once. She wanted to fight with all of her impulses to reject what Tor was offering, but she couldn't. She was done fighting for the day.

Tor carried her like she was a doll, something fragile and cherished. She tried not to be embarrassed by it. It had been a long day, and she was too tired to want to argue for the sake of it.

She had run because she knew he would fuck her senseless, and she loved the thrill of it...of him. It was probably the result of deep trauma, but she wasn't about to analyze it. She didn't care.

Tor's house came into view, and he took her to the bathroom and into the big shower. He kissed her softly and set her down on her feet. She was filthy, her skin stained with mud and moss and with leaves in her hair. Tor was in the same state, and he had never looked sexier.

He waited until the water was hot before tugging her under the spray. Ciara groaned. She hadn't realized how chill her skin was.

"How's your arm? We didn't pull your stitches?" he asked.

Ciara showed him. "No, it's fine. It must be healing because it's not aching."

"Good. I swear I almost had a heart attack when you agreed to fight her," Tor admitted. He soaped up a soft cloth and started to wipe the mud and forest grime from her.

"Why? Did you think I couldn't take her?" Ciara asked.

Tor knelt down on the tiles and washed her legs and feet. He pressed a kiss to the side of her knee. "I'm not good with losing people. I knew Petra would cheat. I hate seeing you hurt in any way."

"Can I ask you something?"

Tor looked up at her. "Sure."

"If wolves choose their mates for strength, why didn't you want to mate with her?" Ciara asked.

Tor stood up, and she got the chance to admire all of the wet tattooed Viking in front of her. Gods, he was beautiful.

"I've never felt anything for her. I've also never wanted to take a mate at all. I figured I would fail at it and become my old man. I've had enough of women leaving me," Tor replied. The admission made Ciara's chest ache.

"And what makes you think I won't do the same?" she dared to ask.

Tor braced his arm on the wall above her head and leaned into her, his fangs showing. "You saw what happened when you tried to run away tonight. I'm serious when I say I'm not going to let you go, bunny. I'm going to do whatever I have to do to make you stay."

Ciara tried to push down her own insecurities and failed. "Give it time, Tor. I'm not the kind of woman people want to keep forever. I'm sure this sudden interest in mating has something to do with the bond and an emotional day. It'll wear off."

"Yeah, we'll see about that. In the meantime, we have a psycho wolf to hunt down." Tor lifted her chin. "After Varg is stopped, we will figure this mating thing out. I'm not going to pretend otherwise." He brushed his lips over hers, a silky soft touch that went straight to her pussy. "Tell me you'll consider it, Ciara."

"I-I'll think about it," she stammered. "I won't hold it against you if you change your mind between now and then."

Tor made a sound between a hum and a growl, his lips gliding down her neck. "That's all I ask. Think about it in lots of detail. Think about how nice it would be to have a mate to worship this gorgeous body of yours whenever you wanted."

His hand gently cupped her pussy and dipped a finger inside. Ciara's leg went around his waist, angling her hips so he could slide further in.

"That's a good point," she gasped. He slipped in another finger, working her open, making her bones turn to liquid. She was about to come when he flipped her, grabbing her hands and pinning them above her head. Her aching breasts were pressing into the cold tiles, and he pulled her hips up and slid his cock inside of her.

"Fucking hell," she groaned, her entire body expanding to make room for him.

Tor chuckled, a gorgeously smug male sound that had her clenching around him.

"My beautiful Wolf Slayer," he growled in her ear. His hands stroked down her slick back. "I'm never going to get enough of you."

He thrust slowly and deep into her, making her rise up on her tiptoes. He clamped an arm around her waist, lifting her up off her toes altogether and making her cry out. He was so deep, she could feel him everywhere, and the bond blew open again. She felt his joy and wonder at being inside of her, and under that, she could sense the feral need he had for her.

"You've been holding back on me," Ciara said, bracing herself against the tiles.

Tor kissed her wet shoulder. "I don't want to break my bunny. The beast in me will always want to take and take. I want to undo you, keep you right here at my mercy."

He changed his angle, and Ciara just about started speaking in tongues. Tor took that as a sign to hit her in the same spot again and harder.

"Oh gods, I'm going to black out with pleasure if you keep doing that," she warned.

Tor tightened his grip on her. "I won't let you fall."

Too late for that, Ciara thought and then cried out as her orgasm blew her brains out.

"Gods, that sound undoes me every time. I fucking love it," Tor said, his voice full of awe. He held her tight enough to bruise and thrust deeply another two times before filling her.

Ciara would die of this feeling. She'd never been so close to another person and still felt like it wasn't enough. Her legs were trembling when Tor released her and washed her again. She was in a complete daze as he dried her off and carried her to bed.

Tor pulled her into his heat and strength, wrapping her in comfortable silence and making her feel so protected and safe. It was something she never thought she would ever feel again.

It's okay for you to give a shit about a man that's not me, Lachie's voice drifted back to her.

It was true that Ciara hadn't cared for any man that she wasn't related to. She was trained to analyze risk, and it always seemed like too much of a big one. She lived a dangerous life that she wouldn't give up.

She knew what it was like to lose people violently and never wanted to inflict that onto another person or have to try and live through it again.

Ciara wrapped an arm around Tor and listened to his heartbeat. "I can't lose you."

"You won't," Tor replied like he knew every worry going through her head. "We go after Varg as a team and get the family involved. We aren't going to do it alone. If I have my way, you'll never be doing anything alone again."

Ciara bit his chest. "Don't be so possessive."

"Rich coming from the woman who actually fought to the death to be in my bed tonight," Tor replied, his laugh a deep rumble in his chest.

"I'm never going to live that down, am I?" Ciara sighed.

Tor kissed the top of her head. "Not while I'm still breathing."

"Monster."

"Keep calling me names, and I'm going to fall in love with you," Tor threatened.

Ciara started to laugh. "You're not okay in the head, are you?"

"Not when it comes to you, bunny." Tor kissed the top of her head. "And I don't want to be cured."

24

The next morning Tor was cooking steak and eggs and wondering if he should follow up with the wolves and Von. As much as he wanted to, he couldn't stay in his cabin shagging Ciara while Varg was still out there. They needed a plan. He needed to head back to Uppsala at least and see if any of the cult were still there.

Staying in bed with Ciara sounds like a much better idea, the wolf inside of him prompted. It wasn't helpful in the slightest. He needed Ciara safe first and foremost, and with Varg at large and the full moon only days away, he needed...

"What are you focusing so hard on?" Ciara interrupted his thoughts.

She walked over to the coffee pot and filled a cup. She was wearing one of his flannel shirts and nothing else. Tor's brain hazed.

"We need to find Varg," he said, shaking all his horny thoughts away. Well, not *all* of them, but it couldn't be helped. She really was stunning, especially when sleep mussed, his scent all over her.

"You want to go back to Uppsala?" Ciara asked, sitting down at the counter and watching him cook.

"At this stage, it's our only lead." Tor caught her staring at his ass, and she only smiled a sphinx smile. He willed his dick not to get hard.

He was only in a pair of sweatpants and having an erection while cooking was a bad idea.

"I'm going to need some more clothes. The rate I'm going through them at the moment is crazy," Ciara complained.

"There was a bag of your gear left on the patio this morning," Tor said and pointed to where it was in the lounge room.

"They dropped it and ran?" Ciara guessed. She frowned. "Wow, they really think we are mating."

We are. You just don't know it, Tor thought unhelpfully.

"The wolves go into a mating frenzy. They get overprotective of their mates and territory, and it's best to leave them be," he explained instead.

Ciara's grin widened. "Mating frenzy, is it?"

"Stop it, seriously, or I'm going to fuck you again," Tor warned her and placed a plate of steak, eggs, mushrooms, and tomato in front of her.

Ciara's eyes widened. "I don't think I can eat all of this."

"Try. You didn't eat dinner last night, and you expended a lot of energy. Your body needs the protein," Tor replied, passing her a knife and fork.

"Are you fussing over me?"

"Yes. I'm allowed to. Now, eat," he insisted irritably.

Ciara had a mouthful of eggs, and something settled inside of him. His stupid wolf instincts were all over the place, and he needed to make sure he was providing for her in any way that he could. The whole thing was a mess, especially because she didn't want to mate him. Not yet.

Tor started eating too, and his thoughts stopped racing so fast. He didn't feel the need to fill the silence, and neither did she. It was comfortable. As much as they argued and she tried to boss him around, they *were* easy together.

Tor's thoughts were starting to get mushy when his phone started to ring loudly. He found it and was surprised to see it was Von calling him.

"Hey, what are you doing awake at this hour?" Tor answered and put the phone on speaker.

"I was getting into bed, and I got an email from my friend

Siegfried," Von replied. He sounded wired, and Tor could just about see him bouncing up and down.

"The Fenris expert?" Ciara asked.

"Lady Ironwood is there too? Why am I not surprised?" Von chuckled. "But yes, Siegfried is the expert. He looked through some of his more esoteric copies of the Binding of Fenris for us."

Tor swallowed his mouthful of breakfast. "Find anything? We were going to head back to Uppsala."

"He found a line that said that once the great wolf was bound, Odin All-Father, buried him in the deepest place in all the lands of the North, a cave of pure darkness, and surrounded him with water," Von replied.

Tor clicked his tongue. "Odin really wasn't fucking about."

"He never did. It's why he was such a fearsome enemy to have."

Ciara had pulled out her phone and was tapping away. "So that reference of the deepest place in the North, I'm assuming, is Northern Europe, yeah?"

"It's an obvious assumption to have. Why, what are you thinking, Ironwood?" Von asked.

Ciara tapped away, her frown deepening. "Okay, so according to Google, the deepest place is actually here in Norway. It's a cave system called Pluragrotta. Oh shit, it's connected to a lake, and look at this, Tor. Most of these caves are filled with water." She held up the phone to him, and he scrolled through.

"It also says how dangerous it is to dive and how narrow the passages are. How would Odin get something as big as Fenris into a place like that? That is if it's the right spot," Tor said.

"He's the fucking All-Father, Tor! He could have used magic," Von exclaimed. "For all we know, he might have had another way in that he did with magic. He could have gotten the dwarves to build something. He's Odin, for fuck's sake. I don't know why you can't just ask him. Aren't the wolves meant to be his private army?"

"Doesn't really work like that. Using magic to hide a passageway makes sense. We'll have to go and check it out and see what we can find. Thanks, Von. We really appreciate it," Tor said sincerely.

"You're welcome, handsome. Don't forget you owe me a story about Odin making a recent appearance," Von replied.

"Talk to Layla. She was the one who found his holiday house and stalked him," Ciara chimed in. They hung on Von as he started to make squawking sounds.

Tor went into his Maps app with one hand while he ate with the other. "Looks like Plura Cave is about a fourteen-hour drive away. Maybe we can get Alruna to portal us to a nearby town where we can get a car and some supplies."

"It feels like a pretty slim chance, to be honest. If Von's friend, who is an expert, had to search everywhere for this tiny hint, then what are the chances Varg would be there?" Ciara questioned.

Tor put his phone down. "I don't know. Something about this feels right. I can't explain it."

"Animal instinct?" Ciara asked.

"Maybe. I doubt Askel was the only shaman Varg has under his command, and if he's using magic to guide him, he might end up at the caves sooner rather than later." Tor rubbed at his chest, a ball of unease already forming. "How about we ask Alruna to send a group of elvish hunters to Uppsala, and we check out the caves? I don't want us all to turn up in force if it's a dead end."

Ciara bit her lip. "I won't cave dive. I don't like small spaces, especially if they involve water."

"Agreed. I doubt I'd even fit in some of those passages," Tor replied. He put his empty plate in the sink and turned on the water. Ciara came up behind him and placed her dish beside his, pressing a kiss into his bicep at the same time.

"I can wash up. You cooked," she said, trying to gently push him out of the way.

"I can do both," Tor replied and shot her a teasing smirk. "You can repay me another way."

Ciara's mouth twitched. "Oh, can I?" She slipped her hand down the front of his sweatpants, and he went hard with the first touch of her fingers around his dick.

"Oh gods," he groaned. He needed to not think about the mating frenzy in case he kicked it off. There would be no hunt for Varg, no one and nothing except her.

Ciara took his curses as encouragement. She turned the tap off with her free hand and twisted him about.

"What mischief...*fuck*," Tor spluttered out as she dropped to her knees right on the kitchen floor.

Ciara pulled his sweatpants down and licked straight down his cock. Holy gods. A small part of Tor knew that the kitchen probably wasn't the place for it, but he'd be damned if he could stop. He threaded his fingers through her silky black hair, the sight of her taking him into her plush little mouth was almost too much.

"Fuck, you're going to ruin me," he gasped, his dick hitting the back of her soft throat.

Ciara pulled off. "That's the idea. Why do you want me to stop?" she asked, the sweetness of her tone totally ruined by the devil in her eyes.

"Never, ever stop," Tor replied, his voice ragged with need.

Ciara stroked his pre-cum down his shaft, the slippery friction making him want to blow too soon. She sucked him back down, and his eyes rolled in the back of his head.

He could smell how wet she was, and it drove him even madder. His grip tightened in her hair, and he began to fuck her mouth like he had always dreamed about. She gagged on him a few times but didn't pull away or show any signs of slowing. He wanted to fill her pretty mouth, but not as much as he wanted to be inside her.

Tor pulled himself free and picked Ciara up, making her yelp in surprise as he dropped her on the counter. Tor ripped open the flannel shirt so he could see her beautiful tits and pressed her down against the timber surface.

"Gods, Tor, get inside of me," she begged, spreading her legs so he could see how wet and ready she was for him.

Tor let out a strangled sound of need, gripped her hips, and guided himself into all of her soft, wet heaven. He leaned down and kissed her breasts, his teeth digging into her pretty pink nipples. Ciara hissed at the sharp sting, her back arching up and pussy clenching around him.

A part of Tor had always worried she would try and kill him one day, and he decided that this was definitely the way he wanted to go. He fucked her hard, unable to hold back the wild urgency to take and claim screaming through his veins.

Ciara's eyes were hazed with pleasure, her short pants and sounds encouraging him to go harder and deeper. Tor grabbed her legs and put them over his shoulders. Ciara's nails scored the counter under her as she cried out the sweetest scream of release he had ever heard.

"You're so fucking gorgeous," he said in awe, his hand pressing over her beating heart. She was so alive. And his. All his.

"I think I love you," Ciara groaned.

Lightning exploded down Tor's spine like an electric shock, and he came with a surprised shout. He was shaking from the force of it, his vision blurring. He lowered her legs and pulled her up into his arms to hold her. Ciara pressed a kiss to his lips.

"Good morning," she said, her expression a little dazed.

"It certainly is," he replied, trying not to laugh. He kissed her instead, his tongue plundering her mouth. He would never get enough of her taste, her warmth, the sated smile she gave him after sex.

Ciara wrapped her hands around his neck and surrendered to it. He wanted to ask if she meant what she said or if it was a post-orgasm exclamation.

Don't scare her and start a fight after sex. Tor wouldn't let it go, and he wouldn't forget.

Ciara pulled back from him with a content sigh. "Pluragrotta it is. We need to get moving. Staying here feels too dangerous."

"You'll always be safe with me," Tor said, a thread of panic in his voice.

Ciara shook her head. "That's not what I mean. I can't keep my hands off you, and it's not the time for a holiday."

"We will need to come back in a few days. It doesn't matter what's happening with Varg," Tor reminded her, tucking a lock of her dark hair behind her ear. "I won't have you vulnerable at full moon."

"Okay," she said, surprising him.

"Okay? No fighting me?"

"Is there a point? If I do turn, I don't want to be in enemy territory or near any of my family," Ciara replied. Her eyes twinkled with all kinds of trouble. "I can always find something else to fight with you about later."

25

Alruna looked at them with a curiosity that she couldn't hide but was too polite to outright ask about. Ciara knew she was glowing from a sound sleep, great sex, and a full stomach and wasn't doing anything to try and hide it.

They had gotten dressed and had headed over to Alruna's to update her on their plans and ask her to open them a portal.

"Are you sure this is a wise idea so close to the full moon?" she asked.

"If you are worried about me shifting, don't be. I've already agreed to come back before the full moon rises," Ciara replied.

Alruna looked at Tor. "You really want to take her from here when you're...in this condition?"

"For Christ's sake, we aren't mating!" Ciara snapped, losing her patience. "It's a bond thing. We aren't in a mating frenzy or whatever else you want to call it."

Alruna's eyebrows shot up. Tor blushed a deep crimson, and the elf queen burst out laughing. "She's actually serious?"

"She is. And she's right. There have been no mating words or promises spoken, Auntie. We will both be fine. Pluragrotta might be nothing. It's a slim lead at best. I only want to rule it out," Tor replied firmly.

After a time, Alruna managed to stop her fit of the giggles and become serious once more. "I'll send the warriors to Uppsala to run down that lead too. This Varg mess needs to be cleaned up once and for all, and I will sleep better at night knowing Linnea is safe and sound." Alruna's magic hummed in the air. "I'll send you to Mo i Rana. It's the town closest to the cave systems where you'll be able to get a car. Only scout the place. If there is the slightest whiff of magic or cultists, you are to tell me immediately. Understand?"

"Yes, Auntie, we'll be good," Tor said and dropped a kiss on her cheek.

"Thank you," Ciara replied because she was grateful as hell for portal magic. She didn't think she would survive a thirteen-hour road trip locked up with Tor. She knew something was happening between them and was refusing to quantify it.

God, you told him you loved him this morning, and he said nothing. Don't get your hopes up too high, her brain unhelpfully reminded her.

Tor had said he wanted to mate her. Maybe that was the same kind of thing to the wolves? She didn't want to think about it before a hunting trip.

Ciara had never lost her head over a man before. That kind of ridiculousness had always been other people's problem. Now she knew that no one was immune to it when the right person came along. She never thought her right person would be a wolf.

Ciara pulled out her phone and texted Lachie. **Following up on a lead with Tor at Plura Cave. I'm FINE. We are not mating. Let you know if we find anything. Don't start any shit with the elves.**

The message bubble danced. *I'll be your backup as soon as you need it. And I'm pretty sure you are mating. You just don't want to admit it. I don't blame you for staking your claim. Tor is still one of the hottest guys I've ever seen and way too good for you.*

Ciara's eyes narrowed. She knew better than to bite at Lachie's teasing, and it didn't help he had pressed on the insecurity she felt the keenest.

How's Apollo? Have you apologized and made up yet? You know he'll never let it go until you say sorry. Life is too short to have an alchemist angry at you. Your life is dangerous enough.

Enjoy your trip. Try not to get stuck in any caves and die while you're there.

Ciara snorted. Just as she thought. Lachie was one of the bravest hunters she had ever seen, but he was so stubborn when he felt he was right. She looked up to see Alruna and Tor waiting for her.

"Sorry. Lachie. I'm trying to get better at letting the family know where I'm going because *someone* has been yelling at me non-stop about it," Ciara said, shooting Tor a wink.

"Gods below, did the lectures actually sink in? I can't actually believe it," Tor replied, aghast.

Alruna laughed at them. "I don't have all day, you two. Am I opening this portal or not?"

Tor took Ciara's hand. "Now we are ready."

She turned bright red but didn't shake him off. His hand was warm and rough, and hers fit into it like it was made for him.

Alruna's portal opened near a road, and with final goodbyes, Ciara and Tor stepped through it and into soft spring rain. Ciara flipped the collar up on her leather jacket to stop another shirt from getting wrecked, and they headed into town.

Apart from the rain, it was a pretty place with a fjord and mountains that made Ciara's breath catch.

"What are you thinking?" Tor asked, hanging onto her hand.

"That I'd really like to see Scandinavia properly without all of the portaling and running for my life," she replied. She let out a huff of laughter. "Maybe Layla was right, and I have been working too hard."

"Hang around after we stop Varg, and I can be a tour guide."

It was an offer she would've liked to accept outright, but she still held back. "You don't think you're going to be sick of me by then?" Tor smiled and gave her a look that had her toes curling in her boots.

"I doubt it, bunny."

Ciara bit the inside of her cheek to keep from smiling and did her best to quieten down all the voices in her head that told her that he wouldn't want her unless she turned into a wolf, that she was too difficult to love because of her spiky personality.

Ciara wouldn't miraculously stop being who she was because she was getting laid. It just wasn't in her nature to be soft and loving like women were always told they should be. She was who she was, and she liked that person. Spiky outer shell and all. If Tor didn't, she would find a way to deal with it when the time came.

Tor stopped walking and kissed her hard. Ciara gripped the collar of his jacket and pulled him closer. It didn't matter that they were getting completely soaked. All that mattered was the heat between them, the bond tugging them tighter together.

"What was that for?" Ciara asked breathlessly.

Tor kissed her forehead. "You were getting too much in your own head, and your energy was changing. I had to change it back before you spiraled."

"I..." Ciara stammered. Well, shit. "I'm never going to be able to hide anything from you, will I?"

"Try not to sound so glum about it. You need someone looking out for you," Tor replied like it was the simplest thing in the world.

"I can take care of myself," she grumbled.

"I know, but you don't always have to. Don't worry. You'll get used to it."

There really was no arguing with Tor when he made his mind up about something. They were stubborn as each other.

It didn't take them long to get to the central part of the town and to find a rental car dealership. Tor was taking care of the arrangements and talking way too fast in Norwegian with the salesperson for Ciara to pick up any words she might know.

Tor was frowning when he walked back over to her with the keys to a Jeep.

"What's wrong?" Ciara asked.

"Apparently, there was a death up at the caves a week ago, and some government department has closed it off to the public. He said that they had hired serious-looking guards on the roads in and out," Tor replied.

Ciara hummed. "Sounds like a coincidence to me. We go off-road and hike in? We can't just turn up in case it's Varg's guys. We'll lose any surprise we have."

Tor nodded. "Agreed. If it's really government, we'll find out soon enough."

26

It was a forty-minute drive out to the caves, and Ciara took the time to dry her hair in front of the car's heaters.

"I'm so tired of being wet," she complained.

"Really?" Tor asked, his mouth twitching.

Ciara smacked him. "Not what I meant, smartass. Get your brain out of your pants."

"It's not in *my* pants, bunny," Tor teased.

"Focus on the road."

Tor saluted her, and Ciara brushed and braided back her hair.

"Can I ask you something?" he said after a while.

Ciara's guard went up instinctively. "Sure."

"Was it true what you said about the first wolf that you killed? Was he really going to try and rape you?" Tor asked.

Ciara's stomach turned. Tor had trusted her enough to tell her about his fucked-up childhood. She could do the same.

"Yeah, it was. I used to listen in on my parent's conversations all the time. I knew the wolf they were hunting liked to kidnap kids and...and play with them before he killed them," Ciara swallowed hard, her mouth too dry. "When I woke up to my mother screaming that night, I knew it was him. It's why the first thing I did was hide my brother. I knew he wouldn't kill me outright like he did my parents."

"You let yourself be bait?" Tor guessed.

Ciara nodded slowly. "Yeah. He didn't succeed in doing much. Just got me to the floor and felt me up. He was distracted enough that he didn't see me take the knife from my father." Ciara could still feel the hot sticky blood soaking the back of her nightgown. "I jammed it right in his eye, and when he let go of me, wailing in shock and pain, I kicked it in as hard as possible. I watched him die, and then I rang Auntie Kenna. She came and got Lachie and me, and we never went back to that house again."

"Fucking hell, Ciara. No wonder you hated us so much," Tor whispered.

"All I could think about was being on that floor covered in my father's blood. I never wanted another kid to go through that because no one would stop monsters from doing what they liked," she replied honestly. "The hating made all the killing easier. It gave me focus. I don't think I'll ever be able to stop hunting. I don't know how."

"If you need to do it, then do it. Just don't do it alone," Tor replied.

That surprised her. Ciara thought he'd try and talk her out of it, give her some advice about getting a life like her cousins always did.

Ciara reached over and took his hand without saying anything. Tor didn't need her to. He only lifted her hand and kissed her calloused palm. If Ciara hadn't already been in love with him, that would have done it.

They turned off the main road, following a dirt trail through a stretch of forest that had come on a satellite map. It looked like it skirted the back of the lake and entrance to the caves.

"If you turn on the full moon, will you hate yourself?" Tor asked.

"It all depends if I'm still myself while I'm shifted. If I'm not and things go bad, I have a plan."

Tor frowned. "What do you mean go bad? What plan?"

"If I turn and become a monster and can't control myself and I hurt other people, Lachie has promised to put me down," she replied.

Tor yanked the car over the side of the muddy road and slammed on the brakes.

"What the hell!" Ciara yelped, putting both hands on the dashboard to brace herself.

Tor was gripping the steering wheel so tight, she thought it would break. Waves of alpha energy rolled out of him. "What the actual fuck, Ciara?"

"We made a promise to each other when we were kids. If we were ever bit, we would do it," she said, trying to keep her voice steady.

"So if you turn, you'll just let him shoot you in the head?" Tor's eyes were glowing with wolf and anger. "I won't ever let it happen, Ciara. You hear me? *Never.*"

"Tor, take a breath. Lachie will only do it if I'm a danger to others. You don't know what I've seen over the years. I couldn't live with myself if I hurt anyone," she said. Years of horror washed over her, and tears filled her eyes. She would kill herself before Lachie could load his gun. "That's what I'm most afraid of. I won't be another monster in the world."

"Ah, fuck, Ciara, don't cry," Tor said, his anger vanishing. He unclipped her seat belt and pulled her into his lap. It only made her tears feel foolish.

Tor brushed them off her cheeks. "Look at me. If you turn, your whole personality doesn't just suddenly change. It's like magic. Whatever is in you will be magnified. You're a good person, bunny. Better than most. You act all grumpy, but under that, you fucking care. You wouldn't do such a dangerous job if you didn't."

"I can't know that for sure. Lachie would never hurt me just because I turned into a wolf. He would need a serious reason," she said.

Tor's hands tightened on her biceps. "It's not going to happen. I promise you."

"But what if I turn completely feral?"

Tor's mouth twitched. "More than you are now?"

Ciara pinched his chest. "You know what I'm talking about!"

"It's going to be fine, Ciara. I swear it." Tor leaned his forehead against hers. "Please just trust me."

"I do. More than anyone in a really long time. It's *hard* for me to admit that, so don't make fun of me, okay?"

Tor smiled and kissed the tip of her nose. "Wouldn't dream of it, Ironwood."

Ciara went to kiss him when something flashed outside his

window. It was a streak of white and brown in a world that was all green.

"I just saw a wolf, three o'clock," she said. Ciara scrambled off Tor and grabbed the gun from her bag.

Tor was out the driver's door, shifted in a blink, and was running through the undergrowth. Swearing, Ciara grabbed the dagger from her bag, took the keys from the ignition, and raced after him.

It had stopped raining. The pine, birch, and fir trees were drenched and still dripping in the silence of the forest. Ciara kept her gun low, watching where she stepped so she didn't end up slipping on the mossy rocks or stepping into a trap.

"Where did you go, Tor?" she muttered. She didn't like being separated from him, and she pushed down the uneasiness. Tor was a warrior. He could take care of himself.

Snarls and snapping branches had Ciara picking up her pace. She didn't dare cry out and made sure she wasn't about to be ambushed from behind. Where there was one wolf, there were more.

Ciara felt a sharp tug through the bond, robbing her of breath and causing a sharp pain in her side.

Tor.

Ciara bolted through the trees until she came to a stream and found two massive wolves circling each other. Crimson was splashed down Tor's side, but it didn't seem to hurt him too badly.

Ciara raised her gun at the other wolf but didn't need to fire. Tor lunged in a lightning-quick move; the brown wolf feinted to the side, but Tor was too quick. He course-corrected, and his massive jaws clamped down on the beast's throat before tearing it free. The brown wolf collapsed, its blood steaming as it spilled across the moss.

Ciara stumbled out of the tree line. "Tor? Are you okay?"

The white wolf nodded and lifted his nose, scenting the air. He bumped his big head against her and gestured to the trees.

"Go. I'll follow you," she said and holstered her gun. "Lead the way."

27

Tor's senses were exploding with the scents of the forest and all the creatures that were moving in it. The wolf he had fought had smelled of the dark, terrible magic that had soaked the ground at Varg's other campsite.

I knew Askel wouldn't be his only shaman. Tor cursed himself. He really hated being right sometimes.

Ciara kept pace with him, stopping when he paused to inspect something. He didn't know how far they were from the car, but it didn't matter. Only the hunt did. There would never just be one wolf stinking of Varg.

The afternoon rolled in, the spring storm returning and darkening the world. There was no fear coming from Ciara. She wasn't afraid of the dark. Tor brushed his body against her, and she placed a hand on his head.

"We keep going. We have to be getting close to the entrance of the caves, and the darkness will give us some cover," she said, her breath pluming in the cool air.

They went slower, Tor leading her around the traps someone had set. They found temporary fencing, chain link panels that locked together and were held in place with concrete blocks. There were warning signs all along them stating that the area had been shut down by the park's department.

"They are really putting on a show, aren't they?" Ciara whispered. They followed the fence until Tor heard voices and drew Ciara back into the underbrush.

She took out a small pair of binoculars and scanned the area. Tor stayed in his wolf form. He wanted the extra senses and to be ready if there were any more scouts.

"Okay, I see a lot of portable gear, like flood lights. The tents look similar to the last camp. Oh, shit. I see Varg," Ciara whispered, her heart rate jumping. Tor could smell her adrenaline, her anger. He needed her to focus, so he nudged her.

"I know, I know. There's a waterway. Oh god, he has an army. There weren't this many last time. It looks like there's a group studying the side of the rock face, but I can't tell what has gotten their attention. It looks like marble. I didn't see this site on any of the caving maps or websites. There's meant to be over two hundred caves in this area alone," Ciara said. She froze and sucked in a breath.

Tor wanted to know what she had seen, but a scent smacked him hard in his snout. It was like honeysuckle and lavender.

Linnea.

Tor's head snapped up, his eyes searching the camp beyond the fence. He saw her, golden braids and all. She didn't look hurt, but she was keeping her eyes downcast, and gods, she looked thin.

Varg stepped out of a tent and lifted her chin, said something to her, and laughed. Red hazed over Tor's vision, his muscles bunching to jump the fence.

Ciara yanked on his ruff. "*Tor.* Stop. You can't go in there alone. Look at me!"

Tor pulled his head from her grip, a low snarl coming out of him as he whirled on her.

Ciara smacked him on the snout, making him yelp in surprise rather than hurt. "Snap out of it! You are not going to get yourself and probably your sister killed by rushing in there like a moron!"

Tor shoved her off and turned back to the fence. Linnea was so close.

"If you race in there without a plan, I'll never consider mating you,"

Ciara said, her voice flat and cold. "If you attack them now, they will kill me, you, and Linnea."

That brought Tor back to reality quicker than the smack on his snout. He could already feel their mating bond, even if she couldn't. He couldn't risk the life of his mate. It was the bond that overrode all else.

"She looks okay. She's been smart enough and strong enough to survive Varg this long. She can wait another night," Ciara said, her hand pushing into his fur. "Come on. We need to go and call in back up. The sooner we go, the sooner we can come back and end this."

Tor nodded and pushed against her. Ciara wrapped her arms around his wide neck. "I know, Tor. I know. We will get her, I promise."

Everything suddenly went quiet. The trees stopped rustling; the small animals froze, and the whole camp hushed. Part of the rock wall was glowing with ancient runes, and a doorway slid open.

Dark, intoxicating magic pulsed from the opening, rolling through the camp and forest and making Tor's fur stand on end. It was ancient and terrible and furious.

Fenris.

Tor didn't hesitate. He grabbed the back of Ciara's jacket in his muzzle and tossed her on his back.

"What the hell?" she muttered. Tor shook, forcing her to hold tight onto his fur.

Then he ran like he had never run before. Ciara was cursing, holding onto him for dear life as he raced through the forest like a streak of pale moonlight.

Tor didn't stop until the car was in view. He halted, his feet skidding on the dirt. Ciara slid from him and collapsed on the ground. Tor shifted, his bones snapping and fur disappearing until he was a panting man once more. He lifted Ciara up, opened the car, and dumped her in the front seat.

"Tor, what the fuck is going on?" she demanded, tossing him the keys.

"We need to get out of here right now," he said, his whole body shaking. It took him three times to get his key into the ignition and start the Jeep. "I felt him, Ciara."

"Felt who? You're not making sense!"

Tor slammed his foot on the gas. "Fenris. They finally found him."

"Fucking hell."

"I saw the glyphs on the rock face. The opening. I felt... I felt him. I can't explain it better than that, but I know. I *know*."

Ciara's hand rested on his shoulder. "Breathe, Tor. We've dealt with gods before. Let's find a hotel, and we'll summon the troops. We need a plan more than ever."

Some of Tor's tension leaked out of him, her touch warming and grounding him. It gave him enough focus to think and stay alert on the muddy road.

Lightning streaked, and thunder boomed overhead. It was as if the whole world knew that something had been disturbed that should never have been.

Tor could only hope they could stop Varg from waking the terrible fury he had felt coming from the cave. If Varg succeeded, they were all going to be fucked.

28

Ciara was doing her best to remain calm despite the waves of anxiety coming off Tor. They got back to town in record time and found a hotel that still had a room available.

"Have a shower and try and calm down. I'll start making some calls," Ciara said, gently pushing Tor towards the bathroom. His eyes were still shining with wolf, his canines a little bit too long. She kissed his dirty face. "Go on, you have blood in your beard. I'm not going anywhere."

Tor nodded and went into the bathroom without a word. Ciara blew out a long breath. She had never seen him so afraid. Whatever wolf sense he'd had that Fenris was in the caves was enough to spook him the hell out. It was radiating through the bond, and Ciara didn't know how to react to it.

They had two days to sort out Varg before they were both out for the full moon. She couldn't deny Tor his vengeance on Varg.

Ciara sent a message to Arne and Alruna and dropped another into the family chat before calling in the big gun.

"What's up, little cousin? Still getting some of that good wolf D?" Imogen answered.

"We found Varg...and Fenris. I don't suppose your better half is keen to test his mettle against another god?" Ciara asked hopefully. "I know he's only really concerned with Wales—"

"We are coming. I swear he's been pouting since he missed seeing the Asgardians last time. Where did you find that dirty mongrel?"

"A place called Plura Cave. You guys will probably get here faster than anyone else." Ciara explained the situation with the camp, Linnea, and the time frame for the full moon.

"We hit them at dawn," Arawan said, and Imogen agreed. "We can't leave it longer than that. If wolves draw their power from the full moon, it will be an ideal time for them to cast any magic to break Fenris's bonds."

"I agree. I just don't know if we can get the people we need in time. He has at least a hundred wolves there," Ciara replied.

"Don't worry about backup. You'll have it. Do you need me to bring you some weapons?" Imogen asked.

"Yes. This was only meant to be a scouting trip based on some random tip of Von's. I don't even have my proper hunting suit with me."

"Okay, we'll take care of it. Text me the coordinates of where we need to portal to. We get this fucker at dawn," Imogen replied before hanging up.

Some of the tightness in Ciara's chest eased up. Arawan was the biggest badass they knew, and if anyone could take on Fenris, it was him. They couldn't expect any divine assistance like last time. Ciara doubted Layla had Havi on speed dial. Ciara messaged everyone the coordinates and hoped for the best.

Fucking finally. Expect us at dawn, Lachlan texted her, and she sent him a thumbs up.

The shower was still running, so Ciara toed off her muddy boots and stepped into the bathroom. Tor was sitting on the shower floor, staring at the wall as hot water sluiced over him.

"We are on for dawn," Ciara said, taking her clothes off and getting into the shower with him. She tipped some shampoo into his hair and began to massage it in. Tor let out a low growl and leaned against her.

"Arawan has promised to come in case of Fenris being awoken. He sounded like he'd be disappointed if he didn't, to be honest. That's death gods for you. He suggested the dawn raid, something about wolves using moon magic."

Tor nodded. "It's the most powerful time. If they are going to break his bonds, that's when they will do it. I don't suppose you'd sit this fight out?"

Ciara laughed and kissed him on the forehead. "No. I'm going to be there. I have part of your strength, and I'm not letting you go into a fight without me beside you. I have my own score to settle with Varg. Where is this request coming from?"

"Today you said you would never consider mating me if I didn't leave. I left. Does that mean you *are* considering it?" he asked.

Ciara's heart sped up. "Maybe? Obviously not right this second, but maybe one day? If we both want it?"

"I didn't hear a no in there, so I'll take it as a win. You should say yes. It would make me feel better," he said, tilting his head back to stare at her with his big gray eyes.

"And I would've felt better if you had said anything after I told you I loved you this morning, but you didn't, so here we are," Ciara said and instantly wished she could take it back.

Confusion clouded his beautiful face. "You were serious?"

"What do you think? You're the only man I've said I love you to besides my bother, and you said nothing back!"

Tor was on his feet in a flash, moving in front of the shower doors so she couldn't escape. "I wasn't sure if you actually meant it or if it was just because you were coming so hard, you didn't know what you were saying."

"I've never come hard enough to let a random 'I love you' come out," Ciara argued.

"You said, 'I think I love you.' It was the 'I think' part that made me question whether you were serious or not." Tor tucked her wet hair behind her ear. "I want to mate you, Ciara Fiadh Ironwood. Do you really think I would want to do that if I didn't also love you?"

"How am I meant to know? Wolves mate for strength. Love has never been mentioned."

Tor took her hand and placed it over his heart. "You're going to talk everything in circles. *Feel.*"

Ciara was about to ask what he was on about when the bond blew open between them. It was clearer than it had ever been, and she felt *everything*.

There was the immense alpha power he didn't show anyone, his worry for his sister, but most of all, there was a thrumming, burning ache of love for her. He wanted to protect her, keep her safe, make her smile, and make love to her under the stars. It was like her whole psyche was being enveloped in his joy and longing and how she felt like home to him.

Ciara placed her head on the groove of his chest and sobbed. She couldn't hold it in and didn't even try. "I love you too," she said.

Tor's arms came around her. "I know. I can feel it as well. I know you're scared, and that's okay too. I want to make you mine, but I'm content to wait until you're ready to accept it."

Ciara went up on her tiptoes and kissed him deeply. She might have a battle ahead and the worry of her turning, but she also had *this* to fight for. It was going to make it worth it.

"You are going to make me beg when the time comes, aren't you?" she said, smiling up at him.

"You can count on it." Tor grinned, as charming as the devil, and carried her out of the shower. He toweled them both off before laying her out on the bed and staring at her. "You are so damn lovely, you know that?"

"Is it because of all my scars?" Ciara teased lightly. She really didn't know how to take a compliment at the best of times.

"It's your scars and your sweet freckles and delicious lines. It's everything," Tor said, leaning down to kiss the skin over her thrumming heart. "And it's all mine, to lick and taste and cherish."

Ciara threaded her hands into his hair as his mouth moved over the curve of her breast. He stroked and teased, mapping her entire body with his mouth.

Their love making had always been so intense and frantic that this gentleness was unraveling her in a whole new way. Ciara fell into the sensation of being loved, she could feel it humming through the bond that he had left wide open. Her whole body was aching to have him on top of her, inside of her. She needed him.

Tor chuckled softly. "We'll get there. Let me have my fill of you. You taste so fucking good."

Ciara was so wound up that his tongue on her core almost made her leap off the bed. Tor's big hand stretched over her waist, pinned her down, and pressed his tongue inside of her.

Ciara's legs tightened around his shoulders, trying to find something to hang onto as he feasted on her until she crashed through her first orgasm in a shuddering cry.

Tor kissed the inside of her thigh in a sucking bruise that would leave his mark on her. For some reason, it made Ciara whimper with want. She wanted him to mark her, to claim her. She didn't want another wolf's teeth marks on her. She only wanted his.

Tor slid up her body. "Don't worry, bunny. When I claim you as my mate, everyone is going to know about it."

"Is that so? You have to convince me to mate you first," she said, her teasing turning into a groan as he thrust deep inside of her. She was so wet that there was no resistance, just him filling her up and making her feel whole.

"You feel like home," she said, not realizing she had said it aloud.

Tor brushed her hair from her face. "You feel like home too, and I'm never going to let you go no matter what happens."

Ciara rolled her hips. "Make me believe it. Make me feel how much you want me."

Tor nipped up the side of her neck and dragged his sharp teeth over her ear. "Oh, bunny, I'm going to make sure you feel me for the next week."

Ciara scratched her nails down his sides, and his control snapped. He lifted her up, gripped her ass tight, and fucked hard into her. Ciara laughed breathlessly, her body racing to meet his, thrust for thrust. Tor pulled her into his lap, but didn't let her take over for a second, dragging her hips up and fucking her onto his dick. She kissed him, her teeth scraping his lips hard enough that she tasted blood. Tor growled, an absolute feral sound, and grabbed her hair in a tight grip.

"Be careful where you sink those teeth or I might do some biting of my own," he warned her. Ciara stretched out her neck to him, and he groaned. "Don't. I can't yet, and I want to so badly."

Tor sucked the spot between her neck and shoulder instead; the thrumming ache of it ran through her, and she cried out. Tor lifted his mouth from her and drove up deeper into her. It was her turn to bite into him, her cries smothered into his shoulder.

"That's it, beloved, bite me as hard as you want. Oh, fuck, Ciara." Tor's words stuttered as she clamped her teeth down hard. His ecstasy smashed through the bond, and they were both coming, their pleasure tangled together so Ciara didn't know what was hers and what was his.

"I love you," she panted against him, unable to let him go.

Tor's arms clamped around her, holding her as close as they could get. "I love you too."

29

The drive back out to the campsite was dark and chaotic. The storm had turned parts of it to mud and blown branches down over it.

Ciara had spent the night wrapped around Tor, waiting for the dawn. There had been no point in trying to sleep for a few hours, so she had cuddled into him and listened to his heartbeat while the rain had lashed the windows.

Whatever happened next, the fight with Morrigan's generals and their followers would finally be over. If they survived, Ciara wanted a holiday. A long one.

They found the spot where they had parked the day before, and Tor turned off the car.

"You ready for this, bunny?" Tor asked, his eyes full of wolf.

"I've been training for a fight against an army of wolves my entire life, sweetheart," Ciara tossed back at him. "It's you I'm worried about."

Tor laughed and kissed her hard. "I might just surprise you."

Ciara didn't doubt it for a second. She wanted to see him really unleash. That would be a sight.

Ciara texted Imogen to let her know they were in place. Almost instantly, a dark portal appeared at the edge of the forest, and Imogen and Arawan emerged from it. Both were wearing armor and looked like they could take on a wolf army on their own.

"Here you are, cousin. Something to keep your hide safe and sound," Imogen said, passing her a bag and placing a smacking kiss on her cheek.

"Thanks for coming, the both of you," Ciara said with a respectful nod at Arawan.

His smile was as sharp as a dagger. "Thank you for giving the Hunt a chance to stretch its legs."

Ciara's eyebrows shot up. "The Hunt?"

"Don't worry about that. Go get your gear on so we can get this show on the road," Imogen said. She looked over at Tor. "You. I want to talk to you."

"Play nice, Gen."

Arawan laughed. "She knows how to do that?"

Ciara left them to argue and went to see what Imogen had brought her. It looked like one of their hunting suits, but it was easier to get on, and the fabric felt odd. She couldn't quite figure out what it was until she did up the zip and felt a magic shield lock into place.

"What in the gods'..."

"Good, isn't it? Charlotte has been tinkering again. This is a prototype," Imogen said, coming around the side of the Jeep. "It doesn't feel like your insides are getting squished into shapewear either."

"You went back to Ireland to get this for me? I'm touched," Ciara said.

Imogen shrugged. "It was nothing. Besides, you're the best person to test it out. We've all been worried about you."

"You have?"

Imogen rolled her eyes. "Of course we have! You're our family, dork. You got yourself bit. You're mating—"

"Nope. I'm not. We have a bond, that's all." Ciara knew that wasn't all they had. Last night she had felt it for herself.

Imogen saw right through it. "You're a dumbass."

Ciara laughed and pulled on a black leather holster with two handguns hanging from it. "I know. I can't think about anything else until this fight is over, and I know whether or not I'm going to wolf out at the full moon."

"Fine, but just for the record, no one will care if you do or you don't. That includes Tor," Imogen said. She tugged on Ciara's braid. "He's in love with you. Like hearts in the eyes, mushy smile when someone says your name in love with you."

"I know. What's wrong with him?" Ciara only half-joked.

"You are very lovable under all that hard badassness. You have squishy insides. I'm happy that he got through those barriers of yours. His dick must've been the battering ram."

Ciara burst out laughing. "Jesus, Imogen. I should never have told you."

"True. But you did. And now I'm never going to let you live it down." Imogen grinned wickedly. "Let's go kill some wolves."

Ciara had four silver blades, two guns, spare ammo, and two full canisters of wolfsbane spray. She was as ready as she was ever going to be.

"I don't know if I should be afraid or turned on right now," Tor said, looking her over.

"Be both," Ciara replied, shooting him a wink. In reply, she felt a sharp stab of arousal through the bond. "Stop that, you menace."

"I can't help it."

They were getting ready to start moving out when three silvery gray portals appeared, and Arne, Layla, and Lachie came through one.

"Finally!" Ciara said and caught her brother up in a hug. "It wouldn't be right to go into a fight without you."

"I can't let you have all the fun now, can I?" he said.

"I hope you aren't starting without us," Layla complained. She was wearing gorgeous elf-made armor.

"Thought you weren't coming," Tor said to Arne.

"Have you ever tried to convince an Ironwood to stay behind when a fight is on?"

"Actually, yeah." Tor laughed. "It's going to be good to have you by my side, little brother."

"And I brought friends," Arne said, pointing to where elves were coming through one portal and wolves through the other.

Ciara's mouth popped open. "The Ulfheðnar. I don't believe it."

"Turns out many were eager to fight beside the Wolf Slayer," Layla said with a smug smile on her face.

"Eager or too scared she would come after them next?" Tor asked with an affectionate smile in Ciara's direction.

Arne chuckled. "Probably both. Does it matter? They are here and ready to fight. I think they are all still feeling ashamed because Ciara called them all a bunch of cowards for not dealing with Varg sooner."

Ciara squeezed Tor's hand. "You should be the one to lead us. Shift. We'll follow."

Tor kissed her hard and deep, uncaring that the elves and wolves were watching. She knew he was claiming her in front of them like she had the day she had fought Petra.

"Try and keep up, bunny," Tor said with a teasing glint in his eyes.

"Try not to step into a trap," Ciara replied.

"I'll take care of the traps," Arawan interrupted and sent a pulse of dark power through the forest. The elves shifted restlessly, and some of the wolves let out mournful whimpers.

"Thanks, Arawan." Tor chucked Ciara under the chin and sent love through the bond.

Ciara nodded. *Love you too. Be safe.*

Tor shifted with a flash of magic and raced over to the other wolves. He wasn't using his alpha magic to influence them, but just for once, he wasn't trying to hide it. The wolves circled him, and Tor turned towards the forest.

"I can't believe you're getting to tap that on a regular basis," Lachie said beside her with a whistle.

"Me neither," Ciara replied, her cheeks pinking.

"Come on, you two, let's go wake up Varg," Imogen said, her eyes turning black in the dawn light.

"Looking forward to it," Ciara replied, and they followed the wolves into the trees.

∽

VARG'S CAMP was already awake and bustling by the time they reached the borders. The wolves went around to the north, the elves to the south, and Ciara, Arawan, and Imogen came from the west. They would pin Varg's back up against the river and give the rat nowhere to scuttle off to.

"He has civilians amongst the camp dwellers, including Tor's sister, so only attack people who attack you," Ciara warned.

Arawan chuckled darkly. "Don't worry, cousin. I'm not an amateur." His power whipped out of him, grabbed hold of the fencing, and tore it to shreds as if it were paper.

"Show off," Imogen said fondly.

Arawan drew his sword. "Try not to be too aroused by my prowess, darling."

"Don't tell me what to do."

Ciara shook her head at them, and Lachie chuckled. Layla and Arne had gone to fight with the elves, and everything felt like the calm before the storm.

Tor's howl echoed through the forest, and her heartbeat tripled. She didn't like them being separated, but she would deal with it.

"Sounds like your boyfriend is kicking off the festivities," Lachlan said. "I got your left flank, big sis."

"Watch your ass. One of us getting bit is bad enough."

Wolves howled through the camp, and Ciara pulled out her long knives. She no longer worried about Tor. She went deep and pulled out the Wolf Slayer.

"Here they come," she said, and wolves raced across the camp towards them. Something opened in the bond, and the dim dawn light shifted to something sharp and bright. Tor had given her his animal eyes.

Ciara laughed as the first wolf leaped for her and found her gone as quick as the wind, her silver blades raking down their side. The wolf's yelps of pain were silenced as Imogen came up behind them and took off its head with one mighty swing of her ax.

"One down," she said cheerily and threw herself into the snarling mass of wolves closing in around them.

Ciara fell into the emergency of the fight, slicing, shooting, and weaving through the battle like a shadow. Her new strength raced through her, making every blow lethal. The shields built into her suit stopped her from getting disemboweled by sharp claws more than once.

Everything became screaming chaos, blood and mud soaking everything around them. Lachie kept pace beside her, his shotgun booming over and over as he filled Varg's cultists full of silver shots.

Varg had so many more warriors than they had seen on their scouting trip the day before, and Ciara tried not to let the thought overwhelm her. They had to keep fighting. She checked for Linnea in every tent she came to but didn't find her.

Arne, Layla, and the elves were pouring down through the forest, pining the wolves in and driving them towards the center of the camp. The world turned to fire as tents caught ablaze. The Ulfheðnar tore through Varg's forces, teeth and claws destroying anything in their path.

Tor appeared from behind a car and shifted beside Ciara and Imogen. He was covered in scratches, but none of them were too deep.

"There's no sign of Varg or Linnea. I think they are in the caves, but they have been sealed up again," he said.

Arawan appeared behind them. "Show me the doorway, and I will open it."

Tor spared Ciara one glance before shifting again, and the two males fought their way in the opposite direction.

"We better follow them so they don't do anything too stupid," Imogen said. A smile lit up her face. "Oh, the Hunt is here."

"How can you tell?" Lachie asked.

Imogen's eyes flashed black again, and Ciara felt the power rolling off her for the first time. She opened her mouth and shut it quickly again.

"Let's just say Ciara isn't the only one with a special bond," Imogen replied.

Strange, haunting horns sounded, and the world trembled around them. The sky split open, and mounted warriors on giant black steeds rode through the nothingness and thundered past them.

"They will clear up the mess. Come on, we have a wolf god to find," Imogen said cheerily.

Ciara stared wide-eyed at her. "What the hell are you?" she stammered.

"One of a kind, bitch. Now stop gawking at me and get moving," Imogen said and nudged her with the butt of her ax.

"This day can't get any weirder," Ciara said to Lachie, shaking herself back into action. She was about to find out how very wrong she was.

30

The sun was rising and making the dirty, rough marble under Arawan's hands glow.

"Definitely Havi's magic on it," he muttered softly. "Complex weaving too. He didn't half do it. If you hadn't already seen the passage open here, I doubt we would have discovered it."

"If some shoddy shaman of Varg's can open it, I'm sure we can too," Tor said from beside him.

Ciara, Imogen, and Lachie had found them minutes beforehand. Arawan was still running his fingers over the groove of stone, a frown on his face.

"It's god magic. Varg might have been willing to sacrifice one of his shamans in order to get it open, but I'm not going to be so stupid. Havi isn't an idiot, and I'm not in the mood to grow back my hands because of a trap," Arawan replied.

"Take your time, baby. The Hunt is dealing with the rest," Imogen said and rested her dirty ax over her shoulder. "I'm going to need your hands fully operational later. I'm feeling very battle lusty right now."

"Gross," Lachie muttered.

"I dunno about that," Ciara said, looking Tor over. He was gloriously naked and didn't seem to give the slightest fuck about it. Imogen waggled her eyebrows at her when Arawan's and Tor's backs were turned. Ciara rolled her eyes and fought the urge to shield him.

"Get your eyes off her man, or she'll end up fighting you too," Lachlan warned, reading Ciara far too easily.

"Ah, there it is," Arawan said, stopping their bickering. His magic made the hair on the back of Ciara's neck rise.

The stone began to glow, and golden runes, unlike anything she had seen before, started to appear as if written with an invisible hand. The rock in the middle of the shimmering archway seemed to go liquid before disappearing and leaving a black opening.

"I'll go first," Tor said and stepped through without hesitation. Ciara followed him into the darkness and found herself on a stone staircase lit with blazing crystal lights. They were similar to the ones she had seen at the Heart of Yggdrasil. Magic hung so thick in the air, she could almost taste it.

"Where are we?" she asked Tor.

"Wherever it is, it's not in Norway or any of the Nine Realms."

Arawan, Imogen, and Lachie appeared behind them. "Oh, Havi, you clever bastard," Arawan said with a smile. "We are in a void space. The Norse call it Ginnungagap."

"Fucking hell," Tor muttered, taking Ciara's hand. "Stay close to me."

"You don't have to tell me twice," she replied.

Time seemed to warp as they followed the stairs down in a steep spiral. Ciara's breath began to plume as the air grew colder with each level they passed through.

"You always take me to the most exotic locations," she teased Tor. "Maybe next time we can have a white sandy beach."

"Only if you promise to wear a tiny bikini," Tor replied.

"I could be persuaded."

Tor paused on the stair. "Can you hear that?"

They all held their breath, and a faint thumping of drums rose up from beneath them.

"Oh yay! I haven't been to a cave rave in *years*," Imogen said brightly.

"Just as long as it's not a Balrog," Lachie replied.

Ciara snorted. "You're getting as bad as Layla. If it was a Balrog, it would be warmer for a start."

"Ice Balrog," Lachie replied.

"Focus, children," Arawan chided lightly.

Tor was already heading down the stairs faster than before. "I can smell Linnea."

"Easy, Tor. We don't know what we are about to charge into," Ciara replied, squeezing his hand. His energy was jittery and making her edgy.

"I can feel Fenris. It's...indescribable," Tor said. His eyes had already shifted.

"It feels like something that should be left sleeping," Arawan muttered, stepping in front of Imogen. She didn't argue, which surprised Ciara. Imogen was never one to let someone get in between her and a fight.

The drumming got louder with every step they took, and a chant began to echo to accompany the beat. The magic building in the air set Ciara's teeth on edge.

"I hope this new suit of Charlotte's stops a magical attack," she said. She didn't know how to wield magic against shamans. Bullets and blades would have to do, but she would need to get close enough.

"She said they would shield against almost everything. She went extra hard because she was still embarrassed about the cuffs failing on you," Lachie told her. "Don't worry, I will jump behind you when the magical lightning bolts start getting tossed around."

"Sounds about right, too," Ciara replied.

Tor held out a hand to stop them. "Let me check. Wait here." He went down the last flight of stairs alone, and Ciara fought the urge to go with him. She barely breathed until he appeared again with a face like a thundercloud.

"Varg, two shamans, six warrior guards," he said, eyes glowing. "They have Linnea chained down in a ritual circle. Arawan? Can you deal with the magic? I don't want my sister hurt because the magic backfired on her."

"I'll take care of it. Hunters, you can deal with the warriors," Arawan said.

"Varg is my kill," Tor replied. He cupped Ciara's chin. "I know you want to help, but please stay out of this one?"

Ciara bit down all the objections she had. The scars on her neck said she had a right to vengeance too. She pushed it all aside. "Do it quickly, no dragging it no matter how much he deserves it. I don't want the fucker getting away on us again."

"He's never going to leave this place, that I promise you," Tor replied and pressed a kiss to her lips.

"Can I have a kiss for luck too?" Lachie asked hopefully, making Tor chuckle and Ciara glare. As a group, they all entered a chamber filled with light.

Varg and the others stood in a circle. Sigils and intricate spirals filled with runes were sketched around them, and Linnea was chained down in the center of the spell. She was on her knees and looked resigned to her fate. She was staring ahead of her at the shadows.

It wasn't until Ciara was fully inside the cavern that she saw what was in front of Linnea. It wasn't shadows at all. It was the black fur head of the largest fucking wolf she had ever seen.

"Fenris," she murmured, fear icing her over.

"B-Big fucking wolf," Imogen replied, her eyes bugging out of her head. They couldn't see the body, which was probably a good thing. From the size of the head, it had to have been bigger than two semi-trailers.

"Let's stop those assholes waking him up, shall we?" Arawan suggested.

Tor's alpha power rolled out of him, thick and hot. Ciara bit down a gasp as it washed over her. He started to shift, and her breath caught. He didn't turn into a wolf, but a battle berserker form like the wolf man on steroids.

"Holy shit, Tor is letting out the beast," Imogen said and nudged Ciara. "Did you know he could do that?"

Ciara shook her head. "He keeps this side of him locked up."

"What a shame. It's rather spectacular."

Ciara nodded. "It is that."

A deep growl of challenge rolled from Tor's muzzle, and the chanting staggered but didn't stop. Varg looked up at them, and his smile was the cruelest thing Ciara had ever seen. Her hand went to the small pocket in her suit that held a canister of wolfsbane. She would more than happily douse the bastard in it again.

"Tor! Run!" Linnea shouted.

"Yes, Tor, run away," Varg mocked. He gestured to the warriors. "Kill the others, but keep that Wolf Slayer bitch alive. I want my revenge on her."

"Did you hear that, beloved? They are going to kill us," Imogen said and cracked her neck.

Arawan unsheathed his sword. "The audacity. I swear you leave the human realm for a few centuries, and they forget who they are dealing with."

"I've missed you guys," Lachie said fondly, drawing his two swords.

Tor raced across the cavern floor and collided with Varg with a roar of fangs and claws. The other warriors shifted and started to run towards them.

Ciara took up her position beside Lachie, and they met the charge head-on. She could feel Tor's alpha power surging through the bond and filling her up with magic and rage.

One shifter came towards her still in human form, and she used all her new strength to kick him hard in the stomach, the shifter went down, winded, and Ciara stabbed him through the top of his skull in one swift downward strike.

"Good one, sis!" Lachie called out before taking the head off another warrior. Imogen was swinging her battle ax with a manic smile of pure joy of the fight. Arawan faced off with the shamans, unraveling their spellwork faster than they could weave it.

Ciara smashed an entire canister of wolfsbane into the chest of the nearest warrior. He screamed, tearing at his own flesh in a panic. Lachie came up beside her and lopped its head off.

"Help Linnea! We've got this," he said.

Ciara raced across the cavern. Tor and Varg were tearing into each other. Varg had fully shifted into his wolf form. His black and brown coat was splattered with dark blood. Tor was bleeding as well but showed no signs of pain.

Ciara dragged her gaze from them and reached the first of the spelled circles.

"Not yet!" Arawan shouted, making her skid to a halt. Dark shadows rose like spears from his hands, and they sliced through the shamans before striking multiple points in the sigils. The spell broke, and Ciara's ears popped hard enough that she flinched.

"Now, get her, Ciara," Arawan said. His black gaze was fixated on the gigantic wolf's head. "What a magnificent beastie you are."

Ciara ran to the sobbing, bloody woman on the ground. "Hey, it's okay now. I'm a friend of your brother's."

"You are the Wolf Slayer," Linnea said. Ciara picked the locks that bound Linnea's hands behind her back.

"I am. How do you know that?"

Linnea smiled through her busted lips. She was finer boned than Tor, but her gray eyes were the same. "He used to talk about you before I was taken. You're probably the only woman he's ever been afraid of."

"Yeah, I'm pretty sure that's worn off," Ciara said with a grin. The locks popped, and the chains unspooled. "Are you hurt?"

"Only superficial. They used my blood to draw their circles. The shamans told Varg that they needed the blood of an unshifted adult wolf to awaken Fenris. It's what kept me alive for the last year," Linnea replied.

"Fucking assholes," Ciara growled.

Linnea's brows shot up. "You sounded so much like Tor. Gods, you're bonded?"

"Ah, yeah." Ciara quickly busied herself with the locks on Linnea's legs. "It's a long story."

"I bet." Linnea rubbed at her legs and feet as the chains fell away. Ciara helped her stand, and they turned to see where Tor and the others were. Arawan was back with Imogen and Lachie, watching Tor's duel with Varg.

"Kill him already," Linnea hissed under her breath. Tears were falling down her hollow cheeks, rage burning in her eyes. Ciara hesitated a moment before she took Linnea's hand and held onto it.

Tor's eyes landed on them for a moment, and Ciara gave him a firm nod to tell him they were well. With a bellow, Tor's alpha power unleashed and slammed into Varg. The wolf howled and collapsed to the ground.

"Oh gods, he's finally making another submit to him," Linnea gasped. "He said he'd never do it without reason."

"Varg has given us all more than one," Ciara replied, her scars pulsing in memory.

Tor grabbed Varg's top jaw with one hand and the bottom with the other. With a roar, he ripped the wolf's head in half in an act of stunning, horrific violence.

"That's my mate," Ciara whispered in complete awe of him.

"He's what?" Linnea squeaked.

Ciara straightened her shoulders. "He's my mate."

Tor strode over to them, shifting down to his human form. He was covered in blood and gore and looked like the vengeful Viking god he was. Ciara let Linnea go, and Tor caught his sister up in a bone-cracking embrace.

"I knew you would find me," Linnea said, hanging onto him. "I knew you would come. Is the Wolf Slayer really your mate?"

Tor lowered Linnea back to her feet and let her go. His gaze shot to Ciara, eyes blazing with love. "Yeah, she is. Let's get out of here before we wake Fenris without the magic."

The others joined them, all of them staring at the giant wolf slumbering in front of them. Ciara could make out the silvery ribbons binding him in place, and she couldn't help but feel a flicker of sadness. No creature should be bound in such a way.

"Now there's something you don't see every day," Lachie whispered. Ciara nudged him with her shoulder, and they shared a smile.

"Let's get out of here," Imogen said, grabbing onto Arawan's hand. "I've already got one beast to handle, and I don't need to adopt another."

Arawan gave her a heated look. "You've never had a complaint handling my beast, darling."

"Gross," Lachie and Ciara said simultaneously and laughed.

Fearlessly, Linnea stepped up onto the dais and placed her hand on Fenris's mighty paw. Tor made a warning noise, but Ciara stopped him from pulling his sister away.

"I'm sorry we disturbed you, Great One. Dream of pleasanter things," Linnea said softly, her eyes full of a strange sadness. She stroked the fur once before turning back to Tor. "Let's go. We shouldn't be down here."

Ciara fell into step beside her as they all made for the staircase. "Are...Are you okay?"

"It's strange. I started dreaming of this place right before I was taken, and I've dreamed of it every night since. I feel like we've stepped into a sacred place that we should have never disturbed," Linnea replied.

"Maybe you need to talk to Gudrun. It sounds like you have the seer gift," Tor said to her. He was watching her like she would vanish.

"It's a good idea. I...I've seen too many strange things in the last year. I'm going to need a Völva or a therapist or both to get my head right again." Linnea shot one last look at the sleeping wolf before heading up the stairs. "Sleep well, Fenris Lokison."

Tor caught Ciara's hand, stopping her from following. "Are you hurt?"

"No. You?"

"Nothing I won't recover from." Tor nodded to his sister's back. "You told her we were mates?"

"It might have slipped out in a moment of weakness when you were acting particularly impressive," Ciara replied, her cheeks beginning to flame.

Tor grinned, wide and joyful. Even covered in crud, he was still the most handsome man she had ever seen. He picked her up and kissed her. Ciara wrapped her arms around his neck, her relief that their enemy was dead and that they were safe overwhelming her. She wanted to fuck him right on the staircase. She let their bond open, and she threw the image at him.

Tor growled and squeezed her ass. "You're such a troublemaker, but I love you."

"Enough to carry me up these stairs?" Ciara's thighs tightened around him, making him laugh.

"You wish." Tor put her down and gave her ass a gentle pat. "Go on, get moving. I want to go home."

"I want to sleep for a month," Ciara said.

"Me too. Unfortunately, you and I have a full moon to get through tomorrow night," Tor reminded her. "And after that? We are going to have the mating talk again."

Ciara shot a coy smile over her shoulder. "Are we now?"

"Yes," he growled. "If I have to pin you down and sit on you while we do it, I will. Don't push me, bunny."

Ciara laughed, and it felt so damn good. "We'll see about that, wolf."

31

The sun was up, and the world was eye-watering bright by the time the door in the side of the mountain opened, and Ciara and the others stumbled out. Layla and Arne were waiting for them with annoyed and relieved expressions on their faces.

"Where the hell did you all go? I turned around mid-battle, and I couldn't see any of you!" she snapped, hands on her hips.

"We are okay, Lay Lay. Keep your knickers on," Imogen said.

Arne looked them all over. "Let me guess? The passage into the mountain wasn't in Norway?"

"How did you know?" Ciara asked.

"I can feel the magic on you. It's good to see you safe and sound, Linnea," Arne said when Linnea came out from behind Tor.

"Big brother," she replied with a smile.

What was left of the camp was in ruins. Ulfheðnar were roaming about with a few of Varg's followers in manacles. A small group of women were wrapped in blankets and being watched over by the elves.

"Linnea! Was he there? Did you see Fenris?" a man demanded. He was being led by an elf, his hands bound behind his back.

Linnea lifted her chin. "It was another illusion of Odin's. It was a dead end." The man looked devastated and was taken away.

"Why did you lie?" Ciara asked.

"They will find a way to keep trying to get back to him. Fenris should be left sleeping," Linnea replied. She swayed a little, and Tor caught her under the arm.

"We need to get you out of here where you can rest," he said, checking her over.

"I believe I can help with that," Alruna announced, coming through a portal with a wide smile on her face. She caught Linnea up in a hug. "Little one, it's so good to see you. Come on, I've had one of the delegation houses prepared for you all. Tor's house is too small to accommodate everyone."

"I'm going to leave you all to it," Imogen said. She hugged Layla and Ciara. "I have a castle to get back to and a death god to shag."

"Is that so?" Arawan asked, a brow rising. Imogen winked at him, and he opened a portal. "Nice to see you all. Be well." He all but dragged a laughing Imogen through the portal, and they were gone.

"I don't suppose the Wild Hunt is still around?" Ciara asked.

Layla shook her head. "They swept through the camp, killed anyone who didn't surrender, and then disappeared again. Creepiest, quietest goddamn slaughter I've ever seen."

"Jesus, I can't believe this is our family now," Lachie said with a shake of his head.

Ciara, Tor, Linnea, and Lachie were portaled to a large house by the lake in Alfheimstod. Alruna had ensured that clean clothes had been provided for them and the kitchen was stocked with food.

"She's going in full mother mode," Tor commented when he saw it all laid out.

"Let her. I want nothing more than a hot shower and a bed," Linnea replied. She disappeared into one of the guest rooms. Lachie went to the other with a tired expression. The post-battle exhaustion was hitting them all. Ciara was in a daze as Tor led her to their room and stripped off her weapons and battle suit.

"Won't Linnea find it weird if we stay together?" Ciara asked, suddenly nervous about the idea.

Tor shook his head. "We are bonded. She knows we are a couple and won't want to be apart. It's really fine, Ciara."

"Okay, I just don't want her to feel uncomfortable."

Tor kissed her dirty face. "Thank you, but it's unnecessary."

They showered quickly and collapsed into bed. Ciara was aching everywhere, but Tor's warm body wrapped around her, and she was out before she knew it.

～

HOURS LATER, Ciara woke with a growling stomach and thirsty as hell. She slid out from underneath Tor's arm, dressed in some of the clean clothes left for her, and went into the kitchen. Lachie was sitting at the counter, drinking tea with a dazed expression.

"Hey, you're up early," he said.

Ciara grunted and drained a bottle of water. "I feel all disorientated. I'll be fine. How are you? You're not hurt anywhere?"

"Bit bruised, and my ass will be aching tomorrow from all those stairs, but I'll live." Lachie frowned, and Ciara knew something else was bothering him.

"Spit it out, little brother."

"You fought like a wolf with their speed and strength. Are you worried about tomorrow night? Or are you looking forward to it?"

Ciara made tea and slid onto a chair beside him. "I think if I turn, I will be okay with it. Tor assures me that it won't change my personality, which was always my biggest concern. He'll help me deal with anything else."

"So you are finally admitting you're all loved up?" Lachie teased.

"Very much so. I know; who would've thought?" Ciara said and laughed a little. "He wants me to be his mate."

Lachie's brows shot up. "Well, well. Not just a bit of fun, after all. I'm happy for you."

"Are you? You're not weirded out that it's with a wolf?"

Lachie put his head on her shoulder. "You've always hated the wolves more than I have, so no, I'm not weirded out. He could be a leprechaun for all I care. As long as he makes you happy, that's what counts."

"You're going to be the only adult Ironwood not shacked up."

Lachie snorted. "And I'm happy to keep it that way. I'm too young and pretty to have a ball and chain around my ankle..." he trailed off, his head snapping up. "We have company."

Ciara turned and spotted the elderly wolf from the council stomping up the stairs to the glass doors surrounding the patio.

"Let me deal with this," she said and went outside. "Can I help you...?"

"Knud. I suppose we didn't get to proper introductions when you were in Ulfheim," he answered gruffly.

"If you are here for Torsten, he's still asleep, and I'm reluctant to wake him," Ciara replied politely.

"I'm not here for Tor. I'm here for you," Knud replied.

Ciara crossed her arms. "Am I in trouble?"

"No, girl. I'm here because you did the Ulfheðnar a good service by proving Petra was in league with Varg, and then you found our enemy and helped destroy him. The council wishes to offer you a favor of your choosing."

"I want nothing from the Ulfheðnar for myself," Ciara replied and slowly uncrossed her arms. "Linnea has been involved with a lot of dark magic, and she's been having visions. I would like you to give her access to Gudrun."

"Linnea has always been welcome in Ulfheim."

"If that was the case, she never would've left. I want you to personally ensure that she doesn't get harassed if she returns to work with Gudrun. She's been through enough," Ciara replied.

Knud's stern expression melted, and he let out a chuckle. "Odin's beard, you really are Tor's mate. That alpha streak in you is a mile wide. I'll make sure Linnea has whatever she needs. Now, another matter, Wolf Slayer. If you turn tomorrow, you will be a part of the Ulfheðnar. Would you consider being an enforcer for the council?"

Ciara frowned. "I already have a job, Knud."

"I know, and we are asking you to keep doing it. The wolves are proud, but maybe you were right. We have become too isolated from the wider world. It shouldn't be left up to humans to hunt down any of our kind that is misbehaving," Knud replied. He scratched at his beard. "You shamed us good, but we need fresh blood to show us another way. Think about it. Your reputation with the backing of the Ulfheðnar will work in everyone's favor."

Ciara nodded. "I'll consider it if I turn, but I'm not going to make any promises. There are things I need to work out first."

"Like your mating with Tor?"

Ciara sighed. "I'm not mating with Tor yet. Gods, you are all so nosey."

Knud actually laughed. "You'll get used to it. Send Linnea to Gudrun tomorrow night. I'm sure you and Tor will want to be alone to deal with your first turning."

"I'll let Linnea know."

Knud held out a hand to her. "Until you make your decision, Ciara Wolf Slayer."

Ciara shook his hand, feeling strange, like she had gotten approval she didn't ask for. Lachie was cooking by the time she came back inside.

"What was that all about?" he asked as he chopped up vegetables to roast.

"They want me to be their enforcer," Ciara replied.

"Well, you are the most terrifying hunter walking the earth," Tor said, coming into the kitchen.

"Hey, I'm right here," Lachie complained.

Tor ignored him and wrapped his arms around Ciara. He was warm and sleepy and looked so adorable her heart ached. Tor sat down and tugged her into his lap.

"What did the grumpy old bastard want?" he asked. Ciara caught him up, and Tor was unable to hide his surprise. "Well, well, looks like you shook them right up. Thank you for asking about Linnea visiting Gudrun. She will feel better going back, knowing she has permission to be there. And we are definitely going to need to be alone tomorrow night."

"Is that so?" Ciara asked, putting her arms around his neck.

Tor nodded. "My sister is safe. Now, I need to deal with the other matters at hand."

"You are not going to drop the mating thing, are you?" Ciara sighed.

Tor nuzzled into her neck. "Never ever. I swear you're only holding out to torment me."

Ciara laughed. "Would I do that?"

32

The following evening, Ciara stood on the patio of Tor's cabin and watched the sun go down over the lake. The forest and the water were so beautiful they made her sigh with happiness. There would be a lot worse places to live.

"Are you feeling anything yet?" Tor asked, coming outside with fresh beers.

"Nothing other than full and happy," she replied honestly.

Tor had recovered entirely from the battle though she was still a bit sore. They had spent much of the day in a conference call with the princes and the Ironwoods, catching them up on everything that had happened. The elves were working to send the displaced women back to their families, and the wolves were dealing with the few remaining followers of Varg's. Ciara was happy to stay out of it and let Alruna and the rest take care of everything.

Linnea had gone off to Gudrun's that afternoon and would stay the night with her. Tor was worried about her, but Linnea wasn't the type to let him fuss too much.

"It's Gudrun for Odin's sake. Nothing is going to happen to me," Linnea had argued before hugging her brother and Ciara goodbye.

Tor sat down on the chair beside her and put an arm around her. Ciara curled into his side and tried to hold onto his calm strength.

"Am I meant to be feeling anything?" she asked him. "Are you?"

"I can sense the energy shifting around us. Like the build-up to a storm," Tor replied.

They waited in comfortable silence, watching as the moon rose over the lake. Ciara got up and walked across the grass to the water, letting the moonlight fall on her entirely.

Nothing happened. There was no fur, or bones, or urge to howl. A lump clogged her throat, and she sobbed.

"What is it? Are you hurting?" Tor asked, resting a hand on her shoulder.

"No. Nothing is happening!" she said, a strange panic overwhelming her. "I thought I would turn, and I'm... I'm still normal."

Tor lifted her chin. "Ciara, I thought you wanted to stay human."

"So did I. But I want you, Tor! You have to mate with a wolf," she said, trying to hold in her tears. She felt like such an idiot for only realizing how much she wanted to be a part of his life, all of it, every aspect she could.

"Ciara, I can mate with whoever I like." Tor placed a hand on her cheeks. "If you want to be a wolf, I'll turn you tonight."

"Tonight? How is that possible?" she asked, eyes widening.

"I'm the strongest alpha the Ulfheðnar have had in centuries, bunny. If I bite you, you'll be a wolf by the night's end," Tor said. He wiped the tears off her cheeks. "Whatever you choose, I still want you as my mate. Please love, say yes."

Ciara stared up at his beautiful gray eyes. Her fears suddenly disappeared, and a deep calm swept through her. "I love you and want to be with you every way I can, Tor. I want to be your mate, and I want you to bite me."

"You do? Are you sure? I don't want you to do it because you feel like you have to. I will want you and love you either way, Ciara," he replied.

Ciara took his hand and placed it over her heart like he had done to her. "Feel." Tor's face shifted as he searched the bond, and he felt all the things Ciara was drowning in—love, desire, longing. She wanted everything. And she wanted it with him. Tor picked her up and kissed her until she was breathless.

"My love," he murmured against her lips. Hot desire rolled through her, and Ciara dragged his shirt off. "Right here on the grass?"

"Yes, right here. I can't wait," she said, pulling her own top off.

"You really are the perfect mate," Tor replied. He pulled her down to the grass and dragged the rest of their clothes off. Ciara straddled him, their skin glowing in the moonlight. She didn't think she had ever seen anything so beautiful. His eyes were fully feral, and she loved it. Ciara sank down on his cock, making them both gasp.

"Fuck, I'm never going to get enough of you," she said, her hands tangling in his hair.

Tor kissed her. "I should hope not, bunny."

Ciara laughed softly and began to ride him. Tor held onto her but let her lead, and she relished the control he gave her. They would probably always butt heads, but he would never force her to do anything she didn't want to. They would keep each other safe and fight side by side.

Ciara could feel the pressure of her orgasm building, her core clutching tight to him. "Bite me, Tor."

Tor's eyes gleamed, and fangs flashed as he shifted into his alpha form. Ciara clutched onto him, unafraid. She fucked him harder, chasing her release. Tor growled out something between his teeth in a language so ancient, she could feel the magic in the words. She bared her throat to him, and Tor's teeth closed down on her flesh as the mating bond began to bind them tightly together. Ciara clung to him, crying out a wordless babble as she came.

Pleasure and pain, love and magic, all melded together until she thought she would die from it. Hot tears were rolling down her cheeks. She was vaguely aware of Tor shifting back down to his human form. His lips kissed over the puncture marks, licking the drops of blood from her skin. Tor stroked her hair and skin, the warm touch bringing her back down and grounding her again.

"Are you still with me?" he asked softly.

"I am always going to be with you now," she replied, resting her head on his neck. The mating bond felt like a living thing glowing between them.

Tor kissed the top of her head. "Thank you for becoming mine, Ciara. I couldn't have asked the gods for a better mate."

"Me neither," she said, kissing him over and over. A rush of magic danced over her skin, and Ciara slid from Tor's lap. There was something pulsing inside of her that wasn't the bond.

"Tor? I feel..."

Tor's gray eyes were so calm. "It's okay, love. It's just the change. Don't fight it."

"So soon?" she asked, suddenly afraid.

Tor kissed her gently. "I told you, I'm an alpha, and it would happen fast. Don't be afraid. I'm here."

Ciara swallowed hard and nodded. "Will it hurt?"

"Only if you fight it. Just let it happen. I'm right here beside you. You're not alone, Ciara. You're never going to be alone again."

Ciara closed her eyes and let the magic overwhelm her. It was like sliding into a warm bath of power. There was no snapping of bones or ripping of skin. There was only heat and magic and Tor's love thrumming through her. Her body stretched, and she went forward onto all fours. She could hear the forest coming alive around her and feel the earth under her. Her senses exploded, and when she opened her eyes, she was no longer human. She looked at her wide black paws in the silvery light.

Tor was staring at her like she was a miracle. He ran his hands through the fur between her ears. "I always knew you were going to be the most magnificent wolf," he said before kissing the top of her glossy black head.

Ciara breathed in his scent that screamed *home*. She wanted to run, to see the world through her wolf eyes. She nipped his hand and then jumped back out of his reach.

"Don't you do it," Tor growled testily. "Don't you dare run away when you're freshly turned, Ciara Fiadh Ironwood. I'm warning you, if you run, you know what will happen..."

Ciara yipped back at him mockingly. She raked her new claws against the earth and bolted. She flew through the trees, knowing he would come for her. In fact, she was counting on it.

EPILOGUE

In Ulfheim, Linnea stared up at the moon and tried not to feel the longing she had in her heart. Hearing the call and not being able to shift was an old pain, but it still hurt like a wound that had never healed. Maybe after tonight, it wouldn't be a problem anymore.

"Are you sure you want to do this?" Gudrun asked her. She was mixing herbs in a bowl, crushing them into a paste.

"Of course I do. If what you say is true, and I have cursed myself not to shift, I want it undone. I want to feel whole," Linnea replied. Her magic abilities as a seer had shocked her, but not as much as Gudrun had earlier that day. Linnea had gone to ask her about her magic, and after Gudrun had inspected her, she had announced that she was cursed.

Cursed by my own magic. Only I could do something so stupid, Linnea thought. She knew exactly why her magic would have done it; to spite her father.

He had been waiting for her to shift so he could sell her off to another family to enhance his own standing in the pack. Linnea had decided she would rather die than be bound to another male. Gudrun suspected that her magic had caused her desire to stay unmated to react and had locked her wolf away. Linnea was going to try and set it loose again, which led back to Gudrun mashing up gods knew what for her to take.

"I don't know if this will work, but this will help remove blocks that have been placed between you and your magic," Gudrun said. She mixed mead into the crushed herbs and offered her the cup.

"You'll stay with me in case something happens?" Linnea asked nervously.

"Yes, and I'll guide you back in case you wander too far away. Find the place where you have locked up your wolf, free it yourself, and then we will see what happens," Gudrun replied. She didn't force Linnea to drink, only watched and waited patiently.

"Here goes nothing," Linnea mumbled and drank the mixture. She lay down on the pallet by the fire and stared up at the hanging talismans and bunches of herbs above her.

Gudrun started to sing softly. It was something that mothers sang to their babies, a lullaby about the first wolves. Linnea hadn't heard it since her mother had kissed her one night and had left her the next morning. She couldn't remember her mother's face anymore, and she wondered if she had locked that away too. Linnea's limbs began to tingle, and her eyes slid shut.

Linnea opened her eyes again, and she was standing in the cavern once more. The chalk sigils were scuffed, and her blood had turned black against the stone.

"Why here again?" she wondered aloud. Why did she always return to the cavern? Before her, Fenris's head rested between his two mighty paws. Linnea sat down beside one and rested her back against it. She wasn't afraid, even though she knew she should be.

"Maybe I dream of you because we are both bound and cursed," Linnea said to him. She rested her head back and softly began to sing the lullaby to the Great Beast.

Linnea started to cry softly, hot tears of anger that her father had frightened her so much that she had cursed herself. That she would never be free of his ghost screaming at her and laying into her with his hard fists. Her voice shook, but she kept singing until the song was done.

Linnea closed her eyes again, and when she opened them, she was back in Gudrun's hut, the fire burned down, and the Völva was asleep on the chair in front of her.

"So much for having magic," she whispered softly before curling into a tight ball and going back to sleep.

∼

DEEP in the caverns built in the void of Ginnungagap, a song echoed around the stone. It curled around the ears of the sleeping wolf, its words speaking of awakening, of shifting, of the wildness and freedom of wolves.

The sleeping wolf breathed in. He could smell blood and woman. *Her* blood. The singing woman's life stained the stones around him. Strange magic was in the air, making his senses twitch with irritation and longing.

In the darkness, the great wolf stirred, and Fenris's blue eye opened.

∼

CHARACTER LIST

The Fae Universe has become so big, I felt like it needed a character list so everyone knows who everyone is. This list has been kept as spoiler free as possible.

THE FAE & THEIR MATES
KIAN - the Blood Prince, mate to ELISE. Rules in England and is technically in charge of all the fae residing in the United Kingdom. See 'Kiss of the Blood Prince' for his full story.

ELISE - Kian's mate, librarian extraordinare and cousin to FREYA.

BAYN- the Winter Prince, mate to FREYA. Lives in a castle in Scotland. See 'Heart of the Winter Prince' for his full story.

FREYA- Bayn's mate, owner of antiquities businesses, viking badass.

KILLIAN - the Night Prince, mate to BRON. Lives in Dublin and gets up to shenanigans with the IRONWOODS. See 'Wings of the Night Prince' for his full story.

BRON IRONWOOD - Killian's mate, eldest Ironwood sister, possessor of a god killing sword.

THE IRONWOODS (in age order)
KENNA - The Matriarch of the family.

CHARACTER LIST

DAVID - The Patriarch of the family.

IMOGEN - Second eldest in the Ironwood family, consort of ARAWAN.

CHARLOTTE - Third eldest in the Ironwood family, and the only magician, mated to REEVE.

LAYLA - Fourth eldest in the Ironwood Family.

MOIRA - The youngest in the family.

EXTENDED IRONWOODS

CIARA - Cousin of the Ironwoods, sister to Lachlan.

LACHLAN- Cousin of the Ironwoods, brother to Ciara.

THE GREATDRAKES (in age order)

COSIMO - The Patriarch of the family, like Valentine, he can use many forms of magic but specialises in glamor and persuasion.

VALENTINE - Oldest of the Greatdrakes, considered a prodigy, he specialises in many forms of magic.

APOLLO - Second oldest of the Greatdrakes, he specialises in alchemy.

BASSET- Third oldest of the Greatdrakes, he specialises in telepathy and psychometry.

REEVE - The youngest of the Greatdrakes, he specialises in transmutation magic, usually in the form of 'trash' every day objects that he can turn into whatever he wants. Mated to CHARLOTTE.

RE- OCCURING CHARATERS

ARNE - An elf from Norway, friends to BAYN and TORSTEN. Prince of the Light Elves and son of VILI.

TORSTEN - an Úlfhéðnar wolf shifter from Norway. Friends to BAYN and ARNE. Brother to LINNEA.

LINNEA - Sister of TOR

ARAWAN - Welsh God of the Dead, ruler of the underworld of Annwn, IMOGEN's consort.

MORRIGAN - Celtic goddess of War. She attacked Dublin but was defeated by BRON. See 'Wings of the Night Prince.'

ALRUNA - Queen of the Light Elves in Midgard, mother to ARNE, mate to VILI.

VILI - Morrigan's third general, HAVI's (Odin) brother, father to ARNE, mate to ALRUNA.

HAVI - the All Father aka Odin, brother to VILI.

LOKI - Trickster god, blood brother to HAVI, Father of FENRIS.

FENRIS - Son to LOKI, wolf god, and first shifter.

GUDRUN - Volvä (shaman) of Ulfheim.

ABOUT THE AUTHOR

I believe that all monsters and villains deserve their happy endings. I prefer my clothes black, eyeliner winged, and books full of hot romance.

Come say hi to me on Instagram, or keep track of all of the gossip early by subscribing to my blog newsletter at:

https://alessathornauthor.com/alessa-news/

Thank you for reading IRONWOOD if you loved it please consider leaving me a short review or a rating on Amazon as it helps other readers find my books.

ALSO BY ALESSA THORN

GODS UNIVERSE
THE COURT OF THE UNDERWORLD
ASTERION

MEDUSA

HADES

HERMES

THANATOS

CHARON

EREBUS

GODS OF THE DUAT
SET

THOTH

ANUBIS

FAE UNIVERSE
THE WRATH OF THE FAE
KISS OF THE BLOOD PRINCE

HEART OF THE WINTER PRINCE

WINGS OF THE NIGHT PRINCE

WRATH OF THE FAE (Box set Audio Book Edition)

IRONWOOD
TRASH AND TREASURE

GOD TOUCHED

ELF SHOT

LUNA CURSED

MERCENARIES AND MAGIC

DARKEST NIGHT
SHARPEST EDGE

IRONWOOD

BOOKS 1-4

ALESSA THORN